No Handbook for the Homeless

No Handbook
for the
Homeless

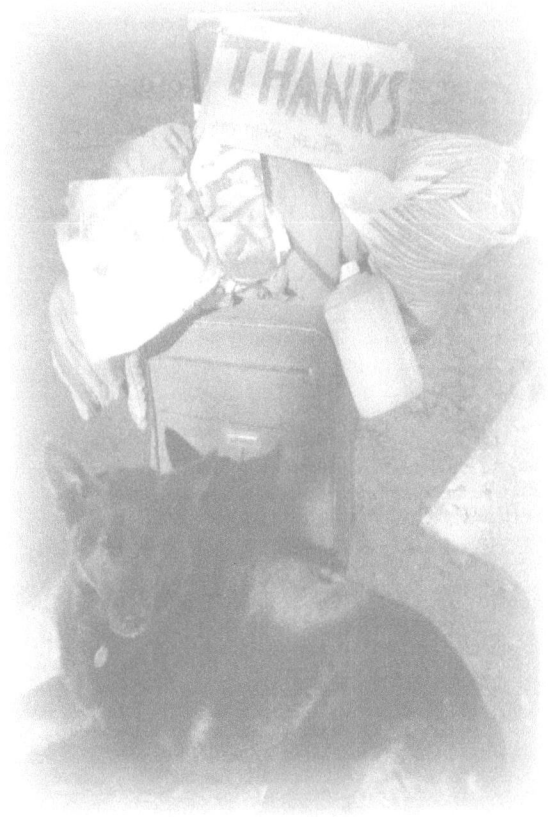

A Novel

Joyce Trainor

SUNSTONE
PRESS

SANTA FE

Sunstone books may be purchased for educational, business, or sales promotional use. For information please write: Special Markets Department, Sunstone Press, P.O. Box 2321, Santa Fe, New Mexico 87504-2321.

Cover photograph by Jeff Toomey
Book and cover design › Vicki Ahl
Body typeface › Rotis Serif
Printed on acid-free paper
∞
eBook 978-1-61139-375-0

Library of Congress Cataloging-in-Publication Data

Trainor, Joyce, 1956-
  No handbook for the homeless : a novel / by Joyce Trainor.
     pages cm
  ISBN 978-1-63293-060-6 (softcover : alk. paper)
  1. Homeless women--Fiction. 2. Marginality, Social--Fiction. I. Title.
  PS3620.R3555N64 2015
  813'.6--dc23

                                        2015009168

WWW.SUNSTONEPRESS.COM
SUNSTONE PRESS / POST OFFICE BOX 2321 / SANTA FE, NM 87504-2321 /USA
(505) 988-4418 / ORDERS ONLY (800) 243-5644 / FAX (505) 988-1025

This book is dedicated to my Dad, who taught me that people's worth is not based on money; my Mom, who laughed at my jokes even the ones that weren't funny; my husband, much more than I deserve. I extend grateful appreciation to Santa Fe author Robert Mayer for his guidance and advice.

1

*F*irecrackers. If it hadn't been for the firecrackers I'd have gone with them. Things would have turned out differently. But no. Two and half weeks left in the school year, last week of May, right before the long weekend and some kids brought firecrackers. Ten years ago it would have meant a trip to the office, a stern lecture and a couple of lunch hours in study hall. Not anymore.

A few kids lingered in my room during the last half of the lunch hour. Finally released from penance by the math teacher for the sin of not turning in homework, they missed the lunch line closing by seconds. Rules being rules, they were refused service and the leftover food trashed instead, leaving the squirmy kids without their only dependable food source for the day. At best, when they arrive home, a box of cheese crackers and hyper-caffeinated soft drink would be dinner. I open my desk drawer and reach for the box of fruit bars and juice drinks I keep for these occasions.

"Hey Ms. Roark, got anything to eat?" Joe-Pablo's lanky frame filled my door. His not really red hair sprawls across his head, and his Bulls' jersey is soaked by sweat, earned by interception of a thrown pass and subsequent chase down through the parking lot of a lunch hour pickup game he was not invited to be part of.

"Hi Joe-Pablo, yeah come in. Miss lunch again today?" I place the box of fruit bars on top of my desk and sighed as he grabs three of the six in there. By now I should know to give them out one at a time.

Efrain, a tiny eighth grader about to hit his growth spurt rushes my door, followed by the clicking heels of the teacher on hall duty he sneaked by to gain entry.

"You know the rules," she says to him, scolding. "No students until the bell rings."

Efrain looks to me for salvation. "It's okay Sue. These guys come in for extra help sometimes." I walk Sue out to the hall.

"As long as they stay in your room, they can't be wandering around the halls." Sue's tone is condescending even though I've got a good seventeen or eighteen years teaching on her. She takes this part of her job way too seriously.

By the time I turn around the boys are at the window, sneaking sips of Coke to some girls gathered right outside the open window. Apparently the boys slipped across the hall to the teachers' lounge and used the off limits vending machine housed in there.

"Can we come in too? It's all hot out here." Andrea's cheap pink glitter nails, poorly glued, catch the noon sun as she reaches her hand through the open window to pass the Coke to Efrain. "We could catch up on our missing work?"

"Please, Ms. Roark, be all cool, okay, please. Let them come in." Efrain asks.

I glance at the stack of papers on my desk I meant to grade during lunch, wonder when I'll ever get to them, then at the sweaty faces of the middle schoolers. After more than twenty years of teaching middle school it still amazes me how they change from scared little kids the first day of seventh grade to tall teens, more at ease in their almost adult bodies, a few months away from High School. The kids I see before me now are a lot more confident in stride and mind then the ones I saw at the beginning of their seventh grade year.

"Sure, why not. I'll tell Ms. Jaramillo to let you in." The boys grin, give each other high fives. I walk to the hall. Sue Jaramillo, the hall duty teacher, is arguing with two students trying to get to their lockers. I call out to her, distracting enough that the students sneak in.

"I've got a couple of young ladies coming in for help, will you let them in? They should be here any minute."

"Are you going to be responsible for them? Your students are always getting into trouble."

I cringe when she says this. 'Aren't they all our students?' I want to say. Instead I smile sweetly, "Of course, I'll be sure they don't get into anything."

The three girls approach the main entrance. Sue looks at me suspiciously, and then reluctantly holds the door open just enough for each girl to squeeze by. She can't resist one last dig. "I'll be checking the bathrooms so don't think you'll get away with anything in there."

The girls roll their eyes as they walk by, saunter down the hall to my room. One tries to stop at her locker. I gently prod her "Not now Katie. Straight to the room, okay?" She closes the locker door, but not before Sue sticks her head around the corner, gives me and them a dirty look.

Loud pops and bangs sound outside, rapid, three, then four, then two more. Kids shout, rush the door.

"Somebody is shooting," they scream. Two more loud bangs, the kids panic. Sue tries to hold them back, keep them outside.

"What are you nuts? Let them in. Let them come in." I push past her, hit the exit bars unlocking each of the six double doors. Kids spill through.

"Walk," I say, yelling over their din, try to remember the procedures drilled into us for this situation. "Homeroom. Go to Homeroom. Quietly, walk." Five more teachers have joined in. We urgently herd kids into rooms, wait for instructions, slow in coming, over the intercom. Kids are already on cell phones, texting frantic parents. "Lock down! This is not a drill!" The instruction finally booms over the hall speaker.

I stride to my room, stop to check the restrooms, pick up two stragglers, close and lock the door, close the windows, draw the blinds, tape the pre-cut paper I keep stashed in the cabinet over the thin sliver of a window in the classroom door and turn off the lights. Less than four minutes have elapsed.

"Quiet, on the floor, under the desk. Quiet." I look at the faces of the students awkwardly crouched under desks and tables. The scared faces of the little kids I saw the first day of seventh grade look back at me. I am gentler now, hold my fingers to my lips and walk silently up and down the rows taking a count. "It's probably just firecrackers," I say to them in a barely audible whisper. I pull the box of free reading books and magazines from the shelf, grab a handful and pass them down each row, find some colored pencils and scrap paper, do the same with it.

A couple of the girls try to talk. I write "You have to be quiet" on the back of scrap paper and hand it to them, mime writing notes on the paper. They get the idea. Half the students start writing notes to each other, playing hangman and tic-tac-toe. Some boys draw pictures of muscle cars and elaborate medieval weapons, pass them around to be admired. I save the giant bag of Smarties and tiny bottles of water for the last hour. It's hot, we can't open the windows. I don't know how much longer I can keep them still. Thank God no one asks for the bathroom. When I think no one is watching I clandestinely reach up and pull the clock from the wall so they can't see it. Doesn't matter, they all use cell phones to tell time now anyway.

Three and a half hours later, maybe a little longer, a full hour past regular dismissal time, after the SWAT team has completed their search, anxious parents park outside the school grounds and school buses line up in a nearby church parking lot. The all clear comes over the intercom. Firecrackers. Those responsible sit in the office, waiting for parents to pick them up and begin a five day suspension. It takes another forty minutes to account for everyone, get the buses boarded and students released to grateful parents.

Teachers and staff are kept at school another hour to debrief. Blank sheets of chart papers with *What Worked* and *Need to Fix* written at the top are posted on walls. Everyone must write two under each or none of us can get the heck out of here. I've been doing this too long I think. I write the same comments I did the last time and the time before that and the time before that: 'Rooms are hot' 'main doors locked', under *Fix,* 'Kids kept safe', 'cooperative students' under *Worked.*

The newbies want to discuss. It's their first lock-down that wasn't a drill. The reality of this responsibility has overwhelmed them. The veterans gather in the back, some complain loudly. "Nothing changes!" "Why get our ideas if you aren't going to act on them!" "Where's the box for this on our teacher effectiveness rating?" one asks exaggerating the sarcasm. Finally, we are allowed out of the meeting room.

It's five-fifty-five the Friday before Memorial Day. I return to my classroom. The smell of twenty five excited middle schoolers locked in a hot dark room all afternoon still permeates the air. If it hadn't been a long weekend I'd risk reprimand and leave the windows open overnight to let the room air out. I'm exhausted, perspiring heavily, gather up those papers I need to grade and collapse into the car for the drive home.

First stop light, I reach for the bag of Hershey Kisses I keep in the middle console; my stress chocolate. They're melted. I put one, soft and squishy, in my mouth still wrapped in foil and suck the chocolate out of it, using my tongue to remove the bits of foil from my teeth, then another and another. Before I get home half the bag is gone.

Sam and the boys are already packed, impatiently waiting to leave when I arrive. "Sure you won't go with us honey?" He asks as he empties a bag of ice on top of the two twelve packs of silver beer cans in the ice chest. "Might help you unwind."

"Listen Sam, the only thing that will help me unwind right now is a long bath and a tall glass of iced tea. I'm just gonna' stay home and take care of Peanuts, grade some papers." I hug and kiss Sam, who pulls me close. "Be good, okay Sam? Don't overdo it with the beer this time." I speak in a whisper so the boys don't hear. Sam winks at me and gets into the truck.

I hug the two boys. Sean, at seventeen, is taller than his older brother, but still carries the baby smooth chin and slim build of an adolescent. Stevie, all shoulders and in need of a shave, a head taller then I, picks me up and swings me around like I'm three years old. "Promise to take good care of my dog, mom? No chocolate or onions, no table scraps. Okay? And don't let him sleep on the bed." Stevie sets me down, roughs the fur around his big black dog's collar.

I wave and close the gate as they pull out the driveway, fishing poles, tent and sleeping bags piled high in the back. "Have fun you guys, see you Monday."

2

People don't think it can happen to them, but it can. One second, one incident, one tiny thing can alter your life. One minute you're Mrs. Middle-class, married, two kids, good job, enough to eat, then B-A-N-G! Those firecrackers changed things forever.

I sat at the dining room table, Sunday before Memorial Day, grading those papers I'd gathered. My family was still on their fishing trip. I glanced at the clock. It was late. If I stayed up and got this grading done I'd have one day of rest this weekend. So I stood and stretched, refilled my iced tea and checked on Peanuts.

I was reading the students' essays, writing comments with a pink pen. I couldn't bring myself to use red, too harsh. I was thinking about the school year about to come to a close and the next one yet to come at the same time. I didn't know it would be my last year teaching.

A tall Hispanic State Police officer and older, graying volunteer chaplain with thick glasses, wearing a gray polo shirt with a yellow Zia symbol, knocked on my door.

"Mrs. Roark? Aileen Roark?" The chaplain spoke first. He was shadowed by the state trooper, who removed his hat as I opened the door.

"Yes, how can I help you?" Were these two selling tickets to a raffle, why were they out so late?

"May we come in? We have some unfortunate news." His voice was soft, low. Great sadness marked his face.

My hands were shaking. I had a hard time unlatching the screen.

"Please come in." Peanuts, Stevie's black Belgian Shepherd, had been sleeping in the laundry room, finally realized we had visitors and trotted out front , a low growl stuck in his throat.

The State Trooper extended the fingers of one hand towards Peanuts who sniffed it tentatively before allowing him to scratch behind his ear. I followed them into the living room, the essays I was grading spread across the dining room table.

"Sit down." I motioned to the two club chairs, and sat on the sofa. Peanuts, believing this a command directed at him, sat in front of me.

I knew the words that would come next, don't ask me how, I just did. They began with "I'm sorry."

I didn't really listen, so I can't really tell you word for word exactly what they said. Sean was in the back of the truck, probably asleep. Stevie was in the passenger seat and Sam drove. It had been a hot day, and somehow in the dark, he must have dozed off or gone too fast or I don't know what. But he rolled the truck.

I sat, silent trying to absorb the news, a million questions spinning in my head, and ten million tears locked inside my heart. Then the news hit me, rolling over me, and I started trembling, my soul an epicenter of pain.

"Mrs. Roark? Are you okay? Can we call someone for you?" The trooper went to the kitchen and came back with a glass of water, wandered into the back hall, in search of a box of tissues. Peanuts followed him.

The chaplain sat beside me and consoled me as I wept. "We are so sorry for your loss Mrs. Roark."

Sean, thrown from the truck bed, died right away even though it took several hours to find his body. It was easily spotted once the sun rose. I pray that's true. It still breaks my heart to think about the tiny baby I nursed and soothed and carried in my heart and womb lying broken and alone on the side of a ravine calling to me in the dark.

Sam died next but not for several months. He walked away from the wreck with two broken ribs, a fractured wrist and a blood alcohol level twice the legal limit. He was arrested. What more can I say? He was drunk, he drove off the road, our youngest died, our oldest in intensive care. Those are the facts. I had to make five calls before I found a lawyer who would represent him. A lot of people think I should have left him. I almost did. Sam and I had been friends and lovers for over thirty years, thick and thin, rich and poor, sickness and health. Besides, who else did I have? I stood by him. The retainer was enormous, the judge set a huge bail, cash only, and the medical bills were outrageous. Sam missed a lot of work as did I. We used credit cards to cover basic day to day expenses. You know the rest.

I never made it back to school that year. Summer was a hazy slow motion blur of hospitals, funeral homes, grave yards and lawyers' offices.

Sam lost his job. Between the alcohol and the legal proceedings, he was counseled by his department head to consider his options. Which he did, opting for early retirement on less than half pay, about three thousand a month minus taxes and insurance, should anything happen to him I was to get half of that or fifteen hundred. We sold the house. It would have been impossible keep the payments, especially since we had remortgaged it to get enough for Sam's legal retainer. We managed to scrape together enough to lease a small plaza style townhouse. Rent was half our previous mortgage. But the bills kept rolling in: medical; legal; funeral; even the EMT's were after us since it was a drunk driving case. Stevie, at twenty six, was uninsured. A couple of months I missed the electric payment. I guess the thing to do would have been to declare bankruptcy, but consumed by the emotions of a grieving mother it never occurred to me that there was a business part of dying.

The injury to Sam's body was small; injury to his psyche was much greater, too great for him to bear. He started drinking almost every day, all day. Overcome with guilt he decided to cash in his chips the night before his trial. I came home to find Peanuts tied to the front porch, frantically scratching at the door. Sam was lying on our bed in a small cramped unfamiliar room with plastic mini blinds shut tight against the day's light; a plastic bag over his head and a helium tank nearby. He had placed a note on his chest with a little yellow sticky post-it. *Forgive me* printed in block letters with a blue pen was all it said.

Not many showed up for his funeral, not even my only brother. My sibling blamed me for Sam's drinking and Sean's death. In turning his back on Sam, he also excluded me.

August came, then September. I left early the first week of school. It was incredibly hard. A half day was all I could manage. The sight of all those hopeful young faces was unbearable. I'd burst into tears at unexpected moments. My students were incredibly compassionate and forgiving. Once, in the middle of a lesson, I choked up, put the chalk down and sat at my desk, head down, not saying a word. Amber, my 'I don't give a fart' homeroom menace, didn't miss a beat. She stood up and led the class reading aloud Chapter One. She knew what it meant to lose everything. I should have taken more leave but I had already used all of my paid days.

I missed more time. The school balked at my bereavement and assigned leave without pay. I filed a grievance to correct it.

After Sam died I couldn't even manage the Plaza Home on my teacher's pay. I had to break the lease to be free of the payment. I downsized again. I still had a car then, and Peanuts. It was hard to find a place that accepted dogs, especially one as big as Peanuts. I put most of the furniture in storage.

Stevie was lost in a forever dream. I would visit every day when I left school. My psyche was battered too, refused to heal.

Stevie, my beautiful golden haired first born son who I cheered in little league and cried when he got his diploma, who I made cookies with and crochet Christmas stockings for and sat in the school parking lot until past midnight waiting for the bus after soccer games, my beautiful boy, lingered. Massive head injury was the diagnosis.

Airlifted to the trauma center, I held out hope for months that he would wake up. The doctors and nurses worked overtime on this one. They saw what I did, a life so young, a body so perfect, a future so bright. But no light shone from his eyes. I tried everything too. Every time they pushed a paper in my face I would sign it: financial responsibility; medical release; legal papers I never read. I just signed believing they would be the key to getting my son back. No expense would I spare. I sold everything I had, my jewelry, my car, opting instead to drive Stevie's twelve year old Subaru. I used the Hardship Provision and pulled money from my Teacher's Pension. Anything, please, save my son. But it was not enough. I fought with my insurance company (What do you mean he wasn't covered?) and the hospital business office, begging for help. I wished someone had warned me it would never be enough.

The hospital legal department finally applied for guardianship. That can't really happen I thought. But it did.

I was no longer able to pay the bill and so not allowed to make decisions about his care. He was after all now twenty seven, a birthday uncelebrated and unremembered by anyone but me. They didn't even notify me when they moved him from the Premium Care unit of the long term care facility. I just showed up one day at four o'clock as I always did to find someone else in his place. Frantic, I ran to the nurses' station.

"Where's Stevie? What happened? Where is he?"

The LPN, a petite, older woman, Rita, with dyed red hair and a heart much too big for the job she had to do, gently led me down the hall and introduced me to the nurse sitting behind a kiosk. Patients who had no other means of support were transferred here. Four to a room, beds pushed against the wall, staff caseloads in line with National Averages. Nurses here were frequently pulled to meet the advertised services for paying customers of Premium Care, leaving Med techs and overworked, inexperienced staff members to make do in the basic care wing.

People told me it was a blessing Stevie didn't see or feel anything, but I didn't feel blessed. They said "You should get on with your life," or "It's God's will," or "They would want you to move on." I don't know why people think these word help. They didn't help me. Things I needed help with were much more concrete. How would I pay the bills? How do I cook for one? How do you change the oil for god's sake? Where do you go when you have nowhere left? I couldn't even figure out how to wash my clothes after I sold the washer and dryer.

People said, "If you ever need help with anything let me know." But when I reached out no one reached back.

So when people ask me "How did you become homeless?" My answer is no one helped and I couldn't get over it. That and those firecrackers.

3

Returning to school full time, when I finally did, was very, very difficult. I realize now I should have been grateful just to have a job, but at the time it didn't seem to be getting any better. In fact, it got worse. More and more of teaching time was taken up by assessments, and most if not all of the time for lesson prep was given over to data sessions, program and department meetings or teacher coaching sessions. Did anybody not get that we needed time to prep lessons, grade papers and meet with students?

With Stevie at the Basic Life Care Center, trying to get out of my lease on the Plaza Home, dealing with Sam's lawyers and worrying over bills, all the while searching for a place to rent that I could afford and would accept Peanuts, I kept getting further and further behind. When I didn't have enough time to prepare a proper lesson I would copy a class set of word searches and pass them out as a time filler. I was not alone among the faculty in doing this. I hated being that kind of teacher, but how on earth did the admin expect anybody to create more hours in a day? I was already spending two to three hours or more almost every night on curriculum lessons and grading. I just didn't have more time to give. I wanted to do something positive with my students, for me more than them.

"Good Morning Students." I greet the middle schoolers as they loiter by the classroom door.

The bell rang. Adolescent kids who only arose half an hour ago and still smelled of Dial soap and toothpaste, now came rushing in from their lockers.

"I want to remind everyone that we have assigned seats."

Two girls with hair-sprayed vertical bangs, got up, roll their eyes in a way only an eighth grader can and move to the correct spot, away from each other.

"Let's start our day with a vocabulary warm up." I turn and begin to write on the chalk board which was coated with chalk dust from yesterday. The school had switched from in house janitorial to contract cleaners. When I complained about the unwashed boards I was informed the contract was for sweeping and emptying trash only, that we, teachers, had to erase and wash our own boards every day and clean the classroom desks once a week or more. During flu season we also had to disinfect light switches, doorknobs, pencil sharpeners, faucets and keyboards nightly. Was this a wise use of my graduate degree I wondered?

"Take the letters a, two e's, h, r and..."

The intercom clicks on. "Mrs. Roark?"

"Yes?"

"Can you send Donald to the office please?"

"He's not here." Five kids shout back at the intercom. I try to shush them.

"Mrs. Roark is Donald here today?" Feedback from the intercom pierces the room. The kids yell and hold their ears.

"No, he hasn't come in yet." I try to continue writing on the board but have to turn around to speak in the direction of the intercom so my voice will be picked up.

"If he gets here will you send him to the office please?"

"Yes I will. Okay kids take out these letters." I continue to write them on the board while the students pull the one inch by one inch tag-board squares from the plastic baggie each has on their desk.

"Take three letters and spell ear." I glance around the room. A few have spelled *are*, that's a little discouraging from seventh and eighth graders, but this is a remedial reading class. I walk around and stop by Amber, help her rearrange the letters. She turns sideways in her seat and helps two boys beside and behind her rearrange theirs, has taken on the role of teacher's helper.

"Now add an h. What word?"

They shout it out. "Hear!"

"Now add S. What word?"

"Hears," they reply.

"Sorry, add S to the beginning of the word."

The intercom rasps on again. "Mrs. Roark is Donald here yet?"

"No, he's not." I try to make my voice high and sweet to mask the annoyance I really feel.

"Is he absent today?"

"Well he's not here."

"Okay, how about Luz. Is she here?"

"Yes, Luz is here."

"Can you send her to the office please?"

"Yes, Luz will you go to the office please?" I repeat back the request to be sure Luz will comply. Luz slams her notebook shut pushing the little tag board letters which start floating to the floor.

"Umbers!" A couple of students chide her.

She picks the letters up and sets them on her desk before walking out the door and slamming it behind her. Luz is known by the assistant principal as a frequent flier with a constant stream of office discipline referrals.

"Okay kids, where were we?" No one says anything. I write *Sh* on the board. "What sound?"

They yell out in unison, "Shear. We spelled shear."

"Great, can you tell me what shear means?"

"Like a cliff, it goes down."

"Good Nathan lets hold that meaning in our thoughts for a minute. Does it have another meaning?"

Luz comes back into the classroom and packs up her backpack.

One of the girls asks, "What happened? Are you in trouble?"

"No, I have to finish my Content Standards pre-test. They said I won't be done until third period and to take my stuff. Do I need a pass?" she asks me.

"No that's okay Luz, do your best." Luz hugs three girls and one boy as she walks out the door, like she will be gone for three months, not three hours.

"All right students, we were talking about *shear*." I move my hand under the word as I say it, emphasizing the sounds. "Nathan thinks it means a steep cliff. What do you think? Does anyone have a different answer?"

"Like when you get your hair cut, my aunt works at Shear Delights."

"Great example of word use Amber. When you cut something like your hair, you shear it. The tool you use is sometimes called shears."

"My uncle lost the wheel on his car. He said the bolt sheared off."

"Good Patrick, that's another..."

The door opens. A food service worker brings in a box piled high with cereal packs, cartons of milk and some oranges but only twelve, not enough for the whole class.

"Can I pass out breakfast?"

"Not now Patrick, we want to finish our lesson first, you said your uncle lost his wheel because the bolt sheared off."

"You should have seen it he was doing about ninety by my house, he was all wasted, and all of a sudden the wheel comes flying into the yard and..." Patrick is animated, using his hands to show the impact of the flying wheel.

"That's great, let's save the rest of the story for later. What about shear, what part of speech it? Does anyone know of another way to spell it? Does that change what it means? Think about Nathan's definition. Is it a noun or a verb or what?"

The kids all put their hands down, start playing with the letter tiles, try different combinations of letters.

The intercom comes on again. "Mrs. Roark?"

"Yes?"

"Is Patrick there? He needs to finish testing too."

Patrick jumps up, stuffs his stuff into his back pack. "I have to have my breakfast before I go." I nod at him. He grabs some food and rushes for the door.

"How come he gets to eat? When can we eat?" Amber says. Her indignant whine grates on me.

"Okay, I'll pass out the food, but I want everyone to get a dictionary and work with a partner to look up the word shear while I give out breakfast. We want to make a word web for the word shear. Find out if there is another way to spell it."

I get the list from the food box, mark off Patrick, and call each student up to get their food. Red asterisks are marked beside six names: "NO BREAKFAST until accounts are brought up to date" is hand printed on the bottom of the form with a bold marker. I walk over to each student with an asterisk, try to tell them privately, so that the other students can't hear, explain they need to pay before the kitchen will send them breakfast and wonder why I got stuck with this task. The students don't make anonymity easy.

"My mom gave them a check!" One says in protest.

"How come they get free breakfast and we don't?" Another asks.

"But I'm hungry now. I didn't have anything today, my grandma's been sick. All I had last night was Coke and Doritos."

One boy, Miguel, passes his box of cereal to one of the "NO BREAKFAST" students.

"You can have mine." He is sincerely concerned about their lack of food.

I'm supposed to keep this from happening. Students on free breakfast aren't allowed to give their food to another. How do you tell a generous kid he can't share with a hungry one? I don't say anything.

"Is everyone still trying to find the word shear? What does it mean? Is it a noun or a verb or adjective or what? Did anyone find another way to spell it? Maybe it's..."

"Mrs. Roark?" The intercom clicks on again.

"Yes?" Several kids get up to throw away empty cereal boxes and milk cartons.

"Is Miguel there? He..."

The kids all start shouting. "We know! We know! He needs to finish his test."

Rosa spills her bowl of cereal and asks to get paper towels from the restroom to clean it up. Miguel, ever the kind soul decides to help her clean up the mess before he leaves for testing.

Buzz. Crap, not the intercom again. How many interruptions is that now? "Mrs. Roark, have you sent Miguel to the office yet?"

"He's on his way now."

Miguel packs up his stuff and leaves. Donald walks in the door. He is perspiring even though it is chilly outside. I want to scold him about being tardy, but I have a hard enough time getting him to come to school, if I do upbraid him he may not come at all.

"Did you miss the bus Donald?" I smile, try to avoid being judgmental.

"My mom was out partying last night and I had to babysit my little niece, we overslept, I had to walk to school. Can I still get breakfast?"

The intercom buzzes. I give up.

"Mrs. Roark? Is Donald here yet?"

I sigh and pass out a stack of word searches.

4

October 1, I had to be out of the Plaza Home. I downsized to a one bedroom apartment, part of a triplex, in a much less upscale area of Santa Fe then I had lived in these past thirty years. I hesitate to call it a low rent district, since everything in Santa Fe was high priced, but in any other town it would be considered one. The apartment had a tiny enclosed back yard and patio. It was the only place I could find that accepted pets and I could manage on my take home pay. I had to have a place for Peanuts. It was small. The furniture barely fit. I tried to squeeze more into the storage locker, it was only ten by ten and stuffed floor to ceiling, but no such luck. I hired a couple of Stevie's buddies, former students of mine, to help me load and unload a rented truck.

"Hey Miss Roark, what do you want us to do with this stuff?"

"I guess we'll just have to leave it on the back patio until I figure it out. Can you carry it through?" I scanned the dining room table and credenza, what was I thinking when I moved them here? There was no way they would fit. Same for the sofa and love seat, love seat maybe, sofa only if I left everything else out; love seat and sofa? No way.

"Sure Miss, but we have to be going soon. Did you still need us to help you return the truck?"

"No, I left my car in the rental yard. I'll drive it over and make the switch."

As the boys walked back through I picked my purse up off the counter and retrieved the hundred dollars I had promised them.

"Here guys, thanks again."

"That's okay Miss, we don't need that much."

"No, you guys worked hard. If it hadn't been for you I would have had to go down to the skate park and hired someone from there. I'd rather pay someone I know."

"Okay, thanks." The two went outside and got into the old Accord parked in front of my new neighbor's place. I walked outside with Peanuts, watching as they drove off, holding the dog by the collar, since it was an unfamiliar place. We started back up the walkway to my end of the triplex. When I was maybe ten feet from the door I let go of Peanuts' collar. He immediately turned and let out a soft warning bark. A woman had opened the door of the place next to mine and started to step out, but took a step backward when she got a look at the big black shepherd by my side.

"Does he bite?" She was in her thirties, spiked short hair and a blue oxford shirt, untucked, hung loose over pleated khakis.

"No...Not...no, he just puts on a good show." I grabbed hold of Peanuts again and managed a closed lip smile, started to pull him inside. She came out and walked the ten feet across the narrow porch to my door, holding the finger of her hand toward Peanuts.

"What's his name?" She waved her fingers in front of Peanuts' nose.

By now Peanuts had tentatively sniffed acceptance of the hand and allowed her to turn it palm up and scratch under his chin.

"Peanuts, his name's Peanuts."

"Hey, Peanuts, I'm Dawn." I thought she was extending her hand towards Peanuts again then realized she was offering it to me.

"Aileen. Aileen Roark." I took her hand and let go of Peanuts collar.

"Welcome neighbor, or neighbors I should say. For a while I was worried those two guys in the Accord were moving in. Not that I have anything against guys."

"No, they were just helping me move. They're friends of my son."

"Oh? Does he live with you?" She peered around me into the open door of my apartment.

I hesitated. I didn't want to spend the next thirty minutes explaining to her. I was exhausted and not really ready to share that much with someone I had just met.

"No, not now anyway."

She sensed my hesitation.

"Sorry, didn't mean to be nosy. I'm right next door. Let me know if you need help with anything. I'll let you guys go, but welcome again." She backed away, Peanuts stepped after her.

"Thanks, I think I'm okay for tonight. But I need to figure out what to do with all my things. Nothing fits. Even my storage locker is full. Right now I have it all piled on the back patio."

"Yeah, I noticed. These places aren't that big. When I moved in I had to get rid of half my junk. If I get rid of more maybe I could move around." Dawn was rubbing Peanuts' head between both hands. I was glad. I'm never sure how people will react to such a big dog.

"I should get rid of things too I guess, I just don't know where to start."

"Have a yard sale," my new neighbor said. "I have them all the time. You can even have one at your storage locker. We can go together on it." Acquainted less than five minutes, she was ready to go into business. I looked around at the boxes inside and out, the furniture on furniture with little room to walk and extended my hand toward her.

"When can we start?"

"Great, great. How about this weekend? I'll get things ready we can start to pull stuff out and organize and by Sunday it'll all be done."

"That soon?"

"Why not?"

Why not indeed, so we did.

Friday after work I pulled it all together. Chairs, boxes of sheets and blankets, sleeping bags, dishes, nick-knacks, books, Sam's collection of LP records , all were piled up on makeshift tables and tagged with colored stickers, my things tagged with florescent orange dots, Dawn's with green.

"I put the ad in the *New Mexican*, also on Craig-list," Dawn pulled out her iPod and brought up the listing. "Great two family yard sale, quality items, LP collection, lots of furniture, no junk. Saturday only, eight to one; early birds pay double."

"Do you think that's enough time? Will people really be here that early?"

"Are you kidding? You don't do yard sales do you, especially in this town." She looked at me incredulous.

"No I don't. The last time I was at a yard sale was the fund raiser for my son's track team. I helped with set up and worked the middle shift. It was pretty slow when I was there."

Dawn pulled out a marker and started to hand letter *Yard Sale* on the side of a cardboard box.

"This is different, for one thing, since we have furniture you can expect everyone and their cousin to be here buying to resell in the consignment shops. Talk about storage lockers, there are people in this town who just buy stuff to keep in their storage locker until they have a sale of their own. That's why you can't price anything to low. The resellers are going to offer you about half whatever you ask so, figure out your bottom line then double it. Trust me it works."

"Should I put a price on everything? What about these candles?" I picked up a small shoebox of holiday candles. There were probably ten or eleven of them, gotten at the annual Christmas gift exchange, or bought from my students' fall fund raising catalog.

"If you really want to get rid of it make a sign 'Candles seventy five cents each or two for one dollar.' If someone wants the whole box say four fifty."

"These probably cost six or seven dollars each, they're brand new." I picked up a white angel, embedding with silver glitter, the top, where the wick was, had a small glass translucent halo that would shimmer in different colors when the candle was lit. It was still shrink wrapped with tag attached.

"Well you can ask what you want, but that kind of stuff doesn't sell unless you mark it cheap. The things that sell are furniture, sports equipment and linens. Clothes? Forget about it. Maybe a few of the nicer things like those Hawaiian shirts and peasant blouses, those you can ask twenty five dollars or more for, then take twelve, they'll sell, but as for the rest be prepared to take it to Good Will."

Dawn helped me price everything. Emotionally it was too hard for me. I removed pictures from frames stored them in a shoe box, wiped off holiday platters, books I'd read to my sons and had hoped to save for grand-kids. Everything I touched made me remember a part of my life I would never have again. I had to block the memories.

Exhausted, Dawn and I shared take out lo-mien and spicy beef with broccoli. I leaned back one last time in Sam's brown leather recliner (marked sixty, sell for thirty) and broke apart the wooden chopstick.

"So how do we keep track of whose is whose?"

"You are green." She reached into the bag to retrieve a fortune cookie before tossing me one.

"I thought I was orange?"

"Oh, ha-ha." She got up and opened the drawer of a two drawer file cabinet, hers, and pulled a manila folder out, tearing it in half. "Right, right you're orange. When you sell an item, take the tag and put it on half the file folder, at the end of the day, you total the green tags and I'll total the orange and we'll pay each other."

"But what about haggling? How do we do that?"

"Did you mark things twice what you'd take, the big things anyway?"

"Yes, mostly."

"Do you trust me?"

"Should I?"

"No, but do you?"

"Yes, if you trust me."

"Then we'll both take up to half the marked price, when you sell it write the selling price on the tag when you pull it."

"What if someone offers less than half?"

"Say no. If they're convincing I'll send them to you to negotiate and you do the same for me."

Peanuts sat in front of her, waiting for more bits of the spicy beef she offered him. The chile made him lap up tons of water. I was surprised he took it.

She stood up. "I think this stuff will be okay, your dog will bark if anyone comes around."

"Does he?" I didn't know Peanuts barked when I wasn't around.

"Yeah, I hear him all the time." Dawn put her hands in her pockets.

"Sorry. I didn't know it bothered you."

"It doesn't bother me, actually it's good. I know when someone's around. But I do hear him."

"Sorry, I haven't lived in an apartment in a long time. I forgot you can hear everything."

"It's okay. The guy who was here before used to have loud parties almost every weekend. Having you in there is kind of nice. That's why I was a little freaked out when I say those two guys in the Accord moving stuff in. A friend of mine was kind of interested in this place but her lease where she lives now, didn't expire until February, your place is a little bigger than the rest."

"Have you lived here long?" I gathered up the empty take out boxes to toss away.

"One year in December." Dawn cracked her fortune cookie and pulled a thin strip of paper from the crumbs in her hand. "You will have new beginnings if you can free yourself of your past. What does yours say?"

I picked up the cookie still in its wrapper, tore open the cellophane, picked the already broken cookie out, feeding the pieces to Peanut and unrolled the tiny fortune tucked inside.

"There will be stormy seas ahead. Friendship and faith will guide you to calmer waters."

How did it know?

5

The yard sale went better than I expected. Just like Dawn said there were a lot of early birds who wanted the furniture. The books sold well, only a handful of nick knacks sold. I was surprised more clothes didn't sell. I had already taken Sam's things to Good Will when I moved; most of what was left was woman's wear. The nicer pieces, more formal dresses and business suits, went first, followed by sweaters and blue jeans. When it was all over Dawn had made one hundred and ninety five dollars and I cleared just shy of three hundred. It didn't seem much for all the furniture I sold, but it would cost me more than that to rent a truck and move them, besides my storage locker was full. I would have all of Sunday to put things away and time, hopefully, to visit Stevie and do a little grading.

I loaded the rest up for Good Will. Dawn poked her head out the door.

"Hey Aileen, can you take a couple things for me too?" She placed two brown paper bags on the table by the door.

"I thought you sold most of your stuff."

"Most of it. I have some blankets. I've been saving them for a blanket drive at work, but I guess they only want new blankets."

I took the bags from her. Each held three or four worn acrylic blankets or quilts.

"Where did you get these?" Two of them were children's bedspreads with cartoon characters imprinted on them.

"Other people's yard sales, at the end of the day a lot of people just give stuff away."

"Why didn't you tell me that yesterday? It would have saved a trip."

"I don't know, didn't think about it I guess. Do you mind taking them?"

"No, it's okay."

I loaded the stuff into the car. After school tomorrow, I thought, if there wasn't a staff meeting, I would hurry to make it by four o'clock, the latest donations were accepted.

Monday after the last bell I rushed to the office to make a few copies. Three thirty, on the dot, I locked my classroom door and hurried to my car for the drive to Goodwill. I got there just in time. A worker came out from the loading dock to help me.

"Is it clean? We can only accept clean items in good repair; otherwise we end up taking it to the dump."

"Yes." I held up a pair of blue twill pants and a summer blouse. "It's all in good shape. I'm not sure about the blankets though, they're from my neighbor."

The woman pulled out the top blanket. It had a large stain in the lower left corner and a rip along the top binding. She quickly stuffed it back into the bag. "Sorry no, we can't accept these, sorry."

"Can I just put them in the dumpster?"

"No, we get charged for pick up. You can try the shelter on Cerrillos Road, they may accept them. They wash everything before they hand it out."

"You guys don't?"

"No we just put it on hangers."

I thought about Stevie's college years. He and his roommates would buy twenty shirts on dollar bag day, then donate them back after they were worn believing they would buy them back washed and pressed a week later.

("Mom it's cheaper than doing your own laundry," Stevie would say. "Boys." I would shake my head in exasperation.)

I refolded the blankets and put them back into the bags. "Do you know if the shelter stays open? It's four now."

"Yes, they don't even open until four."

I drove over there. Three or four dozen men and about a dozen women, a few with kids, lined up along the front wall and around the side of the building. Some were teenagers. Others were older, thin, street weary. They barely glanced up when I pulled into the lot. There were not many empty parking spots. Many cars were packed with sleeping bags, piles of clothes and plastic boxes of towels, pans and tarps. The worldly treasures owned by people who live in their cars. All that would fit anyway.

I grabbed the two bags of blankets from the back of the Subaru and started towards the entrance.

"They're not open yet." A man with dreadlocks and a multi colored crochet beret was sitting on the sidewalk in front of the entrance, leaning back on his elbows.

"I thought they opened at four."

"Four, more or less. They open when they are ready for everyone. Besides you have to get in line."

He looked up at me, smiling, his two front teeth chipped like he had been sucker punched. He tilted his head sideways towards the end of the long line of bedraggled men, women and children that snaked around the front and sides of the building.

I was embarrassed. I don't know why. "I'm not here for that," I said. "I have some blankets to donate. Do you think someone is there?"

"You could knock but they won't open until they're ready." He stood up and looked at the two bags encircled by my arms. "I could take them for you."

"Could you? That would be great. Maybe there's something you want, why don't you look?" I set the bags down on the pavement. Two men stepped out of line and towards us.

"Yes, I'll take a look." He bent down and pulled two blankets from the first bag, handing one to each of the men who had come over. A young woman with two little girls walked up from mid-way in the line.

"Here, sunshine, just the blanket for you." The guy with dreadlocks handed a little girl with deep brown eyes a quilt with yellow unicorns dancing on a rainbow. "And one for you star-bright, a blanket of stars to keep you warm." He gave the other quilt, a plump cartoon bear swinging on a star, to the younger girl who clung to her sister's hand.

"What do you say girls?" their mother said, prompting them.

"Thank you Lenny."

"Don't thank me, thank this nice lady here." Lenny grinned with that chipped tooth grin.

"Thank you, nice lady." The girls clutched their new security blankets and skipped back to the line, their mother trailing behind them.

I smiled. "You're welcome."

They were so young, even their mother was probably no more than twenty four or five. What had happened in their young lives to lead then to the shelter?

A few more stepped from line, two men and a teenage couple with a pit bull mix on a leash.

"Got any more?"

"Any left?"

Lenny reached into the second bag and pulled out the blankets, tossing them underhanded to the intended recipient. The blanket with the large stain was the only one left. He looked at the teenagers.

"You know you can't stay here with the dog."

"We just want to get a shower and something to eat, we'll take turns holding him out here," the teenage girl said.

Lenny nodded. "Is this for you or the dog?"

The couple looked at each other, trying to come up with the answer that would win them the blanket.

"Both."

"Yeah, we share."

"Here then, you probably should wash it if you have a chance." Lenny waded up the blanket and flipped it towards them.

"Thanks Lenny," they said in unison. Lenny made a clicking noise with pursed lips and extended his open palms in my direction.

"Thanks nice lady." A dozen people called out, some sincere others mocking. I waved anyway.

"You're welcome." Got in my car and went home.

6

November, the days blur together. I exist by keeping a routine to keep myself going: Walk Peanuts, school, visit Stevie, walk Peanuts, grade papers, get up and do it again the next day.

Friday morning is a school assembly. Student Council will hold a food drive and this is the kick off. The class that brings in the most food wins a pizza party. We end the day in Homeroom, both to solidify plans for the food drive and distribute report cards. My unruly bunch is not happy to get theirs.

"How come I got a D in History?"

"I have to have two point five GPA to play basketball how do I know what my GPA is?"

The questions go on and on.

"Okay students, you need to bring the report cards back, signed, on Monday. If I don't have them by Tuesday I'm supposed to call your parents," I say in my best serious teacher voice. "And don't forget to bring in a can of food for the food drive."

"What are they going to do with the food?"

"I don't know Luz; give it to the Soup Kitchen I guess."

"What's that?"

"It's where all the bums and dirty hippies eat," Patrick says, his voice loud and annoying.

"What like your Dad?" Donald says, yelling back at him. Patrick's dad is in prison.

"No like your Mom." Patrick kicks Donald's desk. Donald's mom has a drug problem; she comes in and out of his life with some regularity so Donald usually stays with his grandmother.

Donald gets up and starts towards Patrick, fists ready for a fight. I quickly walk between them, "Settle down you two. It's Friday, we start a new nine weeks on Monday, don't start off the grading period in In School Suspension."

The boys glare at each other, I know if I don't do something now the fight will carry over to the bus.

"Come on boys, you don't want this, you used to be friends. Shake hands and apologize." I say trying to cajole them.

They continue to glare and mad dog each other. Miguel, the peacemaker, pats Donald on the back. "Come on bro, he didn't mean anything. It's all good, just say you're sorry."

"He started it," Donald says and snarls his lip.

"Well you both need to end it. Seriously, if you can't I'll have to send you to the office, both of you." I look sternly at them then walk towards my desk, pretend to look for a pen and office discipline form.

Patrick goes first, he extends his hand at an angle, "Siento, dude, lo siento."

Donald hesitates, "Okay then, okay, it's cool, we're cool. I apologize too." He takes Patrick's hand and does the Bro shake. I sigh, hope that really does settle it, and turn my attention back to Luz.

"But in answer to your question Luz the soup kitchen is where a lot of people who don't have anything to eat or are homeless go to get a meal. I was just at the homeless shelter a couple of weeks ago. There were moms with kids and some teenagers not much older than you guys." I fold my arms and half sit on the edge of my desk.

"Why were you there Miss Roark are you homeless?" Patrick doesn't know when to shut it.

"No, not yet, Patrick. I was there to donate some blankets, my neighbor and I had a yard sale and no one bought the blankets."

"They need blankets?"

"Heck yeah." Miguel says, getting up from his seat. "Think if you have to sleep outside, you'd be really cold, like you could freeze to death." He crosses his arms around his body and pretends to shiver. "Maybe we should have blanket drive." Miguel can be so endearing.

"Yes, they did need blankets, and a blanket drive would be great, but the Student Council voted on a food drive."

"Ah, we never win the pizza anyway. We should just do our own drive. We could all bring in blankets." Donald is into it. Several other kids support him.

"Okay guys, I'll tell you what, if the class can bring in at least five blankets..."

"Each? Five blankets each?" Luz looks concerned.

"No, Luz, five total. The whole class, get together and bring in five blankets, I'll buy the pizzas."

"How many?" Donald uncrosses his legs and turns from sitting sideways in his desk to front and center.

"How many what?" I've lost them somewhere. Did they mean blankets or pizzas?

"Pizzas, how many pizzas will you buy?"

"Five. I'll buy five large pepperoni pizzas." If I thought that settled it I was wrong, that's why I love middle schoolers so much, they are always trying to work they system.

Miguel butts in. "I like sausage," he says.

"Okay, I'll get four pepperonis and one sausage."

"Can I bring Cokes?" Luz is excited. If she can keep herself from being suspended she might make the party.

"Yeah and I'll bring Cheetos." Amber, slouching low, puts down the mirror she is always checking her bangs in and sits up straight in her desk.

"Wait, kids, let's get the blankets first." I hold the chalk in one hand and try to calm them down, waving it back and forth like I'm conducting a choir.

"If we bring in more blankets do we get more pizza?" Donald is psyched up.

I do the math in my head. At the six ninety-nine special five pizza's would set me back thirty-five dollars plus tax, three more would bring it up to just under sixty. I still have a little yard sale money left, that should cover it.

"Okay, if you bring in more than five blankets, we can have eight pizzas."

"How many more?"

"Three more, if you bring in eight blankets I'll get eight pizzas, five pepperonis and three sausages. And you can bring coke and chips."

"What about cheese?" Amber asks.

"Okay, okay, eight pizzas." I turn and mark off a box with yellow chalk in the upper corner of the board, write a math equation: 4 pepperoni + 3 sausage +1 cheese= 8 blankets.

"What if we bring in ten blankets do we get ten pizzas?" Patrick would keep going if I let him.

"No, sorry, I can't afford ten pizzas, but if you bring in ten blankets, I'll throw in a bag of Red Vines."

"Do they have to be new?" Luz asks.

"No, just be sure they're clean, and nothing torn or in really bad shape."

"For reals? We get to have a party of we bring blankets?" Donald wants to be sure I'm not leading them on.

"Absolutely." I circle the equation I have just written on the board.

"When?" Luz asks.

"When what?"

"When do we need to bring in the blankets? When will we get pizza?"

"Next Friday. If you bring in at least five blankets by next Friday, we can have a pizza party. You can bring cokes and chips. If you bring in eight blankets, we'll have eight pizzas. I'll bring in a big bag of Red Vines if you bring in ten."

They brought twenty.

7

*F*riday was the day before a long weekend. Monday would be Veteran's day, followed by two days of teacher in-service. For a lot of students these school breaks are hard. School was someplace they felt safe, it was warm, no one was drunk or yelling at them. Many kids acted out the day before a break, but today my students were happy, they had met a goal and were enjoying pizza. Somebody had brought in cupcakes.

"Miguel, can you fix a plate for Mr. Valdez, the security guard?" I have to stand guard over the pizzas or the boys will snag all the slices leaving little for the girls.

"We'll do it!" Luz and Amber jump up.

"Fix a couple for the secretaries too, a slice of pizza, some chips and dip." I say to them, hand them each a paper plate.

"What about a cupcake?" Amber picks up a cupcake. The frosting sticks to her hand and she licks her fingers, still holding the cupcake, then sets it back with the rest, selects a different one. I think about it but don't correct her. After they are gone I'll toss away the rejected cupcake.

"Sure give them one too."

Patrick just couldn't let things go. "How come they get some of our pizza? They didn't bring any blankets."

"Because, Patrick, you want to keep them on your good side." I say. It's time to learn a lesson about real life I think.

"Yeah, they could report us huh Mrs. Roark." Luz, frequent flier that she is, knows the unwritten code.

"That's right. We're not supposed to have parties like this." I say to the students as they stuff giant slices of pizza, folded over like a tortilla, into their mouths.

"But the Student Council and Honor Society have them all the time." Patrick hangs on like a bull dog. He knows the unwritten code too, if you're an honor roll student or your parents have money the rules are not enforced, it's the land of unequal opportunity.

"That's because they're all lambe, huh Miss Roark." Luz doesn't even try to edit herself.

"Luz, we don't say things like that in school. That will get you in trouble." I try not to scold when I say it. A lambe, for those unaware can be translated as a 'butt licker' or someone who 'sucks up'. It is not a nice word.

"But it's true they are. You're not all lambe, huh Miss?"

"Well I try not to be. But I do try to get along with everyone and I want you to take those plates to the office and Mr. Valdez."

Patrick protests. "That's lambe, giving away our pizza."

Patrick, I think to myself, why can't you shut up. But I don't say it, instead I say, "Enough already. I don't want any of you to use that word again. Patrick, just enjoy your pizza." I shake my head. The kids settle down. They are happy. Today will be a good day for them.

Miguel has taken his three slices, but shares two of them with other kids. "When are you going to take the blankets Miss?"

"Today, if I make it in time. I'll load them up at lunch and take them after school."

"Can we go with you?" Luz asks. She and Amber feel empowered. I trusted them enough to give out plates of food to the staff, and now they want to keep the ball rolling.

"I can't take anyone with me. Teachers aren't allowed to take students without a permission slip, especially not in our own cars, but if your parents want to bring you, then that's okay."

"Are there really little kids there?" Amber asks.

"Yes, yes there are, and teenagers, and families."

"Can we put the blankets in your car for you?" Donald, the student who started this wants to see it to the end.

I was reluctant but they seemed so earnest, the blanket drive had been their idea, they had planned it and followed through, they owned it all the way.

"Sure, as soon as we clean up the trash, we can all take a blanket and walk out to my car and put them in."

The kids scurry around. A couple of boys pick up the trash can and walk up and down the rows collecting all the trash. Two girls get paper towels and follow wiping the desks down. The kids line up, not quickly, not without pushing and shoving, but they did line up, manage to each grab a blanket or two and follow me out to my car. I watch them as they each put a blanket in back of the wagon. Amber and Luz take charge of how they are stacked. I think of my own boys, one dead and buried, the other barely living. I hope your families know how special you are I think as I follow them back in and say a silent prayer asking God to watch over them.

8

It was well after four o'clock when I pulled into the shelter lot. As before, most of the parking spaces were full. The line to get in was much shorter, but it was because most were already inside. I walked to the entrance, excusing myself past those waiting.

"Sorry, I'm just here to drop off a donation."

Two volunteers, a man and a woman, stand behind what probably used to be a checkout counter.

"We do need you to wait in line, may not have enough space tonight," the woman says. She is stern, but not mean.

"Oh, no, I'm here to donate some blankets. My students had a blanket drive and I have twenty blankets in my car. I wanted to know where to take them." I juggle the keys with my hand and wonder if I remembered to lock the car.

The man calls over his shoulder. "Adam, we have a lady here wanting to donate blankets."

An older man, thin, with glasses, comes out from the back room.

"Hello. I'm Adam Beverly, how can I help you?" He extends his hand towards me.

"How do you do." I shake his hand. "My class held a blanket drive. They wanted to donate them here. Can I bring them in?"

"How many do you have?" Adam continues to hold my hand with both of his.

"Twenty, I have twenty." I gently extract my hand.

"Wow, they have been busy."

"Yes, I promised them a pizza party if they could collect at least five, twenty is great. I'm very proud of them."

"If you drive your car around back, to the door there, I'll meet you and help bring them in." Adam walks me out the door.

I pull the Subaru around back. Adam is just propping open the door. Lenny, the guy with the dreadlocks and beret that helped me last week is with him.

"Ah, you're back nice lady?" Lenny grins with his chipped teeth.

"Do you two know each other?" Adam takes four blankets and hands them to Lenny.

"Sort of, I was here last week." I stand beside the open wagon back, jiggling my keys again.

"Oh?" Adam looks surprised.

"I was helping her with another donation so to speak." Lenny shuffles the blankets to one hand and extends his arm, bent at the elbow, to accept some more. "You have more blankets for us."

"Yes, my class collected them, I told them how I came here last week and they wanted to donate something too."

"A teacher, you're a teacher and a nice lady?" Lenny follows Adam inside, both with armfuls of blankets. I grab a few more and follow.

"Do you have a name nice teacher lady?" Lenny sets the blankets down on some metal shelving then turns to take the ones I carry. I get the sense his clipped British accent is for show, not for real.

"Aileen. Aileen Roark." We walk back out to the car and Adam and Lenny pile the rest of the blankets in their arms. I close the back hatch.

"Thank you, nice teacher lady Aileen Roark. Tell your students thank you for us," Lenny replies.

Adam hurries in, stacks the blankets and comes back out to shake my hand. "What school did you say you were from?"

I tell him.

"Please thank your students for me. I'll send a letter to them but do let them know how much we appreciate it. If you or your class is interested, we're having a Thanksgiving meal. We always need volunteers and donations. I can get you a flier about it?"

"Yes, that would be great." I'm not really interested but don't want to seem rude. Adam walks inside and comes back out with an orange paper, folded in thirds; *Make this a Thanksgiving for Everyone*. It lists the details of the meal service and what is still needed.

"Thanks, I'll look it over." I take the flier from him.

"Hope you can make it, even if you can't volunteer, everyone is welcome to eat. Bring your family." He goes back inside.

I get in my car. Lenny comes out, uses his foot to push the rock aside so the door will close. "See you Thanksgiving nice teacher lady Aileen."

"Maybe," I say, resting my arm on the car door frame about to pull it closed.

"I'm pretty sure I will." He flashes that chipped tooth grin and gently closes my car door for me.

9

*N*umb. That's the word for it I guess. I'm on automatic pilot, sleep walking through the day and night. Anybody who has been through this will tell you the days are easy. It's the night's that get to you. I got to be good friends with the TV paid programing hosts and audience members, could tell you by name who sold what. I had, in fact, memorized the dialog for some of them. Exercise equipment, weight loss systems, acme creams and cooking devices, I could tell you everything you care to know. Sleep, when it did come was not restorative and I often woke with a headache. Some days I drank four or five cups of coffee before I got to work just to stay awake during the drive there.

Honestly, money was very, very tight. I shouldn't have splurged on that class pizza party, but who else did I have to spoil? I still didn't have Sam's check figured out, was told I had to wait ninety days to file for benefits, which I found out later wasn't true. I kept getting bills marked final notice from lawyers, air ambulance companies, and auto insurance policies for cars I no longer owned. The monument company was threatening to repossess the markers for Sam and Sean's grave. I had made the down payment with a credit card, but was supposed to pay off the rest within sixty days, fat chance of that happening. Stevie had run up a few thousand on his credit cards, as had Sam. I wasn't quite sure what to do. Stevie wasn't deceased, but he wasn't really living either. Companies came after me for Sam's debts. I got calls at work as well as home. Eventually I just ignored them.

All the rest? Bills I had run up? If I could make a payment, even a small one, I did. If I couldn't, I didn't. The late fees and surcharges kept piling up, the interest rate on credit cards tripled or quadrupled, I was no longer a 'Platinum Rewards' customer. At some point, I reasoned, I would start to get the spousal survivor benefit from Sam's pension and would get caught up. But it never, ever, occurred to me, in my worst nightmare, I was one lost paycheck away from joining the line at the soup kitchen.

Daylight hours were short. By the time I got home from school it was already dark. Peanuts and I often took a shortened walk, morning and evening, with a flashlight in hand. I started to take special notice of the smells when we did. First it was green chile roasting, and then wood smoke and decayed leaves, which soon gave way to the morning smell of frost that stings the nose when you first breathe it in. If I was lucky, I caught sight of a sinking pale moon just beyond the Jemez Mountains. Watching the stars shift beyond the dark lavender peaks and red rock mesa to the west was one of the only joys I had left, that and Peanuts' wet tongue waking me in the morning.

Wednesday morning before Thanksgiving was cold and clear but wind was expected later that day. I don't know if it was my imagination or not, but I swear I could already smell turkey cooking as Peanuts and I made the rounds for our morning constitutional. I still didn't know what I would do the next day. When I arrived at school that morning the math teacher extended a last minute invitation.

"Listen Aileen, I don't know if you have plans or not but I want to invite you for Thanksgiving. I have this great cousin, Sal, he just separated from his wife and I know you two would hit it off. Why don't you come?" Seni, in her late forties, had never married. She was always figuring the odds of staff having an affair, with whom and by when, and was right more often than not.

"Boy Seni, you know I love your cooking, but it's just too soon for me to even think about that. I'll probably help out at Stevie's ward. They try and let as many staff take off as they can on Thanksgiving weekend and I know they can always use an extra set of hands at meal times." I would have appreciated the meal, but I was a long, long way from hitting it off with someone. Sam had only been gone a few of months.

"Oh, I guess I didn't realize Stevie had improved so much that he was eating again. Wow. That must make you feel great." Seni stirred a second pack of sweetener into her mega-giant cup of coffee.

"He hasn't. He's still in a coma. I was thinking of all the other patients there. Some of them only need help with dressing and eating, things like that. It's something I can do and still be around Stevie."

I dumped my own coffee, grown cold, into the sink and rinsed the cup before placing it top down on a small paper towel lined tray beside the sink in the teachers' lounge. It was more like a closet, barely big enough for a small table and three, not two, not four, but three chairs and a desk phone on top of a book case that also served as the teachers' mail boxes.

"Suit yourself. But I know you two would get along." Seni headed for her classroom, giant coffee cup in hand. I followed her out the door. My own room was directly across the hall. I seldom took coffee or other foods into the class when kids were present. For one thing who had time?

"I do appreciate the invitation Seni, I'm just not ready to socialize yet. Have a good one."

The bell rang. A sparse group of students filed in from the cold and shuffled towards their lockers.

School would only be in session a half day. It might as well be a full day off the attendance was so low. It wasn't the A students who came today, it was the opposite. For many of these kids, as rough as things were for them at school, home was worse. I brought word board games, a short story to read aloud, a stack of word searches and my hot air popcorn popper. If none of us could have a good day at home, maybe we could have one here at school today.

"Good morning students. Is everyone ready for a long weekend?" I stood in front of the class holding a Scrabble game. Only ten of my twenty plus students were present.

"Are we going to do work today?" Donald got right to the point.

"I was hoping we could play a game of Scrabble or two and read a story."

"Can we sit anywhere? Do we need our notebooks?" Luz was still standing, even though the bell had long since rung.

"Yes Luz, today you can sit anywhere, and no, you don't need your notebooks."

Luz looked content and took a seat three rows over, next to Kateri and Shania.

"Okay students, sit with a partner. Let's play Scrabble. Teams of two, two people keep score."

"Can we have three in our group? We're the only girls?" Shania has already scooted over to allow Luz to share her seat in one desk.

"Sure, why not." Today I'd say yes to almost anything.

"I'll keep score." Miguel jumps up and begins erasing the board. Maybe I can talk him into washing it too.

The students help me push the desks together, we set up the board and I give a quick rundown on the rules.

"Everyone, think of a name for your team, Miguel write it down in columns."

"Can we be any name?" Donald asks. I cringe and think I know what's coming next.

"Anything that is acceptable at school, no gangs or bad words."

"We're Westside." Donald tests my patience.

"No. Sorry, no Westside. Think of another one."

"That's all cheap." Donald flashes his homeboy sign as he says this.

"Stop it Donald, don't blow it today. Just think of another name, okay?"

"Yeah, Donald, just think of another name okay, we don't want to blow it." Miguel practices his English by repeating what I say.

"Fine, then, we're the Homeboys."

"Okay Donald, you can be the Homeboys," I say to him.

The superintendent walks in the door. This is the first time she has ever visited my classroom. Why did she pick today, a half day before Thanksgiving, to do a school walk through?

I am surprised. "Good Morning Dr. Roybal, Happy Thanksgiving." Just grin and bear it I think.

Arms crossed in front of her, without greeting any of us, she walks around the group of desks where I have the students clustered around the game board. The popcorn popper, which I had set up when I first arrived, starts spitting fluffy white kernels into a plastic punch bowl. One of the students must have flipped it on when I wasn't looking. It pulls the superintendent's attention. She is the one who looks surprised now.

"Popcorn?" She looks at me, arms still crossed. "You know we can't serve food in the classroom."

I think about the daily breakfast in the classroom and bite my tongue before I say something sarcastic.

"I do know, but being Thanksgiving I thought it would be okay." I hope none of the kids let it slip about our pizza party a couple weeks back.

She nods, looks around the room again, "This is a small class."

"We have a lot of students out today, about half the class is gone."

"Teachers are gone too I noticed." Her tone is accusatory, like this is my fault.

I try to smile. "We're here."

Donald chimes in, "Yeah, we're here," he says.

Please, oh please, God, don't let Donald mouth off today or flash his gang signs again.

Dr. Roybal doesn't say anything, just circles the room and walks out the door. About three minutes later ten students from another class appear at my door, plop down their backpacks and sit in the empty desks.

"Where are you all coming from?" I ask them, taken aback.

"Mr. Maestas' room, he's gone today and they told us to come here," a student I know only by sight, not name, replies.

"Didn't you have a sub?" I am slightly annoyed.

"Yes, but that lady sent her home and told us to come here."

"What lady?" I ask.

"I don't know, that lady walking around."

"The lady in the blue jacket, kind of short, with glasses?" The annoying one who only shows up the day before a holiday to harass the teachers who are here I think.

"Yes, she said we didn't need a sub, that you could watch us."

I nod, it's not his fault. Another group of eight students walk through doorway. All but two desks are now occupied.

"Let me guess, your teacher is out today and Dr. Roybal sent you here, is that right?"

"Yeah she told Mrs. DeAguirre that she could go home, that the school didn't need a sub for just eight students."

The kids are restless, kicking the desks in front of them, talking too loud. I buzz the office. It takes a while before anyone answers.

"Yes Mrs. Roark, how can we help you?" The secretary is always so cheerful.

"Good Morning, can you tell me if there are any lesson plans for the classes Dr. Roybal sent to my room?"

"Just a minute Mrs. Roark, I'll check." I hear the intercom click off.

The secretary comes back on.

"Mrs. Roark? No, no one seems to be able to find a lesson plan for either class."

One of the guest students speaks up. "We were supposed to watch a movie about comets or something, but the TV is locked up and nobody has a key."

Four more students wander in. There are no more empty desks. I send them over to the teachers' lounge to get the three chairs from the break table and offer up my chair which prompts an argument about who gets to sit in the wheeled desk chair and roll around the room.

"Is the principal here today? Maybe she has a key." I have to shout into the intercom on the wall to be heard above the class din.

"No, she took today off, so did the assistant principal. I'll look around for a key, but you may just have to wing it Mrs. Roark." Her response is barely audible, but Miguel hears it.

"Yeah, Miss, just wing it." Miguel says, mimics me. He is pushing Donald up and down the aisles in my chair.

I look at the kids packed in every corner of my room, the Scrabble game set up and waiting for players, the short story I had hoped to read aloud as readers' theater, the contraband popcorn I can't serve. I pass out the word searches. There aren't enough to go around. Just wing it I think.

"Work with a partner. When you are done finding the words, turn the paper over and create your own word search using fifteen of the twenty words from the list I will write on the board. Then trade with another group and solve their word search."

I grab a wet paper towel, do my best to clean a week and a half's accumulated chalk dust from one area of the board and write twenty words; *Pumpkin, stuffing, turkey, football, parade*; you get the idea. So much for my nice day.

By lunch time, it feels like two thirds of the school is missing, maybe more. All morning long parents have been getting off early from work and picking up their kids. Teachers leave early too. Even Seni saunters by my room last period, which is only twenty five minutes long, and asks me to watch the three students who showed up for her class. I acquiesce, hope she'll return the favor one day and she slips out a good hour early. When the final dismissal bell rings, I stand outside, one of only three teachers still on duty, keep close watch while kids board the bus. Donald, Luz, Miguel and the others all smile and wave at me as it pulls out. A few of the kids I babysat, truthfully that's all it was, wave too. I wave back, pull my sweater up around my neck and head inside.

There are about a dozen pumpkin pies lined up on the counter by the office where the metal security gate is already pulled halfway down.

"Where did these come from?" I ask the secretary.

She is already closing down her computer, switching the telephones over to automatic answering, and locking her desk.

"One of the parents donated them. I guess he runs a bakery and they made extra or something so he brought them to school. Take one, or two or three. Most of the staff has already picked one up." She stashes the attendance rosters in a locking file cabinet and reaches for her coat.

I think about the flier for the Thanksgiving Meal at the shelter still setting on my dashboard.

"What will happen to them if no one takes them?"

"I don't know, I guess they'll just get thrown away."

"Can I have some to take to the homeless shelter? I have a flier in my car about their Thanksgiving meal tomorrow, they were looking for donations."

"Sure, just leave three for the cleaning crew, take the rest."

"The cleaning crew that does such a fine job on my boards and wiping down the desks?"

It was a mean thing to say. I think one of the contracted staff is her nephew.

She shrugs her shoulders, pulls the security gate all the way down, and grabs a couple of pies.

"I'll help you load them."

We walk out to my car, each balancing several pies in our arms, and I open the back, set them on the floor, hope they won't shift too much. The parking lot is empty save for her car, mine and the cleaning crew. She walks over to her car and gets in.

"Have a wonderful Thanksgiving." She waves as she pulls out, anxious to get home and start cooking.

"You too, thanks for the pies." I'm not in such a hurry, have nobody to start cooking for. I walk slowly back to the building, hope the door is still ajar so I won't have to pound on it to get the cleaning contractor's attention.

Patrick, my doesn't know when to shut up student, appears behind me.

"Hey Patrick, where were you today? We missed you." I turn to greet him.

"Did the buses already leave?" He asks me, a little worried.

"Yeah buddy, they did. Where were you?" I already know the answer, he came to school on the bus then took off ditching, hoping to catch the bus home but forgot it was a half day of classes.

"I guess I missed the bus." He looks truly forlorn.

The door is still ajar and he follows me in. "Do you want to use the phone in the teachers' lounge to call somebody?" I unlock the door to my classroom.

"No, nobody's there." Patrick comes in, tries to figure out which is his assigned seat amidst the chaos left by my overflowing classes today. He finally settles on the third seat in the third row even though no one is there to sit in any of the others.

"What happened in here? Why is everything so messed up?" He slinks low in his seat, long legs and high top Converse basketball shoes with holes in the canvas sides, extending four feet or more into the aisle.

"We had some extra students today. The teachers were gone so they came to my class." I start to pack up the pieces of the un-played Scrabble game, straighten the papers. "Don't you have someone that can come and get you buddy?" I remember his dad is in prison.

"No." He sits staring at the desk he didn't occupy earlier today.

I look at him and realize we both have no one waiting for us.

"Patrick, if you'll help me get this place straightened out I'll give you a ride home, but don't tell anyone okay, we're not supposed to." I pat him on the back.

"Okay." His spirit lifts a little, he gets up, starts putting the desks in order, returns chairs, helps me wash the board. "What about this popcorn? Is it any good?"

"Yeah, have some. I was going to give it out, but oh well, it just didn't happen. Here, here's a grocery sack, fill it up and take it home." I hold the bag open while he pours it in, stopping to stuff handfuls into his mouth.

It's close to two o'clock. I turn out the lights and lock the door. Patrick follows me out to the car. It is blustery and I hold my sweater as tight as I can around me.

"Where's your jacket Patrick? Is it still in your locker? It's cold, buddy, better go get it."

"No, I didn't wear one. I'm all right." He gets in my car. I have to remind him to buckle up.

"Where to? Where are you living now?"

"I guess to my grandma's she's up in Seco."

"Seco? Sure thing." I back the car around, look over the seat and check the pies to make sure they are still okay.

I turn the radio on. There are two minutes of music followed by ten minutes of commercials for Black Friday Sales. Some stores will even be open tomorrow, Thanksgiving. I flip it off, try to make conversation. For a kid who doesn't know when to shut up at school, he's not saying a lot now.

"So, having Thanksgiving at your grandma's?" I adjust the mirror.

"No, maybe, I don't know. I'm just kind of staying with my grandma, I don't know if we're eating tomorrow or not?"

Not eating? But I don't say this aloud. "Hey, I've got all these pies in the back. I'm taking them to Santa Fe for the Community Meal, why don't you take one. I'll bet your grandma would like it."

Patrick twists around and sees the plastic covered tins setting on the floor, unbuckles and reaches far over the seat back and grabs one. He holds it on his lap with both hands.

"Thanks."

I notice how grayed his t-shirt is, thin too, almost see through.

"Buckle up, son. We don't want to get stopped okay."

"Oh, yeah, I forgot." He reaches awkwardly behind his shoulder and grabs the metal clasp of the belt, being careful not to upset the pie.

"What's that, a community meal? What's that mean?" He holds the pie up inspecting the sides and top. I can tell he wants to start eating it right now. He probably missed both breakfast and lunch.

"Well, it's at the same place I took all the blankets the class collected. The meal's tomorrow, Thanksgiving. Anybody can come. You don't have to be homeless." I reach up and slide the flier across the dashboard towards him. "Here, this is all the information about it. Maybe you and your grandma want to come. There will be lots of pie. It's free; your grandma won't have to cook. Take it, show it to her."

Patrick looks at the bright orange paper, unfolds it. I think he can read it.

"So where's it at again?" He trying to focus, maybe he can't read it.

"Out on Cerrillos Road, you know, past the McDonald's? I think there's a map on the back."

He flips it over, studies the map. "Are you going?"

"What?"

"Are you going to eat there?" He folds the paper up and stuffs it in his front pant pocket.

I pause a minute to look at the huge white clouds drifting rapidly across the sky and remember Lenny's chipped tooth grin at the shelter door as he said he'd see me Thanksgiving.

"Yes, Patrick, I will be there."

"Turn here."

I barely have enough time to brake before turning onto the rutted dirt road. We bump along. I have to navigate around the washboard and rocks that mark the path. If I wasn't driving Stevie's old Subaru I wouldn't make it. I'm a little worried.

"Are we close?" I ask Patrick.

"Yeah, turn here." He points to my left.

It looks like a wide sandy arroyo. A small trickle of water still flows down one side. No wonder Patrick is always absent when it rains.

We go maybe a half mile, past six or seven pretty beat single wide trailers, some set up on cement blocks with no skirting to block the wind, some with a dozen tires on the roof. No yards really, a few have Pit Bulls tied up or Chihuahuas running untethered in the vicinity, assorted car parts and bent strollers are laying around. If I had to guess I'd say this was an illegal mobile home park. God only knows what they do for a sewer system. I start to wonder about that trickle of water running along the side of the road.

"This is it, right here." Patrick taps the glass.

I stop the car, slide slightly in the loose sand and gravel, back around so Patrick is facing the front door when he gets out. A little girl no more than three is looking out a crooked metal storm door of a falling apart mobile home, the top panel of the glass door panel is missing so it is open to the elements, plastic taped over it flaps loose and flags in the wind. The little girl squeals with delight when she sees Patrick. An older woman, not that old, more like my age, appears behind her and opens the door.

"Hi Grandma, I missed the bus, my teacher gave me a ride. Here, I brought a pie. And popcorn, I got popcorn too."

The woman smiles broadly, takes the pie from him, closes the storm door and waves her hand out the open top half of the door. Patrick hands her the orange flier. I can't hear what he says but he points to me and then at the flier. The woman looks up. I see an O form on her lips and she nods and waves at me again then hugs Patrick.

I assume that means I'll see them tomorrow.

10

Traffic was outrageous. I forgot how bad it could be the Wednesday before Thanksgiving. SUV's with large blue cargo bags strapped to the roof weave in and out of traffic and I am tailgated by huge crew cab pickup trucks most of the way. All I wanted was to get home. But first I had to drop off those pies.

The traffic down Cerrillos Road was no better than the traffic to the north, stop and go five miles from St. Francis Drive to the shelter. It was unexpected when my gas light came on, the extra trip to take Patrick home along with the slow pace and stop lights burned more gas then I thought. With only three bucks in my purse, I pulled into a long line of cars waiting to use the ATM machine. At this rate I'd be running on fumes by the time I got to the machine. I wasn't exactly sure how much was in my account, but when the transaction slip showed a balance of only one hundred and sixty it was a shock. I would have guessed two sixty. Today was the twenty fourth; I wouldn't get a check for another week, December 3rd. I hoped the landlord would let me slide a day or take a postdated check. Of the nine hundred and eighty in take home pay, eight hundred and fifty would go for my tiny one bedroom, a bargain by local standards. I got sixty out, needed to keep one hundred in the account or pay steep fees for every transaction. This week would be a squeaker. Gas and dog food would be my priorities. After I filled the tank and waited in line for almost forty minutes at Walmart to buy a twelve dollar bag of dog food, all I had left were two fives and some change.

A few transients milled about when I got to the shelter, most had already gone inside. I pulled directly around back and knocked on the door. Lenny answered.

"So, nice teacher lady, you've come back to us. Do you have more blankets?"

He wore a bleached and faded pink polo shirt over a long sleeve gray thermal undershirt, tan corduroy pants with the knees almost worn through, at least two sizes too big, cinched in at the waist by a piece of yellow webbing tied in a slip knot. His ever present rainbow beret with thick dreadlocks pushed up under it completed the ensemble. He was, to say the least, interesting to look at.

"No, I brought some pumpkin pies today. Do you think they still need them?"

"I've never known them to turn away pies." That chipped tooth came into view. He walked around to the back of the car with me and helped to lift out the pies.

"Did your students bake these?" He lifted the edge of the plastic to smell the cinnamon and ginger.

"No, a parent has a bakery I guess. He donated them to the school but these were left. I'm sure they're good." I followed him inside with the pies.

"Yes, yes, they will be good. You're coming tomorrow then?" He looked over his shoulder at me.

Adam, the director was at the large metal refrigerator case, checking the supplies. He closed the door and turned to us, clip board in hand.

"Hello, I'm Adam, what have we here?" He must have had that smile surgically implanted, it never leaves his face.

"I'm Aileen. We met a couple of weeks ago. I have some pies to donate."

Adam took them from me and a glimmer of recognition flashed across his face. "That's right, the blanket lady. Well yes, this looks great. Set them over here will you Lenny. I'm trying to sort things out for tomorrow." He placed them on a small prep counter nearby.

"Do you still need help tomorrow?" I asked.

"Oh absolutely, we start cooking at nine thirty and start serving sometime between twelve thirty and one. We can absolutely use more help." Adam shakes my hand, welcoming me and dismissing me in the same motion.

If I was less tired I would have peppered him with questions. 'Should I bring anything? Who else will be here?' Instead I nod, my mind still fixed on how to survive on ten dollars this week. "I've got to get going. My dog and my son are waiting for me."

Lenny walks me back through the kitchen area to the rear entrance. "Will your son come with you tomorrow?" Lenny holds the door for me.

"No, he's in the hospital, long term care. He has a brain injury."

"Oh, I'm sorry." Lenny adjusted the slip knot on his improvised belt.

"Thank you. I try to visit him every day, that's where I'm headed now, and then walk my dog. Well, his dog, but I take care of it now."

Lenny steps out the door with me, gazes at the parking lot and announces, "I'll see you out."

"No, it's okay. I can find my way."

Lenny is slightly nervous. "Please, sometimes people hang out around back that aren't allowed in for one reason or another and cause problems, please, let me walk with you."

I was taken aback. It never occurred to me there would be problems here or that someone wouldn't be allowed in. Outside, three men sat on a curb toward the back of the area, two of them looked pretty intoxicated. They shout at us, crudely laughing. Lenny takes me by the arm and hustles me around to the driver's side of the car blocking my view of them.

"Just ignore them, they're too drunk to know what they're saying." Lenny's grin was gone.

"I couldn't figure out what they said." I say, truthfully.

"Good, you don't need to know. Most of the people here aren't like that, just a few. But they are why we get so much bad press." He closes the door for me. "Be safe Aileen."

"See you tomorrow then." I wave at him as I start the car.

Half a block from home my gas light came on again. The needle on the gas gauge was below empty. How could that be? I just filled it up. Either the light or the gauge had to be broken. I turned into the nearest C store and pulled up to the pump. Five bucks worth just to be sure, would tell me what was happening, that would leave me with the remaining five dollars for the week. Cheaper than a tow truck. When I opened the hinged gas door my heart stopped. The gas cap was hanging loose by the thin plastic strip which keeps you from losing it. Did I forget to screw it back on? I pulled it out and turned it over puzzled. Nicks and scratch marks were all around the edge, it was bent and misshapen. Someone had pried it off and stolen my gas when I was inside the shelter.

11

Thanksgiving, six in the morning. I had given up mechanical alarms shortly after the accident. You had to set them, change the time twice a year, remember to turn them on or off, could hit the snooze button an infinite number of times thereby defeating the purpose of the alarm. I had acquired by default a much more dependable system, Peanuts. Peanuts doesn't care today is Thanksgiving. He wants me up and out of bed like he does every morning. He tries the subtle approach, which is to stand and look down on me, breathing heavily on my face until my eyes open. If that doesn't work he switches to audio, sneezing, loud yawns, a small 'ruff'. I try to snooze by rolling over, which only prompts him to kick it up a notch, pawing the side of the bed combined with the dog breath and yawns, and finally, the tour de force, jumping up on the bed and spinning around until I reach down, scratch his ear and say "Okay buddy, I'm up."

I dress without showering, make coffee, and pour out a generous travel mug of the stuff to take on our walk. On days off like this I try to take Peanuts to the dog park and let him run. But I used five of my last ten dollars on gas yesterday and don't know how I'll manage until pay day, I need to be able to get to work next week and five dollars doesn't even buy two gallons. I zip up my District Two Blue Hawks hoodie, shuffle around inside an old shoe box until I find a pair of gloves, leash up the dog and head out the door, plastic bags stuffed in my pockets for clean-up duty.

Today, the smell of turkey baking is real. It combines with wood smoke and the damp musk of fallen leaves to let you know fall will soon turn to winter. We walk a good two miles, running into the regulars who greet us.

"Happy Thanksgiving." I smile, nod, wonder if it will be a good Thanksgiving for them or not, I know my greeting is a fraud. I pass a guy lying on the ground in back of and half way under a bus stop bench. He's wrapped in a blanket identical to one I took to the shelter. Was there no room for you there last night? I pull Peanuts back so he doesn't bother the man, who opens one eye and lifts his head slightly. "Good Morning," I say to him.

He lifts his head higher, turns to see my face then closes his eyes tightly, sinking his head deep into the pavement and covering it with one end of the blanket, dismissing me and the world from his own, very real, nightmare. Peanuts and I head home.

I shower, fix a piece of toast and decide the most direct route to the shelter and St. Mary Mother of Mercy Extended Basic Care Center, hoping it won't burn too much gas.

I was right. Few staffers are on duty today. Rita, the nurse I usually chat, with is off. Good, I think, she deserves to spend this time with her family. The male nurse, Lynn something or other, is on duty, along with two techs. Is that enough staff for twenty plus patients? How will they get everything done?

Lynn greets me as I enter Stevie's room. He is checking the IV site on one of the four other patients in the room. With five patients the room is crowded.

"I guess you have your hands full today." I unzip my hoodie and take off my gloves.

"Yes, we really do. The admin was trying to get a couple more of our ambulatory patients sent home for the holiday, but it just didn't happen, so we kind of doubled up on beds in a room to make it easier to get to everybody. It's only temporary." Lynn adjusts the flow on the plastic bag hanging from the pole beside the bed.

There is no warm smell of turkey or fallen leaves here, only the acrid odor of bleach used to disinfect the floors and fixtures, combined with the occasional whiff of infected flesh that floats through the air.

"You hope." Only I don't say this loud enough for him to hear.

Four hard plastic metal framed visitor chairs are stacked right outside the door, placed there to make room for the extra bed. I drag one over and squeeze it in beside Stevie's bed and grasp Stevie's hand.

"How 'ya doin' today son? It's Thanksgiving. I'm going to help serve at a community meal today. Did I tell you about the Rasta guy I met there? I don't think he's for real, but he sure plays the part well. I think one of my students is coming too. He missed the bus, sort of, and I gave him a ride yesterday. I think his grandma will bring him. Peanuts is doing well, we had a good long walk this morning."

I pause, look around the room. An older man, long sad face, with grizzly whiskers and gray spotted teeth sits in a wheel chair at the door to the room. He's wearing a torn, once was white t shirt and blue and white checked hospital pajama pants.

"He can't hear you. He's in a coma." He says, snarls at me, elbows resting on the arms of the wheel chair which has the foot rests removed so he can use his feet to walk himself around. He tries to wheel himself into the room but the beds are packed in too tight.

I look at Stevie, trying to blink back tears, want to lash out at this man, but don't. "He's my son. I visit as often as I can. I like to let him know what's going on. I think he might hear me." I try to half smile at the old codger.

"He can't. He can't hear you." He tries again to wheel into the room. Lynn comes in behind him.

"Mr. Martinez, you're not giving Stevie's mom a hard time are you? Let's let her have a visit with her son okay?" Lynn tries to pull Mr. Martinez's chair out of the room, but he flips the brake lever on, locking the wheels.

"When do I get my breakfast? Why are you wasting time on these guys in here, they could care less, they don't even know anyone's here." His voice is gruff, demanding. I can tell it's a cover for being stuck here on Thanksgiving.

Holy Smokes, it's almost eight thirty and he hasn't had breakfast yet? They really are short staffed. I'd be grumpy too.

"I told you, as soon as we make the rounds and give out all the meds, one of us will help you with your breakfast." Lynn tries to appease him.

I look from Stevie to Lynn to the old guy in the wheel chair. "Where's your tray, I'll help you?"

I stand and walk towards him, reach down and unlock the wheel brakes and spin the chair around without saying anything more. He looks up at me, mouth open, startled. After so many years teaching middle school I know how to deal with inappropriate behavior, no matter what the age.

Lynn is surprised too. "It's on the cart near the nurses' station. We only have a few trays to give out yet. It would be great if you could help him."

I wheel him down to the nurses' station where a large double door steam cart is plugged into the wall. I open one side, the smell of overcooked bacon and bad coffee drifts up. Each space is marked with a masking tape label of a room number and name. I scan the labels. Three have Mtz, short for Martinez, printed on them.

"What's you room number?" I open the other side of the cart.

"Why do you need to know that? All I want is a tray."

Well there's not one labeled Mr. Grumpy, I think. "The trays are labeled by room number. I need to know which one is yours." I look over the cart at him.

"Aren't they all the same? Just grab one."

"Okay, if you want melted gelatin for breakfast that's your problem."

One of the two med techs on duty scurries in back of me with a plastic box of medical supplies.

"Twenty eight B, Mr. Martinez, you're number is twenty eight B," he says over his shoulder.

Mr. Martinez's expression changes. He looks worried, like he is not sure what just happened.

"Yup, here it is." I slide the tray out, a domed plastic cover set over a plate of eggs and toast, no bacon, a bowl of oatmeal, a plastic cup of cranberry juice and a round, thick mug of coffee topped by a plastic lid that doesn't fit well.

"Where to Mr. Martinez? Do you want to sit in the day-room, maybe watch the Macy's Parade?"

"The what? What parade?"

"You know the Macy's parade, Thanksgiving, all those balloons? I think one of the high-school bands from Albuquerque is marching in it this year."

A look of confusion pulls his eyes away, like memory he should have but doesn't.

I balance his tray with one arm and use the other to push his chair. "Let's sit in the day room and watch TV while we have breakfast okay?"

"Okay…" He is docile now, can't really get his head around what is happening. I push his chair up to a small square table near the TV screen, set his tray down and turn on the TV. It's already set to the parade. Mr. Martinez reaches for his coffee, tries to pick it up and remove the lid, but his hands are trembling so much he spills it over his tray. Good thing I haven't taken the covers off the other food yet. I take the napkins and mop up the mess.

"Damn it. Damn it." He curses himself.

"That's okay sir, I'll get you more coffee from the nurses station. I know where it is."

Before I go for the coffee, I pull out a piece of toast, place it in his hand and he starts eating it, crumbs catching on his chin.

When I get back, he looks up at me with eyebrows raised. "Did you know today is Thanksgiving?"

"Yes, it is. Do you like the parade?" I help him keep the cup steady while he sips it. He keeps his eyes fixed on the TV. I uncover the eggs, put some on a fork and place it in his shaking hand.

"Damn it." The eggs fall off the fork, back on the plate. I pick them up, guide the fork to his mouth and help him sip the juice.

"So how long have you been working here?" He glances away from the TV.

"I don't work here. My son's a patient here. I'm visiting him. Do you want more coffee?" I stir half a carton of milk into the oatmeal, place a small spoon of the porridge in his hand and steady his elbow.

"Your son? Who's he?" He fights me a little, but not too much, resigned to needing help feeding himself.

"In room thirty, we were just there." I nod towards the hall.

"Those guys can't hear you, they're in comas." He tries to pick up the coffee cup again, it's empty.

I take the cup from him and refill it from the pot behind the counter. When I come back he has spun his chair around and is facing the TV screen dead center.

"Did you know today's Thanksgiving?"

"Yes, isn't it a wonderful parade?" I help him hold the coffee.

He looks at me, confusion covers his face again.

"So, how long have you been working here?"

12

*P*reparations for the Thanksgiving meal were in full swing by the time I got to the shelter a little past ten in the morning. The parking lot, even in the back where my gas had been ripped off, was almost full. I park under a tree, almost over the curb on a side street, facing the wrong direction. I was hopeful this would be more open should the gas thieves try to repeat their sins.

The back door is propped open so I walk in without needing an escort. Lenny's there, dreadlocks once again stuffed under that crochet beret, but this time he's clad in a pair of orange sweat pants and faded green sweatshirt topped by a thin white plastic apron.

"Welcome Teacher Aileen, I am glad you are here." He is carrying a large disposable aluminum pan piled high with freshly peeled yams.

"Sorry I'm late. I stopped to see my son before I came."

"Well, we are happy you are here now. Get an apron, you can help with the sweet potatoes, we need to get them ready to put in the oven as soon as the turkey is reheated."

I follow him through, stop to braid back my hair, wash my hands and pull a plastic apron from the box under the sink. We open cans, add butter and brown sugar and cover with thick aluminum foil.

Four more volunteers are chopping vegetables for a salad, portioning pies and opening industrial size cans of green beans and corn to heat in a giant saucepan.

"Do they bake the turkey here?" I ask one of them, as I stack the prep pans of sweet potatoes on the counter near the ovens.

"No, a couple of the restaurants bake them up for us ahead of time. We slice them up and reheat. You missed out on that job. As soon as the turkey's done we get everything else going."

"Anything else I can help with?" Everyone is busy. I don't know what to do.

"Check with Adam, but I think we have the kitchen covered, maybe in the dining area or serving line."

I walk to the front, find Adam, who has his ever present clipboard and is trying to figure out how many extra tables to set up. Two of the men I have seen panhandling around town are helping to lock the legs on conference tables borrowed from a church for the occasion. Two more men open the door and wheel in a cart of folding chairs and begin setting them up. People are already outside waiting, wanting to be sure they will eat today. A few try to come in.

"Sorry folks. We aren't ready to serve yet, not until noon. Sorry, you've got to wait outside."

"Aw Adam come on man, it's getting cold, can't you see that."

"I know Kev, but if I let you in I'll have to let everyone in and we're just not ready. Work with me on this Kev, okay?"

Kev, reluctantly, backs out, giving a light punch to his companion's shoulder. "Come on, we're still first in line."

Noon, everything is ready, steam tables in place, chairs set up, center pieces donated by the local 4- H club carefully arranged on each table. A guy with a guitar shows up to serenade the dinners. More volunteers from a church group come in the back door, jovial, ready to help serve. Adam walks over and props the front door open, gives a big greeting to everyone in line, shakes hands with people as they walk in the door like he's the host welcoming guests to his home. They come in. Bent elderly men who can barely raise their head, families with six or seven in the group, couples young and old who hold hands and cling to each other, friends, some obviously homeless, some who are lonely and seek companionship as well as food. They just keep filing in the door. Where did all these people come from? Lenny puts me in charge of the green beans. I don't look up for two hours. The church group carries plates for little children and mothers with their hands full, two other volunteers walk around the tables refilling coffee cups and offering lemonade and comforting words .

Around two-thirty it looks like we might run out. Adam surveys the food left, instructs us to give smaller portions, cut the pumpkin pie slices in half, double-up on the rolls of which we have a lot.

"Do you have a car Aileen?" Adam hauls over another saucepan of just heated green beans.

"Yes, why do you need a ride?" I drain the water from a spoonful of the drab green vegetables and gently set them on a plate before passing it on down the line.

"No, I was hoping you could run down the street to the supermarket and get a couple more big cans of green beans and some instant potatoes. If we can do that we might actually make it. Pick up a half dozen bags of salad mix too. Could you do that?"

"Yes, but I'm a little short on cash now. Do you have a check or something?

"We have an open account. Talk to Angelo, he handles it. If he's not there talk to whatever manager is on duty. Tell them it's for our Thanksgiving meal, you'll have to sign for it."

"Sure, you bet." I untie the apron.

Lenny overhears. "I can go too, help to carry everything."

"Okay, if that's okay with you Aileen?"

I must admit I did hesitate. I liked Lenny, but I didn't know him too well and there were those outrageous dreadlocks to think about.

"Sure, that'd be great." I slide the apron off and head for the back door.

Lenny double stepped ahead of me, holds the door open. "Allow me."

The store was less than three blocks away and traffic was very light. It was easy to park up front. Lenny slowed his pace as we walked into the store.

"How is your son? Did he get to eat a turkey dinner?"

"No, he can't really eat, He has a feeding tube."

"Oh, will that be in much longer?"

"Who knows?" I'm a little too abrupt. I feel my gut tense up as it does every time I talk about my family. I race through the store, find the section where restaurant sized cans take up precious shelf space, and load four cans of green beans, two of corn and six giant boxes of instant mashed potatoes into the cart. Lenny follows behind, uncertain of his status. Finally, I break down and tell him.

"He's in a coma. He just turned twenty seven. My husband drove off the road and my son got a major brain injury. I had another son, too. He was thrown out of the truck and died six months ago." I try to stay unemotional, but am not successful.

Lenny slowed his pace even more while I hurried mine. "I'm sorry for your troubles." All he could think to say.

We went to the produce aisle and I threw, literally, some bags of salad mix into the cart. I guess I was running, pushing the cart to the front. Lenny caught up to me.

"It's okay. You don't have to say more."

"I don't talk much about it, that's all. I need to adjust to things, get to where I can tell somebody without freaking out so much." I am nervously twisting the handle of the cart, one of the wheels is stuck sideways making an ungodly squeak as I try to push the cart even harder.

Lenny takes the cart from me. "See if you can find the manager, I'll head to the checkout."

I walk over to the customer service counter which doubled as a cigarette store. A young man about Stevie's age, wearing a white shirt and tie stood behind the counter. He's watching a football game on the one hundred sixty nine ninety-nine flat screen LED TV that would be tomorrow's eighty dollar Black Friday special.

"Can I help you?" He glances up.

"Is Angelo here?"

"I'm Angelo, how can I help you?" he says, turning down the volume on the game.

"Adam from the soup kitchen sent me. We're running low on things for the Thanksgiving meal and he sent me to pick them up. I guess I need to sign or something."

He looks at me, then rises up on his toes, spies Lenny waiting in line and waves him over. Apparently these two knew each other.

Lenny stands on the back bar and rides the cart over like it is a scooter. "Mr. Angelo, how are you this fair Thanksgiving?"

"Wishing I was home watching football to tell you the truth, and you?"

"Be thankful you have a home sir." Lenny is sorry right after he says it, tries to lighten the mood. "Which team do you favor, Giants or Cowboys?"

"Are you kidding? Cowboys will take it easy." Angelo pulls the cans from the cart, scans them, prints out the receipt and a credit slip, has me sign both, while Lenny finds an old box and piles the stuff in.

"How's your turkey supply? Got enough?"

Lenny and I look at each other. "I think we're running a little low, Adam had us cut back on portions, but we'll make it stretch." I reply.

"Good, well Happy Thanksgiving." Angelo nods to the next person in line, waves them over from the cashier's station. "If we can clear the customers out we'll close by three."

Lenny loads everything into the car. "Pull the car around while I take the cart back."

Back in the car Lenny tries again. "Your husband, was he hurt?"

"No, a little, he committed suicide. He couldn't handle it. He was charged with DWI and manslaughter. He just couldn't face it." I was silent as we stopped for the light. When it turned green, I start talking again.

"Stevie's been in a coma since it happened. They didn't think he would make it. I just don't know what will happen. Hope for a miracle or something."

"We can always hope for better things Teacher Aileen, always hope for better things."

I pull right up to the back door of the soup kitchen, Lenny hops out and opens the back while a couple of volunteers came out and unload everything. In the three or four minutes it took me to park and walk back in they already had the canned food in pans heating up, the salad mix being washed and water boiling for the potatoes.

Adam finds me. "Great, thanks Aileen, did Angelo give you a copy?"

I take the copy of the receipt from my pocket and hand it to him. Someone else has taken my place in the serving line. "How can I help now?"

"Second shift of volunteers just took over, so I think we're okay. Why don't you grab a plate and eat yourself."

I was hungry. It was nearly three and I hadn't eaten since that piece of toast at seven this morning. I walk out front and take my place in a long line of people waiting for a hot meal.

"Miss Roark, Miss Roark." Someone is calling out to me from the dining area.

"Miss Roark. Over here." Patrick sits with his grandma and the little girl at the end of a long white table.

"Patrick, Happy Thanksgiving! I'm glad you came." I reach for his grandma's hand and shake it lightly.

"Thank you for inviting us. I didn't know where we would eat today. This is nice, so many people." The woman smiles at me. Even though we're the same age, her hard life has left her deep with wrinkles and worry.

I put my hand on the little girl's shoulder, her face smeared with cranberry sauce. "And who is this?"

Patrick's grandmother pulls a chair out for me to sit beside her.

"This is my niece, Megan," Patrick says as he puts down his lemonade and helps the little girl onto his lap.

"Wow Megan, you're lucky to have Patrick as your uncle, I bet he takes good care of you."

The shy child buries her head in Patrick's shoulder, mashing the pink gel of cranberries into his shirt. Patrick's grandmother beams.

"Oh he does, he's very protective of her, especially now that my daughter and granddaughter got arrested. He takes such good care of Megan."

Patrick casts his eyes down, looks embarrassed. He puts his hand on the arm of an old man sitting beside them.

"Grandpa, this is my teacher." The old man has to turn his head sideways to see me. One of his eyes is clouded by cataracts.

"¿Qué?" He uses the paper napkin to wipe the side of his mouth.

"Maestra, Papí, la mujere es una maestra." Patrick says, speaking loudly to be sure the old man will hear.

"O, sí, sí. Buenos días, Señora." The old man puts down his fork and extends his hand.

"This is my dad, he stays with me too." The woman takes the little girl from Patrick so he can finish his pie.

I thought about that beat up old single wide I saw yesterday. It was hard to imagine all four members of this family, plus Patrick's mom and sister crammed in there. "Boy, you've got a houseful."

"Yes, we do, but Patrick is such a big help." Patrick's grandmother beams at him again.

Patrick gets up to fill his great grandfather's coffee cup. Megan jumps down off her grandmother's lap and toddles after him. I watch as he walks up the aisle, he has to keep one hand on his low hanging pants to keep them from falling down. The shirt he's wearing wouldn't have met school dress code either with eight ball and joker graphics. Can't judge a book by a cover I remind myself.

"I wanted to thank you for giving him a ride yesterday. My car broke down a while ago and I just don't know what I would have done if you hadn't given him a ride." She coughed roughly and took a sip of lukewarm coffee from a small Styrofoam cup. "I had to borrow a car from my cousin to get here today. Since Patrick's mom and sister went to jail, he just hasn't wanted to go to school."

That explained his ditching.

"I guess he missed the bus. It's lucky I was there." I say to her, than look at the roomful of souls who occupy all the other tables. Do they have a story to tell like this I wonder?

"Enjoy your meal. I've got to get mine before they run out of turkey, Happy Thanksgiving."

"Happy Thanksgiving." She grasps my hand and shakes it one more time.

I get back in line. It has not gone down. Unless Jesus shows up with a basket of loaves and fishes, there's no way the turkey will last. I swear to God, no kidding, just as this thought went through my head Angelo from the supermarket walks in the front door carrying a big box with two cooked turkeys wrapped in foil.

"¡Hola, Happy Thanksgiving," Angelo says to all still in line. Adam comes around the counter to greet him.

"Wow, Angelo, wow, where did these come from?" For the first time since I've met him Adam looks flustered, puts down his clipboard.

"We always cook more turkeys than we have orders for at the store just in case. These were left over. We closed at three so I thought I'd drive them over. I've got two more in the car. Can someone help?"

Lenny comes around the counter to help him. "How's the game?"

"Not too good." Angelo frowns. "Giants are up by ten."

13

I was going to have to stay home. I had planned to take a car trip, maybe to Socorro to see the cranes. This time of year thousands of sand-hill cranes, eagles, snow geese and a rare whopping crane blanket the Wildlife Reserve south of Albuquerque. The boys and I used to go. It was our Thanksgiving tradition, carried over into adulthood. We'd make the three hour drive, stop for a Green Chile Cheeseburger at the Owl Cafe, visit the Rock and Mineral Museum at Tech, then head for the Wildlife Preserve to see the dusk flight. It was the one thing I wanted to do without them. I sort of imagined Sean and Sam's spirit with me, and tried to visualize Stevie as floating through the air on the wings of an eagle.

This year I would have to settle for a book from the library and wild cam video on YouTube. I needed my gas to get to school. That five dollars I put in the tank plus the five more I added on the way home Thanksgiving night would barely get me through Wednesday, and only if I was careful, not idling too long or accelerating too fast. Peanuts and I would make do with in town walking.

Friday, while others were rushing and pushing to take advantage of once a year bargains, I rode the city bus to the cemetery, walked inside the rows until I came to Sam and Sean's markers a few yards apart. They were small, but at least they were there, for now anyway. Most months I managed to meet the minimum amount due on my credit card. I found out the hard way when you're late with a payment the *loyal customer* low interest rate triples. I was paying nineteen percent interest on one marker, twenty two percent on the other. And that was just the down payment.

Dry brown leaves filled the cemetery, blown from trees that ringed the perimeter. They crunched under my feet. I could hear a workman with a leaf blower on the other side of the hill, trying to corral them in. I went to Sean's grave first. Mementos left by his classmates leaned against the granite stone: a small trophy with a runner on top, plastic flowers, some had notes or pictures enclosed in plastic bags tied to them; a miniature soccer ball was fastened with zebra print duct tape to a small wreath propped up by a bent coat hanger.

"Hey Sean, looks like your friends came by. The cross country team did well this year. Your buddy Andres took first at State. His picture was in the paper." I told him about my Thanksgiving meal at the soup kitchen, how the store manager, Angelo, appeared with more turkey just as we were about to run out. I left out the part about my gas being stolen.

I sat beside Sam's grave next. I still carried this unbelievable anger against him. But I had long ago learned the power of forgiveness to calm your spirit, and while I wasn't there yet, I was working on it. I told him about Stevie, about my new apartment and helping at the shelter. I did tell him about my stolen gas, as if I expected him to rise up from his grave and take care of it. Was it odd to talk to the dead?

"Not unless they answer."

I jumped up, startled, and brushed the leaves from my pants. "Who said that?"

"Sorry, didn't mean to scare you, just passing by." A tall, older man, a bit disheveled, with a gray beard and two long braids tucked under a cowboy hat, a red canvas pack hoisted on one shoulder, walked down the row of markers, traversing the hill. Where had he come from?

"I didn't mean for anyone to hear that." I was angry more than embarrassed. How dare this street bum eaves drop.

"S'okay dear lady, I'm just passing through. Have a good day." He strode quickly by, tipping his hat, going downhill towards the sound of the leaf blower. I regained my composure, walked quickly towards the foot gate, and waited at the bus stop for the ride home.

14

*I*t was dark Monday morning when I got in my car for the drive to school. I avoided driving anywhere since my Thanksgiving meal, occupied my time by walking Peanuts around town, visiting Stevie, helping Mr. Martinez at the Care Center, who still asked me, everyday, 'So, how long have you worked here?' and reading. The usual holiday specials both on TV and the real ones, like the farolito lighting on the Plaza, were more than I could handle in my new solo life.

Going back to school was a reprieve from my loneliness. I zipped up my Home of the Blue Hawks hoodie, threw my lunch bag on the passenger seat and turned the key. Nothing. No metallic grinding, no clicks or clacks, no whirring, just nothing. I tried the radio, the lights, taking out and replacing the key at least three times. Nothing, great, just great.

I pulled the hood release and walked to the front of the Subaru. I don't know why, I don't know a damn thing about cars. With two sons, I seldom did anything other than put gas in the tank, which I know I had done three times recently, Thanksgiving eve and day. But I did know one thing, you need to have a battery to start a car, and I no longer had one, it was gone. I stood there looking at the empty space, with my hand on hood for maybe five minutes trying to figure out what to do. Then I released the hood, went back inside and dialed the school.

"District Two Middle School, home of the Blue Hawks may I help you?"

"Good morning this is Aileen, I know it's late to call, but I'm having car problems, I'm not sure when I'll make it in, so I guess I'll need a sub."

"Hold on Mrs. Roark, I think you need to talk to the principal, I'll transfer you," the secretary replied.

"Really? I thought I needed to let you know?"

"They're always changing things around here. It's a new policy I guess, hold on a sec. Dr. Roybal showed up this morning wanting to speak with the principal about all the teachers who were out last week."

Uh-Oh, that can't be good. I hoped she remembered I was there. I was on hold, three minutes, five minutes, was about to hang up and call back when the line clicked on again.

"Hello, Mrs. Roark? You're not coming in today?" The principal sounds annoyed.

"Well, I hope to come in, I just don't know when. Someone took my car battery. I need to figure out how to get another one."

"Isn't there someone you can borrow a car from or that can give you a ride?"

"No, I don't know my neighbors that well, and no, I don't have anyone to give me a ride. I just need to call around and find a battery and then figure out how to get it to my car."

"You do know you have used up all your leave time. You've taken a lot of leave without pay."

Why was she giving me such a hard time today? I guessed the superintendent was sitting beside her and she'd taken a scolding about everyone gone last Wednesday.

"Yes, I know, I'm sorry. But my son, they are always calling me from the medical center to take care of something, the doctor wrote a letter about it. Do you need me to get another one?"

"For a car battery? You have a doctor's excuse for a car battery?"

"No, for the other days, for Stevie and Sam. I did give you a copy of the death certificate and obituary for Sam. Did that ever get changed to bereavement? Last I checked it was still posted as leave without pay."

"What are you taking today? Bereavement? We don't grant bereavement leave for dead car batteries"

I couldn't believe my boss was saying these things to me. Was Dr. Roybal giving her insensitivity training or what?

"No. I'm sorry, I just went out to my car and the battery is gone, it's not dead it's gone, I'll be there as soon as I can."

"Do that. The superintendent is taking a very dim view of all the leave teachers are taking."

I hung up before either of us could say more.

Why is she telling me this? Did I ask to have my battery stolen, my son to die, and my other son to become comatose? Was my husband's suicide optional? I thought about the twenty plus years I had worked for the school, coming in sick, hiring sitters when the boys were young, staying late. I had always carried most of my leave to the next year. Now, when I needed a hand up, they suddenly took a *dim view*. Is that why the superintendent sent all those kids to my room last Wednesday? Because of her *dim view*?

I did what I always did when I was about to lose it, leashed Peanuts up and went for a walk.

Eight o'clock, on the dot I started calling around. The lowest price I could find was one hundred dollars with exchange, plus tax, plus service fee. When I explained I didn't have a battery to exchange the price went up even more. Silly me, I thought the environmental disposal fee would be waived since I didn't have one to dispose of, but no, this is charged anyway. Now how would I get the car over there or the battery to my car? One sympathetic parts department clerk suggested I call a tow truck.

"A tow truck? How much will that cost?"

"It depends how far away you are, anywhere from sixty to one hundred and sixty. But you only have to get it here, you can drive it home."

I thought about it. I had one credit card left I could still use and would need to take that one hundred dollars minimum balance out from my checking account, even if it meant service fees.

"Can you recommend one?"

"You can try Phil's Wrecker Service. There are others in the book, but Phil's a good guy, he'll help you out."

I called the number and left a message, within five minutes he called back.

"This is Phil, do you need tow service?"

"Yes, I guess so, I need a battery and the parts clerk said you could get my car there or something."

"You need a jump? Your battery's dead?" There was a lot of static on the line.

"No, it's gone, someone stole it. I need a whole battery." I was practically shouting.

"So you want me to install a battery?"

"Do you do that?" I asked, a little calmer.

"If you buy it from me I do."

"I didn't know you sold them."

"We sell used batteries, fully charged. What kind of car are we talking about?" The phone reception was clearer now.

"Subaru, Legacy."

"I can let you have one for seventy five cash."

God does answer prayers.

"Installed? How much would the tax be? Do you charge that environment fee?" I kept trying to remember all the extra charges the big box auto stores tacked on.

"No, add sixty for me to come over and put it in. Cash, all fees included. No checks, no plastic."

That burst my bubble.

"I can only do one hundred cash, total."

"Can't do it for that, tell you what, I'll go one twenty five total, cash."

I did some mental math. There had to be at least seven or eight dollars in coins in the jar on top of the refrigerator. I had a handful of dollar coins tucked in a little box on my dresser.

"How about one hundred ten." The line was dead.

"Hello, Hello?" I waited, Phil came back on.

"No, sorry. You know a tow alone is going to be almost a hundred."

"I know, but I just don't have cash. Someone stole my gas and now they stole my battery. I can't come up with more."

"What's the most you can do?"

"Maybe..." I had to play my hand right here, I needed to be sure I had enough to pay him, "One hundred fifteen."

"One seventeen, cash. No checks, no plastic."

"Okay, one seventeen." Please God, let me have that much loose change.

"I'll be there in ninety minutes to two hours. I've got a lady with a flat tire on my other line."

The battery was in by noon. Phil said I was lucky who ever took it didn't cut the lead wires otherwise it would have been more. I didn't feel lucky. After I scrapped together the change and hoofed it over to the nearest ATM I had one hundred nineteen dollars and eighty five cents. I carefully counted out the one hundred and seventeen dollars, thanked him profusely.

"I don't know what I would have done without you. My boss was giving me such a hard time about being not coming in. Thank you so much."

"Did you call the police? You might want to check with your insurance about it"

"No, I'm not really sure when it was stolen. My gas was stolen last Wednesday and I only had enough for three gallons. I pretty much just parked it so I'd have gas to get to work. It could have happened anytime since Thanksgiving."

"That's really a shame, really a shame." Phil was wiping his hands on an old rag. "Is that really all you have?" He closed the hood as I handed him the cash and change.

"Yes, things have been tight lately. But I'll get by, thanks to you."

"Didn't I see you Thanksgiving at the Community Meal?"

I looked up at him surprised. I didn't recognize him, but there were so many people. I started to tell him I was a volunteer, did a quick backpedal, I had eaten there.

"Yes, were you there too? Did you like the pie?"

"Oh yeah, the pie was awesome." Phil stuffed the rag into his front pocket and pulled a blue vinyl money bag out from his back, adding the mishmash of dollar bills to it and unzipping the front pocket for all the coins. At the last minute he pulled five dollars out and handed it back to me.

"Happy Thanksgiving," he said.

15

The last half of the semester used to fly by. Basketball tournaments, choir performances, another round of testing and two *Positive Behavior* assemblies paid for by the catalog fundraiser company would regularly supplant the day to day time in the classroom spent learning. The assembly days were particularly hard on my students. Few of them had the family financial resources to purchase the required five item minimum from the fund-raising catalog that would make them eligible for the corporate sponsored fun day. Only eight of my twenty-two homeroom students were on the eligible list. I knew from experience it meant most of the others would soon be sitting on the bench outside the assistant principal's office, discipline referral in hand, as they acted out their frustrations. The days they would miss to In School Suspension, and a few Out of School Suspensions, would only add to their emotional distress, not to mention the impact it would have on their learning.

Out of seventeen school days between Thanksgiving and Christmas Break, nine of them were uninterrupted. Add to that two snow delays and it was the blink of an eye before half the school year was over. But for me, as for most of the students in my remedial classes, the days moved at a snail's pace, even more so in January when we came back from the break.

About a month after Sam died I finally figured out I needed to file for benefits. Three more months, they told me. What? Three more months, fifth day of the month, the deposit will be made. January 5th. Okay, I thought, I don't have anyone to buy Christmas presents for anyway.

When the direct deposit was made for five hundred I was sure someone had made a mistake. I should have checked on it sooner, not waited until the middle of the month. I would have saved myself a tornado of trouble if I had. I gathered all the paperwork I could find, placing it in a manila envelope from work. You know the kind that has a string tie on it and is stamped 'Interoffice' with a place for recipient and sender? Well, I'll tell you where I got it in a minute.

I called and made an appointment, or tried to. They made the last appointment at three.

"But I can't get there until three forty-five." I pleaded with the voice on the phone.

"Sorry, we don't give any appointments after three, most of our staff leave by four and they have to have time to close their files before they leave. Sorry."

So I made it for three. The day before the appointment I filled out a leave form. A new change in policy meant we had to take a half day at a time and I had no time left. Even though I knew it would get me another reprimand, I checked the box for leave without pay, made a copy and turned it in.

Remember that manila envelope? Well I got it two weeks before. The school secretary, who usually hands out paychecks, came into my room while I was teaching and apologetically handed it to me.

"Just set it on my desk." I told her.

"Sorry to interrupt but they told me you had to sign for it." She pushed a clipboard into my hands, pen attached, that read 'I acknowledge receipt of the memo dated date January 14th. I signed it and handed it back to her. The students started chatting, getting up to get water and sharpen their pencils. It was Friday and the last class of the day.

"I really feel bad about this," she said "but they said to be sure you opened it."

I looked at here, exasperated, told the students to go ahead and pack up their things and sat down at my desk.

It took me a minute or two to actually get it open. At least three kids come up to the desk.

"What's my grade?" "Can I still turn this in?" "Do we have any homework?"

But finally, as the bell rang, I pulled the memo from the envelope. It was a reprimand for being AWOL: absent without leave.

"What's this about?" I looked at the secretary perplexed. I had filled out leave forms for every day taken. Early on I sent a letter to both the principal and the Director of Human Resources requesting leave without pay as needed to care for both Sam and Stevie. I had even attached a note from the doctor documenting Stevie's uncertain medical state.

"They told me to tell you there is no more leave without pay, and that I can't release your paycheck for deposit until you sign and return it."

"Who should I talk to?"

"I suppose Superintendent Roybal, but she's already gone for the day."

It would be next Tuesday before I could see her.

"Sorry, no more leave without pay. It was being abused," was her response.

"But I notified you of my son's condition and my husband's appointments. I even sent a copy of the medical report on Stevie." I was upset.

"District policy has changed. We are no longer allowing leave without pay." I glanced around her office. It was bigger than some of the classrooms I had taught in.

"Can I get a copy of the policy?"

She stood up. "It's being revised."

"What about the minutes of the board meeting? Didn't it have to be voted on?" I tilted my head and remained seated. I had been at many board meetings. Three hearings with public comment was the standard procedure to amend policy.

"The board will be adopting the policy at the next meeting. In the meantime they have given me the authority to begin implementing it."

"But what about the minutes, can I get those?" I stayed fixed to my chair.

She blinked. "Look, I am really busy. If you have any further concerns you will need to put them in writing through the HR department." Superintendent Roybal walked around from her desk and opened the door.

Unable to get any real answers I gathered my things and went to the hospital to see Stevie. That was two weeks ago.

Now, I drove nervously to the Retirement Board office, envelope in hand. But this time it held not only the reprimand but Sam's retirement packet. The amount was clearly marked, fifteen hundred and twenty five dollars, monthly, for the surviving spouse.

I parked the old Subaru in a metered space a half block away, twenty-five cents for fifteen minutes. I hoped three quarters would be enough because it was all I had. Actually one was all I needed. It was early February, the Red Buds were starting to bud a fragrant pink, and the first of the crocus sprung up pink and lavender. I admired them wistfully as I walked by the entrance, I missed my flower garden.

I signed in and waited a few minutes before being escorted to a small cubicle. A smiling man, about fifty introduced himself. "Good Afternoon, my name is Eric Smyth, with a y. How can I help you today?" He motioned to a chair perpendicular to his desk.

I pulled it around to face him and opened my envelope.

"Well Mr. Smyth, my husband passed away recently..."

"Oh I'm so sorry," he said, genuinely expressed concern.

"...and I was supposed to start getting half of his benefit. But this first check was only for five hundred and twenty five dollars, not the fifteen hundred and twenty five dollars it was supposed to be." I really wished I had thought this through better, now I was behind two months, January and February, over two thousand dollars I thought I had but didn't.

I handed him the paperwork.

He looked at it quickly, noting the dates and amounts by writing them on a blue notepad he kept by his computer.

"Let me see if I can bring up your file on the computer. Do you know your husband's Social?"

"It should be there on this form." I shuffled the papers and pointed to the space where I had filled it in.

Mr. Smyth entered the number into the system. "Can you give me his date of birth? And the day he passed away?"

I told him, offered a copy of the death certificate.

He was silent as his entered the data and starred at the screen, waiting for the old database to pull up Sam's case file.

"Are these your kids?" I asked as I admired the pictures of kids and teens holding soccer balls, and footballs, one with a baseball glove, tacked by his desk.

"Grandkids, Jesse is ten and Aaron's fifteen," he said proudly. "My daughter just had another one, a girl. I haven't seen her yet. My wife went to stay with them in California. I hope I can take some leave soon and go too." Lucky man I thought.

He continued to smile proudly, but it soon vanished as he saw what was on the screen.

"Someone filed a lean on your husband's benefit. There is a one thousand dollar monthly garnishment against the account."

"Who? When? How was I supposed to find out?"

"I don't know all the details. I can tell you the date of the court order, December 14th of last year and it was St Mary's Mother of Mercy Medical Center. I can give you the name and phone number of the person who handles that. But they all leave by four so you won't be able to get a hold of them today."

I was almost in tears now. How could they just take money away without telling me?

Mr. Smyth handed back my papers and attached a copy of the account summary he printed out. On the top he wrote the name and a phone number for a contact.

"Sorry I couldn't be of more help," he said.

16

It took me a couple of weeks to track down all the paperwork. But there it was. A mediator had assigned us, meaning Sam and I, fifty percent responsibility for Stevie's medical costs. Sam's signature was on the bottom of the paper. Where was I when this happened? Was this an attempt at a plea deal before trial he never told me about or what? The second group of documents was for the garnishment of Sam's retirement; his signature was not on these. In fact, they were dated after his death. I don't know much about this kind of stuff. I needed to find help. Time to use that pre-paid legal I'd been paying into for over a decade. I'd almost canceled it when I found out Sam's legal costs, being a criminal case rather than a civil matter, were not covered by the prepaid plan. I gathered together all the paperwork I could find, clipped it together and made an appointment. At the last minute I put in a copy of Stevie's guardianship papers too.

Parking in downtown Santa Fe is always a problem. This time of year, February, when the legislature was in session, was no exception. I drove around for almost twenty minutes trying to find an empty spot, finally pulling into one in front of the post office, depositing my only quarter and walking the four blocks to the legal firm's office. For thirty-five dollars, and of course fourteen dollars a paycheck for the past eleven years, I got a twenty-five minute consultation. When I walked in the door two minutes late the clock was already ticking. A receptionist greeted me.

"Yes, come in, this is the right place. Do you have your membership card with you?" She pushed a clipboard with a yellow form and pen on it towards me. "Fill in the top half of the form. Cash or check? I'll let someone know you're here."

I took the clipboard, counted out the thirty five dollars and collapsed into a nearby chair.

A rail thin lawyer, exceptionally well dressed in a maroon wool suit and impeccably polished three inch heels appeared in the hallway.

"Mrs. Roark? How do you do, I'm Evelyn Lucero. I'll be working with you today. I see you've already started the paperwork. Bring it with you. Let's sit in the conference room."

I followed her down the hall to a small conference room. Six upholstered swivel chairs were pushed around an oval mahogany conference table. The walls were painted pale coral to resemble adobe, several large Navajo rugs, mounted under glass, graced the walls. It made me yearn for the two I had sold dirt cheap to pay past due electric bills after a third and final notice was sent.

"Please have a seat. How can I help you?" She took the clipboard from me, scanned the form and signed the upper corner.

I pulled the letters and notices from my teacher bag that also held the student homework I would need to grade tonight. "It's a long story, but the two things I need help with are here." I placed the papers in front of me, tapping my hand on top as I spoke.

"I lost my husband a few months ago. I was supposed to start getting his pension benefit, but apparently it's being garnished to pay for our son's medical bills. I didn't know anything about it until two weeks ago. Also, my son's in a long term care facility because of a brain injury and I guess the hospital got guardianship. I didn't know they could do that. I can't make sense of any of this." I pushed the stack of papers across the table to her.

She picked up the papers and began flipping through them pausing every now and then to study something more carefully. I sat quietly watching her, waiting for her to start asking questions.

"If you'll allow me I'd like to make copies of a few of these?" She stood up.

"Yes of course." I agreed.

Good, hopefully I can get some help. I kept glancing at the clock. More than half my time had elapsed. What happens if my time expires? Is it like a parking meter? Do I put in another thirty five dollars? I waited, studying the intricate brown, gray and white pattern of the Two Grey Hills rug that hung on the wall in front of me. I scanned the border of the weaving, searching for the single thread of a spirit line that would prevent the weaver's spirit from becoming trapped inside the complex design. That's what I needed, a spirit line that would release me from this ever turning maze.

Five more minutes elapsed. The lawyer, heels clicking on the polished floor, came back into the room, returning the packet of papers to me and keeping the copies for herself.

"First, let me offer my condolences on the loss of your husband. From the paperwork here it appears that he, and you by default as his spouse, entered into a binding mediation agreement with the medical center over your son's medical costs. Your signature is on one of the forms." She flipped through the stack of papers and showed me one I had signed shortly after Stevie was transferred to the long term care center, only a couple of weeks after the accident.

"This is an acknowledgment by you to accept mediation should any dispute occur, which is what St. Mary's did in seeking judgment. The garnishment was a judgment ex parte, which means neither you, or your late spouse was present and the judge responded to the petition for payment entered by the mediator as requested by St. Mary's. The garnishment is against your husband's pension. To put it simply you and your spouse agreed to accept the decision of a mediator instead of a judge and jury, and when the bill wasn't paid, St Mary's petitioned to garnish his pension as payment, the judge granted the request because no one challenged it."

"What can I do? I didn't even know about any of this?" I flipped through my stack of papers until I found the same form she was looking at.

"Unfortunately, you or your spouse had to file a response within thirty days of the garnishment. At this point I do need to tell you I can't represent you in this matter. Our firm is on retainer as counsel for St. Mary's." She pulled out another paper from the bottom of the stack. It was a list of phone numbers. "Here are the numbers for some legal referral services. It may help you locate someone more able to assist."

"What is that going to cost? I've had the prepaid legal plan for eleven years, this is the first time I've used it."

"And we are happy you have chosen us. But you can understand my position. If you do decide to utilize the referral service, they might be able to steer you to someone who has a sliding fee structure. My best to you, Mrs. Roark." She stood up.

"That's it? I need to call someone else? That's what I got for me thirty five dollars? Call someone else?" How can they get away with this?

"We do our best to meet the needs of our prepaid legal customers. Unfortunately we are not always able to help. Vera at the front desk will give you your receipt. I've already signed it."

"Seriously? That's it? What about Stevie's guardianship?" I stayed in the chair.

"Mrs. Roark I do wish the best for your son. I can tell you that in general the medical center applies for guardianship so they can file for benefits like Social Security disability and any other reimbursements a patient may qualify for. It helps to defray the cost of care provided. But other than that I can't really advise you on this matter either." She stood at the door, holding it open.

"But what can I do? Can I get it back? Can I get Stevie's guardianship back?" I knew my time was up, but I wasn't ready to leave.

"From the paperwork you brought it's unclear if you ever had guardianship over him as an adult. I do have another appointment Mrs. Roark, if you'll excuse me." She left me there alone.

I sat staring at the papers in front of me a good seven or eight minutes, then packed it up, picked up the receipt at the desk and hurried back to the car. At least I didn't get a parking ticket I thought as the expired parking meter flashed. *Violation...Violation... Violation.*

17

When I pulled into the tight parking space assigned to my side of the triplex Peanuts was looking out the window. Every day when I got home from school I leashed him up and went walking, pockets stuffed with plastic shopping bags for the poop patrol. Today I was late and Peanuts was frantic. He missed everybody. He still sniffed the dresser that only a few months ago held his master's clothes, didn't really know where he was, but neither did I. Stevie had gotten Peanuts when he was a freshman in college. I thought it was a mistake, but the two were devoted to each other. For weeks after the accident Peanuts refused to come in at night. The big black dog, gentle as a kitten, would lay out by the gate all night long, alert, attentive, lifting his head high for every car that passed waiting for Stevie to come home, but of course he never did. I was glad to have him now. Evenings when we watched TV he would lie at my feet. Nights, when I put my hand over the side of the bed there he was, and now as we walked, he stayed close by. Every once in a while I would drive over to the dog park and let him run. Today was the first day I didn't go to see Stevie since the accident. I was exhausted, but Peanuts didn't care, so on the leash went and out the door. We were gone an hour. The wind blew gently and you could still smell the earth just starting to thaw after a long winter.

Someone was waiting when we got back, the landlord.

"Aileen, I know you have a lot going on right now, but your check came back." Mel Martinez had been a good landlord. He never bothered us as long as the rent was paid. He handed me an electronic printout of my check stamped Insufficient Funds.

Peanuts sniffed Mel's other hand and softly wagged his tail. Mel reached out and scratched the dog's ear.

"Peanuts really likes you. He misses the boys so much." I took the printout from him and peered at it in the fading light as I unlocked the door.

"Come in Mel." I unzipped my jacket and hung it on the coat rack Sean had made in tenth grade Wood Shop.

"Aileen, I can't stay, but you know there is a fee for returned checks, forty dollars, and late rent fee is fifty. I really hate to do this to you but I do need the account brought up to date by next week. Look, I 'll drop the late rent charge but I owe the bounced check money to my bank." Mel was matter of fact, unemotional, used to dealing with overdue rent issues.

I sighed, as naive as it sounds it was the first time I considered that all the checks I wrote would bounce without the two thousand from Sam's pension I had counted on.

"Well, I'd write you a check but that would bounce too," I said and laughed, he didn't. "I get paid this Friday. Can you wait until then? I'll give you cash."

"Friday then, I can come by right after I get off work." He shook my hand.

"Okay. I usually go to see Stevie at the care center, but I'll walk Peanuts then wait for you."

"That'll work, Friday." He walked out the door, pulling it closed behind him.

If I was a drinking person now would be the time, but I hadn't touched the stuff since the accident. I fed Peanuts, gathered up a load of laundry to take to the Laundromat tomorrow, made myself a grilled cheese and went to bed. Peanuts cautiously put one paw then the other up on the bed, jumped up all the way, turned in two circles and lay down with his back against mine.

Wednesday was uneventful. Routine work, walk Peanuts, sit with Stevie, three loads at the Laundromat, home to grade papers, late to bed. Thursday started routine but around eleven in the morning, a student aid came to my room with a folded yellow message form. I wished they wouldn't send kids with these things. Whatever the message, it was usually personal, either for the teacher or the parent who called. I opened it now as I wrote the chapter and page numbers on the board.

Call Rita at the Medical Center ASAP.

I buzzed the office, waited, no response. Five minutes passed and I tried again, no answer. There was no way to summon anyone to watch my class a minute or two.

"Excuse me class, I have to make an urgent call. You guys be good." I winked at them.

"We will Mrs. Roark." They giggled and jostled each other. If I left the door open I could see them from across the hall where the teachers' lounge held the only school phone teachers had access. Oh how I wished my cell phone payment had gone through but it had bounced too.

I slipped quickly across the hall and dialed the number, surprised when a real person answered, not a Press One loop.

"Medical Center, may I help you?"

"Is Rita there?"

"Who's calling please?"

"It's Aileen Roark, Stevie's mom, I was returning her call."

"Hold please, I'll page her." A medley of Beatles' tunes played over the phone line.

I held the phone under my chin and leaned out the door to check the kids. One of them had closed the door and I could hear yells and banging coming from inside the room. I put the receiver down and raced across the hall.

Deanna, a mischievous thirteen year old was the look out, opening the door a crack before, "Shhh, she's coming, you guys, she's coming."

I opened the door. The little darlings were in their seats pretending to write.

"You kids be good, I'm on a very important call." I slipped back across the hall.

The door slammed again. I was torn. Did I see to my own son or the misbehaving eighth graders? I chose my son. Big Mistake.

I picked up the phone and heard Rita's voice, "Hello? Hello? Is anyone there?"

"Hi Rita. It's Aileen Roark. I got your message. Sorry. I'm at school I'm trying to watch my class too. I had to put the phone down for a minute. What's up?"

Rita was very businesslike, a departure from her usual friendly chatter. "I want to update you about Stevie. He seems to be struggling with breathing and his vitals are not what we like to see. I put in a call to the Doctor. He's supposed to be here around twelve thirty, as soon as he clears his morning appointments. You might want to be here."

I got nervous. "Is Stevie okay?"

"Well, we don't know for sure. I'm guessing the doctor will order some tests. Maybe a culture, he may have picked something up. But if you can come it would be good. Do try to come."

An alarm sounded. Not in my head, a real one; ear piercing horn, lights flashing, kids yelling.

I looked across the hall. One of my students, one of the special needs kids who innocently went along with whatever the others put him up to came running over, waving his arms in the air.

"Mrs. Roark! Mrs. Roark! The kids set a fire. The alarm went off."

The students came pouring out of my room. A stack of notebook paper piled towards the front had ignited a shelf of books. A tall wood bookcase was blazing away. Flames were leaping almost to the ceiling setting off the sprinklers, which, not having been checked for months if not years, spitted and dripped, the flow blocked by a decade of grime and calcium deposits.

I dropped the phone, grabbed the clipboard with the attendance and evacuation plan hanging just inside the class door.

"Out, form one line, walk." I said, shouting as loud as I could over the earsplitting fire alarm. "Let's go." I yelled at the remaining two boys in the room. They ran out pointing the finger at the other.

"Joshua did it."

"No it was Brandon."

I walked them to the parking lot. "Line up single file."

The whole school was rushing to exit, security and administrators looking at each other.

"Who pulled it?" I could see them mouth.

The students all accounted for, I hurried over to the security guard.

"It's my room. The kids set the bookcase on fire. I think you'll need the extinguisher." He looked shocked. He had always been my buddy, stood by me, but this had happened on his watch and in this era of data based performance reviews would be a black mark on his otherwise good evaluation. He scowled, rushed for the building. I could see him grab a red and silver extinguisher as he entered my room.

The fire alarm set off a commotion not only at the school site, but in the community as well. Automatic notification meant the school had less than three minutes to call the Fire Department of a false alarm, which of course it wasn't. It had been a real fire, albeit small one. The fire trucks came, the paramedics came, and the superintendent came. A reporter, alerted by police scanner, showed up with camera in hand. The media attention would bring deep scrutiny to both Fire Department and School Administrators. Everyone was trying to fix blame for the lack of oversight of the school's malfunctioning sprinklers. I was not in their good graces.

The kids were dismissed to the cafeteria for an early lunch while it got sorted out. I walked over to the principal who stood talking with the superintendent, security guard and fire captain.

"I have to leave. Stevie's not doing well. I can come in later or early tomorrow to write up a report. I'm sorry. I got an urgent call and nobody was there to watch my class. I'll come in tomorrow."

The security guard still scowled, looked down, arms folded. The principal looked to the superintendent for guidance.

"No, we need you to come into the office and fill out a report now before you go."

"My son, they called, he's taken a turn for the worse and they called in the doctor. They want me there. I have to go." I pleaded with her.

"You have no more leave. You will be AWOL. I'm not sure you appreciate the seriousness of this situation."

"My son is serious. I need to take family leave."

"You have no more leave. There is no more leave without pay. We discussed this already."

"Sorry, I have to go." And I did.

¤ ¤ ¤

The doctor was standing at the nurses' station reviewing the medical notes when I arrived. He had already been to Stevie's room.

Rita greeted me, "Mrs. Roark, I'm so glad you came. This is Dr. Sanchez; he has taken over for Dr. Vishnu."

Dr. Sanchez barely looked up. "How do you do." He didn't extend his hand but continued to look at the tablet computer he held with both hands.

"Stevie is your son?" He took a stylus from his pocket, tapped the screen twice and began to write.

"Yes, how is he?"

"I'm requesting a transfer to Saint Mary's as soon as transport can be arranged. We want to take a look at his blood work, maybe up his oxygen. I'll refer him to Respiratory for a look. Have you discussed his situation with Family Services? I understand insurance could be an issue, and it's important to have a medical guardian statement in place. I don't see one in this file."

"Yes, the hospital was trying for guardianship so they could apply for benefits under his name. But when did he start oxygen?"

Dr. Sanchez looked over his shoulder at Rita, then back at the screen, using the stylus to scroll across it.

"It looks like Dr. Vishnu ordered oxygen a few weeks after he was transferred here. Also I think we need to follow up on the IV site. We need to be sure it's changed as needed to prevent infections."

"I've never known him to use oxygen before. Rita has he ever used oxygen when I wasn't here?"

Rita shrugged her shoulders. "We have a protocol for priorities when the oxygen is delivered. I don't believe oxygen has been used during my shifts."

"Was he supposed to have it?"

"We follow the protocol that St. Mary's has for his medical care."

Dr. Sanchez frowned.

"What's wrong?" I asked.

"We'll know more when the blood work comes back, but it looks as if he has picked up an infection, probably bacterial. There seems to be some local involvement at the site of the IV, sometimes the infection becomes systemic, it enters the blood stream and then it's really hard to shake off. We can order things but there are limits to what the insurer will reimburse the hospital for, especially if he is receiving indigent care. There are recommended specific protocols that St. Mary's will follow in cases like this."

"Oh," was all I could say. "Well, he isn't getting indigent care. I've been paying for his care myself and St. Mary's started getting most of my late husband's retirement. I just found out when I checked my last deposit." The thought of all the bounced checks and the fees I would have to pay rolled into my head.

"At any rate, I am recommending he be transferred to St. Mary's for a while so we can better address his immediate problems. After that we can look at his long term care plan. I do think you should follow up with the Family Service Office. I would like to see a guardian plan on file and in his chart." Dr. Sanchez flipped the computer's cover closed and slipped it into the front pocket of his medical coat.

"I have some other patients to check on while I'm here, very nice to have met you." He flipped at a stethoscope around his neck and started down the corridor.

"Thanks." I wrung my hands together trying to decide what to do next. Everything was so overwhelming I wanted to shut down.

"Mrs. Roark? Aileen? You can sit with Stevie if you want. We are still waiting for a call back from the ambulance service. They were on a call last time I checked. And the hospital has to approve a bed for him. Would you like some coffee? There is some behind the nurses' station you can have. I'd get it for you but we're swamped right now." Rita put her hand on my arm as she spoke to me, bringing me back to reality.

Stevie's transfer was not approved.

18

Friday. I used to look forward to Fridays. Today I didn't. I owed rent to my landlord, was about to be fired from my job and had to do battle with the hospital over Stevie's care. They say to take things one step at a time, but it was hard to decide which direction to step first, so I leashed up the dog and went for a walk. It was only six o'clock in the morning, still dark, but traffic was light. We walked up the trail by the arroyo. As usual, there were several homeless men just starting to pack up and hoist their bags. I wondered about them, where they slept at night, if they had someplace to get coffee and use a bathroom. It was the first time it had occurred to me I might not have any place to go soon. Surely I could manage for a while in my car I thought, rent a room someplace. There's always tomorrow, the song from *Annie* started to loop in my head. Don't go there, my mind kept telling me, and I pushed tomorrow aside for today.

By the time we got back it was seven o'clock. Normally I would be showered, dressed, and ready to get in the car, headed to school by now, but when I got home last night a message on my answering machine announced I was officially on administrative leave and to report at eight thirty in the morning, to the administrative conference room, to discuss my employment. I made a cup of tea, pulled out my bank statements to see how much I was in the hole for, and turned on the TV. A cold front was expected, spring snowstorm, warnings were being issued.

Several automatic payments; cell phone; natural gas; car insurance; had been taken out first week of the month. I had also written that rent check, bought groceries and dog food, gas, credit cards payment, the typical things one needs these days. But because Sam's check was for five hundred not fifteen hundred, two months in a row, I was overdrawn big time. Not only did I have about nine overdraft charges to my credit union, but I would also owe bounced check fees to everyone else too. For each check I couldn't cover it would cost me almost seventy five dollars on top of the amount I owed the first go around. I thought about the gas station that put people's names on the marque 'Don't accept checks from–', mine would probably be there next time I went by. Christ, I was in the hole for almost two thousand dollars, and that was to cover last month. This month's bills were just coming due.

Remain calm and carry on, I said to myself, tried to channel Winston Churchill. His spirit apparently didn't respond to something as mundane as a bounced checked. I was on my own.

I should get my paycheck today, I reasoned, in fact it might already be in my account. I would withdraw enough to pay the rent, in cash, to Mel, plus a little for groceries then decide where to go from there. At least I would have three weeks to figure things out. I got dressed and let Peanuts out one more time before getting out a rawhide chew. It seemed like a small consolation for being cooped up all day, but maybe it wouldn't take that long.

The wind had picked up outside. I zipped my Home of the Blue Hawks hoodie and pulled some gloves from the pocket, closed and locked the door and headed north for the thirty minute drive to the district administrative conference room.

I was right, it didn't take long. The receptionist/board secretary was sitting at her desk when I came in. She was peeling labels from a computer printed page, and placing them on folded copies of the district newsletter. I had known her for fifteen years.

"Good Morning Della. How've you been?"

She didn't smile. "Good Morning Mrs. Roark (what's up, she always calls me Aileen) you can go into the conference room. The others will be along shortly." She picked up the stack of already addressed newsletters and straightened them.

It was obvious she didn't want to make small talk. I went into the empty room and sat at the second chair on the left of the oval table, where I could see out the window and not have my back to the door.

I could hear Della on the phone, "She's here now. I sent her in. No, no one is with her."

Was I supposed to bring someone?

The wind picked up outside blowing the door open. A scatter of dust and leaves blew in along with a fierce blast of cold air. I realized I was twisting my gloves nervously between both hands, more for Stevie then anything. I should have called to check on him. The whole time I was figuring my bank account I could have called. I set the gloves down on the table. Maybe Della would let me use her phone. I stood up and started toward the door.

Two men dressed in sport coats and ties, the business manager, Brandon Cisneros and Assistant Superintendent Robbie Valentine appeared at the main entrance. I sat back down and waited. I had only meet them each once, but I recognized them from committee meetings and start of school year staff days. Word was when there was dirty business to be done they were the ones who did it. I was about to find out if that was true.

Della greeted them. "Yes she's in there. I'll put on some fresh coffee. What's in there is two hours old."

They came into the conference room and took seats across from me at the table. One had a large brown envelope in his hand.

"Good Morning." I stood up and extended my hand.

The assistant superintendent barely touched it, only half rose from his seat. "Mrs. Roark, I'm sure you know why we are here. Please sit down. You got the message I assume that you were on administrative leave."

"Yes I did. I know Superintendent Roybal wanted me to fill in the report right away over that fire but my son has been hospitalized. I was called to the hospital and had to go. I explained to her I needed family leave. I can fill in the report now." I folded my hands in front of me to avoid twisting the gloves anymore.

"That won't be necessary. You are officially on administrative leave pending termination." The business manager pulled a paper on school letter head from the envelope and pushed it towards me.

"We will be bringing your case before the board at the next meeting. But we don't need the board's approval." Cisneros cleared his throat as he said it.

I glanced at the letter before me: '*This is official notification that you are hereby placed on Administrative Leave pending further action, effective immediately*'. It was signed by Antonia Roybal, Superintendent, District Two.

"What? Look, I'm sorry, my son, I just lost my husband. If you will let me explain..." I tried to push the letter back at them.

"Mrs. Roark, you will have the opportunity to request a hearing after the board meets. We do have another option for you. If you are willing to sign a letter of resignation, we will not initiate termination proceedings." Robbie Valentine was not so sweet. He adjusted himself in the chair, gave a little gasp, like he had heartburn.

"But why? I explained to Superintendent Roybal about my situation, how I would need to take leave for Stevie's medical and my husband's situation. I even gave her a letter from the doctor." My voice was shaking.

At this point Cisneros opened the envelope and pulled out another letter already prepared and waiting for my signature.

"As I said Mrs. Roark, you may request a hearing after the board meets. Our condolences on the loss of your husband and your son, we wish the best outcome for your remaining son, but we cannot have teachers AWOL, the district no longer authorizes leave without pay. We need our teachers in the classroom. If you are willing to sign the letter of resignation we can all move forward and no further adverse personal action will be needed." He made it sound so contrite, like 'how dare you make me do my job and fire you.'

I could smell that fresh pot of coffee dripping in the outer office. Was that part of their contract? Fresh coffee when they came in the door to do the dirty work?

I looked at the letter, short and to the point.

I am resigning my teaching position effective immediately.

I kept thinking back on all the work I had done for these people, usually without added compensation, all the Saturdays and evenings I had given up to take students to science fairs, public speaking contests; workshops and classes on my own dime, meetings with parents when I should have been with my own family.

"No, I want a hearing. This isn't fair. I've worked for this district for more than twenty years. This is the only time I needed to use leave, to take family leave like this. I want a hearing. I can't even get anyone to give me a copy of the Leave Policy. Show me the policy." I pushed the resignation letter back at them. They looked at each other.

"It's being revised." The business manager picked up the letter and placed it back in the envelope while the assistant superintendent drummed his fingers on the table, obviously annoyed.

"Very well, the board meeting will be a week from next Wednesday. In the mean time you are on administrative leave and are not to come on school property or contact anyone within the school system unless you go through one of use. The offer to resign will remain until next Wednesday, at which time we will initiate the formal termination process. I need to collect your keys and any other items, grade book or teacher's edition you have."

They both stood up. I stared at them, dazed by what had just happened. I guess I should have had someone with me. I stood up, took the two keys off my key ring, one for my classroom and one for my desk and lay them on the table.

"The other things are in the top desk drawer, the smaller key will unlock it. Do you want my jacket too?" I smirked at them sarcastically, turned slightly so they could see the middle school name emblazoned on the back of the jacket and walked out. Did these men have no compassion? I was outside about to unlock the car when I realized I had left my gloves on the table in the conference room and went back in.

They were already at the coffee pot, joking and sarcastic. "But, but I've been here twenty years..." rolling their eyes. Valentine was brushing the crumbs of a powdered sugar doughnut from his tie.

They stopped abruptly when they caught sight of me and their faces again turned to stone. Did they practice that look? I started to tell them off, stopped myself, picked up the gloves, got in the car and backed out.

So the rumors were true. These two were the hatchet men. Remain calm and move forward.

19

It was getting very windy. I started the car up again and drove away. I could feel the Subaru being buffeted by crosswinds and had to grip the wheel tightly to keep the car on the road. Several times I slowed to allow huge tumble weeds to blow in front of the car so as not to hit them head on. My worries over money were overshadowed by what had just happened and by my concern for Stevie. Still, I knew I had to take care of business. There was a credit union branch just a few miles from the school administration complex. I pulled into the lot, re-checked the paper I had done my math on that morning and went inside. There were only a few patrons at this hour of the day. It was only nine o'clock and the doors had opened only minute or two ago. I filled out the yellow withdrawal slip and went straight to the teller window. No one was in line.

"Sorry, but your account has a negative balance, no withdrawals are possible." The young lady passed the slip back to me.

"I know I have a couple of overdrafts but a deposit should have been made by midnight last night. My payroll should have gone in. Can you check for me?" I was always pleasant with the bank staff. I have seen people lit into them with a furry when things were seldom their fault. She tapped the keys on her computer, waited, clicked the mouse and tapped the keyboard again.

"No, there wasn't a deposit. The last deposit made was for five hundred on February 5th."

"Are you sure? Can you check my savings? Maybe it went in the wrong account for some reason."

"No." She clicked the mouse again, wrote the number twenty five on a slip of paper and slid it across the counter towards me. "This is the current balance on your savings. You need to maintain a minimum balance to stay a member in good standing."

"Yes, I know, something must be wrong. I need to check with the school and see what's up."

"You may want to meet with one of our account managers regarding the overdrafts." She wrote on a paper again -$3050.00. "It looks like you have exceeded the share account overdraft protection amount."

No way. I owed more than three thousand, not the two thousand I had calculated. I had left off the amount the overdraft protection already covered. I was dizzy and confused. I stood a minute trying to absorb what was happening.

"Thank you," was all I could think to say. "How late are you open?"

"On Fridays the lobby is open until five-thirty and the drive up stays open until six."

"Thank you." I turned and walked away.

Why hadn't my paycheck gone in? I drove back to the District Two Administration Building. When I got out the wind slammed my door shut, rattling the glass of the old Subaru. I didn't try to stop it. Della was still sticking address labels onto newsletters. She looked up, a little worried.

"I need to see Mr. Cisneros or Mr. Valentine. Are they still here?" The anger in my voice was hard to mask.

"I believe so, I'll check." Della picked up the phone and pushed the intercom buttons.

"Is Mr. Cisneros still there? Mrs. Roark is back to see him. Okay, I'll tell her." Della replaced the receiver. "Dr. Roybal says you're to wait here for Mr. Cisneros."

I glanced at the pictures in the little plastic cube on her desk. Our sons had once played on the same soccer team. I calmed down a little.

"Okay, thanks Della. How are things with your family? How's your son's first year of Med School going?"

"Oh, fine." Della turned in her chair to face the other way.

"Aren't you supposed to talk to me or something?"

She turned half around, shrugged her shoulders. A pained look ran across her face.

"It's okay. I know what it's like to be afraid to lose your job. Believe me."

This upset her, she got up from her seat and busied herself wiping up spots of coffee and spilled creamer from around the coffee maker.

Cisneros came out and stood four feet from me leaning on the counter with his elbows.

"What can I do for you Mrs. Roark?"

"My paycheck wasn't deposited. I don't understand. That was for the time I have already worked. I'm still on payroll. I should have gotten paid."

"We are withholding your pay pending inventory of your classroom books, computers and electronics, grades, we need to be sure all school property is accounted for and the appropriate amount withheld for any missing or damaged items."

"You can't do that! I already worked those days. I need that paycheck. How can I check for inventory if you won't let me back in my room?"

"We will take care of the inventory and yes we can withhold pay until all school property is accounted for. It is allowable."

"Please, I need that money. My son, I have bills I owe."

"I sympathize with your situation Mrs. Roark (*I doubt that*), but we have a responsibility to tax payers to be accountable for public property. We could probably speed things up a little if you signed that letter we discussed earlier."

What a freaking scum bag. This was blackmail.

"Do you mean if I sign the letter of resignation you will release my paycheck?"

"Well it would certainly mean we could bring this situation to a conclusion much sooner, don't you agree Della?"

Della looked down beaten. "Can I get you anything Mr. Cisneros? I'm going to go on break otherwise."

"Yes, Della, if you could go to Superintendent Roybal's office and retrieve the brown envelop I left on her conference table."

I stood looking at him with utter disdain. He leaned against the receptionist desk, arms crossed in front of him, smug, contrite.

Della came back down the hall carrying the envelope and handed it to Brandon Cisneros before walking around the back of her desk for her coat and purse.

"Hang on a minute Del; I may need to have you make a copy of something for me."

Cisneros pulled the letter of resignation from the envelope, placed it in front of me, reached over to the plastic photo cube pen holder on Della's desk for a black stick pen, which he placed diagonally across the letter.

I thought about all the money I owed, about Stevie and Peanuts, about the rent. Where would I go if I couldn't pay? I picked up the pen and signed the damn letter.

"I think you made the right choice Mrs. Roark. You should see the money in your account by Tuesday or Wednesday at the latest. Della, can you make three copies of this letter for me, one for Mrs. Roark and one for Superintendent Roybal?"

"Tuesday? I need the money today. I have to pay my landlord. I thought I would get the money today?"

"Tuesday. We have already closed the books today. Monday we will issue the voucher and it should appear in your account Tuesday or Wednesday."

Della quickly returned with both copies and original, handing them to Cisneros, grabbed her coat and rushed out the door.

"Mr. Cisneros, please, I really need that money today." I hated to grovel in front of this man, but risked eviction.

"Tuesday the earliest, Wednesday more likely." He placed the original and one copy of the letter I had just signed back into the envelope. I caught a faint smile, then slight gasp of indigestion, was it me or the donuts?

I looked him in the eye, "How do you sleep at night?"

"Very well, thank you." He said and handed me my copy of the letter. I took it and left, driving slowly through the gated entrance and onto the main highway. I only got a mile down the road when I pulled over onto the shoulder, turned off the engine and started to cry.

The District Two hatchet men had earned their coffee and donuts today, they had broken me.

20

By the time I got home it was not quite ten. I didn't think the time could be right. Like a car wreck, everything had moved in slow motion. I went inside, sat at the tiny table and chair that had once been my breakfast nook but now served as my main dining table/desk/work table and pulled out the resignation letter. It grieved me deeply to end my career at the middle school like this. Maybe things could still be straightened out. But right now I had to figure out how to pay Mel the rent by five tonight.

I flipped through the composition notebook I used to try and keep track of dates, places and numbers so when I needed to fill out yet another form I had all the information in one spot. I had the date of the accident, notes from the meetings with Sam's lawyers, notes from the meeting with the CU prepaid lawyer, questions I had about Stevie's care plan, all the things that were important to me.

I opened the book to a clean page, decided to write an algorithm with plus and minus options.

Problem- Where do I live?

Needs- Place for Peanuts; warm; safe; place to cook and store food.

Possible Solution: Stay in Apartment; Live in Car; Find a cheaper/smaller place.

Then I made check marks beside each choice, and wrote dollar signs. There had to be a logical way to decide this, I struggled with it a long time then decided what I wanted was to stay in the apartment. Which meant I had to have money.

I started a new list:

Options for Money: Write a check? Who would cash it? No money in account Sell Stuff? Get a loan? Borrow from a friend?

Problem was I had no friends left. Most of the friends I had before the accident abandoned me, wrote me off as if I was the one who drove drunk. The few I had left from school had been instructed in no uncertain terms to have nothing to do with me.

I circled sell stuff, remembered the first day I moved here. Dawn, my neighbor, and I had the yard sale. I looked around the place and decided who needs furniture anyway.

21

I would need to act fast if I was going to raise the money. I was too late to put an ad in the paper or online. I'd make a couple of signs and drag stuff outside. As long as it didn't snow I would be okay. If I had more time, maybe tomorrow, I could go to the storage unit and see what I could part with there. But right now I needed to get a couple of boxes to use as sign boards. If I left now, I would be able to stop and check on Stevie. Peanuts was eager to ride, hoped into the car. My neighbor was riding up the street on her bike.

'Hi Aileen, you're home early today." Dawn got off her bike and wheeled it onto the porch.

"Well, yeah, things aren't going too well. I lost my job and..."

"Oh, I'm so sorry. What happened?" Dawn unhooked the box from the back of her bike.

"Things, I can tell you later. I'm on my way to see Stevie and then I'm going to have another yard sale to raise rent money." I didn't see any reason to lie.

"Today? You're having a sale today?"

"Yeah, I told Mel I'd have the rent by five tonight, and well, I don't have it so I'm going to try and get it together by then. I'll talk to you later okay? I really have to get going."

"Let me know, I may have some things to put in your sale."

"Sorry Dawn, I really can't do that this time. I just have to get the rent together or Peanuts and I will need to move out. See you soon okay."

"Okay, later then."

I drove first to the Medical Center. People don't like to call them Nursing Homes anymore. They have all kinds of name now: Long Term Care Facility; Life Care Institute; I even found one called Mindful Living Community. But this one was St Mary's Light of Mercy Basic Life Extended Care Center, a mouthful. The parking lot was empty save for the section marked *Staff Only*. Not too many visitors in the middle of a weekday. Rita was there. She greeted me as I went in the door.

"Do you have any news on Stevie's transfer?" I asked.

"No. Sorry, nothing new to report. The doctor did put in the request. I think he even called the Chief Medical Officer or CEO or something, but the answer was the same. Stevie doesn't meet the protocol guidelines for transfer. We really will do everything we can for him Aileen. The staff in his wing are excellent." She reassured me.

"I know Rita , but there aren't enough of them. I don't see how you can take care of that many patients." I was filled with sympathy for both Rita and Stevie.

"Yes it can be difficult, especially when staff are pulled to another wing or scheduled for in-service." Rita continued to sort through the medications, placing two or three pills into small medicine cups before locking the rest in a wall safe.

"Don't they have to get a sub, like at school?"

"No, as long as the staff to patient ratio is at forty percent of national, they don't bring in anyone. But, I do know they count the staff at training as part of that number."

"You're kidding! How does that help?"

"I don't know, that's just the way it is sometimes." The light on the nurses call board turned on for one of the room.

"Excuse me. I have to see to a patient now." Rita got up and left, carrying the medication tray with her.

I walked down the hall to Stevie's room. Two of the patients in the room were conscious, well at least they had their eyes open and seemed to be watching TV.

Stevie and the other patient, an elderly man in the bed directly opposite Stevie's were both on their sides in a semi fetal position. A white board on the wall behind each read *Turn 1300*, I think it meant both needed to be turned by one o'clock; bed sores were a constant source of infection.

I pulled the metal chair over to the side of the bed where I could face Stevie, re-arranged the tubes and wires that extended from his body which connected him to the unchanging digital monitor slightly above his bed. It was hard for me to see him like this. His face had become ashen, his cheeks sunken and the expression on his face was never changing. His eyes were half open. The few times they did move it was in jerky spasms, not a focused look of acknowledgment. Where was my six foot three strong man?

"Hey Buddy, it's mom. I guess you had a rough night." I brushed what little hair he had with my hand. In order to help in personal care, most of the men like Stevie were shaved clean of hair every couple of weeks.

"Peanuts and I went for a long walk this morning. I had some extra time. He really likes the trail near where we live now. Sometimes he meets another dog and the other owner and I let him off leash so they can run. We're probably not supposed to but boy does he have a blast."

"I saw Jude's mom today. I guess he's doing okay at Med School. You know Jude. You played soccer together for a few years. You guys were great, the All Stars, what a team. This is a world cup year. I'll try to watch for you and keep you updated."

I kept up the banter like this for a good twenty minutes, except it wasn't constant. After every new thought or idea I would wait a couple of minutes, watching Stevie, hoping for some type of response. But no, he just lies there, still. I could hear him laboring to breath. I turned on the call light and a male attendant came to the room.

"Hello can I help you?" He reached behind the bed and turned off the light.

"Yes, I'm Stevie's mom. I don't think I've met you before."

"I'm Orlando, I'm one of the on call staff. This is the first time I've covered this unit."

"Oh, well I was wondering when Stevie would be getting his oxygen. The doctor yesterday said he was recommending oxygen."

"I don't know, I can go and check?"

"Yes, would you please?"

"Be right back."

I got up and stretched my legs. Peanuts was in the car. I couldn't stay much longer. Orlando came back.

"It looks like oxygen is not part of Stevie's current care plan. I did see a note that an order was put in, however there is a follow up note indicating review of chart by the St. Mary's Quality Assurance team found he didn't meet protocol guidelines for oxygen."

I just nodded, sad, tears welling that I willed back, bent over and kissed Stevie on the head.

"See ya' soon son, love you." I left.

I sat in the car for at least ten minutes, hands on the wheel, key in the ignition, dazed. Peanuts sat beside me in the passenger seat. He put his paw on my lap, got up several times, spun around and licked my face. Finally, with a big heavy breath, jumped into the back seat and curled up. I started the car and we headed for the liquor store to find some boxes. You have to try, I told myself, try to keep going.

22

The trick to writing a yard sale sign on a box is it to do it upside down. By that I mean you want to write it so the bottom of the box is on the ground, and put a rock or a brick in it so it doesn't blow. I used an old set of colored markers, most were dry and unusable, but one was all I needed. Three signs, one for each end of the block and one in front of the triplex. By one o'clock I was open for business.

It didn't take long for the first lookers to come in. I had taken all my cookware and dishes out and set them on the counter, I decided to low ball everything. Even if I didn't raise that much money it would be less to pack and move.

Dawn came over from next door with a friend.

"Mind if we look around?" she asked.

"No, of course not, let me know if you see something you're interested in." I was still busy organizing things.

"What about the bedroom? Can we go in there?" They were already in the doorway.

"Oh yeah, almost anything you see, not the pet stuff. I've got to keep Peanuts bed and leash and stuff."

"We just want to look around." Dawn's friend said.

I could hear them talking softly in the bedroom and then the bathroom. I was about to go in and see them when a customer arrived. She went directly to the table I had set my Desert Rose dishes on.

"Service for twelve," I told her. "I've also got the coffee set and a pie platter." I held up the tall pot to show her.

"What are you asking?"

"Boy, for this set? Three fifty, I've seen a single plate for sale for thirty in the consignment shops, so it's a very good price."

She picked up a salad plate, flipped it over, checked the mark and replaced it. "I'd give you one fifty."

I'm not good at poker. My disappointment was obvious. "No, sorry, the price on these is firm. I need three fifty."

She picked up another piece, "Surely you'll take less."

"No. Sorry, no." I re-stacked the dessert bowls.

She spun around in the kitchen, picked up the pizza stone and wheel, "Two bucks?"

"Two's good." She fished the money from her purse and handed it to me before leaving.

A couple more people stopped by. Not exactly busting the doors down. I sold the TV and DVD player for forty bucks, some books and kitchen knives. Dawn and her friend left, saying, "We may be back later."

A woman in a broomstick skirt and thick Peruvian sweater pulled up in a silver Dodge pickup truck. "ReVision Fine Furnishing and Consignment" was hand painted on the pickup's side.

"Hello," she said, greeted me in sing song voice. "Are you open for business?"

"Yes, come in." I held the door for her.

"Do you have prices marked?"

"No, this is kind of last minute Ask. I'll tell you, or you could make me an offer, almost everything is for a sale."

"Are you moving?"

"No, clearing things out is all."

She walked around asked about several pieces of furniture. Her broomstick skirt swished when she walked. No matter how hard I tried I would never be that suave.

"The kitchen table and chairs?" she asked.

"Yes, I can let that go for one fifty."

She stood in the middle of the room and did a three sixty slow spin. The folds of her skirt followed on a three second delay.

"I can give you two hundred for the loveseat, chair, coffee table and kitchen set.

Two hundred? Was she kidding?

I paused before I answered, "Six fifty. I need six fifty." At that I would still be four hundred short of making rent and late fees. If I could sell the Desert Rose set and bedroom furniture I might make it.

"What about three?"

It was almost three o'clock. Mel would be here in a of couple hours, "Five fifty."

"Four hundred, cash?"

I did the same slow spin she had just done, but mine was awkward, halting.

"Okay, four."

She opened her purse and counted out the money, two big ones and the rest in twenties. I was half way there.

"If you can help me I can take the kitchen chairs now, and coffee table. I'll have to send someone back for the love seat and chair." she said.

I cleared the clutter from the coffee table and we lifted the table into the back of the truck, piled the chairs on top.

"Are you interested in bedroom furniture? I have a queen bed set, dresser and night stand, there's a book case too."

"Let me take a look." She followed me back into the house."

"I can give you a hundred for the dresser and night stand if you'll throw in that lamp."

I thought about it a minute. "Okay, what about the bed and bookcase."

"Used mattress sets really don't sell well and nobody is buying bookcases anymore, everyone uses e readers now."

"Can you give me a couple of minutes to get my things out of the drawers? I haven't cleared it out yet."

"Of course, I'll have my crew pick it up when they come for the loveseat and chair."

Great, she paid me the hundred and grabbed the lamp. I was still four hundred short. Mel would be here in ninety minutes. Maybe he'd carry me a couple more days if I paid him what I had. It was worth a try.

I leashed up Peanuts, walked first to one end of the street, then the other and collected the two boxes I had used as signs at each end, then the one in front of the house. Peanuts resisted coming back up the walk way. He had his 'you call that a walk' karma going.

"Sorry Peanuts, that's the best I can do right now." I scratched his belly, which he loved, but he still paced side to side, hopeful there was more to come.

It was easy to take the clothes out of the drawer. I just got a big trash bag from under the sink and put them all in. I'd figure out what to do with them later. It took a little more time to wrap and pack the Desert Rose dishes I had stacked on the table. They had been a wedding gift from my grandmother in law. On our honeymoon Sam and I had stopped by the little apartment she rented in his home town. Already in her 80s, her deteriorating health meant she couldn't come for the ceremony. Next thing I know a box appeared at my door with all her dishes packed inside 'Hope you enjoy them as much as I have'. It seemed like a no brainier to sell them now, I had no one to leave them to. Still, I couldn't let them go for nothing.

I had barely wrapped the last dish when Peanuts began barking, someone was coming up the front walk. Two men, one in his teens and the other probably in his forty's, knocked politely at my door.

"We are here for the furniture," the younger many spoke with a heavy Spanish accent.

"Oh yes, come in".

"Is the dog okay?"

"Yes, but if it worries you I'll put him in the other room."

"Okay good." The two waited at the door while I took Peanuts into the bathroom and closed the door.

They came in, loaded up the living room furniture then the kitchen table. I walked them into the bedroom, and showed them what to take. The older one spoke to the younger one in Spanish.

"The bed too?"

"No, your boss didn't want the bed, just the dresser and night stand."

The teen relayed this info to his senior, who said something back, also in Spanish. I could make out Se Vende -For sale.

"Yes the bed is for sale do you know someone who wants it?"

"How much? How much for the bed?"

I turned to the man, he looked tired, his back slightly bent, old for his years. His eyes seemed hopeful. "Is it for you?" I asked him. "¿Para usted?"

"Yes, for me." He spoke to me directly in halting English.

"For you? Fifty dollars."

He spoke to the teen again.

"He wants to know if he can have the blankets too."

"Yes, he should wash them though." I didn't tell him about Peanuts curled up beside me last night.

"Okay, fifty dollars." The older man reached into his front shirt pocket and pulled out a folded stack of bills, carefully counted out three tens and a twenty, then placed the rest back in his shirt pocket.

At least someone would get a good night rest tonight.

It was down to the wire. If I hurried I could make it over to the storage locker and back with a sleeping bag and air mattress. I leashed Peanuts up again, coaxed him into the car and raced down Cerrillos until I got to the storage yard. The gate was still open, a man was just starting to move some furniture and antiques back into his storage locker. I rolled the window down. "How's business?"

"Today, kinda' slow. It picks up on weekends, maybe not this weekend though, still too cold."

"Do you have to get permission from the manager to sell stuff?"

"Well yes and no. I run this as my business. I have an arrangement with the office. But people do sell out of their lockers. I think the thing is if you don't do it all the time it's no big deal."

"Where do you get your stuff, to sell I mean?"

"Oh, check the want ads, try to scoop other peoples' yard sale. But a lot of it comes from here. People abandon their storage and I buy some of it at auction. You looking to get in the business?"

"No, I may want to sell some of my stuff. Want to take a look?"

"Not tonight. I got to be someplace. I'm meeting my brother, maybe tomorrow."

"If you buy it now I could give you a really good deal."

"I am interested, but not tonight. I can't tonight. Check with me tomorrow." He picked up a tiger oak library table and lifted it over his head, carrying it through the open metal door of his storage locker

I breathed hard, twice, realized it was just what Peanuts did when he was disappointed, gave a half smile and reached back to rub Peanuts nose, which he had rested on my shoulder when I rolled the window down.

"Okay buddy, let's get what we came for."

I carried in the box of Desert Rose dishes, found the air mattress and sleeping bag, closed and locked the storage door and headed home.

23

I was too embarrassed to let Mel come in. The place was mostly empty save for the knick-knacks, books and photos piled on the floor. That and the trash bag of clothes in the middle of the room. I hauled the sleeping bag, air mattress and camp chair in from the car, decided I would set everything up in the living room. When I unfolded the air mattress I realized I left the battery operated pump in the storage locker. I sat in the chair and started to blow. Peanuts looked at me with the erect ears, and tilted head that make animals so quizzical. The air mattress was just starting to show signs of being inflated when Mel's truck pulled up outside. I quickly pushed in the plug to keep any air from escaping and went outside, pulling the door behind me. I didn't bother to put on a jacket and instantly regretted it. The air was cold, the wind made it colder. The front that had been predicted was slow in coming, but had settled in for the night.

Mel came up the walkway, took off his hat. "Good Evening, looks like we're in for a cold one tonight."

"Yes, it has turned cold." I stood in front of my door, arms crossed for warmth.

Mel could tell something was up.

"Mel, I didn't get my check like I expected, in fact to be honest, I lost my job. But I am supposed to get the balance of my pay by next Wednesday. I can give you five fifty now and the rest on Wednesday."

Mel stood in front of the window, turning his hat over in his hands and straightening the brim.

"Aileen, like I said before, I am sorry for all that has happened with you. But I just can't carry you. I depend on the rent checks to pay my bills. When your check didn't clear it set me behind. Now, Aileen, now you owe for two months, January and February."

"I promise, Mel, I can have the rest by next Wednesday. Things have just been so difficult. I need a couple more days to settle things."

He paused again. "Aileen, I just can't. Especially, Aileen, especially being as how you said you lost your job. Even if I let you go until Wednesday this month, what happens next month and the month after? I'm sorry."

I looked at him, pleading, "A few more days. Please."

"No," he said, shook his head, eyes down. "I just can't. Look, I can give you until Wednesday to move out and use your damage deposit for the rent for last month, as long as you leave the place clean. I can give you that. I am sorry."

I nodded my head. "Okay, I'm sorry too. I didn't know any of this was going to happen, I just..., everything keeps going wrong. Thanks anyway." I slipped back in the door before he could see the place was all but empty.

I heard Dawn call to him from next door.

"Mel. Mel, could I see you for a minute?" Dawn and her visitor came out and followed Mel down the walk to his truck. I could see them talking and shaking hands before Mel got in his truck and drove away.

"Well Peanuts, let's see what we can round up for dinner." I looked in the fridge. Standard fare on such occasions was peanut butter or an omelet. I picked the omelet, a handful of spinach, toast on the side. I hadn't eaten lunch, but still, sitting in my camp chair, balancing a paper plate on my knee I could only manage to eat half of what I prepared. Peanut didn't turn it down though. I added it to the cup of Ol Roy I usually fed him, morning and night. When Stevie got him he only fed him specialty dog food, getting it directly from the Vet, and never ever gave him table scraps. I apologized to Stevie in a whisper, like I did every time I slipped people food into Peanuts' bowl.

I kept reliving the day's events: The meeting with the school hatchet men; agonizing over Stevie's care; trying to raise the rent money; finally being told, sorry, too late. It was all too much. I showered, wore sweat pants and a Christmas turtle neck for PJ's mostly because my real PJ's were now at the bottom of the trash bag of clothes I emptied from the dresser. I lay out my sleeping bag on the half inflated air mattress and realized my pillows had been taken with the mattress and blankets. I waded up a towel and pushed it down on the top of the mattress and crawled in. Peanuts kept going back and forth, from the bedroom to the living room, looking for the furniture. His pet bed was still in the corner of the bedroom, beside where the bed had been. I got up, shook out the red plaid cover of the dog's cushion and dragged it into the living room, right beside the air mattress. Appeased, he curled around and settled in.

I lie awake two hours or more. Finally got up and started rummaging around in the medicine cabinet until I found what was left of Sam's sleeping pills. I held the brown bottle in my hand, studying the label. If I took them all I could just lie down and never wake up?

Not tonight, I said to myself. I have to keep going for Stevie and Peanuts, what would become of them if I wasn't here? So I opened the bottle took one pill, crawled back into the bag and fell into a dreamless sleep.

24

Routines are a little hard without stuff. Think about it, if you're used to turning on the TV to watch the Today show, sitting at a table and drinking coffee, whatever, it usually involves stuff. Which I no longer had. But the one routine I did have was walking the dog. Every day, I walked that dog, usually twice. Peanuts didn't care about stuff he just wanted to go for a walk. I didn't even get dressed since I already had on sweat pants, just tied on my shoes, zipped up my sweatshirt and out the door. It was almost eight when we got back. I rolled up the sleeping bag, dragged the mattress into the bedroom and set up the camp chair and used the boxes I packed yesterday as my table. Coffee and oatmeal was all I had. There were a couple of overripe bananas. Any other day I would have taken the time to make banana bread, but today I was anxious to go back to the storage locker and see what I could sell from there. For some reason I had the notion Mel would let me stay if I could come up with the rest of the rent.

I was still wearing the pants I had slept in when I got out there. The first, but not the last, time I would sleep in the same clothes I wore all day. The guy who sells out of the front locker was already set up, bundled in a canvas work jacket and thick black steel toe boots, eating a breakfast burrito. I rolled my window down as I approached him.

"Are you still interested in looking at my things? I have some nice furniture."

"Sure, why not. There aren't many folks out today yet, maybe if it warms up."

"Can we do it now?"

"Now would be great. My name's Dave by the way." He extended his hand.

"I'm Aileen." I shook his hand through the car window. Peanuts pushed his big head over my shoulder and half out the window.

"And this is?" Dave showed the back of his hand to Peanuts so he could discern friend or foe from his scent.

"Peanuts, his name is Peanuts."

"He-eh Doggy, you're a big fellow aren't you." Peanuts allowed Dave to turn his hand over and up and scratch under his chin. Well if Peanuts trusts him I guess I can too.

I pulled the car slowly to the end of the second row of garage doors and stopped. Dave jogged behind. We both met at the same time in front of the door and I bent down with my key to unlock the padlock, Dave grabbed hold of the door and yanked it up.

"Whoa, you do have a lot in here. How long have you had these things".

"Oh, I've had some of them since I was married. Thirty years I guess. Some of this stuff belonged to my in-laws and I inherited it."

"No, I meant how long have you had them here in the locker."

"Oh, I see what you mean. Since last September, we sold our house and moved to a much smaller place. Then I had to move into an even smaller place and now, well, I might have to move again."

"Who's we"?" Dave broke off a piece of breakfast burrito and fed it to Peanuts.

"My husband, we had to sell our house to pay bills when he lost his job."

"You guys split or something. This isn't like you selling stuff to get even with him, 'cause that's bad karma. I can't buy that stuff."

He was serious. I thought about how much to tell him. Where was his level of need to know? Decided it was low on the list and said, "He died last fall, not long after we moved. I'm still trying to pull everything together. Right now I just need to downsize some more." I tried to say it without letting my voice crack but wasn't successful.

"Oh. Sorry. Sorry for your loss. Let me look around okay?"

"Sure, look. Let me know what you might be interested in."

Dave spent about ten minutes, pulling chairs over and flipping cushions. At one point he picked up Stevie's Gibson, strummed a few cords. "That's not for sale. Sorry, that and the mandolin, they belong to my son, he wouldn't want me to sell them."

I wanted to believe Stevie would play them again someday, even though I knew better.

"Well, I can make you an offer on the furniture. I can take it all off your hands for you, today, right now, for three hundred cash, but not the mattress or book case. They..."

"I know, mattresses don't sell well and nobody reads real books anymore."

"You got it, three hundred."

What was it with three hundred? Was this some secret number resellers always offered? That's what the broomstick skirt lady had offered yesterday for the furniture at my triplex.

"Six, I need six hundred for it."

"Three fifty."

Wait, he was supposed to go to four hundred. Dave might be harder to negotiate with.

"Five fifty," I countered

"Three seventy five, final offer."

I did what I did yesterday in my living room, spun slowly around the storage room looking at everything, picturing where it had been in my home, imagining all the times I had sat in a chair, turned on a lamp or put my feet up on the ottoman. I had to have four hundred. That's what I needed to make rent. "Four hundred, I'll let it go for four hundred."

Dave made a sucking noise, his lips pursed, and teeth showing.

"No, can't do it. I can do Three eighty, but no, I can't do four." He had finished his burrito and pulled a torn blue bandana from his jacket pocket to wipe his hands on.

Boy, I did not want to sell for that, but I really needed the money. I would still need $20.00 to make rent. Maybe I could pawn my laptop or something.

"Okay," I said reluctantly, "three eighty."

Dave pulled a brown leather trucker's wallet out from his pocket, the chain was still clipped to his belt, unzipped it and counted out three hundred and eighty dollars, all in twenties.

"Are you going to be around for a while? I can call my partner to help move this stuff if you are, otherwise we can do it Monday."

"No, today is better, I'll hang around."

"Good, I'll go back and see what's happening in the front, then come back and let you know if we can move it out now." He zipped the wallet back up, stashed it in his pocket, blew his nose and walked away. Peanuts started to follow.

"You stay there fellow you're not part of this deal." Dave waved him off.

Peanuts just watched him, a little confused, as was I. We had just made a new friend and now he was leaving. I called the dog back inside, he sat beside me leaning against my leg, still watching Dave as he began to jog across the gravel parking lot. I scratched behind Peanut's ear, and he turned his nose upward and licked my hand, something he seldom did. He always knew the right thing to do.

I turned my attention back to the storage locker. There were still a couple dozen boxes. I had forgotten what most contained. Maybe there was something else I could sell or pawn. I started opening them, pushing aside the dirty white paper that filled the empty spaces between knick-knacks. Most just held mementos: conch shells from our trip to Florida; Disney world souvenirs; one box had at least seven or eight children's Halloween costumes. If I kept doing this I would surely cry again. I closed that box up quickly, pushed it to the back of the locker. Another box held towels, place mats and table cloths, all the fixings for an ordinary life, the one I used to live. I found a box with twin size blankets and pillows from the boys' beds which were now leaning up against one wall. These I can use, and loaded them into the back of the Subaru.

An old Chevy truck with wooden racks attached to the truck bed pulled up and out hopped Dave and another guy who looked just like Dave, only bigger. They were dressed in identical jeans, jackets and black boots. Big Dave pulled a red bandana from his pocket and began to blow his nose. Peanuts turned his head at the sound.

"And who's this?" Big Dave blew again, this time I'm pretty sure it was to see Peanuts' animated expression.

"That's Peanuts."

"Peanuts? What kinda' name is that for a big dog like this?"

"My son named him."

"He shoulda' named him Butch or Blackie or something, not Peanuts. Peanuts is a little wimpy dog's name." Big Dave pulled a zipped plastic bag of jerky out of his jacket pocket, broke off a piece and handed it to Peanuts, laughing as his resealed the bag.

"This is my brother, also my business partner. We'll get this stuff off your hands pronto." Dave got out of the truck and put on some work gloves.

The two began lifting furniture and moving boxes, piling everything in the back of the pickup until I was sure it would topple. They were so in tune with each other they didn't need to speak as they maneuvered things around, they were mind readers, each knew exactly when to lift, turn and set things down.

"I can see the family resemblance," I said, holding Peanuts back.

"Why does everyone saw that?" Big Dave and Dave said in unison.

I smiled at them. What I wouldn't have given for a sibling right now, someone to lean on and pull me through. The only brother I had lived fifteen hundred miles away and had turned his back on me. I hadn't seen him since Mom's funeral six years ago. I let him know about Sam and Sean's deaths, his wife sent a condolence card: 'We are both deeply saddened by your loss.' but she alone signed it. At one point I swallowed my pride and asked for help, called twice, the second time leaving a longer message. If I ever needed family, this was it. He never returned my call.

"Nice doing business with you, Aileen. Take care of that dog now." Dave got in the passenger side and closed the door. Big Dave slid behind the wheel, but not before slipping some more beef jerky to Peanuts.

"You outta change his name to something more dignified, like Rin Tin Tin." Big Dave said, laughed, started the engine and drove away.

25

It was starting to snow lightly when I pulled into the Care Center. Peanuts was still with me. My heart was aching, remembering all the Halloweens and Christmas mornings with my boys. I needed to see Stevie. I knew Rita didn't work weekends, but was surprised that none of the other staff I knew were on duty. I had been coming here nearly every day for nine months. I went directly to Stevie's room. One of the beds, the one that had held the other comatose patient, was empty. There was an unbelievable stillness to the room. Quiet, dark, only the buzz of a monitor marked the silence.

"Hey Stevie, it's mom again." I rubbed his leg. He was in the same position as yesterday. I looked up at the white board above his head, 1300 was still written on it. Did the staff turn him? Was he only moved once a day?

I looked at the empty bed with sadness then back at Stevie. "Hope you had a better night son. Peanuts is with me, he's out in the car, wish I could bring him in to see you. I sold a bunch of stuff today. These two guys who bought it wanted to change Peanuts name to Rin Tin Tin, isn't that funny. They were brothers. They run a resale business out of a storage locker, cool huh. I didn't sell your Gibson though, still waiting for you to play it again."

As always, I paused after each sentence, hoping for some sort of response. A tech and a housekeeping staff came into the room with a small pail and cleaning supplies.

"Oh, we didn't realize anyone was in here." The tech set the supplies down and stood beside the empty bed. "We can come back later. "

"No it's okay. I wasn't going to stay much longer. What happened to that patient? Did he get transferred or move to another room?"

"No, he passed away in the night. They just came for him a while ago," the tech replied.

"Did he have family? Were they able to come?" I already knew the answer to that question. In the nine months I had been coming here only a handful of patient had visitors and most of those who did come, like me, came almost every day.

"No. Not that I'm aware of." He and the other staff started wiping down the mattress, flipping it over and cleaning both sides before starting on the bed frame and night stand.

"What happens when they pass away without family like that?"

"If they have a will or advanced directive everyone tries to follow their wishes, otherwise the deceased is turned over to which ever funeral home has the contract. After that I can't tell you. I do know they usually have to hold the remains for a period of time while they try and find next of kin, but how long I don't know. I think after a while one of the churches or civic groups sponsors a group burial."

"Oh." I looked at Stevie. The thought went through my head that if I had to move they might not be able to find me if they needed to. I needed to be sure I always left an address with them or someplace to call. I pulled a slip of paper from my purse, wrote the address of the triplex on it, my name and Stevie's Mom on the top and gave it to the tech.

"I want to make sure you guys have my address although I am not sure how much longer I'll be there."

He looked at it before putting it in his pocket. "I'll be sure to clip it onto his chart."

"Thanks, I'll be going. See you tomorrow maybe?"

"Maybe, I'm a contract staff. They only bring us in when they have to. They haven't let me know where I will be assigned tomorrow yet."

"Well, if you're here you'll see me. I come almost every day to see my son."

"You are a very loving mother."

No one had called me mother for a long time. I swallowed. "Thanks, I try."

I leaned over and kissed Stevie's check. "Tomorrow son, see you tomorrow," I said, whispering in his unhearing ear.

When I opened the door to the triplex I was startled by how empty it was. My body had been longing to stretch out and sleep but that air mattress didn't look all that inviting. Neither did the camp chair. I was exhausted by the events of the past week. It was all catching up with me. I had a couple more things to do before I could sit down. Number one: find something to pawn. Twenty more dollars and I would have rent.

I pulled my laptop, still in its case, from the second shelf of the book case, sat on the floor, plugged it in and turned it on. I was one of those people who saved everything. There were pictures of weddings, vacations, school events, soccer games, recipes, just so much stuff. Why did I ever save all this stuff, and why didn't I do a better job organizing it? I tried now to move things around, create folders "Family Pictures" "School Stuff", but it was pretty hopeless. The USB memory sticks were in my desk drawer at school. I could kiss them good bye even though they were mine and not the schools. In the end I found a blank CD and copied everything to it still in a disorganized state, ejected the CD and did my best to delete files.

I looked around my disembodied possessions some more. There was an old printer in my closet. I hauled that out. I remembered an old silver tray, a wedding gift, that would still be in the storage locker, why hadn't I thought to find that when I was over there. I'd just have to get in on Monday.

"Sorry Peanuts, I want you to wait here okay buddy?" He whined a bit as I pulled the door closed behind me.

The only pawn shop I knew about was out by the mall. It took me thirty minutes to get there. I had to stop at every light. There were four cars and a couple of pickups out front when I went in. Three men and one woman were clustered at one end of the counter looking over a case of handguns. Another small group was inspecting snowboards that leaned against the wall. Wow, Sean's snow board and boots were in the storage locker too. I'd have to start a list of all the things I could bring in.

"May I help you?" I woman, wearing two or three rings on each finger, spoke to me from behind the counter.

"Yes, I wanted to see if you would be interested in my laptop. It's only a year old. I have the printer too." I lifted the electronics onto the glass counter.

The woman pulled the case up right and started to unzip it, pulling the computer from the inside.

"Do you have the cords and manual?"

"Yes, in the front pocket."

She reached in and pulled out the cord plugging the computer into a power strip secured vertically to the inside edge of the counter, and flipped the computer on.

"What's the password?"

"I'll type it in."

"If you're going to sell it I need the password. We always reset them before we sell them."

"Oh. Sorry, *steviesean two one four,* all small letters."

She typed it in, skimmed through several files, checked the memory, flipped the whole thing over and looked at the back, matching serial numbers to those on the user's book.

"We can give you twenty bucks," she said as she flipped it back over on the counter.

"That's all? This is a really good laptop. Surely it's worth more than that."

"We have a few of these, they aren't worth as much as the owners think they are, the technology changes so fast most people would rather just go ahead and get a brand new one, twenty bucks."

"Okay, twenty dollars. What about the printer?"

"Does it work?"

"Yes, the cords are there too."

"Five dollars."

"You're kidding. Five dollars?"

She shook her head. "We sell them for fifteen to twenty. Printers are another thing people like to buy new."

What was I going to do with a printer if I didn't have a computer? "Okay, five dollars."

"If you can fill out the top half of this form and I'll need your driver's license."

"Why, why do you need my license? I'm in a hurry." I needed to get to Mel's office before he closed.

"We have to verify ID. It's a legal thing."

I pulled the license out, handed it over, filled in and signed the forms and walked out with twenty five dollars. I had done it, I had made rent.

Like a lot of small businessmen in Northern New Mexico, Mel had several things going on. His base of operations was the back half of a rented building on St Mike's Drive. Here, he managed rental properties, ran a commercial office cleaning business and served as a place for wire transfers to and from Mexico. I wasn't sure he would be in, but I had to give it a try. Fifteen inch red and green letters painted on the front window announced the wire transfer service in Spanish, while a smaller sign, *M and M LLP Residential Rentals Management and Office Cleaning Service,* was propped right beside the door.

A doorbell rang signaling my entrance. One wall of the tiny front room was lined with horizontal rows of wood molding on which rested dozens of colorful CD's by Mexican Pop Stars and Ranchero Singers. A portly Hispanic man with a mustache wearing a cowboy shirt and tan Wranglers walked up the short hallway from the back.

"Yes? May I Help you?" He said, heavy on the H in help, like he couldn't quite get his mouth around it.

"Hi, I was looking for Mel. Is he here? I needed to pay my rent."

"No, he's not here. He does not work today."

"Well could I pay my rent? Would you be able to collect it?"

"Wait. Espera. Wait, I will give him a call and see what he says. I work with the cleaning, not the rent."

He retrieved a cell phone from a tooled leather holder on his belt and dialed, speaking in Spanish to whoever answered. He angled the phone away from his face, "Your Name?"

"Aileen Roark, tell him I have the rent now."

He relayed the message and handed me the phone. "He said he wants to talk to you."

"Hello? Mel? It's Aileen. Hey, I have all the rent now. Can I leave it here or meet you somewhere?"

Silence.

"Hello? Hello? Mel are you there?"

Silence.

"Aileen?"

"Yes, Mel, I have the rent."

"Yes, I heard you. Sorry, Aileen, I already have a new tenant. I accepted a deposit last night. Sorry."

"Last Night? How could you rent it so fast? I have the money for the rent now Mel. I can get it to you now, right now."

"Your neighbor, Dawn, has a friend interested. They told me you let them come in to look the place over. I thought you knew. She gave me a check last night for first, last and damage deposit. Sorry Aileen. We agreed to next Wednesday. You said yes, you'd be gone by then. I told her Friday, she could take over the place next Friday. Sorry Aileen, really I am, but like I said yesterday, I have bills to pay too. What happens next month if you can't make rent? Look, if you need help moving things I can have a couple of my people come and help you, gratis. But I've already rented the place."

So that's what Dawn and her friend were talking to him about last night. I felt so betrayed. There was no way Mel would change his mind.

"Yeah, no, I can handle everything, thanks anyway. Goodbye."

"Take care of yourself Aileen, if your situation changes in the future call me. I'll probably have another place come vacant. But right now I don't have any other places in your price range. Take care Aileen."

"Good Bye-Mel." I handed the phone back and left.

26

I had a lot of cash in my pocket, way more than I liked to carry. On the way home I stopped at the Credit Union ATM and deposited all but two hundred of it. It was another of my big mistakes. I should have realized the CU would use it to cover all those overdrafts and fees. But all I could think about now was Stevie and where I would find a place to stay. Find a motel room, Aileen, I told myself, then plan what to do next.

The apartment really was all but empty. My clothes in trash bags along with a few towels and sheets, a lawn chair, a few pictures and household goods. Of course I didn't sleep well that night. I wondered about what to do with Peanuts, considered taking him to the pound. But I had made a promise to Stevie to look after him. If prayers were answered and Stevie somehow pulled through his dog would be the first thing he would want to see. No, Peanuts was on the keep list.

I spent the next three days almost constantly at Stevie's side.

Wednesday, first light, after I walked Peanuts and a quick shower, I shoved everything I could into the back of the Subaru, everything else went to the dumpster. I left the key in the lock and headed out. First stop was the storage locker again. It was cold inside. Both Peanuts and I could see our breath. I found the old wheeled suitcase I used for overnights and sorted through the bags of clothes. A couple of long sleeve shirts, socks, underwear, two pair of pants, a sweater, my Blue Hawks hoodie, gloves. It was too much, wouldn't fit. Try again. I got it down to the most basic. Two pairs of pants, three shirts three changes of socks and one sweatshirt. I tied up a towel and Peanuts' rug inside a tarp. The old JC Penny shopping bag that had become my favorite grocery bag would hold Peanuts dog food and bowl, a plastic cup, a few toiletries and my notebook. If I need something else I can come back for it. I placed all inside the back of the Subaru. It was only ten o'clock, too early to check in at a motel. Maybe, I thought, maybe I could camp. I filled the gas tank, yet again, and took a ride heading north towards Taos.

The sky was blue. Let me say that again, the right way. It can be so hard to describe the sky in New Mexico, but here goes: The sky was brilliant electric neon blue. Even that is an understatement. It had been cold the last few nights, cold enough that ice floes jammed the shores of the Rio Grande. I don't know what it is about a cold night that leaves such a clear, pure blue sky but there it was. Somewhere close to Pilar, along the river, I turned into a river raft take out point. Officially it was closed. But a small beat up truck was parked there, probably fishing.

Peanuts and I got out and walked along a path near the river, making our way through the brush. A man was down on one knee near the river, a pair of binoculars to his eyes. When he heard us, he put his gloved fingers to his lips to quiet us and pointed up river. A blue heron stood on one leg near the middle of the Rio Grande, silhouetted by the red willow branches on either shore. When a trout leapt from the water the Heron spooked, took flight up river and out of sight. It was amazing.

"Wow. That was incredible."

"Oh yeah, I could watch them all day. I do some days." He returned the binoculars to a case fastened to his belt. "Out for a hike?"

His questioned startled me. I wasn't out for anything but to kill time. A hike seemed like a good idea.

"Sort of, I was driving north and my dog needed to get out of the car a while."

"Where are you from?"

Right now I wasn't too sure. "Santa Fe. But, I'm in the process of moving."

"Oh? Where to?"

"I haven't figured that out yet. I lost my apartment and I need to start looking for another place. It's hard to find some place that takes dogs. I may end up sleeping in my car a night or two until I find a place, maybe camp out."

"Yeah, I finally had to give mine up for that reason."

Did he mean his apartment or his dog?

"Do you know of any place to camp? This seems like a nice spot."

"No, not off hand. You could camp around here but the water's off and they still have the bathrooms locked, cold too. If you're in a jam there is a motel down Cerrillos called Queens Quarters. It's not much to see, but it's cheap and they do take dogs. I've stayed there a few nights."

"Thanks, I'll keep that in mind." Peanuts was pulling on his leash. I wanted to let him off to run but not in sight of the bird watcher. I need not have worried, he was as anxious to be rid of me as I of him.

"Enjoy your hike and good luck apartment hunting. I've got to get going myself." He backed away and headed through the brush towards the parking area.

I took Peanuts off leash, and found a sunny rock large enough to stretch out on. I lay there, absorbing the sun's warmth, starring into that obscenely blue sky, and fell asleep.

Peanuts bark woke me. A family of ducks was swimming downstream, looking for a meal. It must have been late afternoon. The sun was blocked by the steep cliffs of the canyon. No wonder I was getting cold. We headed back for the parking area, climbed back into the car and headed south to Santa Fe. Destination? Queen's Quarters.

That guy was right. It wasn't much to look at. He was also right about it being cheap An old style marquee with plastic letters you change by hand, marked the rutted entrance to the old motel. *Wkly Rates 225 up; Dy 45 up, 3rd night free* advertised the price in poorly aligned letters. I parked in front of the office and went in.

"Do you have a room available?"

"How many nights?"

"Weekly would be good. I'm house hunting. I should be able to find a place within a week."

He looked out the front window at Peanuts who was sitting in the driver's seat of the old Subaru.

"How many pets?"

I looked over my shoulder, seeing those big black ears and nose behind the wheel did make me smile. "Just the one."

"Weekly rate on that would be two eighty five plus lodgers tax".

"I thought it was two twenty five?"

"There is an extra fee for the dog. Total with tax would be three hundred and twenty two."

I had a little over two hundred in my pocket, but just deposited what should have been my rent money. I pulled out my debt card.

"Okay, I'll take it." I pulled the card from my wallet.

"I'll need some ID and fill in the guest registration form."

The desk clerk ran my card and I wrote the make and model of the car.

He handed the card back. "Sorry, it was declined."

"Declined? That can't be, I just made a deposit. Can you try it again?"

"I ran it twice already, it was declined. Do you have another card?"

I did, but they were all over the limit. I thought a minute.

"What if I pay cash? Is there a discount?"

"No, we don't offer a discount for cash."

I pulled the bills out of my purse.

"I only have two hundred. Can I pay for half now and the rest tomorrow after I've had a chance to figure out what's going on?"

"No, sorry, to get the weekly rate we have to have the money up front."

"What can I get for two hundred?"

"With the dog, we can do two nights, third night's free, including lodger's tax it would be one hundred thirty eight."

"Isn't it forty five a night?"

"The fee for pets would bring it up to fifty-eight dollars plus lodger's tax. You're paying for two nights, third nights free."

Didn't seem cheap, but I was tired, not in the mood to argue. I looked out the window at Peanuts, panting in the car, pacing from driver to passenger seat, making the car rock.

"Okay, two nights, third nights free."

I filled in the form and he handed me the key.

I had a little over sixty dollar left and a place to stay for three nights.

27

Almost any Walmart parking lot in America, in the middle of the night, is dotted with an assortment of RV's, camper trucks, vans and cars. Most of their owners do not work there. Walmart has become the de facto land of the mobile poor. Average, once middle class Americans, who now reside, temporarily or permanently, in their vehicles, park here. Most stay only a night or two before pulling out, headed to the next free space to park for the night. Some stay a week or more. One recently departed soul spent two weeks slumped across the front seat of his car before anyone realized he wasn't just sleeping.

I thought it was going to be better than it was. Sleeping in your car can't be that bad I thought, but it was. I still believed my checks would start coming, I'd find a place, get another job, and this sleeping in your car stuff would only last a day or two. I did my best to cope. I sandwiched the green wagon between a fifth wheel and Chevy camper van in the Walmart parking lot. The good part was Walmart was open all night, twenty four seven. I didn't realize it then, but access to a bathroom anytime you need one should be a basic human right. Walmart provided that. As long as you kept it low key no one challenged you. The bad part? Exhaust fumes, the whooping calls of teenage and early twentyish men who did donuts in the parking lot at three am, followed by flashing lights of night duty security, and the sound and smell of idling tractor trailers making deliveries. It was cold. I it never occurred to me how very cold spring was in Northern New Mexico. The first two or three nights I wasn't sure I would make it. Three layers of clothes, a sleeping bag, tarp and the ever faithful Peanuts curled up beside me did not keep the chill out of my bones. Uncurling from the back of the car, its' windows heavily coated by frost inside and out, was slow and painful. I developed a semi-permanent bend in my back where the fold of the back seat joined the cargo area into one not really flat surface.

A few days turned into a week. One week into two, then three. If I can just make it until March 5th the little money I did get from Sam's pension would be deposited in my account. I would find a more permanent solution. Surely all the late fees and overdrafts would clear by then. I sold Sean's snowboard and anything else I could find to buy gas and dog food.

Days, I'd drive over to see Stevie, stay hours there, helping with the meal service, sneaking leftovers from the trays for Peanuts (and a few times for me), cleaning myself up in the bathrooms. I'd spend a couple hours at the library, where I could read the paper scanning for jobs and use the computer to apply on line, and, again, have access to a restroom. I preferred the south side or Llano location where parking was free and I could take Peanuts for a long walk in a field nearby. I tried not to leave him in the car too long and would eat meals at picnic tables or park benches, so he could be outside.

Everyone always asks: "Why didn't you get another job somewhere? Anywhere."

The answer: I tried. I applied, sometimes filling out three nearly identical applications a day both on line and in person. But without a permanent address or telephone I was pretty much screwed. One job application asked for permission to check credit scores. I laughed out loud at that one. I had one interview, a state job for program assistant on a grant funded project, but after they checked my references I was shown the door. Apparently, making a phone call while your students set a fire in your classroom is frowned on. The job market for fiftyish women who sleep in their cars was, to put it mildly, damn poor. I used the Medical Center number as a message phone on an a few job apps. I got one call back, but it was two days before anyone connected the message was for me. By then, the position, helping with meal service at a retirement home, for which I used Lynn and Rita, Stevie's nurses, as reference, had been filled.

Ten days at Walmart was all I could stomach. I needed to find a better place to park at night. If only I had friends left, if they still didn't blame me for Sam's drunk driving or if my coworkers had not been directed to have no contact with me, I'd have begged a place to stay. That was a lot of if only's. I had no one left. I racked my brain for a solution. When I spied Lenny, still wearing his brightly colored beret, dreadlocks tucked underneath, with his thumb out on an Interstate entrance ramp I realized the parking lot at the shelter was a good short term solution. I spent a few nights parked there. It was awkward. In less than three months I had gone from a volunteer helping to provide food and shelter to the homeless to sleeping in my car. Adam, the director, didn't blink an eye. I think he may have been on the receiving end at some point in his life too. He seemed to know what to say and how to say. One day I realized the last time I saw Lenny was that day he had his thumb out on the entrance ramp.

"What's up with Lenny? I haven't seen him lately," I asked one of the other parking lot dwellers.

"Lenny? He got busted. He was getting high in the pantry and Adam busted him. He's out for at least six months." Campbell was in his mid-thirties, living out of his truck and doing day labor. His goal was to make enough to head to Oregon, where, he said, his sister lived.

"That long? Did Adam call the police?"

"No, as long as you leave without a hassle Adam doesn't call the cops on you. But he's pretty strict otherwise. So, yeah, Lenny's gone. Sometimes he heads north, to Denver."

"He's such a great guy. I really liked him."

"He'll be fine. He's pretty much got it down. But he stays solo, like me. He keeps to himself a lot."

"Is that a good thing?"

"For him it is, me too. You need to have somebody, you know, somebody who's got your back, but a lot of times you get stabbed in the back instead. Keeping solo most of the time is a pretty safe bet."

Campbell rearranged the thick foam pad in the truck's bed that he slept on at night, picked up and shook out the sleeping bag.

"Does that keep you warm?" I asked him.

"Oh yeah, trick is to get in it while you're still warm, kind of heat it up. Otherwise you have a heck of a time getting it to heat up. And never, ever, let it get wet. It packs it down and you freeze all night." Campbell lit a cigarette, let it hang from his lips as he fluffed up the downy bag and pushed plastic storage boxes filled with toiletries and laundry soap to one side.

"What about you? What's your story?" He kept rearranging the back of the truck, trying to maximize the space.

"What's my story? Oh, I got fired, sort of, and lost my place. We'll get it figured out won't we Peanuts?" I reached down and patted Peanuts side. The dog lifted his head, which had been resting on my foot and flopped his tail once, before stretching out in the late afternoon sun once again.

It was almost four. People were lining up for beds and a meal. I longed to be among the bed group, but there was no way I would leave Peanuts in the car alone all night. When the meal line got down to just three people, both Campbell and I headed for it.

Dinner tonight was courtesy of the Baptist Church Women's Group. Every month, for the last five years, third Thursdays, the congregation's women, young and old, hauled crock pots and Tupperware full of home cooked food to the shelter: Spaghetti, salad, bread, lemonade and cookies. I was thankful for it. Adam greeted me as I made my way through the serving line.

"Welcome, Aileen. It's nice to see you. I hear you're a guest with us now."

"Not exactly, I've been staying in my car a few nights, here in the lot." This time I wasn't embarrassed just in serious denial about how desperate my situation had become. I could see the sympathetic looks of the Baptist women as they ladled canned spaghetti sauce over thick wet noodles.

Adam nodded. "Let me know if there is anything I can do for you."

"I just need to make it until the first week of March. I have a check coming in then."

Adam smiled. He'd heard that one before. "We do have things here besides meals and beds. Once a month, someone from the state comes over to explain their services and how to apply. We help with job placement if we can. Anything we can help with let me know."

"What I really need is a phone, or at least a message phone I can use when I apply for jobs."

"We do that. You can register, fill out a form, and then we keep messages for you here. After you eat go up to the front desk and ask to fill out the telephone contact form. Enjoy your meal." Adam headed towards the living quarters to do a head count for the night.

The elderly volunteer at the front desk cheerfully handed me a form. Her hands shook as she searched around for a pen.

"Write your name here, and any information you can about how to find you if it's urgent." Her voice was as shaky as her hands.

"Like what?"

"Well, I think they want to know where they might find you if they have too, or someone who might know you. Some people have written down Hobo Hill, or Alameda Park. Also they want to know next of kin and where they might be."

"Next of kin?"

"Yes, in case something happens."

My next of kin was in a coma.

"I don't really have anyone. I've been sleeping in my car, here, for the past couple of nights."

"You could put that down, the type of car and license number, where you usually park."

I looked at the form, hesitated, wrote *Green Subaru Legacy Wagon* and the license number, *Sometimes park at shelter or Walmart overnight*. It didn't feel right to put down *none* in the next of kin space, but what purpose would it serve to put down Stevie's name? I left it blank.

"It's really nice of you folks to do this. I lost out on a job because I didn't get the message from my other contact number."

"We try to help, but you still have to check in. They only track you down if it's an emergency or urgent." She took my form and added it to a tan according file with alphabetical dividers.

"Thanks."

I headed outside, two thick pieces of garlic bread in my pocket for Peanuts. That and a handful of kibble would be it. Peanuts and I went for one last walk. I spread my sleeping bag in the back. It was early, barely eight thirty, but I thought about Campbell's advice to get in while you were still warm, took off my shoes and climbed in. He was right. I did stay warmer.

28

Tuesday morning I headed for St. Mary's Care Center, as usual, to see Stevie. I had managed to make myself welcome by helping with meal times, reading aloud to patients who requested it and just plain being useful. I managed a couple of showers there by pretending to spill food or coffee all over myself. I tried it again.

"What I mess I made of myself, if it's okay can I duck into the shower and clean up?"

Fool them twice but not three times. Rita looked at me suspiciously as I picked up the JC Penny tote bag from Stevie's bed side, already packed with towel and clean clothes.

"Aileen, I'm not trying to give you a hard time or anything, but the shower area is for patients. What's up? Is your hot water off or something? Did you forget to pay your bill?"

I sat looking at Stevie, set the bag down. Stroked my son's hair, or what hair he still had. He looked like a little old man curled over on his side, sunken eyes, pale, wheezing , not the young broad shouldered snowboarder who charmed the ladies with his easy smile. I tried to block out what I really was seeing and replace it with the way I wanted to see him.

You caught me, I thought.

"No, I lost my job and my apartment. I've been sleeping in my car the last three weeks. I have to get by a few more days. I'm supposed to get a check. Hopefully I can get a place then. Hopefully."

"Sorry, we didn't know you were having problems like that. What about Stevie? Are you able to cover those bills?"

"Not really, the hospital filed a garnishment notice. They get most of my check, but I still get a little. That and they said they applied for guardianship so they could get reimbursed from Social Security or something."

Rita pulled back the tape that secured the port and line in Stevie's side. The skin around it looked rough, puffy, and slightly inflamed. Rita mumbled something about hoping the supplies would come in so they could change out the port.

"Yes, they do that a lot with Social Security. Hasn't someone from the Family Assistance office contacted you? What about a phone contact? I know the other day we tried to get through at your school. We got that message here, you know about the job? I figured you needed extra money for Stevie's medical. The school told us you were unavailable."

"Unavailable? They told you that?"

"Yes, I wanted to leave a message but they said they couldn't take messages for you."

"I believe that. But I am surprised they said I was unavailable, not that I didn't work there anymore."

She checked the time on her cell phone then slipped it back into her pocket.

"Do you have another phone contact number we can use?"

I thought about the form I filled out at the shelter.

"Yes, you can get hold of me through this number."

I tore a scrape of cardboard from the tissue box beside Stevie's bed. I was the only one who ever used them. I borrowed a pen from Rita and wrote down the shelter's number.

"Are you staying here?" Rita checked her cell phone again. It was nearing the end of her shift.

"Sort of, that's the shelter on Cerrillos, they have a message system. They can get hold of me in an emergency."

"Great, I'll make sure to enter it onto Stevie's file."

"Thanks Rita." I sighed sat back in the metal chair, reached over and held Stevie's curled hand. The skin was soft, nails long, reminded me of a newborn's hand. But these fingers didn't wiggle around in my palm when I touched them.

Rita's eye followed my hand. She tried to veil the look of empathy on her face. It must be really hard to stay upbeat working here, no wonder they have such high turnover.

"It's okay. But back to your original question."

"Sorry, I forgot. What did I ask?"

She looked at me a little exasperated.

"Shower. It's okay if you take one now, but you need to be quick before my shift ends. This will have to be the last time. If my boss finds out I'll get a reprimand."

"Thanks Rita, I appreciate you sticking your neck out for me."

"Good luck with the house hunting."

29

I made it, one more night than March 5th. I would have five hundred and twenty dollars. Seemed like a million right now. Surely I could find something for that amount, a trailer, rent a room in a house, something, even if I had to go to Albuquerque. Just for the summer. By fall I would have a new teaching job, I'd be back on my feet. Everything would be okay. I rolled out my sleeping bag, fluffed up Peanuts rug, made sure to crack the window just a wink. I had gotten used to the sounds in the parking lot, as had Peanuts. The truck camper beside me was playing Spanish Music. I could smell a little pot wafting through the cracked window. Well, that's okay too. Maybe it will help me sleep.

My dreams were vivid, touchable, felt so real. In them I could smell the freshness of the blue sage at dawn along the Chama River north of Abiqui. The sandstone bluffs were just starting their daily march along the color spectrum from deep lavender to blood red. I dream of a smiling young Stevie running towards Sam and Sean, who were calling to him, about to push off in a yellow raft from the river's shore. The gentle thunder of the river rapids echoing off the canyon walls, more like a light drum beat, sounded over the boys' laughter. Peanuts barked, wagging his tail, while I held him back, not letting him jump into the river after the boys. I waved after them, light from a rising sun just above the mesa almost blinding me. I realized I wasn't dreaming. A light was shining into the frost covered window of the car, and a muffled tap sounded on the roof. A Sikh man, bearded, with a blue turban encircling his head, wearing a distinctive sky blue security company polo-shirt and down vest, was tapping on the roof of the car. He was calling my name. Peanuts was barking at him. Had I done something wrong? Had I parked in the wrong place or Peanuts' barking bothered the others? I slid halfway out of the bag and opened the door slightly.

"Yes, is there a problem?" It was cold, difficult to see. A freezing fog had settled over the cars in the lot and diffused the light from the overhead street lamps creating a misty icy haze.

"Are you Aileen Roark?" He shown the flash light down so I could see his face, then flashed it inside the car, stopping on Peanuts.

"Sorry, was my dog bothering someone?"

"No, you've got a call." He reached in, scratched Peanuts under the chin, and called over his shoulder to someone I didn't see. "Hey Max, I found her, she's over here."

"Keep it down out there." Someone from another vehicle yelled out.

"You keep it down dirt bag." Another voice, loud and angry, bounced off the truck beside me. A couple more "Shut Up's" sounded from different vehicles.

A heavyset man I recognized as one of the night staff from the shelter walked over from the other side of the lot. He was speaking into a telephone handset. "Yes, we found her. I'm going to pass the phone over to her now."

I got out of the car, barefoot. Peanuts followed. The Sikh security guard grabbed him by the collar and pulled him back before he could run off. Max handed me the phone.

"Hello? This is Aileen Roark."

They tell me I fell to the ground, wailing, sobbing uncontrollably. I cut my arm on some broken glass in the lot. Max and someone else, who minutes ago had been yelling 'Shut Up', helped me, propped me up on each side and walked me towards the shelter door. People got out of their cars, hugged me. The security guard found Peanuts' leash in the back of the Subaru, took charge of him. Someone, I think it was Campbell, offered me a cigarette. It had been at least twenty years since I smoked. People were talking around me but I didn't understand what they said. All I understood was my beautiful first born son had gotten on that raft and floated down the river with his dad and little brother.

30

*E*veryone tried to help. They brought me cups of coffee. A couple of the homeless ladies helped me into the shower, washed and combed my hair, massaged lotion into my hands and re-bandaged my cut arm. Adam arrived, came outside to where I sat at a white plastic table.

"I am deeply sorry to hear of your loss Aileen, deeply sorry."

"Thank you." I stared at Campbell a few yards away. Even though I barely knew him, he became the unlikely person who had my back. Right now he had Peanuts. He had given up a day of work and bought a giant can of dog food, was sitting on the tailgate of his truck, watching Peanuts gobble it up from a paper plate.

"We do have some special funds specifically to help in these situations. I can offer a voucher for two nights at a motel. It may help while you look at next steps."

"That would be very helpful. Thank you." I was still in shock, staring blankly into space.

Adam glanced over at Campbell and Peanuts then back at me, clipboard in hand.

"Do you have a preference as to motels?" he said.

"The only one I know that takes dogs is the Queen Quarters Inn. Can I stay there?"

"Yes, I think we can arrange that. Do you need someone to drive you somewhere?"

Campbell overhears. "I can do that, ain't no more working today anyway."

"Great, Campbell. Thanks for helping out. I'll call over and arrange that room for you Aileen. Sorry, for all your troubles." Adam got up, patting me on the shoulder as he went inside.

Peanuts jumped easily into the back of Campbell's truck, I rode shotgun. Campbell drove me to the Medical Center, parking out front.

"If it's okay with you I'll wait out here with your dog. Might take him for a little walk."

"Yeah, that'd be great Campbell" I slid out of the truck seat and went inside.

A male nurse I had never met before was sitting behind the duty desk closest to Stevie's room. Neither Lynn nor Rita was on duty.

"No, they both took the day off, called in sick I believe. Can I help you with something?"

"I'm Stevie's mom."

The nurse looked at me puzzled.

"Stevie Roark, he died last night. I'm his mom."

"Oh, yes. The coma patient, yes, he passed away in the night due to the infection in his port. My condolences."

"Can I see him?"

He looked puzzled again. "He isn't here."

"Where is he? I just want to see him. He's my son, I want to see him, I want to say good bye." I was crying, not trying to hold it back, and wiping the tears on my sleeve.

"I'll check, but I believe they released the body to the funeral home already." He pulled a folder from a vertical file fastened to the wall.

"Yes, the Delgado Funeral Home picked up his body early this morning, about five."

I stood at the counter high desk, leaning my elbows on it, hands covering my face, sobbing. I heard somebody behind me, looked low, under my elbows. Grumpy Mr. Martinez in his wheelchair has rolled up behind me. A box of tissues is in his lap. He pulls a handful out and presses them up and into my hands.

"It's okay to cry when somebody dies. Everyone who works here does."

¤ ¤ ¤

Campbell drove me to the funeral home. It was across from a park, so again, he took Peanuts and walked over there. I could watch them from the front window of the funeral home office. I waited a few minutes before a receptionist called my name and walked me to a small room with a table and four chairs. A middle age man in a gray suit came in, offered his hand.

"I'm Arturo Sanchez, Mrs. Roark. I'm here to discuss options with you. You're Stevie Roark's next of kin?"

"I'm his mother."

"Please accept my condolences. St Mary's has us on contract to take care of the patients for whom they have guardianship. We do try to work with loved ones and the next of kin to honor their wishes."

"I'd like to see him. I'd like to see Stevie."

"I'm afraid he isn't here. We are holding his remains at our other facility where we preform cremations. We generally take the remains there until we can determine what services are needed."

Arturo Sanchez let me sit a minute to gauge my reaction. I wiped my eyes on the crumbled tissues I still held in my hand.

"What happens now?" I asked.

"The contract we have with St. Mary's is for cremation. Then we keep the cremains until the next of kin is able to claim them, or we hold a special burial for all those who haven't been claimed."

"Have you already cremated him?"

"No, we do try to contact next of kin first."

"I'd like to see him."

"Let me discuss some options with you first. We have several burial plans or cremation options." Arturo opened a thick professional binder and placed it on the table in front of me, each page had two or three tasteful pictures of flowers, coffins, chapels, followed by a bulleted list. On the back of the laminated pages a price list broke down the cost.

"I don't know how I can pay for any of that."

"We do offer a payment option if you qualify. Would you like me to check?"

"Yes, please."

He filled out a form with my name, social security number and other information.

"I'll be right back, you can wait here, or in the lobby if you like."

"Thanks, I have someone watching my dog outside, I probably need to check on them."

I walked out to the lobby and searched the park across the street. Campbell was sitting on top of a picnic table smoking. He had taken Peanuts off leash and was throwing him a stick, playing fetch with him. For a minute he looked like Sam when he was twenty years younger.

Arturo Sanchez came out to the lobby, rubbing his hands lightly together. "Mrs. Roark, I'm afraid you don't qualify for our payment plan. Do you have any other relatives, family? Someone who can help cover the cost?"

I shook my head no. "What's the bottom price? Is there a no frills option? I'd like to be able to bury him in the same cemetery as his dad and brother."

"We do have one plan. It's just over two thousand plus the cost of the plot. Would you like me to discuss that with you?"

"I'm not sure I can raise two thousand. How long do I have to decide?"

"We can hold the remains for a couple of weeks or so, after that there is a few, per day. We can't release them until we have a payment option in place."

"So you just hold his body until I pay up, is that right?"

"We're very sorry for you loss Mrs. Roark. We can help you contact some organizations that do help with expenses if you need it. The Medical Center Contract does specify cremation for its guardianship patients. We can hold off for a while. But again, there is a charge."

"I just want to see him. Can I just see him? Please?"

Campbell met me beside the truck, held the door open for me. I was still crying, wiping my eyes. Campbell hugged me as I got in. He and Peanuts had walked over to a taco cart for the daily special times two. He handed me one. I wasn't hungry but didn't want to seem ungrateful. I unwrapped a fish taco and took a small bite.

"Did you get things figured out okay?"

"No, not really. I need to think about it I guess. They want me to have a way to pay for it before they'll release his remains to me."

Campbell was quiet as we drove back towards the shelter.

"I've got a couple hundred saved up towards my Oregon trip. Will that help you at all?"

I stared out the window at the passing cars filled with husbands and wives, sons and daughters, sisters and brothers. I had none left, but Campbell still had a chance. Besides, a couple hundred wouldn't even pay for the obituary let alone the burial.

"That is so generous of you Campbell but I'll figure something out. You should use that money for gas and head back to your family up there. I wish I had a brother like you who cared. I bet your sister is anxious to see you."

Now Campbell was silent.

"I've got a son up there too. I was hoping to make a little more. Enough to get set-up, maybe get him to stay with me a couple days a month or something."

I thought of my sons, how I longed to see them, to touch them.

"Just go, he doesn't care how much money you have. Go. See your son, your sister. Just go."

Campbell nodded, pulled a cigarette from his front shirt pocket and lit it. "Suppose you're right." The next day he would set out for Oregon. But right now we were caught in a lane closure construction zone on Cerrillos Road.

"Where to? Motel or Shelter?"

"Shelter, I need to pick up my car."

Sometimes the universe shows us an answer in an unexpected way, like a dope slap across the side of the head.

A silver Camry pulled out suddenly in front of us, cutting us off as we drove through the orange barrel zone. Campbell skidded to an abrupt stop right in front of a used car lot. A large pink and purple sandwich board sign was propped in front: *We Buy Cars.*

31

After I sold the Subaru to pay for the burial and plot, I used the little left to extend my stay in the motel room at the far end of Cerrillos road a few days. The only place that took dogs, Queens Quarters Inn advertised a third night free, a breakfast that was little more than bargain bag cereal and orange punch, and free WiFi, not that I still had anything that could pick up WiFi.

The day of Stevie's burial, Peanuts and I left the motel at 7:30 a.m. and started the long walk up Cerrillos road to the graveyard on the north side of town. I thought about leaving Peanuts alone in the motel room but I was nervous about what he would do. He had been such a trooper. No matter what I asked of him and where we slept, in the car, in a strange motel room, he just curled up by my side providing the only connection with another living thing I had right now. Besides, he had been Stevie's best friend.

We walked slowly, the cars speeding by us. I stopped about five times and found a bench or half wall to sit on, gave him water and let him rest; his chest heaving as he gave a great sigh, it took us two and a half hours to walk to the cemetery. I stopped at Sean and Sam's graves first. Their spots were more refined with grass, flowers and small granite markers that I still hadn't finished paying for. Peanuts sniffed the brown gray headstones, not to relieve himself, but to be familiar with who had been here. I realized this was the first time I had brought him to the grave site. The other times I had come to lay flowers, pictures and birthday cards on their graves Peanuts had sat in the car, windows open, head resting on the back seat.

I lied to the cemetery staff to allow him in. It was the first, but not the last time I would plead his case as a service dog. The first guideline on the cemetery sign: "NO DOGS ALLOWED (Service dogs accepted)".

Being a teacher, of course, I contemplated the correctness of this missive, but was soon jolted back to reality when two cemetery staff pulled up in a golf cart, "Sorry mam, dogs are restricted to the parking area."

"He's a service dog, a seizure alert dog. I really need him with me."

The guard looked dubious.

"Since I lost my sons I've needed him with me all the time, he's the only way I know. I.., things have been so stressful." First rule of telling a lie, say as little as possible and explain nothing.

One guard looked to the other almost rolling his eyes, the other looked at me then at the big black Shepard beside me and shrugged his shoulders. "Service dogs are allowed so I guess it'll be okay."

I nodded thanks almost crying. I don't know what I would have done if they had turned me down.

We walked slowly to the open ground where a small metal canister rested on a wire crate covered with a blue velvet cloth, waiting to be placed in the ground. I rested my hand on it thinking deeply about the boy who had once walked the earth and whose ashes would now become part of it. I didn't hear the footsteps approach. Peanuts stood up, alert, pulling lightly on his lead and wagging his tail. A man in his seventies walking with a can and a woman about my age came slowly towards me. It took me a minute to realize they were here for me, well Stevie really.

The only other souls who came to Stevie's burial were his High School track coach Anavier Alfredo Anaya, Triple A the kids called him, and Lonnie, mother of Stevie's high school girlfriend. Truthfully, I'm not sure how they found out about it since I couldn't afford the obituary notice fees the newspaper charged. Lonnie cried with me as the box was lowered and the grave filled. You wouldn't think a metal box of ashes no bigger than a shoebox required two workmen, but there they were, shoveling away.

"I'm so sorry. He was so special to our family. I know Sonya would have been here if she didn't have mid-terms, honestly I didn't call her. I knew she would be upset." Lonnie wept while she clutched my hands. And I wept right back clinging to her.

"I know Lonnie. Stevie loved you all too. He would want Sonya to do well, you know he would."

"I know, I know." More tears, more tissue.

"Will you be okay? Is there anything I can do?" Lonnie released my hands and stepped back to go.

I could have asked her "Do you have a spare room for a night or so?" But I still had pride then and was too embarrassed by my situation to ask for help from the one person who offered it.

"We're okay." I pulled Peanuts leash closer to me, he sat at my side, leaning into my leg. "Thank you so much for coming. Please give my love to Sonya." We hugged one last time.

"Such a tragedy, Mrs. Roark. He had such a future." Triple A shook my other hand with both of his, while moving his head from side to side. It was hard to tell what he was thinking because of the dark sunglasses and red and white Aggies cap pulled low on his forehead.

"My condolences on your loss."

They both started the walk across bare dirt and gravel to the Green Ford Ranger, parked along the main road, just outside the cemetery fence, got in and drove away.

Peanuts sat, ever faithful, with the leash looped around my arm. We stayed for at least two hours after the grave was filled, I sat down in the gravel beside the fresh dirt, moving small pebbles around into mountains, valleys and roads, like a toddler might. That was the first time I noticed him. I think he had been here before. He seemed to recognize me. The tall man, with a white beard and long gray blond hair in two braids like Willie Nelson, sat on a stone bench near the foot gate, a red canvas pack beside him, his buckskin jacket unbuttoned. He looked over at me, took off his well-worn cowboy hat with its snakeskin band and rust feather, placed it over his heart and nodded three times, bowing his head on the last one.

I nodded back, wiping the last of today's tears from my check, stood up and walked in the opposite direction toward the parking area and the long walk back to the motel.

Wizard sat on the bench holding his hat, watching us, head slightly bowed, knowing somehow I would come back. When I did, he would be there, waiting to guide me.

I was less than seventy two hours away from sleeping in the cemetery's gravel.

32

After Stevie's burial, it took everything, and I do mean everything, physical, emotional and mental to get myself back to the motel more than four miles away. It was the longest, saddest walk of my life. The car exhaust stung my throat. I guess I was crying and gasping for air. I was drowning. It was well after dark when Peanuts and I arrived at the room. The lot was full, even the place reserved for me where only days before the little green wagon occupied the blacktop. I could hear people moving about in the rooms to each side of me, TV laughter spilling through the walls. I had stashed a couple cans of dog food in the room and opened one now for Peanuts. He just sniffed at it at first then lay down and holding the bowl between his outstretched paws, took a mouthful than rested his head on the edge of the bowl. Like Peanuts I knew I had to eat too. I heated water in the room's microwave and added it to a Cup of Noodles, resting a plastic spoon on top of the Styrofoam cover, and spread peanut butter on a slice of bread.

I fully expected to cry more. I had reached the point where your brain goes blank. You're still aware of every sound, every touch and glint of light through the blinds, knew what things were but had no reaction. You're paralyzed by everything that came before. It was in this state that I closed my eyes sitting upright on the lone chair in the room, and passed out.

Just before four in the morning Peanuts woke me with his growl. Someone was trying to open the door. I was petrified, still in a state of shock, unable to comprehend what was happening. Peanuts growl turned into a snarl, then barking.

"Who's there?" I spoke rapidly, wanting whoever was outside the door to know this room was occupied.

"It's me. Open up."

"Who? What do you want?" I tried to look through the spyhole, but in the minimal light outside I could only make out shapes.

"Me! Just open the freakin' door! Why do you have a dog in there?" The male voice was slurred, he began kicking the door and trying to force the knob.

I wished these rooms had phones. I had no way to call the office.

"You've got the wrong room. This isn't your room. You need to leave."

"Wha? Open the door, I'm not frickin' kidding. Stop your shit." He was yelling louder, still kicking the door.

Peanuts continued to growl and bark. I heard another voice. "Hey numbnuts, you've got the wrong room."

I peered out the spyhole again. The figure backed away and leaned against the rail. "What? Oh Fuuaa...," he said as he staggered away.

I could hear laughter from above and footsteps on the stairs. What an ass.

Now I was awake. When I was sure the drunk had left, I opened the door so Peanuts could check things out. He was still on the alert. I slipped the leash on him and walked him to the row of junipers that separated the motel parking lot from the gas station next door. He went up and down the row trying to pick the best spot to relieve himself. We were both startled by movement at the far end of the hedge. A man lay on a large piece of cardboard, a back pack beside him, another box opened out flat lay on top like a blanket. Peanuts growled again, low and long, but I shushed him, pulling him away to the opposite side. A shudder went up my spine. I was seeing my future.

33

I was out of money. Just like that. My bank balance was a negative number, I had used the very little that was left from Stevie's burial to pay for the motel for six days and buy a bag of dog food, and that was it. My net worth was a handful of spare change. Tonight would be my last night in a motel until next month's five hundred and twenty dollars or a miracle. Don't bet your future on miracles.

I got a few hours of sleep after my visit from the drunken motel guest last night. I showered and decided I really had to figure out what I could manage without a car. I thought about trying to spend a night or two in my storage locker but was warned off by the story a guy at the soup kitchen told of trying to do just that, only to be padlocked in for two days until a passing customer heard his yell for help. Apparently, security carries a stash of padlocks, which are placed on any storage unit left without one in the belief the tenant forgot to fasten the lock. With Peanuts I just couldn't risk getting locked in.

Ultimately, I settled on two pants, 4 shirts, a hoodie and 4 changes of socks and underwear. Don't ask why, I just did. This all fit neatly into my rolling suitcase with room to spare. I added a travel bag of toiletries, some matches from the motel lobby (what for? I don't smoke), and a plastic plate, bowl, cup, fork and spoon. In my pocket I carried an old Swiss army knife. It had been a gift to Stevie when he turned twelve. I didn't know what to do for Peanuts. Obviously I need his leash and bowl, but what else? I couldn't carry his 4 foot diameter pet bed with me everywhere. When we lived in the car it set in the back of the Subaru taking up more room than the camping pad I slept on. But I couldn't let him sleep on the ground. I packed everything up in my suitcase, then bundled the rest in a trash bag I swiped from the motel maid's cart and set out awkwardly balancing it on one hip with Peanuts on leash, towards the storage locker. It was a little more than two miles away.

Peanuts and I were both exhausted when we got there. I wondered if Dave and Big Dave were around. I would make them a deal on whatever I could, but they were nowhere to be found. So I just opened the garage door and pushed the bag into the mostly empty locker. The few things that remained , besides Stevie's guitar and mandolin and my dishes, were things like books and platters, LP's, sheets, pillows, mattresses, almost all my clothes and a file cabinet of papers: tax returns, birth and death certificates, you know the usual paper trail we carry through life. I found an old shaggy bathroom rug, a blue plastic tarp and a towel, rolled all these together and fastened them with a bungee cord I pulled from somewhere. My new home I thought as I twisted the bungee cord together. At the last minute I spotted a small envelope of family pictures and pushed it into the middle of the bundle. Off we went.

It was almost dark when I got back to the motel. I went upstairs, fed Peanuts and went down to the lobby hoping they still had coffee or tea to offer. I was dunking a Red Zinger bag in a white Styrofoam cup of almost hot water when the clerk spoke to me.

"Mrs. Roark? Aren't you Mrs. Roark, the one with the black dog?" He was a man in his 60s. I imagine his dream retirement plans were altered by his need to eat, so here he was swing shift at a cheap motel.

"Yes, I'm staying in room two twenty eight." I managed a closed lip smile, I wasn't sure if he was being friendly or doing business.

"You got some mail today." He pulled an envelope out from behind the desk and placed it on the counter.

"Oh? Gee, I'm surprised. Only a few people know I'm staying here." I picked up the envelope. The return address was St Mary's Light of Mercy Hospital. It had an embossed seagull as a seal.

"Will you be extending your stay?" He scrolled through the computer printout of room numbers.

"No, just tonight, I prepaid through tonight." I flipped the envelope over and started to open it.

"The day shift left a note to tell you any future stays we will have to charge an extra twelve for the dog."

I stopped opening the card. "What? Why? He's a really good dog. He doesn't destroy anything, very calm."

"Apparently there were complaints of his barking last night. It disturbed some of the guests."

"He was barking at some drunk from the third floor trying to kick in my door, why didn't they complain about that."

"I'm not sure. I was asked to let you know about the additional charge." He went back to flipping through the printout.

I started to tell him off, almost did in fact. But I was afraid that if I did he'd ask for the twelve dollars for tonight and I didn't have it.

"Of course, no, I'll be checking out tomorrow." I headed out the door with my tea and envelope.

Peanuts didn't bark when I unlocked the door. He must have learned my footsteps by now. I went in, rummaged through the food I still had to find a meager meal, and sat down to open the envelope. Inside was a light lavender card. The front had a lone seagull flying over an ocean stack. How odd. Don't we live in the desert? I opened it.

Sometimes we can't explain what has happened, only accept it was the inscription. It was signed by all the nurses and therapist who had worked with Stevie and a couple of the administrators. I wondered what they actually had to do with his care other than making sure I paid. One signature was larger than the others, it stood out not only for size but also a distinct bold style.

Our deepest condolences on your loss-Sigfriedo Jacquez, was hand written in black ink above an imprint of his name and title: CEO St Mary's Light of Mercy Medical Center.

I wondered if he ever met Stevie, if he had gone in to check on his care. Had he seen where he laid, bed pushed against the wall in a crowded, short staffed room smaller than his office? But I let it go. Instead, I focused on the kind words written by the nurses and staff.

Rita's called out to me: S*tevie has a special soul and place in my heart. I will keep you in my prayers. Rita Rael.* It was the only condolence card I received. I read it and reread it than crawled into bed and went to sleep.

¤ ¤ ¤

Day one or maybe it was day forty five. It depends on how you count it. If you are living in your car are you homeless? How about a motel room? Does that constitute homelessness? I remembered the surveys we gave the kids at school.

Your answer will be kept strictly confidential. Have you or your household experienced any periods of homelessness in the past year? (Please circle your response)

Yes, One day to two weeks homeless

Yes, Two weeks to two months homeless

Yes, more than two months homeless

No, no periods of homeless

Holy Cow! If I couldn't figure out when I officially became homeless how could they? How can anybody?

I stayed in my room until nine fifty nine, one minute before checkout time. I had been packed and ready since eight that morning, but I was still hoping for a fairy god mom to come through my door or Auntie Em to wake me up. I sat watching *The Price is Right* and drinking my sixth cup of weak tea with tons of sugar while Peanuts snored in the middle of the bed. At least I had food for Peanuts.

I looked around the room. Everything I reasoned I needed I had packed in the wheeled black case or cloth JC Penny's shopping bag. The case held my clothes, toiletries, towel, things like that. I used the bungee cord to fasten a sleeping bag, tarp and the rug for Peanuts in a bundle around the telescoping handle. The Penny's tote bag held Peanuts' food and bowl and the composition notebook I had kept all the notes in about the accident along with the papers about Sam's suicide, Stevie's medical care and my lost job. I tucked the condolence card the nurses sent in the back pages along with a family photo and some legal papers from the hospital demanding payment. We, Peanuts and I, started a journey but didn't know the destination.

We walked around for an hour or two then found some shade. Unpredictable spring weather meant days could hover in middle seventies, like today, but nights might drop down to the twenties. I sat down, got Peanuts some water. Wondered where I could get help and headed for the hospitality center. I knew they didn't take dogs, but maybe they knew someplace that would. When we got there only a few cars and an old van were parked in front. The clientele had not yet started to arrive.

I recognized one of the cars, an old cream colored Volvo wagon with one side smashed in so much the driver's door wouldn't open, the other side was tied with yellow nylon rope. To get to the wheel, you had to enter through the back seat and climb over. The kids with the pit-bull mix that I had given a blanket to weeks ago when I still had a home were sitting in the back seat, reading a much worn copy of *The Lord of the Rings* aloud to each other.

"Hi kids." I came around to the side with the open door. Their dog hopped out of the car and immediately wagged what little of a tail he had and sniffed butts with Peanuts.

The boy, obviously a wise guy, looked up from his reading, "Hey it's nice teacher lady! Well I'd get out and sniff butts with you but I think that greeting is species specific."

His partner was not so sarcastic. She slapped him gently and quietly told him to shut up. She leaned out the door and looked up at me.

"Hi. I've been thinking about you, we heard your son died. I'm so sorry, I just can't imagine."

"Thank you, he had been in the hospital a long time." Peanuts, satisfied with whatever he smelled from the pit-bull, turned and nosed the young hobo before giving her a lick. "Peanuts stop that." I pulled him back.

"That's okay, I really like dogs." She petted him on the side, before her own dog, jealous of her contact with Peanuts barged his way between them.

"Do you kids know if anyone is here yet?"

"No, there might be somebody in there, but they don't set up until later so they won't even open the door if you knock or anything."

"I was wondering about the no animal policy. Do they every bend it?"

"No," they answered in unison.

"That's why we stay in the car. Didn't you have a car? A Subaru? I thought I saw you here a couple of times in the lot." The girl answered first.

"Yeah, I did." I scanned the lot, sighed a couple of times. "I sold it. I needed money to bury my son."

I pulled the suitcase, sleeping bag and Peanut's rug bound to the top, close to me and set it upright so it would stand alone. "I need to find a place to stay, I was hoping they might know of someplace that accepts dogs."

"Oh. Sorry about your son and car." Mr. Sniff Butts was feeling remorse for his attitude. I wanted to tell him it was okay. It's the kind of thing my younger boy, Sean, would have said, but I didn't want to explain myself so I just let him slide.

"No, there really isn't a place that lets you stay with your animals. They just try to convince you to give 'em up. Some woman from the Animal Shelter drives over to check in a couple times a week. Sometimes she brings donated dog food and crap."

I looked down at Peanuts, scanned the area where a half dozen men and woman milled about. "Is there someplace people go? I mean is there someplace people can go to camp? You know, like..."

The two finished my sentence, "Like a homeless person?"

I nodded, not able to get anymore words out.

"Well some people go to the Rail Yard, just beside the tracks or in back of the shopping center, like that. But some of those guys are all drugged out so you have to be careful." The boy answered first.

The girl reached across her own dog and began rubbing Peanuts rear. "There's the River Park and over by the Mall, people camp out there. Some people just camp under the junipers off Hyde Park Road."

"If you know somebody, you might find a place on Hobo Hill. Do you know where that is?"

I nodded. I had heard about Hobo Hill for years. It was an undeveloped sloped lot not far from Santa Fe's Historic District. A dozen or so homeless souls had created a tarp and box community on the side of the hill. Once in a while it made headlines, but no one did much to clear it out.

"But I wouldn't try there unless you know someone. They can be kind of territorial."

I thought about it. Seeing these kids made me incredibly lonesome for my family. I decided to head over to the cemetery and visit Stevie's grave, sit a while there and try to sort it out.

"Thanks kids, be safe, okay?" I made the 'I love you sign' with my hand and backed away.

They both climbed out of the car. "You too, be safe." The boy reached into the back of the station wagon and pulled out a yellow dollar store bag.

"Want some cookies?" He pulled a half-eaten package from the bag.

"Thanks, I'd love one or two."

"Take the rest, please." He forced them into my hand. The girl pulled out a six pack of dollar store water in half liter bottles, pulled one off the plastic ring and handed it over.

"Take water too, you can fill the bottle anywhere. Then your dog will always have some. You know you can get some pretty sweet deals at the dollar store, food, dog food and soap and stuff. We go there all the time."

"Thanks kids, I'll keep that in mind. Thanks for the cookies and water, this is great.

Peanuts thanks you too." I took the cookies and water and stuffed them into my cloth shopping bag.

"Be careful nice lady," the girl called out.

"I will. Thanks again." I walked up the street.

"And remember; don't sniff butts unless you're a dog." The boy's voice carried above the Cerrillos road traffic. He was just like my Sean, trying to make me laugh. So I answered like he was Sean.

"Okay, son, I'll remember that. Only dogs sniff butts."

34

A funeral was finishing up when I got to the cemetery. Cars lined the frontage road and side roads in and around the graveyard. They were trying to make left turns into early afternoon rush hour traffic, things were a little chaotic. Peanuts jumped a couple of times when we were cut off by a turning car. I hoped the service dog thing would work again. I needed something to go right.

No one stopped us as we made our way past the huge pile of flowers under a canopy that marked the spot of the dearly departed. It was a stark contrast to Stevie's burial. The only flower arrangement at his grave was the three inch pot of burgundy chrysanthemums brought by Stevie's girlfriend's mom. I spotted them now in the dirt. The metal marker baring Stevie's name, date of birth and death was yet to be pounded into the ground so the flowers were the only identifier. I shook out the rug, meant for Peanuts, spread it out in the gravel beside Stevie's resting place. It would be my resting place too, at least for a little while.

Peanuts and I sat on the rug, not really knowing what comes next. I took out the cookies and water, offered some of each to Peanuts, and I ate a couple too. I tried to remember the good things about my husband, was trying to will myself to force out the pain and sorrow with thoughts about happy times as a family, but it just wasn't working. I sat with my legs folded to one side, arm propped up on my suitcase, staring at the world around me. I guess I zoned out because next thing I know it's getting kind of dark.

Towards the main entrance, a City of Santa Fe Police Department cruiser was parked in front of the now closed and locked gates. How could it be that late already? I didn't remember anyone going around locking things up. Another cruiser pulled in and a female officer got out and walked around to the open window of the first one. They looked my way a couple of times. I turned my attention back to Peanuts. His head is resting on my knee, he is asleep and his paws are moving, jerking, chasing rabbits we used to call it.

That man in the buckskin jacket and red canvas pack seems to appear out of nowhere and starts talking to the two police officers. He removes his hat, smooths the top of his hair and seems to motion towards me before replacing his hat and nodding a couple of time. The female officer returns to her cruiser and both cruisers back around and pull out.

I lie out, flat, half on the rug, half in the gravel with my hands clasped over my chest, waking Peanuts. Should I unroll my sleeping bag now or later I wonder, and then shut my eyes. A 'chink, chink chink' sound, like keys clinking together, keeps getting closer. It must be the maintenance men.

The guy with the buckskin jacket is beside me. "You can't sleep here, dear lady." He squats down on his haunches, balancing himself with one hand, like a tripod, in the dirt. Peanuts raises his head and sniffs the air.

I sit up on my elbows. This is the first time I have seen him this close. He is older than I imagined, probably in his seventies, he's got ear studs all along one ear, and his braided beard is fastened with an old turquoise ring. "Sorry? Are you talking to me?"

He nods. "You can't sleep here, you can't dwell here. Those two officers over there were ready to escort you off the grounds. I convinced them over wise, but you can't sleep here."

"Oh, thank you." I roll up and off the rug, fold it up and fasten it to the suitcase again.

"Do you have someplace to stay?" He stands up when I do, swings an old red canvas backpack over one shoulder, and puts his hands in his jean pockets.

"No. I...no. But if I can't stay here I guess I better get going." I wrap the bungee cord around the roll on top of my bag.

"Do you know about the hospitality center on Cerrillos?"

"They don't take dogs. I was there right before I came here." I start to walk slowly toward the foot gate, the only entrance still unlocked.

"First night?" he asks matter of factually. I realize the clinking sound is coming from multiple necklaces, some silver, some old style love beads, hanging around his neck.

"Excuse me?"

"First night out in the open I mean?"

"Sort of, I've been sleeping in my car, but I sold it to bury my son." I look back at Stevie's grave.

"Sorry." He continues to walk beside me. "I've got a camp over on Hobo Hill. Do you know about that place?"

"I do." I don't know what else to say. This is exactly what the young couple in the Volvo told me about. But what kind of guy tries to pick up an old lady in a graveyard. I keep walking. Part of me wants to go with him, but my good judgment is screaming: *Are you nuts?*

He touches my arm to slow me down. "Look, I'm legit, everybody knows me, even those cops over there, that's why they let me take care of this. Otherwise you'd be in the back of a cruiser by now, and your doggy'd be on his way to the pound."

"I don't know you." I keep walking.

He takes two big steps so he is slightly in front of me, extends his hand, which has a ring encircling every finger.

"Wizard."

I realize he is saying his name, not calling me one and reluctantly take his hand. "How do you do." Up close, it's easy to peg him for the old hippie he is, especially because of the odd smell of patchouli oil, rolling tobacco and sweat that emits from him. This guy is the real deal.

"And you, dear lady, are?"

"Aileen, my name is Aileen." I let go of his hand.

"I'm for real Aileen. I make it my personal goal to rescue at least one damsel in distress every day." He continues walking so he is slightly ahead of me. That's when I notice the cop cars are parked at the Burger Stop across from the cemetery.

Wizard senses right away what I'm looking at. "They're on meal break, they told me they were going to check back afterward to see if you were still here."

I pass him, so I am slightly ahead. A breeze picks up the scent of the flowers from the large stack nearby and I realize how much the temperature has dropped in the last half hour. It will get much colder before the night is over.

"Oh. Thanks again. I appreciate your offer, but I'm not a damsel in distress."

Wizard lightly grabs my elbow so I stop, catches up to me and puts his arm around my shoulder. He seems to struggle to find the right words.

"Dear lady..." he pauses. "Aileen, sweetie, I'm not trying to be cruel here, but you were sleeping on gravel in a graveyard, about to get a free ride in the back of a police cruiser."

I look at him, wrinkles etch his face, and his eyes are deep, deep blue. I burst into tears.

¤ ¤ ¤

There is no *Handbook for the Homeless*. Nobody teaches seminars or gives guided tours that promise to give you the inside scoop on where to flop. You have to figure it all out as you go along. Few of us plan for it. I suppose in today's cliché driven world it means we planned to fail. But how much farther can you fall than sleeping in the cemetery, curled up on your son's grave because it's the only piece of real estate you own. At best, if you find yourself homeless, if you haven't burned all your karma, you will find a spirit guide. More likely the guide will find you.

35

Wizard was a character. A relic of 1960s New Mexico communes that mostly collapsed in the late 70s (some of which were restored for Bed and Breakfasts in the 90s)

Wizard had pretty much done it all. For more than forty years he had farmed, and built and preached peace and love. He had been 'On the Bus' with the pranksters, and carried around the Polaroid snapshots to prove it. For the past decade, since his Teepee, erected on a squatters' field near hot springs in Ojo, was converted by new out of state owners into a rustic weekend getaway, Wizard made it living rough, in the open, mostly in Santa Fe or Taos. He still wore a beaded buckskin jacket with fringe, both summer and winter. He swore it was the same jacket worn by an actor in *Easy Rider* who, he claimed, had borrowed it from him for the movie; he wore his hair in two long gray braids with leather and feather wrapping; a braided beard hung to his sternum, fastened with two turquoise rings tied together with string. Wizard topped the whole thing off with a felted wool Stetson encircled by a rattlesnake skin hatband. At one time he had an intricately carved and beaded leather knife sheath which encased an enormous antler hilt hunting knife, but after several cautions by the police, he no longer wore it for all the world to see.

These days Wizard survived by posing for pictures on the plaza. He'd sit on the benches nearest the old hotel waiting for tourists, many of them foreign, to ask to take his picture. He grinned and told a joke or two, agreed, and would ask if they would help him out. They almost all did slipping a dollar or two into his outstretched hand. On a good day he'd come away with twenty or thirty dollars, on a bad a handful of change. He knew where and when to go for day old pastry, volunteered at the library, and always made sure to visit the cafes during quiet times where his cup was refilled often.

When he found me all I knew about him was that he cared.

Hobo Hill wasn't what I expected. I had envisioned a sort of western slope version of a Hooverville with tar paper shacks and tents. This place looked like somebody didn't keep up their yard. The hillside was littered with plastic bags and tarps, broken pallets, even an old recliner someone managed to get under a tree. You could see and smell the telltale signs of human waste behind and between rabbit bushes and under juniper trees. Peanuts was in heaven.

"My camp's up towards the top, on the side. You want to camp up ground, if there's a slope, and never in an arroyo, you never know when it might rain." Wizard extended his hand and helped me over a low field fence. I don't think it was originally low, but bent down so many times, accordion style, that now it was no more than a foot high. "Mind where you step. There is some broken glass around."

"Darlin' you in there? Got a guest with me." Wizard said, calling into a space under a large juniper tree. His camp was hard to see from the road. Wizard had managed to prop up some discarded shipping pallets in a circle under the base of the tree, covered them all with a camouflage tarp, than covered it by more broken branches. A woman, younger than I by a good ten to fifteen years, poked her head out from a low v shaped opening on one side. She had long unkempt hair, which hung down from a center part. It had once been light brown, but now mostly mouse gray and unwashed. I wondered when I would next be able to wash mine.

"Hello, welcome to the ranch." She popped her head back in. Wizard got down on all fours and crawled in, beckoning me to do the same. I was more than a little uncomfortable, not really sure of what to do with my bag, so I left it outside. Peanuts refused to enter.

The ground inside was covered by two cheap mismatched five by seven rugs that overlapped each other. To one side was an old mattress, bare save for the two sleeping bags spread out on top of it. A pressed board night stand, drawer removed, sat beside it. Books, magazines and old weekly free press papers overflowed its shelves. The rest was pretty much an assortment of plastic storage boxes lined up under a four foot long shelf made from a board stretched across two broken cinder blocks. A row of candles, lit, was grouped on the shelf.

"Welcome, I'm Rochelle, people call me Rocky." She smiled at me, revealing a huge gap where two lower teeth had once been. "Doesn't your doggy want to come in?"

"No, I'm not sure what's wrong, maybe in a little while."

"This is Aileen, Rocky. She's a first nighter." Wizard brought the pack in front of him and reached in, pulling a deli sandwich, the kind made of a whole loaf of soft white bread sold pre-made, wrapped in clear plastic, from a supermarket's cold case. It bore a prominent yellow label showing it was yesterday's stock, now marked half price. "They were just putting these out when I went by the dumpster, so I snagged a couple for us."

Wizard pulled a large folding knife from his pack and used it to cut the sandwich into thirds, handing me a portion.

"Thanks, I actually haven't eaten since this morning." I bit into the sandwich. The bread was soggy and the cheese almost liquid. These weren't just yesterday's, they were two days old, put out with the trash when today's leftovers were marked down. I ate slowly, trying not to let the gummy bread and limp lettuce stick to the roof of my mouth. I stuck my head outside, pretending to check on Peanuts who was curled up beside the door, ears alert, obviously worried, and picked some of the limp vegetables out from under my tongue.

Wizard pulled a half gallon of chocolate milk from his red pack and was drinking from it before passing it to Rocky. "Want some? It's still good. It's dated yesterday, but it's good for seven days after, they just can't sell it past the date."

I was thirsty for something besides water.

"I've got a cup in my bag." I pulled the cloth shopping bag in through the dwelling's opening and rummaged for my plastic ware.

"Don't bother, it'll get dirty and you'll have to wash it out someplace or you'll get ants or flies. Just take a swig from the jug. We don't keep food in here, it attracts pests. Plus, the food spoils too soon. It's best just to eat your fill then pass the rest on."

Wizard was giving me advice for survival the way I'd instruct my students about nouns and verbs. Should I be writing this stuff down? I took the jug of chocolate, drank two large mouthfuls, and passed it back to Rocky.

"And for desert..." Wizard, once again, worked his magic and presented us with a hinged clear plastic box, I believe they're called clam-shells, of red grapes. More than half were spoiled. We picked through them by candle light, eating the good ones and leaving the rest in the box.

I remembered the cookies in my bag. "Here, I have these." I offered the tray to Rocky. She looked at it horrified.

"Rocky is allergic to white sugar and preservatives. We try to stay away from that stuff." Wizard said.

"Sorry, I didn't know." I put the cookie tray back in the bag, tying it tightly with an overhand knot, then back into my cloth shopping bag. I wonder where she thought the chocolate milk came from. Chocolate cows? But it wasn't my place to criticize. These people were the only friends I had right now. As little as they had, they were the ones to invite me in, share their food and shelter with me. Who was I to ever think poorly of them?

Wizard removed the second sandwich from his pack along with a second box of grapes.

"You two want seconds?"

Rocky shook her head no. "No honey bear, I had my fill." She got up on her knees and crept towards Wizard, kissing him on the lips, then rolled back onto the bed and laid down.

Wizard looked at me, offering up the second helping.

"No, thank you, I really was hungry but that filled me up. Thank you."

"I'll be back in a few." He took the leftover food and crawled out of the make shift hovel. I was surprised Peanuts didn't growl at him. I could hear the old hippie talking to someone not far away, couldn't really make out what was said, but did hear several "Thank you's". When he came back his hands were empty.

"How's Mica?" Rocky asked him as he sat on the mattress beside her.

"Not too good, his foots' looking real bad. We might have to convince him to turn out."

"Turn Out?" It was an expression I had never heard before.

"Turn out, means, go to a shelter, get some medical care. People have to 'turn out' there. Turn out their pockets, their blanket rolls, they want to make sure you ain't got any drugs or weapons. If you do they get taken away." Wizard removed his boots and socks. Whoa ,that was a new smell.

"It's important to get out of your boots and socks everyday. Otherwise the fungus and infection, little mites, build-up, it gets into your blood and makes you sick as a dog. That's what's wrong with Mica."

"Oh, I guess I should take mine off then." I started to remove my shoes.

"Well, make sure you're settled first. You don't want to be walking around here without your shoes when nature calls. By the way, always make your latrine down slope from your camp. There's a big Chamisa bush right beside a Piñon with a little trench in between, a few yards down. Now would be a good time."

"Right, I guess it would." I crawled out of the low opening. Peanuts stood up and shook off the dust. I grabbed the leash which I had tied around a branch and took him with me. If it weren't for the light of the full moon I would never have found it.

This is hard, I thought. I had squatted in the dirt camping when the boys were little but my last few years of camping in a travel trailer were considerably less rustic. This was the city. I could hear cars on the road not far from where I now relieved myself, hoped I wouldn't be caught in the headlights. I had a hard time standing up. What do I do for number two? I am way too old for this.

Wizard had pulled my suitcase into his camp when I got back. He and Rocky had gone through my stuff, but it didn't seem to be too amiss. They had unrolled the tarp and placed my sleeping bag on top of it with Peanuts rug right beside. Between their mattress, my bag and Peanuts rug we filled the whole space. I lured Peanuts in with a bit of dog food.

Rocky emptied a small plastic box, told me to put the rest of the dog food in there or the mice would get it.

"Lights out ladies." Wizard bent forward and blew out the candles.

36

It was cold. The beginning of April and snow was in the forecast. A few of the Hobo Hill dwellers lit camp fires, which Wizard tried to persuade them to put out. "We don't want to draw too much attention," he said, admonishing them. "Fly under the radar when possible." But they did provide a source heat and hot water for tea.

"In a while I'll take you down to the plaza and introduce you around. The dog could be a problem though. Depends who's on duty, but some of the patrol don't appreciate the finer qualities of a canine, especially when they belong to one of us."

"I can leave if it's a problem. He was my son's dog. I can't abandon him."

Wizard looked at Peanuts, thinking. He wasn't a dog lover but I couldn't hold that against him, he had treated me well.

"Okay, but be ready to exit stage left if needed." I hadn't heard that since I was a teenager.

We went down to the plaza. I walked a good ten or twelve feet in back of Rocky and Wizard. When we got to the library, about four guys, all with back packs or bedrolls, were sitting on the two concrete benches out front smoking. Wherever they had spent the night, they couldn't wait to get into the warmth of the library. They had a long wait. It wasn't yet seven and the library didn't open until ten. Wizard greeted them by name.

"Charlie, Hajeed, what do you know. Einstein. Floyd." He nodded to each as he spoke their names.

"Wizard, my man, take a load off." Floyd moved his pack aside. Rocky sat down beside him. I stood a few feet away, not certain of my role here.

"I want you to meet a first nighter. This dear lady," Wizard motioned me over "is Aileen".

"Good morning, you survived huh?" Hajeed took a long drag off his smoke and exhaled through his nose.

"Yeah, it was cold, but we managed. Didn't we Peanuts?" I pulled Peanuts lead close to me; I didn't know how he would react to these new faces.

"You think this was cold sister? Last night was nothing. Wait until tomorrow. Snow for sure." Charlie was laughing.

"Don't scare her man, she's scared enough already. She just buried her son." Wizard's voice revealed only a smidgen of the Brooklyn accent he came here with more than forty years ago.

They all sat up straight.

"Sorry lady. Sorry for your trouble."

"It's okay. He was in the hospital a long time." I scratched Peanuts' ear. Maybe I should just move on.

"How old was he?" Rocky was surprised Wizard hadn't shared this information last night when he brought me 'home'.

I looked at her and furrowed my brows. Up until now no one had asked what happened to Stevie. "He was twenty-seven. He turned twenty-seven a few weeks ago. He'd been in a coma for almost a year."

Rocky bummed a cigarette from Einstein. "How'd that happen?" She seemed so even keel, like she was asking about what I had for breakfast or something.

"My husband drove drunk off the road. My younger son died right away, and Stevie, my older son, wound up in a coma." It was easier to talk about then I thought it would be.

"What happened to your husband? Where's he now?" I felt like I was being interrogated.

"He's buried over in the cemetery, there off the highway. He and my two boys are all there. He committed suicide. He was going to trial for what happened, couldn't handle it and cashed it in one day before the trail was to start. I was at work."

I stopped talking, looked down to avoid eye contact. I expected another question, but when I finally looked up Rocky she was puffing away on the cigarette, legs crossed.

"That's where I meet Wizard. I was at my son's grave. I buried him four days ago. Wizard came and rescued me. I guess a couple of city police were about to come after me and he talked them out of it."

Rocky looked me over, put the cigarette out carefully on the cement sidewalk and slipped what was left of it into her jacket pocket for later. "Wizard has good Karma like that. He has radar and picks up on things." She got up, locked my arm in hers. "Come on, let's catch up to Wizard. See what magic he can perform today."

His disappearing act was good; I didn't even know he was gone.

37

I had been to the Plaza well over a hundred times in the more than thirty years I lived here. Every time I came I ran into one or more people I knew, former co-workers, and parents of now grown little leaguers or women from my aerobics class. If I didn't recognize them they did me and a ten minute conversation would ensue. But I had never come here as an oxymoron: Resident Vagrant. This was a first. It was more than a little intimidating to realize I was the person I used to avoid. I kept looking over my shoulders expecting to see someone I knew but it apparently was a 'Not if I see you first' situation. If anyone did see and recognize me, they made themselves scarce fast.

Part of the Plaza had been roped off while the grassy area was refurbished. The remaining sections that weren't covered by pavement each had two or three people such as me, sitting on the ground. Some smoking, some sat talking in small circles. One guy strummed a guitar, a deed that would soon cause him to be asked to leave. Playing music here, unless you were part of an officially sponsored program, was forbidden.

Wizard was holding forth on the southwest corner of the Plaza, in front of an Ice Cream Store and Bakery. In the morning tourists would come for a hot chocolate topped by whipped cream about a foot high and a pastry. Three well-dressed middle age woman, two in broomstick skirts and elaborate cowboy boots, and one wearing a Pendleton Jacket woven with a Native American design were standing with Wizard, who was indeed working his magic. He was, above all, a story teller, and this was his stage. Two of the woman posed with him as the third stepped back and snapped their picture. All three had heavy Texas accents.

"Tell me about this jacket. This looks just like the one that fellow in *Easy Rider* wore. It's fab u lus."

"Oh, you like it? It is the one from *Easy Rider*. Borrowed it from me for the movie. That was my hat too. I lost that one. I was in the movie, don't you recognize me?" Wizard put his hand on the woman's arm and turned in profile.

"Really, you were in the movie, I guess I'll have to watch it again. Which scene are you in?" A woman with bright pink lipstick and purple lizard boots pulled her cell phone from her bag.

"Lots of 'em. I was in more, but they got cut from the final version. They were afraid I would up stage the stars." Wizard held out the lapels of his jacket like a politician.

The women laughed hysterically. "Oh you!!" one of them said.

"Can I try on your jacket?"

"Absolutely, beautiful, and I'll even let you buy me a coffee." Wizard removed the jacket and helped the lizard booted woman put it on.

"Take my picture, take my picture!" She called to her friend, and posed with one boot forward like she was doing a do-si-do. She reached over and took Wizard's hat and put it on.

"One more."

Her friend put it on, posed with Wizard, and the third went into the bakery, returning with a large coffee and pastry, handing them to Wizard.

"You ladies enjoy your stay here." He sipped the coffee. "It's been a real pleasure to visit with you."

"You too." The giggly women headed east on the plaza toward the Cathedral. As soon as they were out of earshot, Wizard came over to Rocky and handed her the coffee.

"Those three were easy; I didn't even have to tell them where I got my bracelet." Wizard pushed up his sleeve to reveal a huge sand cast turquoise bracelet. The blue green rock, flecked with gold must have been 4 inches across.

Rocky held out the coffee to me, it did smell good, but I wasn't quite there yet, by that I mean, I wasn't quite ready to share a communal cup of coffee with someone I wasn't related to.

"Okay, I'll bite, where did you get your bracelet?" I asked.

"This? All the old rock and rollers, you know, like Airplane, Joplin, they all came through here. I was living in an earth family in Llano, do you know where that is?"

"Sort of, isn't it near Taos?" I had heard rumors of all the old hippies in the hills near Taos, but I wasn't sure where exactly.

"More towards Peñasco, on the High Road. There's an old movie theater there. So they decide to do a free jam session. Invite only. At the last minute the drummer craps out, bad trip or something. I had to sit in. After it was over, one of the musicians tells me it's the best drumming he's ever heard and hands me this bracelet."

"Who was it? Which musician gave it to you? Is this story true?" Boy, Wizard could either spin a good one or he really did go back to the summer of sixty nine.

"Why would I make this stuff up? You had to be there. True. True story. I got this from..."

"I have to ask you to keep going with your animal; we're trying to keep animals off the Plaza." A Santa Fe City cop is behind us.

I was surprised. I had been here before with our pets, years ago and never got asked leave.

"Why, he isn't bothering anything? He's on a leash." I challenged the cop.

Rocky locked my arm again, spun me around. "Let's go Aileen, keep walking, I'll explain latter."

Wizard stayed, called out, "Meet me around back in half an hour."

Rocky and I walked west, down San Francisco Street, then headed south towards the State Offices off of Alameda. The Santa Fe River, or what was left of it, bisected this part of the city. A shady park with a walking path bordered one side of the river. A lot of homeless came here. It was a welcome respite from the high desert sand and brown concrete stucco that marked most of a city once made up of thick adobe brick and plaster. The river path turned out to be a good place for Peanuts.

"What was up with that, Rocky? Why did they tell us to leave because of Peanuts?"

I sat on a bench and let go of Peanuts leash. Down here, a little away from the road and people, he was able to walk around unimpeded.

Rocky sat beside me, pulled out what was left of the cigarette and relit it. "They just don't like street people. They use any excuse they can to move us out; it's not the cops themselves. They get pressure from the store owners, especially the ones who run those carts around the plaza. They think we keep people away, especially anybody who has a dog. They blame us for lack of business."

"Don't you stand up to them? Doesn't anybody say anything?"

"It's a lose lose situation if you do. You lose twice, because, one, you're likely to get your ass hauled off and, two; they come down harder on the rest of us after something happens. It's better just to walk away." Rocky finished her cigarette.

"Sorry, I didn't mean for Peanuts and me to be such a problem." I said.

"You're not a problem, Peanuts is a little. He's a good dog and all, it's just a lot harder, and it gives a reason why we shouldn't be somewhere or do something. You can't take them in buildings, you can't let them loose. It's harder that's all."

I called Peanuts over; he came right away, sat beside me, waiting to be petted. I rubbed his chest. "He was my son's dog."

"That's what you said."

Peanuts rolled over on his back, I used my foot to rub his belly. "My son wanted to take him along on the trip he took with his dad and brother. The one they were on when the accident happened."

Rocky sat with her hands folded between her knees, staring at Peanuts.

"I talked him out of it. I said the same things you did, you can't take him in places; you can't let him run loose or leave him locked in the truck. I convinced him to leave him with me, and promised I would take really good care of him. It was the last conversation I had with my son."

Rocky nodded, sighed, stood up. "Better go find Wizard again, no guessing what stories he's telling now."

Wizard, when we found him, was helping to unload crates of lettuce and field greens from the back of a farmer's small pickup. In his younger days he'd show up early in the morning when art and craft vendors were unloading, working for tips to set up, tear down and haul; same for regional bands playing the local venues. These days, two or three times a week, various pickup trucks and vans made their way through the narrow alleys for delivery. Wizard knew they were coming a mile away, not by sight, but by sound and smell. The odd assortment of VW Rabbit Pick-ups converted to biodiesel and dented Ford Rangers bought at public auction each had a distinct engine rumble or squeaky brake that would herald the imminent arrival of today's special and tomorrow's Soup de Jour. Wizard knew some of the organic farmers from his commune years. A few would offer a couple of bucks for help unloading. Truthfully, this was out of a sense of kinship rather than need. Wizard's advanced years made his labor more symbolic than useful.

I started to approach the loading dock to pitch in but Rocky pulled me back.

"Wizard's a great guy, best man I ever hooked up with, but he flies solo when he's working. He thinks of himself as a kind of Robin Hood taking from the rich to give to the poor. So, don't help him, he'd be insulted."

"Oh?" my classic lame response. "Is that where that whole damsel in distress thing came from?"

"Did he do that with you, too? Man, he does that with all the ladies." Rocky said and laughed.

Wizard started to wheel a hand-truck topped by three produce boxes through the kitchen's back door, but stopped short when he saw us.

"Ladies, ladies, go around front, breakfast is waiting."

I looked surprised.

"It's okay, he works deals with them, sweeps the floor or something, but I don't know about the dog. I'll go around first and eat. See if you can tie your dog someplace."

Rocky and I walked around front. A ten by ten foot patio was separated from the street by a small black iron fence. The outdoor tables and chairs were pushed up close to the front window; a thick chain snacked in and through each one. It was nearly seven thirty am, almost opening time. An apron clad worker came out with a key and undid the padlock.

"Do you allow dogs on the patio?" When he didn't answer I tried again.

"¿El perro, bien aquí?" My Spanish was sinfully bad considering how long I had lived here.

"Sí, the dog is okay. Outside," the young man replied.

"Gracias." I entered the little area and started to help set up chairs around the tables the young man was pulling into position.

Rocky was already inside, returned with two small bowls filled with potatoes seasoned with smoked paprika and garlic. Strips of some type of green, probably chard, marbled the potatoes, a poached egg on top of a small slice of a toasted baguette nested in the middle.

"Breakfast hash," she said as she placed one bowl in front of me and passed a fork from her other hand. "Eat up, we need to finish and leave before the real customers arrive."

"What about Wizard? Won't he eat with us?" It didn't seem right to take this food without Wizard here.

"Oh, you know, he likes an audience. He's in back now holding forth with the owner and one of the waiters. Don't worry. They won't let him go hungry."

The food wasn't good, it was great. It had been so long since I had an egg, just an egg, such a simple thing. I slathered the toast with the pats of butter and offered it to Peanuts. His bag of kibble was nearly empty, I had to make it stretch. This was a treat for him too. A couple stopped to admire him.

"What a beautiful dog. Is he a Belgian Shepard?"

"Yes, his name's Peanuts."

The woman stopped to pet him, rough his collar and make a fuss.

"How's the food here?" she asked.

"The best, try the breakfast hash." I finished my bowl and rested the fork on the edge. Rocky sat silent, waiting for the visitors to go inside. When they did she put her empty bowl on top of mine and stood up.

"Aileen, don't take this wrong, okay, I know you're new at this, the owners here are good to us, but only if we don't hassle their customers or panhandle."

"Sorry, I didn't realize I was harassing them."

"Well, you weren't, but most of the time if we talk to someone like that people think we're going to hit them up for money."

"Isn't that what Wizard does?"

Rocky glared. "He's different. People know him, he goes back a long way. But you and me and most of the other street people need to keep it low profile. Okay?"

"Yeah, yes, sorry. I appreciate everything you and Wizard are doing."

"More Wizard then me. He brings people around the way a kid picks up a stray dog, and looks like he picks up a few of those from time to time too." Rocky stared at Peanuts.

I tightened my grip on the leash. "Sorry, I didn't realize. Hopefully I'll be able to pick myself up before too long."

"Well, I've been living like this for seven years, so here's my advice; don't count on it. When things get to the point we're at they only get worse, hardly ever get better. If you want to survive learn to deal with it." Rocky handed me the bowls. "Here, you take the plates inside, take them to the dish tray in the back and put them in the gray bin. I'll hold the dog."

Rocky's words terrified me. Seven years? I need to get this figured out in seven days, a couple weeks tops. I didn't want to leave Peanuts with her, but knew I needed her help to survive, I handed over the leash and took the bowls inside. I didn't notice the sign until I was on the way out. A small card was taped discreetly by the entrance. 'Barista needed. Apply with in'. That's it, my salvation.

I could see Rocky with Peanuts, waiting to the side of the entrance. It'll only take a minute. I waited by the reservation desk for the waiter to come over.

"Can I help you?" he said hesitantly.

"I was wondering if the Barista job had been filled yet."

"Do you have experience?" He scanned me head to toe.

"Not as a Barista, but I'm a quick learner, is the job still open?"

"Wait a minute, the owner is in the kitchen, and I'll see if she has filled the spot yet."

He went into the kitchen. I leaned forward and saw Rocky staring impatiently from the side walk, she beckoned for me to come, did not look happy. I held my hand up, palm out and mouthed "Wait."

The waiter came back. "The owner is too busy to see you now, but said if you want to come back this afternoon, after the lunch rush, between one thirty and two, she can talk to you. She did say to use the back entrance."

"Thanks, thank you, I'll come back." I started to leave when the waiter taped his index finger lightly on the chest high podium to get my attention then spoke very softly.

"A little advice? The owner is a stickler for cleanliness, especially our hands, so you might want to clean up a bit before you come, especially under your nails." Then he quickly grabbed a pot of coffee from a nearby burner and started to make the rounds of the little cafe. I looked at my hands, more than a little embarrassed. A thick layer of dirt and sand had already taken up residence under my fingernails; I realized I hadn't washed my hands in over 24 hours. That thought suddenly grossed me out, I walked out, caught a glimpse of my dirty disheveled appearance reflected it the glass. How had I turned into this poor soul so quickly and who was I fooling? They'll never hire me. I walked outside and slipped the leash from Rocky's hands.

"What took you so long?" Rocky gestured her hands outward, upset, as we started walking west towards the Rail yard area.

"I wanted to ask about a job. They had a card up for a Barista." I walked in front of her, didn't really know where I was going. Rocky yanked me back by the shoulder.

"A job? You ask about a job? Lady are you nuts? After what I just told you about not making waves you go and ask for a job. Are you trying to burn all of Wizard's karma or what? The owner here feeds us at least once a week, twice sometimes. We have to stay on her good side."

I nodded, head down discouraged, and continued to walk. Rocky caught up to me, still ranting about Wizard picking up strays to herself. She was getting less and less patient as the day progressed. When we got to Guadalupe Street I wasn't quite sure where to go. I stopped. and Rocky stopped beside me, looked straight ahead.

"What did they tell you?"

"To come back, the owner said to come back this afternoon after lunch and she would talk to me."

"Well, are you?"

"What?"

"Going back, are you going back?"

"Maybe, I don't know, I would need to clean myself, wash up, and get some clean clothes on. And I'm not sure about Peanuts either."

Rocky changed back into the sweet flower child I first encountered when I arrived at Hobo Hill. The change good cop to bad cop to good cop was so fast, and obvious, I started to wonder if this woman had mental health issues.

"Just find a bathroom somewhere, the library, McDonald's. But you can't take the dog in. Sometimes the park, but they don't always unlock the bathrooms, and the water isn't always turned on at the sinks, and never hot water," she said, still not looking at me.

"Thanks, I just want to try to get a job, if they don't hire me there, I'll start looking around more. When Stevie was alive, well for one I kept thinking I'd get another teaching job, and for another, most of my time was with him or Peanuts or just trying to figure out what hit me."

"I know what you mean." She nodded and started across the street.

A large SUV with Colorado plates narrowly missed us as it turned.

"Freakin' Feaster." Rocky gave them the finger. "Wizard said to meet him over by the Co-op."

"The Food Co-op? The one on Alameda?"

"Yeah, they have a free box out front. We're trying to find Mica some warmer clothes and new shoes."

"Who's Mica?" We kept walking, cutting down to a path along the Santa Fe River. Peanuts kept trying to pull away and drink from puddles of water that spotted the broken sidewalk. "If there's a place to get water I'd like to stop and get some for Peanuts."

"There's a dogs' water bowl outside the Co-op. They keep it filled for people's dogs. It's not that far. It's right by the free box. Mica lives up hill from us. He spreads out under a tarp he has stretched between some trees. Some of the low-life near the rail park, the other end, where it crosses St Francis, attacked him, took his pack and his boots. He lost his pack, all his clothes and other stuff a couple of weeks ago. Wizard found him some shoes, but they don't fit good and he's been wearing them without socks. He doesn't want to take them off. That's what Wizard was telling you about. You have to get out of your shoes at least once a day, and try to keep dry socks on. Otherwise you'll get turned out for good."

"Didn't the police do anything? When that happened? When they took his pack?"

Rocky laughed. "Are you kidding? The only attention we get is when somebody ends up stabbed or dead. No, they didn't do anything."

38

Wizard was already there. Just like Rocky said, a large metal bowl was filled with water a few feet from the door.

"How are the ladies this morning? Did you enjoy your breakfast Aileen?"

"It was great, thank you, I really do appreciate it."

"Aileen applied for a job at CJ's." Rocky got right to the point.

Wizard looked surprise, and not in a good way. "Really? And did you get it?" Wizard stood behind Rocky massaging her shoulders.

"No, not yet, I have to go back this afternoon. I need to clean up first and find someone to watch Peanuts."

"Well, you can probably clean up here. There's a restroom in back you can use. They don't give us too much grief. The Salvation Army has showers, but I'm not sure about the ladies shower. Maybe Rocky can fill you in on that." Rocky pulled away from Wizard, annoyed.

"Any chance we can head up to the hills today? I'm suffocating here."

"Sure Rock, let me see if we can get Mica taken care of and then we can head up, maybe catch a ride or something. Aileen, you can manage can't you?"

"Yeah, thanks, I can. I just need to clean up." I still didn't know what to do with Peanuts.

"Rocky, grab hold of his leash a while. I'll see what I can pull out of the pile for Mica."

Wizard already had a pair of shoes in his hand, and was sorting through some sweaters."

Rocky, reluctantly took Peanuts' leash as I pulled my suitcase around, took out a towel, soap, and clean shirt and pants, a bit wrinkled, but valet service wasn't available today. As I zipped up the case, a tall bearded man, about sixty wearing torn jeans and an old forest service shirt came out of the store with two cloth bags of food.

"Wizard, my man." The two clasped hands and gave a quick hug.

"Geo, how's it going brother." Obviously old friends. "Hey, I want you to meet my old lady. Rochelle." Geo hugged her, kissing her on the check.

"Where are you staying now? I haven't seen you in over a year, what are you up to?" Geo stood back eying me and Peanuts.

"Got a camp over off Hyde Park Road. You know me brother, always working it. How about you?" Wizard stood rocking his heels, hands in pockets.

"Gia and me still up near Truchas, big garlic farm, spring onions, mostly for stores and restaurants. Keeps us going. Come up, you and your old ladies." He winked at me.

Old Ladies? Did he think I was part of the family?

"Can't wait, in fact if Rock had her way we'd be there now."

"Why not? Let me make a stop at the feed store. I'll be back. You can ride up with me."

"Great, I need to get these to a fellow traveler first." Wizard held up a thick sweater, some socks and a pair of well-worn boots gleaned from the free box, destined for Mica.

Rocky looked elated.

I hurried into the store. Wizard was right. No one bothered me as I cleaned myself up and changed. I wish I could have taken a full shower, but I was better than before. I took extra care to scrub my hands and nails. When I came out Wizard was gone and Peanuts was tied to the bike rack, my wheeled case beside him. Someone had put a few dog bones on the ground beside him. He just sat there waiting for me to give him the okay. Good Dog.

40

I learned pretty quickly to tell time by two things, well three really. One, St. Francis Cathedral bells still chimed the hour. If you were anywhere near the plaza area, you could count the chimes. Two, traffic at certain hours of the day was predictable. Three, the direction the homeless were walking. I knew it was twelve thirty, and lunch service was over at the soup kitchen when I saw the men and woman walking, slowly, toward park benches, shade trees and other places, to find respite for the afternoon hours. Shelters would not open their doors until four or five o'clock. The slow steady stream of unshaven men and woman without makeup or heels meant it was time to head to the cafe. I would need to tie Peanuts up out back. I was praying for this job. I had to find a place to sleep indoors again, and to do that, I needed money.

Peanuts and I made our way up San Francisco Street and turned onto the narrow side street that accessed the alley. About midway down the gray-green dumpster of the cafe jutted out into the graveled lane. The back door to the little cafe was propped open slightly with a rock. I knew I couldn't take Peanuts in there but I wasn't sure what to do with him, decided he would be safer out front, walked around to the front, looped his leash through one of the metal bars that made up the front patio enclosure and went inside. Always hope for the best. The same guy I talked to that morning was still there.

"Hello again. Still at it?" I smiled, tried to be charming and friendly not terrified and desperate. I had to get this job.

"Oh, so you did come back. I think Susie is expecting you to use the other entrance. Her office is just inside the back door." He wasn't smiling, but at least he wasn't rude.

"I know, she was, but I didn't have any place to leave Peanuts right now, it was short notice, I hope it's okay, I tied him outside."

"Yes, well, customers do leave animals there, but not for long, usually just for take out."

"Do you think I should tie him someplace else?"

"Don't you have someplace to leave him? I mean when you work?"

"I'm in a pinch today," I lied. "It's really hard to find someplace that takes pets you know."

"I guess it'll be okay, I'll try to keep an eye on him. Go ahead and go through." He lifted the hinged section of the counter so I could walk through, past the prep area and down the hall. The door to the office was slightly ajar. I could hear talking on the phone, someone calling in an order. I tapped lightly on the door. A woman in her forties with lightly graying hair pulled back into a pony tail wearing a white shirt and black apron stamped with red and green chiles poked her head out. She still had the phone plastered to her ear, and motioned me in, pointing to a small chair perpendicular to her overflowing desk. A white board with a work schedule took up most of the opposite wall, the rest of the office was a conglomeration of motivational posters 'Be the change you want to see' with a picture of Gandhi, 'One world to share' in bold letters across the earth from space, and more. Here and there a Gladys cartoon taken from a Daily desk calendar was taped to a lower corner of a poster. I sat on the edge of the chair and tried to take in the display. If I was a kid with ADD, I'd be spinning circles right now, too much visual stimulation.

"Susie." She finished the call, set down the phone and extended her hand.

I took her hand, shook it lightly. "Very nice to meet you, I'm Aileen."

"Aileen?" She held onto my hand, and reached across with her other picking up a pen.

"Aileen Roark, thank you so much for seeing me today."

"Yes, well, we are looking for a Barista for the afternoons, part time and as a sub. Right now I've got my lead, Herman, I believe you spoke with him earlier, working seven days a week all shifts. That and the summer tourist season is almost here. So, tell me about you. Have you worked in the food industry?"

"When I was in college, it's been awhile. I did work-study in the cafeteria. When I was teaching I used to help out with lunch service when they were short staffed."

"You're a teacher? Tell me about that." She was writing as we talked but I don't think it was about me.

"I taught for District Two." I wasn't sure how much I should tell her, technically I resigned, but it sure felt like being fired. "I had to take some time off for family reasons, and well, the school year is almost over, so I need something for the summer."

"You're looking for summer work then?" She pulled a pink sticky note from a stack by her phone, wrote my name and *pt-sum* on it.

"Right now I'm looking for something, yes, for the summer. I do hope to get back to teaching next fall, but things are pretty open at the moment." This wasn't a lie.

"What I have available is part time, afternoons, at the coffee station, doing basic beverage prep, occasionally helping out with plating if needed. Tell me about your coffee experience." At least I had lasted this long in the interview.

"Honestly, Mr. Coffee is about the level of my skill right now, but I'm a quick learner. I'd really like the chance to work here. Such a great environment and very high quality food." Compliment the boss, I thought nervously, make her want to hire you.

"Well, we try. We have been voted best local food two years in a row. Come around front. Let's see what you can do."

Thank you Jesus, I was about to get my chance. I looked out the window at Peanuts, he was lying down with his big paws extended in front of him, but sat up when he caught sight of me.

"Oh pretty dog." Susie lifted her head to see out the window. She turned toward Herman, who was using a clean white towel to wipe down the espresso steam jets. "Whose is he?"

Herman raised his eyebrows and tilted his head towards me.

I cleared my throat. "Um, he's mine. I'm between places right now and it's hard to find a place that takes pets. Sorry."

"No, it's okay, I love dogs. I run a dog friendly patio, but if you do work here you'll need to find someplace else to leave him." Susie walked me over to the sink down the hall. "This is our hand wash station. All employees wash their hands at the beginning of shifts, and after any breaks." She turned the water on and pushed up her sleeves, I did the same. Susie grabbed a clean black apron from a row of hooks hanging to the right of the sink and handed it to me.

Taped to the shelf behind the work station were two pages enclosed by plastic page protectors, each had a list of the coffee and tea drinks and a direction for its prep. Susie walked me through a small latte, grinding, steaming and a swirl. She put a lid on it and set it aside. We talked about the amounts, the procedures, how the order is taken and set out for the customer or wait staff. By this time two customers had come in, Herman took the order, Susie made one drink, than stepped me through the second. Two more drink orders, same steps. After about eight or nine lattes she left me on my own.

"Herman will be right here, ask if you need anything."

"I've got the job?"

"We'll see how you do today. Of course I'll pay minimum wage for now. We can talk about tips and such if this works out. Consider this a trial basis for both of us, okay?"

"Yes, thanks, thanks," I wave of relief and hope filled me, maybe I could pull this off.

I worked for nearly three hours. There were more than a few mess ups. Herman was patient, but not infinitely so. You could tell he was getting tired of doing two jobs, and just wanted some relief. In between customers Herman took me back to the kitchen and introduced me to the cooks, all of whom spoke only Spanish. The evening staff arrived. Only one introduced himself.

"Hi, I'm James, and you are?" He asked as he pulled a black apron over his white shirt.

"Aileen, I'm auditioning for the Barista job."

"Ah, well break a leg. Didn't I see you with Wizard earlier?"

I was embarrassed and ashamed for it. Wizard was the only one to reach out to me, and here I was embarrassed to be seen with him. I kept my answer short. "Yes. What a character he is."

James looked me up and down before responding. "Yes, he is," and walked away.

Susie came out and spoke to Herman, who shrugged his shoulders and nodded. Then she walked over to where I was busying myself by wiping the espresso machine with a clean white towel.

"Okay Aileen, we'll see you tomorrow. You'll need to bring a copy of your birth certificate, social security card and other id. We have to have copies of all that stuff now, federal rules you know. Be here by 1:30, I'm going to start you on the smoothies and some other things, about four hours tomorrow?"

"Great, wonderful, thank you so much." I was smiling, thank God, I had a job. I took off my apron asked Herman where to put it or if we took it with us.

"No, there's a laundry bag in the back, put it in there. Black pants, white shirt is standard. Can you manage that?"

"Yes, I do have a white shirt and black pants. When do we get paid?"

My question startled him. "Friday, checks are issued on Friday. But you may not get your first check this Friday. It depends on getting in the forms and things. Susie has to get the paperwork to the bookkeeper in time to issue a check."

I would never make a good poker player. Herman could easily detect the disappointment on my face. He reached into his aprons' pocket and retrieved a roll of dollar bills.

"We're supposed to put tips in a shared jar at the end of the shift, but no one will say anything about a couple of ones. Buy yourself a coffee." He peeled off four ones and handed them to me.

"Thanks." I guess I had misjudged him. "What I really need is a bag of dog food and I've got to find someplace to leave Peanuts."

Herman reached under the counter and pulled out a large plastic barrel with miniature dog bones in it, took three out before replacing it and handed them to me. "If you have to bring him, it's better to tie him out back, he'll be okay there. Bring your own water dish."

I thanked him again went out and untied Peanuts. The dog had been so patient. I had left him there for nearly three hours. I headed towards Hobo Hill, hoped I was still welcome.

¤ ¤ ¤

No one was home, if you can call it that. Wizard called it his dwelling. Most of the other residents of Hobo Hill called it their camp. Being part of Wizard's entourage was a trip. Literally. You never knew where you were going, who you would meet or what you would do.

I remembered Rocky and Wizard climbing into the back of the pickup, wondered if they would be back or if I was intruding too much. I need not have worried. Within a few minutes Wizard appeared, Rocky following, along with two other men. One, skinny as a guitar string and just as tightly strung, limped beside her. He was about Wizard's age, his back bent like an old man's. A canvas duffel, something that might have once held baseball bats or soccer balls, bounced up and down diagonally across his back when he walked.

The other man, thirty or so, maybe younger, short and stout, with a shaved head, bore no expression. He had on a new blue wind jacket and black and white running shoes. His tan bargain store pants bore little signs of wear. I was too naive to know his uniform was that of someone recently out of prison. Given a new set of clothes and little else, he was expected to make his way back into a society that had written him off after a third strike when he was still a teen. Now, twelve years later, without family, friends or support of any kind, he was expected to magically acquire a set of skills that would allow him to rebuild his life without resorting to crime. Fat chance of that happening.

"Dear lady, you are still with us. I thought you might have joined the ranks of the enslaved, er, employed." Wizard put his arm around my shoulder and grinned. The others were likewise amused.

"You don't really want to sell your soul for the almighty dollar do you sweetheart?" The other old geezer came around to my left side, put his arm around my waist while swinging the duffel off his back and onto the ground. It was extremely discomforting.

"Maybe. I'd like to earn enough for a place to sleep and something to eat." I pulled Peanuts closer to me, trying to politely extract myself from between the two men. My mind was racing, who were these people and how did I end up here? How do I get myself out?

"Aileen, this is my old compadre, Ty. We go way back to my days up in Truchas."

"Further than that brother, we first met at Llano, don't you remember? You were in that family up there. Tried to grow pot on Forest Service Land?"

"Shh, she doesn't need to know all that, Ty. She doesn't even know where Llano is." Wizard dragged a beat up truck's bench seat out from the back side of a juniper tree. Where did he get all this stuff?

"Take a load off friend." Wizard motioned to the newest member of the group, who looked around, a little confused, hands in pockets.

"Thanks." He sat down on one end of the truck seat's torn blue cover.

Rocky sat beside him, pulled out a joint and lit it, offered it to him. "Here Champ, this will help whatever ails you."

Again, the newbie, which I was just two days ago, looked over his shoulder nervously.

"It's medicinal honey." Rocky reassured him.

Wizard ducked inside his tarp covered dwelling and pulled a cracked plastic chest cooler from inside, opened it to retrieve 3 mismatched beers, tossing one to Ty before handing one to the young ex con.

"Here you go Champ, bet it's been awhile since you had one of these."

He took it from him, scanning the can at arms' length before popping it open. "Yeah, it really has been a while. Thanks." Champ, his newly acquired name, started to relax.

Wizard offered me the third beer. I shook my head no. "Thanks, I was just going to try and find something for Peanuts' dinner. I did get a couple of bucks from working today. I want to be sure he gets fed." I relaxed the leash and took two steps away.

"I'll go with you. I know where we can probably get some eats for him and us." Wizard handed the third beer to Rocky and tipped his hat to the others. "Gentlemen, Lady, I'll be back shortly with some grub."

Wizard and I walked carefully down Hobo Hill. Several times he stopped and greeted someone I didn't even know was there. Two were well hidden, lying on cardboard beneath a Juniper tree. Another had created a sort of brush hut with fallen branches woven together and was sitting inside drinking from a pint of MD 20 20.

"That stuff is not too good for you guv, take it easy." Wizard said to him.

"That's what they all say, Wizard, don't you stomp me too." The imbiber did not appreciate the caution.

Wizard took my arm and hurried us past him, speaking softly to me.

"When you see someone with that stuff just keep walking, you don't know how much they might have drunk already or what they might do."

Right before we reached the road Wizard spotted Mica, they guy he checked on last night, sitting on a block wall that separated the next yard from Hobo Hill.

"Mica, how's the new shoes and socks. Did you change them out yet?"

"Yeah, I did, thanks, Wizard. My feet are still pretty rough, but I do notice a difference." Mica coughed a couple of times and reached down to rub the calf of one leg.

"Look at me buddy." Wizard, knelt in front of him, looking at Mica's feverish glazed eyes, reached over and in a super gentle almost motherly way, smoothed back Mica's thinning hair. "Still might want to think about turning out buddy, get you a bed at Pete's or something, looks like the fever still has hold of you."

"Nah, ain't going to do it man, this'll clear up."

"Suit yourself Mica. Take it easy okay buddy?"

"Easy as pie." Mica collapsed in a coughing fit.

Wizard and I walked away, up the street on to Paseo, past the cemetery where we had first met and my family was buried and towards the chain supermarket on the corner. Two to three times, Wizard turned and walked backward trying to keep an eye on Mica.

It felt awkward walking with him again. I was still stinging from my self-reproach when James at the cafe had questioned seeing me walking with Wizard. I needed to make small talk, take my mind off of it.

"I do know where Llano is, up past Peñasco, high in the hills there." Wizard slowed his pace to let me keep up with him. Older than I by a good twenty years, all the walking he did kept him in top shape.

Wizard laughed. "Are you still on that? Yeah, we had a commune up there. Boy, talk about dwellings, we had everything you could think of. Teepee, old school bus, glass bottles cemented into a dome. It was great. I remember that bottle house, called it the Singing House. Some of the worker bees hadn't ever worked a day in their life before that, didn't take too well to criticism. They would stack those bottles up and wouldn't let anybody tell them you had to face the bottle in. When the wind would blow, especially in the spring, that house would sing like a flute choir from the air pushing across all the empty bottles. Those days are gone that's for sure."

"How about you, what was your dwelling like?"

"My dwelling?" He looked at me, amused. "Well, darling lady, let me tell you about dwellings. There are different kinds, not just where we lay our body down to rest, but where we rest our soul, our spirit. You can have the biggest, fanciest million dollar adobe home on the east side, and your spirit can still dwell in poverty, your soul can be homeless. Me? I'm not homeless. I've got the whole fricken world to dwell in. My soul rests easy in its own dwelling."

I stayed quiet. I never went in much for this meta-hippie spiritual stuff. Wizard kept looking at me, waiting for my response, all I could come up with was my classic lame. "Oh."

"Oh." He repeated it back to me. "Aileen, the way to find a home is to build one. I'm not talking about with bricks and wood. I'm talking about finding a place for your mind, body and spirit to dwell in peace, among friends and people who care about you and that you care about. When you have built that place, find that place to dwell, you'll know you'll be home. Dear lady, I am home, not homeless." He made a bow in front of me tipping his hat, the fringe on his leather jacket swinging back and forth, like a street performer.

"Oh." I said it again. Boy, this guy sure knew how to make you feel humble.

He looked up at me, returned his hat to his head, and took Peanuts leash. We were a few feet from the entrance and he stopped. "Watch and learn dear lady."

Several people pulled up from the parking lot, got out and started towards the door.

"Could you help us out with some dog food? A can or a quarter, anything would help?"

Two women stop and pet Peanuts. One reaches in her bag and pulls out a dollar bill, handing it to Wizard.

Wizard kept at it, approaching other groups of people. Most handed him something. Some offered a handful of change. One gave him a five dollar bill. The first group of people came out of the store. A man gave Wizard a bag of dog food. Another couple came over and presented him with a white plastic bag that contained two cans of dog food. Within about twenty minutes, we had several cans of food, a five pound bag of kibble and over twenty dollars in cash. Wow was he good.

I leaned against the building with Peanuts. Wizard strode over, carrying the bags of dog food.

"Here, give him some now."

"Now, you want me to feed him now?" We were under the portal by the front door, traffic only a few feet away. Not the best place to feed your pet.

"Yes, now, it's important that people see you feed him so they know we were sincere when we asked for the food. Otherwise they'll think we were trying to rip them off. It's a karma thing Aileen."

"I know, I know, find a place for my soul to dwell, right?"

"No, just find a place to feed him so everyone can see."

A took one of the plastic bags, folded it over so that it would stay open, and opened a can of dog food and dumped half of it into the make shift bowl. Peanuts gobbled it up.

Several cars drive by slowly, occupied by the do-gooders who had furnished Peanut's meal. They smiled and waved as they drove by, watching the big black dog finish off the rest of the can. I smiled and waved back.

"Not too big a wave dear, just enough to let them know you appreciate it, they don't want to get too friendly with us." Wizard barely lifted his hand to acknowledge the couple who had given him a five.

"What? What about that caring lecture you just gave me?"

Wizard laughed. "You'll figure it out some day Aileen."

41

It was still below freezing at night. A light frost made my early morning walk downhill from Wizard's encampment slippery. Several times I grabbed Peanuts to keep my balance. When it's cold like this most of the homeless are up early moving around, looking for a hot cup of coffee or sun warmed wall to relieve the ache in bones and joints. I was no exception, neither was Peanuts. It was the first morning I noticed him favoring his rear leg. I checked it for thorns or wear to his pad, but finding none decided he and I suffer from the same malady: old, cold and sleeping on the ground.

I was cold, hungry, needed a shower but surprisingly upbeat. Tomorrow would be better than today. That Barista job would pull us both through. I would need to go to my storage locker, find my social security card and birth certificate which I kept in a locking file box. I could visualize the box's exact location, on top of containers that held shoes, linens, Christmas decorations and school pictures of my kids. I was betting I still had a pair of black pants and a white shirt in one of those boxes, clean, that would serve as my work uniform.

It would take two hours or more to get there, then two hours back. We started our long walk, stopping at the skate park, where a couple dozen day laborers, homeless teens and street folk were picking up cups of coffee and potato and egg burritos given out by a local immigrant rights group. I waited in line with the rest. The volunteer hesitated before handing me a small white Styrofoam cup of black coffee and a wax paper wrapped folded tortilla.

"Surely you have someplace else to go to get breakfast." She scrutinized me and my dog.

"No. Not today anyway." I smiled slightly, pulling my wheeled case tight behind me.

"We're really here for the day workers. Can't you find services out at the Soup Kitchen on Cerrillos?"

I look at her, 'Not here. Please, don't give me a hard time. I just want a cup of coffee and something to eat, please?', but this was all said in my head, not out loud. Instead I nod a couple of times, could feel the cold tears welling up in my eyes, blinked them off, said "Thanks" and moved out of line, coffee in hand. When we were out of sight, I stopped and drank all the coffee, tore the tortilla in half giving part of it to Peanuts, and stuffed the rest in my tote bag for later.

It had warmed up considerably by the time we made it to the storage lockers. Only thirty degrees when we left, now past ten, it was almost sixty. Only two cars were parked in front of the office. Peanuts and I walked through the gate and headed up the second row, where the ten by ten rented storage room held the last of my earthly possessions. I retrieved the key ring, which held only two keys, from the side panel of my wheeled case and reached down to open the lock.

Wait, this was not my padlock. Puzzled, I backed up a bit, scanned the lockers beside mine. Was I in the right place? The right row? But this was not my lock. We went to the office.

"You can't bring that dog in here." A snarly, bearded man wearing a Marathon Mud Bog t shirt emblazoned with a cartoon character of a woman sporting impossibly big boobs covered with mud stops me before we get through the door. A small TV screen mounted on the wall was showing a story about WWII. Three small screen in screen pictures displayed the security camera feed in and around the facility.

"Sorry, I just need to find out about my storage locker. There's a different lock on it."

"Can't bring him in here. Can't wait on you with the dog." He turned his back to me, adjusted the screen.

I back out, park my wheeled case and loop Peanuts' leash around one of the handles. He could easily have pulled the case with him should he choose to take off, I was counting on him staying.

I go back in and try again, work hard to smile even though I don't feel so cheerful.

"Hi, I came to get some things from my locker and there's a different lock on it. I 'm sure I've got the right locker." I still have the key ring in my hand."

He already knew my unit number. "Number one twenty-eight, rent's past due. Lock is changed because the rent's past due. You owe..." he brings up a file on the computer, prints out a page with the account summary on it, "two hundred and forty dollars," passes me the printout.

"What? How can that be? I may be a little late, but I can't possible owe that much," I say, rattling the past due bill in protest.

"Well, there's the returned check fee, forty five dollars."

Oh yeah, I forgot about that.

"The late payment fee, twenty five dollars, you're behind two months, so that's time two, and you'll have to pay for lock replacement." He's pretty snotty, he knows he has the power in this situation, doesn't need to pretend to be polite to me.

"What? I just need to get in there and get my stuff."

"And you can, soon as the account's brought up to date."

I look outside at Peanuts, he is sitting ever so nicely and his nose touches the window glass when he sees me looking at him.

I'm desperate. I need to get that birth certificate and Social Security card.

"Please, I need to get in there, just for a minute. I need to get my ID and papers. I'm supposed to start a new job and I need them to get paid. I'll pay you, but I have to get paid first. Please."

"This ain't a welfare office. You can get in there when your account is brought up to date. You have ninety days from the date the first payment was missed to bring it up to date."

"I can, I will pay, but I need those papers first so I can get a job. Please."

"No, sorry, can't help you." He turns his back to me, changes the channel on the TV.

"Please!" Can't he hear the desperation in my voice?

I wait, he ignores me. He's good at this, must have had lots of practice at it.

"What happens after ninety days?" I finally ask him.

"Read the bottom of your bill. We sell off the contents of the locker to pay off the amount due."

This time I can't blink back my tears. I turn, walk out the door and take hold of

Peanuts leash. He nuzzles my hand, aware I am upset. We walk a lot slower, back to the plaza area. Both of us are limping.

¤ ¤ ¤

CJ's Cafe is busy when I tie Peanuts out back. I cleaned up best I could in a City Park restroom, have to wear the same shirt I had on yesterday. Hope the apron will cover any spots. Herman puts me to work right away, wiping tables, restocking the creamer and sugar stations. Eventually he calls me back to the espresso station and takes orders beside me while watching me pour, giving me hints on how much foam, how much espresso. It is two hours before it slows down. Susie, the owner comes out from her office, talks quietly to Herman. I think I got the thumbs up.

"Okay Aileen, looks like we can use you. Let's go back to my office and get you started on the paperwork."

I follow Susie back, unsure what to tell her. She pulls out the tax form, hands me a pen and the form, then reaches into a file for a second form, verification of something. It has a list of different types of documents, of which I only have a Driver's License as picture ID, no passport, no birth certificate and no Social Security card.

I don't lie, but I don't tell the whole truth either.

"I haven't been able to get them from my storage locker yet."

"But you do have them." She is stern.

"Yes, but I can't get them right now."

"When do you think you can?" Susie is not the type of person who likes to have her time wasted.

"Well, I'm not sure, a couple of weeks?" I say, hesitate. I'm thinking if I can get a paycheck I can start to pay off the amount I owe.

She looks me over, lips tight together, taps her fingers on the table. Her phone is blinking, either she has a call waiting or has put someone on hold.

"Listen Aileen, I'd really like to make this work. I think you could fit in well with our staff, but I have to have those documents before I can bring you on board. Tell me again when you think you can get them?"

"Honestly, I'm not sure. They're locked in my storage locker and I can't get to them."

Susie goes out to the front of the restaurant, comes back with some cash in hand, two fives, a ten and a twenty.

"This is to pay for your time yesterday and today. Come back when you have the paperwork in order. I always need good help, especially over the summer months. I wish you well." She pushes the blinking light on her phone and picks up the receiver.

I have been hired and fired on the same day.

Reluctantly, I walk back towards Hobo Hill, stopping at the grocery store for dog food, buying juice, bread and bologna, some bananas and a box of granola bars to share with my hosts. Wizard doesn't ask what happened. He passes the bananas around and hands Rocky the bread and bologna so she can start slapping sandwiches together.

42

*P*eople say they love New Mexico's four seasons. The subtle change of a clear blue sky in winter highlights snowcapped adobe walls. Autumn means red chile ristras hang from pickup trucks parked at road side stands in contrast with the brilliant yellow of cottonwood trees that line the Rio Grande. When summer arrives, huge white clouds build to unbelievable altitude, mirroring the mountain peaks beneath them. But during New Mexico's unpredictable spring the thing that blows you away is wind.

It was a spring day, late April almost May, I'm not sure of the date. I had been under Wizard's wing for almost a month. The plan to get the next check and find someplace to rent was dissolved by the reality that I still had past due drafts and bank charges hovering over me like a tormenting demon. My grief in Stevie's death mentally masked the deplorable conditions of living in cardboard boxes or on the side of arroyos under elm trees. If I wasn't with Wizard and his crew, I was sitting in the cemetery beside Sean's or Stevie's grave. Wizard came around to collect me at sunset two or three nights a week. I never told him where I was, he just knew. Each time, he would patiently take my hand and Peanuts' leash and quietly lead us out the foot gate. "Can't dwell here Aileen, this is no place for the living."

Today the wind blew. Hard. I couldn't ignore the sand, grit and exhaust fumes that blasted every inch of my body filling my hair, eyes and mouth with dirt. Sitting in the cemetery was impossible. I wandered on my own. Even when I took cover behind a dumpster or under a portal the wind found me. Worse, a spring storm was expected. By late afternoon a cold drizzle waxed and waned, creating pockets of fog around the Santa Fe River Park. Snow and freezing rain would move in by sundown.

Wizard, Rocky, Mica, and two other street dwellers had taken shelter under a bridge near Guadalupe Street, not far from the Rail Yard. Peanuts and I joined them. One of the street dwellers pulled a bottle of Jose Cuervo, probably stolen, from under his sweatshirt and offered it around. I held it in my hand, part disgusted, and part wanting to take a long swig and forgot everything.

Wizard made my choice easy, reached in front of Mica and took the bottle from me before I could tip it up.

"She don't need that brother, she's cool, but that stuff ain't good for her. Or you." Wizard passed the bottle back to its owner.

"Who made you boss, boss?" Rocky laughed and took the bottle from him, making her eyes pop while she swallowed my share and hers.

The others laughed too. Wizard wanted to take the booze away from Rocky, but instead got up and headed topside where a thin kid in his early twenties, a back pack hanging from one shoulder, walked rapidly towards him. I followed, pulling my wheeled case behind me. After that first night, when I was pretty sure the others searched through my stuff, I made a point of always taking it with me.

"Wizard, dude. Wizard! They're clearing out Hobo Hill. They've got cops there and some guys with a trash cart. Dude, they're taking everything. There's a tractor with a blade." The kid was frantic, waving his arms.

"What? Now?" It was one of the only times I saw anger flash through Wizard's eyes.

"Yeah man, now. You got to get over there."

Wizard ducked back under the bridge. "Rock, Mica, come on, we've got to go, they're gonna take our stuff. Let's go!"

Rocky was drunk. "You go, Boss." She laughed, took another drink from the now almost empty bottle.

"Go ahead Wizard. We'll catch up in a while." Mica had a buzz going too.

Wizard slung his red pack up and marched with a purpose, followed by the kid, then me and Peanuts. We went up Alameda, cut across the Plaza and headed north on Washington Avenue. Several of the city officers who were permanently on patrol in the plaza area, smiled and nodded at each other, stifling a laugh as they pointed at us when we walked by. They knew what was going down and were amused by it.

By the time we got to Hobo Hill it was all over but the paperwork, which a couple of city officers and sanitation department workers were filling out. Two Hobo Hill dwellers were being escorted, hands cuffed behind their backs, to separate waiting patrol cars. Apparently the two tried to make a stand, resulting in their arrest. The recliner, mattresses, tarps, blankets, and a few white plastic chairs protruded from a trash trailer parked nearby. Wizard shook his head in disbelief and approached one of the officers, whom he knew.

"Why? Why are you doing this? Why?" Wizard asked.

The officer pointed to a mustached man who stood akimbo near a new blue Ford SUV with a *City of Holy Faith* emblem painted on its side. The official had his jacket zipped tight to the chin to keep out the wind. When Wizard approached him, the man looked towards the uniformed officers, slightly alarmed. But when one cop shrugged his shoulders and turned away and another found an excuse to enter her cruiser, the jacketed city administrator re-took his stance, legs planted, arms and hands resting at his waist.

"This has always been private property. We are assisting the property owner to be in compliance with city zoning. This is not public land, and even if it was, camping is not permitted within city limits."

Wizard continued to stand in front of him. "This was our home, man, our property. You can't just take property."

"This was an eyesore, a health hazard and an illegal dump. We have legal standing in working with the landowner to remedy the situation. If you have further issues you need to take them through the appropriate channels at city hall."

The mustached man in the jacket gets in the city owned SUV. I can see him as he sips coffee, fogging up the windows and watches the remainder of the cleanup. Wizard flings his hat at the car window, which prompts the city police officer to walk over and persuade us to move on. Wizard watches as the tractor starts dragging a rake across the slope of the hill, pulling up trash, toilet paper and bottles. He looks over at the two other Hobo Hill residents now in the back of the cruisers. It starts to rain.

I stand by him, put my hand on his arm, the way he did with me when we first met.

"Sorry, Wizard. Sorry. This isn't right. You'll have to go down to city hall and file a complaint or something."

"That isn't going to change things Aileen. Nothing will change until people start treating us like human beings." Wizard hangs his head, trying to figure out his next move.

"Let's get out of this rain," he says finally.

The kid and I follow him back to the Plaza area. We meet up with the under the bridge bunch all in various stages of intoxication. Mica is propping up Rocky as they head towards us. A steady rain and wind pounds us. We duck under a portal by one of the stores. A salesperson stands on the other side of the glass door and pulls out her cell phone. Wizard leads us back towards the river park where we take refuge under yet another bridge from both the wind and rain.

"Did they really take everything?" Mica gently lowered Rocky to the ground, leaning her against the bridge support. It is crowded here. The wind starts to blow the rain sideways and I try to use my body and wheeled case to block some of it so Peanuts doesn't get wet.

"Yup, every fricken can and candle. Gone, hauled away." Wizard sits on the hard ground beside Rocky, cradling her head and shoulders, trying to keep her dry too.

Mica starts coughing. The cold and wind have finally gotten to him. He had seemed to be on the mend after his last bout of illness, but is not able to fight off the fever that now plagues him.

"What do we do?" Mica asks, expecting, as does everyone else, that Wizard can work some magic and make it all better.

Wizard gently strokes Rocky's hair, sits silent a while.

"I know a place. This guy I did work for said I could use his garage once in a while, it's up top of Alameda though. It'll be a haul up there. Rest a while, see if the rain stops."

It was a haul. We were soaking wet by the time we got up there. The wind had to be at least thirty miles an hour, maybe more. Every now and then lightning would streak the sky. The accompanying thunder would spook Peanuts. Three times I had to pull his leash in tight to keep him from bolting.

"Are you going to let your friend know we're here?" I was so naive.

"He's out of town. I know where he keeps the key. Wait here, I'll open the door. Stay around back, so the neighbors don't see you. I don't want to get him in trouble for letting us stay here."

We hover close together, pushed up against the stucco on the back wall of the garage. Wizard returns and leads us in through the side door.

"I'm glad you found the key." The others look at me, roll their eyes.

I take off my wet sweatshirt and try to twist the water out of it. Peanuts shakes, spraying wet dog drops everywhere, but especially on Rocky who is just coming off her drunk and not in a good way.

"Get that damn dog out of here!" She tries to kick him but is still unsteady, slips on the now wet concrete, hitting her head. The light from a lightning strike outside the window reveals a large goose egg and thin trickle of blood on her forehead.

I fumble on the wall for a light switch. Wizard is aghast.

"Turn off the light! Now! Turn it off!" He says, yells at me. I do but not before revealing the two large SUV's and one empty spot inside the three car garage.

Peanuts begins to bark at the rounds of thunder.

"Aileen, shut that dog up." Wizard speaks harshly to me for the first time.

I pull Peanuts close to me, find a space on the opposite side of the garage, un-rope the tarp and rug from the wheeled case and lay them out for Peanuts and I. Next round of lightning I hold him down, keep my hand across his snout so all he can do is whine a little.

Mica calls out, "You've got to shut him up!"

I finally figure it out. "Are you sure it's okay to be in here?"

"Just be quiet okay. Don't turn on the light, keep the dog still. We'll be okay." Wizard is not very reassuring.

We sit like that in the dark. I'm on one side with Peanuts, shivering, with the tarp and a half wet sleeping bag pulled around me, and Wizard sits with Rocky, Mica the kid with the back pack and one of the two under the bridgers on the other side. I can hear them talking very softly, but not enough to know what is said. It's late, raining hard. The occasional burst of snow is reflected out the window with the lightning. I drift off, half asleep.

Peanuts low growl wakes me. He is up, on his feet, alert. Blue and red flashing lights play across the sole window. Wizard is at the garage door, locking it. Mica is locking the side door. They both motion me to the area between the two cars and hold their fingers to their lips to silence me. Rocky and the other two men are already crouched low between the two cars. We all press together, trying to make ourselves small and invisible. I can hear two male voices outside and the static of a police radio.

"Any response at the residence?"

"No, doesn't appear anyone is home."

I hear someone rattle the garage door. Peanuts growls again, but very low. Wizard makes a sudden move, mouths the words: "Shut him up."

I try to pull the leash closer, but instead the loop slips off my arm and Peanuts rushes for the side door, the handle of which is now being jiggled from the outside. Wizard and company look absolutely horrified.

One of the officers is outside the window, shining a light inside trying to look in. Peanuts lunges for the window, jumping up, barking and snarling madly.

"Jesus H Christ!" I hear one of the officers yell. "It's Cujo."

The other starts to laugh. "Need to change your pants partner?"

You can hear them talking on the radio.

"Residence is secure, neighbors probably heard a large dog that's locked in the garage. Nothing seems amiss. Have animal welfare come out tomorrow and do a check on the animal, make sure it's being cared for."

We wait a long while for the cop car to pull away. Slowly we begin to crawl out of our hiding place. The others turn their backs to me, complain as loudly as the circumstances allow.

"Fricken dog. I ain't going to jail because of no fricken dog."

"Stupid bitch's dog almost got us busted."

I'm afraid they will attack me. Wizard once again intervenes.

"Aileen, the dog has to go. We can't have him with us. They're right. He almost got us all busted. Wait a couple of hours than you'll have to leave with him, take him to the shelter or something. He can't stay."

Peanuts doesn't know he's the bad guy. He thinks he's the hero dog that scared away the bad guys. I pull him over to the tarp and rug and he lies down, sighs and falls asleep. I don't.

It's nearly light. A cold frost covers the windows, and for a while the wind has stopped blowing. I rub Peanuts side to rouse him, pour a small amount of water in his plastic bowl and roll up the rug and tarp while he laps the water. Without saying anything, I head toward the side door. Wizard is the only one fully awake. The others are sleeping along the far edges of the garage so they would be difficult to spot should anyone come back with a flashlight, looking in the window.

Wizard walks to the window, stands back to the wall, and looks out sideways to be sure no one else is outside then nods to me. I unlock the side door, and he follows me out, we stand behind a large Juniper tree while Peanuts relieves himself.

"Come back after you've found a place for the dog. I can figure this out, it may take a while. You can always ask around the library. Or over by the mall, find out where we've landed."

"Or the cemetery, no? Isn't that where you hang out? Picking up ladies in the cemetery?" I don't know why I am mad at him. None of this is his fault. The expression on his face tells me the sarcasm truly hurts him.

"You're not the only one who needs help now and then you know."

I look down, embarrassed. This man has kept me, and Peanuts, alive for the past few weeks. I nod, tug on Peanuts leash and head up the driveway. "Sorry."

"Thanks for everything Wizard, really, thanks."

"Where are you going?"

"Don't know. I'll figure it out too."

"Peanuts?" Wizard scratches him behind the ear, one of the few times he ever paid attention to the dog.

"No, I can't let him go. I promised my son I'd take care of him. I have to find a dwelling place, like you have, only one that takes dogs."

Wizard tips his hat, "Mind, body and spirit dear lady, a place to dwell for mind body and spirit. Don't forgot."

43

Once upon a time I had a home. It was beautiful. We were constantly changing and updating, replacing tile and bathroom fixtures, never quite satisfied with the way things were. One year we added one of those sun rooms. You know the kind, modular, with glass on three sides and overhead. It was my favorite place to sit and read on a Sunday afternoon, especially a blustery one when the wind outside would drop the temperature fifteen or twenty degrees. Inside, warmed by the sun, it was February in Phoenix.

One such Sunday, as I sat with the paper, a loud thud made me look up. A bird had flown into the glass. It took me a minute to realize I was witnessing the furious pursuit of a small wren by a large hawk. Stunned and on the ground, the little bird didn't stand a chance. I watched in horror as the hawk swooped in and grasped the grey and white wren in its talons, alighted on a nearby branch and commenced to shred the poor thing to bits.

Unable to look away I saw two more wrens take perch above and to either side of where the hawk now feasted. They stood watch, helpless, refusing to allow a member of their flock to die alone.

44

It had been at least a week, maybe longer, since Wizard had given Peanuts and I our marching orders. I struggled, constantly looked over my shoulder, afraid of my own shadow, didn't know who to trust or where to get help. If not for Peanuts, I'm sure I would have gone completely nuts. We found respite under Piñon trees, near freeway exits, in back of shopping centers, and behind garages. Wherever I could find a place to lay down my tarp and bag, and Peanuts rug beside, I'd close my eyes, try to rest and not think too much about my circumstances. Closing my eyes had become my only coping strategy. A couple more weeks, I kept telling myself. In a couple of weeks, you'll have money, rent a room, have some relief.

I guess I was still too much of a snob because I didn't socialize much with the others. I thought I was somehow not like them, but I was wrong, we were exactly alike. Still, some greeted me and let me in on the sweet deals to be had in dumpsters around town when the stock changed. A guy named Danny, who started his nose dive into homelessness when the local high end cast metal foundry shipped its jobs overseas some years back, relayed that a good pair of brand new but last year's model running shoes, just donated, could be procured at the Salvation Army, but, he admonished, I better act fast. When you wear the same pair of shoes day in and out, you begin to realize the value of a second pair. I leashed up Peanuts and headed north on St Francis Drive.

Traffic was heavy. It was approaching tourist season and more and more visitors were making the trek to the City of Holy Faith, oblivious to the un-domiciled residents who hunkered down on the streets.

I could hear sirens, lots of them, as I headed up the Santa Fe River Park pathway along west Alameda. About half a dozen homeless men and a couple of women rested on benches or stone ledges, drinking coffee from Styrofoam cups and eating bread sandwiches; a thin slip of potted meat spread between stale white bread.

A guy with a heavy plaid jacket over a florescent orange sweatshirt and two pair of pants, carrying a heavy aluminum frame pack walked rapidly up the path. I didn't know him by name, but his face had become familiar, like someone who frequents the same grocer. He approached two bench sitters excitedly.

"Didja hear? They found Mica." He bent his elbow, using his thumb like a hitchhiker wanting a ride.

The two bench sitters uncrossed their legs. One offered the messenger a cigarette, eager for more news. I strained to listen, but really wanted those donated shoes and I kept walking. When we got to the dirt ramp leading to street level, Peanuts and I made the climb, bumping my suitcase over the rocks on the path.

More homeless, gathering in small groups, looked north where three city police cruisers, a crime scene van, an ambulance and an unmarked detective's car quartered off the area near a small rock encrusted pedestrian bridge.

I stayed on the far side of the street, walked past the flashing lights and yellow tape and crossed over to gain a vantage point above the fray. Wizard was pacing, restless, almost desperate, in the dry riverbed.

Police, uniformed and not, stood about the area while a man in a disposable white hazmat suit knelt over a body on the ground covered by a blue tarp then nodded towards a couple of waiting EMTs. Wizard tried to follow them as they brought a gurney, but was held back by two uniformed officers, one the female officer I saw my first night on the streets. They were firm but not harsh, restraining him gently. As the EMTs started the trek up the path with the tarp covered body, Wizard broke through, striding towards them, and walked alongside. He placed his hand on top of the stone cold body that once held Mica's mind and spirit, keeping watch over a member of his flock, until they reached the waiting ambulance.

45

It was the last day in May, a year since the accident. Stevie had been gone almost three months. I still visited his grave every day. But where else would I go? When you are homeless you tend to wander place to place unless you set up a schedule for yourself, establish a routine.

I continued to have the delusion it was all a mistake. Fooled myself to believe that the problems, financial, emotional and legal, which weighed me could be lifted and I would pull through. I'd find some sort of shelter, get a job and restart my life. Every time I closed my eyes I'd imagine sleeping in a bed again. You can do it, hold on and survive a while longer. I convinced myself it would happen. Closing my eyes, a lot, and finding a routine helped me stay sane.

Part of my new schedule was to spend mornings at the Street School. It was a project to help homeless teens complete a High School diploma. Besides education, the Street School aimed to provide social services, health care and a safe place to spend the day. Most of the kids here were smart. Too smart for their own good some would say. School work was easy for them, school itself though, things like getting there, staying there, interacting with adults and peers was not so easy. Without projects like this many would just drop out of school if not society. It was the committed staff, not the program itself, which made them want to show up every day.

One of the teens, a rebellious skate boarder with more tattoos than I could count, overheard me lament about not being able to take Peanuts with me everywhere I wanted to go. On my next visit he proudly handed me a blue and white dog vest with the words *Service Dog* stamped on it.

"Try this Miss. It really works."

He was right it did. Peanuts pulled at the vest at first, but after a while he gave up and ignored it. As long as I put the vest on him we could go into stores, restrooms, almost anywhere really, unchallenged. Still, I didn't put it on him 24/7. I figured that would be pushing my luck

Most weekday mornings, about nine thirty, Peanuts and I would make our way towards Cerrillos Road, now the main corridor for the 'real' Santa Fe. About three miles from the Plaza area, sandwiched between a tattoo parlor and a Thai noodle bar, the Street School announced its presence with graffiti style letters painted on the windows by the teens enrolled there. About once a month the volunteer staff would spray the windows down and allow the kids to start over.

I had known about it since it opened. Now it seemed a way I could put myself out there and avoid too big a gap in employment history. I was still imagining I would be able to line up another teaching job by fall, especially when my eyes were closed.

Peanuts and I walked the well trafficked road stopping frequently for turning cars and delivery vans. I kept smelling diesel exhaust mixed with lilacs and sage, an occasional whiff of green chile or carne adovada cooking enmass at the nearby Coralinda's New Mexican Bistro. Peanuts paused, lifted his nose and sniffed the air when we walked by, me too.

Today was the last day of spring session. After a one week break summer session would begin. It wasn't quite like the last day of school I was used to. Still, the teens were in a celebratory mood. Someone brought doughnuts and pouches of fruit punch to mark the occasion.

Peanuts and I were greeted by three teens, all with assorted piercings: eyebrow, lip, and nostril. One boy had eight sharp studs along the ridge of his ear.

"Hey, Miss Roark, how's that service dog thing going for you?" he asked as he rolled back and forth on his skate board.

"Great, Leonard. So far no one has called me on it. Thanks." I pulled the cereal box cut away on one side like a file box off the shelf. It held the students' notebooks, which I spread out on the table.

"Aw come on Miss Roark you don't really expect anybody to do work today do you?"

"Well, maybe a little. Why? What were your plans today?"

"Just chill, it's the last day."

I smiled at him, wishful for the celebrations I was used to on the final days of school. One of the girls, with a small cross hanging from a chain that pierced her eyebrow in two places, broke off half a doughnut and began feeding it piece by piece to Peanuts. He loved coming here and the kids loved him. One of them tied a tennis ball in the bottom of an old sock and tossed it across the room. Peanuts brought it back to them, eyes dancing, paws forward in a 'let's play' stance. They all loved it. Leonard, still on his skate board grabbed one end of the sock and Peanuts pulled him across the vinyl floor.

"Way cool. Way cool Peanuts." Leonard said, laughing.

"Hey, can we take him outside and try this on the sidewalk?" Shawna, the girl with the pierced eyebrow pleaded with me.

I was hesitant.

"Please, promise we won't let him get away, or get in the street, please?"

"Okay, just be sure he doesn't run into traffic."

"Cool, cool, cool, let's go Peanuts."

The three of them grabbed more donuts, the end of Peanuts' leash and made for the door.

I smiled watching them even though it was painful. It reminded me of my own boys. I was lost in this emotion when Erin Torres, the Street School director, walked out of her office in the back and came to my side, touching me on the elbow.

"What great kids, no?" I said to her.

"Yes, they really are." She was quiet a minute. "Can we sit down and talk?"

Uh-oh, this can't be good. "Sure. What's up?"

I sat sideways at one of the long conference tables, my back to the wall. Impulsively I began trying to smooth down my unkempt hair and pull the wrinkles out of the t shirt I'd worn day and night for the past three days. I turned my head to get the best view of the kids outside. They were taking turns being pulled on the skateboard by Peanuts.

"Do you remember when you filled out the volunteer form? You listed your teaching license on there?"

"Yes. Why, is there something wrong?"

"To be honest, yes. We ran the routine background check through the Education Department and it came back as Hold: License Revoked."

"What? When? I don't know anything about it." I was incredulous.

"Well, I called. You've been such a great volunteer. The kids really respond to you and I think you have a lot to offer. But we can't jeopardize our status here Aileen. It's something that needs to be cleared up before you can continue here." She was unapologetic.

"What did they tell you when you called?" I was still in disbelief. How did this happen?

"Apparently the school you worked for requested the Education Department revoke your license based on child endangerment, also that you had failed to give proper notice when you left."

"That's outrageous. I would never do anything that would put a student in danger, I didn't know about any of this." I was shocked.

"Why don't you tell me what happened. What's your side of this?" She folded her hands on the table in front of her.

So I did. I told her the whole story, losing my son and husband, taking leave without pay, which the school labeled AWOL, getting a phone call from Stevie's nurse and finally my students setting the books on fire.

"To make it worse, when I tried to collect my last pay check District Two made me sign a letter of resignation, not termination, or they would have held my pay. I was evicted, for God's sake, bouncing checks, had no food, didn't have anywhere to go. I had no choice."

Erin was sympathetic but firm. "It's something you'll have to get cleared up Aileen. I'm sure you can get a hearing. Why don't you call the Education Department, you can use the phone here." She motioned toward her office door.

I glanced outside where Peanuts and the teens continued to play.

Erin could see my concern for the dog. "I'll keep an eye on things. Besides, I'm going to call them in. I need them to complete a semester evaluation before the end of the term, which is today. I hope the others make it in."

I stood and walked back to the office, sat at Erin's chair and pulled the phone book from the narrow ledge below the one way mirror that framed her desk, allowing whoever was in there to keep an eye on things in the front. It took me a while to find the right number. It shouldn't be that complicated but it was; first you had to find the government section, then state government, then the Education Department. But wait there's more. After you found the Education Department, you had to find the right Education Department: Higher Ed; NM Activities Association; Vocational Ed; finally, I located 'Education Department Licensing' and dialed the number.

You have reached the New Mexico Education Department Certification and Licensing Division. Para Español empuje uno; if you have a question about becoming a licensed teacher in New Mexico press two; if you are renewing a license press three; if you want to check the status of your application press four.

And so it went, through three or four more options, none of which said *to find out why your license was revoked.* Finally the options ended and the recorded voice said *If you want to talk to a department representative press star,* so I pressed star.

I could see out the one way mirror. Erin was standing at the entrance, door open, trying to gather the three, along with Peanuts, into the room.

"One more, one more." They kept pleading.

I could hear the ringer on the end of the line. Another phone loop started: *If you know the number of the person you want to speak with enter it now. To hear the list of extension press two, to return to the main menu press three, to speak with an operator, press four.*

I pressed four, and waited and waited.

Your call will be answered in the order received, please stay on the line.

So I did, at least seven or eight minutes longer, hearing the *Your call well be answered...* bit twice more before a real person answered. "How can I help you?"

"I need to find out about my teaching license. I just found out it has been suspended and I wasn't aware what happen." I tried to not let my voice shake.

"Hold on, I'll transfer your call." Then click, back to the main menu. This happened a second time. Finally, when I got the main menu a third time I pressed two just to get to speak with a person.

"This is Ben. How may I help you?"

"Hello Ben, my name is Aileen Roark. I just found out that my license was suspended. I don't really know what's going on. I need to talk to someone about it."

"Was this a new license application?"

"No, I've been teaching for over twenty years. I have a license, but apparently it was suspended. I need to know what happened, who filed the suspension request and why. I only learned of it today."

"Let me try and connect you with another department, we only handle initial applications here. I'll transfer you."

"Wait, please, I keep getting put back on the main menu. I need to talk to a real person. Isn't there someone I can talk to in your office?"

"I think you need to talk to someone in License Renewal, I'll transfer you."

"Promise I can speak to a real person?"

"I'll do my best." Ben pushed whatever button one pushes and I was put back in the main menu loop for the fifth time today.

This time I pressed four.

"This is Ben, how may I help you?"

"Ben? Didn't I just talk to you? This is Aileen Roark again."

"Oh, I must have transferred you back. My mistake, I'll transfer you again."

"Wait Ben, I pressed four, status of my renewal application, isn't that what I got?"

"Well, I'm covering, they're all on break. I can take a message and have someone call you back." I could hear him sipping coffee between questions.

"Really, Ben, please? I need to know who requested my teaching license suspension and why. Can't you check that for me? Name is Aileen Roark. Check? Please?"

There was a long pause, a sigh and then "I'll need your license number and the expiration date."

"I don't have my license in front of me. Couldn't you just use my name? Aileen Roark- R O A R K."

"How about the last four digits of your Social Security number."

I recited them to him.

"Are you Aileen Roark?" he asked.

"Yes, that's me. Aileen Roark." This would be funny except I was the one involved.

"It looks like Dr. Antonia Roybal, Superintendent of Schools for District Two put in a request to terminate and revoke your license in February. The reasons given were Child Endangerment, Class Abandonment and failure to give required notice when terminating employment. Request was approved March fifteen of this year."

"How can they do that? Don't I have to be informed? Can't I appeal, tell my side? How is this allowed?"

"The file indicates a letter was sent by registered mail to you at twenty sixteen Nuevo Rio, and it was returned as undeliverable."

"That was my old address. I haven't lived there in almost a year."

"Did you put in a change of address with the Department?"

"No. No, I had a lot going on."

"The letter was sent to the address on file, it was returned."

"Well how do I appeal? What can I do?"

There was silence, then another sigh on the other end of the telephone.

"Request for a hearing had to be made within ten days of the Notice of Revocation. Which would have been March 25th, you're about two months too late."

"But I didn't get the letter."

"That wasn't the Department's fault."

"Seriously, how do I request a hearing? How do I protest this?"

"You can't, you missed the deadline."

"What? Wait, isn't there someone higher up I can speak with? There has to be a way." I'm sure my voice was increasing in pitch. It always did when I was annoyed, no matter how hard I tried.

"Well you can talk to the Division Director, but I know her and she is going to tell you the same thing I did."

"Can you transfer my call anyway?" I tried really hard not to sound whiny.

"Sure."

Silence, a click :*If you know the extension of the person you want to speak to enter it now.* God was I screwed.

I sat at Erin's desk, looking through the one way glass, rubbing my temples, wondering what to do now. I wouldn't be able to get a teaching job, or any other type of job unless I could get this sorted out, but I just couldn't deal with it. I had slept in the open for weeks now, had not had a shower in several days, relying instead on wash ups in public restrooms, and hadn't really had a meal either. If I could just get some decent rest, a bath, a hot meal, maybe I could figure this all out.

The Street School teens were filing in. There were about ten all together today. Erin managed to persuade Leonard, Shawna and their companion to come inside. Shawna got a small plastic ice cream tub from the art supply center, walked to the back and filled it from the bathroom sink before setting it on the floor by the door for Peanuts, who lapped it up loudly then collapsed onto the floor with a contented moan. When she turned to come out, she was looking straight at me as I sat at Erin's desk, rubbing my head.

"Are you okay Miss?" She came into the office and stood beside me.

"Yes, just some unfortunate news. I'll get it sorted out."

"Are you sure you're okay?" She was surprisingly concerned

I stood up. "Yup, thanks for caring, really, I'm not trying to be funny. Hey thanks for taking care of Peanuts too. You guys are so good to him."

"He's a great dog." She looked over at him, concern still on her face.

"Shawna, you're not the one who is supposed to worry about me, I'm supposed to worry about you. Go do your work. Erin is waiting for you." I gave her a playful scolding, wagging my index finger in front of her face.

"Whatever." She smiled, pushing my finger aside.

I followed her to the front room.

"Did you get it sorted out?" Erin asked, before she passed pencils to the kids, who, by now, had found their favorite spot either at the table or one of the two sofas pushed against the wall.

I looked down at the floor, hands in my pockets. "No. No, I guess I missed the deadline to file an appeal, so I need to figure out what to do next."

I gathered my cloth shopping bag, tied it onto the telescoping handle of my suitcase, and whistled softly for Peanuts.

"Hey! Where are you going Miss? We were just kidding about chilling all day. We're ready to work now." Leonard was concerned.

I smiled at him, lips closed, wanted to go over and push the long hair from his eyes and reassure him, but I didn't want to embarrass him so I looked away. I missed my sons so much.

"Are you mad at us or something?" One of the other kids flipped a pencil up at the ceiling, trying to make it stick point first into the white ceiling tiles.

"No, you kids are great. I know you're going to make it. Just keep working okay. Stay cool, take care of each other." I looped Peanuts leash through my hand.

"You're leaving us?" another said, calling out in surprise.

I nodded, didn't want to say anything else. "Be good, okay?"

The kids turned towards Erin for answers. "Miss Roark has some things she needs to take care of. When she does she'll be able to come back and help us again."

Erin held the door open while I wheeled my stuff outside, went out with me then pushed the door almost closed so the teens inside couldn't hear.

"As soon as you can get a letter or something, some official verification that your license has been restored, or at least the child endangerment issue has been resolved, as soon as you can get that come back. You understand a lot of people don't want us to succeed. They want to take it over, contract with some out of state group to run this place.

Having you as a volunteer here with that issue hanging over you would only give them more ammunition to yank our funding and close us down. Sorry Aileen, truly I am."

I nodded, of course I understood. I understood that sometimes, even when you do everything right, when you treat others with respect , courtesy, kindness and caring, sometimes none of that matters. I understood that what mattered was the money.

46

By midnight five days from now, the meager money that mattered to me, five hundred and twenty five dollars from Sam's pension should appear in my account. With that I would find a motel room for a couple of weeks and sort things out. I had to find a place to keep myself a few more nights and a way to feed Peanuts. First task was finding a place to rest in the shade for an hour or two. The City Park, about two miles away seemed like a good option. The temperature was starting to climb. Today our goal would be to stay cool, not warm. Peanuts was already panting thanks to the workout the kids at the street school had given him. I was starting to perspire in the two layers of clothes I wore most of the time. I paused for a minute at the turn up Alta Vista, past state offices I had once worked summers in, to take off the gray hoodie that had become my second skin. As I rolled it up and tried to stuff it into my already over packed home on wheels I could hear the distinct rolling "click- click- click" of a skateboard coming from behind me.

"Miss. Hey Miss. Wait up." It was Leonard. He had abandoned his black players sweatshirt, and now just wore a dirty white t-shirt with the his version of *The Scream* hand drawn with purple and black markers curving from back to front on the shirt. A plastic grocery bag hung from his belt loops. Leonard expertly stopped the board and flipped it up, catching it in one hand right beside me.

"Hello Leonard. What's going on? Are you done already?" Peanuts licked Leonard's fingers and waged his tail.

"Where are you going? Why did you leave?" He reached into his pocket and pulled out some pizza crusts wrapped in a paper towel which he offered to Peanuts. No wonder the dog licked Leonard's fingers, they were coated with the dripping grease of pizza.

"Oh, buddy, I guess there's a problem with my teaching license. Ms. Erin is worried it might cause the school to lose funding. It's not you guys. That's not the reason." I shook my head softly and tried to reassure him.

"But where are you going? Now I mean."

"Well, Peanuts and I are just going to hang for a while. Then I'll figure out what to do next. You don't need to worry about it."

Leonard pulled a can of Red Bull energy drink from his other pocket, popped it open and started to walk with me, balancing his skate board on his shoulder as he walked.

"Miss you're not the only one who cares what happens to someone else you know." His frankness surprised me.

"Leonard you're great. I know you're going to make it, you're smart, funny and you care about others. Stay in school, get your GED. Peanuts and I will be okay. I'm supposed to get my check this week. I'll get a place for a while and then try to pull it together. We just have to get through today and tomorrow and a couple more days and we'll have a break. I'll make it and so will you." I was barely convincing myself.

Leonard looked down, reached over his head and scratched his shoulder, scowling, while he listened to me. He put his skate board down, pointing it in the opposite direction, untied the blue plastic bag from his pants loop and handed it to me.

"Here Miss. They had pizza. I snagged you a couple of slices and a juice pouch. I snagged some extra pepperoni for Peanuts too. Peace out Miss." He stepped on his skate board and gave a push off with his foot, ruffled Peanuts fur backwards as he rolled off in the opposite direction.

Peanuts whined, longing after him. I knew what he was thinking, same as me, he looks like Sean. I had to tug the leash to turn him around. The dog looked back twice before heaving his chest. For both of our sakes, I needed to find a place to rest, figure out my next step, sit in the shade and eat. The park was nearby. I pushed on towards it.

It took me longer than I thought to get there. Traffic was awful. I forgot what it was like once the tourist season started. We had to cross two major intersections. At both, even though we had the walk signal, we were invisible to turning traffic. Peanuts was still skittish around cars. You would think all the walking we did he'd have gotten used to it, but he didn't. We stopped at the train park. It isn't named the train park, people just call it that. Years ago someone donated an old locomotive for display. When my boys were little you could still climb on it, but now it was fenced off by 8 feet high chain link, with keep out signs attached. I used to come here when I lived up the road. I'd bring the boys to the tot lot, sit and read while the boys enjoyed the climbing structures and the chance to play with other kids. Now Peanuts and I sat on a bench outside the fenced play area and watched the preschoolers at play. I pulled my wheeled suitcase up, untied the cloth shopping bag from its handle and took out the small empty margarine tub I used as Peanuts' water bowl. I looped the end of the leash around one of the bench legs and entered the fenced in area to fill the water bowl from the fountain there. I waited while two tow haired girls filled tiny bottle caps with water from the fountain for their stuffed animals. I took a long drink, filled Peanuts' water dish and a plastic liter bottle for myself while speaking softly to the girls.

"Looks like your bears are thirsty. Do they have names?" The two ran back to their mother clutching their bears. I smiled and lifted my hand to acknowledge her, closed the gate behind me and set Peanuts' bowl in front of him.

Peanuts was thirsty. It was a never ending task to find a place for him to get water and rest. Not to mention the struggle I had finding a public restroom where I could take him in with me. The service dog apron did help, but I had removed it at the Street School so Peanuts could play unhampered by its strings with the teens. After he had his fill of the water, I left my suitcase parked by the bench, hoping the mothers in the play area would be enough deterrent to anyone who looked suspicious from bothering it, and took Peanuts with me to the concrete block restroom, poking my head in the door to be sure it was empty before entering, dog in tow, to relieve myself. When I came out, a City of Santa Fe police cruiser rounded the corner of Letrado Street at the east side of the park and pulled into a spot a few yards away. I didn't get it that I was the one who looked suspicious.

I took off one of the two shirts I had on and stuffed it into the suitcase, sat again on the bench and took out the pizza, tearing off a piece of crust for Peanuts. The Police officer entered the Tot Lot and was approached by two of the mothers. They were looking over at me. It still didn't register that I had been the reason for the call.

I bent down and picked up the margarine tub, shaking out the few remaining drops of water and returned it to the cloth bag, to which I added the blue plastic shopping bag that held the other slices of pizza. The officer left the Tot Lot, and approached me, hands resting on his belt as he stood slightly to the left of me.

"Good Afternoon." He was polite but business like.

"Hello." I stayed sitting down, looking up at him and doubling the loop of the leash around by wrist.

"Do you have children or grandchildren playing here?" His hands stayed at his waist as he rocked slightly on his heels.

"No, just enjoying the day, is there a problem?" I held my free hand up to my eyes to shield the sun, trying to gauge his expression. He didn't have one.

"We have been getting complaints of panhandlers, and undesirables camping in the park, it's a special concern near the play area."

I nodded my head not saying anything, looking sadly at the mothers who gathered behind the orange plastic tube slide and looked over their shoulders at us, refusing to make eye contact with me.

"Do you have some ID?" The officer continued to stand to my left, bending his head slightly to look over my wheeled case with the sleeping bag roped to the back.

"Yes, yes I do, I'll get it." I unzipped the front pocket of my suitcase and pulled out the plastic sleeve that held my license along with my ATM card and credit cards from accounts that had long ago become delinquent. I handed it to him.

"Could you remove the ID from its holder please?" He continued to rock back and forth on his heels.

I did as asked, handed the license back to him. He held it in front of him with both hands and started back towards his cruiser. "Wait here please."

"Should I walk over with you?" I stood up, as did Peanuts.

"No, wait here, don't leave." He looked at Peanuts, for the first time noticing his size. "Please keep your dog leashed."

I wanted to say 'Can't you see he IS on a leash', but I didn't, just sat back down, with my head down. Oh, now I got it, the mothers in the Tot Lot called me in. I panicked, trying to decide if I should run away. What if the school had made a police report for the Child Endangerment thing? What if the background check the officer was running turned out to be a problem? I stood up, turned my head, searched for a place to hide, to find safety. The mothers lined up, backs to me, obviously trying to avoid watching my life unravel. There was no place to go. No escape. I closed my eyes, blinking back tears, sat back down on the edge of the bench, packed everything up and wondered what would become of Peanuts if I got hauled off to jail.

The officer got out of his car, came back and handed me my license.

"Is this your current address Ms. Roark.?"

"No, no I don't have an address right now. I've been staying here and there." I tried to make my voice as unemotional as his, used me sleeve to wipe my eyes. There was a very small sense of relief he didn't get the handcuffs out.

"Please keep your dog on the leash. We have been receiving complaints about dogs running free in this area. You understand we need to keep this area safe for families. Also, there is no camping in this area. The park closes at ten o'clock except for special use permits. It would probably be better if you found another place to rest and water your dog." He held a postcard size paper in his hand.

"Okay. I understand." I placed the ID back in the plastic sleeve with the other cards, pushed them into my pocket, stood up and pulled the suitcase handle all the way out, getting ready to leave.

"Here's the address of the Community Service Center on Cerrillos Road, if you need help finding shelter you may want to try there. I do know they don't open until four." He handed me the paper. *Hand Up* was printed in block letters along with a hand drawn map.

"Thank you for your cooperation on this matter. I'll be doing close patrols on this area for a while." He watched as we walked back towards the street, passing within a couple of yards of the gossiping young mothers, one of whom lifted her hand to the side of her face to avoid having to look at me. I used to be part of that. My mind was spinning with the day's events, how had I fallen from grace so far so fast.

It was after three o'clock. I was hungry. All I wanted was a place to sit and eat the slice of pizza Leonard had given me and rest. Like Peanuts, I never got used to walking all day. I walked the half mile slightly up hill to the Rose Park. Small, but shady, one end was filled with rose bushes that also ringed the park. A few people milled about; government workers on break; nearby residents trying to find respite from the heat. There was no playground here, only a half dozen benches and picnic tables. A couple of other homeless souls sat and smoked at one of the tables that was chained to a concrete square on the fringe of the park. Heavy backpacks were leaning against one end of the table. I nodded towards them, recognized them from the line at the soup kitchen. They nodded back, motioning me over.

I waved them off. "We're just going to sit a while and take a load off. I'm not having a good day."

"Is anybody?" one said and laughed.

"Amen to that brother since the tourists arrived you'd think we were serial killers or something. Can't sit anywhere for more than five minutes without a hassle." He leaned back, moving one leg over the bench, straddling it, smoke billowing from his nose.

"Well, I'm going to rest a bit." I waved them off again and pulled my suitcase close.

Peanuts and I found a tree with some bare dirt under it. I unrolled the sleeping bag, sat down. Peanuts stretched out beside me. The pizza, cold, kind of smooched together and congealed, still tasted good. I hadn't eaten all day. I drank the juice pouch, left Peanuts lying on the sleeping bag and got up to empty the trash. A couple drove up in a silver SUV with Texas plates, the back packed with suitcases. They began walking two greyhounds in the park, not far from where I rested. They let them off leash, threw two Frisbee in different directions and the dogs ran, flying across the grass to retrieve them. After two or three more catches, one of the hounds, back hunched, did his business near a rose bush. Neither of the two humans with them made any attempt to clean it up. Peanuts lifted his head and watched but quickly lost interest and laid it back down.

"You got the right idea buddy. Let's mind our own business and take a nap." I patted him on the side and stretched out on top of the open bag, using my wadded up sweatshirt as a pillow. I only meant to rest a minute, but with the heat of the day and a full stomach, I was soon in dreamland. They were sweet dreams too, floating in a canoe with both boys, my husband waving from shore, calling us over to a campfire. It was serene. Then panic set in, he's screaming at us, standing over us, yelling. But this was only partially a dream. When I opened my eyes half an hour had passed.

A woman in a white shirt and black capris pants was standing over me, for real, yelling.

"You dirty hippie! You can't just let your dog do his business. That's filthy! You dirty hippie!" She was yelling directly in my face above me.

"What?" I propped up on my elbows, looking and feeling stunned. Peanuts was still by my side, leash looped around my wrist, but standing now, dancing from foot to foot, looking from me to the woman screaming in my face.

"You can't just come here and let your dog do his business. You dirty hippies are ruining our park. We don't want you here. I reported you. You can't just come here and do your drugs. I called you in." She was still yelling, getting in my face. She reached out to push me but I rolled back before she could make contact. Peanuts lunged for her but I pulled him back before he made contact too.

What was this lady talking about? I was fast asleep and next thing I know all hell broke loose. The police cruiser pulled up. The same city police officer that chased me out of the train park, approached.

"Ms. Roark." He nodded towards me and turned toward the screaming woman. "Are you the one who called? What seems to be the problem here?"

I stared at them in disbelief. How could this be happening?

"These dirty hippies, they come into our park, they think they own the place. They do drugs. Look, over there at that table. Look, you'll see, her friends were doing drugs. They threw the butts on the ground." She pointed toward the now empty picnic table where the two guys had been smoking earlier. I guess they could have been smoking pot too, I thought it was hand rolled tobacco.

"I don't know what she's talking about. I've been resting here with my dog since I left the other park."

The officer held his hand out to me, palm first. "Wait, I'm not done hearing what this woman has to say."

"She was with those filthy bums over there, doing drugs. I saw her with them. They can't come here to our park like that. They stink up the place. She let her dog poo over there. It's right there you can see it." The woman pointed towards the rose bush where one of the Texans' greyhounds had defecated.

"That wasn't my dog. Some people were here earlier. Really, we've just been resting here in the shade."

The officer tried not to lose patience, walked over to the rose bush and peered at the fresh turds. He had an expression now, it was something like 'I can't believe I became a cop to investigate dog poop.' The woman in the black capris followed him, arms crossed in front of her and continued to rant about Dirty Hippies.

The officer pulled back from the rose bush and walked a few feet towards the picnic table, talking a knee and using the tip of a pen to push a hand rolled cigarette butt around before standing up and returning to where I was.

"That wasn't my dog, really. He's been beside me the whole time. I don't know what she's going on about."

"Are you calling me a liar you dirty whore?" The woman was in my face again. She pushed my shoulder. I didn't step back in time, she made contact and I lost my balance. Peanuts lunged for her again, but I was able to grab him around the middle and pull him hard towards me. The officer stepped between us.

"Calm down, you need to calm down." At least he was addressing the woman not me.

I stood up, started to protest. He again held his hand up to me in a kind of stop signal then said, "Walk with me." We headed towards the picnic table.

The woman in capris followed behind. The cop turned around.

"You wait here," and pointed towards the tree where my sleeping bag was spread out. She pouted, stomped her foot and spun around.

When we got to the picnic table the officer stood in front of me, put his hand on my shoulder and turned me slightly so I could no longer see my accuser.

"Ms. Roark this is the second complaint I've had to respond to in less than four hours about you hanging around in parks. Can you tell me your side of things?"

I shook my head, my eyes tearing up.

"When I left the train park I came here. I just wanted to eat my lunch and rest awhile. There was a couple with two greyhound dogs. They had out of state plates. They let the dogs run around the park, one of them pooped by the rose bush, not my dog. After that I fell asleep. I don't know what she's talking about."

He nodded his head. I could see him look beyond my shoulder I started to turn my head, but he drew my attention again.

"What about the two guys, your friends, where were they? How are they involved in all this?"

"I don't know what she's going on about. There were two men here, setting at this table, smoking. I didn't think it was marijuana, just home rolled tobacco. I said hello to them that's all, I didn't even sit with them or anything, just hello and a wave." I stared at the ground where at least two dozen cigarette butts littered the ground under and around the picnic table.

"So they were your friends?" He motioned to the now empty benches at the table.

"Acquaintances. Not really friends. I barely knew them. They're just guys, sitting in the shade trying to rest a while, like me."

"There is no camping in the park Ms. Roark, in any park in the city of Santa Fe, camping is not allowed and you must clean up after your dog. I could cite you for both camping in the park and a dog at large..."

"It wasn't my dog. I wasn't camping. I told you, I..."

"Ms. Roark let me finish please. The best way to resolve this is for you to pick up the cigarette butts. They do appear to be tobacco not marijuana, and clean up the dog excrement, and you can't stay here. You'll have to leave. I believe that will resolve this situation with the local over there."

"But I don't smoke. It wasn't me smoking and it wasn't my dog."

"Ms. Roark I'm trying to resolve this situation so that it works for everyone. As I told you at the other park we have been getting calls about campers and panhandling in parks from the locals, we are trying to address that. If you agree to what I asked of you, you and your dog are free to walk away."

I looked at him silently for a moment then knelt down, humiliated, and started to pick up the cigarette butts.

"I'm local too you know." I said it softly but loud enough for him to here.

"Excuse me?"

"I'm local too. I live here too."I looked up at him but didn't say anything else. For the first time I saw concern in his eyes.

"Do you still have the paper I gave you?"

"Yes, I do. I'll walk over there soon." Soon as they take dogs I thought.

He watched over me for at least ten minutes while I picked up every single cigarette butt within a twenty foot radius of the table. There were thirty-four of them, only a handful where home rolled, most were Marlboro. It took several trips to the trash can with my hands full of dirty filters to get rid of them.

I stood up and walked toward the dog poop, I remembered the blue plastic bag I had discarded earlier and went back to retrieve it shaking off the cigarette butts I just deposited. I bent down to pick up the stinking doggy do-do. Peanuts gave it a good sniff as I reached for it. The Officer positioned himself between me and the capris lady, kind of like a human barrier, but it meant that he had his back to her and I was looking her way.

I was on the ground tying a knot in the bag of poop, looked up, and saw her with my cloth Penny's bag. She was taking things out and throwing them on the ground.

"Hey!" I stood up and started to yell. "Hey, that's my stuff."

The officer instinctively put his arm out and blocked my way.

"She's got my bag. She's throwing my things around."

When he turned around, the capris lady instantly stopped emptying the bag.

"Wait here," he said, and walked quickly towards her. I could hear him talking to her but couldn't make out what everything she said. I heard 'dirty hippies' several times and something about drugs. The officer took the bag from her and placed it on top of my sleeping bag. The two started towards his cruiser and he motioned me to gather my things. I walked over, Peanuts leash still looped around my wrist, and stopped to pick up the things she scattered across the grass. A tooth brush, wash cloth, plastic spoons encircled by a rubber band, socks and stash of brown paper towels used for emergency toilet paper, but the thing I looked for wasn't there, my composition notebook. What had she done with it? I raced around the park. That book was not only my diary but my filing cabinet. All the papers from the hospital, pictures of my boys when we were happy family, the only things I had left to remind me of them were tucked in the notebook's pages.

Frantic, I called out to the officer, "My notebooks gone. She took my notebook." I ran towards them.

The officer stood sideways to me. "Did you remove a notebook from this woman's bag?"

"I don't have her notebook." Capri lady smiled smugly and wobbled her head, neither yes or no.

The officer was fed up.

"I didn't ask if you had it I asked if you removed it. Did you take a notebook from this woman's bag?"

His irritation was soon tempered by the knowledge that one negative letter to the editor on his watch could derail his future. His tone returned to one devoid of emotion.

"If not, I'll need to go back and review the cruiser cam video and see if we can discover what did happen to it."

Capris Pants, smirked, anger in her eyes, unfolded her arms and tottered toward a rose bush, its coral pink buds barely starting to bloom, reached to the center slightly scratching her arm on the thorns. She yanked out my black composition notebook, throwing it at me.

"Here you dirty hippie and don't come back."

At that point the officer put his hand on her elbow and escorted her to the front of his cruiser and used a stylus to fill in information on his tablet computer. Several times he put his hand on the woman's upper arm so she would look away. I gathered up the paperwork of my life, rolled up my sleeping bag and prepared to leave. Almost as an afterthought, I flipped through my notebook to be sure everything was there. It wasn't.

A family photo made into a Christmas card the year before the accident, all four of us smiling in identical forest green turtlenecks in front of a snow wet adobe wall framed by braided strands of red chile, the last remnant of a happy family I had, that photo card was missing. I checked again and again, three times. No card. Desperate I raced to the rose bush from which capris lady had extracted my notebook. There, scattered among the pastel yellow- red blossoms, were the torn pieces. How could someone be that hateful?

I gathered up as many of the torn photo's pieces as I could find and stuffed them into the pages of the notebook, took the rubber band from around the plastic spoons and used it to bind the notebook's pages together sealing everything inside, all the while giving scornful glances over to the officer. I stood a minute trying to decide where to go.

"You need to be on your way Ms. Rorak," the officer said over his shoulder, while capris lady, obviously placated, smiled and flirted with him.

47

We found shelter a few more nights in an alley that borders the cemetery, after my encounter with capris lady I needed to be close to my family even if they were dead and buried. I walked around, wondered if Wizard was nearby, and wandered up the path to where several other homeless folks had left the remnants of their life behind. When it got to be late and no one appeared, I spread out my tarp and Peanuts' rug and slept. Now, not more than six in the morning, I packed up and headed towards the mall, hopeful I could find a restroom open.

Next was an ATM. Finally. The full five hundred and twenty dollars was in the account. It had taken two months, my last paycheck from school and the money I raised by selling the furniture to clear out all the bounced checks and fees. I still owed for my storage locker, on credit cards and of course for Stevie's medical. But at least I could control who got paid first. Sort of. St. Mary's was still garnishing most of Sam's check.

Even though it was well before noon, Peanuts and I made our way to the Queens Quarters Inn. I'd get a room for at least a week, try and regroup, make phone calls. Maybe pay on my storage locker and get my ID back so I could find a job. Now, I thought, now it will be all right, I'll pull it together, start over.

The room rates were no longer posted on the rolling lighted sign out front. A small 'ding-dong' sounded when Peanuts and I entered the office. A new clerk staffed the desk.

"Hello, may I help you?

"I know it's too early to check in, but can I go ahead and pay for a room and check in latter?"

"How many nights? How many guests? The dog is staying?"

"I want the weekly rate. Just me and the dog."

"We do have a room available. With the dog the weekly rate on that would be six hundred and seventy five."

"What? I stayed in March and it wasn't even half of that."

"Rates go up after Memorial Day."

"By that much?"

"Yes, we have summer rates between Memorial Day and Labor Day."

There was no way I could afford that much. "What's the daily rate?"

"With a dog, for one person, one seventeen, plus tax."

"Wow, is that third night free?"

"No, we only offer that during the off season."

"When's the off season?"

"From Labor Day to Memorial Day we offer lower rates. Do you want to book a room?"

"No, I didn't realize the price had gone up, I guess I'm going to look around." I backed my case towards the door.

"You won't find a lower rate in Santa Fe during the summer months. There is a central reservation number you can try, but this time of year, if you can find a room, it's a safe bet it won't be less than a hundred a night, and an extra charge for the dog." He wasn't being mean, just factual.

"Thanks, I guess I'll take my chances."

"If you do change your mind, come back around three, by four we will probably be full."

How was I going to afford a room? Three nights would wipe out most of my check for the month. We walked around, tried at least seven other places. Most didn't accept pets or had such an outrageous rate I couldn't afford it. Sure burst my bubble.

It was almost two o'clock. I bought dog food and a few packs of juice and cheese crackers from the supermarket. At least Peanuts would enjoy a can or two of food. Reluctantly I made my way back to the Queen's Quarters Inn.

"How much for three nights again?" I asked.

We slept, I showered, slept some more, showered again using every bit of the little tiny soaps. I washed all my cloths in the beat up coin-op machine found in a closet marked guest laundry, folded them and repacked my bag. I had fifty dollars left after three days. Not enough for another night's stay. But I was clean, had slept in a bed and Peanuts was well fed and rested. At 9:59 a.m., on the third day, Peanuts and I headed out the door. Peanuts stopped in the doorway, gave a little sigh while looking over at the bed I let him sleep on. "Look on the bright side fella, it's not raining or snowing and it's pretty warm outside."

Reluctantly, he followed me out the door and we headed towards the rail yard.

The guys at the Rose Park were right. It was a hassle in the summer to be here. Traffic was heavy, you got hassled and harangued by merchants, tourists and residents who blamed you for every little offense whether it was caused by you or not. Being ignored, which happened the rest of the year, would have been better. I was going from being humble to being angry. Not a good place for a dwelling as Wizard would say.

Peanuts and I walked along the Rail Runner tracks, cutting east near St Francis to the Rail Yard Park. A farmers' market is going on, people everywhere. I looked longingly at the fresh vegetables, remembered my own tiny garden. Even if I buy some of the produce I have no way to store, wash or prepare it. I kept walking. Peanuts and I find a bench and sit a while. A young homeless couple, she with long dirty blond dreadlocks, he with a goatee and green plaid golfers hat pull out a guitar and tambourine and start to play, case open, hoping for tips. Within five minutes a city officer on a mountain bike rides up, after which they pack up their instruments and walk away. Music, like everything else here, was timed and scripted, required a permit, and had to be in keeping with the ambiance of the Santa Fe Farmers' Market experience of travel magazine fame. It was only a matter of time before I was encouraged to move on too.

I watch a couple of buses pull up, followed by courtesy vans from hotels and casinos picking up tourists from the Albuquerque Rail Runner. Could Peanuts ride the train? If he could and we made it to Albuquerque maybe I could find a job and a place to stay. Peanuts bobbed his head trying to avoid the service dog vest, but I managed to pull it on him. He paws at it, wants to get it off, finally sighs, sits beside me. A couple of Public Safety officers are walking our way, time to get a move on.

"Come on Peanuts. Let's go."

We walk across the tracks to the line of casino and hotel courtesy vans. Third van down the line is painted with red white and blue triple sevens. It has a banner fastened to the back that promised a complimentary meal voucher and twenty dollars in free slot play. A large map marked the location roughly in the middle between Santa Fe and Albuquerque with the slogan 'Stop Half Way and Play'. The driver smoked and chatted a few yards away. Ask forgiveness not permission, I tell myself. Peanuts and I get on the bus.

¤ ¤ ¤

It wasn't the first time I'd been here. Sometimes Sam and I'd make the stop after the boys' soccer tournaments. The post-game appetite of teenage soccer players challenged the profitability of an All You Can Eat buffet. Sam and I would try our luck.

Sam would say "Sometimes you win, sometimes you lose. That's why it's called gambling."

Today I was gambling I could make it all the way to Albuquerque for free, with a large black Shepard, a suitcase topped by a sleeping bag and tarp and snag a free meal, too.

Ten minutes south of Santa Fe on I-25 the driver notices me, or more precisely, Peanuts. Without comment, he keeps watch from the large rectangular mirror angled backward above his head. Forty five minutes later the bus pulled to the expansive circular drive of the casino's first entrance. I wait while the eight other riders, laughing and excited, walked up the aisle, off the bus, and through the double doors of the darkened casino. Peanuts and I are last. Two Native American men in security guard uniforms approached me.

"Good Afternoon." Unfailingly polite, they wait for me to respond.

"Good Afternoon." I smile at them, pull my case in back of me, shorten Peanuts' leash until it's not more than half a foot.

One walks in back of me while the other stands front and side, looking Peanuts over, studying the blue service dog vest.

The older of the two crosses his arms and steps between me and the casino door. "We welcome service animals into our establishment, but we ask you keep them under physical control at all times."

"Of course."

He continues to inspect us, especially Peanuts and my suitcase, considers his words carefully. Sometimes you win, sometimes you lose, but sometimes you break even. I was about to break even.

"Our courtesy van leaves the front of the Casino on the hour, alternating between Santa Fe and Albuquerque. I can reserve a space for you and your service animal on the next van going in your direction. Will you need a seat on the van back to Santa Fe or on the next van, which will be going to Albuquerque?"

I had been found out. In the most polite way possible, without creating a scene, he was telling me to be on my way, ASAP.

"The Albuquerque van is the next van?"

"Yes, it will be leaving in approximately fifteen minutes."

"That's the one I should probably take then."

"We will be sure you have a seat. Let me have someone bring you a complimentary soft drink to enjoy outside, with your service animal, while you wait."

These guys knew how to frame it. No meal or twenty bucks in free play for me, I wouldn't even make it inside. At least I'd get that ride to Albuquerque. I swallowed hard.

"That would be wonderful," I said.

¤ ¤ ¤

"This is your stop"

The van exited I-25 at the first Bernalillo exit and turned into the Rail Runner parking lot. The driver looked at me, his sunglasses reflected by the mirror, and said it again.

"They told me this was your stop."

"Don't you go all the way into downtown Albuquerque?" I asked.

"We do, but," he took off his sunglasses so I could see his reflected eyes, "this is your stop."

What could I do? Peanuts and I got up, pulling the suitcase in back of us. The driver took the handle of the case from me as I guide Peanuts down the steps and onto the sidewalk. The driver follows, but leaves the case on the bottom step. I want to look around him, but he put his arms out, blocking the door.

"They wanted me to ask for the dog's jacket."

"What?"

"The dog's jacket. My boss told me to ask you for the dog's jacket. They said they didn't think you were supposed to have it and wanted me to ask you for it."

"I need my suitcase."

He looks down at Peanuts, then over his shoulder at the case.

"The dog's jacket."

I furrow my brows, if I protest he will surely hop on the bus and drive away. But there it was, he knew he held the cards on this one. I kneel down, unfasten the service dog vest and wade it up in my hand.

"I need my case."

The driver reaches back and pulls it onto the sidewalk in front of us but keeps his hand on the handle. I reach for the handle, he jerks it back.

"The dog's jacket. "

I hold the Service Dog vest out with one hand and reach to pull the suitcase away with the other. The driver takes the vest without letting go of my case. Instead, he gives a tug, jerking it back a second time and pulling me forward. This was too much for Peanuts. His huge mouth open, baring his teeth, he snarls and lunges at the driver who releases the telescoping handle and falls back onto the courtesy vans steps. I grab my suitcase, tighten Peanuts lead and run, not stopping until the other side of a fence, far from the drop off point. The van pulls out of the parking lot. Peanuts' blue Service Dog vest is rolled up in a ball on the dashboard.

"Good dog, Peanuts. Good dog."

48

Bernalillo is north of Albuquerque. Like most metro areas, it was part of a conglomeration of villages and small towns surrounded by commercial development. Peanuts and I walked parallel to the train tracks, but the gravel and brush soon drove us to find a street to follow. Fast food restaurants, convenience stores and small strip malls replaced most of old Route 66, Main Street of America. If I stayed on it I would eventually end up in central Albuquerque, where, I hoped, I would find food and shelter.

It was later than I thought. Since becoming homeless I had no sense of time. I got up when it was still dark, found a place to sleep when it got dark and ate when and where I could find food. Right now I was hungry. An old style Lota Burger with an outside walk up window, probably one of the original hamburger stands built in the sixties came into view. Peanuts and I cross the busy intersection and stood in line.

The Junior Burger would set me back five bucks. If I spent anymore I wouldn't have enough for a room. I gave Peanuts more than half and glanced at the receipt, it was past eight. The sun began to set over the barely discernible ancient volcano cones that dotted the mesa to the west of us. I needed to find someplace to spend the night while there was still some light.

We traveled south, continuing to parallel the Rail Runner Tracks, the Interstate and old Route 66. At some point Route 66 took a western curve towards a busy six lane interchange. I hesitated. If I kept to the road I would get to Albuquerque. But the traffic, businesses and terrain would be difficult to deal with in the dark. I had to find a place to lay down the tarp and Peanut's rug. I took the lessor curve, back towards the Interstate.

A field, empty save for tumbleweeds and rabbit bush, separated Bernalillo from the next flagging village. The field looked promising. Maybe I could find space, away from the road, where the tall weeds would mask my camp. I followed the cracked sidewalk that bordered the field. Twin bell towers of an old adobe church came into view, followed by another empty field, than a cemetery, also overgrown with weeds. If this was Santa Fe I'd find shelter just outside the graveyard's fence.

We had to cross back over the Rail Runner track to reach the edges of the declining enclave. Near the ungated crossing the remains of a splintered wood sign, the kind a Chamber of Commerce might put up with symbols for Toastmasters, BPOE, and 4H, lay half covered by sand and construction debris: *Welcome to Las Manchas, Home of the Águilas.*

Peanuts and I found a spot under a jumble of Siberian Elm trees that lined one side of the neglected cemetery. Looking north we could see the adobe church and abandoned u shaped red brick school beside it. West, the Rail Runner was within home-run range. Beyond that the tops of cottonwood trees along the Rio Grande bosque were raining tiny white puffs onto the landscape. The river couldn't be more than three miles away.

I unpacked the tarp, spread it out with Peanuts rug on top and unfurled my sleeping bag. My plan was to stay hidden and hope no one would hassle us. You could tell this had once been a thriving community. Now, sandwiched between the Interstate and the Rail Runner tracks, only a few houses and mobile homes were still occupied. It had definitely not been included in anyone's master plan. Las Manchas, I played the word in my head: Las Manchas, the spot; Man of La Mancha; Out Out Damn Spot; a spot on one's character; a spot of hope; chasing an impossible dream. I sat leaning against the fence, legs bent, resting my head on my folded arms across my knees, closed my eyes and drifted off.

¤ ¤ ¤

"Good Evening." The deep voice with a Spanish accent pulled me back.

Why hadn't Peanuts barked? I kept my eyes closed, didn't want to know who it was, or why he was here. I had enough confrontation for one day. "Please just go away," I said, barely a mumble, to myself.

"Good Evening. Are you all right young lady? Do you need help of some kind?"

Young Lady? Who would call me young lady, and why hadn't Peanuts barked? I reluctantly opened one eye. A stout elderly man, dark complexioned, with tightly curled salt and pepper hair wearing a Priest's collar and black polo shirt stood in front of me, pressing on a cane. Peanuts is leaning into his leg, getting his ears scratched, wagging his tail slowly.

Peanuts how could you, hero one minute, traitor the next. The dog lay down, rolling to his back, begging for a belly rub.

"I'm Father Rico. This is our church." He motioned to the adobe bell towers west of us. "I noticed you over here by our little cemetery, you and your dog. I had a dog like this when I was a boy." Father Rico used his cane to scratch across Peanut's chest.

"Sorry, I didn't mean to intrude. I'll be on my way." I stood to gather the bag and tarp.

"You have someplace to be?"

"No, but I don't want to intrude on you. Thanks, I'll be going."

Peanuts is firmly planted beside Father Rico.

"From time to time we have travelers come here. There is an old cot in that shed over there where you are welcome to take shelter for one night." Father Rico points with his cane to a small wood shed about twenty yards from the side of an old gymnasium. "I'll go and unlock it. If you feel you want to stay there for one night, it will be open."

The dog tries to follow him.

"Come here Peanuts. Stay!"

I gently pull the leash. It took me ten minutes to re-roll my bag, tarp and Peanuts rug and use the bungee cord to secure them to the handle of my suitcase. I watch as Father Rico walks away from the open door of the shed to the church yard where an adobe half wall separated the church from the squat building that served as his residence.

"Well Peanuts, that's the best offer we've had all day." I carefully follow the narrow path through the weeds from the cemetery to the shed. It is barely light enough to see inside. An old style army cot is set up, slightly off center, surrounded by boxes. Some, without lids, appear to hold old textbooks. A metal wind turbine spins unevenly from the peak of the shed, exhausting the stale air. I pull Peanuts inside and leave the door half open, lie down on the cot, staring at the shadows made on the walls by the full moon as the metal blades of the turbine spiral above me. I unhook Peanuts leash and he lies on his rug beside me. Home for one night.

Peanuts' ears pick up. Father Rico appears in the doorway carrying a paper plate covered by a brown paper towel and a mayonnaise jar of red fruit punch.

"I thought you might be hungry." He hands me the plate and jar, and pulls a folding lawn chair from between two boxes, unfolds it a few feet opposite me and sits down.

"Oh, yes, I thought you might like to use this too." He removes an old metal flashlight from his pocket, flicks the switch, but has to hit it with his palm a couple of times before it turns on. Father Rico places the flashlight on the floor, light pointing up, illuminating the front half of the area.

Father Rico migrated to New Mexico in the sixties as a young man by way of a rocky boat ride from Cuba to Florida. One of dozens of Catholic Priests and Brothers either imprisoned or about to be when Castro came to power, his family scraped together what little money they still had control over and secured him a place on a fishing boat, leaving at midnight for the ninety mile crossing over rough water. An overabundance of Spanish speaking priests in the Miami area meant the twenty-something Father Rico would soon take another journey, by train, west, where small Spanish speaking parishes eagerly awaited him. For over forty years Father Rico moved from small town to city, back to small town , never staying more than seven or eight years. On the eve of his seventieth birthday he would be reassigned once again, and the waning parish of St. Ursula would become his home as he entered his senior years.

I took the plate of food from him and sat opposite him on the cot.

"Thank you for this, for all of this. Peanuts and I appreciate it."

"Peanuts eh? Well, Peanuts, you certainly are a fine looking dog." Father Rico reaches into his pocket again for a couple of dog treats, feeding them one at a time to Peanuts, "And you are?"

"Aileen, my name's Aileen." I take a bite of the cheese sandwich.

"Aileen? Do you have a second name?" He continues to fuss over Peanuts.

"Aileen Roark. My name is Aileen Roark." I hurry to swallow before I answer.

"Miss or Mrs.?" He looks at me solemnly, leans to one side of the metal chair and folds his hands in front of him.

"Mrs." I hesitate, feel a need to explain. "I'm a widow." It is the first time since Sam killed himself I spoke those words.

"Ah well, Mrs. Roark, you are welcome to spend the night here. It may get a little warm, so you might want to leave the door open. I unlocked the girls bathroom of the old gym should you have need of it, it's on the south side of the building."

"This is a school?" I stare at the boxes marked by grade and subject. "Is this where you keep the supplies?"

"It was a school, a very fine school. St. Ursula Elementary Mission School our mascot was Los Águila, the Eagles." Father Rico stands and picks up a small spiral bound workbook labeled *Third Grade Spelling.* "We always had champions in the spelling bee and our basketball wasn't bad either." He flips through the book.

"They aren't open any more then?" I sip the red punch, remembering how sweet the stuff is.

"No, the school closed, let me think, at least eight years ago, maybe nine. Times have changed, the children all grew up, the area changed. We have fewer families. Now we have our church to keep us busy, but for how long I don't know."

I stand, brush the crumbs from myself and looked around for a trash can.

"Here, I'll take that. I'm sure you are tired, rest. In the morning, you can start your journey again. Good Night Mrs. Roark." He snaps his fingers lightly towards Peanuts. The dog obliges, wagging his tail, sits beside him, leaning his head into Father Rico's hip. Father scratches him under the chin.

"And you too Peanuts, Good Night."

¤ ¤ ¤

The cot wasn't bad. It was warmer in Albuquerque, the storage shed more sheltering than the banks of the arroyo's and vacant fields where I'd been sleeping the last couple of months. Peanuts slept well too on his rug beside the cot. It was the first time in a long time he got up and nosed my hand wanting to go outside. I stretched, slid open the half closed door and stood outside with him while he ran, unleashed, through the empty field that separated the cemetery from the churchyard. He kept looking at the church and old school buildings, wagging his tail expectantly. I ducked back into the shed and gathered a clean set of clothes from my suitcase, toothbrush and plastic cup and headed for the bathrooms, Peanuts at my heels. Inside the bathroom someone had laid out an old towel and sliver of soap on one of the stained square sinks that ran along the wall. I took advantage of the situation, spent at least twenty minutes cleaning up. The sound of Peanuts lapping water from the toilet bowl in one of the stalls startled me. I peeked around the partition in time to see him lift his head, water dripping from his snout. "Seriously Peanuts?" He drops his head again for another round.

I rolled up the old clothes, tucked them under my arm and headed back. My wheeled case was propped up outside the now closed door of the shed. Bummer.

I stand with my hand shielding my eyes from the morning sun and survey the area. Last night, when I lay out my tarp and Peanuts rug along the cemetery's edge, it had been almost dark. Now, in the light of day, I clearly see abandoned buildings, some half torn down, dotting the area. Between the church yard and cemetery are the stubs of trees and leafless vines from an old vineyard, arranged in neat rows. An acequia, lined by cracked concrete, jutted perpendicular to the mother ditch, the rusted wheel of the head-gate silhouetted against the weeds. A few fruit trees, apple, peach and plum, overgrown, broken branches touching the ground, bordered the edge of what had once been a playground. All that was left was the large gray metal frame of a swing set with one chain hanging down. The lower metal bar of a double teeter totter was attached to one end of the play structure. Broken boards of a bench lay beneath. I bet this was once someone's grand estate. I envision the old orchard and field of chile where piles of concrete construction debris have been stacked and tumbleweeds taken root between them. Along a gravel roadway one road over, four or five modest houses with detached metal garages line up, their backyards abutting the steep embankment by the Interstate. My attention was drawn by the sound of a Rail Runner Train to the west of the cemetery. It was easy to see the faces of the riders on the commuter train making their daily 60 mile trek to Santa Fe. Las Manchas, the spot, had become the equivalent of the town between the tracks, bordered by the air brakes of tractor trailers on one side and the warning horn of a commuter train on the other. In Santa Fe, local residents and merchants petitioned to have the train's warning horn silenced. The poverty stricken residents of Las Manchas held no such clout.

Peanuts jolted me back when a prairie dog popped his head out of a nearby hole and the black Shepard almost pulled me over trying to reach it. Much to Peanuts chagrin, another popped up a few yards away, then another. It was like Whack a Mole. I resisted the urge to let him off leash and pulled the barking dog back towards the shed.

The sleeping bag and Peanuts rug had been neatly folded and placed on the edge of a small concrete pad at the entrance to the shed. A heavy padlock sealed the door. On top of my suitcase a white Styrofoam cup, covered by wax paper secured by a rubber band, held lukewarm black coffee, beside it, also wrapped in wax paper, two slices of toasted white bread with a fried egg in between, and a banana. Beside that lay a brown paper bag half filled with dog kibble. I sighed. I would have liked to stay longer, find Father Rico, thank him, ask him for a few more nights, and offer to help clean up the place or something. But it was obvious, the accommodation was one night only. Under the modest breakfast Father Rico left a folded purple flier detailing services available at St. Vincent de Paul in downtown Albuquerque, in the margin was a hand drawn map and a note.

God speed your journey Mrs. Roark. I'll keep you in my prayers and ask you keep Las Manchas and St. Ursula's in yours.- Fr. Rico

I drank the coffee standing up, tore the sandwich in two, giving the larger of the pieces to Peanuts, and ate the other in three bites. We headed out, banana and dog kibble, our lunch, in my cloth shopping bag, and began to follow the map Father Rico had drawn for us. Wind picked up ahead us swirling a dust devil high into the air. I closed my eyes, covered my mouth with the edge of my shirt, bent my head down to block the dust and made my way through the whirling sand.

49

It took two days of walking to reach the shelter in downtown Albuquerque. I wasn't too sure about the map, stopped whenever I found a park or a place to rest for a while with Peanuts and could find a restroom. Access to a bathroom, as in Santa Fe, was a continuing struggle. Peanuts was pretty happy to have the kibble Father Rico left for him. I mixed it up in an old plastic bowl with half a hamburger patty, the ninety nine cent kind you get on the value menu. When it got dark again, I found a place behind a wall that separated the road from an empty strip mall. Ill trimmed juniper and Arizona Blue Cypress provided limited cover, but enough, I hoped, we wouldn't be disturbed. Peanuts was restless. The sounds and smells of Albuquerque were foreign to him. He would raise his head and ears each time the sound of someone's voice floated in our direction.

Middle of the night, three a.m., a sharp pain in my belly woke me. I probably shouldn't have shared the saved half hamburger patty between myself and Peanuts. Where's a damn bathroom! Who would let me in with Peanuts at this hour of the night? I staggered out to the road. A gas station was open across the street. I could already see the sign, *Bathroom for customers only.* A small drive up cigarette shack was a block down *No restrooms.* Other places were closed up tight or posted *Customers only,* we were turned away. I walked around the unoccupied mall clutching my side. I was desperate. Behind a dumpster no more than four feet from the wall, a large piece of cardboard as cover, I had to heed nature's call, right there, squatting on the ground, behind that dumpster. It was the most humiliating experience I ever had. I went back to the sleeping bag, put my head on my knees, hugged them close to my chest, and cried silently. Peanut sat beside me and licked the salt off my face. I put my arms around his neck, hugging him. When would this end?

First light, and I do mean very first light, the sun a tiny crescent rising above the Sandia Mountains, we set out again, arriving at the shelter just before four in the afternoon.

¤ ¤ ¤

The thing that surprised me most about the homeless men and women I encountered in Albuquerque was the number of them. Almost every intersection, most parks, walking along roadways, hanging out by convenience stores, a man or woman with a pack or shopping cart, wearing several layers of dirty torn clothes, sat, stood, leaned or lay trying to find a place to exist in this vast universe. A few smiled or gave a small wave of kinship. Some were obviously under the influence of whatever they could find, and some could be seen pacing, talking to themselves, upset or agitated by the real world that surrounded them or the alternative reality that played out in their head. A few were limping, coughing, and ill. It was the latter two groups I prayed the most over. I was of sound mind, relatively good health and I was having a hell of a time trying to take care of myself. How were they able to cope?

The line at the St Vincent de Paul Help Center was a reflection of what I had seen since leaving Las Manchas. Six or seven dozen people, mostly men, a few women, stood in line, waiting to see if they would get a bed for the night. I learned later a separate facility accepted families with children. At winters end, about the last week of March, the extra beds meant to keep us from freezing to death had been deactivated. Anything above twenty-eight degrees was deemed survivable. Limited space was available, dormitory style, this time of year, and competition was steep. Anyone drunk or on drugs was turned away. If you had stayed too many times in the last two weeks you were turned away. If, like me, you showed up with an animal, you were turned away. I found this out after a two hour wait.

I stood in line with the rest, Peanuts pulled close to me. He was uncomfortable with this new setting. A few guys commented, petted him. Several told me "They won't let you in with a dog, but sometimes they give out vouchers if you tell a good story." I nodded thanks and we waited. A tall man with thinning reddish hair, and a patch over one eye wore a red vinyl vest over a work shirt and pants, a hand radio clipped to his belt, walked the length of the line patrolling our ranks. He was friendly but not overly so. At least twice he took the arm of a man, and once of a woman and gently escorted them away, reminding them of the house rules, probably over pot, or tipping a bottle in line.

I was close to the front of the line when he approached me.

"Haven't seen you two around before?" He stood a few feet to the side of me and adjusted his cap.

"No, I just came down from Santa Fe two days ago." I pulled my case behind me as the line moved a few feet. People were being let in by two's and three's, each time a group went in the whole line surged forward six feet. Two more groups and I'd be in.

"I'm pretty sure they won't take the dog. They may offer to call an animal shelter or something." He rocked on his heels, looking down at the ground, lifting his foot and inspecting the sole of his shoe in back of him.

"I guess somebody did tell me that. But I was hoping they might make an exception. He's a really good dog. Father Rico referred me here." I rubbed Peanuts ears, bent down slightly and pushed his rear down so he would sit beside me.

The radio on his belt clicked on.

"Gilbert, come in." A man's voice, broken by static, emitted from the radio's speaker.

The man with the eye patch, Gilbert I guess his name was, unhooked the radio, bringing it in front of his lips sideways.

"Go ahead."

"What do the numbers look like out there?"

Gilbert stepped back a few feet and surveyed the end of the line.

"Got about thirty five maybe thirty six still in line."

"How many female?"

Gilbert looked at me, hesitated, and scanned the line again.

"Approximately six women, one has a canine."

"Did you tell her we can't accept animals?"

"Yes, but she wants to talk to you about it, said Father Rico referred her."

"Got it. Male side is full. We still have four beds on the female side. Send the women in and we'll figure it out."

"What about the woman with the dog?"

"We'll talk to her, but let her know we can't take the dog."

Gilbert clipped the radio back on his belt. "I guess you heard that?"

"Yes, I heard. I was hoping they might put me in touch with another place or something?"

"Well, go to the front and wait, I'll let the other women know." Gilbert walked a few yards down the line and called out, "Sorry gentlemen, no more beds on the male side. Try again tomorrow. Male beds only may still be available at the Methodist up the block. If the women will come to the front of the line, there is still room on the female side."

I watched sadly as the men shuffled away in different directions, heads down, slow to react, knowing it meant another night in the open, under an overpass, or in a drainage or parking garage. I wanted to pay attention, see where they went so I would know too, but Gilbert was holding open the heavy iron barred door that covered the inner steel door. I grabbed hold of my case, grasped Peanuts leash snugly and went in. Two of the other women were sitting along a bench to one side of the room. I walked over and sat beside them. One, a woman in her forties, was wearing a pair of bright pink sweat pants under a longish denim skirt. A two wheeled metal mesh shopping cart stuffed full of clothes and blankets was parked to her immediate left. I and Peanuts were on her right.

"You're new." She had really bad breath. Mine wasn't so great either. I was lucky to find a place to brush my teeth once a day.

"Yes, I was in Santa Fe until two days ago."

She sat on the edge of the bench, hands folded on her knee, looking straight forward. Her hair was about chin length, light brown, streaked with gray, frizzy, and hadn't seen a comb in two or three days.

"It gets bad there when tourist season starts." She seemed to be talking from the side of her mouth. Her words slurred together. "You know they won't take dogs."

"Yes, everyone tells me that. I wanted to see if they can send me someplace or give me a referral or something."

"They won't. All they'll do is try to get you to give up your dog, and if you say yes they still won't promise you a place to sleep." She reached into the top of her cart, pushed aside three dirty quilts, pulled out a blue plastic grocery bag, untied two knots from it, lifted another yellow grocery bag from that, unknotted it, finally reached in and retrieved a white fast food bag. From this she pulled out three cold French fries and spoke gently to Peanuts. "Here luvy, want a treat?"

Peanuts, to my surprise, was hungry enough to stand up, lean over and take them from her, laying the fries between his paws before eating them. Now I really felt guilty. He never ate French fries, especially not cold ones. He must have been very hungry.

"Thank you. Peanuts thanks you too." I loosened up the leash a bit and rubbed Peanuts head. It's hard to make small talk when you're homeless, like 'Did you see the news last night?' Or 'Where did you get those shoes?' are questions you would never ask. But I had to try something, she was making a gesture.

"Have you stayed here much? How is it?" I studied the room. It was pretty Spartan save for a small plant stand topped by a plaster statue of Mary, Mother of Jesus on one wall while a poster print portrait of John Kennedy graced the wall beside it.

"S'okay." She lifted her shoulders, repacked the bags and quilts in her cart. "They don't have as many spaces now that winter's over. About half the time I get in and half I don't."

I sat silent a while, noting the three woman ahead of us gathering their things, they would have a place tonight. If what I overheard from Gilbert's radio was correct that meant only one more bed. I looked sadly down at Peanuts. "Well buddy, looks like we're on our own again tonight."

"Scuse me?" The French fry lady began smoothing her hair, but it was way too little, way too late to make a difference.

"Oh, I overheard that guy outside, Gilbert I think? There were only four more beds on the female side. So I guess I'm out for sure."

She stared at me, weaving side to side, then back down a Peanuts. "Do you have a camp yet?"

If it hadn't been for my time with Wizard I would be clueless what she meant. "No, we stayed in back of a strip mall last night, towards Bernalillo, but I don't really know where we'll end up tonight."

We were summoned to the interview table. A woman wearing a dark blue skirt and a white blouse was motioning us forward. She may have been a nun.

"Well, if I don't make it either wait for me, I can show you a place or two. I'm Alice by the way," but it came out all bunched up like 'Imalicebyway'.

Each of the three of us sat at a plastic folding conference table across from a shelter worker. Another man, wearing a priest collar and light colored sport shirt paced in back of them, occasionally stepping into an alcove and talking into the hand radio he held in the palm of his hand.

The lady I thought was a nun sat in the chair in front of me.

"Let me tell you right off the bat two things: one, we can't accept animals here, we just don't have the facilities for it and two we only have one bed left." She was matter of fact but not upsetting, she had practice saying no.

"Yes, Gilbert, the security guard, told me when I was outside. I was hoping maybe you could put me in touch with some services or something. Father Rico referred me."

"Oh? Are you a member of Father Rico's parish?"

The worker beside her broke in, "I thought they sold that old church."

"I think they were trying to. Father Rico is still there, but I thought it was in an unofficial capacity." She leaned back in her seat and called out to the priest in the alcove, only he wasn't a priest.

"Brother Michael."

Brother Michael pulled the hand radio away from his mouth, "Yes?"

"This woman said Father Rico refereed her to us."

"Did he?" He put the radio away and took three steps stopping near us.

"When I got here, or there, Las Manchas, Father Rico let me stay in one of the old sheds, gave us some dinner." I pulled the flier Father Rico had written on from my pocket. "He gave me this."

"Is Father Rico saying mass?" The nun turned to Brother Michael quizzically.

"I don't know exactly what his role is anymore. Officially I think he's retired, but they were letting him stay at St. Ursula's more as a caretaker. Apparently they tried to sell it a couple of times and the deal didn't go through."

It was my turn to butt in, "Selling that great old church? What about the school?"

"Those old adobe churches are costly to maintain, and the school has been closed for at least eight or nine years. A relative of one of the original Las Manchas families tried to negotiate buying everything, wanted to combine it with family holdings nearby and develop a live work condo situation. The cemetery was the hold up."

"The cemetery? Why the cemetery? People still worry about living near a cemetery?" I pictured the neglected graveyard where I first rolled out my sleeping bag.

"It wasn't the cemetery itself. It was the land. The archdiocese didn't want to release the land where the cemetery is located if it meant moving the grave sites."

That's good then." I gave a silent cheer. What if someone wanted to move my sons to build a condo?

"Maybe. If it goes to bankruptcy court, they may be forced to sell anyway." He took a deep breath, looking over the nun's shoulder at the flier I had given her. "It's nice to know Father Rico is still thinking of us. I'll have to give him a call. But what about you? Do you want us to call the shelter to pick up your dog? It's an excellent facility. The volunteers are great with the animals, and work to find new homes. We can call them. They'll send someone over and pick him up?"

Alice, drew my attention, frowned and shook her head no.

"No, I'll be all right. Thanks anyway." I stood to leave.

"Wait, hold on a minute." The nun got up from her chair and used a key on a flexible blue cord around her wrist to unlock a metal storage cabinet. She shook open a brown lunch bag. A couple of packs of cheese and crackers, a single serve can of beans and weenies, an applesauce cup and a spoon were added to the bag. The nun closed the cabinet, pulled a bottle of water from a box on the floor and walked back to me, reaching across the table with the food.

"We don't want to send you away without something to tide you over. Also," the nun took a tri-folded paper from a small box on the table and pushed it into the bag, "there's a list of services available in Albuquerque. You may find a program that can help you in some way. Do come back if you change your mind about the dog."

"Thanks, but I made a promise to someone I'd take care of him. Thanks for the food."

Alice was breathing into a hand held breathalyzers the shelter worker pressed to her lips. Oh, that's why her speech was slurred. I went outside and waited. Less than three minutes later Alice came through the door holding a brown paper bag like mine, mumbling under her breath, which was getting worse by the minute.

I did think about it, but like that first night on the streets of Santa Fe when Wizard offered his hand, I had no place to go and no idea what to do next. I'd only known Alice ten minutes and that breath could knock a buzzard as the saying goes, but she offered help, liked dogs, it was getting dark and I was clueless. I followed her.

Six blocks, three stop lights and an Interstate underpass later she finally spoke to me.

"What'd you say your name was again?" But it came out "Whatsayurnamegan."

"Excuse me?" I couldn't understand her.

"Name. Your name." She was talking out of the side of her mouth.

I caught up to her. "Aileen, I'm Aileen."

"Pleasedtomeetcha." She pulled her cart up over a curb. A wheel got caught in the street drain and it tipped, spilling half the contents into the gutter. Alice was stationary, puzzled, looking around her, turning from the waist, back and forth.

I pulled my case unto the curb, looped Peanuts leash around it. "Sit."

I stepped back into the street, dodging several cars and started to gather her things, stuffing them into the cart in no particular order. "I've got it Alice."

Alice stood there, pulling her fingers through her hair, distress on her face, dazed. Maybe she wasn't intoxicated, just confused. I pulled her cart over the curb and helped her to step up to the sidewalk.

"Here you go." I placed her hand on the handle of the cart and took up my own wheeled chariot. "Where to?"

It was past eight o'clock, in a few minutes it would be completely dark.

"This was, this way; we have to wait until the buses stop running." She pulled her cart behind her, once again and began the trek east, up Central Avenue, the old Route 66.

"Oh?"

She ignored me.

"Are we going to another shelter?" I was worried where we'd end up.

"Ha-ha, that's a good one. Yeah, we're going to a shelter." She had a distant smile. Every time she opened her mouth that foul odor came pouring out. It was better she didn't say much.

We walked east, kept going. A couple of times I wanted to sit and rest.

"I have to rest Peanuts; he's still not used to going this long." I sat on the edge of a wall surrounding a grassy area near UNM. Two homeless men were lying in the grass, propped up on their backpacks about thirty feet in back of us.

"Hey, Alice, who's your friend?"

But they said it in a mean way.

Alice waved a hand in front of her face. "Ignore them." She spoke again out of the corner of her mouth, pretend it meant only I could hear her.

I started to open the lunch bag and get out a pack of crackers, but Alice stopped me.

"Not here." She rolled her eyes, and nodded backwards in the direction of the men.

"Can I give Peanuts some water? Is that okay?"

She closed her eyes and nodded yes, then she started to repack her cart, taking out a dozen knotted plastic bags, some scarves, belts, three cheap quilts, a couple of empty trash bags , sweat pants, another skirt, three sweaters. She folded and packed and repacked until satisfied.

After Peanuts had his fill, I put his bowl and the water bottle back into my cloth shopping bag, wedging the lunch sack in between. Was I imitating Alice in the way I carefully replaced everything? A frightening thought. We started up Central. An incline lead us to the Knob Hill area. Dozens of people, real people, like I used to be, enjoying a Friday summer evening, took great care to avoid us. They waited in doorways until we passed, or would scurry to the other side of us a good ten feet, avoiding eye contact. A beautiful Harlequin Dane sat with his owners on a tap room patio. The aroma of pizza and freshly poured beer got into my head. Two years ago I sat on this patio, my family, Stevie, Sam and Sean, around me, being a normal person, doing what normal people do, enjoying pizza and beer on a summer evening. Peanuts stopped to sniff at the couple's black and white hound, both wagged tails at each other.

"Nice dog." I said, forgetting for a moment in time I wasn't part of this world anymore. I reached across the patio wall to scratch the hound's ear.

The Dane's owner pulled the huge dog away, dragged his chair to the other side of the table glaring at me with a nasty look.

Alice took my arm and pulled. "Snob Hill," she said. "Keep walking."

The consignment stores, microbreweries and antique shops gradually gave way to tattoo parlors, used car lots and painted over store fronts with *XXX PRIVATE ROOMS* scrawled on the windows.

Cheap motels, once the mainstay of motoring tourist heading west, lay in various states of disrepair. I few were boarded up, but you could see places where boards had been pried loose to allow nightly trespass. We weren't in Kansas anymore. But we were across from the fairgrounds. Everywhere I looked a lost soul, some with shopping carts piled high, others, with nothing but the clothes they wore, sat on the edge of parking pylons, or leaned against the side wall of closed businesses, heads down, already in a state of semi-sleep.

Alice headed for a bus stop shelter; it was enclosed on all four sides by clear Plexiglas with large openings on both ends of the front panel to allow egress from either end. The fake glass was scratched and marked with graffiti depicting exaggerated cartoonish genitalia, and distorted letters of gang tags. We went inside the enclosure. Trash accumulated in back of the hard plastic bench, which, like its surroundings, was marred by deeply carved graffiti.

"Thisit." Alice plopped down on one end of the bench.

"Here, we're staying here?"

"Yeah, buses stopped, soskay." Alice pulled her cart in front of here, got out the lunch sack and sat back, crackers in hand. "I should have eaten before but I wanted to get here before it got too late, otherwise someone else would claim it." Her words were still slurred.

"I know what you mean, I'm hungry too. So's Peanuts." I pulled the last of the kibble Father Rico had given me out of my cloth bag and poured it out for Peanuts. It didn't seem like much. I added one of two packages of cheese and crackers to it.

"I'm supposed to eat regular, but can't. I've got the sugar diabetes. Supposed to take shots too but don't know where they think I can get those." Alice opened the can of Beanie Weenies and spooned out a mouthful.

That explained the bad breath and confusion. Her blood sugar was haywire.

"Isn't there someplace you can go, a clinic or something?" I popped open my own can of beans, the pieces of bacon fat and gummy liquid that floated on top were disgusting, like eating a can of worms.

"Nah got to have insurance. That's how I got in this mess anyway. I was working but they cut my hours and I didn't have a health plan. Then when I got the diabetes I couldn't afford the insulin. I kept blacking out at work, and they lay me off, said I was drunk. Like now, at the shelter, they think I've been tipping it you know, but I just need to eat." Some of the beans and tomato juice dribbled onto her lap.

"Can't someone help you? Isn't there someplace you can go for medical care?" I remembered a friend, a fellow teacher, who was thrown in jail for public intoxication when what he really needed was a sandwich and orange juice. The other prisoners stole his shoes and his self-esteem before he could get anyone to come and bail him out.

"Haven't found it yet. Besides, got to have a real address before they let you sign up. Otherwise, if you live rough, they don't want to claim you. Think it's somebody else's problem." She occupied herself with the applesauce.

Alice pulled a folded quilt from the top of her cart, placing it under her, and wrapped another around her legs, sitting on the ends.

I ate half the can of beans, poured the rest into Peanuts bowl, decided to save the applesauce for tomorrow. I did have some money, could have bought a hamburger, but I was afraid to let Alice in on this. We had just met. A few of the transients I encountered in Santa Fe would have hit you over the head with a large rock to get their hands on five bucks.

The traffic was getting lighter and lighter. Every once in a while somebody would honk and yell an obscenity directed at us or at one of the other homeless that had taken refuge in the area.

"Now what? Do I just lay out my sleeping bag under the bench?" I packed what was left of the food into my bag and started to unhook the bungee cord that held my tarp and sleeping bag to the top of the suitcase.

"Nah, Nah, you can't lay down. You have to stay sitting up or they'll come for you." Alice pushed her hand into the side of her cart and pulled out two long colorful scarves, handed me one.

"Here you tie this around yourself, like this." She worked the scarf through the slats on the bench, trying them high on her abdomen. "This keeps you sitting up, even if you fall asleep."

"Do you have to do that, can't you just lie out?" My feet hurt from so much walking. I wanted to lay back, take my shoes off and put up my feet.

"If you fall over or lie on the ground the police will come. That's how I lost my doggy, Bingo; he was a cute little guy. I fell asleep, next thing I know the police are here and they had me on a stretcher. Took my dog to the shelter, when I tried to get him back they said I needed to pay all sorts of fines, get him licensed, I just..." Alice's chin quivered, she sighed. "I just had to leave him there."

We sat silent a while. "Is it okay if I put Peanuts rug out for him?"

"Yes, I don't think that'll attract them, maybe even protect us from the leeches."

"There are leeches here?" Was she serious?

"They come and steal your stuff while you're asleep. You have to be careful. I lost my sleeping bag that way, stole it right off me while I was asleep." Alice used a webbed belt to fasten the metal cart to her ankle, then folded her hands in front of her and rested her chin on her chest. "Good night."

"Good night Alice, thanks for helping us." I was amazed how fast she fell asleep.

50

I spent the next eight days and nights hanging out with Alice. She walked me all over central Albuquerque, up town, down town, cross town. She took me to the parks where, at last, I could lay out during the day, shoes off, catching a nap; warned me about the leeches, and who they were, how to avoid losing my stuff to them. I pretended to find five bucks, went to a dollar store and got Peanuts some food, and Alice and I a bag of cereal and small carton of past dated milk, which was breakfast and lunch. We visited four different meal sites. Two, both run by churches, had shelters attached to them. I didn't even try to get in, didn't want to be told once again, that an animal shelter could pick up my dog. Alice tried, but like that first night she was turned away. For breakfast, Alice took me to a public parking lot downtown where an elderly nun passed out fried egg sandwiches from an iron grated half door, blessing each one of us as we came to the front of the line. The Egg Lady, they called her.

We were both starting to smell pretty funky. Washing at a sink only helps so much if you can't get your clothes clean. A night at shelter would mean a shower, a bed, a place to wash out a few things. On the ninth night I couldn't stand myself anymore. My skin itched, feet were swollen and hurt. My hair was a mess. I was sun and wind burned and my clothes stank. Like Alice, I had a bad case of halitosis. I had to find a place indoors for the night.

Steer Inn, an old Route 66 motel, was a block away from the bus shelter where we spent our nights. A large cut out of cattle horns extended up from the roof of the office. A lighted sign, the kind on wheels someone has to go out and change the clear plastic letter tiles by hand, was parked in front. A mish mash of different size letters and numbers announced: *Day 23.95+tx Wk 145 & up*

I still had twenty five bucks in my pocket. Maybe I could convince them to accept it. It was about nine-thirty, dark, a quarter moon hung low in the southern sky. I left Alice sitting at the bus shelter, pretended to take Peanuts for a walk. Alice did lift an eyebrow when I pulled my case behind me. If I could get a room I'd come back for her.

The unpainted cement block lobby was dark. A man in his thirties, deep circles under his eyes and bulging blue veins on the back of his hands, sat on a stool in the darkened lobby watching TV. A torn vinyl loveseat, a high counter that served as a desk, and an old style vending machine, the kind you pull a mechanical knob from the bottom to make your selection were all that occupied the dimly lit lobby. A rusted metal display rack stood on one end of the counter, mostly empty, it held four or five pamphlets for the Balloon Museum, Old Town tours and restaurants known for their green chile cheeseburgers. The door was locked. I tapped on the window glass to be buzzed in.

"Can I help you?" The guy quickly put out the cigarette he had been smoking.

"I wanted to see about a room for the night, do you have one?"

"For you?" He looked me over, then Peanuts.

"Yes, me and my dog."

"How long?"

"Just the one night. Tonight. Do you have one?"

"The rate is twenty three ninety five plus tax, the dog is an extra five bucks, altogether it would be thirty two dollars."

I looked outside, it was dark, an old Chevy Corsica, scraped down to bare paint along one side panel, bottomed out on a hole as it pulled into the motel parking area. I could hear the occupants yelling. You'll never know unless you ask, I thought, but I had to ask carefully.

"Do you give discounts?"

He looked me over again. "Maybe."

I kept going. "Would you take twenty bucks, cash, no credit card?"

He wobbled back and forth on his chair. "Thirty. Cash."

I thought again. Twenty five was all I had, but I really, really needed to sleep inside tonight.

"Twenty five?" I was shaking.

"Okay, sure. Got it?"

I reached in my pocket pulled the money out, held it in my hand.

"Do you need me to fill out a registration form or something?"

"No, that's okay." He pulled a green plastic motel key ring with one key out of a drawer under the counter, lay it down in front of me. "Number twenty two."

I lay the money on the counter beside the key, picked it up and went out the door. As the door was closing behind me I grabbed it and went back in. "What time's check out?"

He had relit the cigarette, and let it hang from his lips. His wallet was out, and he was putting the money I had just given him into it. He chuckled a little, smoke coming from his nose and took the cigarette from his mouth, pinching it between his thumb and index finger, flicking the ash on the gray green linoleum floor.

"Check out?" He asked and smirked with a flat lipped smile, amused by my question. "Check out's ten thirty. Just leave the key in the door."

The room was awful, truly, sincerely, awful. The door didn't close properly leaving a gap on three edges that let bugs, light from nearby streetlights, and foul smelling air into the room. The thin red carpet was torn in several places and rubber backed yarn tangled in Peanuts' feet as he walked over it. The toilet was low, small, hadn't been cleaned and was slow to flush. There was no tub. Instead a metal shower stall with peeling green paint and a too short shower curtain occupied one corner of the bathroom. Smooth white bath towels, no bigger than dishtowels, hung on a metal rack under the single window which was broken and held together by foot long lengths of duct tape. Did I mention the smell? Dampness, mold, decay. For the next twelve hours it would be home. I took off my shoes and socks and plopped down on the bed, which was propped up on one corner by a block of wood. Peanuts jumped up beside me and we both fell asleep.

I could hear sirens very close by. It felt like a dream. I had a hard time shaking it off. Peanuts was on the floor, a couple of soft low barks, nosing my hand. I opened my eyes, remembered where I was. Alice! I forgot to go back for Alice. I jumped up, grabbed the key from the fake wood dresser nailed to one wall, and ran outside still barefoot, pulling the door closed behind me. Peanuts was scratching at it, whining.

"I'll be right back Peanuts, sit, stay. I'll be back." I'm not sure he found my words comforting. I ran to Central Avenue. Two police cars and an Albuquerque Fire Department ambulance were parked in front of the bus shelter. Oh Christ, they were loading Alice onto a stretcher. She must have forgotten to tie herself upright.

"Sorry, Sorry, Sorry Alice, I'm so sorry." But no one was around to hear me. I took a few steps backwards, leaned against the side wall of the Steer Inn, tried to blend into the darkness, and watched as they loaded her into the ambulance, and kept watch as they pulled away. I was still watching when two men crept out of their hiding place and proceeded to go through her things, taking what they wanted and leaving the rest lying on the ground in back of the bus shelter with the rest of the trash.

"I am so, so, sorry." I walked back slowly to the room. Peanuts sat up, ears erect, in the middle of the bed. I sat on the edge, reached over and rubbed his back.

"I blew it Peanuts, I lost the only friend you and I had in this city. Sorry to you too."

I sat like that maybe twenty minutes. An odd chemical smell came wafting through the openings around the door giving me an almost immediate headache, making my eyes itch and burn. I took a shower. At least the water was hot. The sliver of soap was barely enough to get me clean. I used the little that was left to wash out socks, underwear and two t-shirts. If they weren't dry by morning I would pack them up in the trash bag which I had removed from the small bathroom wastebasket before anything had been thrown into it, a trick Alice showed me.

It was past midnight. I turned on the TV, flipped through the channels, lie back down on the bed and fall asleep again.

¤ ¤ ¤

It was June 20th. I would need to make it another two weeks before I got a check again. Then, the five hundred and twenty five dollars would buy me three weeks at the Steer Inn. That would see me through most of July. Right now I was broke. I fed Peanuts, filled both of my liter plastic soda bottles with tap water, brushed my teeth and headed out, wheeled case in tow.

"Where to now, buddy? I think we're too late for the egg lady. Let's head towards downtown. Maybe someone knows something about Alice. At least it's mostly downhill." Truth be told I was glad to have Peanuts; it's hard to spend your day without saying anything. With him by my side I at least had someone to talk to and keep my going one more day and night. But I wondered how long I could stretch that bag of dog food. I had used up the last of all my money on that one night at the motel. I patted him on the head. "You're a good dog Peanuts, you're a good dog." He wagged his tail, licked my hand and stayed by my side.

It was going to be a hot day. When we passed the bank sign on Menaul, it was eleven fifteen and already eighty nine degrees. We would need to find a place to sit out the day in the shade. I tried to remember one of the parks near downtown. If I kept walking, we'd be there by around 1:30, too late for a lunch from the nearby shelter and too early for dinner. I turned south on University. One of the shelters Alice had introduced me too was in an old gas station converted first into an evangelical church, then again into a Welcome Center for the needy. According to Alice, this was the place with the most relaxed rules. Maybe I could get in with Peanuts for a noon meal. We made it just as the doors were opening.

A tall black woman, a blue cotton scarf tied around her head stood holding the door open and greeted me as I approached.

"Welcome sister, come, you can sit on the side. We have tables there for the overflow." With an exaggerated wave of her arm she ushered me and Peanuts to a small outdoor area on one side of the old garage where a five foot high yellow mesh fence cordoned off a section set up with four square metal picnic tables, benches attached. A large and very smelly trash can sat in the middle.

"I'm Sister Frankie. Welcome to our church." She had a slight British accent.

"Thank you. I'm Aileen and this is Peanuts." I pulled Peanuts close in. He wanted desperately to sniff at that trash can. It was hot, no shade, but not unbearably so. "Can I still get lunch?"

"Of course, we barely started to serve. Sit, please, I'll bring you something." She tapped the top of a metal table near a side door. I sat down parking my suitcase beside me and pulling Peanuts under the table so he would have a little shade. It's kind of tough being a black dog in the summer sun. We had been sitting for less than five minutes, when a two men and a woman came and sat at the next table, one of them had a dog on a leash, who also plopped down under that table. They had heavy packs, which they helped each other out of and propped up along the fence. I nodded at them. They seemed familiar, but I wasn't really sure how I knew them.

"Nice dog." I told them. "It's nice to have a place to come where they let dogs in."

"Yeah, Frankie and Mike are the only ones in town who have a place like this. Everyone else just turns people with dogs away." One of the men said.

"Who's Mike?"

"Mike is Frankie's brother, they run this place. I think they're from Rwanda or Kenya, someplace like that. Came to start up a church or a church brought them here or something. Don't really understand it all. But, well, they're here and so are we." The woman replied then got a t-shirt from her pack and went inside with it to change from the heavy sweatshirt she was wearing. One of the men got up and went in the side door.

The third man spoke to me from his seat at the next table. "Hey, ain't you Alice's friend?"

"Yes, Alice was showing me around." I didn't know if I should tell him about last night. "She got sick and the ambulance came for her."

"Yeah we heard. Guess they were trying to get her into a program, like a residential program."

"Really? She didn't mention it."

"Well it's for alcoholics. I'm not sure she wanted to go."

"Alice didn't drink when I was with her." This was true.

"Not in front of you anyway."

"No, really, she said she was diabetic. Don't they have programs for that?"

He laughed. "That's a good one. No, I think she got a bed in a treatment center. Probably be there three or four months." The man licked the side of a rolling paper, twirled it into a cylinder around tobacco, sealing the edges.

"How do you know this stuff?"

"Word gets around." He pushed the now rolled cigarette behind his ear and stuffed the bag of tobacco into his pants pocket when Sister Frankie came back outside carrying a paper plate and Styrofoam cup of orange punch. She was followed by the other homeless man who had come in with his friends, carrying two plates, a cup, and holding the rim of a second cup of orange punch carefully between his teeth.

"Here you are. Enjoy your meal." Sister Frankie placed the paper plate in front of me. A florescent pink hot dog on a bun, large spoonful of boxed macaroni and cheese and thin slice of watermelon was on the menu today. The homeless woman had changed into the tank top. She came outside with her own plate of food and sat down.

I touched the edge of the plate, spinning it so I could see the food. "Thank you. This looks great." Some of it looked great. It had been years since I'd eaten a bright pink hotdog, I think it was at one of the boys' little league games. Sister Frankie sat down beside me.

"We must pray and give thanks for our meal together." I looked at the trio at the next table; they nodded at me, folded their hands, and bowed their heads.

"Lord, we thank you for the nourishment You have given us, and for the beautiful day that You have made and for each other that we may help each other as we travel our journey in service to You. In Jesus name, Amen." Sister Frankie opened her eyes, smiled brightly and stood up. "Enjoy. Enjoy."

Amen and thank you Lord for Sister Frankie.

51

I didn't know what else to do so I hung with the crew from Sister Frankie's Welcome Center. We walked to a park off of Twelfth Street, not far from I-40. Maybe a dozen other homeless were already there. Smoking or sleeping on their sides with their packs curled under their head, some shared a bottle of cheap vodka. A few were shooting up. I walked to the other side of the park, wanted to avoid the spent needles that were barely visible in the grass and the drunks who could barely stand up. I parked my wheeled case beside me, unfurled Peanuts' rug for him, lay down and closed my eyes. Next thing I know Peanuts has jumped up and is snarling, pulling my wrist with the leash. One of the guys I met at the Welcome Center is running away, dragging my suitcase behind him. Christ!

"Stop." I jump up and run after him, or more like Peanuts is pulling me after him. The man is half way across the park. If he crosses the street with my stuff I'll never see it again. Peanuts is still barking, snarling and pulling me with the leash. A tree branch trips me and Peanuts breaks free. The large Shepard is almost on the guy and he lets go of the suitcase. Peanuts continues to chase him into the street. Car brakes squeal. I close my eyes fearing the worse.

Horns honk, I hear yelling. Peanuts is okay, but dodging cars in the middle of the road. I can see the suitcase thief on the other side of the street, walking rapidly away. I hurry over to the curb, two cars stop for me while I jog to the middle of the road and grab the end of Peanuts leash and walk him back to the curb where the suitcase is sideways in the gutter. I tilt it back up, and we walk to a nearby bench where I put my arms around Peanuts, burying my face in his fur.

"Peanuts don't run again buddy, I need you. You're a good dog buddy." I cry, cling to him and rub his chest and side.

After that we kept to ourselves. Stayed solo as Campbell called it. I'd sleep on cardboard spread out on the sidewalk beside help centers or near churches. Sometimes we'd find a soft grassy spot in a park, but we were always dodging police and security patrols. On more than one occasions I was told to move on. I always saved half of whatever I got to eat for Peanuts. I still had part of a bag of dog food and I'd mix the egg sandwiches or half hot dog in with it and sit on the ground beside him while he ate. I was grateful for the big dog, a reminder of better days before and yet to come.

When my July check finally came in I made my way back to the Steer Inn. I milled around outside, waiting for the same night clerk and paid cash for three weeks in a dirty cramped room that smelled of bad sewer pipes, always the same room. As long as I could still feed Peanuts, it was okay. I'd buy a big bag of food and tie it to my suitcase. He stayed by me, giving deep sighs when we'd pack up and move on. But he always wagged his tail when I set the plastic food bowl down, wondering what new delight I had mixed in with his supper. Same for August, it meant I only had to sleep outside for nine or ten days each month. Still, those nights were hard. I'd lie on the sidewalk outside shelters, prop up at bus stops, spread cardboard under bushes near highway exits, anywhere I could find where I wouldn't get hassled. But, I had to be vigilante, least the leaches, as Alice had called them, stole the little I had.

September came. The nights were getting cooler, dipping into the forties. I knew I needed to try and figure something out. We'd never make it through the winter. September 5th I did my usual and paid cash for three weeks at the Steer Inn, same smelly room. If I hurried I could make it to the dollar store and back before it closed. I left my suitcase parked right inside the door and unleashed Peanuts. He immediately jumped up on the bed and stretched out, head on pillow.

"Take a nap buddy. I'll be right back with dinner."

I left Peanuts inside, headed to the Dollar Store for a bag of dog food and peanut butter cheese cracker packs. The ten dollars I had left would barely be enough to keep Peanuts fed. I'd still have to beg at soup kitchens and help centers for my own meals. I made my way back up Central to the Steer Inn, struggling with a thirty pound bag of cheap dog food balanced on my hip. I had gotten so used to the sounds of living on the streets the sound of police sirens barely registered. When I saw at least five police cars, a crime scene van and three news crews crowded in the parking lot of the Steer Inn I panicked, raced towards them, dropping the bag of food.

Two uniformed officers were stringing yellow police tape around the entire perimeter of the motel. Motel residents, bedraggled, worn and weary, some without shirt or shoes holding toddlers in diapers, stood near the street. A couple of community service officers were corralling them. I ran up, trying to lift the police tape and make a dash for my room. Two uniformed officers jogged towards me holding me back.

"Can't cross the line. You need to stay back." One took my arm and escorted me back under the tape.

"Please my dog, my dog's in my room. I need to get him." I said, pleading with them. One officer spied the bag of dog food I had dropped on the pavement.

"Hey Sergio, this lady said her dog's in her room, want to check on it?" He said to another officer standing near the crime lab van. I watched as he unclipped the radio from his belt and spoke into it.

"Please, I just need to get him. He's a big dog, he might bite someone."

"We're taking care of it. Calm down." The officer tried to appease me.

A man wearing white paper coveralls and a face mask came out of the room two doors away from mine and walked towards my room, using a pass key to unlock the door.

"Please, he won't let anyone but me get him." I again tried to get under the police tape but the officer grabbed my elbow and pulled me back. I could hear Peanuts barking and snarling as the guy in the white coveralls slammed the door shut. The officer near the van waved me over.

"You got sixty seconds to get him."

I ran for the door, grabbed the leash and my wheeled case and pulled Peanuts from the room, running back towards the office. "Thanks."

I never found out who called in the meth lab. So that's what smelled and made my eyes burn. Red Cross workers came offering vouchers and a list of motels that would accept them. Two nights was all I got. In total, kids and babies too, there were fourteen of us left without a roof over our heads.

"When do you think we can move back in?" I ask the Red Cross volunteer as I take a seat in the folding chair set up inside the RV. The interior is outfitted like an office. File boxes line the sides, held in place by a long thin metal bar that hooked on one end.

"No, that's not going to happen. It's my understanding the place is condemned and will be torn down after the evidence is collected. Seems it was already condemned. We're not sure why it was still open." She folds her hands on the desk in front of her; glances down at Peanuts then back up at me.

"But I paid for three weeks. Can't I get that back?" I ask. That was all the money I had, what I didn't pay towards the room I used for Peanuts' bag of food.

"Do you have a receipt?" She adds my name to a list on a clip board.

I shake my head slowly. I never got a receipt, it was always cash. Never signed anything, the night clerk never even asked my name. I thought back on my first night here when I innocently asked about check out time and he laughed at me. "No, no receipt." I say in a hoarse whisper, clearing my throat of the dust and choking smell of chemicals that lingered in the area.

"We're still trying to find the guest register maybe that will help." She lay the pen down and looked across the desk at me.

"I don't think you'll find one. I don't remember anyone writing anything down." I slide back on the folding metal chair. What would the people with little children do? Where would we all go?

"A canceled check or credit card statement maybe?" She is sincerely trying to help.

I gaze out the window of the remodeled RV, it was past midnight. There were still three police cars and a hazmat truck parked nearby. At least I had Peanuts with me, and his bag of dog food.

"No, never a check or credit card. Cash only. Cash and you got a key, no registration forms or receipts." I sigh loudly enough that Peanuts, curled at my feet, lifts his head and looks up at me, impressed.

"Sorry, really I am, but a voucher for two nights is all we can do. Check back with us in a week or so. Maybe we'll know more." She tears out the middle yellow copy from a half page carbon-less copy form, adds it to a thin stack beside her on the desk.

"Here's the list of motels that accept our vouchers. Present the voucher, they'll fill it out, you sign it, they'll keep the original and pink copy, and you keep the green one as your receipt." She stapled the forms to a list of motels with address and phone numbers listed.

"Do you know if any of them accept pets?" I hold the papers in my hand scanning the addresses.

She took the form back from me and circled two, *This Side of Heaven Motel* and *Rest Inn*. "I'm not too sure about *Rest Inn* anymore I think the policy may have changed," she said.

52

*P*eanuts and I spent the rest of that night on the bus stop bench down the block from the Steer Inn. The same place Alice and I used to tie ourselves upright so we wouldn't fall on the ground if we went to sleep. It was a cold night. The summer had been so warm, I had forgotten how much the temperature dropped at night and how the cold hurt and made my joints ache. I could barely stand up. I could have used an aspirin or four. Winter wasn't even close yet. I pushed the thought from my mind.

I took me four hours to walk from the bus bench where we'd spent the night to the *This Side of Heaven* motel. Of course we stopped often. A city pocket park tucked into a neighborhood off of San Mateo was a welcome relief from the heat. As cold as the nights had been, days still climbed into the eighties. Peanuts and I lay on the grass, letting the damp ground surround us and dozed for a half hour or so. When Peanuts stood up suddenly I knew, once again, something was up. A police cruiser had parked near the curb about twenty yards away and a uniformed officer was getting out of the car. Deja vu all over again. I grabbed my suitcase and Peanuts leash and hustled myself out of there before she even had her hat on.

I turned on Gibson by the military base, heading east. This was one of three areas around town where small cheap motels were dispersed between used furniture stores and fast food spots. The *This Side of Heaven* motel should be in the next block.

"Come on Peanuts, we'll be there soon." He was walking slower, hanging his head down. The heat was getting to both of us, but I didn't want to rest again until we were checked in. I could spy the pale blue sign with fluffy white letters meant to resemble clouds less than half a block away. A NO VACANCY sign in red neon was turned on under it. "No way," I said aloud. "No way." But it was true. We went in anyway and asked. There was no room in *Heaven* for our weary feet or souls.

The *Rest Inn* was right beside the Interstate. A convenience store and gas station occupied the space diagonal to it. Beside that was Burger King. The constant drone of cars along the Interstate was calming, like white noise, it canceled everything else out. Peanuts and I went in the office and stood at the counter. A Hispanic man, only a few years younger than I, stood behind the desk. His hair was that great shade of salt and pepper that marks the beginning of middle age. He wore a red polo shirt that was stretched tight across his huge chest and arms; a two inch slash up the underarm seam of the shirt was the only thing that allowed him to even put it on. Must be a body builder or something. A *Rest Inn* ID tag hung from a lanyard around his neck. *CJ CHAVEZ NIGHT MANAGER*

"May I help you?" he asked as we came in the door.

"Hi." I pulled Peanuts behind me and reached in my pocket for the crumbled up voucher, setting it on the counter in front of him. "I wanted to see about a room for two nights."

He smoothed out the paper and inspected it. "We do accept Red Cross vouchers but don't accept pets. Sorry." He pushed it back across the counter towards me.

What was I to do? I blinked a few times. Beg, I thought, get down on your hands and knees and beg.

"Please. I know they told me you might have changed your policy, but I just lost my other room and I need a place to stay." I flipped the voucher over to reveal the list of motels, and pointed to the circled ones. "There's only you and *This Side of Heaven* and *Heaven* didn't have a vacancy. Please." I folded my hands in front of me like a beggar.

He made a sound halfway between a cough and a laugh, thought I was trying to be funny, but he turned serious again right away. I could see his bulky arms and shoulders tense up as he looked again at the voucher. He turned to his computer, using the mouse to scroll down the screen.

"I do have one nightly rental room, ground floor, two nights only. We don't accept pets anymore, but I'll make an exception owing to the voucher, but just for these two nights." He pulled out a registration card and placed a pen on top of it.

Finally, for two nights we'd be in from the cold, and Peanuts anyway would have something to eat. I wonder what dog food tastes like? I filled out the form and signed the voucher, passed it back over to him.

"Are you the day manager too?" I said, trying to make conversation.

"Night, day, whenever they need me." He tore the green copy of the voucher, my receipt for the stay, set it on the counter and placed a key on top of it. "Welcome to the *Rest Inn*, Ms. Roark."

The room was a lot nicer than the Steer Inn. For one thing it was clean. The door closed tight against the world, had a good lock on it, a small kitchenette with a microwave and some cooking pans and plates took six feet of space along one wall. If only I had something to cook. I feed Peanuts. He almost immediately got up on the bed and went to sleep. I took advantage of a real bath tub, not a shower and soaked off weeks and weeks of street grime. I was hungry, but those cheese and peanut butter crackers and some hot water would have to do. I couldn't think of anything else tonight, pushed Peanuts away from the center of the bed, crawled in and slept like a colicky baby. I only left the room to walk Peanuts around the perimeter of the motel a couple of times. He was just as happy to stay inside too. He was getting old. At almost nine in calendar years, he would have qualified for Social Security in dog years. Our two nights at the Rest Inn were over. I didn't want to go. I thought about not leaving, just squatting here until I got dragged away, but I knew Peanuts would be taken to who knows where, and he had already been through enough, I couldn't do that to him. I rolled my sleeping bag around some just washed cloths, and used the bungee cord to attach the whole thing to the top of the suitcase; I wanted the space inside the suitcase for that large bag of food I bought Peanuts. It was too big to fit. I poured some out into the plastic trash bag I had taken from the bathroom wastebasket and added it to my JC Penny tote bag, then stuffed the large bag of kibble and Peanuts rug inside the suitcase. Peanuts took a special interest in the packing of the dog food. He was such a good guy, ears alert, tail wagging as he sat beside me.

"Okay Buddy, time to go again." I attached the leash to his collar and we walked out the door and to the office. The same man who was there when we checked in was on duty again. CJ Chavez came around the counter and opened the door for us.

"Thanks, that's very kind of you." I went inside followed by Peanuts. "I guess I'm checking out." I set the key back on the counter "What's the CJ stand for?"

"I beg your pardon?" He raised his eyebrows at me, my question annoyed him.

"On your badge, what's the CJ stand for? Colossal Jabs?" I made a little left -right boxing motion with my fists.

He ignored me, more annoyed. "I hope your stay was satisfactory." He picked up the key and walked back around the counter, entering the room number into the computer. "That's it, you don't need anything else."

"Sorry, didn't know it was a sensitive topic. I was just trying to be friendly"

"It's not a sensitive topic; it's just none of your business. I don't get paid to make friends with people." I sure set him off.

"Sorry, didn't mean to offend you." I thought about it a minute, this guy had let Peanuts stay. I couldn't walk away like this. I turned back around and started to open the door. "Look, thanks for letting my dog stay. I don't know where we would have gone otherwise."

"Probably where ever you're headed now." He said as he stood back up again.

"What?" I spun around. I don't know if he meant it sarcastic or not, but it sure sounded like it. "Why do you say that?"

"No reason, have a nice day." He sat back down, pretended to be busy on the computer.

I stood at the door, glancing outside, not really wanting to leave or knowing where to go.

"Is there something else I could help you with Ms. Roark? Otherwise I have things to do."

53

I wandered around Albuquerque like all the other untouchables with no place to go. I did have a little money, two dollars to be exact. I was saving it for my absolute last resort. When I needed to buy more food for Peanuts at least I could get him a couple cans. We made the rounds of the soup kitchens and welcome centers. If I was lucky I managed two meals a day, usually breakfast and lunch, never dinner. I fed Peanuts in the evening, he seemed to settle down more and sleep afterward. We slept on benches, in alleys, under low slung juniper or cypress trees at the entrance to business parks. I watched to make sure who was around, and used the bungee cord to secure the suitcase to my wrist before I stretched out. Most of the time I didn't lie down, I sat up with my back to whatever I could find, a brick wall, a tree trunk or a sign post. It was difficult sleeping this way. I appreciated Alice's advice about tying yourself upright. A couple of times I fell over, hitting my head, raising a large bump. If I had done that at home, I would immediately have found an ice pack and called the nurse help line but who did I call here? The longer I stayed on the street the worse I looked. Dirty, unkempt. If I had a chance to rinse things out someplace I did. I had other clothes, but at this point everything was filthy.

It was about September 20th. I say about because I had lost track of the days. If I could get a meal at the soup kitchens it was a weekday. If they were closed up tight, it was Sunday. If I could get a lunch but not breakfast, it was Saturday. A couple of the Hospitality Centers passed out packs of juice, applesauce and crackers on Friday night to help you tide over until Monday. At least I still had food for Peanuts, I'd tell myself every night as I watched him eat, petted his side, and curled my feet under him to keep them warm.

One day, I think it was a Tuesday; I made my way through the downtown area, looking for a meal at the Methodist Church. A kid, no more than eighteen was leaning against the wall off an alley, barely able to stand up. He was staggering from side to side. He was so young.

"Son, are you okay. Do you need some help?" I stood a few feet away from him as he staggered again into the wall.

"Talk to me son." I put my hand on his shoulder. For a brief moment in time he looked at me, terror filled his eyes. Then they rolled back in his head and he fell to the ground, convulsing. I ran to the nearest business and opened the door. "Call 911, someone's unconscious in the alley. He needs help." No one moved, they all stared at me. I heard a voice to the side of me

"Some transients, probably drunk or on something."

I screamed at them. "He's just kid, call 911," I said and ran back to the alley. Another woman, also a street dweller was on the ground beside the kid, doing chest compressions. What astonished me was the ease with which she did them, like she had done it before.

"Wake up!" She screamed at the boy as she used two hands to push on his breastbone

"Wake up, the police are coming." She may have been his mother. I knelt down beside her, Peanuts in back of us, nervously pacing, and we took turns pushing firmly on the boy's chest.

A small crowd gathered at the end of the alley. Did they not know we could hear them?

"Just some hobos."

"Some tramp's kid passed out drunk in the alley"

"Shame they spend all their money on drugs and booze, no wonder their homeless."

It took forever for the ambulance to arrive. It backed into the alley and two paramedics got out, one took over the chest compressions while the other pulled a small vial from a nylon medical bag, and measured out a dose, injecting it into the kid. No response. Then he hurried back to the ambulance for a defibrillator. No response. They put a bag on his mouth, asked the mom to pump the bag while one kept up the chest compressions. When a police officer arrived, they loaded him into the ambulance. His mom jumped in beside him.

I stood up, pulled Peanuts close to me and approached the officer. "I think they left their things over there." I pointed to a duffel bag and rolled up tarp stashed in a corner.

The cop looked where I was pointing and nodded. "We'll take care of it. You can move along."

I walked through the crowd of onlookers. Some made crude remarks. One held his nose waving his hand in front of it.

"Couple a real dogs there," he said as Peanuts and I walked by.

"One of 'em needs a bath, and it ain't the one with four legs." another said. This made the crowd roar with laughter.

How dare they! How dare they judge me or any of us. Wasn't I the one who tried to help? Hadn't they witnessed a mother desperately trying to save her son? And all they could do was make crude jokes. I turned around and flipped them off. Back in the alley I could see the cop lifting the rolled tarp and duffel bag into a dumpster.

It turned cold, rainy. Peanuts and I took shelter in a parking garage. That lasted a couple of hours. Security kicked us out. I pulled my bag, wet, behind me, used the tarp as a raincoat. I finally settled in a corner between a parking barrier and the side of a building and used the handle of the suitcase to hold the tarp over us like a tent. An old cardboard box, opened flat under us, Peanuts and I settled in for a very cold, rainy night. The good part is no one harassed me. The bad part is it was probably because no one else wanted to be out in this weather either. By morning everything was wet. My sleeping bag, Peanut's rug, and the suitcase were soaked through. I was glad I had put his food in plastic trash bag or that would have been wet too. I shook off as much water as possible and spread everything out, hoping it would be dry enough to lug around after I visited the Egg Lady for a fried egg sandwich and coffee.

Peanuts and I stood in line with the rest, all of whom looked as cold, wet and miserable as I did. The line was moving slowly. I hoped they wouldn't run out before I got up front. I needed that hot coffee to warm me. A commotion started in back of me, lots of yelling and confusion.

"They're dumping our stuff. The damn city is dumping our stuff." An old guy in a plaid wool jacket, bearded and gray is hoping around, waving his hands in the air. "Better run for your packs and gear or they'll be gone."

More than half the line took off running in all directions. I stayed in line with less than a dozen others confused by what was happening.

"What's going on?" I called towards the bedraggled messenger." Who's doing what now?"

"The damn city trash trucks, they're going up and down the streets loading all the packs they find into the trash truck and crushing 'em." His lower jaw jutted outward; if he ever had dentures they were gone now.

"My bag, the dog food, how can they?" Why were they doing this to us?

"Better hustle, they's already cleared two streets." His eyes were wild with rage.

Peanuts and I ran the two blocks towards the parking barrier where I had spread my things to dry. Too late, the trash truck was half a block up the street. I could see my blue tarp and Peanuts' rug on top of the load as the bucket tilted up, ready to be crushed.

"Stop." I ran, yelled after the truck, "Stop, wait, my things, please?" I ran as fast as we could go.   The workman hanging on the side of the truck laughed. The truck clanked, revved its motor and made a jerky start, continuing up the block.

A biblical verse came to mind, something like to those who have much is given, those who have not everything is taken. All I had was taken. It was gone, everything, gone. No sleeping bag, or tarp or dog food or change of shoes or clothes. The only things I had left in this world were the few things I carried in my JC Penny shopping bag: a plastic dish for Peanuts food and water, my black and white composition notebook and the plastic sleeve protector that held my ID and useless credit cards. Why I saved them I don't know. The only card I needed, the debt card tied to Sam' retirement account, I kept in my back pocket. I stood in the street a long time, watching as the truck turned the corner, and witnessed the same scene as I had just played in two more times, before the truck turned again. Gone, all gone.

We, Peanuts and I and ten or so other homeless, made our way slowly back to the Egg Lady, most of us in a state of shock. As little as we had, we desperately needed it to survive. There was some low mumbling, a few angry tirades, but mostly just silence. We stood in line, dragging our feet, had lost all we owned, couldn't afford to lose a meal too.

The Egg Lady was especially compassionate. A lot of "God bless you" s could be heard. When I got to the front of the line she passed me an egg sandwich and coffee, and reached in back of her, took two dog bones from a coffee can and pushed them out the metal slot towards me. "I will pray for you, God bless you." She touched her hand to my cheek.

It rained on and off all day. I went from overhang to overhang, hopelessly wandering, wanting to find a place to stay dry. At noon we made our way to the Methodist Church for the noon meal. Usually I tied Peanuts to a post, ran in, got my Styrofoam box and ran out again, but today I lingered under the front entrance with Peanuts, trying to stay out of the rain. When the line slackened I hoped to take him in with me just long enough to pick up the food and make haste out. I stood at the door, glancing in every time the door opened to check on the line.

A young church volunteer walked towards the front and held the door open.

"You can come in." She smiled at me.

"I...I've got the dog." I held up the leash so she could see Peanuts curled up in back of me as I leaned against the wall.

"It's okay today. Come in the foyer. I'll bring you something. We can't leave you in the rain like that." She held the door wider then pulled a sweater tight around here from the cold outside.

Peanuts and I stood inside the tiny foyer. Religious pamphlets were carefully fanned out on the entry way table. A small wooden box with a padlocked lid was nailed to the wall. A sign taped to the side: *Please help make sure no one goes hungry*, with a clip art drawing of a soup kettle and loaf of bread underneath it. A senior volunteer, barely able to unbend his back, dragged a metal folding chair out to the foyer, placing it beside the ancient metal radiator, which was on and warm.

"Rest a spell; somebody will bring you a plate." He patted the back of the chair. "Were you one of the ones who lost their gear this morning?" He tilted his head sideways so he was able to look up at me.

"Yes." I sat down on the chair, pulling it even closer to the warmth of the radiator. "Yes they took my bag and tarp and things. I spread them out to dry from last night's ran, and I saw the truck crushing them."

"Sorry for your troubles." Peanuts wagged his tail at the old gentleman while the guy scratched the dog's ears. "There's a fella from the legal aid coming over at one o'clock. Those that lost their gear can stay and hear what he has to say."

The young woman came back carrying a red plastic bowl of chile beans with a tortilla folded on top, in her other had was a large Styrofoam cup of hot chocolate.

"Is Les filling you in on what's happening?" She asked as she handed me the bowl.

"Yes, I did lose my stuff. I would like to stay and talk to the legal aid person. Do you think it's okay if I stay here with my dog?" I sipped the hot chocolate, held it to my face and let the steam of it warm me.

"I think it' s okay today, as long as you don't bring him into the food service area I think we'll be okay."

I set the hot chocolate down on the floor, balanced the bowl on my knee and tore the tortilla in half, giving it to Peanuts. "Mostly what I lost was Peanuts food; I had a big bag of it in my suitcase. Do you know of any place that helps with that?"

The two volunteers looked at each other. "Nobody to our knowledge helps with that sort of thing." The young woman spoke first.

"There's the Animal Shelter." Les said. I knew he was just trying to be helpful, but I didn't want to hear it. "You could take him to the shelter? I know someone who will pick him up for you if you want to do that?"

"No." I shook my head and gave Peanuts the other half of the tortilla. He lay down and held it between his paws as he ate it. "No, I've had this dog a long time. I want to try to keep him if I can find a way to feed him."

"Well, maybe this fella who's coming can help you out." He put his hands behind his back and returned to the dining room area.

I sat by the heater in the foyer eating my beans. When there was no more than a couple of spoonful's left in the bottom of the bowl I put it on the ground and let Peanuts have the rest. I wasn't sure he would eat them but he stayed working at the bowl, licking every bit until it was gone. I spied a half-eaten bowl in the trash, sneaked over and grabbed that for him. He ate it too. It was going to be hard to keep such a big dog fed. At one o'clock, on the dot, a thirty-ish man wearing a field coat, rain dripping from the sleeves, came in the door. The woman who had welcomed me in rushed over to greet him.

"Thank you so much for coming David." She shook his hand and guided him into the dining room area. The meal service had already been halted. Volunteers were wiping down the tables and putting up the metal folding chairs. About twenty of us stayed. I pulled my chair away from the radiator so I could hear.

"Greetings," the young lawyer said, trying to get everyone's attention. "I'm here today to speak to those of you who had your things taken by the City of Albuquerque."

Loud, angry comments could be heard around the room.

"They got no right to do that," one transient said.

"What do they want for us to freeze to death? Is that how they want to get rid of us?" A woman in the company of a man in a wheelchair climbed on a chair, you could hear the desperation in her voice.

The young female volunteer stood to the side of the lawyer. "Okay everybody, let's calm down and hear what David has to say. He's not the one who took your things; he's the one here to help you." Everyone sat back down and was quiet. "Dave, you have the floor"

"Apparently the downtown merchants petitioned the City of Albuquerque for help regarding the number of homeless people in the downtown area." David's voice filled the room.

"Where do they expect us to go? Snob Hill or something?" An angry voice yelled from the back, those around him shushed him.

Dave continued his presentation. "The merchants feel your presence is interfering with business, keeping people from coming to the downtown area."

"Why now? With winter coming? We lost our sleeping bags and coats. How do they expect us to stay warm?" Someone said.

"Why now? Well, to my understanding two reasons. One, the Balloon Fiesta is coming up soon and they want to make the city more tourist friendly."

"Sounds like Santa Fe." I said to no one in particular. A few in the back of the room heard me and turned to look.

"Two, apparently there have been some drug overdose deaths in the area lately, one a teenage boy, and it has brought some negative publicity to downtown Albuquerque." Dave took off his glasses, which had steamed up due to the temperature change. Outside, the rain started back up again with a fury.

Oh God, oh God, that kid I found. He died? He was so young. His mother was right beside him, pounding on his chest, how could that happen? I closed my eyes tight, buzzing and ringing in my ears, it felt like my brain would explode. I was going to pass out. I bent forward put my head on my knees. Peanuts sat up and licked my face. The elderly volunteer, Les, walked over and put his hand on my back.

"You all right?" he asked, nervous concern surrounding him. "Let me get you a drink of water." He found a paper cup and filled it from the water fountain.

I sat up, sipped the water. "Thanks," I said, but I don't think he heard my whisper. "Thank you," I said again, clearing my throat.

Les nodded at me, pulled another chair around and sat beside me, petting Peanuts under his chest. I didn't hear much else that was said. At the end a paper was sent around. If you lost something to the trash truck you were to sign the paper and give a description of what was lost, there was a space for an address and phone number. What nonsense. If we had addresses we wouldn't be here. I took the lead of others who had signed. General Delivery, I wrote.

The blankets were all gone before I got to the front of the line. There were six of us, still waiting, hoping, for a blanket or sleeping bag. The ones scrounged from the backs of volunteer trunks and storage closets at the church were not enough to go around. Instead we got a plastic trash bag.

"If you cut a hole in the bottom you can wear it like a rain coat," the kind hearted Les said. "I'm gonna call around and see if we can get some more donated, maybe by next Monday or Tuesday."

"Oh." As in oh I forgot it was Friday and there was no meal service tomorrow and I will have to spend a cold rainy weekend with no sleeping bag, rug for Peanuts, tarp or dog food. "Thanks anyway," was what I said aloud.

It was still raining when Peanuts and I left the church. Most of the others were already making their way to shelters and favorite camps. I had none. But I knew I couldn't stay downtown. Between the merchants and the police there was no safe haven to be found here. I made my way to a city park where a Ramada covered some picnic tables. There were already four people hanging out there. Peanuts and I dashed through the rain, making it under cover just before the rain turned to hail. Lightning and thunder struck nearby making Peanuts jump and bark.

"Do you think we're safe under here?" I said to the group sitting at the middle table. One had his head down on the table, trying to sleep. A woman sat beside him, rubbing cheap lotion into her hands. The man across from them leaned with his back to the table watching the hail bounce off the sidewalk nearby.

"Safe as we are any place else in this god-forsaken town." He pulled a blue foil pouch of tobacco from his pocket and started to roll a cigarette. Uh-o. Last time this happened I wound up on my hands and knees picking up someone else's cigarette butts.

There was a small play enclosure with a single covered bench to one side. I decided to make a dash for that. "Think I'll head for that bench, don't want my dog to bother you good folk," I said to them, dragging Peanuts behind me as we dodged the hail. Without my suitcase or tarp to carry it was easy to manage him. I took the trash bag Les had given me and stretched it across one side of the bench, sat on the ground behind the bench and bag and pulled Peanuts beside me.

"Hope this holds up buddy," I said to Peanuts as hail bounced off the dark green plastic.

It stopped raining about six that evening. I pulled off the trash bag, shaking off as much of the water as I could and found a Dollar Store. I left Peanuts tied to the post outside, went in and bought two cans of dog food, all I could afford with the two dollars I had left. I could have gotten three, but the less expensive ones required a can opener, which I did not have, so I had to settle for the seventy-eight cent ones with the pop top. Peanuts was excited when I got out, whining a little. He had come to associate my trips to the dollar store with food. I went around back, where a three sided cement block wall enclosed the shipping and receiving area, found a cardboard box to flatten out and sit on and fed the dog a can of food.

I knew it would be a cold night. I gathered up half a dozen copies of the free weekly shopper papers, stuffed them in my cloth bag along with the dog food and bowl and turned west on Mountain Avenue until we came to a park, directly across from the Natural History Museum. I used to visit here with my sons. The Dinosaur Museum, they called it.

There was minimal cover here. I let Peanuts off leash so he could run a bit. A handful of kids anxious to be outside after a day cooped up by the rain began kicking a soccer ball around. Peanuts tried to chase after the ball the way he used play with Stevie on the soccer field. The kids were terrified of the huge animal. I had to run and grab him, put him back on his leash. We left the park. I did not want any more confrontations. We crossed the street and walked the back road behind the museum. Sitting on a bench in front of another museum, directly beside the first, I watched as the traffic slowed and the lights in the buildings around us were turned off and doors locked. The clouds had gathered again and thunder rumbled across the valley. I needed to find shelter.

A row of pine trees bordered one side of the outdoor lot. The lower bows of some of the bigger trees hung almost to the ground, barely touching it. It would provide good cover from the rain, but I worried about lightening. I'd have to risk it. Peanuts and I crawled under one; I spread out the cardboard for us both to sit on, leaned against the tree truck, wrapped the plastic bag around my shoulders, covered my legs with the newspapers, fed Peanuts the other half of the first can of dog food and tried to sleep.

I felt the growl before I heard it. My head was resting on Peanuts chest, and the deep rumble in his throat went all the way back to his tail. It was more a snarl then a growl. "What's up Buddy?" I whispered to him, smoothing back his alert ears. "Somebody out there?"

A flash light's beam shown through the tree branches. A security guard and a patrol officer were lifting the branch closest to us. "Who's in there? Identify yourself." One of them said.

Peanuts growled and snapped making them jump back. In the dim light I thought I saw one reach for his gun, but it was only pepper spray. Still not something I wanted to mess with.

"It's okay, it's okay. I've got him. It's okay." I tried to appease them.

"Come out slowly and restrain your animal," a female voice said.

I crawled on my knees under the branches, keeping Peanuts leash as tight as I could and still let him walk out with me. He continued to growl and snarl. The hard days and nights on the street were starting to have a negative impact on his usually sweet temperament. He growled more, barked at everything and was jumpy. Most mornings he limped heavily until the sun warmed his bones. Tonight he was exceptionally snarly. Funny thing, I was the same way.

"He's protective. Doesn't take too well to uniforms." I got up, my knees and hands wet from the ground and scowled at my interrogators. "It's okay Peanuts, sit." I had to say it two or three times before he complied.

"Do you have some ID?" The officer asked, as she shown the light first at Peanuts then at me. I memorized the name on her badge. I had been stopped so many times, I wanted to remember who had and hadn't harassed me: Officer F. Doe.

I pulled the plastic sleeve from my cloth bag, took out the driver's license and handed it to her.

"Wait here," she said.

"Don't worry Officer Doodoo, I know the routine." I probably shouldn't have said that, but I couldn't take it anymore. Everywhere I went I got harassed. What worse could they do to me that hadn't already been done, no family, no home, no car, no food not even a crackled old blue tarp. She gave me a dirty look, walked over to her car and got in. I waited while the security guard kept his light shining in my eyes.

"What the hell are you doing here?" he asked roughly.

"Needed a place to spend the night. What's the matter afraid I'll steal a pine cone?"

"This ain't no campground, ain't no homeless tramps half way house either." He shown the light on Peanuts again, "Or dog pound."

"Nah, it looks like someplace they send wannabe cops." I couldn't believe I said that.

The patrol officer came over with a small clipboard. "I'm going to cite you for vagrancy and trespassing. You will have thirty days to respond or pay the fine, if you do not respond a summons will be issued. Do you understand?"

I really wish I had kept my mouth shut.

"Sorry, yes, I do understand." I pulled Peanuts leash even tighter, forcing him to lean into my leg. "If we just leave now, can you not write the citation?"

"You are trespassing on Museum property. I'll leave it up to Museum security whether I proceed with the citation, either way you'll need to be on your way."

The guard crossed his arms in front of him and stood at an angle to me so he could address us both, he was talking to the officer, but his comments were intended for me more than her.

"Hell yes. Like I told this tramp, this ain't no homeless campground. We can't have her kind lying around trashing the place. Hell yes cites her." He shown his flashlight back under the tree on the cardboard, newspapers and trash bag I had left there when I crawled out.

"Look at that, trashed already."

"Wait, I'll get all that out of there." I started to kneel down ready to crawl back under.

"Remain here." The officer pointed to a spot beside her.

"But I need to get that stuff out of there."

"Did you not here me? Remain here." Officer Doe was stern.

What could I do but stand head down. It was kind of like getting a parking ticket but for humans. I had been in a no parking zone, and she was about to slip a ticket under my wipers. I tried my best to stay silent.

"Is this your current address?" She asked as she filled in the form.

"Well da, if that was my address I wouldn't be standing here now would I officer DoDo." I mumbled. What was wrong with me? I couldn't keep my mouth shut.

"What did you just say?" She was glaring, angry.

"Sorry, I, sorry, current address is General Delivery. Sorry." Please God, please just let this be over.

It started to rain again, the only thing that saved me. Neither Officer Doe nor the security guard wanted to get wet over someone like me.

"Sign here." Officer Doe held the clipboard in her hands as I used her pen to sign my name. She hurriedly tore off the top copy handed it to me and started to dash back to her cruiser.

I knelt down, wanting to retrieve the plastic bag and cardboard from under the tree.

"Leave it." The security said, yelling at me. "If you know what's good for you, leave it be."

54

We wandered around all weekend. The nights were very, very cold. I found more cardboard to lie on and cover up with. I only had that one can of dog food, which I gave Peanuts for breakfast. None of the usual places for a free meal were open Sunday. I tried to find discarded food in dumpsters and trash bins, but as Wizard had shown me, groceries seldom culled outdated food on weekends. I did something I had never done before, shoplifted. It was easier than I thought to slip the yellow can of beef chunk sirloin in gravy into my cloth bag and slip out the door. Peanuts was the one who almost gave it away. As usual he jumped up and wagged his tail when I came out of the store, prompting a long glance from the cashier. I untied him and headed for a park.

"This isn't going to work buddy." I said as I dumped the can of dog food into his plastic bowl. "I can't keep stealing food for you." I sat on a picnic bench beside him, petted him as he inhaled the mashed up mess. When he was done he sat directly in front of me and pawed my leg, asking for more.

"Sorry bud, the cupboard is bare." He whined and licked his lips. I knew what had to be done. We walked up Lomas Avenue, past the Interstate, kept walking, cut through the Fairground parking lot. It was late afternoon when I reluctantly walked in the door.

Peanuts was cowering. I didn't have to pull him close to me; he stood touching me, crouching low.

"May I help you?" A middle age woman sat behind the desk wearing cute kitty print fabric cut into volunteer vests.

"Yes, I need to ..," hesitated, Peanuts again pawed at my leg, anxious. "I can't keep my dog I need to drop him off."

"You want to surrender your animal?" The volunteer stood up and looked over the counter, leaning forward in order to get a good look at Peanuts. When she sat back down the judgment in her eyes was obvious. "You are giving up your animal is that right?" She frowned at me.

"Yes, I can't keep him anymore." I reached down and scratched Peanuts ears, trying to calm him down.

The cute kitties' woman called out to the back room. "Don, we've got a surrender here."

Don came out looked at Peanuts, then at me. He at least had empathy in his eyes.

"Let me see what space we've got, we're pretty full, especially for a big dog like that." He went through a set of double metal doors. When he opened the second set a barrage of barking dogs echoed through the lobby.

The cute kitty lady placed a form and a pen on the counter. "You'll need to fill out this form, sign and date it and there is a thirty dollar surrender fee."

I picked up the pen and immediately set it down. "I don't have thirty dollars".

"We are a nonprofit organization; we can't take in animals without some way to provide for them. We depend on responsible pet owners to care for their animals and if they can't we depend on them to support our organization so we can."

"If I had thirty dollars I wouldn't be here," I told her. I could feel tears on my checks.

"You shouldn't have adopted an animal unless you could care for it."

I studied the pictures on the bulletin board behind her of dozens of dogs and cats waiting to be adopted, and the scant handful of pictures of animals already placed, and then glanced down at Peanuts.

"Thanks for your time." I didn't have to pull Peanuts out of there, he pulled me.

The kennel worker came back out to the lobby. "Where's she going?" he asked the cute kitty lady, as I opened the door.

"You know those types, try and get everything for nothing. She's keeping the dog."

This still didn't solve our problem. Should I steal another can of food? Try another shelter? I walked across the street, sat at a bus bench and watched as two small children climbed the red plastic tube slide at a McDonald's two driveways away. The little girl dropped her hamburger in the gravel. When they left I hurried over and grabbed it, giving half to Peanuts. I was tempted to eat the other half myself, but wrapped it up and put it into the cloth bag for Peanuts' dinner. I cut in back of the businesses, up the alley and past the back of the shelter. That's when I noticed the fenced in kennel area at the back of the shelter, enclosed like a box with chain link fence, two half doors connected to the back of the shelter. A small sign wired to the gate said: *Night and weekend drop off, emergencies only please.*

¤ ¤ ¤

Peanuts and I hung around the fairgrounds all day. We joined at least a dozen other transients, who were lying on the grass, sitting on pylons or benches and under trees. When a security cart would come around, we would get up, en masse, and move to the other side of the fairgrounds. We did this several times, like a game of cat and mouse. When two City of Albuquerque officers on mountain bikes rode onto the grounds we looked at each other. They couldn't catch all of us. The younger, faster ones, would make their escape off grounds, the older, sick or lam, some on crutches, would be caught and frisked, told not to come back. Peanuts and I both hobbled a bit showing our age, but we were still more limber than some, managed to cross the street and head for Central Avenue before the officers could catch up to us.

I had to find a place to rest. Peanuts pawed at me, became stubborn. "Oh Peanuts buddy, I know you're hungry. I'm so sorry. It'll be okay soon. Promise. Hang with me Buddy." He didn't have a clue what I was talking about.

We sat across the street from the Animal Shelter most of the night. Peanuts was restless, knew something was up. I dozed a couple times, was jolted awake by the honking of a car when it went by. When did harassing the homeless become a form of entertainment? The traffic got heavier. I'm guessing it was between five and six in the morning. I crossed back over the street and walked up the alley to the Night Drop enclosure. We stood outside the gate a while, probably half an hour. I played everything out in my head. When a truck pulled behind us in the alley and stopped at a neighboring business I knew I had to act. Now or never, I opened the gate and led Peanuts inside.

A heavy gray metal door with a small ventilation grate cut in it opened to a holding area. About four feet square, a small drain was in the middle of the concrete floor. There were two units like this side by side. I knelt down, burying my head in Peanuts' fur, hugging him. I could feel his ribs.

"I'm so sorry Stevie, so sorry son. I tried." I unhooked Peanuts collar, threw the other half of the hamburger inside the concrete kennel room, shoved Peanuts in and closed the door. He immediately started to whine and scratch at the door, desperate to get out.

"It's okay, buddy. It's going to be okay, Peanuts. You're such a good dog. Be a good dog." But my voice did not console him. He continued to whine and dig at the door. When a few more cars pulled into the alley in back of the place I wiped the tears away and hid in back of the nearby dumpster. Peanuts continued to cry and bark, desperately calling to me.

It was fully light now. Two compact cars pulled up front. The kennel worker got out of one and a different volunteer than I had encountered yesterday climbed out of the other, walked to the front door and unlocked it. Peanuts howls filled the parking lot.

I could hear the woman tell the kennel worker "Sounds like we got a drop off last night."

A minute or two passed before they came around from the back. The animal care tech, holding a thick black leash, opened the gate to the drop off area. I had a clear line of vision as he unlocked the kennel door and slipped the loop around Peanuts' neck. Peanuts was cowering, walking low to the ground. For a brief minute the black Shepard caught sight of me, jumped a little, gave a gentle "woof" and wagged his tail expecting me to rescue him.

"What a beautiful animal," the woman said, rubbing Peanuts' sides as the kennel worker led him through the gate. "Why would someone abandon a great dog like this?"

55

*P*eanuts, my wonderful canine companion, my only friend in the world and last remembrance of the family I once had was all that had kept me going. Without him there didn't seem much point. To anything. I sat in one spot for hours, hardly moving. It didn't matter if it was cold or windy or sunny. I sat until somebody told me I couldn't be there anymore. I thought about going to a soup kitchen or shelter, but didn't seem much point in that anymore either. Some street folk I had met at the Welcome Center stopped a couple of times and talked to me.

"Didja eat?" one said as he sat beside me on the edge of a planter near the University. I shook my head no, kept looking down.

"I think they're still serving at the Southside Kitchen. You could make it if you left now." His concern is unexpected.

I still didn't speak, pulled my shopping bag up on my shoulder and started to shuffle off in the other direction. I say shuffle because that's what it was. I hardly lifted my feet, just kind of pushed them along in the gravel. He quick stepped beside me.

"Here, I got some of these extra. Be good to get something in your stomach." He pushed a plastic sleeve of cheese and crackers, half gone, into my hand and folded my fingers around it. "You'll be all right, just got to keep going, put one foot in front of the other."

Darkness came. It was late. I didn't realize I had made it all the way uptown, past the fairgrounds and the shelter where Peanuts lay on a rug in a heated concrete kennel. I did think about him when I walked by, but I knew it was better. He had more than I did. I walked another couple miles, slowly. It was past midnight when I used Peanuts' leash to tie myself upright to a bus stop bench so I wouldn't fall off if I fell asleep like Alice had instructed me. I did not bother to cover up with cardboard or discarded newspapers. I don't think I slept so much as passed out.

The sound of the first city bus of the morning stopping in front of me roused me. I sat more upright slowly. The City bus driver, door open, looked me over. I could see him radio in as he pulled away from the stop. Can't stay here, I thought, he called the cops on me.

I had problems standing up. It took me a minute to remember I tied myself down last night. Even untied I struggled. It was so cold the night before I couldn't feel my feet and could barely move my fingers. You reach a point when you are out in the cold you don't realize you are cold. People do crazy things, like undress instead of cover up. I wasn't there yet, but pretty close to it.

I shuffled off toward the center of town again. I didn't think about where I was going. Just shuffled, head down, arms close to my sides. Cars honked at me when I failed to look up and stepped in front of them at intersections. Do me a favor okay, run me over.

It was ten o'clock in the morning when I got to the Central Albuquerque Community Library. They had just opened. People, mostly homeless, like me, were staggering in. At least it would be warm. I could try and thaw a little. I found a single chair with wooden arms at the end of a book stack in the fiction section. I grabbed the book closest to where I sat and opened it. I wasn't going to read it I just needed a prop in case I was questioned. It was the first time I had taken shelter in a library although I met lots of people who did. Peanuts had not been welcome here, so while I occasionally sat on benches outside, I rarely ventured in. Before too long my chin dropped to my chest.

Next thing I know a young guy, mid-twenties maybe, with an unkempt beard and three earrings in one lobe wearing a green camo army coat, a pack slung over one shoulder is kneeling beside me, using three fingers to poke my arm and push me upright.

"Hey, hey." He poked me again, pushing me to wake up. "You can't sleep here." He spoke directly in my ear.

"What?" I'm still in a daze.

"The library, you can't' sleep in the library, if you do, they'll call the police on us and everyone will be kicked out." He has stopped poking me, but remains on one knee beside me.

"Oh, I didn't know." The feeling is just beginning to return to my feet, but it comes back as searing pain. The same pain pulses through my hands and fingers as I am finally able to un-bend them.

"You can't sleep here, can't bother the people checking out books and you have to stay out of the children's section. Otherwise they'll kick us all out." He does not smile. He is telling me this to help himself survive, not me. He rises and moves to a bench two book stacks down, pushes his pack under it and opens a newspaper, like me, pretending to read.

I sit with my arms on the wooden armrest, staring out the window, the open book on my lap. A security guard walks the aisle looking for any infraction then moves on. I feel my head start to nod. I need to get some water and wake up a little more. The restroom is nearby. I duck in, take my time washing my hands and splashing water on my face. When I come out, another homeless soul has taken up residence in my chair. I wander through the library, spot an empty bench, go over and sit down. I should have looked closer. If I had I would have seen the yellow cartoon mouse with big ears and glasses, his round black nose stuck in a book, painted above it.

I'm on the floor when they come for me. I don't know how I got there. I assume I went to sleep and fell over. An Officer Marquez, on one side of me, lifted me up by my arm. The security guard is on the other side, and has hold of my arm and elbow. They hustled me out the door. The same young man in the green army coat who warned me earlier glared angrily at me and shook his head.

Officer Marquez doesn't ask me anything yet. He loads me into the back of his cruiser, but not before he takes my shopping bag from me, places it on the passenger side of the front seat. It smells back here. Bad. Like vomit and piss and unwashed bodies and disinfectant. At least it's warm. Officer Marquez sits in the front of the cruiser and starts to play twenty questions with me.

"Are you injured or ill?"

"Have you taken any drugs, legal or illegal?"

"Are you under the influence of alcohol?"

"Do you have any ID?"

"In the bag, my ID's in the bag," I say.

"Do I have your permission to search this bag?" He holds it up.

I nod my head.

"I need you to give verbal consent. Do I have your permission to search this bag?" He holds the bag up again. I realize he is doing this for his lapel camera.

"Yes, you can check my bag," I say to him, but my tongue is thick, my speech slurred.

He finds my driver's license, enters the number into the on board computer.

"You're Aileen Roark? This is you?" He holds up the license so I can see it. I must admit, I don't look anything like the smiling well groomed woman pictured on my driver's license.

"Do you have any outstanding warrants or arrests? Anything like that you want to tell me about?" He is waiting for the information to go through and come back on the network.

"Parking ticket," I say mumbling.

"Do you have a vehicle?" He looks around the library lot.

"No, not a car parking ticket. In the back of the notebook. There's a citation."

He holds up the composition notebook. "This, in the back of this?"

I'm not going to be a smart aleck today. "Yes, that's right."

He flips through until he finds the citation for trespassing and vagrancy from a few days ago. By this time the ID has cleared and he folds it along with the citation together and puts them back in the bag.

"I'm putting this all bag in the bag. Okay? Do you see me putting it back in the bag?"

"Yes," I nod. "I see you putting it all in the bag."

He keeps playing twenty questions. "Where did you spend the night last night?"

"When was the last time you ate?"

"Is there anyone I can call for you?"

That's twelve, eight more questions to go to reach twenty.

"Okay Aileen, I need you to sit back. We're going to take a ride," he says to me.

I close my eyes. The only way I can cope. Just close my eyes and not see anything. I don't want to watch myself get driven to jail. I don't want to picture myself in the back of a police cruiser. I don't want to remember where I am or how I got here or who I used to be. Officer Marquez puts the car in gear and we pull out of the library lot. Several times during the ride he speaks to me.

"Are you still with us Aileen?"

I nod my head.

"I need you to answer me," he says. His voice is firm but not angry, like my teacher voice.

"Yes I'm still here." I need to keep my mouth shut tight and not let myself say 'where else would I be?'

And "Open your eyes Aileen, all right? I need to make sure you're okay?"

"I'm okay." I open my eyes and see him looking back at me in his rear view mirror. Ten minutes later he starts talking to me again.

"You can't go back to that library for thirty days, okay? You're kicked out of there for thirty days. Today's September 25th, so let's just say after Halloween. You can remember that can't you? After Halloween you can go back to that library, but you can't sleep there and can't go in the children's area. Do you understand Aileen?" Officer Marquez continues to drive, making several turns, stopping at red lights.

"Yes." I keep my eyes closed.

"Open your eyes and tell me you understand."

"Yes, I understand."

"Tell me, when can you go back to the library? And keep your eyes open when you do." He keeps peering at me in the mirror.

"In thirty days. After Halloween, I can go back but not the children's area and no sleeping." This cop thinks I'm stupid or something. He must have gotten through his twenty questions by now. I close my eyes again and lay my head on the back seat.

"Right, good, you got it. Okay we're here." He pulls the car to a stop.

I don't sit up or open my eyes, don't want to see the police station or jail or wherever we are, can't bear to think about the disdainful glances of onlookers when I am hauled out of the back seat of a police cruiser.

Officer Marquez comes around to the outside of the car and opens the door.

"Okay Aileen, this is your stop. I need you to open your eyes and exit the vehicle."

When I do, there's Sister Frankie, standing at the curb outside the Welcome Center with a blanket to wrap around my shoulders.

56

Sister Frankie was incredibly kind and compassionate. She never judged. "Aileen, we must be prepared to accept the gifts God gives us, you are stronger than you know." She sat beside me offering hot tea and soda crackers.

I didn't feel gifted. No pun intended. I think what she meant was the cop could have taken me to jail, but he brought me to the homeless shelter instead. Sister Frankie bent the rules, let me shower and sleep during the day that day. The next day, and the next I had to join the line and wait for a bed and plate of food.

I stood in line waiting, four o'clock, with the rest of the street dwellers. A blue Saturn, lowered, with small wheels, pulls up beside us as the line of hopeful souls looking for a bed for the night snakes around the sidewalk. A teen boy rolls down the passenger window, stands on the seat so the top half of his body extends through the open window and tosses a pack of lit firecrackers at us. The men and women in line jump and yell as the fire crackers pop and explode at their feet. Some are so disoriented they can't comprehend what is happening and begin running away, trying to find a safe place to hide. Damn firecrackers.

¤ ¤ ¤

This is where I came in.

When I was a kid, until about my mid-teens, there were no multiplexes. Theaters would have consecutive showings of different movies. Usually it was a double feature, sometimes a triple. This made for some strange pairings. A horror movie with Vincent Price might be on a bill with a musical about rainbows and unicorns. You could come in or leave at any time. If you came late, you would sit through the second movie, and watch the next one up until the point where you came in.

This is where I came in.

But don't leave yet, it's a triple feature.

<h1 align="center">57</h1>

Being homeless usually means you are friendless too. If you had friends, or family or even close acquaintances you probably wouldn't be homeless. Somebody, even if they didn't like you all that much, would take you in, give you a garage to sleep in, try to connect you with service or something, as much to ease their own guilt as anything else. When I finally lost it all I didn't know it meant losing friends too. It was a real slap in the face, a rude awakening, a bolt of lightning, a blow deep down in your soul when you figure this out. But when you do it isn't anger you feel, it's incredible loneliness.

I tried to talk to people, find out what I needed to know, but soon learned they aren't really all that interested in my welfare and don't particularly care to converse. The first time I lost all I had it was a learning experience. I didn't know how painful loneliness could be. I discovered I could survive without talking to anyone for days on end. I didn't like it, but I did it. I started to understand why you see street people pacing around repeating things; they're waiting for someone to answer them. I learned to tell how long someone had been living rough based on how often they talked to no one in particular and what they said.

One guy must have been on the streets more than a decade. He was tall, way too thin, had given up both shaving and haircuts and walked with that particular lift in his step that comes from balancing a heavy gear bag on one arm twenty plus hours a day, seven days a week. Bert, someone told me, had once been in the Marines. I thought they took an oath to never leave a man behind, but here Bert was, left behind as clear as the sun is bright. I was a little afraid of him owing to his size and wild appearance. It was a judgment I struggled with considering my own deteriorating looks. I was way beyond a little lipstick to freshen up. I hadn't changed clothes since the City of Albuquerque did their sweep of the downtown a month ago and confiscated all unattended bags, including mine, stashed by the homeless until needed. Where do you put your stuff when you have nowhere to put it?

Anyway, Bert, after he got his coffee in the meal line, would blow roughly on it, take a sip and say "good coffee good coffee", than spin around, take three steps and repeat "good coffee." He would do this until he had downed all the coffee or until someone agreed with him, "Yay, Bert, good coffee."

One of the volunteers at the soup kitchen had figured it out. As soon as he saw Bert get his coffee, while he was still blowing on it, would ask, "How's the coffee today Bert?"

And Bert would reply, "Good. It's good coffee."

Then he'd sit down with his cup, satisfied and drink the rest without comment. For Bert this was the only thing that still connected him to the world and validated his humanness. All the other words he had spoken, all the conversations, hopes, dreams, memories or fears, even just talk about the weather had failed for lack of a second.

Once, the regular crew wasn't there to serve us the evening meal. A special group of DJ's and TV anchorman had been brought in along with a film crew to get the small town celebrity community service thing on camera. It was publicity for the kickoff of the fall food drive. A Girl Scout troop had used crayons and colored markers on some of those white textured placemats you still see in a few dinners. They were decorated with rainbows and pink flowers, blue trees with yellow butterflies and a smattering of words like *Have a nice day, Enjoy your food* or my personal favorite *We (heart) you* with little smiley faces in multiple pastel colors. The placemats lay neatly arranged on most of the tables.

I shouldn't be so cynical. The publicity bit did bring in donations of food and cash. For a few weeks our bowls would be fuller, and you got two slices of bread or two buttered rolls instead of one. There were days we only got half a slice of bread and watered down soup if the cupboards were bare.

Anyway, the regulars weren't there to serve. Bert is next in line, gets his plate and his coffee from a grinning Channel 8 News Weatherman Joe, blows on it, takes a sip and says "Good Coffee." He takes another three steps and repeats and does the usual. Trouble is he's blocking the camera. As long as he's there, they can't get a good shot of the rival station news crews in full make up, smiling at each other in the spirit of cooperation with these big brightdentistwhite teeth made all the more obvious by the lack of dental care in the local clientele, serving soup to the homeless. The cameraman and producer tried to navigate around him. But Bert spins, takes three steps, sips his coffee and says "Good Coffee" and is in front of them again. The producer glances around to see where to set up a better shot; Weatherman Joe is starting to look a little stormy; the rival anchorwomen are looking a little distressed, worried they might have to stay longer than expected, leaving little time to retouch their make-up before the newscast. But Bert just takes another three steps, sips and says "Good Coffee."

The cameraman reaches out to gently nudge Bert out of the way and you know what happens, he spills the coffee. Bert is not pleased. He has forgotten how to express himself when he is unhappy, doesn't know what to do or say, and is just raising his arms above his head softly vocalizing "Aw-aw-aw."

When I am in a food line I always try to position myself beside women with children even if it means I end up at the end of the line. As hardened and out of touch as many of these men are, they seem to hold a special reverence for mothers with children. I've seen guys who out on the street would get in a fist fight over a couple slices of pizza left in the trash give up their buttered rolls, cookies and fruit cups to kids sitting in the dining area. They would do magic tricks for them like pulling a penny from behind the kid's ear, or fold a paper napkin into an origami crane, showing the kid how to pull the tail and make the crane's wings beat. I think it was because they knew how incredibly hard it was to live on the streets, and had the ultimate respect and empathy for what lay ahead for these young kids. Standing beside the mothers and kids in line meant I wouldn't have to hear the profanity or vulgar comments that would fly across the room when children were not within earshot. That and the women and kids smelled way better. Sorry but it had to be said.

So there I was sandwiched between two mothers who had five kids between them. I was only about eight from the front of the line, and it looked like Bert might upset the whole applecart and the food line would close, we'd be literally sent to bed without our supper; the news crew would set up a shot at another shelter across town; donations would not pour in and everyone would be eating canned tomato soup and stale crackers for the next few weeks. Unless someone did something and fast, this would cause a chain reaction of events so distressing that the whole center might have to close. The old timers would conspire with the young guns to beat the crap out of Bert sometime in the next few days. Factions would develop. People would be so emotionally unsatisfied by the meager rations provided, turn into grumpy unhappy souls, provoke fights, steal each other's packages of peanut butter crackers, someone would get stabbed, the police would be called and the shelter would be forced to close its doors because of the excessive number of 911 calls. Don't laugh, I've seen it happen.

Someone had to act fast to avoid this series of unhappy events from unfolding. I didn't see any Marines bursting through the doors. I took a deep audible breath, stepped out of line, grabbed another cup of coffee from Weatherman Joe, reached up and placed it in Bert's hand, saying "How's the coffee today Bert?"

Bert blew on it, took a sip, said "Good Coffee. Its good coffee," and sat down.

I patted him on the shoulder and went to the back of the line. Now there were about thirty people ahead of me. The shot the producer had been waiting for of the star weatherman and rival station young anchorwomen offering up soup and fruit cups to homeless mothers and children was made. It would be on the ten o'clock news. I was not in it. Donations would pour in, a chicken would find its way into every pot and we'd have lots of smiling new faces cheerfully serving us in the near future. The Channel 8 News crew packed it up, hands were shaken, gratitude expressed, and those of us still in line had to wait even longer to get about half the food the others received. The celebrity servers, unaccustomed to portioning the meals, had generously filled plates, leaving little for the ones still to be feed. I watched sadly as Sister Frankie emptied the last of the hot water pot into the soup, stirred in two small cans of Veg Al and Brother Mike took a knife and cut the last seven rolls in half. I got about two thirds of a cup of soup, half a roll and no fruit cup. By this time the coffee pot was empty too, so I filled my cup with water from the sink.

The women with children, having been afforded the privileges of entering the living quarters ahead of the others, left the dining room. I had no safe harbor. I reluctantly walked to the end of a rectangular table that was mostly unoccupied, sat down, said a prayer, and began to eat, staring into space and trying to think of nothing in particular lest I fall into utter despair. I was surprised to not hear the usual barrage of name calling and harsh hacking laughs echoing through the room. It was really kind of quiet. At some point I glanced around the room and became aware that some of the guys were looking over their shoulders at me. One of the old timers got up from his place, walked over to me and set his buttered roll on my plate. At the same time, one of the young guns, a real gangster with tear drop tattoos and blue boxer underwear showing about a foot above his belt, walked over from the other side of the room and set his fruit cup in front of me.

I looked up at both of them and stuttered "Thanks, thank you." Both nodded without saying anything, turned and walked away.

Now if I could just get them to pull some pennies from my ear.

¤ ¤ ¤

I became a soup kitchen regular. Sometimes I'd get a bed, sometimes not. When my three days that week were up at the Welcome Center I moved to the next shelter, then another one. Without Peanuts I was able to line up for a bed and breakfast, same as the rest. One more night, but just one, I pulled cardboard and plastic bags, stolen from public trash cans, around me. I woke up to a heavy frost that had formed on top of my tiny camp under an abandoned tractor trailer on a little used frontage road by the Interstate. When I peek out from under my man-made hovel, the cold thin air was filled by three or four hundred hot air balloons. One, shaped a like a cow, its pink udders swaying side to side in a slight breeze, floated almost directly above me. It was surreal.

It was October 5th, payday. I left everything there, trashing up the place, as the security guard at the museum had said and made my way to the Rest Inn. *Mnthly No hskeeping, 485 + tx* the carefully aligned letters of the marquee announced. I would be in from the cold. This time I got a receipt.

58

I had more or less settled into a routine at the Rest Inn. It didn't sink in what no housekeeping services meant when I rented the room. All I knew was that at four hundred and eighty five dollars, plus twelve dollars tax, my five hundred and twenty five dollar check from Sam's pension was enough to keep me from sleeping behind buildings and pooping beside trash bins for a whole month. It was a surprise to find my room didn't come with sheets or towels, nor did it have toilet paper or other consumables, not even light bulbs. That first night I rushed down to the office, sure a mistake had been made, only to be greeted by the night Manager, CJ, (Cesar Jesus I would find out later), Chavez. The thing you couldn't help but remember about this guy was his huge muscular arms and a tattoo that fanned up above his shirt collar onto his neck.

"May I help you?" He swiveled his desk chair around and stood up behind the counter.

"Yes, my room, I'm in three o eight, I don't think it's ready. I mean the bed isn't made and there are no light bulbs. Can someone get it ready or can I get a different room."

"And you are?" He tapped his fingers on the counter.

"Mrs. Roark, Aileen Roark. I rented the room this afternoon. I needed to pick up a few things first and I barely went in the room a little while ago." It sunk in pretty fast that my dirty clothes and limited access to hygiene changed how people reacted to me. I always pictured a proper middle class teacher with clean clothes, combed hair and a husband and two kids, a look that was gone forever. In my current ragged state few people wanted to acknowledge me at all, let alone pay attention to what I said. It was a surprise when Cesar listened. Even if this guy had a rough exterior, he treated everyone with respect.

"Yes Mrs. Roark I do remember you now. Let me bring up your registration."

"I registered about five o'clock, and paid the monthly rate. Don't you have another room?" I spoke rapidly, I was tired, wanted a bath and something to eat.

Chavez raised his eyebrows and gazed from the screen to me and back again. "Well Mrs. Roark, you paid the monthly rate, single room with kitchenette, no housekeeping. Is that not what you wanted?"

He was matter of fact.

"No, I mean yes. That is what I rented. But the room doesn't even have light bulbs, or sheets and blankets let alone kitchen utensils. I stayed here before and the rooms had everything." I said, loud and demanding, my impatience obvious. I was taking out my frustration on this guy.

"Ah, nightly, am I correct?" His mustache rose on one side and he crossed his arms in from of his chest, doing his best to stay professional and not tell me off.

"Yes, that's right, I stayed here before for two days, my room had everything. "I said, yelling.

"Yes, I remember you, had a Red Cross voucher. Nightly rate is for full housekeeping, but you didn't pay the nightly rate, you..."

I cut him off, unbelievably annoyed. "I know what I paid. I thought no housekeeping meant no maid services not no toilet paper."

He was annoyed back, barely able to keep his voice down. "It was on the guest registration form, which you signed, the monthly rates you were quoted, paid and which is listed on your registration form specifies that all consumables and basic housekeeping goods and services are the responsibility of the guest, is there anything else I can do for you? If not I do have things to do."

"But the room doesn't have a TV; I can't even turn on the lamp above the bed."

"You rented the basic furnished room with no housekeeping. It does not include cable or other amenities, do you wish to upgrade?"

I glared at him. Of the five hundred and twenty five dollars I had this morning four hundred and ninety-even went for rent. I treated myself to a ninety nine cent burger and baked potato for lunch and I spent another twenty at the dollar store on oatmeal, rice, a couple of cans of mixed vegetables, Raman noodles, tea, dish soap and tuna fish. I had a buck fifty left in my pocket.

"No, I don't care to upgrade, but I didn't realize the room would be so, so, um basic."

"I can offer you a refund provided the room is still clean. I would need to hold half your rent as a deposit until tomorrow when housekeeping staff checks it. Would you like to vacate the room and get a refund?" He started to open the cash drawer, pulled my registration form from the thin stack in the file labeled *Monthly Rental Agreements*.

A refund? Where would I go? By now all the beds at the shelter would be filled. I didn't know where I could find a warm spot to sleep or what I would do. I had to make this work.

"No, No." The resignation in my voice was obvious. "I don't want a refund."

"Then what do you want Mrs. Roark? This isn't exactly a 4 star accommodation you know." He gave a closed mouth forced smile, straightened the papers in the folder by tapping the edge loudly on the counter top. He looked at me hard like I was the enemy.

I glanced around the tiny lobby, at the dirty carpet and the torn vinyl of the sectional seating, small TV bolted to one corner of the room, the broken lower corner of the front window cross-crossed with duct tape, and began to say something sarcastic. "Really? Could have fooled me. Especially the excellent staff," I said under my breath.

"Excuse me? " Cesar stood up, scowling at me.

I glanced outside again, "Nothing. Sorry to bother you."

I walked slowly up the stairs to my room. On the second metal landing, a young woman with thick black hair pulled back the curtain of the corner room. She caught my eye, smiled and waved shyly as I continued up the flight and rounded the corner. All I could manage was a small nod and a single finger, raised in acknowledgment. She continued to watch from below as I unlocked the door to my room and went in.

Instinctively I flipped on the switch, but, of course, there was no light. If the blinds were tilted ever so slightly thin beads of light reflected off the sign outside and some of he light from an overhead streetlight on the corner reached into the undersized room. I pulled a small round table and a desk chair close to the light by the window and opened my cloth tote bag and carefully pulled the food out, lining it up on the table in front of me.

I wanted it to last a week or more, but without a can opener or anything to boil water in all I could do was look at it and wish. Finally, I picked up one of the Cup of Noodles and tore away the cellophane, walked over to the mini-kitchenette in the corner It was only about four feet from one side to other, but packed into that space was an ever so small sink, single burner, wavy metal drain board and an under counter refrigerator. The foot wide shelf jutting from the wall above was bare, save for some old weekly Bargain Bizarre newspapers. In the other room I had stayed in here a microwave, set of plastic dishes and utensils in a small white plastic drawer bin occupied this space. I'd been counting on that stuff to get me through. Now, I would have to figure out where to get some plates and forks, not to mention a can opener and pan. I had a couple of leftover plastic spoons and a plastic soda cup in my bag. I laid these on the counter and thought about what to do next. I turned on the hot water and let it run until it was as hot as it would get, filled the Styrofoam cup of noodles to the line, closed the lid and hoped, if I let it set a few minutes longer, it would soften the noodles enough to eat.

At least I was safe, indoors and had a place to sleep, but for how long? I tried not to focus on the future, just what to do in the next few minutes. Clean clothes and a bath came to mind. If I washed my clothes out in the bathtub, and hung them over the chair surely they would be dry by morning. (Wrong).

While my noodles softened. I filled the tub with hot water, took the dish-soap, undressed and climbed in. Hair, clothes, body wash, cheap dish soap was the go to for trying to clean up. For a dollar you got a huge bottle, orange scented, that, while it didn't leave your hair smooth and silky, or your skin soft it did get it clean. I didn't have a towel. All I could do was use my dirty t-shirt to towel off. I placed my clothes in the bathtub water, squirted in more dish-soap, and twisted and rubbed everything, rinsed it twice and wrung it firmly before draping everything over the back of the chair.

It was freezing in here and I was stark naked, with wet hair, and I was hungry. I had no blankets or sheets. I turned the ancient metal heat/cool unit under the window as high as the temperature setting would go, made sure the blinds were twisted closed and prayed it would warm up a little more.

The noodles never did soften up. I ate them crunchy, and salty, followed by two large cups of water. I took the papers down from the shelf, opened them flat and used them to cover myself in sections as I lay on the bare mattress. As long as I didn't move, they stayed in place. So there I lay, flat on my back, naked save for the newspapers, staring at the light fixture with no bulbs in it, hoping my clothes would dry, listening in the dark to the cars and big rigs with their outlawed Jake Brakes filtering through from the Interstate outside, finally falling into a restless sleep.

About two or three in the morning I was awakened by the cold. All the newspapers except the one right on my stomach had fallen to the floor. I gathered them up, shifted again and started the careful task of arranging them so as to provide the most coverage. As I sat up to lay the papers around my feet and knees, I heard the dull thud of foots steps, more like running steps on the metal staircase and landings. Farther away at first, the sound moved closer until they were very nearby. Someone was running laps around the place, going up one stairwell, running the length of the outdoor walkway, then moving up to the next floor. I predicted, correctly, the stairs directly to the right of my room would be next. I stayed tuned in, trying to figure it out. Without any way to cover myself, I was reluctant to get up and look through the blinds, so I stayed as silent as I could, waiting for the sound of the running footsteps to fade away before I lied back down to sleep.

Twice more that night I would shift position and find my meager bedding had fallen off. And twice more I would hear the sound of footsteps running the length and width of the modest motel. The third time, I dropped out of bed, on all fours, crawled to the window and stood up, my back tight against the wall and tried to peer through the edge of the window blinds to see who exactly was using the place for track practice. A caught sight of the back of a man with broad shoulders, wearing wind pants and a dark blue hoodie with the hood pulled tight over his head jog past my room. Quietly I checked the door to make sure it was locked and re-set the puny chain that was supposed to act as extra security. I thought I saw the man turn slightly at the sound of the door lock turning, so I stood absolutely still until I saw him do an about face and go down the metal stairs at the end of my floor. Ever so slowly I dropped again to my knees and crawled back to the mattress. A wet spot had formed at the head of the bed where my wet hair, which was still damp, had soaked the gray and blue striped cover. I moved to the other end, lay on my side and pulled the newspapers around and over me, again falling into an uneasy sleep, wondering: Who was that hooded man?

59

Morning doesn't come slowly at the Rest Inn, it comes in a rush. Lights appear, horns honk, people move about. You can hear shouting as the guests and monthly residents such as myself, open and shut their doors and load their cars. When closed, the thin plastic mini blinds did prevent someone from looking in, but they did a poor job of keeping the day light out. Last night I couldn't adjust them to let in enough light, but now light filled the room before I was really ready to start my day.

I had no idea what time it was, but I did know it was early. My plan was to get dressed and head downtown to the hospitality center, hopefully get a cup of coffee. Maybe they could help with towels and a blanket. But when I picked up my thin khaki pants from the back of the chair they were still soaking wet, so was my shirt and jacket. Still without any dry clothes to wear, I pushed the chair closer to the wall heater, checked to make sure it was on and turned to high and turned the hot water tap on, hoping that it was hot enough to make tea.

It was the first real chance I had to look around my new home. Last night, it had been too dark to see anything, and besides, I was totally focused on trying to get clean and get warm. Now in the filtered light, I could see what I had signed up for. The room was basic. My students would have called it generic or 'all cheap'. A wooden chair with torn orange vinyl seat held my drying clothes, the round table on a single pedestal had seen better days, cigarette burns marred its edges, and a single long scratch divided the table into unequal halves. The cheap flake board bedframe and nightstand were covered in the same imitation wood grain vinyl as the table. Unlike the nightly rentals here, no cheaper by the dozen framed pastoral art prints graced the walls. They were painted a faded mint green and were dotted here and there with the spray of a shaken can of RC Cola. I would have lots of time to study these dots over the next 24 hours, that's how long it took the clothes to dry. I would look at those sticky spots, imagining what shapes I could make by connecting the dots. It was an odd way for a fifty something woman to amuse herself, but I couldn't exactly leave, or even open the blinds to gaze outside since I was still almost completely naked. I spent most of that first day sitting either on the bed or in the chair, reading and re-reading the newspapers which only a few hours before had served as my bedding. The walls were thin and you could hear almost everyone's business as they walked around outside.

I could hear the amiable chatter of a woman and man discuss the weather and the need for more heat in the rooms, bits and pieces of a conversations as someone walked by. Eventually I pulled my cloth bag out again. I had already arranged the food on the shelf above the kitchenette. The bag contained only the few items I always carried, my composition notebook and colored pencils, some extra paper napkins I had pocketed from various fast food establishments and a white plastic litter bag with Smokey the Bear's round eyes and ranger hat outlined in three colors. The paper napkins proved to be especially handy now. I pulled the stack out and balanced it carefully on the edge of the bathroom sink.

I opened the white plastic Smokey bag and poured all of its contents onto the round table, a glue stick, small rounded scissors, six inch ruler and a couple of unsharpened pencils and pencil sharpener, school supplies, donated to the shelter by the local civic club. I had found the bag on the ground, abandoned by its intended recipient the morning after they were distributed. I picked each item up, examined it, set it back on the table. They reminded me of all the years I asked kids to bring in these very items and all the projects we had used them for. I sat a while looking at them, sad, angry, resigned. I don't know all the stages of grief but it felt like I was grieving for my classroom and students.

It finally dawned on me the glue stick could be used to glue the sections of newspapers together. Great, a blanket, in one piece, albeit made of paper. I assembled two newspaper blankets three sections wide and four long, enough to cover me twice. Tonight

I would sleep better and not see or hear that hooded runner again. Was he even real? Or just something I dreamed. Then realized I could make a paper poncho of the newspapers too, kind of like the exam gowns you in doctors' offices. I don't know why it mattered to me so much to be covered up, I was the only one here, but I did feel some degree of civility returning as I slipped the paper poncho over my head.

I spent my first day at the Rest Inn, dressed in a newspaper poncho, eating wet but still crunchy Ramen noodles, drinking weak lukewarm tea, and living vicariously through other people's conversations gleaned through the thin walls.

The second night in my new home saw a more restful sleep. The glued together newspaper blankets did provide some warmth. That mysterious hooded runner wakened me in the night again. When morning light shown translucent gray through the blinds and the sound of trucks once again dominated the Interstate, I was determined to not spend another day sitting naked in this room. Even thought my pants and sweatshirt were still a little damp, I put them on, emptied my bag and headed out the door. I was starting to get used to the constant diesel exhaust smell that settled down from the I 25 overpass, it was worst in the morning , right before the sun came up. I practiced taking shallow breaths, mouth closed, to avoid the sting from the fumes in the back of my throat.

No breakfast today I guess. I did have a buck fifty. I could either buy a dollar breakfast sandwich at a fast food place or try and find a thrift store and buy a pan to heat water in, if I was lucky maybe even a light bulb or blanket, if I could find the right thrift store. I knew what I was looking for; but wanted to find the quickest way there. Back under I-25, up hill towards Menaul, a corner mall, which at one time held a Safeway and chain discount store, had been taken over by an Ice Cream Shop, cell phone store and a large second hand shop called *Remember When*. The store advertised itself to benefit a local non-profit group. It was only eight thirty, a half hour before the resale shop would open. I walked up and down the windows. Old mannequins were dressed in donated clothes department store style. Oranges, gold and deep greens the dominate colors. Some glass shelves between each figure held dish sets, silver trays and figurines. It reminded me of my Franciscan ware left behind in my storage locker. Would it be featured in a storage locker sale?

It took a little searching but I finally made out the price tags twelve dollars for the corduroy blazer, fifteen for the rust plaid skirt. The dishes were harder to see, but I did see one serving piece marked twenty five. Well, probably the more expensive stuff is in the windows, the cheap stuff is in the back I reasoned. I walked up and down the side walk twice. My stomach was growling and I needed the can to boot. It was too light outside to hide behind the dumpster. If I could just hold on a couple more minutes the store would open.

A man about my age pulled up in an old BMW. He was dressed casually in better quality clothes, not the thin fabric and uneven stitched seams that mark discount chain apparel. I imagine that he gets the pick of donations. I waited for him to go in. It took another five minutes for him to turn the lights on and unlock the door.

"Good morning, are you open?"

"Yes, almost." He looked up at me as he read from a small clip board by the cash register and scowled.

"Is there something specific you need?" He was curt, a little huffy.

"Um, right now I need the restroom." I was polite, smiled at him.

"Restrooms are for customers only." He did not smile back.

Another woman, petite with snow white short hair came in the door. She balanced two lattes in a cardboard tray with one hand and had a Lhasa Apso in the other.

"Sorry I'm late. Penny just insisted on coming." She fluffed up the dogs fur and set the lattes on the counter.

The manager, if that's what he was, took the little dog from the woman, "And how are you today Penny? Did you come to work with us today?"

Is this guy for real? He just treated a three pound floor mop better then he treated me.

"Please, I do plan on shopping, but I need the restroom first." My gut was clenched, as I pleaded with him.

Annoyed, he put the pampered dog down on a pillow lined basket in back of the counter.

"First door on the right behind the beaded curtain." He picked up one of the lattes. They sure did smell wonderful.

I walked through the store. It was packed with clothes racks, sorted not only by size but by color and style as well. I saw the kitchen items arranged on two large dining tables, they too were displayed in groups, not by purpose, but by the coordination of color and shape. The beaded curtain that masked the restroom door rustled loudly when I passed through it.

I resisted the urge to stuff a bunch of paper towels and toilet paper in my bag when I was done using the can. I didn't want to get the manager anymore annoyed then he was already. What if I needed to negotiate a price? I came out and made a beeline for the housewares section. Before I was five feet away the woman who had come in carrying the Lhasa Apso hurried into the restroom. She didn't close the door, instead I heard the sound of aerosol air freshener being sprayed. The smell of the lavender scented disinfectant spray soon wafted in my direction. I turned my head towards her but she avoided eye contact, instead pulling on the lapels of her wool blazer to straighten her jacket, she marched by me. I swear she had her nose in the air, really, just like you see in the movies. The manager walked around the counter.

"What is it you're looking for?" He held his hands in front as if in prayer. I'm sure he was praying I'd get the hell out of his store.

"Oh, I need a pot to boil water in and a blanket." I surveyed the housewares area again, trying to spot a pan, not too big, that would fit on the ever so small kitchenette burner in my room at the Rest Inn.

The man walked to the other side of the table and picked up a heavy stainless steel pot. "Something like this?"

"Yes, that's a little big, but that's the idea." I reached over and took it from him. "This one is eight dollars."

"Holy cow, if I had eight bucks I'd go to the dollar store and buy a whole set." Oops, I didn't mean to say that out loud. It just slipped out.

If he was a little huffy before he was really huffy now.

"This is not a junk store. We do not sell cheap imported trash. We are a quality re-sale shop, all our proceeds go to charity I don't think we have anything in your price range." He was snotty.

"All of your proceeds or all of your profits after you get paid? What's your cut?"

"I'm afraid I must ask you to leave." He pointed to the door.

I couldn't resist one last jab, "You're wrong you know this is junk. The stuff you're wearing is made in the same sweat shops as everything else. Have a nice day."

Before I was out the door the Lhasa Apso lady made a show of spraying disinfectant into the air again. What a couple of arrogant asses, they deserved each other.

This was not where I needed to shop, I wandered around town and tried to think of all the places I could that sold second hand. I passed a few consignment shops, a for profit re-sale store, they either weren't open or had prices out of my range. Nobody hassled me in them but they didn't go out of their way to welcome me either.

If you're down on your luck and need clothes or stuff there's something you need to know about thrift stores. The least expensive ones are run by churches or charities devoted to helping poor people, like the Salvation Army or Good Will. They have good prices; the clothes are organized by size not color. They are not trying to turn a steep profit for paid board members. It was at one such place, St Gregory's of the Valley Episcopalian Thrifty Boutique, I now found myself. It was housed in a small shed towards the back of the church parking lot, open only two days a week, twelve to three, staffed by volunteers, they welcomed all through their doors.

"Good Afternoon." A sweet voice greeted me as I walked in the door. Was she talking to me?

"Good afternoon." I smiled back at her.

"Nice fall weather isn't it?" She was talking to me.

"Yes, it is." I looked around the small shop, clothes were folded and stacked on tables, a length of rope had been stretched from wall to wall and assorted wire and plastic hangers held jackets and dresses and weighed it down until it sagged almost three feet in the middle. "Do you have any pots? Cooking pots?"

"Why yes we do," still a melodious soprano, what a sweet lady. "We have some right over here." She walked with me and picked up a plastic bin from the floor balancing it on top of a stack of old blue jeans. "Look through and see if you can find what you're looking for."

"Are the prices marked?"

"I believe everything in that bin is fifty cents. But if you find what you want bring it up front and I'll check it for you." She headed back to the front of the store and began to pull used plastic grocery bags from a larger bag, smoothing them and folding them neatly.

All right, this might turn out okay after all. I pulled five pots, most were dented or hand large gouges in the finish, about half way down, a bit of copper showed through, I grabbed the handle and pulled it up. A heavy copper bottomed pot, it bore only one small dent. It did need cleaning, but hey, so did I.

"How about this one? Is it fifty cents?" I think the desperation in my voice showed.

She came over, picked it up, handed it back. "Oh, I could probably let that one go for forty cents."

Thank you, Jesus, for bringing me here.

"I'll take it. Do you have any blankets?"

"No blankets, but we do have a couple of bed spreads and quilts." She came back, lifted the bin of pots down to the floor, walked four steps to the back wall and pulled up another plastic bin. In it were three bedspreads, one worn thin with a large tear separating the lining from the front, the other was little more than a crib blanket, but the third was just right. I felt like Goldilocks lost in the forest, except instead of bears and bowls of porridge, this one had Power Rangers. Red Ranger to be exact.

"How much?" I held it open, checking for stains or rips, it had none.

"Two Dollars." She returned to the front of the store, but turned around and stepped towards me when I called out.

Even if put the pot back I wouldn't have enough for this, I started to fold it and put it back in the bin.

"One fifty?" She asked sweetly, looking over her glasses that had fallen to the front of her nose.

"No." I shook my head sadly. "I only have a dollar to spend."

"Sold," she said, and helped me fold it back into its compact shape.

It was the first time I had smiled in months.

"Thanks, it, I, just thanks."

"Oh, that's why we're here."

I walked with her to the front of the tiny shop and put the quilt and the pot on the counter, reached in my pocket to retrieve the dollar bill and change. She pulled a cash box from under the counter and used a key from around her neck to open it, put my money in and handed back a dime. As I was stuffing the quilt and pot into my cloth shopping bag I spied two rows of nick knacks on shelves by the door. Hidden behind Christmas ornaments, souvenir spoons and flower vases were two glittery snowman candles; one was brand new. The other candle had about a fourth of the snowman's top hat melted to one side. I picked up the latter.

"How much?"

She looked at me smiled broadly and said "Ten Cents."

I could hug her. I put the candle in my bag and handed her the dime. "You wouldn't happen to have any matches would you?"

"Just wait." She walked back to the counter where the cash box had been stowed and pulled out a gallon size zip-sealed bag stuffed with matchbooks.

"We find them all the time in the pockets of donated clothes." She reached in and picked out two of the bigger packs, opened them to be sure they still had matches and brought them over to me.

"Thank you so much, this is great, exactly what I needed." Tonight would be a lot different than the past few nights. I'd have candle light, a blanket and a pot to heat a can of soup.

She reached over to the nick knack shelf and grabbed the second snowman candle stuffing it into my bag. "Two for one special today." Then she opened the door for me.

"Be safe. Come back and see us. Come for bag day, third Wednesday of the month all you can fit in a bag for three dollars."

I do believe in miracles.

I started to walk everywhere with my head down. Not out of shame but out of hope. I was hoping I would find a few coins, dropped from pockets or purses. The best place to look is outside a convenience store, or near vending machines. Once I found a dollar bill stuck between some tree branches downwind of a coffee drive up window. If I could find another one, I might get to that bag day sale at St. Gregory's.

60

Every other day I would find the Rest Inn housekeeping staff, all of whom spoke only Spanish, and beg for the leftover soap slivers and old newspapers discarded in the rooms.

Fewer and fewer rooms needed cleaning as the motel made the gradual transition to weekly or monthly rentals without housekeeping services. But there was still the occasional unwary traveler or unlucky local who needed a cheap place to spend the night. For them, the Rest Inn, as run down as it had become, was a welcome respite from on otherwise unwelcoming world.

My friendship with the downstairs neighbor with thick black hair, MaryIsabelle, was just getting started. After the first couple of days she shyly approached me. Two mornings a week I would greet her and we would visit a few minutes before she got on her bicycle, riding to her regular group sessions at the Community Mental Health Center. There she and others who were sidestepped by bi-polar or other psychosis met regularly to help each other navigate a path in life that would keep them out of jail and at least half a foot in reality.

Sometimes we would share a cup of tea, all I had to offer. But MaryIsabelle might have snack cakes or stale donuts brought home from her last session. She was the one who told me that CJ stood for Cesar Jesus. It was he who made the nightly run through the complex. Three times a night, he would lock the office doors and run the steps, balconies and parking lot of the Rest Inn checking for malcreados.

Talking with MaryIsabelle could be a little dicey. I was never sure which one of her I was talking to. As long as she took her meds she was pretty even headed. But if she forgot and skipped a dose or two she was likely to slam the door in your face and lock it. Today was such a day. I bypassed her door and headed over to the other building in the complex where I saw the housekeeping cart parked outside a group of rooms on the ground floor.

"Buenos Dias Lettie.¿ Como Esta Usted?" My Spanish was barely passable

"Buenos Dias Señora, Bien, bien y Usted?" she was sorting through the linens, counting out sheets and towels.

"Bien, Gracias. Tiene...mmm...newspapers, papel? ¿Periódico?" (Jeez what was the word for newspapers?) I used the formal verb when speaking with her; I was one of the few here who did. I'm not sure if she appreciated it or just thought I didn't know any better.

"Sí, dos, Albuquerque Journal and uno màs, no se." She motioned with her chin to the small trash can on the middle shelf of her cart.

"Gracias Lettie."

"¿Le gusta leer Señora?"

"Sí, me gusta leer. Yo una Maestra de leer in la escuela in el norte."

"Sí, muy bien. ¿Donde? ¿Que escuela?"

I was embarrassed; I was living hand to month in a cheap motel, begging for leftover soap and newspapers. How could I explain my past life as a teacher to her?

"Oh, en el norte. Pero, no màs, no more. Gracias por el periódico, hasta luego."
I grabbed the paper and hurried off.

The Journal was a week old, from last Thursday. It didn't matter, without a TV or Radio, even week old news was new to me. Besides, when I was done reading it I could carefully fold it into strips and weave them together into mats and baskets. I had three so far. It gave me something to do besides try and spot constellations by connecting dirty spots of exploded cola on the motel room's walls.

I took the papers back to my room, boiled some water and made tea. If I put the tea bag directly into the pot of hot water I got two or three cups out of one bag.

The third section of the newspaper was the local features section. Thursday's issue was devoted to pets; animal advice column, stories of dog heros, or people who ran animal sanctuaries. It was one of my favorites. I flipped to the second page of the section and there in the bottom left corner were the pets of the week, one of them, a beautiful black Shepard, was my Peanuts.

I kept starring in disbelief, read and reread the caption. They had renamed him King. He did look like one; he sat up straight, ears erect, looking into the camera, always eager to please.

Meet King, he looks to be a Belgian Shepard, about nine or ten years old. Good manners. But don't let his size fool you. This big guy is a real sweetheart. We can't believe someone would abandon such a great dog in the night drop box. Make this royal canine part of your family. Call or stop by the Midtown Animal Assistance Center for more information.

Blinking back tears I tore the picture from the paper, folded it and placed it in the pocket of my hooded sweatshirt as I put it on. Maybe If I called I could get him back, maybe if I talked to the managers here they would see what a great dog he was and make an exception: maybe, maybe, maybe.

I checked my pockets, a dollar and some change was all I had. Would it be enough for phone call? I went down the stairwell and asked the first person I encountered, an older man, Mr. Gonzales. He carried a small coffee and white Burger King bag I'm pretty sure held his morning sausage, egg and cheese sandwich. I had watched him make the slow trek, down the stair and across the street every morning since I had been here.

"Good Morning, Mr. Gonzales. How's the coffee today? Do you know if they have a pay phone in the lobby?"

He paused, leaning hard on his cane, "Coffee's hot, that's about all I can say for it, but it does come free with the sandwich. Do you know when I first moved here they used to have coffee in the lobby all day long and we had a coffee maker in our room right near the bathroom mirror? But, no, they had to take out the office phone. People kept breaking into it for the change; once upon a time every room had a telephone too. Anyway, everyone uses a cell phone now, don't you have one?"

"No, I don't. Do you have one I can borrow?"

"I would let you borrow it but the batteries' dead. If Cesar is still in the office he lets people make calls on his phone for a dollar if it's not long distance. You could try there." He walked past me and fumbled with the lock to his room.

"Cesar? The man who works in the office?"

"Yes, didn't you meet him? He's always there. He lives here. He has a room next building over." Mr. Gonzales reached into his jacket pocket in search of his key.

"Yes, I have met him, I just wasn't sure of the name. Thanks, enjoy your breakfast."

"You too Mrs. Roark, come join me sometime. I go over every morning at eight thirty." Mr. Gonzales smiled at me as he closed his door.

If I spent my dollar on the call there was no way I would have the three needed for the bag day sale. I hesitated outside Mr. Gonzales door. It wasn't quite nine o'clock. I wasn't sure Cesar would lend me his phone. We hadn't hit if off so well the first couple of times we crossed paths. But I had to find out about Peanuts. I swallowed my pride, something I had gotten good at, and went down to the office.

Cesar was still there, but the second shift was too. They sat together reviewing the motel guest register.

"Yes, can I help you Ms. Roark? Anything else you care to complain about?" Cesar looked up from the computer screen; at least he remembered my name.

"I need to make a phone call. Mr. Gonzales said you lent your phone sometimes."

"Is it local?" He looked me up and down, doing a sobriety check. So many of the motel residents came into the lobby intoxicated Cesar had developed his own under the influence detection system.

"Yes, it's local." I pulled the dollar bill from my pocket and pushed it over to him.

He took the phone from his pocket, turned it on and handed it to me, leaving the dollar bill on the counter and went back to the computer screen.

"Don't leave the lobby," he said.

A couple of other people had come in to check on rooms and pay rent, it was kind of noisy. I squeezed myself into a corner, pulled the newspaper clipping from my pocket and dialed, trying to shield myself from the chaos.

"Midtown Animal Services, may I help you?"

"Yes, I wanted to find out about a dog in last week's paper, the black Shepard, Pea- I mean King, is he still available?"

"King? No, he was adopted by a wonderful family. They were so happy to get him, such a great dog. But we have so many other great dogs here. Why don't you come down and have a look?"

"Oh, I, um, I had a Shepard that looked like that one. I wanted to find out about him, was he at the shelter long?"

"No, we had him about three or four weeks. He was left in the night drop box, a little skinny, but such a sweet guy the staff here just loved him. When did you lose your dog? Did you check with the other shelters?"

"It's been awhile. I just wanted...I was hoping...I...well thank you. I'm glad he found a good home."

I hung up before she could say anything else. I couldn't help but tear up, again blinked them off, took a deep breath, forced a smile with closed lips, turned around and passed the phone back to Cesar who had just finished the review of the computer guest registration.

He looked me over again. For the first time since I walked in the door he didn't seem annoyed.

"Is everything all right?" He peered at me over the top of the monitor, his concern unshielded.

"Yeah, it's great. I'm fine, thanks for the phone."

The dollar bill was still setting on the counter; he picked it up and handed it back to me.

"I never charge for bad news."

I tried to give it back to him. "It wasn't bad news, it..., well, it was good news."

"Then why are you crying?" He pushed the dollar back towards me.

"Tears of joy."

"You don't look too joyful."

"It's okay, really." I pushed the dollar back at him. I couldn't help it, more tears fell I couldn't blink them away, used my sleeve to wipe my eyes and started to walk away.

"Wait. Two minutes. I'll let you use that dollar to buy me a bowl of chile at Wendy's for breakfast".

I don't know why but I waited.

He grabbed his hoodie jacket, clocked out and pushed the door open.

"After you."

Wendy's was about six blocks away. I hoped all he wanted was a bowl of chile because that was all I could afford. Including my change I had exactly one dollar and seventeen cents in my pocket.

It was hard to keep up with him. I thought I was used to walking everywhere, but this guy ran everywhere. It was almost impossible to talk or answer his questions, for one he was always ahead of me. For another, I was out of breath.

"So, how are you adjusting to the Rest Inn?"

"Good, good. I am glad to have a door that locks." I spewed that last part out rapidly and quickly caught my breath.

"Aw, that's what most of our guests say." He had his hands in his pockets, looked back over his shoulder as we crossed a side street.

"MaryIsabelle tells me you were a teacher." We were on the other side of the street. The morning traffic had thinned so he stepped from the curb and jaywalked, more like a jog, across the intersection against the light.

I hustled to keep up with him. "Yeah, I...was...I...taught...middle school. But...not now." I was out of breath and barely made it across before a group of cars passed by, none of them slowing for us.

"It's okay; you can save your life story for later."

Whew, I was off the hook and out of breath.

We got to Wendy's in record time. There was only one other customer in the place. A worker was wiping down tables and sweeping up from the morning traffic, two others worked behind the counter. None of them looked to be more than twenty years old.

Cesar took off his jacket and threw it on a table close to the entrance; he wore a white t-shirt under a blue work shirt that had the arms cut off. Man he had big arms, most of the skin on them covered by tattoos.

"You go order while I hit the can." He headed down the hall towards the restrooms.

I walked to the counter and ordered the ninety nine cent chile from a teenager who probably should have been in school. I resisted the urge to scold him.

"Do you want our ninety nine cent frostie or fries with that order? Anything to drink? For here or to go?"

"Just water, that's all, for here."

He put an empty tray on the counter, placed a paper place mat on it, reached behind and got a small cup, no bigger than a bathroom cup, the kind you get from plastic dispensers, and placed in on the tray.

"Water's available with the fountain drinks. Your order will be right up." I handed him my dollar and change. I had five cents left.

"Thanks." I picked up the cup and walked to the dispenser, half filled it with ice and then filled it to the top with water, and wished I had a second cup, I was thirsty too. When I turned around Cesar was sitting at the table. He held his cell phone in front of him thumbs working the numbers, peering at the screen, looked up at me and nodded.

By the time I got back to the counter the bowl of chile was setting on the tray. I grabbed a spork, asked for some crackers and took it to Cesar, setting it down in front of him. He flipped the phone off and returned it to his pocket.

"I hope you like water."

"It's my beverage of choice." He looked at the single bowl on the tray. "Why aren't you eating too?"

I didn't t have a good lie so I told him the truth. "I only had the one dollar. It's okay I had tea before I left."

He seemed annoyed again, took his wallet out of his back pocket, pulled out two dollars, walked to the counter, and returned with another bowl of chile and cup of water, which he set in front of me. "I hate to eat alone."

We sat in silence for a while, eating the chile, crunching the crackers in and pushing them around. He wasn't talking now, I felt awkward. I refilled both water cups and came back to the table.

"Thanks for letting me use your phone. I really appreciate it. I was looking for a pay phone but there aren't many around anymore."

"You're welcome." He took his phone out again and flipped it on, laying it on the tray beside his bowl of chile and took a long drink of water, emptying the cup.

"I was just wondering what makes someone like you, who seems well educated, you don't seem to have a drug problem or anything." He looked me over again, checking for signs of impairment.

I stopped eating, put my spork down and folded my hands in my lap, staring down and anticipating the rest of his question. Oh god, here it comes. I wasn't ready to tell this guy my life story.

"What makes someone like you spend their last dollar to call the Midtown Animal Shelter?" He held up the screen of his cell phone revealing the outgoing call's number.

I looked up at him, startled. This wasn't the question I was preparing for. They say the truth shall set you free so I gave it a try and pulled the newspaper clipping, folded to show Peanuts' picture, out of my pocket placed it on the table beside the cell phone.

"This used to be my dog. I couldn't afford to feed him anymore, plus the hospitality centers for homeless won't let you in with a dog, I couldn't take care of him. I took him to the shelter. I had to leave him in the night drop box because I didn't have the thirty dollar surrender fee. I wanted to find out what happened to him. He was a really good dog. "

I hung my head again; tears flowed down my nose landing on the paper napkin beside my bowl of chile. I picked it up and dabbed my eyes before crushing it in my hands, holding it between them.

"I do remember him. You had a voucher from the Red Cross, couldn't get into Heaven I believe." Cesar rearranged the cups and bowls on the orange tray. "So what happened to him?"

"He was adopted by a family. It's good, it's not bad. He was, is, a good dog."

Cesar leaned back in his chair and got his wallet out again. He opened it to the plastic insert that held his driver's license, and pulled a small picture folded in half out from behind his license. He unfolded it on the table, smoothing the tattered edges, and then pushed it across the table to me. A much younger smiling Cesar with even bigger arms and wearing an identical blue work shirt with the arms cut out leaned against an adobe wall, holding a chubby Beagle, rubbing his belly.

"This is Blue." Cesar said. "He was a great dog too. My sister was supposed to watch him for me. I was, um, indisposed. She got tired of his barking and took him to the pound. By the time I got out, I mean by the time I could take care of him again, he was already gone."

Cesar hung his head, reached across the table and placed his two hands on top of my folded hands, and we both stayed like that in the Wendy's booth, starring into our empty bowls of fast food chile and the pictures of each other's good dogs placed beside them.

The kid who had taken our order walked over. He had been listening in. He carried a red tray on which sat a small order of fries and two chocolate frosties in the same size small bathroom dispenser cups we drank our water from.

"Can I offer you a complementary order of fries and a frostie?" He offered the tray to us, genuinely concerned.

Cesar raised his eyebrows a bit amused and lifted the two Frosties from the tray. I took the fries. "That's very kind of you," we said together. When the kid smiled and walked away Cesar and I looked at each other and tried to keep from laughing. Here was a teenager, probably a high school dropout, neither of us knew, offering condolences in the form of a bag of fries and chocolate soft serve. It was the best gesture either of us had received in a long, long time. Gotta love that kid.

We finished our meal in silence, gathered up the trash, put the pictures back in our pockets, waved to the kid who waited on us and walked out the door.

"Are you headed back?" Cesar asked me as he turned south towards the Rest Inn.

"No, I want to go the library, check out a book now that I have an address. Hey, thanks again for the phone and for the chile." I put my hands in my pockets and backed up a couple of feet.

"Not to mention the complimentary fries," he said, laughing then turned and jogged away.

61

It was November 10th, Wednesday, and the Day before Veteran's Day. I had been living in one small room, furnished with one bed, one table and one chair, at the Rest Inn for one month and three days. I counted because I had to know how many days to feed myself on twenty seven dollars a month. I had dutifully paid the rent on the fifth day of the month, four hundred eighty five plus tax, which meant I had another month of not sleeping on the ground. I was hopeful that today, the second Wednesday bag day sale at the St Luke Presbyterian Thrift Store, I would be able to get a change of clothes, a real plate and bowl, even a towel, all for the grand sum of three dollars. That was contingent on it all fitting in one brown paper bag. When you have nothing you become keenly aware of how even something as simple as clean socks and a towel can make a huge impact on your quality of life.

I had worn the same set of clothes for more than two months. I washed things as best I could in the sink. Soaking things in the sink didn't really clean them. The dirt had embedded itself in the fibers and was muddied and blended together to create a new shade of gray. But it did make them smell better. I had to be mindful about what I washed and when. That first night, when I washed everything at the same time I was left without anything, and wrapped myself in a newspaper poncho waiting for my clothes to dry. I wondered who was wearing my old clothes. Were they slowly decaying in a landfill or were they waiting to be added to someone else's three dollar bag?

It took me a while to figure out I didn't need the entire red and blue *Power Rangers* comforter on the bed. It was long enough to pull over my head. The first few days I used a corner of the quilt as a washcloth, cleaning myself at the bathroom sink with a squirt of dish soap, then spread the blanket out carefully hoping it would dry. After a couple of nights with two wet corners on the bed, I knew I'd need another solution. I got the idea to tear a small strip, not more than a foot, from one end of the comforter and use it as a towel. It worked, though not well. Now I could take a proper shower and not have to drip dry.

I sat in my single chair, wearing a more or less clean but damp shirt and socks, writing in my notebook, trying to budget three dollars for bag day. I was down to the twenty dollar minimum balance required to keep an account open. Since my account at the Credit Union had dipped below the two hundred dollar mark, I had lost three dollars to service fees, I had already made two of the three free withdrawals, and only had one more left. I needed to be accurate. Otherwise I would find myself paying my rent money to the bank in service fees and then I'd be sleeping on the street again. The service fees never fazed me when I was working, but in my present financial state every dollar made a difference in whether I would eat today or not.

So there I was, with my dirty thin cotton khakis and almost dry muddy yellow T-shirt, deciding that the thing to do to get by was to eat out, by that I mean eat in the soup kitchen. If I was lucky I might get a food box. I had never been eligible for a food box before because I had no place to cook or store the food. But now I did, maybe I could get one. It meant I might scrape together the three dollars for bag day.

I checked the tuna can I used for change: one quarter, two dimes, two nickels and six pennies. It's a start I thought. I put the change in my pocket, repacked my JC Penny cloth shopping bag and opened the door. It was a little after eight in the morning. The traffic jams were just starting to clear.

MaryIsabelle's door was open. I knew this meant Cesar had not worked the night before and MaryIsabelle had company. MaryIsabelle's bi-polar disorder and clinical depression garnered a monthly disability check and supply of antidepressants which kept a constant stream of street people visiting her. Cesar, when he made his thrice nightly rounds would shoo them away. But last night no one came by to serve as MaryIsabelle's bouncer. She had three guys in there, all in various stages of intoxication. From the smell of things, they were huffing.

Rooms on the second floor, where she was, were a step up from third floor's *basic no housekeeping*. The room was bigger, had two chairs instead of one, cable TV and a microwave. Housekeeping was optional and MaryIsabelle had opted out. She sat in one of the two chairs drinking value pack brand orange soda from a shared three liter bottle and eating pork rinds. The TV was blasting away. The look on her face said this was a down day.

"Good Morning." I greeted her as I passed by her door. She looked up. One of her eyes was bruised. I paused by her door.

"You okay?" I peered into the room.

The guys in there immediately turned their attention to me. I had seen them around. These were the homeless your mother warned you about; drunk or on drugs most of the time they would steal anything even if it was nailed down. Their drug of choice was inhalants and I don't mean nasal spray. Spray paint, gas, any kind of aerosol, it was cheap, easy to use and didn't get you arrested. But it rotted your brain, permanently, the original zombie maker.

"Hey, Blondie, come in and join us. Why you so stuck up?" One of the zombies waved his arm at me. Jesus, he looked bad. He had deep black circles under his eyes which were unbelievably yellow, a thick haze of red lines twisting through them. His clothes were a mated mess. I'm no one to complain about having clean clothes but my god, he looked as if he had pissed his pants several times and never bothered to try and clean them up.

"Sorry, maybe another time. I was just leaving."

"Hey, where you gooooooo-ing. You going to school or something? Teach ABC? Hey come teach us." Zombie one, aka Simon, amused himself at my expense.

"Yeah we want to learn don't we Benny." Zombie two kicked a pile of clothes on the floor. Under it was another drug out Zombie, Benny.

Benny appeared to be unconscious but he wasn't. He might as well have been, he was clueless to what was happening around him. He sat up slightly and swayed forward and back still high from sniffing the gasoline he kept in a jelly jar in his pocket. He took it out for another whiff.

"Lay off her Jerome, she's a friend of mine, okay." Even on her bad days MaryIsabelle had a since of loyalty.

Jerome got up and grabbed the bag of pork rinds from her hand, tearing it down the side which made them spray out in all directions of the cheap motel room. Truthfully, you couldn't tell, there was already so much garbage, spilled cereal and food wrappers on the floor, half a bag of pork rinds was barely noticeable.

"Oh she your friend huh? How come she don't want to party with us, huh?"

"Stop it Jerome! Look what you did. They're all over the floor."

"You still hungry? Here have some." Jerome grabbed a handful of the crumbled food off the floor and smashed it into MaryIsabelle's face, laughing.

I didn't know what to do for MaryIsabelle. I couldn't leave her here with these guys, but they were so far gone you couldn't predict what they would do. I had to find my best big mean teacher voice.

"You gentlemen need to clear out, that's enough." I took a cautious step into the room. Jerome took a step back, surprised, but quickly recovered.

"So what you gonna do about it Blondie." Simon smirked at me.

I spoke directly to MaryIsabelle. "I'll get Cesar."

She was blinking back tears, but remained motionless. I didn't wait for a response. I backed out of the room and walked rapidly towards the stairwell, hoping I could find him. I knew which room he stayed in, but there was no telling if he was there. I didn't know if he would help or not. I could hear the guys laughing and taunting MaryIsabelle. I wondered if she would ever get the help she needed for her bi-polar so she wouldn't welcome scum like that into her life.

She was yelling and weeping. "Stop it, cut it out." The three men kept taunting her.

When I heard the door to her room slam closed I double timed it over to the next building, second floor corner room, next to the mechanical area. It was as far away as Cesar could get from the office, and isolated from the rest of the rooms by the whirring of heaters, coolers, ventilators and just plan stuff that kept a place like this from melting into the asphalt.

I banged loudly on his door "Cesar, it's Aileen. Please, are you in there? Cesar?" I kept banging on his door.

"What?" There was an angry yell from the other side of the door.

"Cesar, MaryIsabelle needs you."

"I'm off, go to the office." He was more than a little annoyed.

"Please, Cesar. She's got those glue sniffers in there. Please, she's got a black eye. I'm worried what they might do."

"What do I look like a hero? Call the police."

"Please." I pleaded with him. "I don't have a phone. She needs help".

There was silence on the other side of the door.

I closed my eyes and leaned my forehead against the door jam. The vibrations from the traffic on the interstate nearby seemed to transmit through the asphalt and up the wall. It was strangely comforting, like a vibrating fingers bed box for your brain.

"I thought you said you got a bonus if the police weren't called all week."

I heard a little movement. The door opened and Cesar came out, pulling on his shirt and slipping on his shoes. He tossed his phone at me "That's for back up only, if you have to, call 911." He jogged across the concrete balcony that connected his building with the next. "You are such a pain Blondie."

I followed after him, but couldn't keep up. A couple of the regulars noticed the commotion, and wishing for a fight to mark the day's entertainment, followed along.

Cesar started pounding on MaryIsabelle's door. "Open up Mary, I need to inspect the premises." Cesar's voice was stern and loud, but silence followed.

"Look I'm coming in. Don't make me use my pass key." He jiggled the handle.

The hinges moaned as the door slowly opened. The three zombies filed out, like the three witches of Macbeth, the first two sneering and presenting three middle fingers of their hands like a trident, shaking them sideways in a gang threat inches from Cesar's nose. I know he wanted to pound them into the pavement, but stood resolute and silent while they dragged past him, pulling up their pants and spewing obscenities as they walked along the landing and down the stairs.

MaryIsabelle stepped out from behind the open door, her head down, in a daze. Her left eye was swollen, puffing out above the eyelid, blocking her vision. Cesar looked at her then around the littered room, pausing at each pile of trash, spoiled food or dirty clothes on the floor. He turned towards me, lifting his index finger in front of my face. "You, you get this place cleaned up." He flipped me his key ring, "The door next to my place, get the cleaning stuff, get it cleaned up, pronto. ¿Comprende Blondie?"

"Thanks," I said to him as he walked by me and handed back his phone.

He took it from me, frowning. "Make sure she's okay." His tone softened.

"Yeah I will, I'll take care of it, thanks again."

He nodded and shook his head at the same time. "Next time just call the police." He walked back to his room calling over his shoulder "Leave the keys in the office."

I went into MaryIsabelle's place. She stood motionless in the middle of her room, subdued by her circumstances.

I put my hand on her shoulder, pushed the hair away from her eye with my other hand, and said "Let's have a look at your eye." The place still smelled like the gasoline and solvents the three zombies had been sniffing. I left the door open in hopes it would air out.

I guided her to the chair she had been sitting in a few moments ago. We had an audience of three on lookers, people of limited means and unforeseen circumstance who made the motel their home.

One of them, Mr. Gonzales used one of his crutches to push the door all the way open and looked in with concern "I'll get some ice," he said and shuffled down the balcony toward the ice machine which only worked half the time. He returned with a large chunk of ice cubes melted together wrapped in a clean but worn dish towel, clutched in his fist beneath the crutch hand-grip

Mr. Gonzales, like me, had once been a teacher. Now in his eighties, and nearly blind by diabetes, the modest pension he received combined with Social Security was barely enough to pay for his rent and buy food, let alone provide the insulin and supplies he needed. He had retired in the days when twenty grand a year was considered good money. Problem with that is his pension was half of what he made then, about ten thousand a year, less health insurance premiums, which consumed over two hundred a month. It's hard to imagine someone blaming this man's very modest educators' pension spiraling the country into bankruptcy.

"What else can I do?" he asked, while I held the ice pack to Mary-Isabelle's eye.

"Do you have any quarters for the washing machine?" I asked. Mary-Isabelle nodded and pointed to the drawer of her night stand. Mr. Gonzales maneuvered himself over and took out a zip sealed sandwich bag which held about five bucks in change.

"Maybe you could do a load of laundry." I placed MaryIsabelle's hand over the ice pack, pressed it there so she would hold it on her own.

"There's some detergent in the bathroom," she said, more mumbled than spoken outright, moving her jaw sideways. She had been hit there too.

I stripped a dirty pillow case off the bed, began to pick up clothes and towels from the floor. I tried to separate the colors, like I used to do picking up my sons' bedroom floor, but when the case was three fourths full I gave up and stuffed everything else in.

Junior, a developmentally delayed man in his twenties and pals with Mr. Gonzales, who also called the Rest Inn home, took it from me. Junior worked part time sacking groceries at the chain store supermarket a few miles away. Three weekday mornings and one weekend a month he boarded the city bus and rode it to the store where he worked a five hour shift. If Mr. Gonzales needed help getting to a medical appointment it was Junior who accompanied him, acting as his eyes, helping navigate the bus steps and opening doors. When Junior needed help banking, budgeting and scaring away zombies who wanted to steal his pay check; it was Mr. Gonzales's crutch he leaned on.

The two of them took the pillow case and bottle of cheap laundry detergent along with the bag of change, down the corridor towards the closet room which held two coin operated washing machines and one large dryer.

"I've got to go and get the cleaning supplies. I'll be right back, MaryIsabelle."

"I'll stay with her." Our third audience member made her presence known.

Cherie was about forty but looked sixty. An unlit cigarette hung from her lips. She pulled the second chair up beside MaryIsabelle, throwing her pack of cigarettes and lighter on the table as she sat down. She grabbed the remote and tuned in *Let's Make a Deal*, picked up the lighter, shaking it a few times to get it to ignite. I didn't know Cherie well. She seemed pretty stable right now and I needed to go get those cleaning supplies. I nodded thanks and dashed along the walkway to retrieve a large vacuum cleaner, broom, mop and some spray cleaner and rags from the supply closet. I pulled the door closed hard behind me to make sure it locked. The sound of Cesar's cough came from the room next door. I hurried back to the other building.

"Did you take your medication today MaryIsabelle?" I gently prodded her.

"No. It's on the shelf near the sink." She was pointed at two empty prescription bottles resting beside the microwave.

"These two are empty. Do you have anymore?"

She looked distressed. "I think there might be a few in my purse." She reached across the table and pulled a red and yellow leather purse with stylized tulips stitched on it towards her and started to rummage through. I am not sure what exactly she pulled out of it, but she popped whatever it was into her mouth.

I found a plastic soda fountain cup in the sink, rinsed it as best as I could and filled it with water. She took it from me, tipping up the cup and swallowing. I busied myself wiping down the tables and counter, straightening things as I did.

A picture frame set on the night stand bore red and pink hearts and lady bug spotted edges. Two red haired little girls, their curls embraced by green ribbons smiled in the photos. The five by seven inch photograph was of a type done by an itinerant portrait salesman. This one had come from a Kmart; the stores watermark was still visible around the edge.

I picked it up to admire it. "Cute Kids."

"Those are my daughters, Fairy May and Melody June."

"What beautiful names." I placed the picture carefully back in place after giving the glass and table top a good wipe down.

"Thank you."

I was curious to know where they were but it was obvious she was reluctant to share. Okay. I had never shared with her either. I went first.

"I had two sons. Stevie and Sean, they died in a car accident." It was as much as I could get out.

Cherie looked up from the TV, surprised.

"Oh, sorry. How long ago did it happen?"

"It's been about a year and a half since the accident. Sean, my youngest, died at the scene, but Stevie passed away last spring. He went into a coma for a few months before he died."

"I'm so sorry. You must really miss them." Cherie lit another cigarette.

"Yeah, I do." I kept cleaning, picking up trash, scrubbing gunk from the floor. I never talked about the boys, but that didn't mean I didn't think about them. Every morning, every night and every noon, and the times in-between too, were filled with thoughts of my sons. Early on I had trained myself to function with these memories operating as a continuous reflection in the background, like reruns of a TV program always on with the volume turned low.

Cherie quickly went back to watching contestant two try to guess the cost of an ATV. MaryIsabelle's meds were starting to kick in.

"My girls are with a foster family. This nosy old witch at my last place kept calling Child Services on me. They didn't have anything on me, but that nosy witch and all the neighbors were jealous of me and lied. They even got me kicked out of my apartment."

I got up from scrubbing the floor, stretched and walked over to check her eye, the swelling was slowing down, but now bright red and purple bruises circled her eye, extending halfway to her jaw.

"Can you see all right?"

"I get to see them twice a month." Either she misinterpreted my question or wanted to tell me more. "I'm going to get them for Christmas. I'm going to get a lawyer and sue and get my kids back. They lied, they all lied. As soon as my next check comes in I'm going to make a deposit on a new place, and I'll have room for them. I'm getting them for Christmas."

I didn't know what to say to her. I had only lived near her a few weeks, but having seen the mess in her place, the worst of her bipolar days when she forgot her medication and the ebb and flow of losers and crack heads in and out of her room, I probably would have called child protective services too.

Cherie continued to chain smoke while I cleaned.

"You missed a spot over there," she motioned with her chin, not bothering to remove the third cigarette she had lit this morning from her mouth while she shook the match to extinguish the flame.

I wiped down the surface. Everything was sticky with food waste, and coated in a mix of dust and the ever present diesel exhaust that drifted from the Interstate.

It took me two and a half hours to pick up the trash, vacuum and clean. You wouldn't think such a small room would take that long, but boy was it dirty. The last thing I did was strip the sheets from the bed and head down to the laundry closet where Junior had set up a couple of flimsy metal folding chairs. He and Mr. Gonzales were playing war with a deck of Casino cards on top of an overturned box. The two cans of Coke setting on the concrete beside them were already decorated with polar bears in Christmas attire. Junior and Mr. Gonzales had used some of MaryIsabelle's change in the vending machine to buy them. The decorated cans could have been early holiday fare, but it was more likely they were old stock, leftovers from last season. The impoverished dwellers of the Rest Inn would seldom complain about the postdated, flat and stale offerings found in the complex's several vending machines.

"Mr. Gonzales, maybe you should try diet soda."

"Oh that stuff taste's awful, besides, my sugar's good this morning. I can tell because my hand isn't shaking." He held his hand out; it was shaking like a cold Chihuahua. Was this how he checked his blood sugar?

"Be careful Mr. Gonzales. I think Cesar would throw us all out if we have any more excitement around here today. "

"Don't worry about him, he likes everyone to think he's a bad hombre but he's really a softie." Mr. Gonzalez winked at me, or tried to. It was more of a blink with both eyes.

"Do you have enough for another load?"

Junior pulled the zip-lock bag from his pocket. There were four quarters, one dime and two nickels left. Unfortunately the machine cost one twenty five, and that was just for the washing machine. I pulled the change from my pocket, added my only quarter to the stash and put the linens in to wash, emptying the last of the detergent bottle into the slowly filling wash tub.

"Hey Junior, take the dry clothes back to MaryIsabelle's and see if Cherie is still there and can fold them, ask her if she has a couple more quarters for the dryer." The wind was starting to pick up, signaling another round of fast moving storms would move through the valley.

Junior took the clothes from the dryer in one large armful, dropping socks and dishtowels on the way, trailed by Mr. Gonzales, who deftly used his crutch to pitch up the dropped laundry, catching it in midair. I watched them move along the balcony. Today would be a good day for both of them, they had a purpose and had each other, later they would share a frozen pizza and watch sitcoms, Junior would fill in the parts. Mr. Gonzales couldn't see, and he in turn would explain the jokes Junior didn't get.

Junior jogged back towards me "She say she take care of things."

"Who? Cherie or MaryIsabelle?" I asked.

"Cherie. She say she take care of sheets and stuff."

"Great, thanks Junior."

"Okay, see you later."

"Yeah, see you later buddy. Don't forget your chairs."

He picked them up, turned over the box, and discarded the coke cans in the five gallon bucket that served as a trash can in the laundry room. I watched him walk away and wondered what would happen to him if he didn't have someplace like this to stay. Would he be forced to live on the streets as I had?

There was an unwritten rule at the Rest Inn: never ask anyone how they landed here. If they wanted to tell you, okay, but don't ask. The motel was not on anyone's top ten list. That doesn't mean we weren't profoundly grateful to be here. I know I was. I was pretty sure Mr. Gonzales, Cherie and Cesar were too. The doors lock, there was a warm place to lay your head at night and space to prepare a modest meal. Not luxury living, but it sure beat squatting behind a dumpster to take a crap when it was thirty degrees outside just before you lay out your cardboard for the night beside the receiving door in back of a strip mail. Thank you, Rest Inn.

I took advantage of the cleaning supplies to do my room too and hauled the stuff up to the third floor. It was already after noon. If I hustled to clean this place I would still have an hour to make it over to the Better Day Hospitality Center and try to collect a food box.

I made quick work of my own place. I especially appreciated the vacuum. I used it to vacuum the mattress flipping it over to get both sides. Visions of dust mites had filled my head those first few days I slept here. When I was done, the whole place smelled of pine cleaner and bleach. That smell was never so enjoyable. I let myself smile as I pulled the door closed and lugged all the gear back to the mechanical room.

When I dropped the keys off at the office, Cherie and MaryIsabelle were waiting out front.

"How are you feeling MaryIsabelle?" I pushed the hair away from her eye.

"Oh I gave her some of my Tylenol three, it really helps with the pain" Cherie lit a cigarette from what must have been from her second pack of the day and it was only a little after noon.

"It looks worse than it is, really. Thanks for cleaning up my place. I know it needed it, it was hard to get started." MaryIsabelle was much calmer and able to focus on the world around her.

"That's okay. Where are you two off to?" I was curious. I never knew these two to be friends before.

Cherie blew a smoke cloud through her nose and answered a little too fast.

"We're going for the buffet at the Casino. I have enough points on my card to get it for half price. They have barbeque on Wednesdays."

"Want to come? The Casino bus is on its way to pick us up." MaryIsabelle was sincere.

I remembered my last ride on a Casino bus. "Thanks, maybe next time, I'm a little short on funds right now."

"You and me both." Cherie coughed, laughed and took a drag on her cigarette all at the same time.

It was a three mile walk to the center. If I went west on Central, through the downtown area and across the train tracks, I would have a more direct route, but would have to pass through the no man's land of homeless who made claim to the area around the railroad tracks and frontage road as their kingdom. I had learned to pass through quickly to avoid confrontation. The intersections along this route were prime territory for passive panhandling, the only kind allowed by law.

Passive panhandling meant you couldn't physically go up to someone and ask for money, you also couldn't make a sign that asked for money directly. You could stand on the median, or sit on the street corner, but you could only have a bowl or tin can set out in front of you, and the signs would have say something like *God Bless* or *Hungry* and hope the passerby would know what you were after.

When you walked through this part of town you had to be careful lest someone think you were trying to muscle in on their spot. I had never panhandled except for watching Wizard work his magic in Santa Fe. But I saw the aftermath of it all the time. For every dollar collected, the beggar endured ten dollars' worth of thrown beer cans, flipped cigarettes and obscenities along with spinning gravel and games of chicken. Don't people have anything better to do?

I crossed under the Interstate. Someone was standing on each side, hoping to get a few coins tossed at them. I knew one of them; he frequented the same soup kitchen I did. "Any luck today?" I asked him.

"Nah, nothing. I might move over to Menaul. More traffic this time of day."

"Good luck." I nodded towards him as I made my way west.

The guy on the other side of the Interchange looked a lot like Bert. It took me a couple of minutes to realize it was Bert. He had a pink mermaid sleeping bag folded and tied to the aluminum frame of an old style backpacker's pack, on the outside an extra pair of Converse high tops with ragged holes in the canvas sides was tied, and loose socks hung from the back. I was pretty sure the socks had recently been washed in the closest public fountain, and were hanging there to dry. The whole pack was propped up against the I-25 sign a few feet from where he stood.

I hadn't seen him in a month. He was pacing back and forth, occasionally saying something to himself. He held up a small sign to about every third car that just read

Veteran. A pick-up truck stopped long enough for the driver to hand a five dollar bill out the window. Good, Bert, of all people needed it.

I gave him a small wave as I took long strides trying to make up for lost time; he hesitated and raised his hand halfway, hardly a wave, more an acknowledgment.

My hands were white and cracked from all the cleaners I used that morning and I wondered where I could find an open bottle of lotion. One of the department stores at the mall might have testers out. I tried to remember the last time I had any lotion or cosmetics of any kind. I still used dollar store dish soap when I took a bath and as shampoo. I longed for the gift baskets of soap and lotion infused with the scent of white gardenias, my boys always gave me for Mother's Day. I tried to remember the last time I had any and carried this memory in my mind, walked on oblivious to my surrounding. I'm convinced a guardian angel prompted me to look up. I was inches away from bumping into Simon, one of the zombies Cesar chased out of MaryIsabelle's place this morning. The thug made a sudden stomp, flagging his gang sign in front of my face to frighten me. He yelled something obscene, then, "You'll get yours bitch."

I stepped aside and around him. The Hospitality Center was in sight. I made a beeline for their door. Fast.

The Center was housed in a falling apart brown metal portable classroom erected on what had been a parking lot for a closed parochial school. Someone bought the site hoping to turn it into an upscale office condo redevelopment project, but the finances dried up and the bank pushed the owners into foreclosure. Homeless souls would break into the building looking for a place to spend the night. Black smoke stained the edges on some of the boarded up windows, the result of fires built for warmth.

The city, in an attempt to address the problem allowed a community agency to open an outreach food pantry in the one portable building that still met code. A mesh metal ramp led to the front door. A refrigerated truck sometimes parked to the side, especially this time of year when lots of turkeys and pumpkin pies would be donated.

It was 2:55 p.m., five minutes to closing. Ten people were in line to fill out the paperwork needed to request a food box. After you got through this station, you were ushered into a back room where you stood along a wall until 'next' was called. Volunteers collected the form, took a box or a bag from the shelf and began walking the isles of the makeshift warehouse, filling the box or bag according to your application. Family of four with small children would get boxes of cereal, granola bars and juice packs. Single elderly, were given soft foods, jars of applesauce, instant oatmeal and soup. If fresh fruit was available it was placed carefully on top so as not to bruise.

Two more came in after I did. We were called up to the long white folding table together. An overworked volunteer patiently explained the rules to us.

"To qualify for a food assistance box you have to have an address and place to keep and prepare the food. You can't sell or give it away; patrons are limited to one box every two weeks if food is available. We want to make sure you have tried for more permanent food assistance so here is the address of the nearest Human Services office where you can apply for food assistance, and other types of benefits like Medicaid." As she spoke her head bobbed up and down, reflecting the light of the overhead florescent in her glasses.

The volunteer handed each of us a form. The blank look on the face of the woman in line with me spoke volumes. She didn't have a clue what comes next. She was in her mid-sixties, neatly dressed and seemed a little embarrassed to be here.

"Do you need some help with that? I can help you if you need it." I touched her elbow gently as I spoke to her.

She looked relieved. "I forgot my glasses; I can't see that tiny print. Do you mind?"

My years as a teacher clued me in. 'I forgot my glasses' was often used to cover up an inability to read and write. I was pretty sure that was the problem now.

"Not at all." I took the form from her and started reading the boxes. "Name? Address? Do you have a kitchen or access to a kitchen? Number in household?"

"Just me and my husband, I guess you could count the cat," she answered with an uncomfortable laugh.

"Have you applied for or received a food box within the last month? If so, when and where?"

"No this is the first time I've applied. Seems like the money runs out before the month does." She adjusted the buttons of her coat and sighed.

We all nodded in agreement. My stomach growled audibly, surprising even the food worker. I hadn't eaten anything except a single slice of bread with half a plastic packet of jam for breakfast.

I handed the form back to her and pointed to the signature line. "If you take this back up to the table they'll tell you if you qualify."

"Thanks. I really appreciate it." She still looked bewildered, but cautiously walked over to the volunteer who was reviewing a stack of forms already filled out.

The other member of our little group was waiting too and looked at me hopefully. "Did you forget your glasses too?" I asked him playfully.

"No, I just don't write all that well. My hands shake so much I can't hold onto a pencil anymore. Could you help me too?"

And it was true, the paper rattled as his hands trembled. I smiled and reached out to get it from him. When we had filled out all the questions I held his elbow to steady his arm as he signed it.

"Next." The volunteer called them up to the desk.

I turned to my own paper work, began to write. A few more hopefuls had come through the door and were dutifully given a form and a rule run down. As I was on the last question Mr. Shaky Hands and Mrs. Forgot My Glasses walked back through the door, each carrying a brown bag with a couple of slightly bruised bananas on top. They were followed by the center director.

"Sorry ladies and gentleman, we won't be able to fill any more food boxes today. Please come and see us next week. You can try the St. Vincent Hospitality Center on Menaul; they may still have food available. Sorry once again."

I looked at the form in my hand. It was shaking. My hands were trembling, so was my lip, so were my shoulders. I was hungry, cold, dirty and about to cry. I probably cried more in the last two years than all the other years put together.

I got up slowly, not saying a word, turned and walked out, wiping tears from my eyes with the sleeve of my sweatshirt. I stuffed my hands in pockets and started the slow trek back east through the downtown area, past the civic plaza and empty storefronts, back to the intersection where less than an hour before Bert was holding up his sign. I passed at least twenty men and four women who were obviously street dwellers. None of them looked healthy. I could see myself in them like the ghost of a life that once was, a thin bony hand pointing at a headstone.

Bert was gone but his *Veteran* cardboard sign lay on the graveled slope of the Interstate ramp. Like I said, I had never done this before except for the brief stint watching Wizard, but never say never. I needed to eat. I ambled over, still hesitant, picked up the sign and flipped it over. The other side read *Thanks* in thick black letters.

I walked a little further back from the Intersection so I wasn't at the corner, pulled my hood on my head, and held the sign up. The light changed a half dozen times before anyone stopped. A couple, probably in their early seventies in a tan sedan pulled to the curb lane, rolled down their window and handed me a dollar bill,

"Thank you." I took the bill and put it in my pants pocket. They were obviously of modest means.

"God bless you child, we'll keep you in our prayers," the woman said to me. The light changed and they pulled away.

A small blue SUV stopped one lane over. Three giggling high school girls called out to me, the girl in the back rolled down her window and held out a five dollar bill. I stepped off the curb and approached the back window, but at the moment I said "thank you" she pulled the bill back in, flipped the switch to roll up the window and the car pulled away. All three girls inside were laughing hysterically, leaving me out in traffic as cars and trucks sped by. The teen in the front passenger seat held up her cell phone and I realized they had been filming the encounter.

A couple of empty beer cans landed at my feet, another soared above my head. But I kept standing there; ready to start talking to myself. Another car stopped, a couple with a small baby in the back, the man held out a plastic grocery bag with apple juice boxes and a pack of orange cheese snack crackers.

"Maybe this will help," he said. He looked familiar; might have been one of my former eighth graders. I pulled my hood tighter over my head and hoped he didn't recognize me.

"Thanks, it's great." I turned away rapidly, pretending to move towards another car. He idled a little longer than he needed to before finally driving away.

I was thinking I should probably call it quits when a man in his forties, driving a silver extended cab pick-up pulled into the third lane over.

"Hey! You want to make some money?" He called out the window. I waited for two cars to pass before making my way towards him.

He reached down where I couldn't see, pulled out his wallet and waved a ten dollar bill in front of the steering wheel where I could see.

"Come on, I know you want to make ten bucks." He beckoned me.

I held the sign under my arm and walked to his window. He grabbed my head from behind, pulling my face into the cab. He had unzipped his pants exposing himself to me and now wagged the ten dollar ill in his lap

"Want this? You know what to do. Come on, this can be yours."

I jumped back, almost into the path of an oncoming car about to throw up.

"Come on, you know you want it." He waved the ten again.

I ran back to the intersection, grimacing, terrified, wondering what to do. How could I get away? Tires screeched as two cars slammed on their brakes to avoid hitting me. An Albuquerque Police cruiser was third in the line of cars stopped in the west bound lane.

The light changed to yellow, the pervert in the pickup floored the car and sped off, heading south up the ramp and onto the Interstate.

The cruiser turned its lights on, I thought it was going to take off after the truck, but it was me he was after. As the city officer pulled to the intersection he rolled his window down and sternly told me to meet him on the other side, pulled through the intersection and into the parking lot on the northwest corner. The asphalt and graveled lot was shared by a store front car title loan office and a pancake house. The people in the pancake house glanced through the windows, expressionless, as the patrol car, lights flashing, pulled into the lot. For most of the establishment's patrons, this was an everyday event.

I thought about running away. The majority of my encounters with law enforcement had not ended well. But my last one, when Officer Marquez delivered me to the shelter, probably saved my life. I had the crazy idea this patrolman was on my side too. I waited for a turning car, made sure I had the walk signal, and head down, trembling, approached the dark blue Dodge Viper. The uniformed officer opened his door to get out.

"That guy in that truck exposed himself to me." I was out of breath, panicked.

"Is that right?" He didn't look up; adjusted something on his uniform. I looked for his badge, Officer Encino.

"He showed me a ten dollar bill and when I walked over to his truck he pulled my head into his cab and he had his pants unzipped."

I was so distraught and upset the words came out in a high whiny pitch without any pauses; I must have sounded like a lunatic.

"Listen, I observed you holding the sign up and stepping off the curb into the roadway. I could cite you for jaywalking as well as panhandling."

"But that man! He tried to get me to..., he pulled my head into his cab...he exposed himself to me." My voice was shaking so badly I wasn't sure I was making sense.

"Well that would be your word against his. We are having problems with aggressive panhandling in this area. Let me see your sign. We're getting complaints of people disrupting the flow of traffic. Do you have some ID?" Officer Encino pulled a clip board from his front seat.

I was incredulous. How many other women would have to endure that pervert in the pickup? What would have happened if I he had grabbed me and pulled me into the truck? Would I have been left for dead in an empty field somewhere on the city's edge? Did this cop not care or not believe me?

Officer Encino took the sign from me and flipped it over, "Are you a veteran?"

"No," I said softly. "I found the sign. I was using the other side."

"Do you have ID? An address?"

I still had my cloth bag, pulled the plastic sleeve out of the back of my notebook and slid my driver's license into my hand. He took it from me, told me to sit down on the gray parking barrier, and went back to his cruiser, checking my ID.

I sat on the concrete pylon, knees bent, arms folded around them, head down, the acrid smell of fast food grease mixed with the exhaust fumes that gathered under the interstate made my throat itch. I was thinking of all the times I had seen this play out before my eyes: Men and woman with backpacks or sleeping bags I had seen sitting on the ground or parking barriers, police lights flashing. I always assumed the street person had committed some crime, a wanted criminal on the lam, drunk, high on drugs, creating a disturbance. Now I was part of this drama and I knew different. My only crime had been to ask for help.

Officer Encino came back. "Do you have an address?"

"The Rest Inn, I have a room at the Rest Inn, off of Menaul."

"I know where it is. What's in the bag? "

"You can look; it's a notebook, some pencils and stuff." I started to stand up and hand it to him.

"Stay seated." He held his hand out flat, like he was telling a dog to sit. "I have your permission to search the bag?"

I sat back down; put the bag on the ground beside me.

"Yes, you have my permission to search my bag."

He picked it up; it took him all of ninety seconds to go through it. He handed it back to me and told me I could get up.

"Here's your ID. I don't want to see you panhandling in this area again. Next time I will write you up for it."

"What about the guy who grabbed me?"

He sighed. "If you want to file a report you can do so at the main police station, or a substation. You'll need to have a complete description of the vehicle and driver, time, and any possible witnesses. But to be frank, I observed you panhandling and stepping out into oncoming traffic, jaywalking. If you put me down as a witness that is what I would swear to. I don't want to see you in this area again."

I picked up my bag, walked over to the traffic light pole, pushed the button and waited for the walk signal.

The police cruiser idled a minute or two before heading out, turning west towards the downtown; Officer Encino continued to check his rear view mirror as I walked across the road. He kept the cardboard *Thanks* sign.

62

That was it, my first and last experience with the will work for food crowd. I had a dollar, some prayers, some juice and crackers and ten years' worth of humiliation and abuse. How did people do this? Was their need so great they would endure so much abuse for pocket change?

I walked slowly under the Interstate stopping mid-way under the bridge. The tractor trailers and semi's rumbled, non-stop, above me. There must have been seventeen or eighteen in a row, drowning out all other sounds. I was glad. I didn't think I could endure any human voices right now. If I could have packaged that sound and carried it around with me I would have. I needed it to block out the world. When the rumbling stopped I waited a while longer, trying to think what to do next. I could go by the dollar store. With the little change I had and the dollar from the first couple I could get another bag of rice or a box of oatmeal. At least it would be something hot and last a couple of days. I would hole up in my room at the Rest Inn, drinking hot tea and reading the three library books I had from dawn to dusk since I still had no light bulbs.

There was a lull in traffic. I heard a soft moan coming from the drainage which amounted to little more than a slope about five feet down from the sidewalk on the east side of the bridge. I stopped, turned slowly, twice, trying to hear it again. I walked forward, continuing to listen carefully and decide which direction it was coming from. Almost on the other side of the underpass I spied someone curled in a fetal position at the bottom of the drainage. Were they drunk? Sleeping? Passed out? I was afraid. Where was that cop? Would he believe me if I ran after him? Or would he dismiss this as another blip in the life of the homeless?

I walked down the embankment, cautiously side stepping through the broken glass and gravel, whoever it was started to moan again. About two feet away I spotted round pools of blood in the gravel. Oh my god it was Bert.

"Bert, buddy, Bert you okay? What happened?" I knelt beside him, trying to see where the blood was coming from.

He was clutching his stomach. "They took my stuff. They took my money; it's not right, not right."

His shirt and jacket were soaked through with blood. He seemed to be bleeding from three places in his abdomen. I put my hand on them trying to stop the blood, but I must have applied pressure in the wrong place because the blood started to come out faster.

"Bert we need to get help. I need to get help." I tried to stand up and go back up to the roadway, but Bert grabbed my arm, pulling me back down by him.

"They took my stuff. It's not right, need to stop; it's bad, not right." I took off my hoodie sweatshirt, wadded it up and pressed it into his abdomen.

"Help! We need help, please, can't anyone hear me?" I yelled as loud as I could. No one came.

"Bert we've got to get you some help. Can you stand up buddy? Can you walk up?"

Somehow I got him into a standing position, the blood that was covering his abdomen, now streaked my clothes. I put one arm under his shoulder, the other hand held the sweatshirt to his stomach. He used his one free hand to hold his side. I managed to get him up to the sidewalk I was afraid to let him go.

"Help, please help!" I yelled at passing cars.

I tried to flag a few down, they kept going. Did they think we were a couple of drunks holding each other up? Why didn't anyone stop? I looked up the street, desperate. Mid-Town Medical Center was less than two blocks up and across the street. I had gone there at least three times when my boys were young, twice for broken bones, and once for a football concussion. If I could get Bert there we could get help.

I dragged him, walked him, cajoled him, "Come on buddy, we can do this. Bert we've got to keep going." All the while I was trying to get someone driving by to notice us. I don't know how but we made it through the doors of the emergency room. I lowered him into the first chair inside the door and called out,"Please he's hurt."

The other patients in the emergency room stared blankly. No one came out from behind the glass to help us. I went over to one of the three partitioned desks set behind wire reinforced glass and rapped on the glass "Please, my friend's been hurt. He's bleeding."

The receptionist pointed to a sign on the wall behind where I was standing. "You have to sign in, a nurse will see you."

"Please, he needs help".

"Sign in, a nurse will see you," she said it louder, like I didn't hear the first time.

I looked around distressed until I saw the orange clipboard hanging on the wall, ran over , grabbed it, signed *Bert* under the name column since I didn't know anything else *Injured bleeding* under reason for visit *VA* for insurance. I didn't know for a fact he was a veteran, but it was better than leaving it blank. The clock on the wall read five twenty five, our arrival time.

Bert sat bent over, about to pitch forward out of the chair. I went back tapped the glass again. "I signed in, please he needs help. He's bleeding, he might pass out."

The receptionist turned to a man dressed in scrubs standing in a small corridor behind her, said something like "Can you check this one out." I couldn't hear it all, next thing I know he's comes out from behind the heavy metal door that leads to the treatment area.

"Where's the patient?"

"Over there by the door, he's bleeding."

"What happened?" He reaches into his pocket for a pair of blue latex gloves, which he puts on before he touches Bert.

"I don't know. I just found him like this near the Interstate. I couldn't get anyone to stop and help us."

The med tech gently moves Bert's shoulders up until he can see the bloody weatshirt, removes it but immediately pushes it back into Bert's stomach.

"Hold this." He takes my hand and places it over the sweatshirt. "Press hard."

The EMT quickly runs back into the treatment area and returns with a man and woman wearing green scrubs and blue latex gloves. One is pushing a wheel chair. The woman kneels in front of Bert, and takes over for me while the two guys, one on either side of Bert, maneuver him into the wheel chair.

"What happened?" the female nurse asks.

"It looks like he's been stabbed, at least 3 wounds I could see," the first tech answers as he backs up the chair.

They rush him back through the doors. I stand there confused, not knowing what to do, my clothes and hands covered in Bert's blood. Suddenly completely exhausted, my knees buckle and I can't stand up anymore. I sit in the chair Bert just vacated, blood stains and all, lean back and close my eyes.

I hear a rap on the glass nearby, look over to the partition, it's five forty five. I've been asleep or in a daze for a good twenty minutes. It's almost dark outside.

The receptionist calls me over "We need you to fill out these forms." She pushes them through the slot at the bottom of the glass.

"I can't answer any of these questions. I don't really know him that well. Is Bert all right? "

"Do the best you can to answer them."

I only write his name, for an address I put the New Start Hospitality Center, for insurance I write VA again.

I slid the form back under the glass. "Is he going to be okay?"

The receptionist checks the forms, "What about these questions?"

"I don't know his next of kin or if he takes medication. I don't really know him. I just...we...we eat at the same soup kitchen."

She looks at me suspiciously then pushes the forms under the glass again.

"Read, sign and date the last line so we can treat him."

The last line is the financial responsibility statement.

"I can't sign this. I don't have any way to pay for it. I don't really know him."

"Well we need a signature before we can treat him."

"I'm sorry, I can't, I..."

A police cruiser, lights flashing but no siren, has pulled into the emergency lane beside the door. Officer Encino, the same officer who an hour before told me he didn't want to see me again gets out. Christ, I've got to get out of here.

"I need to wash my hands is there a restroom nearby? I've still got blood on me." I try my puppy dog look on the receptionist.

She motions to a hallway at the other end of the waiting room. "What about a signature?"

"I'll be right back."

As I stand a security guard comes through the metal doors that lead to the treatment area. I pretend to hold the doors open for him.

"Thanks," he says and walks past me toward the entrance to greet Officer Encino.

I slip through the doors and head down the treatment area hallway trying to look behind curtains for Bert but I can't find him.

The next hall over has an arrow hanging from the ceiling that points to x-ray. Years ago I brought my boys here to get their arms x-rayed. If I remember right there is another entrance from the other side of the hospital, almost directly into a parking garage. I hope they haven't remodeled. I try to stay close to the walls and avoid cameras.

I'm right. There is an entrance on the south east corner of the building. I'll be able to exit here, cut through the parking garage and walk east through the university before circling back towards the Rest Inn and avoiding Officer Encino.

I say aloud as I jog through the parking garage, "Sorry Bert, I guess I left you behind too."

The blood has dried on me, making my clothes stick to me, and now I have no hoodie to block the wind, it's probably discarded in a medical waste bag back at the emergency room. Even some of my hair has been stiffened by blood, and sticks out, unkempt.

I exit the garage; rush hour has about subsided so I don't bother trying to find the crosswalks at the intersections and jog across the street, not even looking to see if a car might hit me. I gotta get home.

There are quite a few students on campus, and smatterings of homeless lying on their backs in grassy unused corners of the campus. If anyone has noticed my extreme appearance they don't acknowledge it. I half jog, half walk through campus, trying to stay in the alleys, behind buildings, out of sight.

I turn down a small utility access street behind a dorm; hear familiar voices, harsh, rough laughter. It's the three zombies. One of them has Bert's pink mermaid sleeping bag pulled around his shoulders and over his head and a small plastic bag in his hands with what looks to be silver spray paint coating the bottom. He takes a big whiff from the bag, staggers back then begins pacing in circles repeating things. "That's my stuff, that's my stuff; give me coffee, give me coffee," trying to imitate Bert. The other two are sitting on top of an industrial transformer box, opening miniatures of Jack Daniels and Jose Cuerva, about a dozen tiny bottles, all empty, are scatters on the cement in front of them. Oh God! Oh God! One of them is wearing the Converse high tops Bert had tied to his backpack. The pack is thrown on the concrete alleyway, its contents strewn in a ten foot circle around the zombies. Shit Shit Shit! What do I do?

I back away, trying not to make a sound, and run, dodging traffic, gasping to catch my breath, until I am at the Rest Inn, bound up the steps two at a time without stopping. Inside my room, my hands shaking, I close and lock the door, put the flimsy security chain on, prop a chair in front of it. The blinds were down, but angled slightly open to let in what little light remains, I turn the rod to adjust them closed, turning the room dark gray, like an old black and white horror movie.

I've got to get out of these clothes, got to get cleaned up. The only light I have in the bathroom is from the snowman hostess candle which is three fourths gone. Trembling, it takes me four of the six matches I have left to light it.

I fill the sink with cold water, turn the hot water on in the tub so it can fill up and strip down to nothing. Bert's blood has soaked through to my underwear. I put everything into the cold water of the sink, squirt value right orange essence dish soap on top and begin kneading and scrubbing the clothes together, turning the water brown red. I let it drawn, fill it with more cold water and start massaging it into the clothes again. Three more times I fill the sink, add the clothes and a squirt of soap before the water runs mostly clear.

The blood has dried on my skin and hair. I squirt more dish soap into the hot water of the tub and use my foot to kick around a few suds and climb in. The water is too hot, but I get in anyway, frantically trying to wash off the blood, grime, and stink of the day, using my hands to cup water over my head and wash my hair. I sat in the bathtub crying until the water turns cold. I drain it without getting out and fill the tub again, staying in until that water is cold too. Finally getting up, using the torn strip of bed spread to dry myself off. I have the same dilemma as my first night here, soaking wet, cold, no clothes. At least I had a candle and the rest of the bedspread. I wrapped it around sari style, wring as much water as I can from the clothes in the sink and spread them out over the chair and towel bars, hoping they wouldn't take two days to dry this time.

My stomach growls. From fear or hunger I'm not sure, probably both. I think it's about eight o'clock, twelve hours after I opened the door this morning. Twelve hours since I've eaten anything. The cloth JC Penny's bag is lying on the floor by the bathroom where I dropped it, blood stains on both sides. I dump everything out onto the mattress, and place the bag in the sink to soak. Two cheese crackers and a five ounce apple juice is dinner.

Wrapped in the Power Ranger comforter, I lie on the bed and pass out.

¤ ¤ ¤

Someone's banging on my door. Oh God, is it the Zombies? Did they see me run and come after me? I roll from the bed, as silently as I can and try to stand sideways against the wall to see who's there. The banging starts again.

"Open up Blondie, it's me. Open up. I need to talk to you." It's Cesar.

"What do you want?"

"Open up, I need to come in and talk to you." He is jiggling the door handle like he did at MaryIsabelle's.

"I can't let you in. I'm not dressed."

"Open up, I don't care what you're wearing. I need to talk to you."

"Cesar, I can't. I can't right now, tomorrow. I'll come to the office in the morning."

"No, now." He uses his pass key, pushes in on the door breaking the chain, but the chair keeps him from opening it more than a couple of inches.

"What the...? Turn the light on."

"I can't, I don't have light bulbs. I washed my clothes and they're not dry, I don't have anything to wear, I'm wearing a bedspread. Please, I'll come by in the morning."

"Wait here." Cesar's head disappears from the door.

"Oh yeah? Where would I go, to a toga party?"

"You are such a friggin pain Blondie," he says, yelling back over his shoulder.

I walk over and close the door. He comes back, knocks twice, rapidly, opens the door a couple of inches and pushes some clothes into the room.

"Put these on. Come down to the office. We need to talk."

There is an old pair of UNM wind pants and a gray Purdue sweatshirt. They are both three sizes too big. The pants are so big I knot the side of them to keep them up. The sweat shirt hangs to mid-thigh.

"Got any socks?" I say, but he has already gone done to the office.

The cold concrete stings my feet, frost has already set on the railings. I walk barefoot down the stairs and think it must be two or three in the morning. A Dr. Pepper lighted clock behind the office counter tell me it is barely past eleven.

"What's up?" I look quizzically around the tiny office lobby.

Mr. Gonzales and Junior are sitting on the plastic sectional chairs in the office. Cesar is behind the counter. They are watching the TV bolted to the ceiling in one corner of the small room.

"You're on TV, Miss Aileen. We seen you on TV." Junior is pointing to the screen where a Chevy Truck commercial reminds me of my nightmare panhandling.

"What are you talking about?'

"You in some trouble Aileen? Anything you need to talk about?" Mr. Gonzales is looking at me with concern.

"I had some, some unfortunate experiences today. Why? What's going on?"

Cesar flips his computer screen around so I see it. He has downloaded a news segment from Channel Eight's ten o'clock news. One of the anchorwoman who helped serve food at the soup kitchen a few weeks before was reading from a teleprompter as a grainy video from Midtown Medical Center Emergency room loops in the background. It's of me, walking back and forth from the reception desk to the waiting room.

Police are looking for this woman in relation to the stabbing of a homeless Veteran about five this afternoon. She apparently brought him to the hospital before abandoning him when police arrived. The veteran, forty- six year old Bert Angelos, was stabbed multiple times in the chest and abdomen, is in critical condition at Midtown Medical Center tonight, fighting for his life. Police ask if you have any information regarding the stabbing or the whereabouts of the woman shown in the video you contact Crimestoppers at the number shown on the bottom of the screen.

"Well Blondie should I call or are you going to tell us what's going on." Cesar pulls out his phone.

"Hey! Is there a reward?" Junior looks at me grinning, "That's pretty cool if there's a reward."

"Shh, Junior, no, there's no reward. Ms. Aileen is just going to tell us what's going on, and then we'll figure out what to do." Mr. Gonzales sits back with his arms folded in front of him, crutches propped up beside the chair.

I turn away from them, leaning the side of my head against the front glass, looking up at the Interstate. It is dark, late, dozens of cars speed by on the roadway above. What I wouldn't give to be in one of them right now.

I shake my head, hesitate.

"I found him beside the Interstate, in the drainage. I tried to help him, I yelled for help but no one would stop, no one cared. I got him to the hospital."

"Do you know him? The report on another channel said you seemed to know him." Mr. Gonzales's voice was loud, excited.

"No, maybe, a little. We ate at the same soup kitchen sometimes. I would give him coffee, talk to him a little. That's all."

"So why did you take off when the police arrived?" Cesar spoke sharply, direct and to the point.

I sigh. The whole story comes out: no more food boxes; panhandling with Bert's sign; the guy in the silver pickup; Officer Encino pretty much telling me to get lost; and finally my escape through the parking garage. I turn quiet, afraid of the glue sniffing zombies.

Throughout the whole confession Cesar remains still, but doesn't take his eyes off of me. He picks up and drops a pencil a couple of times, letting it bounce off the counter. But otherwise he sits in absolute silence taking in what I say. He has his internal lie detector turned on.

"What is it you're not telling me? There's more, you're afraid of something." Was he a mind reader now? Was I telegraphing that much?

"Yeah, there is more. When I was coming back, cutting through UNM, the three zombies..."

"The who?"

"The three zombies, those paint sniffers you chased off from MaryIsabelle's place this morning, they were hanging out in back one of the dorms. They had all of Bert's stuff. I think it was them. Bert kept saying 'they took my stuff."

"Did they see you?" Cesar stood up straight, tensed. He was worried.

"No, I'm not sure, I don't think so."

Cesar shook his head, looked down, thinking.

"She's going to need a lawyer." Mr. Gonzales said and used the tip of his cane to mute the office TV.

"I don't trust lawyers, lawyers are how I became homeless, how I lost everything I had. Besides, I can't afford one."

"I know one. He'll work with you." Cesar picks up his phone and begins scrolling through the numbers, pausing once or twice before he hits dial.

Billy James Dean, Esquire, answered the call.

63

The Castillo family had roots in New Mexico going back five centuries. At a time when the British and Dutch were struggling to build settlements on the east coast of the New World, the Spanish had already established trade routes and roads, appointed governors, and built elaborate mission churches. They established a capitol city north of Santa Fe around 1598, beside the confluence of two rivers near Española, a place then called San Gabriel. The Spanish claimed title to thousands of miles of land, the northern most reached into present day Colorado. The Spanish were led by a harsh conquistador named Don Juan de Oñate. The rebellious men of Acoma Pueblo would bear the brunt of his wrath by having their left feet cut off. Four centuries later, the left foot of a bronze statue of Oñate, erected smack dab in the center of Ohkay Owingeh tribal land, would have its left foot cut off in the middle of the night, a modern protest to past injustice.

A secretly planned rebellion lead by Po'pay from Ohkay Owingeh, successfully drove the Spanish from the northern land which the Europeans dubbed New Spain in 1680. The Spanish returned again just eleven years later, led by the equally harsh Don Diego de Vargas, to reconquer the land they believed contained Cibola: Seven Cities of Gold. The Native people who offered up fierce resistance to European invaders were concurred not by military might, but by diseases for which they had no weapons. Prior to the Spanish coming to what is now New Mexico over forty thousand Native people lived in relative peace. By the time of the Pueblo Revolt, they numbered less than a third of that.

The Castillo family had been there from the beginning. Serving as alcaldes, both judges and mayors, then territorial leaders, modern times would see the Castillo's become engineers, lawyers, and educators. Tall, with smooth dark skin and thick wavy hair, even the women were said to be exceptionally handsome. The young Genoviva Castillo, like her ancestors, was both intelligent and fiercely independent, entering college at sixteen and graduating at twenty, she reluctantly took a secretarial job on the hill in Los Alamos with a secret government lab during World War II. A charming young army driver named William Dean swept her off her feet and the pair eloped when Genoviva's father baulked at the union. She refused to heed her father's advice a second time after the war ended and accompanied her husband to his home in Ohio where the dark skinned Catholic bride was treated like a second class citizen by the pale Protestants of the mid-west. Tearfully, she returned to her family's home near Española, baby in arms. The pudgy boy with red hair was an enigma in the community. People would look at the tall handsome Castillo's clan then at young William James Dean and say "What Happened?"

It was Billy's voice I heard when Cesar handed me his cell phone.

"Hello?" It had already been a long night, it was about to get longer.

"Hello, this is Billy Dean, who am I speaking with now, please?" A man's deep voice was without emotion or accent.

"This is Aileen Roark." I stood, leaning against the office counter, hand on one ear to try and mask the noise of Interstate traffic outside.

"Aileen Roark. Is that with an A or an E?" He was writing this down.

"A, Aileen with an A." I turned away so I wouldn't have to look at the video of me walking around the emergency room one more time.

"Spell your whole name for me. Then give me your date of birth." Billy Dean slowly recited it back to me to be sure he had it right.

"Cesar gave me a little info, but you tell me, in a paragraph, not a novel, what's going on." He was matter of fact.

I did my best to summarize it. How I found Bert lying in the exit ramp drainage, bleeding. No one would help, dragging him to the hospital and fleeing through the parking garage.

"Why did you run away?" He emphasized the word *you*.

"The police came. I was afraid I would have to pay for Bert's care. I was scared of going to jail." I spoke rapidly. I could see myself, disheveled and worn in unfamiliar clothes, reflected in the dark glass of the office door.

"You were afraid the police would arrest you if you didn't pay for the victim's care?" The way he said it made it seem silly.

"No, I, no. The same officer who was at the hospital stopped me a couple hours before for panhandling. He basically told me to take a hike and he didn't want to see me again. I was trying to get away before he saw me." This was true.

"Okay. So you took this guy to the hospital. He was bleeding. The police officer who stopped you earlier came to the hospital and when he showed up you took off, is that correct?"

This sounded right, but it was so late and I was so confused I wasn't sure. "Yes, that sounds right."

"You hesitated."

"I had to think about it. It's all so confusing."

"And you had nothing to do with the victim's injuries. He's just some guy you found and you were trying to help, you never saw him before tonight." Billy was accusing me of something.

"Yes...No. I don't know. I do know him, sort of. I was acquainted with him. We both ate at the same soup kitchens sometimes. I was friendly with him sort of. It's difficult to explain."

"Try. Try to explain it." There was silence on the line while I composed my thoughts.

"He's a veteran, kind of shell shocked, talks to himself. I tried to help him once, at the soup kitchen. He would talk to me sometimes and I was friendly back. But we weren't friends, just knew each other that's all."

"But you knew him well enough to drag him to the hospital."

"I wasn't just going to let him bleed to death. No one would help us. I tried to get someone to stop and help. No one would."

"And you have no idea how he wound up there, how he got hurt?"

"Well...," I was really confused now, almost crying again. I needed to find a way out of this.

"There were these guys. They were in the alley behind a dumpster at the university.'

"What guys, how many, who were they? How did you get from the hospital to the University?" He was firing question at me in rapid succession.

"These three guys, they were here earlier with MaryIsabelle and..."

"Wait, who's MaryIsabelle and where is 'here'?"

"She stays here at the motel, she's a friend of mine and..." How was I going to explain everything? It was late. I was tired and scared. "MaryIsabelle has a room at the Rest Inn, near my room. The three guys were with her, but they were harassing her, bothering her, I got Cesar, he chased them away. That was this morning."

"This morning? I thought all this happened this afternoon."

"Yes, it did, but, oh God, it's just that, it's been so wild. I can't explain it."

"Look Aileen, you can explain it to me or to the police. Which do you want? Give me enough I can call the police and let them know, with some certainty, you were a Good Samaritan, not a participant, and we tell them you will come in and give a statement in the morning." Billy was getting tired too.

"Okay, okay. The same three guys who were harassing MaryIsabelle this morning at the motel were in the alley at UNM this afternoon. I ran through campus when I left the hospital, through the parking garage because the police were parked out front. The three guys, at UNM, had Bert's stuff, his backpack and shoes. Bert kept telling me they took his stuff. I ran away because I was afraid, of the police, of the hospital making me pay for Bert's medical bills and of the three guys in the alley. I ran back to the motel and hid in my room until Cesar came and got me."

"How did Cesar know about it?"

"It was on the news. The security video of me bringing Bert into the emergency room was on the news. Cesar saw it and recognized me." I was crying. This was another nightmare.

"Okay, calm down. Is Cesar there? Can I talk to him?"

"Yes I'll put him on." I passed the phone to Cesar, went into the small bathroom beside the lobby, got a paper towel and blew my nose.

I could hear one side of the conversation through the bathroom door. Cesar was saying yes or no, then "Will do." He knocked on the bathroom door.

"Blondie, Billy Dean wants to talk to you again." Cesar said.

"Hello?" I calmed down a little, the terror had lessened. On Cesar's recommendation, I was putting myself in the care of someone I had never met.

"Aileen Roark?" A born lawyer, he left nothing to chance, wanted to be sure it was me.

"Yes, it's me again." I was tired, my voice cracking, small, like I had a sore throat.

"Here's the plan. I'm going to call the police and let them know I represent you. I'm going to tell them you were just trying to help the victim and will come in tomorrow and make a statement. That way they will stop looking for you." At last I had a way out.

"I'll be down tomorrow morning, we'll meet in person. I'll get your complete statement, we'll make sure it's okay, then go down to the police station and you will make the same statement again to them. In the meantime, stay out of sight, off the street. Don't talk to anyone else about this. Understood?"

"Yes, I understand." Now the big question, "I don't know how I can pay you."

"There is a fee. I generally work with my clients to figure out how to be compensated for my services. It's usually to our mutual benefit. I almost always figure something out. I'll know more when we talk tomorrow. For now don't worry about the fee. What we want to happen is to clear up the current situation then we'll take care of the rest. Okay?" Billy Dean was more reassuring. Cesar had said he would work with me, and I had to believe him, there wasn't anyone else I could trust.

"Get some sleep. I'll be there by eight tomorrow."

¤ ¤ ¤

First light the next morning I got up, though I hardly slept, took another bath and put on the same too large sweat shirt and pants Cesar brought me the night before, made a cup of weak tea, and sat on the bed, staring at the spots on the roughly painted wall. I played out the events of the day before over and over in my mind. There were so many what ifs. What if I hadn't tried to help MaryIsabelle? What if there was food at the food pantry? What if I hadn't panhandled, or just kept walking when I saw Bert? What if? Would they really put me in jail this time? I had come so close before even though I hadn't done anything wrong. You're being paranoid I told myself.

Billy Dean was knocking on my door. I peered out the side of the blind, without opening it, making sure who it was. I could see him, a man about five foot eight, stocky, with tightly curled reddish gray hair, beard and mustache all of which needed a good trim. He was wearing a brown tweed blazer, yellow shirt and red tie. He had a cardboard accordion file in his hands and a pencil behind his ear. Scowling, he knocked a second time. I would have made him for a census taker, not a lawyer.

I opened the door.

"Aileen Roark? Are you Aileen Roark." There he was again, making sure who he was talking to.

"Yes, are you the lawyer?" I stood with the door all the way open.

"Billy James Dean. Yes, we spoke last night. May I come in?" He was already walking into the room. Instinctively he reached for the light switch.

"Oh, sorry, I don't have any light bulbs." I twisted the blind open.

"Only a little, don't let anyone see in." He looked me up and down with a critical eye then took the single chair at the tiny wobbly table in the corner of the room. "Why don't you go ahead and change, then we can go someplace to get your statement. Someplace with light."

"I don't have anything to wear." I was honest with him. He took it the wrong way.

"It's okay, it doesn't have to be anything fancy, but not sweat pants. A skirt and blouse perhaps?" He pulled the pencil out from behind his ear, opened the accordion file folder.

"I really don't have anything. I only have one set of clothes and I washed them out in the bathtub last night, they had blood on them. They're still not dry. Cesar gave me this to wear yesterday when he came to get me."

"Oh. Oh. Well, I see. Well, then, let's go across the street to that Burger King, get some coffee. I'll buy." He closed the folder, replaced the pencil and opened up my door. "After you, but you might want a jacket, it's still a little chilly out."

"I'm okay. I used my jacket to stop Bert's bleeding. I left it at the hospital." I grabbed the plastic key from the kitchenette counter and headed out the door and down the steps. MaryIsabelle was up.

"Good Morning Aileen." she called out. The bruises on her eye and forehead were already changing from purple to yellow.

"Good Morning MaryIsabelle. Feeling okay today?" I waved at her as I walked down the stairs.

"Great, doing great. I saw you on TV this morning." She was smiling like a Cheshire cat. Would she turn me in?

Billy Dean looked up at her as we rounded the staircase to the ground. "Is that the woman you spoke to me about last night?"

"Yes, she has some problems too. She goes for therapy." I was a little worried.

"What kind of problems?" Billy was hurrying across the lot. He waited at the curb for traffic to clear.

"You know, your personality goes back and forth, runs hot and cold. She had her kids taken away I guess, because of the men she was letting stay with her and stuff. I don't really know all the details." The traffic had stopped and we crossed over to the Burger King parking lot.

"Good, don't. You don't want to know the details. If you do you become part of it." Billy held the door open for me. I had my arm in front of my face, trying to block the wind. I kept thanking God I didn't have to sleep in the open the night before. Bad as it was living without lights, or sheets or anything at the Rest Inn, at least I wasn't on a piece of cardboard on the sidewalk in twenty degree weather.

Billy stood at the counter, returned to the table with two coffees and two breakfast sandwiches, pushing one of each across the table to me.

"Thanks." I said starting to un-wrap the sandwich.

"It's okay, at some point this will be paid for you know." He had already taken a bite of his, now retrieved a large yellow pad from the accordion file and the pencil from behind his ear.

"In that case, I better not." I re-wrapped the sandwich and pushed it back towards him.

He looked surprised, pushed it back at me. "Please, we're not on expense vouchers yet, please, eat it, have the coffee. I meant the whole situation paid for, not just coffee and fast food." He took a sip of his coffee.

I nodded, un-wrapped the sandwich again and started to eat. It tasted good.

"Okay, start with yesterday morning, you got up, yesterday morning, opened the door to your room, went out and then what happened?" Billy had finished his sandwich, began taking notes as I spoke.

I told him everything I could remember; the zombies at MaryIsabelle's; getting Cesar; cleaning up MaryIsabelle's room; cleaning my room; seeing Bert; seeing one of the Zombies; being turned away from the food pantry; panhandling with Bert's sign; the man who exposed himself to me.

Billy Dean stopped me there. "And the police officer, when he stopped you, he didn't offer to take a report?"

"No, I told him. He said he didn't see anything except me panhandling and he didn't want to see me again. He told me if I wanted to file a report I had to go down to police headquarters and do it, but he wouldn't back me up." I sipped the still hot coffee.

"He said that? He said he wouldn't back you up?" Billy Dean was taking copious notes now.

"Not exactly, he told me what he would swear to was that he saw me panhandling and I caused a disturbance."

Billy looked thoughtful, "Hmm, well go on."

I told him the rest, finding Bert, calling for help, getting him to the hospital and having to fill out forms, then sneaking through the double doors when the police arrived. When I got to the part about the three zombies I hesitated, looked around the room to see who else was there.

"What's the matter, expecting someone?" Billy Dean looked around the room too.

"No, those guys, the zombies, from MaryIsabelle's, they're bad news. If they would do that to Bert, what will they do to me?"

"They're never going to know. We are not going to mention them in your statement."

"But don't I have to tell the police? How else will they find out who did it?" I had finished my coffee and was swishing the grounds around in the bottom of the paper cup.

"They have already received an anonymous tip. I got Cesar to get their names from MaryIsabell and we called it in to Crimestoppers. Hopefully, they have already picked them up."

"Won't I have to testify at trail or something?"

"Doubtful. Usually, in situations like this, there is a plea deal. One turns on the other and they end up testifying against each other. We are sticking to the truth, which is that you found the victim already injured, helped him to the hospital and took off because you were afraid of the police due to your previous encounter with them that day. End of story, no cutting through parking garage or campus, you say you left the hospital and went back to the motel, period, No more details. If they ask, you answer the question asked only, with as short an answer as possible, don't volunteer anything. But, really, they won't ask. You were a bystander who tried to help. That's it."

"Okay, I can do that. When do we go in?" I picked up the trash from the table, stuffed it into the coffee cup.

"We need to make a stop first. Find you something else to wear." Billy repacked his file folder and we went across the street and got into his old Jetta, ended up at the SaveMart second hand thrift store.

"Something plain, basic; dark skirt, white shirt, some flats. Can you find that?"

I walked the row of 'bottoms' pausing two or three times before pulling a black wool wrap around skirt from the rack. I thought it was my size, but it swam on me. All the walking and irregular meals had made more of an impact on my body then I realized.

"How's this Mr. Dean?" I cinched it up, pulling the ends tight around my waist.

"Great, that's it, now find a shirt. Plain, white or light colored shirt." He pulled one from the rack. "Try this one on. And it's Billy by the way."

I pulled it on over the sweatshirt I was wearing, it was tight. I took it off and handed it back to him. "Too small."

"Too small over that sweatshirt maybe. Go into the dressing room and change." He handed it back to me, headed for the shoes.

"I don't know. Maybe back at the motel."

"Why not here? I want to go directly to the station." He crossed his arms, stopped in front of me.

"I don't have everything I need to get dressed." I thought about my wet things hanging on the rack in the motel bathroom.

"What else do you need?" I was going to have to spell it out to this guy.

"I need something to wear under it, you know, personal stuff." I was embarrassed, looked down.

"Oh, duh. Sorry." Billy was genuinely apologetic. I wasn't the type of client he usually dealt with. "Look, here's a ten, the skirt's two bucks, the shirt's one, can you get shoes and whatever else you need for ten? Maybe even a sweater or something?"

I nodded.

"Yes? Then get it, change, meet me in the car. I'm going to sit there and make some calls, but hurry. I want to wrap this up so we can move on to the next step."

"Next step?" I held the skirt and blouse in one hand, the ten he had just given me in the other.

"My fee, remember?" He winked at me and headed out the door.

¤ ¤ ¤

The interview at the police station was just what Billy said it would be. I made a statement, said as little as possible. Answered a few questions, signed the hastily typed statement placed in front of me after Billy's careful review and we were on our way.

"Now what?" I asked as he pulled out of the police lot spot.

"Now? Nothing. If they need you, believe me they'll find you. But they won't. I checked and they have at least one of those guys, the zombies as you call them, in custody and he is ready to deal. So nothing." Billy looked in his rear view mirror before backing out.

"Can you give me a ride back to the motel?" I looked down the street. Three street dwellers, all of whom I had met at the soup kitchens, were walking away from the substation. When it starts to get this cold out, some turn themselves in, just for a warm bed and a meal.

"Are you in a hurry?" Billy glanced at me as he merged into traffic.

"No, I thought you were." I was worried, what would I have to do to pay for all this.

"I rent space from a colleague in Albuquerque, use their conference room when I need to. I was hoping we could go there." He adjusted his collar in the mirror before we changed lanes.

I swallowed, paused, then "Okay." Dear Lord, what had I gotten myself into?

We pulled into a small office building off of San Mateo. Double doors lead to a large open reception area. A round desk occupied the middle of a foyer where a petite woman jumped up and came around the counter, hugging Billy as we came in the door.

"Billy. It's so nice to see you. I thought you had forgotten about us." She gushed after him.

"Can't forget about you Celina, you're my eyes and ears down here. And beautiful eyes they are. Ears are kinda cute too." Billy laughed.

"Oh you flirt." Celina put her arm around Billy's waist and looked up at him. "How's Yolinda?"

"Great, she sends her best." The two finally released each other.

"Tell her I said hello. The room's all ready. I put a recorder in there and some coffee in case you want it. I signed it out until noon for you. Do you think you'll need it longer than that?" Celina was behind her desk, checking a dry erase monthly calendar.

Billy was scanning me from head to toe, again.

"No, noon should do it." He ushered me into the conference room and motioned to a swivel chair on this side of the table. He took the other side so he could see out the door.

I didn't know what was about to happen. I had to ask. "Why are we here? Why did you bring me here?" I looked over my shoulder nervously.

"Why? This is where you tell me your life story, and then we figure out how I get paid." He poured a cup of coffee for both of us and turned on the recorder.

I talked for about an hour, maybe longer: my marriage and sons; the accident; my job. He asked lots of questions about the accident, took notes. When I got to the part about selling our house to pay Sam's legal fees he stopped again.

"Who was your lawyer? How much did you owe them?" he asked. Then "It's too bad you sold your house, despite what you see on TV it's really hard to take that away from you. Somebody should have had you file for bankruptcy."

Billy stood up. It was eleven thirty.

"Let's take a quick break, come back in and talk some more." He picked up the two empty coffee cups and placed them in the sink beside the coffee pot in one corner of the room.

I walked out to the lobby, found the restroom, grabbed some paper towels and stuffed them in my pocket, thought about stealing the light bulb. The public restrooms I usually frequented used the long tubes of fluorescent lights, not standard bulbs like in here, but Billy had been there for me, it didn't seem right to take from him now. I went out into the foyer.

It was warm, the lights here had a soft glow, and I watched the news on a TV in the lobby. Bert was mentioned, as was the arrest of one of the zombies. The video of me in the hospital waiting room was no longer part of the story. Five minutes later Billy and I were sitting across from each other again.

"Okay, Aileen, talk to me. What happened after that, after you sold your house and after your husband died?" Billy turned the recorder back on.

"Well, I was teaching middle school in district two and they fired me. My son was in a coma and I had to take time off. I used up all my leave. I got a call my son had taken a turn for the worse and had to leave and they said I couldn't take leave without pay anymore. So I got fired and then I couldn't pay my rent and I had to live in my..."

"Stop. Stop, let's talk about that. The district fired you. You needed to take leave because of a family member's illness and your employer fired you, is that right?" Billy sat up in his chair, clicked his pen.

"Yes, technically they made me resign. They forced me to resign, then they filed a complaint against my license and I couldn't get another job." I measured my words, wanted to say the truth the right way.

"They forced you to resign. You had to take time off because of an illness of a family member and the school forced you to resign." Billy was writing furiously on the yellow legal pad.

"Yes." I wasn't sure what he wanted me to say.

"Yes. That's what happened." He looked directly at me, nodding yes when I did, trying to find holes in my story. "Did the school know about your son's illness? Had you made a written request for leave?"

"Yes, I even got the doctor to write a letter. When my husband died they made me take leave without pay and not bereavement leave, then they said I couldn't take any leave."

"Who said? Who told you no more leave without pay? Do you have copies of anything? Any documents?" Billy Dean was writing dates, times, who was present, what they said. He wanted a play by play of everything.

"They sent the school secretary to my room with a reprimand, made me sign it. I have a copy of that and the letter of resignation". I reached into my cloth shopping bag and pulled out the composition notebook. In the back I found the envelope that held both the reprimand and the resignation letter, along with a copy of my leave requests, one of which had a copy of the doctor's verification of Stevie's comatose state. I passed them over to Billy Dean.

"Wait; did I just hear you say they sent the secretary to the classroom to sign a reprimand? Were you teaching at the time? Were students present?" Billy certainly was animated. He was waving his arms, pushing his hands out, making sweeping motions with the pen and paper.

"Yes, it was during the school day, right at the end of the day and yes the kids were present. The secretary said I wouldn't be paid if I didn't sign. So I signed. I tried to see the superintendent, but she was gone for the day. When I did get to see her she said the policy had changed, but I couldn't get her to give me a copy of it. She just said it was being rewritten." Now I was animated. Past the grief and shock of losing my family, the outrage over what had happened to me came out.

"You specifically asked for a copy of the policy and she didn't provide you with one. Is that correct?" Billy was jotting things down, got out his cell phone and pulled up a calendar.

"Yes, I asked twice actually, once when that happened and again the day they forced me to resign. The assistant superintendent and business manager met with me told me I was on leave. I asked for a copy of the policy and said I wanted a hearing, I wouldn't resign. They said the same thing as the superintendent. When I went to withdraw money from my account to pay my rent, my pay had been withheld. The business manager told me if I signed the letter of resignation it would speed up my pay. I was way behind on my rent; I had bounced a ton of checks because my pay wasn't deposited so I signed. But it was too late, my landlord had already rented out my place and I had to move. I wound up in a motel, then sleeping my car."

This time Billy was silent the entire while I spoke. He wasn't writing now, but I did notice him checking the recorder twice to be sure it was on.

"Witnesses, tell me about witnesses, especially anyone who you trust to stick up for you." He was intense, his face red, almost sweating.

"Well, there's Della, the school secretary. Our kids went to school together. She was there when they made me resign. She made copies of everything for them. I think she would tell the truth about it." I hoped Della wasn't that intimated.

"Good, good. I think that's it. That's what we want to pursue. They fired you for taking leave related to your son's medical care. That's it. That's how I get paid."

"How? What do you mean?" How was my being fired going to help him get paid.

"First I write a letter, see if they bite. District two has caused you grievous injury by forcing you to resign for taking leave to address issues related to your son's illness. You didn't just lose your job, you lost your home, you way of life. What they did is a violation of federal law. Let's see if they bite, offer to negotiate or settle. If not, we'll go to the next step." Billy seemed satisfied.

"What's the next step?" I was clueless.

"File suit. We file suit for compensation. Look, let's be clear, I play hardball in situations like this. It's why I'm able to help people like you. When we win, and we will win something, I get forty percent, and you get sixty. Okay Aileen? That's what we'll do, but I need you to say yes. I can't pursue this unless you agree." Billy pulled a form from his file, filled in some dates, wrote some sentences and passed it over to me with a pen.

I looked at the form. This reminded me of the day I got fired. If I signed would that undo everything that had happened?

"You can take your time, but we have to vacate the room in two minutes. If you need more time than that you'll have to come up to Santa Fe. I don't have anything down here for a while." Billy was packing up the recorder, clearing everything else from the table.

I signed the paper.

64

I slept better the next couple of nights. I wasn't convinced I would see any money from Billy Dean's plan, but at least I wasn't a person of interest anymore, had a new set of clothes, and Billy had convinced Cesar to put light bulbs in my room. I hid in my room at the Rest Inn for the next couple of days, but this time I was clothed and had enough light to read both of the books I had checked out of the library. The change from the thrift store, which Billy refused to take back, was enough to buy a box of oatmeal and some noodles from the dollar store. But after four days, even that was gone. I would need to make my way out into the real world again in search of a meal.

It was a cold Friday morning. Not that I had a calendar or any way to know what day it was. I judged by the traffic, both on the streets by the motel and on the Interstate. Busy meant it was a weekday. Not so busy, a weekend, with Sunday being the slowest day of all. Frost covered the cars in the lot as well as the balcony railing. I was grateful for the both the sweatshirt Cesar had given me and the sweater, thin as it was, that Billy Dean had paid for, but even with both on, I was still cold. It was mid-November, night time temperatures were in the low twenties, and twice so far this year had dropped into the teens, there was no way I would have survived on the streets without shelter. Now, I needed to find food.

I made it downtown, to an alley by a church and small convent. I might be able to pick up a fried egg sandwich given by the nun affectionately known as the Egg Lady. I was surprised no one had lined up by the padlocked metal frame door where the Egg Lady passed the sandwiches and filled coffee cups through a six inch square cut in the mesh. I was either really early or way too late. I sat on the edge of a concrete pylon that divided the small graveled parking areas. Somebody had to be around soon.

A man wearing three coats and two pairs of pants was shuffling along the street, close to the curb but in the street not on the sidewalk. Cars honked at him, but he just kept going like he was deaf. His left foot, up to his knee, was encased by a black foam boot, you know, the kind that closes with Velcro tabs. People who have foot injuries wear them. Anyway, he was pushing an empty wheelchair. It wasn't exactly empty, three or four blue Walmart bags, stuffed to the top with clothes, paperback books and plastic containers were tied to each side of the armrests. When he was about thirty feet from me I called out to him.

"Good Morning." He turned to look, unsure if I was his enemy or his ally.

"Morning." He continued to push the chair, pausing only a minute to look up.

"Hey, do you know if the Egg Lady has given out all her sandwiches yet?" I locked my arms around my chest trying to stay warm.

"No, she don't do that no more. Them bureaucrats made her stop." He angled his chin towards the eight stories Public Utility Building that shaded the one story convent for all but two hours of the day.

"What? Why?" My hands and arms dropped to my side.

"Said she was attracting too many bums and riffraff, too many vagrants." He stopped, stood up straight, looked around the parking area, a mischievous smile on his face. "I don't see anybody like that around here, do you?"

I stood up too.

"No, no vagrants around here. No bums either. I'm not sure about riffraff. "I surveyed the mostly empty graveled lot. "Don't really know what one looks like."

This amused him. "No, me either, me either." He shook his head and continued shuffling along pushing the chair, turning north onto Central, yelling over his shoulder, "I'll let ya' know if I seen any of them riffraff."

No egg sandwich for me today. I headed west, towards downtown. If I could wait around until lunch time, the Baptist church served an indoor meal most days of the week. I had only been there a few times. Dogs were usually not allowed, and up until a month ago, Peanuts had been my constant companion. I started walking the busy downtown avenue. Business people were scurrying into offices, gathering up the paper and mail as they unlocked and entered buildings. I bet I could do their jobs, I thought. Maybe I should put on my new skirt and shirt, clean myself up and apply. Who are you kidding Aileen, there is no way anyone would give you a job, for one thing how would you explain the last eight months I could just picture the interview.

Oh what have I been doing since my last job? Well I took a sabbatical to learn how to crap behind dumpsters.

Yes, I was charged with vagrancy, but I have a good lawyer, he's getting ready to sue my previous employer, why do you ask?

My last position? Well I took so much leave I was reprimanded , then the kids set fire to my classroom and I was forced to resign or they wouldn't pay me and I was being evicted from my apartment so, yes I did quit without notice.

I shook my head and laughed out loud, like a crazy person. A group of people, dressed for success, walked by, giving me a wide berth. I turned and stared at them. Hold on Aileen, get it together, you've got to pull it together, find someplace to sit down, clear your head. Round concrete planters were spaced every few yards along the street. I found one, a few feet in from the corner and sat on the edge, trying to gather as much sun as possible and warm up. It had to be almost nine now, maybe nine-thirty. I sat thinking of the week's events. The aroma of fresh roasted coffee drifted my way and I turned my head towards the scent. A small store front espresso shop was kitty corners from where I sat. I watched as customers went in and out the door, sipping from tall white paper cups and carrying small bakery bags. What I wouldn't do for some of that right now. I flashed on Wizard, what would he do? I stood up, straightened my clothes and crossed the street.

Dino's Coffee was no more than twenty feet wide and maybe thirty feet long. A single glass door with the hours *7 to 4 Monday Saturday*, painted in gold letters, rising above a stylized cup of coffee like steam was framed on both side, inside and out, by iron and wood tables with black iron chairs. Two more tables, with two chairs each were pushed along one wall. Old advertising signs, mostly made of metal, filled the indoor space. A string of red chile Christmas lights outlined the wooden order counter and glass bakery display case which occupied most of the back of the shop. On one side, a door painted red, framed by blue led to the single unisex bathroom. I waited, just out of view of the barista, who turned out to be the owner, until everyone was gone, then went inside. Tall, with brown hair and beard, he was probably ten or fifteen years younger than me. He wore a dark blue apron and Dino's Coffee cap. He was cleaning up the spilled grounds and wiping down the espresso steamer when I approached him.

"Good Morning." I said sheepishly.

"Good Morning, can I help you?" He looked up suspiciously as he refilled the milk pitcher.

I cleared my throat, wasn't sure what to say or how to say it. I really needed Wizard right now.

"I was wondering if I could wipe down your tables, sweep up or something for a cup of coffee." I tried to smile, but my teeth were chattering partially from the cold and partially from being nervous. I expected him to curse at me and kick me out.

Dino looked at me, still perplexed, then grabbed a second white bar towel from a small pail under the counter and handed it to me. "Sure, why not, wipe the tables down and clean up the cup and lid area, I'll pour you a cup."

I took the towel without saying anything else, went table by table, throwing away crumpled napkins, lids, plastic stirrers, picking up paper form the floor, and wiping everything down. I proceeded to clean and sort the lids, cup sleeves and sugars packs; brown, white, sweeteners; placing each neatly into the small square box they were meant to occupy.

"Do you want me to catch the tables outside too?" I asked without looking up.

"Yeah, that'd be great." He was restocking the bakery case, leaning inside to move the muffins forward.

I went outside, it was still cold, the wind was blowing furiously making wind chill no more than about fifteen or twenty degrees. A man and woman, each wearing a long wool winter coat, went inside, ordered at the counter and sat at one of the tables I had just cleaned. I wiped and re-wiped, the chairs and tables outside, pushing the chairs in around each table, until the customers came out, lattes in hand. I went back in, setting the bar towel on the counter and waited.

"How's that?" I stood patiently while Dino counted the bills in his cash drawer. Is this guy going to stiff me for the coffee?

"If you'll clean the bathroom I'll through in a day old pastry."

I nodded, headed towards the bathroom without saying anything.

"The supplies are in the cabinet just inside the door." He called after me as another customer came in the door.

I spent maybe twenty minutes scrubbing everything down in the tiny single seat bathroom, sweeping, restocking the toilet paper. I didn't stuff my pockets with paper towels, which was my usual modus operandi. I replaced the cleaning supplies in the storage cabinet, and went back out into the coffee shop. Dino was just finishing up with a customer.

"Do you want to check it?" I stood to one side of the door, leaning with my hands in back of me against the wall.

"Yeah, sure." He passed the customer his change which was quickly added to the large tip jar on the counter, walked around, held the door to the bathroom open and looked in without going in. Dino surveyed the shop's tiny WC, went halfway in, still holding the door open, and checked the supply cabinet, making sure I didn't steal his cleaning supplies.

"Looks good. Nice job." He walked in back of the counter, grabbed a large cup and placed it in front of me. "Help yourself from the pots there."

I filled my cup, added the luxury of real half and half, placed a lid on it and took a sip. Boy was that good.

"Here you go." Dino pushed a white paper bag towards me.

"Thanks." I peeked inside, two large carrot pineapple muffins smiled up at me. "Thank you," I stammered and headed for the door.

"Wait." Dino called after me. I stopped. Had I forgotten something? "Wait." He picked up the tip jar, fished around inside for two one dollar bills.

"Here." He handed me the money. "Come back tomorrow. Same time."

Everyone needs a reason to get up in the morning. For me, having someplace to go for a good cup of coffee was extremely motivating. Four or five days a week I would get up, shower, and make my way to Dino's Coffee. I usually got there between eight and eight -thirty in the morning, Dino's busy time. I'd wipe tables, take out trash and clean the bathroom. In return I'd get a large cup of coffee and a day old pastry or two. Sometimes Dino would give me a couple bucks from the tip jar if it had been a busy morning. Once, Dino asked me to keep an eye on things while he was out back, locking the cash register as he went. When he returned he was surprised to see a ten dollar bill setting on the counter.

"What's this for?" he asked, holding the bill up to the light like it was play money.

"Somebody came in for two latte's so I made them and made change from the tip jar. I wrote it down there, beside the register." I kept wiping the tables.

"You made the lattes? Where did you learn to do that?" He used his key to unlock the register and put the ten in.

"In Santa Fe, I worked a couple of days in a coffee place up there. But I didn't have all the ID they needed to work, so I didn't stay on." I swiped the rag on the seat of one chair. Somebody had smeared jelly from a pastry on the cushion and it was a mess.

"Show me." He stepped back from the espresso steamer, opened his arms out.

"What?" I rinsed the rag in the pail of hot soapy water.

"Show me, come over here and make a double shot, show me how you made the drinks for that customer." Dino motioned towards the coffee grinder and steamer.

I went to the back sink, washed my hands, walked back around the counter measured and ground the coffee, packed it into the strainer, let the steam build up and made the coffee. "Do you want a latte? Americano? "

"Latte, double shot." He stood in back of me, arms leaning back, watching everything.

I steamed the milk, added the two shots in a paper cup. "Want a swirl?"

He picked up the cup, took a couple of sips and set it down. "Nice pour. You know I can't afford to pay you. I don't have a real job. But if you want to work for tips and a cup of Joe, informal, we can do that."

<h1 style="text-align:center">65</h1>

Saturday before Thanksgiving I made my way back to the Rest Inn from Dino's coffee, four day-old pastries and a large coffee to be reheated on my single burner tomorrow morning, in hand, and five bucks in my pocket. People who don't think five dollars a week can make a difference in someone's life have never been truly destitute. With those few extra dollars from Dino's I could go to the Dollar Store and buy a jar of peanut butter, loaf of bread and tube of toothpaste. On bag day at the thrift store I got socks, a radio, and a real towel and can opener. It was like winning the Powerball.

I was surprised to see Cesar in the front office; he seldom worked days and almost never weekends. When I went by he waved me in.

"Hey Blondie, haven't seen you around much lately." He had a bag of roasted Piñon and was carefully cracking them with his teeth, discarding the shells into a Dr. Pepper can that set on the counter near him. He held the sandwich bag of nuts open and offered me some. Like sunflower seeds, I never quite got the hang of manipulating the pine nut shells in my mouth to avoid swallowing them. But I took a handful anyway to be polite.

"Got Thanksgiving plans?" He cracked another nut and spit some of the shell out onto the floor.

"Thanksgiving? I hadn't thought that far ahead, I guess I'll probably find something to do that day." I had thought about Thanksgiving, planned to spend it at the Salvation Army, but I wasn't going to tell Cesar that.

"Some of us are getting together. We're going to order one of those take out turkey dinners from the grocery store, and then everyone bring one thing extra. It's six bucks each." Cesar grabbed some more Piñon from the bag. "Want in?"

"Who's we?" It would be nice to be able to eat here.

"Me, Mr. Gonzales, Junior, MaryIsabelle, Cherie. Maybe one more. Pretty sure there'll be enough food. What do you say?"

I pulled the five from my pocket. "I've got five. I can give you the other dollar Monday." I hesitated, what if I didn't get tips Monday? "Probably, or Tuesday."

"Blondie, Blondie, Blondie, always a day late and a dollar short. Aye chica, who am I to deny you turkey and pie on Thanksgiving. I'll cover you, one dollar." He took the five from me, pulled an envelope from a drawer under the counter and added a one dollar bill from his wallet and my five to it.

"Okay, you're in. We pick up the meal before noon Thanksgiving Day. Plan on it."

"Thanks Cesar, I will pay you back."

"Forget it Blondie. Amigos sin dinero, eso quiero, que dinero sin amigo, no vale un higo." He went back to cracking Piñon nuts with his teeth.

"What does that mean?"

"It means I needed a sixth person to pay for the meal. See you Thursday."

Wednesday was busier than usual at Dino's. Everyone was gearing up for the long weekend. Dino did ask if I had someplace to go for Thanksgiving. I think he was relieved I was eating with neighbors; it unburdened his conscious for not inviting me. He need not have worried, the ten dollars he gave me from the tip jar was more than enough to put me in a celebratory mood.

"If you can, come in early Friday morning. I'm going to open at five for Black Friday. Should do good business, pre and post shopping coffee. I could use your help." Dino packed up the last of the day olds into two small white bags. Two muffins and three thick slices of pumpkin bread, each tightly wrapped in clear plastic, breakfast for the next five days.

"I will absolutely be here. Thank you and thank you for the tips too." I packed up my cloth bag, put on both sweat shirt and sweater and headed out the door. It was only two, and already the temperature was dropping. "Happy Thanksgiving Dino, I am thankful for the chance you've given me."

"Likewise, Happy Thanksgiving." Dino began stashing cups and lids under the counter, stocking up for Friday.

I walked east, past the Civic Center. A small man, not more than five foot two or three, dressed in a beat up long army coat, sleeves pushed up above his wrists, paced back and forth in front of the parking garage exit gate. Two other men, one passed out, sat on the pavement nearby. I knew what they were doing, waiting until four when they could line up for a bed at the shelter. If they were turned away they'd seek shelter inside the parking garage for the long weekend.

On impulse, I handed the walker the bag of pumpkin bread slices.

"Something to tide you over. Happy Thanksgiving." I quickly walked away.

Nobody said anything. But when I looked over my shoulder, two of them were stuffing the moist orange bread into their mouth and gently nudging the guy who was passed out to sit up before tossing the bag into his lap. Tomorrow, I said silently to them. There's always tomorrow.

Tomorrow did come. I had a radio to listen to, a real towel to dry off with, blankets and someplace to eat that didn't involve waiting outside in the cold or listening to a lecture about Jesus dying for my sins before the loaves were broken. I had debated what to bring as my Thanksgiving meal contribution, ultimately decided on deviled eggs. For a little over a dollar I could boil a dozen eggs, mix them with some relish, mustard and mayo packs scavenged from fast food places, and call it an appetizer. Talk about thrifty. About nine- thirty I made tea and opened my door. MaryIsabelle's blinds were half open and I could see her moving around. I took the bag of banana muffins and a mug of tea, headed down the stairs to her room and tapped lightly on her partially open door.

"Happy Thanksgiving." I pushed open the door, closed it behind me. She was sitting on her bed, watching TV. It had been a couple of weeks since I cleaned her place. It was back to its old state. I pushed aside a stack of mildewed towels from the kitchen chair and sat down at her table.

"Haven't seen you for a while. I kind of got a job. Pays nothing, literally, but the bennies are sweet." I held up the bakery bag. "Here, I brought you a muffin." I took one from the bag and passed it over to her. I couldn't tell if this was one of her good days or not.

"Thanks, I didn't get to the store yesterday. I got held up at my lawyer's office." Her hair was uncombed and wet; I guessed she just got out of the shower.

"Is everything okay?" I searched for a clean paper towel to wipe a sticky red soda spill from the table.

"I fired my lawyer, he's garbage. I was supposed to get my kids, you know, he was supposed to get my kids back for me and he didn't do anything about it. I fired him. I'm going to court on my own. He is so worthless." MaryIsabelle was swaying back and forth on her bed, pulling on her wet hair.

"What did he tell you?" I got up a third time, found a can of coffee and grabbed the glass carafe of her coffee maker. A blue green spiral of oily three or four day old liquid swirled on the top of what coffee was left. I let the water run hot, scrubbed it out, and then put another pot to brew.

"That I wasn't following my plan, I missed my sessions and wasn't doing what I needed to do to get them back. It's his job to get them back. I don't see why he has to stick his nose in my business like that. He's the one that needs to do his job and sue to get my kids back." The more she talked about it the more agitated she got.

I wanted to say 'Well are you going to your sessions? Are you taking your meds?', but I knew right now she needed kind words not a lecture.

"I'm sorry things didn't work out yesterday. I know how much I miss my kids; you must miss your girls a lot, too." I found an almost clean mug, gave it a good rinse and poured a cup of coffee for her, found a comb on the bathroom sink, pretty grimy, scrubbed it with a bar of soap, and came back out and started to gently comb out her hair. She calmed down.

"Shall I turn the TV on? Do you want to watch the Macy's parade?" Deja vu all over again.

We were watching huge balloons float down the street. Dogs and Cats seemed to be the theme, *Snoopy, Underdog, Garfield, Felix*. When the camera panned the crowd and paused on a three rosy checked little girls, MaryIsabelle's shoulders dropped three inches or more. I quickly flipped off the TV.

"Still doesn't match the Albuquerque Balloons." I tried to lighten the mood. I was braiding her thick hair into one tight French braid. A sharp knock on the door. "Expecting anyone?"

"No, see who it is, don't open it." MaryIsabelle was more afraid then I had seen her before. What else happened yesterday?

I peered out the small peep hole, where the distorted face of Junior smiled back at me and waved. How did he know I was looking? I opened the door.

"Hey Junior. Happy Thanksgiving."

"Happy Thanksgiving." He answered back, hands in pockets. "Cesar say to find you, he say you need to go for the turkey now."

"Me? He said I need to get the turkey?" This was news. "How am I supposed to get there?"

I still had the comb in my hand, walked over to MaryIsabelle and handed it back to her, she finally acknowledged Junior.

"Hi Junior. Are you off from work today?" She stood up for the first time since I had been there this morning, walked to the kitchen and poured herself more coffee. "Want some?"

"No thanks, I already ate with Mr. Gonzales; he took me to Burger King." Junior turned back towards me, the door was still open. "He say you need to go and get the turkey now.", then backed out the door.

I leaned out after him. "Where is he?"

"Who?" Junior was walking backwards across the balcony.

"Cesar? Where's Cesar now?" I stepped outside, it had turned cold and windy again and I crossed my arms in front of me to keep warm.

"In the office, he's waiting for you." Junior was already on the second landing and headed towards the first.

"See you later MaryIsabelle, I need to see what's going on." I started out the door. MaryIsabelle looked back with these unbelievably sad eyes. I walked back in and hugged her.

"Keep the faith. I know you love your girls."

She nodded, walked over to her bed, sat down, then picked up the remote and turned on the TV to the Price is Right, holiday show.

Cesar was sitting in the office with Mr. Gonzales watching a pregame football show. A bag of barbeque flavored potato chips, Junior's contribution to the meal, a store bought sugar free apple pie in a box with a clear plastic lid , Mr. Gonzales's purchase, and a crock pot of red chile with potatoes, Cesar's specialty, were lined up on the counter.

"Here's our driver." Cesar looked up from the TV as the static of an electric doorbell chimed when I opened the door.

"Me? I'm the driver? When was this decided and what exactly am I supposed to drive."

"You're the only one with a license. You need to go and get the turkey, if you start now, you should get there by eleven thirty." Cesar couldn't be serious.

"You're kidding right? What am I supposed to drive that golf cart out there?" I pointed to the three wheeled Cushman the housekeeping staff used parked in front of the office.

"You got it." He was serious. "You probably want a jacket or something. It's getting colder."

"I can't drive that, get real. I don't think that thing is legal. What if I get stopped? What am I supposed to say it's a turkey emergency?" There was no way I was going to drive that thing to the supermarket.

"Look Blondie, if you want to eat, you have to go and get the meal, Junior can't drive, Mr. Gonzales is legally blind, if I send Cherie she's likely to take the money and go to a bar someplace, she may already be loaded. You're all we've got."

"What about MaryIsabelle, what about you?" Why did he expect me to take care of this?

"I'm working, can't leave." Cesar turned the volume down on the TV and started for the door. "MaryIsabelle has her own problems, she got into a tussle at her lawyer's office yesterday and he called the cops on her. She's lucky she's not spending Thanksgiving in jail."

Cesar was already pushing the cart out of its spot.

"There's no reverse. Park so you don't have to back up or you'll have to push it."

Mr. Gonzales, came out of the office, he was bundled up with in his overcoat, scarf, and leather gloved, he held his cane and the envelope of money in his hand. "I'm going too." He got into the tiny seat up front.

Great, now both of us would get in trouble. "You can trust me; I won't run off with the turkey money." I was surprised they didn't have faith in me.

"Mr. Gonzales is your alibi if you get stopped."

Mr. Gonzales reached in his pocket and brought forth an old prescription bottle. "I need to pick up my prescription. It's an emergency." He had a good poker face.

Cesar unzipped his faded black canvas jacket and handed it to me. "Take this, you'll want it. I put an ice chest in the back and a couple of bungee cords to hook everything down with. You'll do okay."

I was dubious, but slid in next to Mr. Gonzales and looked for a key. "No key, just push the button." Cesar reached in front of the triangular steering bar and pushed a bright orange button.

Nothing. I got out of the cart.

"Battery's dead." Mr. Gonzales remarked.

"I know that." Cesar was pretending to be smart ass. He pulled keys from a large ring hanging off his belt and unlocked a storage closet to the right of the office. Among the brooms, trash carts and stacks of broken TV's about ten car batteries, all different brands were lined up along one wall. Was one of them taken from my old Subaru I wondered?

"Where did you get these?" My eyes were wide; I think I knew where they came from.

"Motel owners don't want me to ask too many questions. We trade them for rooms. Every so often they come and pick them up." Cesar unhooked one from a battery charger, carried it out to the cart, made Mr. Gonzales stand up and switched out the battery under the seat.

"But they could be stolen." I was getting more uncomfortable about this whole plan minute by minute.

"No!" Cesar feigned surprise. "Don't ask, don't tell Blondie, those are my instructions and good advice." He reached in and pushed the orange button, the engine hummed. "Two pedals: go and stop. When you are ready to go push down hard, let up when you get started. Stop, take your foot off the go pedal and let it coast until it almost stops, and then push the stop pedal, otherwise you'll skid sideways and roll. Got it?" He saluted me.

I jammed the go pedal and the cart lurched forward. We were on our way. Cesar jogged alongside of us a few yards.

"One more thing. You may need to walk or push to get it to go uphill, too much weight with both of you." He jogged in a circle back to the office.

Seriously?

¤ ¤ ¤

The supermarket was not more than six miles away. But the ancient Cushman, with both of us riding, could only manage about eight or nine miles per hour. Still, it was better than walking. If possible, I drove through the mostly empty parking lots of strip malls and gas station/convenience stores, but for a good two or three miles the only way to go was on the road. Traffic was light. I finally managed the stop procedure. The first two times we had to stop for a red light I almost did flip the cart, but I soon learned the feel of the pedals, and kept a pretty steady pace.

It was cold. I pulled the hood of Cesar's jacket over my head. It kept falling off. Next stop light I reached in back for a red bungee cord and wrapped it around my head and the jacket, fastening the hooks slightly off center on top of my head to hold the hood in place. I put socks on my hands to act as gloves. Even Mr. Gonzales, nearly blind as he was, did a double take when he saw me and stifled a laugh. A block and a half from the store I heard the *whoop whoop* of a police car. There were no mirrors in the Cushman; it took me a minute to realize it was me who needed to pull over. I turned in at the next curb cut and we wound up in front of a tattoo parlor. To my surprise they were open. A couple of guys stood just inside the door of the shop and watched, chuckling. The ABQ police officer pulled in back of me, lights flashing. Any other time I would have been embarrassed, but I had endured so many humiliating experiences with the police this was routine.

"Let me do the talking." Mr. Gonzales spoke from the side of his mouth.

We waited in the Cushman for at least five minutes, before the officer got out of his car and walked up beside me. He looked tired.

"Good Morning Officer. Happy Thanksgiving." Mr. Gonzales was jovial.

"Good Morning to you sir." He acknowledged Mr. Gonzales then addressed me, "I need to see your license and registration."

I looked over at Mr. Gonzales, reached into the back of the cart for my shopping bag and pulled my plastic ID protector from it, handed it to the cop.

"Could you remove it from the plastic for me please? And your registration?"

I took the license out and handed it to him, looked over at Mr. Gonzales and raised my eyebrows. "I'm not sure where the registration is. It's a borrowed, um, cart."

The police officer nodded at me, started back toward his car.

Mr. Gonzales spoke up. "Officer, this lady is helping me out, I need to pick up a prescription and have no other way to get it. No buses today, Thanksgiving. I'm sure everything is in order. We wouldn't be riding around in weather like this if it wasn't an emergency."

Mr. Gonzales reached into his pocket and pulled out the empty prescription bottle. Another police cruiser pulled in back too. The second officer, older and heavier than the first, got out, walked around to Mr. Gonzales's side and peered into the back of the Cushman.

"Didn't know there were any of these left."

I could see the two tattoo artists inside the shop, shaking their heads and laughing. I'd be laughing too if it wasn't me about to be arrested. The first officer said "Sit tight," and continued back to his cruiser.

The second said, laughing, "I think we can catch up to 'em if they run off Joe." He kept standing to the side of Mr. Gonzales who still held the prescription bottle in his hand.

Ten minutes went by as I sat, waiting for them to do whatever it was they did. Officer One called out to Officer Two and they both walked to the back of their cruisers, talking it over. It was easy to imagine what the gist of it was. Vagrancy, twice, the incident with Bert, the child endangerment charges from the Education Department. If they searched the cart they were sure to find the stolen car battery, add receiving stolen goods to the list. I put my head down on my arms. Wonder if they served turkey in jail.

The first officer came beside me, his metal ticketing case in hand, pulled a carbon less copy from inside and started to write.

"I am going to issue you a citation for operating an unregistered and unregisterable vehicle in the road way and not having proper safety equipment, seat restraints, mirrors, and windscreen. You can accept the ticket, sign it and be on your way. If you choose to contest the citation you will be taken to the detention facility for arraignment and a hearing will be scheduled and bond set. Do you wish to accept the citation?" He was filling in boxes on the form, still had my license under the metal bar at the top of the clipboard.

Mr. Gonzales had taken out his wallet and was shuffling through the cards and IDs in it. He paused on a Red White and Blue laminated card with a picture of a police hat as a watermark and *TO PROTECT AND SERVE NEW MEXICO UNITED LAW ENFORCEMENT ASSOCIATION* printed in bold letters along one side. In the middle of the card was Mr. Gonzales's name with large gold star and GOLD STAR SUPPORTER printed under it. He reached in front of me flashing the card out my side of the Cushman where Officer One was writing the ticket.

"Here, here, officer. Does this help at all?" Mr. Gonzales tried to wink at me but blinked both eyes instead.

The officer stopped writing, put his thumb and index finger on the red, white and blue card to steady it in Mr. Gonzales's shaking hands, and then looked over at Officer Two for guidance. Number Two walked around the back of the Cushman and positioned his body sideways, took the card from Mr. Gonzales, flipping it over in his hand. Aha, I thought, I know what you're doing; you're blocking the dash cam. Officer Two bent forward and reached across me returning the card to Mr. Gonzales.

"You're supposed to show us this before we start to write the ticket." Officer One looked at the carbon less copies in his hand, crossed off and initialed the citation box, wrote *warning only*, tore out the yellow copy and handed it to me with my license.

"Have a nice day".

We were on our way again.

¤ ¤ ¤

Our turkey dinner was waiting for us. It looked like ours was the last one to be picked up. Last Thanksgiving, Angelo, the store manager in Santa Fe showed up with the extra cooked turkeys at the shelter.

"Do you every cook extra just in case?" I asked the clerk.

"In case of what?" A sour faced middle age man in a red work apron pulled a wine carton box from the almost empty deli case. It held our turkey, three quart size containers of mashed potatoes, gravy and stuffing and a plastic bag of dinner rolls.

"What about the pie?" I placed the box in the shopping cart. A few obviously homeless slowly walked the aisles. Window shopping or shop lifting, I thought. And trying to stay warm.

"Just take one from the display. Pay up front." He certainly wasn't friendly.

Mr. Gonzales and I walked the aisles too. He decided we needed more for our feast, a can of cranberries, three cans of corn, and two large cans of yams. On the spur of the moment I added a can of pressurized whip cream; he peered over his glasses at me.

"Cool Whip, we want Cool Whip." He told me.

"Don't you like this? It's real cream?" I held up the can for him to see.

An announcement came over the intercom: "Attention customers, our store will be closing in ten minutes, at twelve noon, so our employees may enjoy Thanksgiving with their family. Please make your way to the front of the store with your purchases."

"No. Cool Whip. Put that back and get Cool Whip." He was lecturing me. I got the message, pulled the frozen topping from the glass case and started towards the front of the store.

"Wait, we need plates." He called to me.

"How are we going to pay for this? I don't have any money and the money we collected only pays for the turkey and sides." Dollar signs spun in my head.

"Not to worry, I have my charge card." He patted his wallet.

We got in line. Right before Mr. Gonzales swiped his card he hesitated and asked me to get him *Tic-Tacs*. I reached for *Certs* minis.

"No, not Certs, *Tic Tacs*."

There were none at the checkout. The patient cashier sent me to aisle three, where four different flavors of the little mints occupied a section beside candy bars and sugar free gum.

"What flavor Mr. Gonzales, peppermint, spearmint? Fruit?" I shook a box to draw his attention.

"The white ones." He replied loudly.

"Peppermint?"

"Are they white?"

"Yes." I looked the box over carefully.

"Then that's the one."

I hurried to the checkout, handed the mints to the cashier. It took a little while to pack everything into the ice chest, and I struggled to lift the heavy container onto the rack then stretch the bungee cord to hold the box and ice chest in place. Mr. Gonzales had to hold the pumpkin pie on his lap. I forgot Cesar 's warning about no reverse and needed to push the cart backward, out of the shopping cart rack where I had parked it as close to the store as possible to avoid theft. It was heavier than expected. I pushed the orange button, the engine hummed and I stomped the go pedal. Mr. Gonzales put his hand on my arm.

"What about my *Tic Tacs*?"

"They're in there, in the ice chest." I reassured him. Why was he so focused on *Tic-Tacs*?

"I need them." He squeezed my arm lightly.

"I made sure they're in there. I'll get them out when we get back."

"No, I need them now. Stop the cart. I want them now."

Wow, this guy had a real addiction to *Tic-Tacs*. "All right, Mr. Gonzales I'll get the *Tic-Tacs*."

I stopped the cart, a little too abruptly; we jerked forward knocking the ice chest off the rack. I pushed and tugged it back into place, lifted the lid and found his *Tic Tacs*. Then I used all the bungee cords to really secure the chest in place, and started out again. Mr. Gonzales struggled to open the small plastic box, unwrapping the white film from around it, prying open the top, finally succeeded.

"Want one?"

"No thanks." I had never met anyone so focused on a mint.

Next he pulled the prescription bottle from his pocket, dumped half the box of *Tic-Tacs* in it, closed both and put them in his pocket. The ride back seemed quicker. I didn't realize it when we were coming, but we had been traveling slightly up hill most of the way to the store. Now, going back it was downhill, the cart moved faster. It also meant I had to really baby the pedals when we needed to stop. I didn't want to risk the mashed potatoes and gravy spilling over everything. We cleared the second to last light and the terrain shifted to slightly uphill instead of down. The already slow golf cart slowed even more until it was barely moving. I remembered Cesar's other warning about walking up hill. The weight of the turkey and groceries, along with the battery being run down meant the old cart had minimal power left.

"Okay Mr. Gonzales, you take over, steer, press down on the go pedal. I'll get out and push to help us along." I pulled the hood down from my head so I could see a little better.

He scooted over, occupying the middle of the seat, holding the metal steering bar with one hand. I had to place his foot on the go pedal. The problems with his feet meant he had little feeling left in them and only minimal movement from his knees on down. I got out and started to push. It was mostly clear sailing, but slow going. I pushed from the side, every now and then reaching over to correct his steering. As we topped the incline I stopped pushing and told him to let up on the go pedal. My plan was to get in while the cart was still moving slowly and pretty much coast the rest of the way home. Problem with plans is things don't always go according to plan, and this was one of those times.

Instead of letting up Mr. Gonzales pushed down. The cart lurched and hummed and hit top speed of twelve miles an hour going downhill. I ran hard, but there was no way to keep up.

"Let up Mr. Gonzales, lift your foot up." I yelled at him as the cart gained speed.

"It won't stop. I can't make it stop." He yelled back.

A furniture store parking lot was just ahead on the right, it was higher than the road way, the uphill incline of the entrance should slow him down enough so I could catch up, it was our only chance before the next large intersection.

"Turn right Mr. Gonzales. Turn right and let up on the pedal." I said, screaming and out of breath. I leaned forward with my sock covered hands on my knees getting ready for one last all out run.

He did it. He turned the cart just enough to start the uphill trek into the parking lot, took his foot off the go pedal and grabbed the pie before it flung itself out of the cart. I raced along the road and into the furniture store parking lot, jumped in the cart, aimed it even more uphill and gently applied the stop pedal. Not gently enough. The cart skidded, tipping to one side like in a keystone cop movie.

"Lean left, hija," Mr. Gonzales said as he thrust his body in the opposite direction, clinging with one arm to the side of the cart and the other to the pie.

We leaned; the cart righted itself and came to a sliding stop. I put my head back and closed my eyes, breathing deeply to recover from the run.

When I opened them again Officer One and Officer Two were getting out of their cruisers which were parked just to the west of the furniture store. They had seen the whole thing. Both walked towards us, shaking their heads. One took off his hat and used it to smack the other across the chest.

"Everyone okay?" Officer One asked as he put his hand on the roof of the cart. He was eying the box of food in the back and the bungeed ice chest on the rack and took a particular interest in the pumpkin pie Mr. Gonzales held on his lap.

"Yes, thanks, we're fine." I smiled. "The cart lost power and I had to push it uphill. We're okay, thanks." I started to push the orange button and get the cart going again.

Officer One stopped me. "Hold on, I want to make sure you got your prescription sir, so you won't have to go out again. Do you have your prescription sir?"

Mr. Gonzales reached into his pocket for the bottle, handed it to Officer Two.

"Yes, thank you, yes I do have it. We'll be on our way, thank you so much for your kindness." Mr. Gonzales, after attempting to butter them up, tried to reach for the small brown bottle and take it back.

Officer Two opened the bottle, shook it a little, and gave it a sniff. "These look like *Tic-Tacs*."

"You know, I said the same thing hijo, the same thing. But there you are." How could he say that with a straight face?

The radio on Officer One's belt squawked.

"Unit forty seven, come in, Unit forty seven."

Officer One stepped back from the cart and pushed the button on the black microphone clipped to his shirt.

"Unit forty seven, responding." He bent his chin down to speak directly into the microphone.

"Accident with injuries northwest corner of Menual and San Mateo, are you able to respond?"

The looked at each other and eyed us again, wishing they could issue tickets for dumb luck. Officer Two handed the prescription bottle half full of *Tic Tacs* back to Mr. Gonzales, and jogged back to the cruiser.

"Unit forty seven responding, in transit to the scene."

Cesar came out and met us when we pulled into the Rest Inn lot, unhooking the ice chest, stacking the box of canned food on top of it and lifting all with one of his powerful arms.

"Any problems?"

Mr. Gonzales took off his thick glasses, wiped them with the end of his scarf, pulled what remained of the box of *Tic Tacs* from his pocket and offered one to Cesar after popping one in his own mouth.

"Not a one, señor, not a one," he said.

66

I slept pretty well that night, even though the wind was howling outside. We had stayed together until almost nine, filling our plates to reheat in the microwave. After round one, we played cards, and listened to New Mexico Music on KANW. Junior, Cesar, Cheri and MaryIsabelle danced the cumbia as best they could in the confines of the office. They tried to teach me, but gave up after I banged into the TV, temporarily knocking out the cable. An occasional customer was quickly registered and sent on his or her way with a sliver of pie and key to a room. Two shots of Peppermint Schnapps, Cheri's contribution to the potluck, were enough to send me into lala land for the whole night. Cesar's four in the morning run woke me. The first time I heard him racing up and down the staircase and balconies all night. When did that guy sleep?

I dressed quickly, bundled with everything I could find, even wrapping the bedspread around myself like a poncho and headed down to Dino's Coffee shop.

Dino was right. It was busy. I made the coffee while he took orders, accepted payment and barked out names and drink orders for pick up. Four hours later, about nine am, it finally slacked off. A well-dressed middle age couple with three women in their late teens and twenties came in for hot chocolates and chai tea. They pulled their chairs around one of the tables and waited, sipping their drinks as each used the bathroom. The one male in the group, a salt and pepper haired Hispanic man, came out last, gathered up his coat, helped his wife and daughters into theirs and lingered by Dino's shop display of caps, cups and travel mugs: *Stocking Stuffers* the chile shaped sign above them read.

Dino started to wipe down the counters. "Okay Aileen, I think that does it, if you can take a minute and clean the restroom that would be great."

"Of course." I slipped off the Dino's Coffee apron, placing it on the wooden coat rack, the base of which was carved to resemble a T-Rex, by the back door and headed into the restroom. It wasn't too bad considering how many people had been through. The trash needed to be emptied, the paper towels replenished. A quick wipe down and I'd be on my way. At the last minute I decided to give the sink a light scouring. That's when I spied the ox blood red leather wallet on the floor behind the toilet. I reached down and grabbed it, opening it up to see what was inside. Wow, wow or wow. There was almost a thousand dollars in here. Somebody was going to have a miserable Christmas if they didn't get this back. I unsnapped the front pocket to check for ID. A New Mexico Driver's license with a picture of the patriarch of the family that was just here starred back at me. I put down the cleaning supplies and rushed out the door.

"That family, the man, they were just here, which way did they go? He dropped his wallet in the bathroom." I was flustered. I'd be lying if I said I didn't think about keeping it. A couple of months ago, when I was sleeping on cardboard and concrete in back of buildings I probably would have, but today, my stomach was still full from yesterday's Thanksgiving feast and I had slept well in a warm bed, I needed all the good karma I could earn. I headed out the door after them.

I could hear a Salvation Army Bell Ringer on the corner and turned towards the sound. I recognized his overcoat first. The dark tan cashmere was the mark of an obviously well-heeled man. I ran down the block, red wallet in hand until I caught up with him as he opened a car door for his wife.

"Sir, excuse me. Sir?" I called out. He stopped and turned back, spied the wallet in my hand and instinctively patted his pants pockets.

"Sir, I think this is yours, you must have dropped it in the coffee shop." I handed it to him.

He immediately opened the wallet to the money compartment and flipped through the bills then turned to me a bit stunned.

"Thank you, thank you so much." He held the wallet in his hand still open to show to his wife and daughters already in the car.

"You're welcome." It was cold I was without a coat; I started back towards Dino's "Merry Christmas," I said over my shoulder as I rushed down the street.

"Miss, oh Miss." Now the man is chasing me, a ten dollar bill in hand. "Miss thank you for returning the wallet to me. I appreciate your effort in tracking me down." He pushed the ten into my hand.

I grasped the ten. This was unexpected. "Thank you."

"No, thank you and Merry Christmas."

I passed the Salvation Army Bell Ringer and, without giving it too much thought, I walked over and stuffed the bill in. That should pay for a few more meals, maybe buy a little more karma. I walked back to Dino's and gathered my things.

67

The next few weeks passed quickly. Having a job, even if it was only for tips and coffee, made a major difference in my life. I looked forward to getting up and getting dressed. I wasn't constantly focused on finding a something to eat or a place to sleep and stay warm. I started to read more, go for walks on purpose and not because I had nowhere to go and nothing to do. I wanted to make more of an effort with MaryIsabelle. I knew she was hurting. At least three mornings a week, after I got back from Dino's, I'd sit with her. Sometimes we'd watch TV. Sometimes she'd show me the things she bought in preparation for getting her girls back like sets of sheets with lollipops on them or cartoon character juice glasses. She kept talking about them, where they would live and how she would be taking them to Disneyland. Other mornings she was difficult, cussed at me, accused people of stealing from her. They may have been. Some of the people I watched go in and out of her room could only be described as unsavory. I struggled with this. When I was at my lowest point I carried that label too. I had the police called on me three different times for the crime of being a homeless person in need of a bath and a place to sit.

Two days before Christmas I went by her place with a couple of day old giant molasses cookies shaped like pigs and a carton of eggnog from the dollar store. As usual, her door was slightly ajar. I tapped lightly.

"MaryIsabelle, are you here? Can I come in?"

She was sitting at the table, a pile of boxes and wrapping paper in front of her.

"Hi Aileen, come in. Check out all the things I got for the girls for Christmas." MaryIsabelle was excited, laughing. I had never seen her so happy.

"Look, isn't this adorable?" She held up a pink and white striped sweater with tiny candy canes on the sleeves arranged in the shape of a heart. "I got two, one for each of them. And look, look Aileen, a matching one in my size." She held up an adult sized version of the sweater.

I laughed with her. "Those are so sweet. I know you and the girls will look adorable in them."

"And check this out." She held a small red and green plastic reindeer, when you lifted its tail chocolate candies dropped out underneath.

"Isn't that wild." She pumped the tail and showed me how it worked three or four times.

There were dolls, board games and pajamas with slippers that looked like bear feet. She must have spent her entire disability check on these things.

"I need to get them wrapped up by tonight so my girls won't see them. I have my last hearing tomorrow and then I get my kids back. I have another place lined up after the first of the year, a three bedroom house. We all get our own bedroom. The girls are going to love it. They can walk to school."

"That's wonderful MaryIsabelle, you must be so excited." I found two glasses, washed them, even though MaryIsabelle insisted they were clean, used a paper towels to dry, and poured each of us eggnog.

"Let's toast." I handed her a glass, "To Fairy May and Melody June and a wonderful New Year." We clinked glasses and saluted each other.

"Can I help you wrap some of this?" I surveyed the mess of paper, bags, tags and tape.

"No, but maybe you can help me find the Christmas stockings. There's a bag around, I bought two already stuffed but I wanted to add a couple of things." She took a bite of the molasses cookie.

I searched through the bags until I found them. They were made of red netting with a felted heel, toe and cuff. Inside were coloring books, crayons, glittery barrettes with ribbons and other small toys. I handed them to MaryIsabelle.

"Great, I got them both jump ropes. They love to jump rope, and those reindeer. Did you see a bag with some pins in it?"

"Pins? You mean Christmas pins, a snowman and elf?" I had noticed them, and searched through the bags again until I found them.

There were three pins altogether, an angel, an elf and a snowman. The latter were enclosed by a tinsel wreath and had a red nose that lit up when you pushed it. Mary put the elf in one stocking, added a purple vinyl jump rope and candy pooping reindeer, then packed the other stocking with the same purple jump rope, reindeer and added the snow man pin.

"Look at this one Aileen." She tore the plastic wrap off the third pin, an angel, slightly larger than the other two, and pinned it to her sweatshirt. When she tilted the halo the wings lit up. Tinny electronic versions of Christmas carols played as the lights on the angel's wings and halo shifted color in time to the music. "This is so cool."

It was hard to know how to respond, not something I would wear, but to each their own.

"That is different, I like the way the colors keep changing." I tried to be jolly. "Are you sure you don't want more help?"

"No, I've got it all planned, what paper to use with each toy and ribbons and everything. I can't wait to see the look on the girls' faces when they open all this. I want to get our picture taken wearing those pink and white sweaters. Oh Aileen, this is so wonderful." She picked up a bag of star shaped ribbons and bows. "Thanks for the eggnog and cookie. "

"You're welcome." I stood up to leave. "And good luck tomorrow, I know how excited you must be."

"I am, I am. I can't wait to spend Christmas with my girls. Merry Christmas." She hugged an enormous fluffy purple puppy.

¤ ¤ ¤

Christmas Eve day was cold with the promise of snow. The storm would come from the east, meaning Albuquerque metro would get the wind and cold, but most of the snow would dump in the East Mountains and Tijeras Canyon making travel on I-40 treacherous. Traffic on I-25 would increase as truck drivers sought alternate routes home to avoid spending Christmas huddled at a truck stop waiting for the all clear.

The routine of my days had helped me cope with my loneliness. It wasn't until I was on my way to Dino's I realized I had friends, sort of, to share a present with. In my mind I played out my gift list; Cesar, Junior, Mr. Gonzales, and MaryIsabelle. I debated about Cherie, but I seldom saw here and thought maybe a card would do. In my BH (Before Homeless) days I would make a cookie plate, add some homemade fudge and baggie of chile spiced pecans and enclose the whole thing in red cellophane. I couldn't do cookies, no oven. But I could toast some nuts and seeds, maybe manage some homemade trail mix with dollar store bargains. I made a mental list of the nuts, butterscotch chips, mini pretzels and store brand oat cereal I could afford.

Dino's shop was bustling. I made twice as many coffees as usual. Dino was swamped helping panicked office workers, mostly men, with logo aprons, caps and mugs needed to save face at the office gift exchange. People were merry and gay. Dino had tuned in the twenty-four hours of Christmas radio station and even introverts hummed along when Elvis's soft velvet voice purred Blue Christmas. We stayed until 1:15 p.m. when Dino locked the door and posted a hand lettered sign announcing the early Christmas Eve closing.

I quickly wiped down the counter and headed for the bathroom to mop, scrub and empty the trash. When I came out, Dino was dividing what was left of the pastries into two boxes "One for you, one for me." He closed up the boxes, placed a pound of Dino's Dynamite Morning blend, already ground, on top of the box and walked around the counter with it in his hand.

"Aileen, you've been such a great help. Really, when you walked in that day wanting a cup of coffee I was sure you were trouble. I don't know why but something told me to give you a chance, and boy I'm glad I did." He hugged me and handed me the coffee and pastries.

"I'm glad you did too Dino, it changed my life. Seriously, this has been a god-send to me. Your coffee gives me reason to get up in the morning." I hugged him back.

"It's good, but not that good." He laughed and walked back around the counter, picking up an envelope and bringing it to me while I put on my sweater and sweatshirt.

"It makes it all the harder to tell you this."

Oh God, I was being fired, on Christmas Eve no less, and it wasn't even a real job. I looked down and buttoned my sweater before responding. Why was it that I got so tongue tied a really lame 'Oh' was all I could manage.

"Oh?"

"I'm closing the shop. Today is pretty much it. My lease is up the end of this month, and a new Starbucks is opening on the corner this spring." His voice was filled with melancholy.

"No more Dino's coffee then?" I pulled the hood of the sweatshirt up, tried to tuck the edges into the sweater so the wind wouldn't knock it off. I was trying to not let him see my tears.

"Well, not here anyway. A buddy and I are going in on a food truck. We'll do coffee drinks, sandwiches, wraps, that kind of thing. Our target date is February 14th, a big Valentine's Day special grand opening."

"My birthday." I looked up at him, smiling sadly.

"Really, your birthday? If you track me down I'll give you a free wrap and latte. Who knows Aileen; this could be the start of something even better for you."

"I'm sure you're right Dino." I picked up the pastry box and unlocked the door. "Merry Christmas and good luck with the food cart."

Dino was right behind me, "I almost forgot your Christmas bonus." He handed me the envelope. "Merry Christmas Aileen, take care of yourself."

I stuffed the envelope in my pocket and walked out the door.

The dollar store was packed, wall to wall people. A sign on the door announced a six o'clock Christmas Eve closing. It was three now, if I hurried I could be out by four. I found most of the things on my list. I had to sub peanut butter chips for the butterscotch and a large jar of peanuts was the same price as two ounces of pecans. The good part was they had baggies with red and green chiles on them. I picked up a ten pack of cheap holiday cards, no bigger than index cards, while I waited in line at the cash register. The whole thing set me back eight bucks, a real extravagance when your total food budget a month is less than thirty dollars.

The temperature had dropped into the teens by the time I made it back to the Rest Inn. My original plan was to make the trail mix and deliver the bags and cards to the intended recipient. Afterward, I wanted to visit Old Town for the Luminaria tour, maybe attend midnight mass at the old mission church, something I had always wanted to do with my boys but never made the time for. But when I got back to my room my hands, feet and knees were so cold I couldn't move them anymore. With my thin sweatshirt and socks for gloves, there was no way I would be able to make it downtown and back in ten degree weather. I ran a hot bath, made a cup of noodles and turned on the radio. The Nutcracker Sweet serenaded me as I mixed the bags of salty and sweet snack food together then measured them equally into the festive plastic bags. I wrote everyone's name on a card, added a brief note telling them how great they were and put all back into the plastic dollar store shopping bag for delivery.

Around eight o'clock Christmas Eve I made the rounds. Junior and Mr. Gonzales had just gotten back from a movie. Junior ran down to his room and returned with a box of, what else, *Junior Mints*, and handed them to me. "Merry Christmas Ms. Aileen."

Mr. Gonzales gave me a hardy hug, "Let me buy you breakfast next week, Burger King, my treat."

"You don't have to do that Mr. Gonzales. I just like making things for my neighbors for Christmas." I stood at the top of the stairs.

He called out "And I like taking my neighbors out for breakfast, isn't that right Junior?"

"Yeah, he buys breakfast all the time."

"Merry Christmas." They called in unison.

I knocked on MaryIsabelle's door next. No answer, but the light was on inside. I knocked again, tried the door, nothing. She must be with her girls someplace. Good for her. Cesar was next.

Cesar had turned on the No Vacancy sign and was sitting behind the desk watching TV in the office.

"Merry Christmas, Cesar." I pushed open the door. A blast of warmth from the heating duct greeted me when I went it.

"Merry Christmas, Aileen. That's my gift to you, for one whole day I will call you by your real name." He laughed. He had stashed what was left of the Thanksgiving Day Peppermint Schnapps under the counter for just this occasion. He pulled it out now, along with a disposable plastic bathroom cup and poured me some. "Saluda, Aileen."

"Cheers." I took a big sip. That'll warm my finger and toes. "Gee, all I have is trail mix." I handed him a bag and the Christmas card. He opened both, taking a handful of the mix and reading the card.

"Well that's real nice Aileen, real nice." Except the real was more like rrreeeaalll, ong and slow, like he had been drinking, which he had. Cesar propped the card up on the counter with a half dozen other cards already displayed there.

I took another sip of the Schnapps. "Have you seen MaryIsabelle? I knocked on her door, but no one answered."

"She's in there. She just doesn't want to see anyone." He refilled both our cups.

"Why? She was so happy yesterday, all she could talk about was being with her girls and how she would get them back today." I never drank, so when I did it went to my head almost immediately, my nose got red and my face flushed.

"Get them back? No. No way. They were taken away." Cesar popped open a *Pepsi*, poured it in with the Schnapps. I wondered what that tastes like. I held my cup out to him and he obliged.

"I know they were taken away, but she said she had a hearing today. She told me she was getting them back and they were moving into a house after the first of the year. I helped her stuff their Christmas stockings." The Pepsi and schnapps wasn't half bad.

"It wasn't a hearing to get them back; it was a hearing to take them away, permanently. The hearing she had today was a termination of parental rights hearing. The only part of what she told you that's true is the moving part. She hasn't paid rent in weeks, she's being evicted."

"How can that be? She had all kinds of presents and clothes and things for them. Why would she do that?" I set the cup down, my vision was blurry. I would never have passed a field sobriety test.

"No se, Blondie, er, I mean Ai- Ai- Aileen, why do people do anything?" Cesar burped.

I looked at him confused. A car pulled in to the guest registration spot.

"Are you okay to work Cesar?" I got fired today, I worried he'd suffer the same.

"Work? Me? No, I'm just watching the office so Ned could get something to eat. I'm off for three days." He burped again, turned off the NO VACANCY sign, picked up the bottle of Schnapps and baggie of trail mix and staggered towards me.

Ned came in the door, fast food bag in hand, "Thanks Cesar. Appreciate it."

"No problemo primo." We were outside, it was freezing cold, and a very light snow was beginning to fall. "I'll walk you to your room." Cesar said as he put his arm around my shoulder.

"Maybe I should walk you to yours." I propped him up and headed for the other building, second floor. He unlocked the door, grabbing hold of the doorjamb.

"Can you make it from here okay?" I let go of him.

He peered from under his arm "You're not coming in?"

"No, Cesar, No. You're drunk, you know. You don't really know what you're saying." I was drunk too, but not as far gone as he was.

"Es verdad, chica." He entered his room clinging to the door as he closed it. "Feliz Navidad, Amiga".

"Merry Christmas, Cesar." I headed to my room, closed and locked the door and fell into bed.

68

*I*t was almost seven and barely getting light when I woke. Cesar being off, there was no thrice nightly run on the stairs and balcony to wake me. I'm sure the Peppermint Schnapps last night had something to do with it too. I peeked out the window. Not a creature was stirring Christmas morning. A dusting of snow, barely enough for Santa to get his sleigh around in, covered the cars in the parking lot and edges of the balcony. No foot print or tire tracks marred the white crystals. It looked like I would be the first one up at Rest Inn this Christmas morning. I missed church the night before. If I hurried I could make it to the eight o'clock service. I waited to make coffee, planned on making a large pot later and enjoying the pastries Dino had given me when I got back. I opened the door and stepped outside.

A light wind blew snow in my face. I could hear the tinny sound of electronic Christmas carols echoing through the complex, and wondered if MaryIsabelle had dropped her angel pin with the lighted wings someplace nearby. The wind kept sending spirals of the already fallen snow up the stairwell as I headed down the concrete and metal steps. I turned the first landing and there was MaryIsabelle, with glittery ribbon barrettes in her hair, wearing the pink and white striped sweater with candy cane hearts on the sleeves .The silver angel twinkling red blue and green was pinned to her chest playing Angels We Have Heard on High. She was swaying from the end of a purple jump rope that was looped around her neck, hanging three feet below the top rail.

The police thought she had been dead about three or four hours, maybe longer. The TV news came; someone pounded on Cesar's door to let him know, he stood watching with the rest of the bystanders from the next building not wanting to make himself part of the story of a lonely young woman who spent Christmas at a cheap motel she was about to be evicted from, while two different TV stations filmed the aftermath. Ned, one of two new front desk clerks, was pulling a double shift, and had the burden of calling the motel owners before the media did so they would have a prepared statement ready.

I didn't cry until much later, after all the authorities had spoken to me and MaryIsabelle's body carried away. For the third time since I rented my room at the Rest Inn, I closed the blinds, locked the door, and hid under the covers. It is late afternoon Christmas day when I get up again. It was already dark, probably between five-thirty and six. I filled a pan with water for that cup of coffee I promised myself twelve hours earlier. Someone tapped on my door. I ignored it, they tapped again. I didn't want to know who it was or care. I didn't look out.

"Go away." I said as I stood by the tiny single burner trying not to watch the water boil.

"Blondie? Aileen? It's Cesar." I heard him try the door knob. "Want to open the door for me?"

"No, no I don't." I turned on one light, the one in the bathroom, and let its dim light filter out into the rest of the room. The shadows made by the chair and table played out in my head. The room was empty and I wanted it that way. I half expected Cesar to use his pass key like he always did when denied entry to a room. "Please Cesar, just go away. I don't want company now."

The familiar sound of his footsteps on the landing and stairs drifted under the door. as he jogged back to the office I made a cup of coffee, turned on the radio and sat in the half dark, listening to an NPR holiday special reading of Dickens' *A Christmas Carol*. I remembered it was originally meant as a ghost story. What ghosts will haunt me this Christmas night?

Probably an hour later I again heard Cesar's distinctive walk-jog on the landing and another tap on the door.

"Blondie? We've got a bucket of chicken in the office." He spokes through the door.

I didn't answer.

"Junior and Mr. Gonzales are there. We're watching videos. Come down and join us."

I still didn't answer.

"Come on Blondie. Yell, cry, say something. I need to know you're okay." His voice was getting louder. "Don't make me use my pass key."

I walked over and opened the door. He looked at me, took off his jacket and put it around my shoulders. I let myself be led down to the office.

"I thought you were off for three days?" I finally spoke to him.

"I was, but the new guy didn't show up to relieve Ned, so I'm back on tonight anyway. It's okay, double time you know." He lifted the trap door that allows entry behind the counter and pulled the swivel desk chair out for me to sit in.

Junior was rewinding an old VCR tape to the beginning of *The Lone Ranger*, the original episodes in black and white, a thrift-store find Christmas gift from Mr. Gonzales.

Mr. Gonzales struggled to stand up. He picked up a paper plate from a stack by the office coffee pot and spooned out coleslaw, added a biscuit and reached into the red and white cardboard bucket on the counter, turned toward me, "Regular or Extra Crispy?"

69

MaryIsabelle had family. That is the saddest part. Her bi-polar disorder and struggles with depression had driven them apart. No longer able to mandate treatment or cope when she didn't get any, MaryIsabelle and her family had alienated each other so greatly that only MaryIsabelle's death would unite them again and help them remember the beautiful young woman who was their daughter, sister, niece and a confused but loving mother to two young girls. None of us was invited to her funeral. Services were private, a family spokesperson relayed. Still, for the next few weeks, I prayed a special prayer every Sunday for her everlasting peace; a prayer that whatever devils tormented her in life would not follow her in death.

Her room was sure cleaned out quickly. Motel management's new policy was to shift back to daily rentals, with less focus on the monthly and weekly residents. The hope was that fewer guests of the lowest social economic class would become permanent residents of the beat up old motel. People like Mr. Gonzales, Junior and I were allowed to stay, albeit at increased rent. I went from having thirty five dollars a month for groceries to twenty five. If it hadn't been for the sixty dollars in my Christmas Bonus from Dino's I don't know what I would have done.

MaryIsabelle's bicycle and trailer were still padlocked to the bottom of the stairwell two weeks into the new year. No one got around to telling her family or anyone else it was here. One clear Tuesday morning as I made my way down to street level Cesar stood over the bike, a pair of bolt cutters in hand.

"What are you going to do with her bike?" I asked, putting my hand on the plastic grips of the handlebars.

"Goodwill, sell it, don't know but it can't stay here forever." He snipped the lock and pulled the bike away from the metal post it had been chained to and leaned the bike in my direction. "Want it?"

"I couldn't take MaryIsabelle's bike Cesar. That doesn't seem right." I let go of the handlebars, letting it fall towards Cesar.

"Why not? What's not right about it? You were the only real friend she had. Who else should have it?" He pushed it back towards me.

"I don't even know if I can still ride these. I haven't ridden since..." I hadn't ridden since the boys were in elementary school. "I haven't ridden in a long time."

"Try, here try." He pulled the bike around into the parking lot. "Hop on." He patted the seat.

It was a very wobbly start. I out and out fell once. Cesar jogged along beside me and caught me a couple of times before I hit the pavement. Some of the new guests, nightly renters unable to save up enough to pay for a week or month of room rent because they spent most of their money on drugs or booze, came out and laughed, making crude remarks from the second floor balcony. One stern look from Cesar was enough to send them running back inside. Even they knew better then to take him on.

The bike helped a lot. Instead of spending all day walking to a soup kitchen or the library, I could ride in less than an hour. When the weather wasn't too cold or windy, I would take longer rides, along the bosque, or north towards the Sandia Tram. It gave me something else to do now that I had no job. I was at a high point in Albuquerque, the foothills above the ice arena when I gazed out over the cityscape and came to the realization I could apply for new ID and Social Security Card and get a job. It was kind of like an 'oh how stupid you are' moment. I had an address. I had a way to get to the office.

I could use the computer at the library to download the forms. For the first time in a long time I felt hopeful, like I hand a plan that might actually work. I immediately started the ride downhill to the closest library branch. Wouldn't you know it, closed due to a water line break. Tomorrow, I said to myself, tomorrow.

I stopped at a different dollar store than usual and got a pack of spaghetti, can of sauce and box of tea bags. Three bucks bought dinner for at least four days.

Someone new was staying in MaryIsabelle's old room. They had been there a week already, three boys, all very polite, who didn't look old enough to be alone. The youngest, about thirteen or fourteen, was in the parking lot throwing a Frisbee with Junior when I got back.

"Hi Junior, how are you today?" I waved at him as I propped the bike up at the bottom of the stairs.

"Good Ms. Aileen, doing good. Josiah showing me to play Frisbee." Junior was excited. This is good, I thought. Mr. Gonzales is a great friend, but I was glad Junior had someone to do things like throw a Frisbee with. "Watch this Ms. Aileen," he said.

Junior threw the Frisbee to me. I was surprised I could still catch one. I threw it back to him, then to Josiah, and back again. My fifty something year old body was not up to playing with these two. I tossed it to Josiah one last time, "See you later boys, I'm going upstairs to cook spaghetti."

Josiah held the Frisbee, took a couple of steps towards me. "Spaghetti? You know how to make Spaghetti?" He looked so innocent when he said this.

"Well of course. Doesn't everybody?" I laughed at him, he reminded me of my former students.

"My mom used to make us spaghetti." He was so matter of fact.

"I'll bet it was good." I spoke softly, like I would to my students when they had problems, trying to leave an opening for them to share more.

"I liked it. All we eat now is hamburgers. My brothers got jobs at Burger King and that's all we ever have." Josiah seemed annoyed.

"Is that who you are staying with? Your brothers?" I recalled seeing the other two boys, one tall one not so much, all three with light brown hair and eyes, none needed to shave yet.

"Yeah, we stay here. My brothers are trying to save enough for a real place." Josiah tossed the Frisbee back to Junior.

"So you're in school here?" I was a teacher after all. I had to ask.

"No. Not yet. Pretty soon maybe." He caught the Frisbee and tossed it back to Junior.

"Hope so. I'm Aileen by the way. I live on the third floor." Were these kids runaways? Waiting for some adult to come back for them? Why were they here? Something was amiss "If you and your brothers need anything let me know."

Junior threw the Frisbee hard and it veered off to the side of the building. "I'll get it," he said and hustled around the corner.

Josiah followed me as I headed up the stairs. "Can I help you carry that bag?"

"Sure buddy. Here." I handed him the bag, even though there wasn't much in it.

He looked inside. "That's a lot of spaghetti for one person." He was pleading like a lost puppy.

"Josiah, would you like to have some spaghetti with me for dinner tonight?"

"Can my brothers come too?" His face brightened immediately.

"Sure, you bet." There was no way I could turn this kid down.

"Do you ever make it with meatballs? I sure like it with meatballs." He was grinning ear to ear. "Hey Junior," Josiah stuck his head over the rail, "This lady's making us spaghetti and meatballs for dinner."

"Oh cool Ms. Aileen, I'll tell Mr. Gonzales."

How did I get myself into these things?

I sent Junior, on the bike, to the supermarket where he worked with a list and one of only two twenty dollar bills I had left. Another can of sauce, bag of frozen meatballs, I would have liked a salad too, but I was on a very tight budget. I settled on a bag of carrots. At the last minute I added a carton of milk to the list, I hadn't bought one since I became homeless. The mother left in me wouldn't let me serve anything else to the teenagers. Junior assured me he could manage, and that his co-workers would help him find things on the list. He returned with everything I asked and a chocolate cake in a plastic dome with a yellow discounted bakery item sticker on it.

"What's this?" I asked as I emptied the bag.

"My boss gave it to me. I tell him we're making spaghetti dinner and he gave it to me." Junior and Josiah were standing in back of me in the tiny kitchenette watching me try to fill a small pan with water from the miniature sink. I'd have to cook the noodles in three or four batches with this size pan.

"Junior, go see if Mr. Gonzales has a bigger pan I can borrow, would you please? And see if you can find some paper plates. I won't have enough plates and forks." The two scurried out the door.

Next thing I know Cesar's at my door. "What's this I hear about a spaghetti dinner? You didn't think to invite me." I couldn't tell if he was kidding or not.

"Cesar, I'm so sorry. I didn't know this was going to be such a big deal. It started out with that kid, Josiah, then his brothers, then Junior and Mr. Gonzales. Of course you can come too. I just hope there will be enough to go around."

"In that case you do need these." He pulled a pack of paper plates and box of forks from behind his back. "What else do you need?"

"I sent Junior to borrow a pan from Mr. Gonzales, I've got some carrots and Junior's boss sent a cake." I tried to imagine how I could stretch everything to feed seven people.

"How about bread, need garlic bread?" Cesar was reading the label on the bag of meatballs.

"Bread would be great." That should be enough to fill everyone up.

"Just so you know, I think they invited Cherie too." He put the bag of meatballs back down on the counter.

"As long as she doesn't bring booze, those are teenagers you know, not adults. I'm a little worried about those boys."

"Yeah, me too. I probably wouldn't have rented to them, but I'm not the one who makes those decisions." He leaned against the counter, picked up the bag of carrots, opened it and rinsed them in the sink.

"Are they alone? How did they get here?" I broke some of the noodles into the boiling water.

"Lost Boys." Cesar opened the single drawer in the cabinet. "Don't suppose you have a peeler?"

"No, I just use the edge of knife." I handed him one. "What do you mean Lost Boys? How did they get lost?"

"Lost Boys, you know some of those polygamist sects, one man many wives? Well that means there aren't enough women to go around. When the boys hit adolescents they get dumped in someplace like this."

"No! How can that happen? I've heard about lost boys. I thought it was an urban myth, you know, like pit bulls in elevators."

"It does happen. I think these three are from Texas. Some man brought them in about two weeks ago, paid for a month upfront, cash, and left."

"He's coming back?" How could someone just dump their kids like that?

"Don't think so. Think they're on their own."

"Shouldn't we call someone? Social Services or someone?"

"What do you think will happen? They will get adopted by some rich family and live happily ever after?" I could see torment in Cesar's eyes. "That's the myth, the fairy tale. They'd be placed in different homes, might be a good home, but it might not, even get institutionalized if there's not enough beds for older kids. They're better off together. The older boys already found jobs. They'll save enough in a month or two to move out. If they're really lucky one of their mothers will have enough guilt to come looking for them."

"Josiah can't be more than fourteen, he should be in school." I was getting angry. How could someone treat their sons like this?

"I don't think he's ever been in school. Home schooled is my understanding." Cesar found a bowl and placed the carrots, washed, scrubbed and cut into sticks, in it then added some cold water. "If you think he should be in school, why don't you drag him down and enroll him?"

Junior and Josiah walked in the door without knocking carrying two bigger pots. "These okay Ms. Aileen?"

"Great Junior, thanks. Set 'um on the table for now, I've got to make room here." I told him as I set aside the jars of spaghetti sauce.

Cesar bit into a carrot stick, "When's dinner?"

Dinner was a modest success. It was hot and there was enough of it. The three brothers dragged chairs up from their room, Junior brought a couple of folding chairs from the laundry room and everyone else sat on the bed. At Mr. Gonzales insistence we tuned in the oldies station.

Jebidiah, the oldest of the three brothers was especially courteous and polite. He seemed overwhelmed by what was happening. His two younger siblings were constantly asking him if something was okay. Like "Is it okay if we ask for seconds." or "Is it okay if I play Frisbee with Junior again tomorrow?" .At seventeen, he was too young to take on the role of parent to his little brothers. Jericho, sixteen years old, the in between brother was quietest. Depending on how you looked at him and the expression on his face he would transform from being Jebidiah's identical twin to being Josiah's. The bond between the brothers was deep.

"Ma'am, can we help with the dishes?" Jebidiah asked as we finished off the last of the cake.

"That is very thoughtful of you but I can manage, there are only a few." Truthfully there were only the pots I cooked in, everything else was disposable. "You fellas must be tired from working all day."

"It's all right ma'am. Jericho's working early shift tomorrow. I go in later. But thank you for your concern." I wasn't used to kids being this polite.

"Have you thought about school? High School?" I gathered up what was left of the plates and cups while Josiah held a trash bag open for me.

"No ma'am. We were all home schooled. Our moms taught us but we're too old for school now." Jebidiah took the full bag of trash from his brother and tied a knot in the top.

"No you're not. You could still go. I used to be a teacher. You could all go." These boys were going to need convincing. "Especially Josiah, he'd probably be in eighth grade. I could find out about it for you?"

"I don't know ma'am, Josiah was never that into our school work. His mom always had a hard time getting him to settle down." Jebidiah was so serious, unexpected in one so young.

"Why don't you let me check on things? Josiah would probably do well once he got used to it. Besides, don't you worry about him hanging around here all day without you two around?" I was trying to be sweet, not scolding.

"I do think about him being alone here all day, but Jericho and I need to work so we can get a real apartment. Maybe when we find a place you could check on things for us."

"At least let me find out what school he would go to. Is that okay?"

"I suppose so." Jebidiah wrinkled his brow. "I do thank you for the meal though. I was getting pretty tired of hamburgers too."

70

Wednesday I had two things on my to-do list, twice what I usually had on it. One: find out how to apply for a new social security card. Two: check on a school for Josiah. I thought the Social Security card would be easier than the school, I was wrong. When I got to the library I found out they didn't open until noon on Wednesdays. When did that happen? About six or seven homeless men milled about out front, waiting for it to open.

"Aren't you the lady who helped Bert when he got stabbed?" One man approached me.

"Yes, that's me. Did I meet you at the shelter?" He looked familiar.

"Yeah, I remember you. Bert used to walk around talking about coffee all the time. You got him a cup once. He calmed right down after that. How's he doing?" I did remember this man. He was the one who shared his buttered roll with me at the shelter. Almost six months later and he was still wearing the same clothes. He kept his mouth open most of the time, even when he wasn't talking, struggling to breath with each word he spoke. If he hadn't been homeless he probably would have been lugging around an oxygen tank.

"Bert? He was stabbed pretty badly. But I guess he's doing okay. My lawyer told me they found a bed for him at the VA. I haven't seen him since it happened."

"Did they catch the guys who did it?" His teeth were a peculiar shade of brownish green which was a little distracting.

"Um, I know they got one, I'm not sure of the rest." I blinked, trying not to focus on his teeth.

"So you saw who did it." He seemed angry, reminded me of Wizard.

"No, I never saw who did it. I found him already hurt beside the Interstate." I hesitated, the thought of the three zombies still terrified me and I didn't know if they were in jail or what. "I guess the police got a tip someone had his stuff. That's about all I know."

"Whoever did that to Bert should have the same done to them." He made fists with both hands.

It was still twenty minutes to noon; I really didn't want to talk to this guy anymore.

"Nice to see you." I lied to him. "I've got to run and check on school for my nephew. He just moved her from Texas and I'm not sure where he's going to go yet. Take care." I hoped on the bike and rode away before he could say anything.

I started toward the Rest Inn. My plan was to find the nearest school, any school, and ask.

I rode about eight blocks before I came upon a middle school. 'East Central Middle School: Home of the Bears' the scrolling marquee announced. I rode my bike up the side walk, leaned it against the building and tried the door. It was locked. A sign was posted on the door 'Visitors and Parents, please press here for admittance.' An arrow pointed to a silver intercom mounted to the wall.

Buzz "Hello how can I help you?"

"Hello, I'm trying to get information for my nephew, he's new to Albuquerque and I'm trying to see what school he will go to." It felt awkward telling my story into a faceless box.

"Where does he live?" I thought they were going to buzz me in, not give me the third degree out on the side walk.

"Right now he's staying at a motel until his family finds an apartment." Not a lie.

"It may be better to get him enrolled at a school near the apartment they are planning on renting. Do you know what general area of Albuquerque they'll be in?"

"No, not sure really." I paused, hoped they were still listening. "It may be a while before they move in. I was hoping to go ahead and get him started in a school anyway."

"Are you his guardian?"

"No, just...just trying to help his family. They all work so they're busy." This was getting me nowhere.

Buzz. "Come in, I'll give you some paperwork to take to them."

The enrollment packet was pretty typical: a registration form for the office, a nurse's form, a counselor's release form, a home language form, a school lunch application, a federal lands survey form. I understood why parents hated filling them out; it was the same information on each of the forms. If you had limited English skills or struggled with literacy, there was no way you would understand what it was all about, even if they were translated into Spanish. Getting Jebidiah to fill these out would be tough. I'd have to fill them out, guessing at the information, and convince him to sign them. In the end, I pulled all but the registration form and the nurse's form. My career in teaching had vested me with the knowledge of what would get Josiah accepted and what we could ignore for now.

I rode back to the library, parked the bike and went in. Two kiosks with six computers each were lined up in front of the checkout desk. Only half were in use. I stopped at the reference desk and spoke to a cheerful volunteer.

"Yes, we have some free. Go ahead and use that first one." She walked over to the kiosk with me and made sure the computer was on and working.

A male librarian approached from a back office; he was thin, slightly balding and had a pair of bifocals that slid down his nose. He tucked his chin forward to peer over the lenses.

"Computers have to be signed up for in advance. Did you sign up for use?"

"No, I haven't signed up yet." Why was this guy giving me a hard time half the computers were not in use?

"Sorry, Vince, I thought it would be okay, we don't have anyone signed up until three this afternoon. I didn't think anyone was going to be using these."

Vince pushed the glasses back on his nose, looked down at me then back at the volunteer.

"We don't want people to get the idea they can just come in at any time and use a computer. We have a policy on computer use, the patron has to read and sign for use. Have you signed the computer use agreement? First priority is to job applicants and those applying for unemployment"

"I've been using them for a couple of months already. I just didn't sign up today." Boy, talk about a stickler for rules. "I need to find out how to get a copy of a birth certificate and Social Security card. I can't get a job without that."

"Isn't it okay if she uses one since no one is signed up?" At least the volunteer was on my side.

Vince the librarian looked at me sternly, "As long as she signs the signup sheet beforehand, and, you understand, you can't just come in here and use a computer anytime you want to, this is a one-time only deal. Fifteen minutes, maximum."

Sign up had always been for thirty minute blocks, this didn't feel right, but if I gave this guy a hard time he would give me one. "Thank you; I do appreciate your bending the rules for me." The past year had turned me into a lambe as my students said.

Social Security card replacement looked easy, sort of. You needed a picture ID, which I still had: my New Mexico Driver's license, but you also needed proof of citizenship, NM Driver's licenses were not accepted as such, and I would need a birth certificate.

The birth certificate was another matter. The state of my birth referred to the county, which referred to the vital record office. Each page took a long time to load. I kept watching the clock, expecting Vince at any time to come out and boot me off the computer. I finally got to the page I needed. Twenty-four dollars and fifty cents, no checks, money orders only, notarized signature on downloadable and printable form, three to five weeks to process. The two page form would cost me three dollars to print at the library. Including the cost of the money order, getting a copy of the birth certificate which would get me a replacement Social Security card which would allow me to get a real job would set me back about thirty-five dollars, fifteen more than I had. Discouraged, I logged off, thanked the volunteer and went back to the motel. Maybe I would have better luck getting Josiah into school.

Getting him into school proved easier than keeping him there. Like a lot of kids who had limited reading and writing skills he was almost immediately pegged for Special Ed. It wasn't that the teachers didn't know how to help him, it was they couldn't. The only way to get him the smaller classes, personal attention and special resources he needed to catch up was to get him into a Special Education program, otherwise he was regulated to the thirty minutes, three times a week of "Anykey" tier two intervention.

Most teachers love computers. They love the opportunity they provide to students to expand their learning, the resources and diversity in learning they add to the curriculum, but they despise, and I do mean despise the "Anykey" programs for-profit educational companies have pushed into the schools under the guise of improving test scores. Many of the companies have strong ties to elected officials. "Anykey" works like this:

Read this passage (or math problem) and answer the questions using information from the passage.

Question 1 is presented.

Is it A? B? Or C?

If the student chooses B, an incorrect answer: *NO that's not right, try again.*

The student answers C: *No, re-read the passage and try again.*

Final choice, the student answers A

Yes, that's right, good job. Press any key when you are ready to go on.

Students learn all right. They learn they don't have to read the passage at all, just guess until they get it right and finish a half hour lesson in ten minutes or less, leaving them twenty minutes to search for videos of shark attacks and car crashes on the web. Josiah, instead of getting the individual instruction he needed was forced into "Anykey" tier two intervention. He saw lots of shark attack pictures, some of which he printed out and brought home, excited to show his brothers the cool stuff he did in school today.

The school kept sending notes home with him.

Please verify Josiah's former school, we have not been able to find an address and we can't get school records forwarded.

Josiah's teachers would like to set up a conference. Call the school counselor to set up an appointment.

Josiah is not bringing paper and pencil to class. Please make sure he has the supplies he needs for learning.

I was tempted to respond to that one. "We will get Josiah his school supplies as soon as we decide which meals to skip so we can pay for notebook and paper." But I didn't.

But the note that got him suspended from school wasn't from the teachers or counselor, it was from the nurse.

Josiah needs to bring in documentation he has received the listed immunizations before he may attend school

The list was stapled to a form: Pertussis; Chicken Pox; Measles; Rubella; Hepatitis; and on and on.

"Did you boys ever see the doctor or go to a clinic where you lived?" I asked Jebidiah as he tried to make sense of the form.

"No, if one of us got sick one of our aunts or our mom would take care of us. I don't ever remember seeing a doctor." Jebidiah still smelled of the fryer grease he stood in front of for eight hours a day.

Jericho chimed in, "One of the girls fell and broke her arm, they took her to the doctor and put a cast on it, but that's about the only time I remember."

"I think you can take him to the Health Department and they can get him started, but someone is going to have to go with him, sign for him. I'm not sure what else you'll need." I had already looked up the address of the Public Health Office and written it at the top of the form for him.

"Maybe you can call from work tomorrow and find out, but they used to only give shots on Fridays. You all could go in, Jericho too."

It was Wednesday.

"I don't know about that. I don't know if I want us to go there. What if they give us a hard time?"

Jebidiah was still dubious about Josiah's attending school. He knew, as did I, at some point they were going to find out he, his brother's guardian, was only seventeen.

"At least call. Josiah will have to stay home until it's taken care of." This was discouraging; I had worked so hard to get Josiah to go to school.

Jebidiah nodded and filled his plate. Spaghetti Night became a weekly event at the Rest Inn. Cesar would give me five bucks, and Mr. Gonzales three and I'd kick in two.

Everyone appreciated not eating from the microwave one night a week. Any leftover, which was not often, was packed for lunch the next day.

"I'll call for you Jeb; I can call tomorrow after I get back from my appointment." Mr. Gonzales knew education was the only way these boys would pull themselves out of poverty. "I'll even find out about getting you and Jericho into a GED program if you want. I'll call and let you know what I find out tomorrow night."

Josiah and Jericho looked around the room, from Mr. Gonzales, to Jebidiah, to me, uncertain what their future would hold.

71

It was February 5th, my payday more or less. First thing I did was pay rent, sure to get a receipt. Ned, the day clerk was on duty. Ned was a nice guy, but didn't live at the Rest Inn and would put in his eight hours and leave, not interested in the daily struggles of the residents at the Rest Inn. He didn't care who rented a room, as long as they had cash or credit card and picture ID, they got keys to a room, no questions asked. Today was no different, while I was in the office paying rent three different daily renters came in, one obviously intoxicated; another couple, the woman familiar to me from the food pantry was escorted by a well-dressed man I had never seen before, probably would have preferred an hourly rate; and the third, two middle age men driving a beat up red two seater convertible. No telling what brought them here. Cesar's advice, Don't Ask Don't Tell, entered my mind.

Ned had me wait while he issued the latter room keys. "Here you are gentlemen, enjoy your stay." He gave them keys to a room on the first floor.

"We want to be able to see our car," one said.

I watched as they pulled the sports car into the space directly in front of room one seventeen, middle section of the second building.

"Are they day, week or monthlies?" I asked as Ned entered my rent payment.

"Two days, but it's none of your business, mine either really." He handed me the computer printed receipt that meant I wouldn't be sleeping in a shelter or at a bus bench for at least another month.

"Guess you're right, see you later." I went outside. It was cold but not unbearably so. A good day to pedal to the library and fight over a computer again. Maybe I could finally get my birth certificate taken care of.

Josiah was riding MaryIsabelle's bike in the parking lot.

"Hello Josiah, doing okay today?" I walked in front of him, wanting him to stop and return the two wheeler.

"Hi Ms. Aileen." He pedaled around me, didn't get the hint or didn't take the hint about the bike.

"Your brothers working?"

"Yeah, they both work late today." Josiah pedaled in between the parked cars trying to get as close as he could without crashing into them.

It occurred to me I could take Josiah to the library with me.

"Hey buddy, I'm going to the library, want to come along?" I asked him.

"The library? Books and stuff?" He raised his eyebrows at me.

"That's right, books and stuff. Want to come?" I forgot the library is the last place a kid his age wants to go.

"Naw thanks anyway. I'm supposed to stay here, Jebidiah said not to leave the parking lot." He continued to swerve in and out of the parked cars, playing chicken with himself in the rear view mirrors. "Okay if I ride your bike? It's kind of boring here."

I thought about it. The walk to the library would take me about forty minutes, the ride fifteen. Oh well, it was a nice day for a walk.

"Sure buddy, just be safe okay?" I set out on foot.

Vince, the cranky librarian, was off today. I could use the computer unhindered. Success, I got the birth certificate request forms printed, filled out, notarized, bought a money order at the convenience store and put the whole thing in the mail. Of course, now I was broke, would have to hope for a food box or eat in soup kitchens, but, with a little luck, I'd have a job before next month's rent was due.

It was six in the evening before I got back. MaryIsabelle's bike was lying down in the parking lot in front of Building Two. I picked it up, looked around for Josiah, more than a little annoyed with him for leaving it where it could easily be backed over. He was nowhere to be found. I leaned the bike in its usual spot at the bottom of the stair railing and went up to my room, poured the left over spaghetti into a pan, watering down the sauce to stretch it, and settled in with a library discard pile mystery.

Close to ten o'clock Jericho knocked on my door.

"Have you seen Josiah?"

"Hi Jericho, last I saw him was this afternoon, about three. I invited him to the library but he didn't want to go. Why, can't you guys find him?" I still had the paperback in my hand.

"No. Me and Jebidiah got off work half an hour ago and we can't find him, he was supposed to stay here at the motel." Jericho looked worried. "He's never been on his own like that before."

I set the book down, grabbed my sweatshirt. "I'll help you look for him." We went out the door. "He was riding the bike when I left. I found it out in the lot." We walked around to the other side of the building. Jericho walked beside me, calling Josiah's name.

"Where's Jebidiah?"

"He walked over to the school to see if Josiah was there. He's pretty worried about him. Josiah was mad about school because Jebidiah told him he couldn't go anymore." Jericho stopped, surveyed the lot. "I don't know what to do?"

"Let's go to the office, if Cesar's there, I know he'll help us look."

Cesar had just come on duty. "What can I do for you fine people today?" He was cheerfully reconciling the day's receipts, looking over registration forms.

"Josiah's gone. We can't find him." Jericho was panicked, his face red, speaking fast and loud.

"Josiah? When's the last time you saw him?" Cesar put down the stack of receipts.

I put my hand on Jericho's arm, tried to calm him down. "He was riding MaryIsabelle's bike in the parking lot when I saw him about three this afternoon. He didn't go to school today. Jebidiah walked over there to see if he could find him. I got back about six and found the bike in the parking lot."

"Where, where in the parking lot?" Cesar rolled up the computer forms and slipped a rubber band around the bundle.

I told him. He immediately walked into a back room. I could see him forwarding and rewinding the security videos, pausing several times.

"Bastards, bastards! Call the police Blondie, now, do it." Cesar ran from the office and I dialed 911, telling them a child was missing at the motel then followed Jericho to Building Two in time to see Cesar pounding on door one seventeen, the red sports car parked out front.

"Open up, management. I need to inspect your room." He was yelling at the door.

"Not now, come back later." A muffled voice sounded from the other side.

"Now, I'm coming in. I'm using my pass key. I need to inspect the room." Cesar unlocked and pushed the door.

I could see one of the men Ned rented the room to, shirtless, trying to hold the door closed and secure the flimsy chain. "Not now, come back later."

"Now!" Cesar grimaced and pushed the door open, breaking the chain and knocking the man to the floor. The guy was no match for the ex-boxer.

There, on the bed was a semi -conscious Josiah, wearing just his boxers. Beer cans and pizza boxes, used to lure the young teen into the room, lay on the floor. The other man, also shirtless, sat on the bed beside him. Cesar took one look at what was happening, pulled back his massive arm and let fly one powerful blow. BAM! The guy was dead before he hit the floor.

"Call Billy Dean," Cesar said right before they cuffed him and loaded him into the back of the police cruiser. "Call Billy Dean and tell him what happened."

72

Things changed. That's an understatement. Josiah was placed in a foster home and the older two, Jericho and Jebidiah, got shipped off to separate residential programs for teens, like Cesar said would happen. I never found out if the state sought out the man who abandoned them. The Rest Inn, without Cesar's presence, became a haven for drunks, drug deals and prostitutes, both male and female. Police cruisers, lights flashing, visited at least two or three times a week, occasionally twice in one day. There was even a shooting after a high speed chase veered into the parking lot in pursuit of a stolen car.

A City of Albuquerque community services worker came to talk to Mr. Gonzales and Junior, and got them into a city sponsored housing program. I was left on my own, being neither disabled nor elderly, there was no program to help someone like me. The only resident of the Rest Inn I still knew was Cherie. Since I was not a source for booze or smokes, she seldom spoke to me. I started propping a chair in front of the door whenever I was in the room. My only hope out of this was that birth certificate and Social Security card, without them I wouldn't get a job. I checked at the office twice a day for mail or messages, even on Sundays. Nothing. Days moved in slow motion, nights in low speed stop motion animation.

March 5th, rent day. I got a money order from the Credit Union, afraid if any one saw me with cash they'd think I had more and come after me, and scurried to the office. Ned, now the manager, printed out the receipt.

"By the way, you've got a message." Ned walked from behind the desk, window cleaner in hand and started spraying and wiping the door where grimy finger prints distorted the glass. He reached in his shirt pocket and took out a business card, a pink sticky note with my name and room number on it affixed to the front, Billy Dean's handwriting on the back. *Call Me ASAP.*

"When did you get this? Was he here?" I flipped the card over in my hands.

"Don't know, I just noticed it. Must have been when I was off. If you hadn't come in I was going to tape it to your door." He continued cleaning the glass.

"Can I use a phone?" I stood at the counter, anxiously shifting my weight.

"Sorry love, business use only." Ned pulled the vinyl loveseat away from the front window and made a face as he looked at the dirt behind it. "Euwooo."

What would Wizard do?

"What if I clean the lobby for you? Sweep, mop, finish the windows, can I use the phone then?"

Ned looked at the muddy footprints on the lobby floor and layer of dust on the counter. He handed me the spray bottle and rag. "Have at it."

It took me forty minutes to clean the pocket-sized lobby. I don't think it had been touched since Cesar was arrested. Ned asked me to do the bathroom. "Bathroom? If I do the bathroom I want two phone calls, one now and one later when I need it again."

"Hard bargainer," he said. "Deal."

Ned dialed the number and passed me the receiver. I reached in back of the counter for a pen, he scowled but said nothing.

"Hello, Billy Dean? This is Aileen." Whew, a real person, not voice mail.

"Aileen Roark? Is this Aileen Roark I am speaking to?" Billy asked.

"Yes, it's me, Aileen Roark. I just got the message." I held the card in my hand.

"Yes, well, it's short notice now, but I need you here tomorrow. We got a bite from the school. I rattled a few cages and I think I've got a deal. I've got a meeting set up tomorrow here in Santa Fe to finalize things and I need you here."

"Really? I'd given up on that. Good. Great. What's the deal?" Even a couple hundred bucks could pay the deposit on an efficiency apartment and get me out of here. I regretted paying a month's rent.

"One hundred and ten thousand, about two years pay more or less. Remember the agreement is sixty-forty, so your net would be about sixty six thousand."

I'm stunned, shaking, holding the edge of the counter to keep from collapsing. Did I hear him correctly? A cherry top, lights flashing pulls up outside. Two men on the first floor landing closest to my room jump over the rail and run, cops in pursuit.

"Say that again please?"

73

$\mathcal{B}$illy Dean met me at the South Capital Rail Runner station. I wore my black skirt and white shirt, like he told me to. I carried my cloth JC Penny bag, which held an old soda bottle filled with water, my last pack of cheese and crackers, and my composition notebook which I no longer left in my room, fearful anyone entering when I wasn't there would take it along with all the precious photos and memories I had tucked in the notebook's pages.

"Aileen, good to see you. You're looking well." He shook my hand. Billy was dressed in his typical tweed sport coat and khaki pants. "I need to fill you in on what's happening. We have a meeting at the Santa Fe Administrative Offices at ten o'clock. It's nine now and..."

"Wait, Billy, that's the wrong district, I taught for District Two, to the north, not Santa Fe." What a letdown. How could he negotiate with the wrong district? My stomach churned.

He laughed. "No, no, no, District Two arranged to borrow a conference room for this meeting, neutral territory." He could see the relief on my face.

"Anyway, let's walk over for coffee at the bakery. I'll fill you in there." We walked a block to the shopping center, passing the natural foods market, the dollar store and cafeteria. I used to eat out of these dumpsters I thought as I walked by. Billy directed me to a table, lined up at the counter, returning with muffins and coffee. I glanced out the window, the daffodils and crocus in the planters that surrounded the patio were just coming up. I sat back abruptly when I spied Bobby Valentine and Antonia Roybal getting out of a car. Billy glanced over his shoulder to see what I was looking at.

"Friend of yours?" he said.

I took the cups from him as he sat down with his back to the door. "They're the ones who fired me." I set the coffees down.

"Ignore them, don't look at them. When we get into the meeting don't make eye contact, don't shake their hands and above all, don't talk to them. If you need to say anything I'll let you know, otherwise don't talk to anyone. Remain silent." Billy added two packs of sugar to his coffee and stirred.

"Okay then." He opened the cardboard accordion folder that served as his brief case and pulled out a file, a copy of the agreement I had signed months before and several pages of handwritten notes on yellow legal paper.

"We have an offer on the table. They tried to low ball us, but I tightened the screw. We could have gone the way of federal court since this was a clear violation of the Family Medical Leave Act. Also they violated their own policy regarding leave and bereavement leave, and withheld your pay, a violation of Wage and Labor laws. I think this is the best we can do." He pushed a typed letter to me to read. The bottom line was two years pay. I read it over, twice, while Billy sipped his coffee.

"Problem?" Billy took a bite of the muffin, crumbs tumbling down his shirt and tie.

"Maybe," I read the letter a third time.

"What? What's up?" He used a napkin to brush crumbs from his jacket.

"I want my job back. I want to teach again."

Billy thought I was nuts. "That's not part of the offer. I'm not sure we can do that." He shuffled through the pages of notes. "You can get a different teaching job, take some time to recoup, get back on your feet and line something up with another district next year."

"They put a hold on my license, filed an official reprimand. I can't get a teaching job without a license." Despite Billy's admonishments I glared over at Roybal and Valentine, who was laughing like the day he fired me.

Billy reached across the table and took both my hands. "Aileen, look at me. Don't look over there. Look at me. Don't let them upset you." He squeezed my hands lightly until I shifted my gaze. "I don't think I can get your job back for you. Judging by the malice in your eyes when you look at those two I don't think you want it back anyway. I might be able to get them to rescind the license hold and letter of reprimand. You can find a job someplace else. But this is a good offer. As your lawyer I recommend you accept it."

I thought about it, ate half the muffin, closed my eyes, tight, and opened them. "Okay."

"Okay? Yes? Good, finish up and we'll head over." Billy placed all the paperwork back into the accordion file. "Remember, don't say anything. Do what I do, have some water in front of you or make sure you know where the nearest fountain is. When you feel like you're going to say something, take a drink of water. Keep sipping until the urge passes."

The meeting went okay. Not great. Okay. I had to sip a lot of water which meant half way through I urgently had to get up and pee. Billy was able to persuade the lawyers for District Two to remove the hold on my license and reprimand. Valentine and Roybal balked. One of the lawyers left the room with them for a private conference and they relented. When they came back in we all signed. I stood up to leave and Billy again grabbed my hands pulled me back into the conference chair.

"Wait," he said to me in a whisper. "Wait until they leave. Then I'll walk you back to the station." He poured more water into my cup.

I sat with hands folded on the table while Billy smiled at the other group between sips of water, waiting for them to pack up their files and exit the room.

When they were barely out the door I took a deep breath and started to get up again.

"Not yet." Billy said, pushed the still full cup of water towards me.

I looked around the room. "How's Cesar?"

"Cesar?" Billy sipped from the glass of water in front of him once more. Was he trying to avoid talking about Cesar or was he truly thirsty? "Cesar will be okay. We got the charges dropped. But his parole was rescinded so he's still in jail."

"I didn't know he was on parole." I swivel in the chair to look at Billy who finally put down the glass of water.

"This was his second manslaughter charge. The first was eight years ago. His sister was having problems with an abusive boyfriend and he walked in on them. Pretty much same thing. We got a plea deal on that. Sad part is he would have been off parole next January. I'm still working on it. Haven't given up yet." Billy's expression changed, his inability to secure Cesar's release dragged on him.

Now I took Billy's hands. "If there's anything I can do for Cesar, anything, if you need money to get him out, well, now I've got some."

Billy smiled at that. "You're too nice Aileen. Too kind. If the world was made up of people like you, I wouldn't have a job." He stood up, walked into the lobby, came back smiling. "All clear, let's go."

I wasn't ready to go back to Albuquerque. I wanted to visit the cemetery where my sons and husband were buried. I had twenty dollars cash. Billy told me to give it fifteen days for the settlement to get processed, the money would be sent to his office. He would handle the deposits. Still, I felt flush, went by the market and bought a six dollar bouquet of flowers to be split between the three graves. It was a strange feeling walking the streets of Santa Fe as I headed for the north side of town. I lingered places; the River Park; the Plaza; and Rail Yard. I saw some people I knew from both before and after being homeless. They looked at me with faint recognition, but no one approached or made an effort to say hello.

It was early afternoon when I got to the graveyard. Like at the planters outside of the bakery, the crocus and daffodils were just starting to peek through moist earth. Patches of green grass emerged in stark contrast to the muddy paths that led into and out of the cemetery. I visited each of the boys' grave sites, Sam's grave last. I wanted to say something to them but not know what, I lay flowers by each marker and sat on a bench, letting the sun warm me and looked up at the mountains . I could trace the white fingers of snow at the ski basin. Wizard appeared beside me.

"Dear lady." He stood in front of me blocking the sun.

"Wizard," I jumped up and hugged him. "Wizard," all I could say.

He sat beside me in silence as I stared up at the sky.

"What brings you to these environs?" His voice was hoarse. He looked older than I remembered. The winter had not been good to him.

"I'm here for a meeting with my lawyer. It's a long story, but the end of it is I can start looking for a job again, teaching. I wanted to visit my family before I head back." I used my chin to point to Sean's and Sam's graves.

"Ah, well you have good news then. The universe smiles on you." He pulled the red canvas pack off his back and placed it on the ground under the bench we both sat on.

"And you? Still rescuing damsel's in distress at the cemetery? What do you do, hang out here all day waiting for one to show up?" I didn't mean it in a bad way, but he took it so. He tensed up.

"You're not the only one with someone to visit here you know." His tone was solemn.

I put my hand on his knee. "Sorry, Wizard, Sorry. That wasn't a very nice thing to say."

He nodded, took off his cowboy hat and dusted it on his leg.

"How's Rocky?"

"Took off, didn't like the weather. Went south, Arizona maybe?" He used both hands to place the hat back on his head.

"Sorry, Wizard. I know how much you cared for her." I could smell the mix of decaying leaves and wet cement as the sun warmed the ground around us. Every now and then the scent of patchouli oil would drift over from Wizard's direction.

"Likely she's right to go where it's warmer. Sleeping on the ground's getting harder and harder. It's not getting down it's the getting up again." He chuckled, more like the Wizard I remembered. "Where do you dwell now?" He looked squarely at me, arms folded in front of him.

"Now? Albuquerque, staying at a motel. When I get back I'm going to look for someplace else. I want someplace they can't kick me out of, where I can settle in for a while."

"You want to find someplace to dwell that's good for mind, body and spirit, like I told you. It's not just four walls and a roof. You need a place that fits your soul Aileen. Find a place like that. Otherwise you'll never have peace." His hair was grayer than ever, his face deeply lined, but his eyes were still that intense blue that matched the sky.

"I'll keep that in mind." I picked up my cloth shopping bag. "I've got to catch a train back to Albuquerque. Want to walk along?"

"You bet, dear lady."

If no one wanted to acknowledge me on the streets of Santa Fe, everyone noticed Wizard. I forgot how well known he was. People came up, shook his hand and joked with him. By the time we reached the Rail Runner Station at least a dozen people; merchants, street people, just plain folks, even a city councilor, hailed us. The Rail Runner train was ready and waiting when we finally stepped up to the platform.

"Take care of yourself Wizard." I hugged him again as I lined up with the others, mostly tourist, to board the train.

"And you dear lady. Remember what I said, a place to dwell, mind, body and spirit." He took his hat off tipping it in my direction as I climbed the steps onto the train.

74

The hum and sway of the train lulled me to sleep. I had vague dreams, mostly mixed up memories; my sons and the lost boys eating spaghetti together; Father Rico, the priest who helped me when I first came to Albuquerque, tossing a ball to Peanuts; in one vignette I rode a hot air balloon over a bell tower that sat atop a casino while a raven squawked beside me sailing high on the winds, directing me to a rooftop. It was in the middle of this last dream I was jolted awake when the passenger across the aisle dropped the book she was reading while gathering her things. We were stopped at Bernalillo. The same place I was dumped by the casino bus and made to surrender Peanuts' service dog vest almost a year earlier. I sat back and gazed through the window, moving across the aisle to the newly empty seat. I wanted to see if I could find Las Manchas and the church and shed where Father Rico had offered me shelter. Maybe I should look here for my dwelling as Wizard would say.

The train ran slower these few miles, like it was moving through a time warp. And it was. This part of the Albuquerque Metro Area was a blast from the past, a journey along the real Route 66, not the cartoonish landscape found on post cards and souvenir shot glasses. Tiny old adobes with corrugated roofs sat beside livestock pens where pigs and goats were being fattened for the next matanza. Forty year old mobile homes, bought when Richard Nixon was President and proclaimed them eligible for HUD financing as a way to house the poor, were packed into cramped mobile home parks with low slung power lines. Nearly every yard had at least one car or truck up on blocks, frequently two, of the same make, year and model as the one in the driveway; the poor man's parts store. A couple of old style diners advertising cheese enchiladas, Christmas, with an egg on top or three rolled tacos with a side of beans, survived among the Title Loan and Payday storefronts and 'We Buy Gold 'pawn shops. The dual bell towers of St Ursula's rose above the mud and gravel landscape as the train approached. I thought I saw Father Rico walking alongside a man in a wheelchair on the unpaved road beside the old cemetery. What a muddy mess that must be. Both men glanced at the train as it went by, I waved and they waved back but I doubt Father Rico could see me or would remember me. From here you could see I-25 and the Sandia Mountains to the east. I tried to focus on the glint of sunlight on the aerial tramway that led up the peak, but a large sign painted on top of a roof right below the Interstate caught my gaze. A huge black raven sat at the roof's peak, cleaning its feathers. The uneven brush strokes of the hand painted sign were obvious even from this distance - *4sellhse70KOBO*. This wasn't a dream. It was the answer to a prayer.

¤ ¤ ¤

I had to try hard to look hard. I don't know if that makes sense or not. What I mean is, I had to stop being nice to people at the Rest Inn, stop talking to them, or evening smiling at them. Once in a while someone would say something to me. I'd answer in as few words as possible so not to engage them. When some young gangsters passed me on the stairs "What's up?" they'd lift their chin to me, and I'd have to tilt my head slightly and respond, "Same old, same old," or "Not Much," and keep going. It was the only way to survive or they might take offense and take revenge.

When I got back from my trip to Santa Fe, copy of the settlement letter folded in my pocket, it was hard to be hard. I had to slow my step and drag my feet on purpose. I traversed the sidewalk towards the stair landing passing a guy, barely in his twenties wearing a gad-awful orange hoodie and pants at least three sizes too big for him. He was leaning over the driver's side window of a blue Crown Vic. The wheels told me it was an old police cruiser picked up at auction. The car backed up and pulled out when I walked by leaving Orange Pants standing there, staring straight at me. Dear god, I did not want to talk to this guy. I tried to frown and look down, too late, he made eye contact.

"What's up?" He hiked his pants up with one hand and used the other to take the cigarette from his mouth with two fingers. "You're not around much today. All dressed up too. Looking for work or something?"

Why would he ask that? Is he keeping an eye on my place or what? Why did he want to know if I was looking for work? Did he think I had money? Think fast, Aileen, think fast, this kid could be bad news, just like the zombies.

"No, I had to go to Santa Fe; meet with my lawyer." I said it in as much of a monotone as I could manage.

"No shit. Who's your lawyer?" He took a deep puff on the cigarette, flicked the ash on the hood of a parked car.

"Billy James Dean."

"Oh yeah, Billy Dean, he's all right. He took care of my primo, got him a pretty sweet deal, he didn't have to spend, only, about , I don't know, a couple months at county, then he got him out on a bracelet." This was more information then I wanted to know. The kid took another deep drag on his cigarette. "So how'd it go?" he said as he exhaled smoke from his nose.

"Sorry?" I looked at him on purpose for the first time. Had I misjudged him?

"In Santa Fe, with Billy Dean, how'd it go?" He had to walk feet splayed outward so that his pants wouldn't fall down.

Don't blow this Aileen, don't tell him you got a settlement, your teaching license back and will soon be flush with cash and out of here. I've never been that good a liar. No water around to sip. I let the saliva build up in my mouth, swallowed hard and shrugged my shoulders, deeply furrowed my brow, worked hard to look hard without saying anything. The kid bought it.

"Yeah, I'm down with that." He came walking over like the do-dah man and did a bro shake with one hand while holding his cigarette between his fingers and hiking up those hideous orange pants with the other. It was really, really hard to look hard.

74

The telephone number I had written down was incorrect, scribbled in back of my composition notebook as the train regained speed. I had wasted my second phone call on a wrong number.

"Care to clean the bathroom again?" Ned's grin was contrite.

I hadn't told him or anyone else at the Rest Inn, about my settlement and didn't plan to. Resident after resident had been cast out of the motel, which claimed exemption to providing notice of eviction or termination of rental agreement saying they were subject to Lodger Occupancy code and not Landlord and Rental laws. I planned on taking them for their word and simply turning in my key the day I left.

"That's okay Ned; I guess I have the wrong number anyway." I handed him back the receiver and hopped on MaryIsabelle's old bicycle. I started to ride, but thought better of it. It was at least ten miles away. I honestly wasn't sure I could make it there and back at all let alone before nightfall. Instead I rode to the library, used the computer to search for places nearby, both for rent and sale. If I had a job, that sixty-six thousand would make a nice down payment. It would also pay a lot of rent. It made sense to move into a furnished apartment, get a new wardrobe, a haircut, maybe a car, than start my hunt for a teaching job. I could move away, to Las Cruces, or Farmington, out of state even. Find a job in a small rural school district. Possibilities were endless. So why did I keep thinking about Las Manchas and the beat up house beside the Interstate? I knew the answer to that: Billy James Dean.

His admonishment- *It's too bad you sold your house, despite what you see on TV it's really hard to take that away from you,* was embedded in my brain. If I had a house, a real house, four walls and a roof, with plumbing, and a yard, owned free and clear, I'd never sleep on the street again. I feared going back out on the street. I had seen too much hunger and suffering, witnessed too many deaths, been hassled by the police more than I could count. My bones held the memory of cold chilling pain after a night spent lying on pavement with nothing but a piece of cardboard to cover up with. Never again, I pledged to myself, never again. I waited for the settlement money to appear in my account and boarded the Rail Runner for the twenty minute ride to Bernalillo, taking the bike with me.

It was the end of March, sunny, warm, and windy. Grit found its way into my mouth, eyes and clothes. By the time the two bell towers of St Ursula were in sight, I felt like a giant piece of sandpaper. I crossed back over the Rail Runner tracks and headed up the loop road that connected the church, school and cemetery with four houses and a couple of vacant lots that completed the circle. Dirt roads leading in and out of the loop connected with similar neighborhoods, all of which needed quite a lot of work. The handful of roads that were paved had been crudely done with black asphalt leftover from government jobs by contractor nephews or cousins. Las Manchas residents were used to taking care of their own problems, and street maintenance was one of them. I rode by the house. You couldn't see the sign and phone number up close. I had to ride back around the circle toward the train crossing before I got a line of vision on the rough 4sell sign and phone number. I wrote it down, correctly this time, then proceeded back around to the house, leaned my bike against the front fence, opened the gate and walked to the door. Before I had a chance to knock someone called out to me.

"Can I help you Miss?" It looked like the same man in a wheelchair I had seen Father Rico walking with. He positioned his chair a few feet away on the other side of the fence. The elderly man wore a VFW cap and blue zip sweatshirt. One foot was missing at the instep, and covered by a foam boot, the other foot fitted with a heavy duty shoes such as diabetics wear. A small dog trotted behind him, followed by a raven, who was trying to chase the dog.

"Hello. I saw the sign on the roof and was wondering if this place was still for sale?" I smiled at him. I could feel the sandy grit slide between my lips and teeth.

"Is you one of those people from the real estate company?" He frowned, placed his hand on the wheels of his chair ready to wheel himself away.

"No, I was passing by a couple of weeks ago on the train and saw the sign. Is it still for sale?" I took a couple of steps towards the fence.

"Did Beulah send ya'?" He pushed his chair back from the fence a few feet. The raven started to hop in front of him. The little dog began chasing the raven.

"Sorry?" I again tried to smile but had to move my mouth and tongue around to try and expel the dirt then used my hand to wipe it from the corners of my mouth.

"Beulah, did she send you over here to check on the place?" The man was still frowning.

Just when the little dog was about it nip the raven, the black bird jumped up into the air and cawed at it, causing the pooch to bark and run in circles. The guy in the wheel chair gave a whistle and the little dog jumped onto his lap. The raven flew to the roof of the porch I was standing under and looked down on me, pacing back and forth across the length of the roof.

"No, I don't know who that is." I wonder what this guy is up to. Having a nosy neighbor was one thing, but I wasn't even moved in yet. "I'd like to find out if this place is still for sale. Do you know how I can get a hold of the owner?"

"It is and you're looking at him." The man relaxed his frown, set the little dog on ground and extended his hand over the wire fence. "Names James Duboski and this here's Little Dog."

"How do you do Mr. Duboski, I'm Aileen Roark." I took his hand and shook it lightly, then turned and looked back at the house. "Do you think I can look around inside?"

"Hang on. I'll go and get the key." He backed up and headed for the ramp that led to the deck of the double wide mobile home next door.

Up close you could see what was not obvious from a distance. This house was really a nine by forty foot trailer to which a large adobe great room was added along one side, the whole thing covered in stucco to resemble a single unit. A corrugated tin roof with an uneven pitch was erected over both. The trailer and great room were situated lengthwise on the half acre lot, a simple gravel driveway extended front to back along one side, beginning at the street through wrought iron double gates that had at one time been painted silver. A sturdy portal was erected on wood posts extending about six foot to either side the front door, which opened into the adobe great room. A screened in porch was attached to the back. I walked around the outside of the place, inspecting the broken tiles embedded in circles of cement to form walkways around the yard. An old camper set up on a wooden platform was parked to one side and a wood and metal shed, half collapsed, lay not far from it. The remnants of flower and vegetable gardens dotted both front and back yard. An acequia, which flowed with cool mountain snow melt, crossed the back of the property, a small gate allowed the water's diversion into the furrows that led to fruit trees, grape vines and rose bushes. I smiled imagining it, turning slowly in a circle I envisioned the trees in bloom and the sweet smell of the lilacs that marked the property line of the house to the south. Could I find peace here? Could this be my dwelling?

I could hear Little Dog and the raven fusing at each other again and walked to the front yard. Dub was unhooking the gate, wheeled himself up the walkway and handed me the key.

"Been a while since I's in here, reckon' everything's still okay." He watched as I struggled to get the key to work. "You probably have to work at it a bit to get it to unlock." He was more at ease, seemed friendlier. He had a small VA tote bag hooked on the back of his chair and reached around and grabbed it, grasping it with one hand." I got all the paperwork on everything here. You can take a look at that when you're ready."

I nodded at him as I juggled the key in the lock, eventually finding the sweet spot that allowed it to turn and open. I held the door for him and we both went inside.

The great room was just that, one large nearly empty room. There were only two windows, one at the front and one on the long side. A door at the opposite end led to the back porch. A bare concrete slab served as the floor, and the walls were un-stuccoed adobe, the mortar between the bricks rough and uneven. An old wood stove, the sole source of heat, was installed not far from the front door. The only electricity in the room came from two outlets along one wall that amounted to holes cut in the side of the trailer and an outlet box inserted, connecting it with the trailer wiring. One corner in the back of the great room, about a six by six area, had been partitioned off with plywood. I thought it was a storage closet, but when I opened the door a low toilet and tiny sink were affixed to one wall, in the opposite corner of the bathroom was a metal shower stall. Mr. Duboski, unable to get his wheel chair through anything except the front and back doors sat a few feet away watching me.

"Everything works, just can't check it, I got the water turned off so as not to freeze up. Oh, but hot water, there ain't none. If you buy the place I'll see to having the hot water heater replaced. Electric's off too, but it all works." He sounded hopeful. "Was you planning on moving in here yourself?"

I came out of the bathroom and stood beside him. "Yes, I've been renting a room in Albuquerque, but want to find something more permanent."

"You and your husband I reckon." He still grasped the VA tote bag in one hand.

"No, just me." I stopped telling my life story a long time ago. When the topic of my family came up I changed the subject. "Can I look inside the trailer?"

"Go ahead, I can't get up those steps, but you go ahead and look around on your own." He wheeled his chair over to one of the windows and sat in the light of the sun that streamed in through the glass. Even thought it was warm outside, it was cool, almost cold in here without the wood stove's heat.

"Them boxes in there, I can find someplace for 'em, might take me a while though."

I climbed three steps fashioned out of stacked cement blocks, to what had once been the trailer's front door. The door had been removed to allow direct entry to the kitchen area. Everything in here reminded me of the sixties: the rose pink and yellow linoleum on the floor; the small nosegays that dotted the wallpaper; even the sink was yellow. At least it's cheerful I thought.

"Does the stove work?" I stood in front of the narrow electric drop in range and played with the knobs. Duh, well of course it wouldn't work now, there's no electricity.

"Well, two of the burners do, but not the oven. Reckon I could replace that too if need be." Mr. Duboski said from the bottom of the stairs. "Fridge works though, cold as can be, makes good ice."

I turned in the narrow corridor kitchen to spy a short, fat, old style refrigerator the kind you need to defrost. Might have guessed, it was yellow too. I continued on to the breakfast nook which connected with a small living room. It was piled high with boxes. Down the corridor were two tiny bedrooms and another bathroom this one with a tub, sink, and toilet, all yellow. Every room, including the bathtub had boxes, bags and plastic storage tubs stacked waist high or higher. A thick layer of dust covered all. I took my time walking back to the adobe great room. For a while I stood in the living room and breakfast nook part of the trailer, closing then opening my eyes, imagining the space, first empty, then filled with furniture, not boxes. I could dwell here I told myself. Definitely, I could dwell here.

"Well Mr. Duboski, can we talk price?"

He grasped the VA bag with both hands, twisting it closed and looked up at me suspiciously, "Are you sure Beulah didn't send you?"

75

I got the place for sixty two thousand. My first offer, of fifty five was countered by sixty six, my counter being fifty eight and the final agreed upon price of sixty -two. At that price I would have to live without a new water heater or stove. Mr. Duboski, or Dub as he told me to call him, would make sure the electricity was on and the water flowing. Oh, and I also had to put up with the boxes for a while. That was okay by me. I didn't have furniture anyway.

The big disappointment was that I didn't have much of my settlement money left. After the paperwork was transferred, fees paid, acequia fees and every other kind of thing that needs doing I had next to nothing in my account. What I did have would be used to pay taxes on the place. I could live without electricity if I needed to, squeak by with cold water, but as they say, death and taxes are for certain.

Moving day, three days before my rent at the Rest Inn would be due, I dragged out MaryIsabelle's bike trailer, salvaged from the dumpster when Cesar was still night manager, used a coat hanger to secure it to the bike and piled in everything I owned. Sad to say, there was room to spare. Ned was in the office reconciling the night's receipts when I walked in with my key, laying it on the counter.

"Can I help you love?" He didn't even look up from the computer screen.

"I'm checking out Ned." I had worked so hard to look hard while at the Rest Inn, I didn't even have to think about it anymore.

"Honest? You're checking out?" He looked up now; the surprise on his face was obvious. "What, did you lose your monthly benefit or something?"

Oh like that's the only reason I would leave this place? But I didn't say it out loud, just continued to stand in front of the counter without expression. "No, just checking out. Can you print out my receipt please?"

Ned pushed aside the stack of forms from yesterday, picked up the key and entered the room number into the computer. "Let's see, you've been here six months."

"Yes that's right. I should still have a couple days left; I believe I'm paid through April 5th." I stood sideways, wanting to keep an eye on the bike and trailer outside.

"Yes, I can see that. Well, it tells me you get a refund, thirty-eight fifty. We usually put it through as a credit on your card."

"Don't have one, always paid cash or money order. Can you issue a check or cash?" Having a little money in my pocket would certainly be nice. I could treat myself to take out from one of those old diners. I could taste the sopipillas already.

"Um, I can do cash." Ned unlocked a small drawer, took out some bills and two quarters and counted them out on the counter.

"Is that it?" I put the money in my pocket, buttoned up my sweater and put my hand on the door, ready to high tail it out of there.

"Yes, that's it." He stapled the receipt for the refund to the computer printout. "Good luck to you."

"You too Ned, if you stay here I think you'll need it more than I will."

If I kept a steady pace, kept my breaks short and stuck to the back roads I'd be there by dinner time, even with the wind working against me. I did have to stop a couple of times to re-attach the trailer. Mid-day I found a Wendy's ordered a baked potato and bowl of chile for lunch, splurged on a chocolate frostee and thought about Cesar the whole time. At one intersection a woman wearing a dirty sweatshirt, kind of like I used to wear, stood with her dog and a sign that read *God Bless*. I circled back around took a ten from my pocket and handed it to her. I could wait for sopipillas.

I could tell people were watching me when I unlatched the gate and rode my bike through the driveway at Las Manchas. You know how you can feel eyes on you sometimes? I caught sight of the woman next door peeking through the curtains and Dub was sitting on his deck, watching the brilliant pink and purple western sky. One thing about the spring winds in New Mexico, the dust they kicked up into the air made for some magnificent sunsets.

Dub probably wouldn't have noticed me but for the raven. The large black bird alighted on the closest fence post and sent up the alarm.

Dub looked over and waved. "Starting to get set up?"

"Yes, it's good to be moving in." I closed the gate behind me and walked the bike and trailer under the portal.

"Well when you get ready to move the big stuff, Rae, lives t'other side of you with his Grandma, he kin give you a hand. I asked him to clean up the chimney for ya. And he said he'd paint up that sign now the place is sold. He's a pretty good guy." Dub wheeled down the ramp and sat on the other side of the fence watching me. The raven flew back up on the portal roof, his talons clicking as he walked across it.

"Thanks, but this is about it. I'll be starting fresh." I lifted out my blankets from the trailer, held them on my hip as I struggled with the key. "Who's your friend?" I titled my head towards the raven.

"Aw this guy's just a pest. He thinks he has to find out what's going on everywhere. Right now he's waiting for Little Dog to wake up so he can bother him; he's asleep under the deck." Dub took a dog treat out of a bag that hung from the wheelchair's handle and tossed it on the ground. "So when you planning on moving in?"

"Tonight. Got everything I need right here." I hoisted up the blankets a little to show him.

The raven flew down from his perch and picked up the dog bone then flew across the empty field towards the twin adobe towers of St Ursula Mission Church, spreading the news of my arrival.

298   ¤

It didn't take long to unpack. About five minutes in fact. Despite the cold water, I dared a shower and put on clean clothes. A gusty wind blew outside and tree branches swayed with it, brushing the roof. It was okay. Everything was okay. I boiled some water and made a cup of noodles for dinner, sitting on the cement steps that lead from the great room to the kitchen. Unlike the Rest Inn, I had light bulbs. I sat under the converted porch light that jutted from the trailer into the great room surveying my abode. My immediate problem was where to sleep, even though it was barely eight o'clock, I was tired. The ride over had been exhausting, and the last few weeks at the Rest Inn had been emotionally draining. Even if I had to sleep on the floor tonight, I was looking forward to bedtime.

The great room was colder than the trailer side which itself was not too warm. If I had known the lack of hot water extended to lack of heat in the trailer I might have renegotiated that deal, but things are what they are. I decided laying out my blankets on the great room floor would be easier than moving boxes around on the other side.

I barely sat down with my cup of noodles on the second step when there was a knock at the door. When you close one door you have to open another I thought, and turned the nob to allow no more than a glance out.

"Father Rico." I flung the door open. "Father Rico, it is so nice to see you, do you remember me."

"Of course, of course I do. You have returned to Las Manchas, Mrs. Roark." His sturdy frame filled the doorway as he stood waiting for an invitation inside.

"My goodness, where are my manners, please, come in." I stood aside and welcomed him into the empty room.

He glanced at the Styrofoam cup of noodles on the steps and pile of blankets laid out on the floor.

"I won't stay long tonight Mrs. Roark; I just wanted to welcome you back to Las Manchas." He reached in his pocket and pulled out two bananas and a tuna fish sandwich wrapped in wax paper.

"So you won't have to cook tonight," he said as he handed them to me. "And where is your dog?"

"Peanuts? I don't have him anymore." I hadn't thought of Peanuts in months, the pain of having to abandon him at the shelter was something I purposefully blocked out. "I couldn't feed him anymore so I had to take him to an animal shelter."

"Pity, he was a beautiful animal." Father Rico took one of my hands in both of his, patting it lightly. Then he looked around the room again. "I can't stay you know, it's Holy Week, and lots to do, but I do have something else to help you feel at home."

I followed him outside. A beige sixty four Mercedes sedan was parked just outside the driveway gate. Father Rico walked to the back, opened the trunk, and pulled out the same cot I had slept on nearly a year before. He handed it over the top of the fence to me. "Welcome to Las Manchas Mrs. Roark. I hope to see you sitting in the pews at St Ursula soon." He opened the driver side door of the Mercedes to get in.

"How did you know I was here?" I slung the cot over my shoulder, eternally grateful. "A little bird told me," Father Rico said before he closed the car door.

76

This isn't the end. It isn't the beginning either. It's just part of the story. I was still poor, had nothing but a roof over my head. That first week at Las Manchas I pretty much sat. I sat on the cot, on the steps leading to the kitchen, on the floor leaning up against the wall, outside on a cut down tree branch. I just sat. Nobody, nobody could tell me to move on.

Monday, a full week after moving in, I got up, made tea and sat. Now what do I do with my life. I could hear that pesky raven walking on my porch again. Boy he sure has gained weight. He sounds more like an elephant than a bird. When I heard a loud thud, I put my cup of tea on the step beside me and went outside. Somebody was up there.

"Can I help you?" I called out.

"Morning." A kid in his twenties wearing olive green Dickies slung low on his hips and a black hoodie with torn and oil stained cuffs walked over to the edge.

"I'm Rae." He slid off the porch roof onto the ground landing on his feet in front of me and extended his hand.

I gave my classic clueless response, "Oh?"

"Your neighbor, Dub, sent me." He still held his hand out.

"Oh! Yes, Dub told me. I forgot." I finally took his hand. "I'm Aileen."

"Nice to meet you Aileen." He moved a ladder from one side of the porch to the other.

"Trying to get this for sale sign painted over. Not that Dub got a ton of calls. I think you and my Aunt Beulah were the only ones." He climbed back up, moved a bucket of white paint and a long handled paint roller to the house roof line.

"Sorry, I didn't know a family member was interested." Wow, I hoped my new neighbors wouldn't hold it against me.

"Are you kidding? If Aunt Beulah bought this place I'd be the one to move. Anyway she offered Dub crap for it. She didn't think anyone else would come along and want it. He was about ready to sell it to her too, if you hadn't showed up." He dumped the paint into a tray and began to roll over the large letters on the roof, leaving huge uneven stripes. "I can redo this sometime over the summer, but I wasn't sure if you were going to have the roof replaced or not."

"Oh, should I?" It never occurred to me I'd need to do anything that major.

"Well, there are a couple of leaks, but nothing that can't be patched. But eventually, you're going to want to put a new one on." Rae climbed slowly to the ridge and started to paint down over the top half of the letters. "How's that? See any place I missed?"

"No looks good, thanks." I didn't have a dollar to offer this kid, not even a cookie or cup of coffee. Don't think he'd want a bowl of oatmeal. "I hope you'll take a rain check on what I owe you, I'm a little short on cash right now."

He handed down the paint and roller to me, used the ladder this time to climb down.

"Heck no, you don't owe me anything. My nina and me are happy to have somebody here after all these years. Nobody's been in there since Dub started using his wheelchair, couldn't get around anymore with the steps and all." Rae took back the roller and emptied what little paint was left in the tray back into the paint can. "That's when the VA helped get the double wide next door. I built that deck for him and ramp so he could get up and down on his own."

You're a man of many talents. Are you a carpenter?" I helped him collapse the ladder.

"Mechanic, got a shop next door. Just opened it a few months ago thanks to my Aunt Beulah. Word is getting around. I get a little busier every week." He was grinning at me as he hoisted the ladder on to his shoulder and walked towards the rock wall that separated my place from his.

"I thought you just said you didn't like her." This was confusing.

"Don't, but the jokes on her. She's had plans for your place, got it re-zoned for mixed use. She was mad as heck when I opened the garage here. Didn't think any of us would know what the rezoning allowed." Rae levered the ladder over the wall into his yard. "Anyway, glad you're here. If you ever need help with anything, till the garden or something, let me know."

Garden? Who said anything about a garden.

"Ditch crew will be coming through this week, clean out the ditch. When they open the gate on the acequia I'll come over and show you." He picked up the paint bucket and roller, set them on the rock wall. "In fact, my nina and I are going to Belen later to get some manure, I got a friend who runs sheep and alpaca down there, good for the soil. I can bring you some?"

A garden would be nice. "Great, yeah, that would be really great. How much does he charge?"

Rae looked at me mischievously. "Charge? For sheep crap? Nah, he only charges rich people." He hopped over the fence. "Welcome to Las Manchas."

A little over three weeks later, when I pulled the first of the radishes from the ground and picked a handful of spinach to add to my cup of noodle soup, I cried. Two weeks after that purple and gold beets formed round domes on top of the soil and wild asparagus stalks lined up along the ditch bank, I cried again. Early June, bright red strawberries planted years ago all along the rock wall were the size of walnuts, tender and ripe, my eyes turned into Niagara Falls. I packed some berries into cottage cheese containers and walked the circle stopping at Dub's house first. That pesky raven followed, begging for the spoils. On more than one occasion I had to shoo him out of the garden.

"Dub? You there?" I called out as I walked up the ramp. I need not have worried, Little Dog sounded the alarm.

"Why good morning Missy, nice to see you getting all settled in. We been watching you work the soil." Dub opened the metal screen door and held it for me.

"Brought you some strawberries." I set an overflowing plastic container on the counter. "Did you plant these?"

Dub reached for one, popped it in his mouth without washing it. "You bet. Sweetest berries this side of the Missouri. Them plants came all the way from Minnesota. My ma dug 'em out of her garden one summer I went for a visit. About the only thing she give me worth anything. Those plants rode out on the train with me."

I could see the memories in his eyes.

"Well that was a great gift. Look, it's still giving." I picked up the carton and rinsed it in the sink before setting it an arm's reach of him. "Do you want some sugar for them?"

"No, they's sweet enough, and I'm not supposed to have sugar on account of my diabetes." He popped a couple more in his mouth.

"Do you think your neighbors want some too? There are way more than I can eat. I picked plenty." Little Dog scratched at the door until I let him out. The raven was waiting for him, dove at him two or three times making Little Dog turn circles trying to catch him. I leaned against the kitchen counter and watched the show.

"Anselmo and Penelope? Why yes, they always did like 'em, used to trade tomatoes for 'em. Hold on, let me get my hat and I'll go with you." Dub wheeled over to a row of hooks along the back wall, grabbed a VFW hat, and wheeled towards the door.

"Isn't it a little early for tomatoes?" It was the beginning of June, warm but not hot. I didn't garden much, but I knew enough to know it would be weeks before tomatoes were ripe.

"No, the little ones, you plant 'em. Anselmo used to start 'em on his window. Best around, old family seed. Can't buy those." Dub wheeled out the door and smoothly rolled down the wooden ramp to his driveway, then circled the chair back and looked up at me. "Ain't you coming?"

I tried to push his chair but he waved me off. "This is how I get my exercise," he said. We hadn't gone a few yards before I heard a voice from behind me. "Wait my friends, I'll go with you." Father Rico came up behind us. Where had he come from?

"Hello Father, nice to see you out and about today." Dub greeted him warmly. "You was a little under the weather I guess."

"Just a spring cold, this sun is helping." Father turned his head towards me." Well Mrs. Roark, how are you settling in? I see you've discovered Dub's berries." He eyed the box I carried with four more plastic tubs overflowing with strawberries.

"One's for you Father, I have lots." I handed him one and he popped it in his mouth.

"Nothing like a fair June day, fresh berries and friends to share it with. We are blessed." Father walked between Dub and I. "Nice to have you join us on our daily walks?"

"I didn't know you did? Walk, that is. I wanted to share some of these strawberries." I had become so cloistered in my house and yard I had stopped noticing what went on around me.

"Me and Father try to get out most days, long as the weather holds." Dub reached over and picked a strawberry out of Father's hand and tossed it high into the air. The raven swooped out of nowhere and caught it. They both laughed.

Anselmo and Penelope's gate was already open. A late model white Chrysler was parked in their driveway. "Guess we should come back, they got company." Dub said.

"It'll be okay Dub. Mrs. Roark has to meet her sometime. There is no time like the present."

Father took another tub of berries from my hand and knocked on the door. A tiny man, bent with the years, hobbled on a cane to the door and came outside. Three hens came clucking towards him, expecting to be feed, and leading about a dozen tiny yellow chicks.

"Aye, Padre, Dub, bienvenidos, have some coffee." He greeted Father Rico warmly motioning us inside.

"Not today, my friend, we wanted to drop off some strawberries. Have you met your new neighbor, Mrs. Roark?" Father offered up the tub of berries to Anselmo.

Anselmo's eyes grew wide and he quickly closed the door behind him and walked a few feet away with us stopping beside the car. The hens followed him.

"My niece is here you know." He looked over his shoulder to see if he was being followed.

"Yes, yes we know, saw the car. But she has to meet her sometime." Father put his hand on his friends arm for courage.

"Call her out, call Penelope, I'll do the introductions."

Anselmo hesitated then slowly hobbled back to the door "Nellie, tenemos visitors, ven aca."

A tiny woman, equally bent, used a walker to push her way out the door. "Buenos días Father Rico, Dub, cómo estás?" Her soft gray-brown eyes twinkled when she saw the berries her spouse held.

"Qué bonita." She, too, popped one in her mouth. "Muy dulce, delicioso."

"Señora," Father Rico addressed the little lady, "Señora Romero, esta es Mrs. Roark, su vecino nuevo."

The woman extended her hand softly towards me, "Bueno dias Señora Roark, bienvenido a Las Manchas."

A woman, close to my age, but only a few inches taller than the frail couple I had just been introduced to, watched us through the door. She did not look pleased. Even though it was a warm day she wore a heavy skirted business suit, stockings and heels. They clicked as she walked out the door, scattering the hens and their brood in all directions. Her hair was cut short, heavily frosted, streaked with an off shade of yellow and red, which were supposed to be highlights.

"Beulah." Father greeted her enthusiastically. "You are just in time to meet the newest resident of Las Manchas." He opened up his arms, trying to welcome her to the group. She crossed hers in front of her chest shutting us out, frowned and stood a few feet away.

"Good day to you Father. Anselmo tells me you have been coming around to check up on them." It was more accusatory then friendly.

"Of course Beulah, I good priest always checks on members of his parish." Father Rico was good at what he did. No matter how unfriendly the reception, he always kept a positive slant.

"You don't have to check on them. I do that. I make sure they have what they need, so you needed bother." She had yet to address me.

"Ah Beulah, I have to take care of their spiritual needs too you know my dear woman. You are a good niece to them, bringing them groceries and such, but I am right here. Besides I enjoy my visits with your Aunt and Uncle. Surely you can't object to that." Father offered her some strawberries, which she pushed away.

"No thank you." She said curtly then opened her car door, keys in hand.

"Wait; let me introduce you to Mrs. Roark." He called after her.

Beulah stood beside the open car door, looked me up and down with disdain, got in the car and drove away without saying anything more.

"Well, we tried didn't we?" Father shook his head.

That night, right before sunset, someone knocked on my door. Anselmo stood under my portal holding a cut down milk carton with nine small tomato plants popping out. "For the strawberries," he said. "Come by if you want some chile plants or some mint root, I've got those too." Then the old man reached into both pockets of his windbreaker and pulled a tiny yellow chick from each one, passing them gently to me. "They'll be good layers," he said.

77

Between dumpster diving and yard sales I managed a bare minimum of furniture for my simple dwelling. A cast off metal futon couch, left curbside by graduating students, a modest table with one broken leg and a couple of stools, you get the idea. A few nails, and paint from the dollar store and little by little I had a place to sit and sleep besides the floor. I moved the cot Father gave me to the back porch. The futon, while not exactly a feather bed, was at least more comfortable then the cot. On warm afternoons I'd lay on the cot out back, reading. It was one such hot afternoon, middle of June, I heard Billy James Dean's voice calling out to me.

"Aileen Roark? Aileen are you there? Aileen Roark?"

I jumped up, walked to the side of the house. "Mr. Dean, welcome. What brings you here?" I opened the side gate and ushered him thru. He looked around the place curiously.

"Is this what you spent your settlement on?" He sounded doubtful.

"Yes, let me give you the tour." I guided him around the back yard.

"What made you buy this place? Not rent an apartment or something?" He held a quizzical look on his face.

"You did. You said it was too bad I sold my house that it was really hard to kick someone out and take it away. I wanted a place no one could take away." That annoying raven was in my garden, picking at my pea vines. I picked up a stone and threw it at him.

Billy was mildly alarmed. "That was a casual comment, not intended to be legal advice."

"You mean someone could take this away?" Now I was alarmed. Was that why he was here? Was someone trying to take away my home?

"Well," he said, except he dragged it out slowly. "In certain situations, given the right set of circumstances, it might be possible. But," he hesitated again, looked the place over once more, "unlikely."

I sighed, relieved. "You had me worried. I thought that's why you were here."

"No, no, not at all. Actually I'm here to ask a favor." He looked around for a place to sit. All I had to offer was a white plastic lawn chair, slightly cracked. I wiped it clean with a rag and he sat down, I sat on a tree stump beside him.

"Do you remember when you offered to help Cesar? Did you mean it?"

"Mr. Dean, to be honest, I spent my settlement money. I don't have any left. If I had known Cesar needed it I would have saved some for him. I am so sorry. But I'll do anything else I can to help him."

"Billy, call me Billy. No, not money. I need to find him a place to live. He has six month left on his original sentence, the one he was on parole for before. I got him out on parole again. But," Billy Dean hesitated, "with some pretty significant restrictions. That's why I thought of you. Frankly Aileen, you're the only client I have who isn't really guilty. That's what I need for Cesar, someplace he won't' be around other felons, or drugs or guns or mayhem. You came to mind immediately."

My classic response: "Oh?"

"It's only six months, till next January. You don't have to do anything except provide a place for him to live. Everything else is taken care of." Billy was standing up.

"Is it okay with Cesar? Does he know you're asking me?"

"He's out front in the car. We can go ask him."

78

When the end of July came around and I still didn't have a job offer I knew something was up. School would be starting in just two weeks. In some places teachers were expected to report August third. Since mid-May, when vacancies began to be posted for the fall semester I had ridden my bike twice a week to the library and filled out dozens of on-line applications. I had a new Social Security card, a copy of my birth certificate, duplicate transcripts, everything in page protectors bought for a penny each at yard sales. Something was up, only two interviews and no offers.

I took a cold shower, the only kind I had, put on my nicest shirt and pants and hopped a bus for the Success Academy, a charter school for homeless or near homeless teens. The interview had gone well. I was honest about my struggle with poverty and homelessness. I had a nice letter of reference form the Director of the Street School in Santa Fe where I used to volunteer. When I left the interview I thought I had nailed it. So when I was never called back it was a huge disappointment. Maybe, I reasoned, I never got the message. I listed both Cesar's phone number and Father Rico's for messages. Both denied any calls came. I got off the bus at the closest stop and walked through the high chain link fence, waited by the door to be buzzed in.

"Yes can I help you?" A male voice came over the intercom speaker.

"Yes, I'm Aileen Roark. I interviewed for a teaching job here a couple of weeks ago and I wanted to follow up, maybe talk to Mr. Sanchez or Ms. Dias?" I never got used to talking into the side of a building.

"Wait, I'll see if they are available."

I recognized a few of the street people who sat around. I took two steps toward the fence and greeted them. Only one spoke to me.

"Aren't you Aileen? Bert's friend?" A wiry bearded character in a torn tax service T shirt said when I hailed him.

"You bet. Last I heard he had a VA sponsored apartment or something?" I remembered sitting beside these guys at the soup kitchen.

"Yeah, I heard. He still shows up to eat sometimes. You're looking well." He scrutinized my clean clothes and lack of a rolled up tarp or bag.

"Pretty well. I'm trying to get a job here. I interviewed, but no one called back so I'm trying to follow up." I nodded towards the entrance.

"Very nice, a lot of the younger ones have been going there. They miss it over the summer. Wish they had someplace for us "senior citizens" to go during the day." He used his fingers to make hand quotes around the "senior citizens".

"Maybe someday." The intercom buzzed on the side of the building. "Got to go, take care of yourself."

"You too, good luck with that." He took some long strides, joined a group of three other men and headed west, towards the downtown area.

Mr. Sanchez greeted me right inside the door. "Mrs. Roark, what can I do for you?" He wasn't unfriendly, but he wasn't too excited to see me either.

"Hello Mr. Sanchez. I wanted to follow up on my interview. I was pretty excited about teaching here. Have you filled the position yet?" I stayed cheerful. Always remember, I told myself, you have to make the people like you or you'll never get hired.

"Yes, Mrs. Roark, we have. You did seem like a strong candidate, but," he looked over his shoulder it see if anyone was within ear shot then lowered his voice, "there were a couple of issues with your background and license."

"Oh?" There I go again. Can't you think of a better response then that Aileen?

"Well, for one thing you don't seem to have a current license. We ran the standard check with the State Education Department and they have no record of you having a current license."

"That can't be." I protested. I had to pick my words carefully here. "I did have an issue last year with my license, but it was cleared up. I was assured it was cleared up." Oh boy, did District Two renege on their agreement to remove the hold and child endangerment charge?

"I'll leave that to you to take care of, but, also, your background check didn't go through. There's an outstanding warrant somewhere. Sorry, really I am. The committee was excited about bringing you on board, but you understand, we have to check everything." Mr. Sanchez held the exit door for me. There was nothing more he wanted to discuss. "Good luck to you Mrs. Roark. If you get things straightened out, come back and see us. We could use you as a sub."

It took forty five minutes before another bus came along and I could ride home, then a half hour walk from the bus stop to Las Manchas. I almost could have walked all the way. It was unbearably hot. When I walked in the door, dripping with sweat, Cesar was adding ice to a large jar of sun tea.

"How'd it go?" He handed me an old pickle jar filled with the cool brew.

"Not good. I guess I've got a warrant." I slumped down on the cement block kitchen steps and held the cool jar to my forehead.

Cesar sat down on the step beside me, pulled his phone from his pocket, scrolled to Billy Dean's number and passed it to me. "Join the club."

¤ ¤ ¤

Father Rico started a neighborhood farmer's market in front of the church every Thursday afternoon. Only a handful of vendors came. When we moved to the west side of the church, where we could be seen from the Rail Runner train and passing cars at the busy intersection things picked up. Cesar turned out to be quite a good gardener. He knew when to plant, when to weed and water, and didn't mind doing the squash bug squish as he called it. He placed boards under the zucchini plants and pumpkin vines and early morning, when the sun was barely up, he'd jump up and down on the boards. There were probably two dozen or more squished bugs every morning. Glad it was him, not me, the smell was awful.

It was the middle of August, prime harvest time. Cesar carried two long boards and I tied two crates to my bike trailer, and we set up a stand in the shade of the church's tower. This week we harvested green beans, yellow squash, a few cucumbers, tiny carrots and a bushel of heirloom tomatoes grown from the plants Anselmo had given me. In another week we'd have tons of corn. It wasn't much but the fifty or sixty dollars we earned made a huge difference in our budget. 'Bread and Beer Money' Cesar called it.

I was placing handfuls of green beans into a brown lunch bag when Billy Dean called back. Cesar handed me the phone.

"Aileen Roark? Is this Aileen Roark?" Billy asked.

"Yes, Mr. Dean, it's me."

"Aileen Roark."

"Yes, it's Aileen Roark, Mr. Dean." It was hard not to be annoyed even though I knew he was doing this for me as much as him.

"Billy, call me Billy. I had my assistant do some checking on your situation. District Two did what was agreed and pulled the hold. However," he took a deep breath "however, apparently your license expired during that period of time and now the Department insists you reapply as a Level I teacher, apparently you have to take a test now or something, maybe retake a class. I wish I had better news about that, but unless we take them to court over it they won't bend."

I was silent.

"Aileen Roark? Are you still there?" Billy spoke rapidly as always.

"Yes Billy, I'm still here. What do you think I should do?" This was very disappointing.

"Frankly, I don't think the court fight is worth it. We could go that route, but by the time it got heard and ruled on you could have done everything needed to get another license."

I really didn't want to restart my career as a Level I teacher. The pay average was just a little over what you could make as a waitress with tips. And there was no unpaid overtime.

"What about the warrant?" I asked him. "What did you find out about the warrant?"

"Yes, were you every cited for vagrancy or trespassing?"

"Oh," I said.

79

Twice a year New Mexico Game and Fish declares free fishing day. It's a day when everyone gets to fish without a license, usually mid-September and mid-April. When I saw the very small announcement in the weekly free paper, and noticed the Rio Grande was on the list of free fishing waters, light bulbs went off in my head. I went to tell Cesar.

He was out back. The camper that served as his bedroom had literally come apart at the seams, exposing pink insulation and white plastic mesh. Cesar's solution was to cover the whole thing in tin roofing panels salvaged from a collapsed shed. He had anchored 2 by 4s to the camping trailer, and was now using a cordless drill borrowed from Rae to attach the roofing. But the power pack battery had run down so he was mostly turning it by hand. He was wearing his usually uniform, an old work shirt with the sleeves cut off.

Back in the days when he was the night clerk at Rest-Inn, I thought this was some sort of fashion statement on his part. It wasn't until I got to know him better that I learned he cut the sleeves off because his biceps were so massive from years of training as a boxer that most sleeves were much too small for his arms.

I brought him a glass of water, still his beverage of choice, shoved the folded newspaper under his nose with the Free Fishing Day headline circled.

Ever Mr. Cool, he barely glanced at in.

"What makes you think I want to spend my Saturday catching fish Blondie? Have you ever been fishing? What are you going to catch them with your hands? A worm tied to a string? Ah, talk about dumb blond."

"I'm not blond and yes I have been fishing, but since you aren't interested I'll talk to Dub he's got fishing gear stashed in one of the trailer's closets."

"Tell you what, if Dub wants to go I'll go with you, but only to be sure you don't push him in the river."

"Oh sí, well don't trouble yourself".

"No trouble. No trouble at all."

He went back to screwing the metal roofing into the side of the camper.

I went over to the apple tree. Its branches hung heavy and low, almost completely enclosing the two white plastic chairs we had placed close to the trunk which had been nearly split in two by a lightning strike years ago. A sort of outdoor room, the shade served as a respite on hot days. In another week or so the apples would be fully ripe. I would dry some, sell the best and use the rest for apple sauce which I would freeze in sandwich bags from the dollar store. I picked three apples that seemed to have the least number of worm holes

"Heads up," I said to Cesar tossing an apple in his direction. He tried to catch it with one hand, but had to release the drill to use the other, pressing his chest against the corrugated metal to stop it from falling to the ground.

"You throw like a girl Blondie."

"Yeah, well you catch like one."

I hurried to the fence before he had a chance to throw it back at me. There was a place in the fence where we had fashioned a rough gate by cutting the field fence in one spot and curling the loose ends on each side to some long branches pruned from the apricot tree. The whole thing was kept closed by bungee cords. It didn't look pretty but it worked.

Dub was sitting on his deck, His little dog was curled up at his feet, or where his feet used to be since most of them had been cut away. Dub sat, arms crossed over his stomach,

Bataan Survivor cap on, staring down, looking up occasionally to watch the big-rigs speed by on I-25, one hundred and fifty feet above us. The raven was nowhere in sight today.

I called to him as I crossed the yard.

"Morning, how're you doing, Dub?" I sat on the edge of the deck and passed up an apple.

He looked the apple over, noting the worm holes. "We used to get great apples from that tree. It must be fifty years old." He rubbed the apple on his sleeve polishing off the dust before taking a bite. "We'd pick em by the bushel full, haul down to Basinger's market. People used to come looking for them. Of Course they weren't as wormy. You should have sprayed. There used to be some stuff in that old shed. Bet you could find it."

"I'm pretty sure that stuff is illegal now Dub. People don't mind the worms so much now. They just think it's organic. Pay more for them that way."

That made him chuckle. "How come it's illegal?" He took another bite.

I scratched Little Dog under the chin. "It was killing the eagles, made the eggshells so thin the mother bird would crush them first time she sat on them."

"There's plenty of eagles. I see them flying above the river couple times a week." He reached behind him and pulled some old binoculars from a cloth bag hanging from his wheelchair and passed them over to me.

I raised them to my eyes, one eyepiece was cracked so I had to squint to compensate, scanned the sky above the river slowly. No eagles but the cotton woods were starting to change and that raven was there spiraling in circles in the air. Soon there would be deep shimmering gold leaves for miles along the bosque, like a river of gold under a deep blue sky.

I passed the binoculars back to Dub, who immediately put them to his eyes and began to scan the river.

"Well the reason I came to call was to invite you fishing. It's free fishing day this Saturday and I was kind of hoping you would want to go and maybe we could share your gear."

"Fishing huh? I can't recall the last time I went fishing." He sighed wishfully. "Well you're welcome to the gear. But you might need to spiff if up a bit. I don't see how I can climb down to the river with these feet."

"Cesar said he'd go, but only if you did too. He wanted to be sure I didn't push you into the river."

Dub chuckled again, folding and unfolding his hands, looking at them each time. Little Dog sensed Dub's excitement. The shaggy canine got up and circled several times before jumping up with his front paws on Dub's knee. "Well Blondie, can we take some sandwiches and lemonade?"

"You bet. I'll make it sugar free. And why does everyone call me Blondie.".

He was grinning, hard to do with so few teeth. "Send Cesar over and I'll help him with the gear."

Cesar had finished the patch job on the trailer by the time I got back. Now it looked like a chicken coop on wheels. Oh well, at least it was paid for.

Cesar went to Dub's that evening, though I believe it was more to watch the football game then to check fishing gear. Dub was the only one in Las Manchas to have cable TV, which meant he was the only one to get all the NFL games. It was not uncommon for Rae, Cesar, Anselmo and even Father Rico to pay a visit on football night. Las Manchas football night might involve a twelve pack of cheap beer, pretzels and a couple of those giant sandwiches you get in the cold case. The one time I went over I learned right away they really didn't want me there,

Cesar had come back looking for some salsa

"Hey Blondie, can you whip us up some of that salsa you make with the fresh tomato, not too hot though, maybe only two chiles." I pulled some fresh tomatoes from the fridge and dumped them into the blender. It would be another week or so before we got a frost and I was furiously picking and freezing as much of the garden produce as I could.

"I'll bring it over in a few minutes." And I did.

It wasn't that they were rude or anything, it was the opposite. They were painstakingly polite, until the first bad call on an out of bound failure to make the first down or some such thing. I didn't know priests used profanity. Leaving the salsa on the overturned crate they were using as a table I made a hasty retreat and never went back. I never liked football anyway.

The next morning Cesar came in the back door, reached for his favorite cup from among my mismatched yard sale mugs and yawned.

"We checked out the gear. It's good to go, but there are only two rods and I need to rebuild the reel, a little machine oil to clean up the rust. Rae has two sets of tackle and Father thinks there are some stashed in the back of a storage room of the old school. I'm going to go by later this morning and see if we can find it." He gulped his coffee. Years of eating on the run had allowed him to drink even the hottest coffee without flinching.

"That's more than we need don't you think? I don't think you're allowed to have more than one pole in the water at a time."

He looked at me, mouth open, shoveling in corn flakes with eyebrows raised.

"They're going too."

I was surprised. "Really? That's great."

"I think Penelope is coming too. Anselmo doesn't want to leave her alone for too long at the house."

"Terrific, what about Rae's grandma, Priscilla?"

He hesitated, "No, no I don't think so." He took another bite of cornflakes.

And that is how the Amigos del Las Manchas Neighborhood Association got started.

80

Saturday came and everyone was up bright and early. Father Rico would pick up Penelope and Anselmo in his old Mercedes. The rest of us, Dub, me, Rae and Cesar would squeeze into Rae's truck. I would drive. We made bologna and cheese sandwiches. They could double for bait, Cesar explained. I picked some apples and made powdered lemonade in an empty gallon water jug, sugar free as promised. I visited the dollar store and managed some plastic cups and plates and packed everything into my cloth JC Penny's shopping bag. Anselmo and Penelope brought a package of oatmeal cookies, the generic kind that comes frosted in a flimsy plastic tray. Dub brought a hug plastic jar of cheese puffs and Rae brought potted meat and crackers. Father Rico, who was always full of surprises, brought the beer.

I imagine we were quite a sight. Dub in his wheelchair, Penelope with her walker, and Anselmo bent over so he constantly looked at the ground. Father Rico wore his collar with a T-Shirt over that read St Ursula's Elementary, a picture of an Eagle in flight printed across it. Cesar, as always wore a work shirt with the sleeves cut out. Rae, well he is just Rae, but he had taken to wearing his pants below his buttocks gangster style and his belt hanging loose and low. Me? I was in my men's khakis and a Route 66 Casino T-shirt, all bought at a thrift store on bag day.

We found a spot down river from the Pueblo boundary where a narrow trail had been bushwhacked through the weeds. The river itself was only about three miles from Las Manchas, but to get here we had to cross the railroad track, circle twice in a roundabout to find us able to turn right, and travel about a mile up a little used utility access road. I parked at a wide spot on the road's shoulder. We got Dub's wheelchair down from the back of the truck, Cesar lifted him into it. He still had a boxer's arms. He had set up a make shift gym for himself under the apple tree with some cement blocks tied to a railroad tie. Like a prisoner in an exercise yard, he spent at least one hour a day lifting the weights and doing chin ups on a lower branch.

Cesar placed a box which now held most of the food onto Dub's lap and while Little Dog ran circles around his ankles, began the careful task of pushing Dub to the river. It had rained the night before and the path was muddy in several spots.

"Watch for snakes." Cesar warned Dub.

"They're more likely to bite you than me buddy. I'll just make them mad."

They passed into the head high weeds.

Father went next carrying most of the fishing gear, the twelve pack of beer and lending an arm to Anselmo. The two of them seemed to be trading fish stories in Spanish. I'm not sure exactly what they said, but I'd guess it to be a wager. Rae and I followed last, one on each side of Penelope, helping to steady both her and the walker. I had the bag of sandwiches and lemonade swinging from my arm. Rae had three of those folding stand up chairs like I used to take to my kids' soccer games slung over his shoulder.

"It's too bad Priscilla couldn't make it," I said.

Penelope said something in Spanish under her breath.

Anselmo and Father turned their heads and looked at Rae and then each other.

Rae hung his head and replied "Yeah it's too bad."

Penelope mumbled again. Was it something I said?

Awkward. I didn't yet know about the two sisters' long standing feud.

Father reached in his pocket and fished out a Susan B Anthony dollar. Turning half around he said "First one to catch a fish gets the dollar."

"That's as good as mine so just give it to me now," Rae said, bragging.

"Don't be so sure of yourself, gangster." Cesar's voice boomed out from the weeds and willows, even though we couldn't see him, he wasn't that much further ahead.

"You both need to be taught a lesson and I'm the one to do it." Dub's voice trailed Cesar's.

Father and Anselmo joked with each other in Spanish a few feet ahead of me.

With only a few stumbles and scratches and tree branches in the eye, we made it to the river.

The water was down, but clear and fast even though it had rained the night before. The sky was that clear electric blue you see only in New Mexico; sparse large flat bottom clouds extended miles into the atmosphere. It was cool now but would soon climb into the eighties, hot for mid-September.

We struggled down to the bank, leaving Dub on higher ground and Penelope sitting in one of the chairs beside him. Rae ran back up the trail to the truck to retrieve an umbrella from in back of the seat which he propped up between Dub and Penelope giving them some protection from the sum.

The other two chairs were for Anselmo and Father, although Anselmo, ever the gentleman, kept trying to surrender his chair to me.

Cesar, I and Rae scrambled up and down the bank baiting the hooks and helping the others to cast. By one o'clock we had caught nothing, the clouds were gathering and we reasoned we only had an hour or two left before it rained. So we passed around the food and lemonade. The beer had already made the rounds. Filling our plates and our hearts with fellowship and fresh air, we baited the hooks one last time with the cheese and bologna left from the sandwiches.

Suddenly, Penelope calls out, "Ay da Dios! I've got one!"

"Reel it in slowly Nellie." Anselmo tells his spouse, excited beyond compare.

Penelope stands up, but, without the walker to steady her, pitches forward half walking half falling into the river. Anselmo drops his rod and shuffles in after the love of his life but is soon knocked off balance by the current and is lying sideways in two foot deep water. Rae, Cesar and I all rush to pull them out, but the rocks are slippery and we fall.

Dub, stuck about a foot above us tries to navigate down the slippery muddy back and tips over backwards in his chair. He is lying on his back with feet in the air.

Only Father doesn't panic. Even with a couple beers in him he knows what to do. He pushes himself up, looks up to the sky as if for guidance and slowly wades into the water toward Penelope who is now sitting upright in about 18 inches of water still holding her fishing rod with two hands. She is about six feet from shore. Father wades out, reaches down and pulls her to her feet and walks her gingerly to shore. Then he grabs hold of a tree root, pulls himself up to where Dub is starring into the heavens half covered in mud with Little Dog licking at his ears. Father carefully bends down and rights the wheel chair. Cesar, Rae and I help each other up. Rae and Cesar pick up Anselmo, who is now soaking wet, and carry him to shore.

Somehow, Penelope has managed to keep the fish attached. She pulls up a brown trout about 8 inches long letting it flop on shore,

"I win," she says grinning like a three year old. Father laughs and pulls the Susan B Anthony coin from his pocket.

Rae bends down and starts to remove the fish from the hook.

"Who's going to clean him?" Penelope asks.

"It's too little to eat Tia. We need to through him back."

"What do you mean too little to eat? I don't eat that much."

"Rae's right Nellie, you need to throw him back," Anselmo says, teeth chattering, trying to wring water from his shirt. Cesar nods in agreement than hustles up the path through the brush to the truck hoping to find a towel or some shop rags so everyone can dry off.

Penelope grumbles something in Spanish again, but nods her head in agreement.

Rae takes the little fish in both hands, wades into the river and releases him. The trout immediately swims to the middle of the river a little up stream.

Like a bad movie, a large winged shadow passes over us and a piercing call fills the air.

"Águila," Father Rico says and everyone nods in agreement.

The eagle flies to the middle of the river, feet first with talons extended, picks up Penelope's trout and heads for the sky. 'Ay da Dios' indeed.

81

*C*esar is taking his time getting back. At Father's suggestion, we collapse the chairs and lock the fishing poles, and, soaking wet, head back up the trail. I go first, in back of Penelope, with hands on either side of her walker, helping her lift, making slow progress towards the road.

Father is next, Anselmo grasping his arm, teeth chattering, taking careful deliberate steps behind us.

Rae next, pushing Dub in his chair. The chair gets hung up on a few rocks on the trail and they have to navigate the last few yards backwards, with Rae pulling the chair up over the obstacles. Little Dog has opted to ride this time and Dub places him in the box which contains the discarded plates and beer cans. Little Dog immediately begins rummaging through it trying to find the last bits of bologna and cheese.

The clouds have gathered and are touching. A strong breeze blows, shaking the weeds and reed around us. Soaking wet and without the sun to warm us, everyone shivers. Penelope and I make it to the clearing where the trail starts. Two police cars are there. The Sandoval County Sheriff's SUV pulls up, lights flashing but no siren, parking diagonally in front of Rae's truck and kicking up dust. I stopped dead in my tracks, terrified, wondering should I run up to the cars or in the opposite direction back to the river. Being homeless has taught me not to trust the law. What's up? What's going on?

I catch sight of Cesar lying face down in the gravel beside the truck. His hands are pulled in back of him, encircled by plastic zip ties that sub for handcuffs. I open and close my eyes in disbelief.

Beulah gets out of the Sheriff's SUV.

"You see, you see," she says excitedly, hands waving in the air. "A murderer, find out what he's done to them. He probably threw the weapon in the river. Make him talk." She is pacing back and forth on the other side of the truck still not having caught sight of us.

Father and Anselmo have caught up to me.

"Beulah," Father calls out. "Beulah calm yourself, nobody's been murdered, no one is dead."

Beulah runs around the side of the truck, followed by two deputies, who continue down the embankment toward Penelope and me, and grab hold of my arms, pulling them in back of me and taking hold of the walker.

"You! I should have known you were behind this. Call an ambulance, they've been drowned."

"Cállete Beulah," Anselmo says, yelling up the hill, lifting his head as much as he can. "The only one who should be drowned around here is you."

Father shushes him quickly. "Let her go officers. This is all a misunderstanding. We were on a picnic and doing some fishing. There is no crime here, let her go. Let them both go."

Rae and Dub appear, moving backwards, through the weeds. By now Little Dog has found a discarded beer can and is proudly holding it in his mouth. He jumps from the box, off Dub's lap and runs up to Beulah, who has always hated him, and drops it as a peace offering at her feet wagging his tail.

The deputies look at Father, at Little Dog and Beulah and finally at the Sheriff who has positioned himself between Cesar and Beulah

The Sheriff calls down to us, "You folks all right? Anyone hurt?"

"Of course they're not all right. Can't you see? Call an ambulance, arrest them both." Beulah is shouting in the Sheriff's ear.

"Never better Sheriff. Never Better" Dub responds.

"Everyone's all right." Father says as he continues to assist Anselmo up the incline before another deputy reaches down and takes over.

The sheriff nods to the deputies, who let me go and help Penelope and Anselmo to the top, leaving me, Father and Rae to push, pull and carry Dub up the steep embankment to the truck. If they would let Cesar go his strong arms would make quick work of it, but the stronger arm of the law continues to hold Cesar, cuffed, face down on the ground in the dirt.

Earlier that day Beaulah stopped by to check up on her aunt, finding her home, and Rae and his truck gone she thought she finally had the leverage needed to wrest control of the land holdings. Prime real estate near the Rail Runner and Interstate exit, she already had the architect's plans, waiting for the day she held title. She could see that day in sight as she rehearsed what to say to the Judge regarding Rae's violation of probation for driving on a revoked license.

When she stopped at Penelope's to find that house empty, she was puzzled, and Dub and his nasty little dog that bit her ankles were gone too. Believing them to be at church, they only place they went without someone taking them, she drove to St Ursula's to find the church doors locked, something that had never happened before. Father Rico was not answering the bell that acted as guardian to the parsonage living quarter. The sheriff was summoned. Beulah directed them to my door. "Search the place," she demanded. "She's got a murderer living there."

A search was begun. Two deputies cruised the roads near Las Manchas in an ever expanding circle, looking for the old pickup and any sign of us. Tribal officers were notified and joined in. The sheriff questioned Priscilla in hopes she would provide a clue to our whereabouts, but Rae never informed his grandmother where we would be.

A keen eyed young tribal officer spotted the truck tire tracks in the rain cleaned dirt of the access road. Driving slowly he came upon both the truck and Father Rico's distinctive Mercedes parked beside a river path with Cesar lying prone on the front seat, door open, searching under the seat for an old towel.

Calling for back-up, having already gotten the word on Cesar's two priors for manslaughter, he approached the truck with gun drawn and ordered Cesar out, cuffing him face down, aware that at any point Cesar could have taken him out with one powerful uppercut.

That's when we showed up.

"This is all a misunderstanding, Sheriff. We can clear this up. No one is hurt, no law has been broken." Father Rico, remembering his own arrest and imprisonment in Cuba fifty years ago, remained calm trying to persuade the sheriff.

"You can't just let them go." Beulah's ranting drowns everyone else out. "They can't just come in here and do whatever they want. Arrest them, arrest him." Beulah points to Cesar, still face down in the dirt.

A deputy, who has been sitting in one of the cruisers waiting for confirmation on our ID's, gets out of the car and walks over to the Sheriff. Handing me back my license, he tells the sheriff in a low voice "The only thing that came back on her was one misdemeanor for vagrancy and trespass."

"Vagrancy?" the sheriff says loudly, looking me up and down then locking my eyes in a stare down. I hold his gaze, not offering any explanation. Father is right, we haven't broken any laws.

The tribal officer bends to the ground, and helps Cesar, his arms still behind his back, to his feet.

"Well Sheriff, this is my collar but your jurisdiction, do I turn him over to you or let him loose?"

"Arrest him." Beulah continues to demand, dancing around in front of the Sheriff. She is the oldest daughter of the oldest daughter and used to being in charge and being obeyed. "Arrest him."

"Take him in." The Sheriff nods to the two deputies.

Incredulous, Cesar, Father and I all say in unison, "On what charge?"

The Sheriff pauses for minute, kicking the dirt, than glances at the fishing gear.

"Fishing without a license."

The three of us look at each other, and say in unison again, "It's free fishing day!"

"Look in my front pocket Officer Peña, please, just look." Cesar leans forward, trying to puff out the front pocket.

"What are you playing at? Just arrest him." Beulah continues to bounce nervously up and down in front of the Sheriff.

Officer Peña reaches into Cesar's shirt pocket and with two fingers removes the newspaper article, roughly torn and folded with the headline circled *New Mexico Free Fishing Day Set*.

"They're right." He says handing the paper to the Sheriff, and pulling a Leatherman from his belt to cut the zip tie.

It took a while to sort it all out, but we finally got home. The sheriff decided I was the only one sober enough and a licensed driver to drive either the truck or the Mercedes, and offered to call a tow truck as an alternative.

"No. No I'll manage." I was relieved that was to be my biggest problem that day.

The Sheriff gave Beulah a ride home to pick up her car, which she used to take Priscilla and Anselmo home, but not before taking them to the emergency room to be checked out, where they were pronounced cold, wet, but in other wise good shape.

I drove the Mercedes first. Father sat in the back. We loaded Dub into the passenger side and his wheelchair into the trunk. The plan was for me to take these two home then ride my bicycle back to pick up the truck while Cesar and Rae, along with one of the deputies, waited. After dropping Dub and Little Dog off, making sure they were in the house and the gate secured, Father and I started down the quarter mile dirt road that led past the graveyard to the church. As we reached the cemetery gates the Mercedes gave a loud backfire, sputtered, shuddered and died. I tried to restart it but to no avail.

"Just leave it here, Mrs. Roark. I'll come back for it Monday with Rae. It probably just needs adjusting or the air cleaner replaced."

"Monday? Don't you want to pick it up tomorrow Father?"

"Tomorrow is Sunday Mrs. Roark, the Lord's Day and Holy. We don't work on cars on Sunday." He looked at me with surprise I would suggest such a thing. We got out of the car and started walking towards the church parsonage.

"Come to Mass tomorrow Mrs. Roark, service starts at ten."

"Aw, but I'm not Catholic," I said, reminding him

"The Lord welcomes all into his house Mrs. Roark, come and rejoice in your community. Give thanks for his blessings of friendship and peace."

He grasped both my hands in his and shook them.

It took about another half hour to bike back to the bosque and pick up the truck along with Cesar and Rae. The deputy was still waiting with them, leaning against the front fender of his car so the dash mounted camera would catch everyone's actions. He was not too pleased that he had to baby sit these two malcreados, it was past time for his meal break, and he would miss out on the evening burrito run at Tio's Tacos. He even followed us home to make sure we would not cause any more disturbances. What had we done but enjoy a day of fishing?

The sun was setting, and dark clouds covered most of the sky. Thunder began to rumble in the distance and would soon fill the valley with a fireworks display to rival the Fourth of July. The darker it got, the more brilliant the lightning strikes. Cloud to cloud, cloud to ground, the strikes surrounded us.

I sat on the flagstone portal watching the show from the wooden bench I had fashioned out of two logs and a piece of two by ten salvaged from the shed. Cesar came through the door, having taken a shower in his camper first. The one advantage of living in the camper was that it had a tiny propane water heater. Not much, but enough for a quick shower. I still had not managed to save enough to get a water heater, so the only hot showers I got were from the black Solar Camper's Shower, which I dutifully hung from the beam under the portal every morning so as to catch the best sun. As the cooler nights approached, I knew this would not last much longer, and thought about having a small electric hot water tank installed, but again, money was the barrier.

Cesar was not too happy of course. He let his displeasure show by not saying anything. He went to the kitchen and fried slices of Spam, folding them into two flour tortillas around roasted green chile and tomato. He came outside and handed me one before sitting on the other end of the bench. I made tea in a quart jar and we both sat silent, eating the Spam burritos, watching the lightning, passing the lukewarm tea jar between us like it was moonshine.

Finally, I said "Sorry."

Cesar sipped his tea, finished eating, wiped his hands on his shirt, stood up and opened the screen door. "Me too. "

Thunder boomed and lightning flashed a hundred yards in front of us, near the cemetery's gate. More lightning continued to pummel the sky in rapid succession, like a strobe light, making everything look animated. A large white stream of mist and fog arose over the graveyard. Eight feet tall and at least five feet around, the thin mist hung a few feet off the ground and moved slowly through the graveyard, grazing the tops of the tombstones. I stared in disbelief. Was I seeing a ghost? I couldn't stop watching as the spectra dissolved into nothingness. I scanned the cemetery, the sky continued to flash and thunder rattled the ground. The gray black silhouettes of crosses and spires amidst the high weeds and overgrown tree branches of the cemetery were shadowed by each lightning strike. Some of the tumble weeds were as tall as a man. I had to look twice to be certain what I was really seeing.

"Did you see that?" I asked aloud of Cesar who was gazing from the other side of the screen door just before he closed it.

"See what Blondie?"

"Nothing. Nothing, just the lightning." I wasn't sure what I had seen. I sat staring into the night another hour. Finally, I too went inside and lay down, drifted in and out of sleep. All night long, with each rumble of thunder, the Ghosts of Las Manchas called me from the graveyard. "*Remember us,*" they whispered over and over in my dreams.

82

Sunday came, the morning passing slowly. The rainstorm the day before had cleaned the air and left the sky the purest blue I had ever seen. I thought about Father Rico's invitation to attend mass, but really I wasn't Catholic. I had never been comfortable with the formality of Catholic mass. My prayers were informal and urgent, not memorized or premeditated, something akin to 'Please God let me be warm tonight'. Still, Father Rico had a sincere concern for the welfare of his parish and I was part of it Catholic or not. He was also one of the few who had offered me and Peanuts shelter when I needed it.

Cesar made himself scarce Sunday. The confrontation with the law following our fishing trip disturbed him. I'm not sure where he went. I walked the wet red sand and gravel road around Las Manchas, stopping at the graveyard. What had I seen last night? The rock work that framed the entrance was crumbling with a dozen or more large rocks scattered near the gate. A few of the headstones had toppled over or begun to sink and lean into the soil. And the weeds were everywhere. What souls rested here? When did the live? When did they die? Who loved them?

I stepped inside the gate, stopping at the first headstone. The weeds had grown in front of the marker obscuring its inscription. I knelt down in the wet sand and pulled the larger ones, touching the engraved letters when they were revealed.

Beloved Mother, Augustina Duran, August 3 1905 – October 20, 1977.

I thought about the inscription. Beloved, someone had loved this woman, had cherished her. Who? Where were they now? Was no one left to clean her grave?

I kept pulling weeds, brushing the soil clean with my hand. Several times thorns or burrs embedded themselves in my skin, prompting a slight curse and hand to mouth to staunch the blood. I stood up, surveyed my handiwork. Something made me think of the local custom of leaving a stone on the grave marker, a way to let others know you had been there. I found a small smooth blood red pebble, no larger than a marble, and balanced it carefully on the top of the headstone.

"Rest in peace Augustina," I said softly.

I moved to the next grave. Tumble weeds taller than I and at least four foot wide completely enclosed the three foot stone carved spire which leaned slightly to the north. If it hadn't rained the night before I never would have been able to pull them out. The nettles stung my face, and brought an angry red rash. If I had gloves or tools this would be easier, even a heavier work shirt would have helped. The last tumble weed was stubborn. Two sturdy tugs barely loosened it. My arms were already scratched, despite my long sleeves, so I reached into the middle with both hands and pulled with my full weight, falling backwards on my butt.

Laughter. Not from me, from behind me. Cesar and Father Rico were leaning on the edge of the northern rock wall, watching me.

"Careful Mrs. Roark, that tumbleweed will get the better of you." Father called from over the fence.

Cesar, using one hand, pommeled over the fence. In two steps he was beside me, helping me up from the dirt. "What's going through your head Blondie? Do you think you can bring back the dead? Does this have something to do with the ghost you saw?"

I brushed the dirt from the seat of my pants. "You did see it."

Father tossed a small bottle of water to Cesar who handed it to me. It was cold and tasted good. Sweat dripped from my nose as I used my sleeve to wipe away the dirt.

"What ghost? What are you talking about?" Father Rico asked.

"Last night, during the lightning storm, a white cloud floated up from the ground then drifted through the graveyard. I saw it so clearly. It drifted right above the graves." I used my hand and arm to trace the path of what I had seen through the air.

"And you think it was a ghost? Mrs. Roark I think the heat has gotten to you. If you could see your face, it's bright red. You should wear a hat." Father shook his head, scolding. "Still, I am grateful for your interest in our cemetery. At one time we had a volunteer group from the church that met to clean the grounds once a month, but, times being what they are, those that have the time are too old to do much of the labor, and those that are young do not seem to have the time."

I scanned the cemetery. It would take a very long time and a lot of work to clean this place up. Both Father and Cesar read my mind.

"Remember what I told you yesterday? Sunday is the Lord's Day. We do not work on Sunday. Leave your labor. Tomorrow, if Cesar is willing, we'll see if we can get the old mower going and at least mow down some of these weeds." Father walked toward the foot gate, half off its hinges and pushed it open, motioning me out of the graveyard.

Rae's truck, as usual driven by his grandma who could barely see over the steering wheel, skidded to a stop just in front of the gate where the old Mercedes broke down last night. Where was it now? I was about to ask when Rae pulled himself out the open window and sat on its frame. You could see the yellow plastic grocery bags piled between them.

"¡Hola neighbors, what's going on? Someone die?"

"No, Blondie here has decided she needs to clean up the graveyard or ghosts will haunt her." Cesar jumped back before I could swat him.

"Oh, so you saw it too." Rae was nonchalant. Apparently seeing ghosts was an everyday occurrence around here.

I turned toward him, speechless.

Father walked over to the truck's open window and spoke to Priscilla in Spanish. He opened the driver's side door and helped Priscilla to the ground.

"Your grandmother is reminding me that all of your ancestors are buried here Rae, your Padrinos and Tios."

We walked together, all five of us, through the gate. Priscilla leaned heavily on Father for support. He used his cane to push aside the larger weeds. We trailed her to the fourth row of graves. Stumbling and unsteady, she stopped at a simple granite stone and pushed away the weeds.

"Mi espouso está aquí, tu tocayo Reynaldo. Muy guapo, muy fuerte." Priscilla looked lovingly at the headstone and struggled to bend forward to pick something up. Father knew what she sought, reached in front of her and picked up a small green pebble, it may have been smoothed broken glass, and handed it to her. She gently placed it on the headstone, smiling sweetly. "Qué lástima que no tenemos flores."

"Mañana señora, mañana, I will come and mow the weeds. Then you can bring flowers." Cesar picked up a pebble too, as did we all, to place on the headstone before returning to the truck.

¤ ¤ ¤

It was barely six when I got up the next day. Daylight hours were growing shorter and shorter. I took my time making tea and oatmeal. Even though I had a little more money these days I had become accustom to the meager morning rations that could be purchased from the dollar store. For less than three dollars I would eat my morning meal for a month. About twice a week I would indulge my love of coffee and brew a pot, but today was a tea day. I wished for a TV, decided to add it to my list for the next bag day at the thrift store, or be on the lookout for a curb side find.

First light, I put on my sweatshirt, gathered my thrift store garden gloves, rake and hoe and walked to the Las Manchas Cemetery. The weeds I pulled yesterday lay scattered between the first two headstones. I imagined a game board's twists and turn. Start just inside the gate, finish at the end of the last row, far corner from where I stood. Start here. I leaned the hoe against the rock wall and began raking. If I raked the loose brown weeds first, the still green ones would be easier to reach. Empty miniature liquor bottles, beer cans and fast food wrappers were hidden under the mat of decaying vegetation, more debris then I noticed yesterday. This was going to take a lot longer than I thought. Still, time was something I had to fill. I picked up a cast off orange baseball cap, shook it heavily, and pulled it down snugly to shade my face from the rising sun.

The Rail Runner commuter train rolled by. The tracks were close enough to count the passengers and see most of their faces. One or two looked over at me as I lifted my hand in a kind of wave. One waved back.

I kept working. Judging by the sun it was probably close to ten. I reasoned I would work until about noon, hope the black solar shower bag I hung every morning from the portal would be heated up enough by then to get at least a lukewarm stream of water, clean myself up then ride to the library. I was thinking about what book to read next when Cesar and Rae showed up, a mower and more tools in the back of Rae's truck. Cesar was driving. I worried for Rae, I knew he had lost his license due to DWI, somehow, he managed to find someone to take the wheel, usually his grandmother, but she was approaching 90, and any day now would probably have to stop acting as chauffeur.

"Morning Blondie, any more ghosts?"

"Will you leave it alone Cesar. I'm trying to help out a little here. What if your family or loved ones were buried here? You'd want this place kept up."

Cesar lifted the mower down from the truck and looked at me sideways, a serious side of him I rarely saw.

"How do you know they're not?"

"Oh, sorry, I didn't know." I took my newly acquired hat off held it in my hands and scanned the rows of headstones, pondering which ones he was related to.

"You are so gullible Blondie." He and Rae both laughed as they took the gas cap off the mower and filled the tank with fuel.

Rae pulled out a weed whacker and walked slowly around the perimeter of the graveyard, along the fence line, cutting down the taller weeds. Cesar started in the opposite direction, about three feet in from the rock wall, doing his best to cut the overgrown brush with the old mower. Twice both Cesar and Rae stopped to refill the gas tanks. It was slow work. Several times broken glass sprayed out of the mower when Cesar ran over a hidden tequila or vodka bottle. After the third time, he came and got my rake, told me to take a break, and walked the length of the side he was trying to cut down, carefully checking for more glass bottles.

"There are cokes in the back of the truck. Nina sent them." Rae called out to me. I hopped into the bed of the Ford and opened the ice chest that two days ago held the beer for our fishing trip. There weren't any real Cokes in it, but around here every soda was a coke. I reached in and pulled out a store brand ginger ale in a Kelly green can, closed the lid of the ice chest and sat down. The sun was almost directly overhead. I didn't plan on working all day, but these two were ready and willing. I'd stick with it as long as they did.

The weed whacker stalled. It was quiet here in the middle of the day. Even though we were surrounded by commerce the little enclave seemed to have natural sound barriers.

From where we were now, even the traffic from the Interstate seemed muffled. I heard a shuffling sound, like someone dragging something on the gravel road, stood up, held my hand to my eyes to shield them from the overhead sun and scanned the area around us. Dub came wheeling himself through the gravel, a little red child's wagon tied behind him. Little Dog pranced along beside it.

"There's Dub." I hopped down from the truck bed and started towards him; Cesar put down the rake and jogged over too.

"Afternoon folks, neighbors. I thought you might like some lunch." Dub pulled the child's wagon beside him and took a small laundry basket from it, setting it on his lap. He reached in and pulled out a narrow bread bag filled with five or six pickle loaf and cheese sandwiches, handed it to Cesar, before grabbing some slightly bruised bananas from the basket which he passed to me.

"I never turn down a meal Dub. This is great." Cesar handed me the bag, then wiped sweat from his face with a blue bandana he pulled from his front pocket.

"You pull them out of there Blondie, you're the only one who's wearing gloves, and your hands should be mostly clean. I got gas all over mine."

"There's some paper towels in here too folks, but I only had a jug a water to drink, it's still in the wagon." Dub pulled back a checked dish towel to reveal the roll of towels and gallon jug of water. I took off my gloves and set the bananas and sandwiches down before picking up the towel and water, dampening half the towel with the cool water from the jug and lightly wiping my hands. I dampened it a second time and handed it to Cesar to do the same.

"This is terrific Dub, how did you know we were over here?" I tore a towel from the roll and used it to grab a sandwich from the bag for Cesar. By now Rae had made his way over and I handed him a sandwich too.

"Oh, all the racket of them mowers and weed cutters, I looked over when I first heard 'em and figured out it was you bunch. What made you decide to clean this place up?" Dub juggled a bag of ginger snaps on his lap. Little Dog jumped into the wagon, not wanting to walk home.

"Blondie here, she's been seeing ghosts." Cesar had devoured the first sandwich and used the towel to reach in the bag for a second one.

"Is that right? Ghosts you say?" Dub smoothed Little Dog's curly fur across the sides of his chest.

"Come on Cesar, you saw it too. I'm not really sure what I saw Dub, I just wanted to do something to help out. I didn't know it was going to turn into a big deal. Priscilla's husband is buried here, she seemed happy we were cleaning the place up."

"Well I'm happy too. I used to come regular to do what you folks are doing, but in this chair I just can't get around like I used to. My wife and daughter are here too." Dub let go of Little Dog and grasped his hands together in front of this abdomen, resting his elbows on the arms of his wheelchair.

"Is it muddy in there? Or real sandy? Do you reckon I can manage to get my chair through all those weeds?" He looked hopeful.

Cesar shook his head no.

"Not today buddy, we're working at it, maybe in a week or so it will be cleaned up enough for you to get in there, but I wouldn't try it today." Cesar finished his second sandwich and reached for a banana.

Dub was crest fallen.

Rae knelt down to the side of Dub, placing his hand on Dub's shoulder. "My Nina is going to come next Sunday with flowers; do you want us to pick you up too? We could all come over after Mass?"

"Yes, I would be grateful for that. That's very kind of you." Dub looked out at the cemetery, his eyes mapping the position of the headstones.

"It's kind of you to bring us lunch man; otherwise we would have had to eat this guy's cooking." Rae rolled his eyes at Cesar.

"Back to work everybody. This isn't a government job you know. We don't get long lunches." Cesar finished the banana and drained more than half the water left in the jug.

We picked up our tools and I started to rake again, working first the perimeters, than making a plan to clean row by row. When the Rail Runner train made its evening run, we were barely starting the second row of headstones. The sun was starting to set and gleaned in my eyes. I looked at the train, thought I recognized the same passenger's face from the morning, waving at me as the commuter train sped by.

83

Thunder came rolling across the valley Tuesday morning. A late season monsoon meant the already late sunrise was further delayed by a low gray blanket of clouds that held a threat of more rain. In the west, fall rain was steady, unlike summer's fast and furious downpours. Fall showers ebbed and flowed over hours not minutes. It was the kind of day that makes you want to sleep in, which I did. When I finally pulled myself up and off the futon sofa that served as my bed, I realized how sore I was. Ten hours of bending, weed pulling and raking had done a number on my fifty some year old back. I reached for the aspirin. This was definitely a coffee day.

I sat on the bench under the narrow portal, sipping coffee and staring at the graveyard. I could see progress, but like a little knowledge, a little progress can be a dangerous thing. When you clean one section, the rest looks twice as bad. The sorry state of the of the adobe mission church and old school buildings became even more obvious. It would take a major investment in time and money to bring them back to their former grandeur. Time I had, money I didn't, that and a twenty five year old back. I sighed and went inside for another cup.

Cesar knocked lightly on the back door, came in and lifted a cup off the narrow shelf above the sink topped by a dish towel that served as a dish drying rack.

"I could smell it out back; I do like a cup of coffee in the morning." He filled it to the top, shook the pot to be sure a second cup would be forthcoming, and leaned against the counter. "You're up late this morning Blondie."

"Yeah, my back's kinda sore. I didn't realize we had put in more than a ten hour day yesterday until I got back last night. What about you? Are you ready for another day of yard work?"

"I'm always ready. Ready, willing and able. But," he paused and gulped the black coffee savoring the taste in his mouth before he swallowed, "I promised my man Reynaldo I'd help him lift an engine and start a rebuild. Besides, you don't want to work in this rain, too muddy. Wait until tomorrow or even later this afternoon, if the ground is wet it will be easier to pull some of the taller weeds."

"You're right, I guess I'll haul a couple of boxes over to Dub's and help him sort through them." I was a little more than half way through the pile of boxes that occupied the larger of the two bedrooms on the trailer side of my home. Dub had been pretty close to a hoarder. He had offered to just have someone haul all the boxes into his new double wide, but it was easy to see this was only postponing the inevitable, not dealing with it. At least once a week, sometimes twice, I'd carry over a couple of boxes and sit with him while he opened and sorted them. Sometimes he'd ask me to put something in storage, I'd look over his shoulder , say "Sure Dub", then have Father or Cesar take it to Good Will. Most of these boxes hadn't been touched in years. Still, both Dub and I enjoyed the social interaction. He'd pull an old white ceramic *Coors* ashtray from a box; tell me the story of how it was acquired, what bar, who was with him and what was playing on the jukebox. But most of the stuff we uncovered leaned more towards trash than treasure.

"Why don't you let me carry a couple of boxes over for you since your back is out? Any particular ones you want me to take?" Cesar drank his coffee fast and was already on his second cup.

"No, just grab a couple. Let me brush my teeth first and then I'll meet you over at Dubs." I rinsed my empty coffee cup and turned it top down onto the dishtowel covered shelf. When you have been homeless and living on the streets, even something as simple as brushing your teeth feels like a luxury. I took a long time brushing each side twice, tasting the mint of the paste in my mouth. Wow, who would think brushing your teeth could give you a rush.

Cesar was walking down the ramp that led to the three foot deck which served as Dub's entrance. "He's inside waiting for you; I set the boxes down on a chair by the kitchen table. I'll be over at Rae's if you want me to bring more."

"Thanks Cesar, you're a real gentleman." I smiled at him as he jogged out to the street.

"Don't say it so loud. It'll spoil my reputation."

A light rain started as I closed the door of Dub's double wide behind me. Something was wrong. The top box, a blue and white banker's box with a separate lid, had the top off which was leaning against one of the table legs. Dub was sitting beside it, head down, his back to me, and didn't lift his head. He held something in his lap. I know he heard me come in.

"Hey Dub, everything okay?" A walked in front of him, pulled a white plastic chair from the table and positioned it so I could face him. He held a small olive green box in his hands, army issue. His hands and shoulders were trembling. Should I check his blood sugar?

Dub sat silent, suddenly spun his wheelchair around so he was flush with the table, slamming the box down on the red and gold plaid vinyl tablecloth, putting his other hand to his forehead to hide his eyes. He was crying. I pulled the chair closer so we were side by side, reached over and put one of my arms over his shoulder and rested the other on top of the hand that covered the box.

"This here," he paused, "this here box," he took a deep heaving breath. "Bad times Missy, bad times."

I sat awhile waiting for him to say more, then got up and found a clean cup on the drain board and a carton of orange juice in the fridge.

"Dub, maybe you should have something. Your sugar could be out of whack." I lifted his hand from the green box and placed the plastic cup of OJ in it. I had to help him hold it and guide it to his mouth, he was shaking so much. Some of it spilled in his lap. I got a dish towel from the rack that hung off the sink cabinet's door, and lay it across his knee, letting him grab it himself to dab at the wet spots on his pants.

The box still sat on the table. I resisted the urge to immediately pick it up.

"Can I see it?"

Dub was silent.

"Please?"

"Suit yourself." He shrugged his shoulders, and continued to dab at the wet spots.

I picked up the box, inspected the outside, it was really just a sturdy cardboard box with an attached lid that was covered in military green canvas. A round brass snap secured the hinged lid. No more than five or six inches square and about an inch and a half high, I shook it lightly side to side for a clue to its contents.

Dub watched me, immeasurable sadness crossed his face.

"Can I open it?"

Dub nodded, grasped the dish towel between his hands, twisting it tightly. Dark, dark circles enclosed his blood shot eyes.

There wasn't much inside: Two sets of military dogs tags; three military metals; a page torn from a three by five memo book, different handwriting filled both sides and a small black and white photo of a tall skinny young man, not more than sixteen, standing in old style military issue white boxer shorts, a cigarette hanging from his lips. I picked up one set of dog tags.

"Yours?" I held up metal tabs. Dub reached over and took them from me, rubbing them between his fingers.

"Yup." He continued to rub them, feeling the impression of the letters and numbers stamped into the metal.

I pulled the second set of dog tags from the box, set the box down, and brought the small steel tags closer to my eyes so I could read them.

"Thems belong to Priscilla and Penelope's brother, Antonio. Him and me was in the army during the war." Dub tried to focus on the second set of tags I now held.

"You were in Bataan." I knew this from Father, who seldom shared information about his parishioners with others but when I moved into Dub's old adobe enclosed trailer Father felt I had a right to know.

"Yes. Yes I was." Dub took the second set of dog tags from me, held them together in his hand, jiggling them together to hear the sound. I wasn't sure how far to press him. I picked up a military medal pinned to a ribbon. It was one I had never seen before, a solid black stripe in the middle of the ribbon, framed narrower stripes of red white and blue.

"That's a POW award." Dub reached and took it from me. "You know what POW means doncha?"

"Yes, it stands for Prisoner of War."

"That was not war Missy." Dub shook his head, rocking softly side to side in his wheel chair. "That was pure Hell on Earth."

I didn't speak, didn't know what to say. I had heard and read about the surrender of US troops to the Japanese in the Philippines, had visited the museum and been present when posthumous medals were awarded at a Veterans' Day ceremony, but nothing was as moving as the seeing the man who sat in front of me now.

Dub wheeled his chair towards me, lifted the box from my hands. He pulled out the picture.

"Can't believe it to see me now, but this was me. I weren't really old enough to be there. I was just a kid, sixteen, near seventeen. My Mom had married a man up 'ta St Cloud. First thing he does is move us, me and my sis and mom over to Duluth. Him and me didn't take to each other much. When the war started up a bunch of fellows from my school all went and joined up. So he tells me if I want to join up he'll sign for me, make like I was older you know, so that's what I did."

"Were you scared?"

"No, not at first. Lots of the fellows were young like me. They sent a bunch of us together to be support for the tanks, taught us how to work on 'em, how to judge what was wrong when something happened. Only thing is, when we got over to the Bataan Peninsula, there's no tools, nor parts of any kind. What equipment we did have was too old to be of much use. It got to be tough going." Dub kept a tight hold on the box, looking deep into it, a photo album of all the pictures no one took.

"We was runnin' low on everything, ammo, medicine, we already had low rations. Then one day our CO calls us all together, tries to explain it to us, makes us put all our guns in the back of a big wagon, knives too. Before we know it, the Japs are there, all around us, yelling and pushing everyone together. We didn't have time to get anything, no mess tins or anything. Some fellas didn't even have their boots on. Japanese didn't care. Right in front of me, this fellow tries explaining to 'em how he needs to get his boots and such, and this Japanese just takes his bayonet and stabs him through the neck. I was a pretty big fella, not too many put up to box me on a Saturday night, and I was a goin' to help him, go after that Japanese Soldier and make him pay, but my CO and a couple of the other fellows grabs hold of my arm and makes believe we're all marchin along, tells me to shut up or I'd be lying in the dirt too. I'd never seen nothing like that before, no sir, never. We'd walk for days and miles, no food, no water. If anybody fell the Japanese soldiers would just do what they done to the fellow that wanted his boots. Guys, young guys, seemed strong like me, they'd just fall down and die or be killed and we just had to leave em lay, no proper burial at all. They'd just run over 'em in the dirt and leave 'em lay."

"There was this fella, Spanish he was, turned out to be Antonio. He was a few years older 'en me. He and some other Spanish fellas, they's all from here, from New Mexico, they ended up in front of us in the line as we walked. There really weren't much to him, he was at least a head shorter 'n me, and we was all getting skinny. We was a walkin' and all a sudden Antonio falls, two guys in front of me they just march right over him. Well I don't know what took me, but when I get to him I just reached down and picked him up, carried him on my back like he was my little sis. That's the way it was after that. If the Japs suspected I was carrying him and come over I'd put my head down low so Antonio's stuck up. We had to keep a close march, if the Japs had seen us they'd did us both up dead as that. I carried him all day until we got a little rest. Then we just march side by side. Stayed together, like we was brothers. Being he was older 'n me and knew a bit of the language he could understand a little of what was going on. The things we saw ain't nobody have a right to do or see, ever. He'd try to tell me when to look away, when to keep my head down so I didn't stick up so high above the rest and draw attention. When he seemed like he was about to go down again I'd just swing him up on my back."

I pulled my chair closer, tried to reach out and hold his hand. But he brushed it off, took out the notebook paper with writing on both sides.

"This here is how I come to live here." He smoothed out the edges of the little paper, looked up at me for the first time. "Do you read Spanish?"

"No, a little, but not much." I squinted at the tiny writing on the first side of the paper.

"When they finally stopped us, put us in a camp if you can call it that, things were even worse than when we were marchin'. Everyday there'd be half a dozen or more in our section just drop dead. They'd catch something, come down with the cholera or something. Oh we had doctors, but they didn't have anything to give us, so wasn't much they could do."

I got up and rinsed out the blue plastic cup at the sink, filled it with water from the five gallon water bottle that set on a stand in the corner. Dub put the medals and dog tags back in the box and handed it to me before taking the water. The small lined paper and his picture still rested on his knee.

"When somebody'd die, first thing we were supposed to do was search the body. Didn't like to do it much, but if anybody had something they weren't supposed to have, a little old pen knife or some cholera medicine or something, well those Japs would make the rest of us pay on account they couldn't take it out on the dead man. So this Spanish fella, he dies and me and Antonio have to check his body. Well, he's got this little notebook tied to inside his leg, and a couple of those ink pens tucked up with it. Antonio takes one look and quick as that grabs that thing and stuffs it in his pants before anybody can see it."

Dub lightly slapped his hands together.

"Is that a page from the book?" I reach over and tap my finger on his knee.

"Yes. Soon as he had a chance Antonio gives that notebook to the Spanish CO. He takes one look at it and panics, rips out all the pages with writing, shred them into tiny pieces. The dead man been keeping a record of everything that was happening to us, kind of like a diary, was even drawing pictures of camp, and a little map. That Spanish Corporal he tells me 'this will get us all killed like you pulled the trigger yourselves. The enemy doesn't want no written record what so ever of the things that happen here, we've got to keep the record in our heads and tell it when the times right or none of us will make it." He tells me and Antonio that we have a responsibility to make sure one of us gets back to tell the story so they don't surrender a man ever again."

Dub was shaking again. I didn't know if it was his blood sugar or the memories. I got more OJ and half-filled the cup.

"No, I don't need that now Missy."

"You don't have to keep telling me the story Dub, it's okay"

"Somebody's got to hear it. I been keeping it in my head all the time now, and like that Spanish Corporal said there's still them that don't want to hear it, want to deny any of it happened, but somebody's got to tell the story."

I got my own cup of water and sat down again. Little Dog is scratching at the door to come in; I got up and opened it.

Cesar is walking over carrying two more boxes. I hold the door for him. He sees the boxes delivered that morning mostly untouched, right where he left them, looks at me with raised eyebrows "I guess you're not ready for more?"

I cleared my throat a little. "Dub was telling me about his time in Bataan, and how he met Priscilla and Penelope's brother Antonio over there."

"I did not know that, Dub. I knew you were in Bataan, but I didn't realize you served with Priscilla's brother." Cesar turns a chair around sitting on it backwards right next to the door.

"Yeah, me and Antonio, we stuck together much as we could. The ones around us called poked fun on account of our looks and size being so different. Well, we was different, but we helped each other, it was the only way."

"Dub just told me about how the CO from New Mexico wanted them to tell their story when the time came." My voice was shaking now too.

"He did, yes, he said we needed to be sure the ones that died were never forgot and that those in charge never surrender any of us again." Dub used his hands to rock his wheelchair back and forth mindlessly.

"Is that what the paper is about? Your story?" I nod towards the paper.

"Do you read Spanish Cesar? I know you can speak it." Dub looked over to where Cesar sat.

"No buddy, I can read it a little, but I'm not that good at it. Why? What do you need translated?"

"Well there's this paper." He handed it to Cesar.

Cesar pretended to focus on the tiny writing on the first side then flipped it over to the other, read it and looked at Dub in admiration. "Is this Antonio's writing?"

"One side of it is, t'other's mine, but I never could get anybody that said they knew how to read the Spanish."

"Have you showed it to Father Rico? He could read it to you." Cesar leaned back in the chair, bracing himself against the wall.

"No, the only ones that even seen it are you all, Antonio's father and me. "

"Didn't Antonio's father read it? To you I mean." I took the cup from Dub's hands and set it on the table.

"No, he just read it silent. That's when he got me set up in that little place there, where you're at now Blondie, 'cept we had a little wood house on it, no bigger than the trailer side. Give me a place to live and a job. More like a dad to me then that man my mom married."

(Why was I Blondie when Cesar was around but Missy when he wasn't? Now was not the time to ask.)

"Is it okay if I take it over to the Parish Hall and show it to Father Rico? I promise to take good care of it and maybe he can tell us what it says." Cesar stood up, gently smoothed the paper and placed it in his wallet.

"Suit yourself. Don't do nobody any good just settin' in a box. I'll be gone soon and no one will ever know anyhow."

"How did you get the paper Dub?"

"That CO I told you about, he tore out all the empty pages of that little notebook and told each fella to write a note to their family on one side. We was ta pass it to another to write on the other side. If one of us was to die, the other was to deliver the note to the family of the dead man when things were over." Dub crossed both arms in front of him, tucking his hands, thumbs up, in his underarms. His head dropped so much his chin touched his chest and he shut his eyes tight, pursing his lips, trying to keep from crying again.

Cesar and I looked at each other. We both knew the answer to the question one of us needed to ask, but neither of us wanted to be the one to ask it. Cesar broke the silence.

"Was it hard to find Antonio's family here in New Mexico?"

Dubs eyes stayed closed. "Findin' New Mexico wasn't a problem. You could catch a train drop you off right there in Albuquerque from just about anywhere in the US. But nobody much could tell me where Las Manchas was, 'course I was sayin' it wrong, kept calling it Dela Manchy. In those days, right after the war, all the soldiers could walk everywhere and people'd just give you things. I'd be walkin' along and someone come up to me and gives me apples, or some cookies or something. Got a kiss from near every pretty girl too, boy I'm tellin you." Dub opened his eyes, almost smiling.

"So when I got off the train wasn't much to get a ride. But no one seemed to know where I needed to get to. Finally this fella, he's driven a milk truck, well a wagon, out here they's still usin' lots of wagons instead of delivery vans, anyway, it was getting dark and he was coming in from his run, he tells me, 'Soldier, come spend the night with me and my wife, in the morning you kin ride my route, I think I know the place you want.' So that's what I did. We'd go and pick up the milk bottles and stop at every little store and coffee shop 'tween here and there. I'd help carry in the fresh bottles and pick up the empties."

"So anyway, we get to where the church is now and the milk wagon man tells me 'I think this is the place you're after.'"

"A priest comes out to pick up the milk for the children at the school. The school wasn't much then, just two rooms, one for the little ones and one for the big. Wasn't Father Rico either, he didn't come along 'til, I don't know, the sixties or seventies sometime I guess. It was Father Jorge. I ask him 'Is this Dela Manchy?' and he says it back to me the right way. 'That's it, that's the one!' I tell him and I get down from the milk wagon with my duff. I asks him 'Do you know the family of Antonio Romero?', and he tells me he does and what's my business, so I get out the paper and says I got to get this note he wrote before he died to his family. Father Jorge looks me up and down and asks did I know Antonio and I tell him I was beside him when he died. Just like that Father Jorge walks me over to the Romero's place. It was right there, opposite to where the cemetery is, big old house, all spread out and low. There were apple trees and grape vines all in between. It's all gone now, burned down same time my place did, but it was a grand place then." Dub wheeled himself to the window and looked out toward the cemetery.

"When we get there, Father Jorge calls out Antonio's dad and he invites us in, brings us some apple juice and the two start conversing in Spanish. After a while Father Jorge tells me to show Antonio's dad the note, so I do. He sits there reading it over and over. Then he folds it in two and hands it back to me. 'Thank you, thank you' is all he can say." I figured my jobs done and I get up to go and turn to Father Jorge and ask him does he know where I can get a bed for the night. Right then Antonio's dad grabs me by the arm and pulls me back, puts his arm around my shoulder and tells me "your place is here, you can stay here" and I been here since.

I got up and stood beside Dub. "Sounds like you found the right place to be, Dub."

"Oh, I did, I did. Found work on that milk truck, and Antonio's dad got me set up right. Meet my wife right here at one of the girls' weddings. We had it good. Finally bought this little bit of land from the Romero's. But I always had it in my head it ought to be Antonio dancing at his sisters' weddings, not me, not me."

Dub wheeled his chair back from the window and over to the table. He picked up the box one last time, rummaged through it then closed the lid and set it aside, staring at the table for a good five minutes.

I started picking things up around his place even though I knew his VA paid home care aid would be coming soon. After a little while Dub spoke at me.

"Hey Blondie, suppose you could make Cesar and me a couple of those cheese and chile dogs you're so good at? You know the ones with lots of onions."

How could I saw no?

84

Thursday, October something, I didn't really pay attention to the date except the day I got Sam's pension check. I have never gotten over how perfectly clear the sky in New Mexico is, even on a cold blustery day like today. The brown and gold leaves of the cottonwood and elm trees were falling in mass from the scrubby trees that surrounded the cemetery. I waited until the sun was warm, about ten o'clock, before I started my assumed job of caretaker for the Las Manchas graveyard. Now, beside the weeds and trash I had tons of fallen leaves to clean up. I raked in piles, hoped Cesar would show up and help me find and fill some trash bags, or borrow Rae's truck and haul it all off. Just before noon Father Rico walked over with a cheese sandwich and jar of red punch for my lunch. It was the same meal he had served me that first night with Peanuts, when we were just off the casino bus from Santa Fe.

Cesar and Rae had done a hasty repair on a small granite bench just inside the cemetery, propping up one side with some cement blocks. Father Rico sat there waiting for me to join him.

"Sit, rest, and enjoy a meal break." He handed me the sandwich wrapped in waxed paper and pulled an apple from his bulging jacket pocket. I thought the apple was for me, but he took a bite, sat back and crossed his arms in front of him. "You're making good progress. The fruits of your labor are rewarding."

"Yes, I had to go through and re-rake the rows we already did because of the leaves, but at least you can start to see it. Maybe I'll have it done before the first snow." I drank half the sweet punch and took a bite of the sandwich. I'm glad he put pickles on it, the cheese was pretty dry.

"Well I have good news Mrs. Roark, good news." He took another bite of the apple.

"You found a buyer for the church property." I finished half the sandwich and started on the other.

He stopped chewing, turned towards me alarmed.

"Now what makes you think St. Ursula's is for sale?"

"Do you remember when I first came here and spent the night in that shed? You sent me to St. Vincent's Hospitality Center." Dub's raven flew down from a telephone wire; I tossed it a crust from the sandwich.

"Yes, I do, you had that big dog with you, Donuts was it?"

"Peanuts, his name's Peanuts." It felt awkward to talk about Peanuts; it made me remember my boys, the life I used to have.

I started to take another bite of the sandwich, lost my appetite. "Anyway, the staff at the center told me they thought you were only taking care of St. Ursula's until it could be sold. They said a family member, I'm guessing that's Beulah, wanted to build condos or something, but the church wouldn't sell the cemetery."

"You know quite a bit then. Beulah was trying to buy up the property. I convinced the church to let us stay open, to keep the church and school all together and that to sell now while the market was low was bad business. I have always had faith that we would pull through. And now we have help. More specifically, you have help." He took another bite from the apple, pulled a piece of apple peel from between his teeth.

"Oh? Besides Cesar and Rae?" I tore off another crumb and threw it to the raven.

"I had a call yesterday from a woman who works in Santa Fe. Seems she has been watching you work when she passes by on the train every day, said you waved at her." Father tossed the apple core to the raven, who picked it up and flew back up to the top of the telephone pole where it kept watch.

"Her employer and coworkers had been looking for a project for the National Day of Service Volunteer Challenge. They picked our little cemetery here." Father sat up right, his hands on his knees, turning in all directions like he was seeing both past and future.

"That is good news. Who is it? Are they going to help do the work or something?" I took another bite of the sandwich, chewing slowly, needing to take a long drink of the red punch so the bread didn't stick in my mouth.

"The woman and some others will be coming by this afternoon to have a look at things. The volunteer work crew will be here Saturday. She wants to bring a photographer with her, do before and after shots. It's a good thing, a company out of Santa Fe. Maybe when they see our need they will bring more help to the rest of St. Ursula's." Father stood up, a look of hope on his face. "Take the afternoon off won't you? We don't want our before shot to look too good."

He pulled six more apples from his jacket pocket, "But you could make a pie for me, so I have something to serve my guests."

"I'll make it, but you'll have to bake it. My oven doesn't work."

"I can do that." He dusted his hands off on his jacket front, headed back down the road towards the church yard.

The solar shower bag was barely warm. But warm enough for me to clean up a little after my morning's work. I pulled on a clean shirt and pants and climbed the three steps to the yellow kitchen on the trailer side of my home. I improvised a little, emptying all the packet of sugar I had collected over the past few months, drizzling syrup on top of that, but did manage a descent pie. Cesar came into the kitchen as I was rolling out the top crust.

"Pie? You're making pie? You've been holding out on me." He looked longingly at the tin as I crimped the edges with a fork.

"It's for Father Rico. He'll have to bake it, this oven doesn't work."

"You need an oven? You mean you'd bake pie if you had an oven?" Cesar was leaning against the counter, picking at the apple peels I had piled on the counter, awaiting the chickens or the compost pile.

"I used to bake things. They were pretty good too, cookies, pie, bread."

"What if I rebuild that old horno in the backyard? Would you use it? Make pie?"

"The horno? I've never used one. I'd have to find out how to use it."

"I know how. My aunties used to have one. My uncle built them. I helped him a couple of times. I'll bet I can find some adobe from that pile by the churchyard and get that sucker stuccoed up in a couple of days. You'd have to wait for the mud to dry and cure, but you'd be in business in a week or so."

"Hey, if you do that I'll make you two pies."

"How about three?"

"Okay, three, apple, apricot and pumpkin."

"Do you know how to make pastelitos? Or empanadas?"

"Yes, actually, Cesar, I do. I do know how to make them." I thought about the flat prune pies, and dark pumpkin and raisin filling of the empanadas. It had been awhile, but I could figure it out.

"But right now I need to get this over to Father Rico. Some people from Santa Fe are coming to check on the cemetery. This groups wants to help us clean it up, I guess they saw us working from the train. "

"You, they saw you working." He popped another apple peel into his mouth. Now how did he know that?

"I'll take it over." He grabbed his well-worn jacket from a hook near the steps that lead down into the adobe addition.

"Oh, but Father will need to bake it, put it in the oven."

"I can take it, just write it down. I was going over anyway."

I wrote time and temperature on a scrap of paper, torn from a brown paper bag, used the rest of the bag to tuck around the pale pie crust. "Be sure he preheats the oven."

"I can do this Blondie. I can handle it." He took the pie from me. "Don't wait up."

"What?" Where would he go? I knew it was none of my business; we weren't anything more than roommates

"Don't hang out waiting for me, I may be awhile." Cesar smiled, balancing the pie with one hand as he went down the steps.

"Are you sure you're going to Father Rico's to bake that pie?"

"Blondie, don't you trust me?" He had a mischievous look on his face.

"No."

I did worry some, but not much. A glance out the window at the vacant lot of weeds that separated my place from the church and cemetery told me all I needed to know. Cesar walked across the lot, pie in hand, straight to the black iron gate of the adobe wall that surrounded the parish living quarters. Father Rico came out to greet him and the two walked back inside.

I had plenty to do. Even though I had been living here almost seven months, there was still a lot that needed attention both in and out of the house. Today, I would try to caulk and seal around windows and doors. Three or four weeks from now would see major cold and snow. Since I had only the wood stove for heat, I needed to be prepared. Still, I was grateful for my place, modest as it was. It sure beat sleeping on the pavement behind a bus stop, tied to a bench or on the side of an arroyo.

Several times I glanced up to see half a dozen cars parked by the church and school. One, a dark blue Crown Victoria, parked directly beside the gate, and three men, each wearing the distinct coat and collar of the clergy, exited the vehicle. This was turning out to be a big deal. I hoped it was to discuss saving the church not selling it.

85

Saturday was clear and cold. Cesar, who always rose early for his daily run, was in my kitchen brewing coffee.

"Up and at 'um Blondie, eggs are on. Coffee's almost done." He was flipping eggs, rinsing out a coffee cup for me. How could anyone be so cheerful at this hour of the morning?

"What's got you going so early Cesar? Someone giving away free beer or something." I sat up on the edge of the folded down futon where I slept in the large adobe addition, where most of my life played out now and days.

"Very funny." He poured two cups of coffee, walking down the steps and over to where I was trying to unkink my back.

"Did you make this coffee all by yourself Cesar? " I mumbled after taking a couple of sips of the pale brown Joe.

"Who else?"

"You auh'ta be ashamed of yourself." I walked up the three steps to the kitchen and poured it back into the pot. "Maybe I'll have tea."

"Is that anyway to treat someone making your breakfast?"

"Sorry, Cesar, sorry. You're right. It's just that I like my coffee a little stronger, that's all. Besides I usually have tea on mornings like this." What I didn't say was 'why are you making me breakfast?'

"Like what? Mornings like what?"

"You know, regular days, when nothing is happening." I plug the kettle in, rinse out my cup and fumble open the top of the old cocoa tin I used to hold dollar store tea bags.

"Not today Blondie, we're working today. That group from Santa Fe is coming to clean up the cemetery. We need to be over there before they are." Cesar is scrapping scrambled eggs onto two tortillas, adding a whole roasted green chile to each and a good dash of pepper and tobasco, before rolling them into cylinders. "Maybe you'll like this better than the coffee."

I take a bite of the thick warm tortilla.

"These are good eggs." I say to him.

And they were good, as was the green chile. I never learned to roast green chile so perfectly that the skin peeled off without shredding the chile, but Cesar had it down. I take another bite, wiping my chin with the paper towel he wrapped around the burrito.

"What's up with the urgent need to do yard work? That's not like you. Has Father Rico absolved you of your sins if you do this?" I chide him, take a sip of tea.

"Church doesn't work that way Blondie." He is already through his own burrito and pouring his third cup of weak coffee. "But in answer to your first question this is a paying gig for me."

"What? When did this happen?" My nose was starting to run as the heat of the chile caught up with me.

"At that meeting the other day. Father Rico convinced the group that's sponsoring this that the job required a head honcho and the church needed a handyman to spruce the place up a little. He convinced the diocese to kick in for a couple months work. That's me. "Cesar rinses his coffee cup, dries his hands on his shirt and leans against the sink.

"Why are you just now telling me?" It felt like a slap in the face. I could have used that money too, and I was the one who started the cemetery cleanup. Cesar had made breakfast to soften me up before telling me. My disappointment was obvious.

"Escaped my mind I guess." Cesar stands in front of me, places his hands on my shoulders.

"Come on Blondie, I can't live on your charity forever. At some point I have to pull it together and move on. January I'll have finished parole and I need to be ready." He tries looking me in the eye, but I bend my neck low to avoid it.

"Blondie?" He puts one hand under my chin, extends the other, and bends his knees to look up at me. "Amigos? Qué no?"

I sigh deeply, reminding myself of Peanuts whom I missed dearly, then finally allow myself to look at Cesar.

"Qué sí, amigos." I take his extended hand, give a fist bump, and rinse my cup in the sink.

"Get dressed. Meet me over there. I promise to go easy on you." No wonder he was cheerful, he had become my boss.

¤ ¤ ¤

There were a lot of people. No, not a lot, there were a whole, whole lot. I hadn't seen this many people in one place since the lines at the soup kitchens and shelters. Thirty or forty employees plus spouses, kids, siblings and whoever else they could convince to give up a Saturday in October were organized by Cesar into task groups. Mowers, rakers, gravestone levelers, even fence menders all wearing gold and purple baseball caps emblazoned with *Amigos del Las Manchas* on the crest, were hard at work restoring the cemetery to its deserved dignified glory as final resting spot of the beloved.

I had to wind my way around the cars parked on the road and church lot. Father Rico was there, as was Dub, just inside the foot gate in an area I had already raked and weeded, speaking with a man and woman, one of whom balanced a large video camera on his shoulder. It reminded me of Bert spilling his coffee at the soup kitchen. I recognized the cameraman as the same one filming that day. Had it only been a year since that happened? It felt like a lifetime.

Right now Dub and Father were being interviewed. Dub spoke of his wife and young daughter, lost during a flu outbreak. He spoke of his regrets in not being able to get his wheelchair through the rows to visit their graves. Father lamented changes to the parish, the need to restore the church, his wish to keep it open as a vital part of Las Manchas and New Mexico history and expressed his deep gratitude to the businesses that sponsored the cleanup.

I stood to one side watching, wondering what to do. Cesar came up behind me, placed a purple and gold cap on my head.

"Do you believe this? It took us all day, all day Blondie, to do what has taken them half an hour so far. This is just amazing." Cesar adjusted his own cap, pulled a pair of new leather work gloves from his back pocket and put them on.

"This is great." I looked over my shoulder at a group of young men who had improvised a block and tackle to right a fallen headstone. There was no way I could have done that.

"What do you want me to do?" I brought out my own gloves and put them on, noticing the holes in a couple of the fingers.

"You? I'm pretty sure they want to interview you, better not get too dirty yet." Two volunteers approached him, asking for advice regarding a section of the fence that had been knocked down.

"Don't go too far." He called over his shoulder as he followed them to the back of the cemetery.

I had to do something. I felt obvious, useless and out of place. I grabbed a rake and started to level a load of gravel someone had dumped on the path, smoothing it into a walkway, my head bent down, trying to blend in. A woman's voice made me look up.

"Hello, I'm Allison Jimenez, aren't you the lady who waved at me when I was on the train?" She was about forty, a little over five feet tall, and wore bright orange red lipstick which matched her nails. I always wondered how anyone could keep their lipstick and nails looking so perfect while doing yard work, but somehow she did.

"Yes, I believe so. I did wave a couple of times at someone on the Rail Runner. Are you the one who made all this happen?" I pulled my cap back so I could see her face better.

"Oh yes, I do some of the PR for the company. We always do something for National Day of Service. We wanted to find a project to really involve everyone this year. Something we would be able to see the results of right away and bring our families too.

I saw you working here, what? Three or four days in a row, and I thought, that's it, that's what we can do." She gushed, using her hands to tell the story too. Enthusiasm was her middle name.

"Three, I worked for three days. I started the fourth day, but that's when Father told me about the volunteers. He told me to hold off, leave some for you all to do." I smiled at her. Maybe I should find some lipstick next time I was at the dollar store. I couldn't help looking at hers.

"Isn't Father Rico the greatest? And Cesar, I was so glad when he told me about Cesar. He is just what we needed to pull this off." She would have been good at charades. She crossed her hands over her heart when speaking of Father Rico, than held them wide, mimicking Cesar's broad strong arms.

"Yes, they're both great." I used my hands to grasp the rake tightly trying to hold in what I really felt: a twinge of jealousy mixed with guilt. Jealous? Cesar and Father Rico were getting all the accolades, but I was the one who started this. Guilt? How could I be jealous of an eighty year old priest and an ex con who saved a boy from abuse? "Well, thanks for all your help. I guess I need to get to work too." I went back to raking.

"Mrs. Roark, come, speak with us." Father Rico was motioning me over to the main gate, where four volunteers on ladders were taking down the cemetery sign to be cleaned and polished. The cameraman was filming them.

Allison Jimenez took the rake from my hand, and guided me by the elbow over to the female reporter who stood beside Father Rico. "This is the lady that got it all started. The one I told you about? I saw her working out here all by herself, trying to get this place in shape, and I mean, WOW, she was ready to do this all on her own."

"Okay, let's get set up, I'll ask a few questions, how long you lived here, how you got involved in this project and what you hope to see happen. Take a minute to freshen up while we get the shot set okay?" The reporter was kind, but to the point. She walked over the to the cameraman and the two discussed the best location for the shot, in the end deciding to stand in front of the first row of gravestones, with St Ursula's bell towers framed in the background.

Allison Jimenez took off the company jacket she was wearing and helped me into it. It was too small, but she tugged it down, pushed the too short sleeves up to my elbows and showed me how to stand so the company logo was fully visible during the interview, then she smoothed my hair down, and adjusted the *Amigos del Las Manchas* cap on top of it.

"You look great." She framed my face with her thumb and forefingers, backed away and gave me the thumbs up.

Just before the interviewer walked over, Father Rico whispered "I wouldn't mention the ghost incident. People might get the wrong idea about you, if you know what I mean."

"But I did see something Father, right there, where everyone is working. That's what made me start this in the first place."

"I believe you that you saw something, but not everyone will understand, so please, Mrs. Roark, if you care about St. Ursula, your neighbors, please don't mention it. If we can get the right attention paid to us, we could get even more help. Telling everyone you saw a ghost will not get us the right attention. Please." He frowned.

The interviewer came up, got my name, introduced me, and BAM first question: "What made you decide to clean up this old neglected cemetery?"

86

It was Monday night, a slow news night, when the segment aired. Allison Jimenez called Father Rico to let him know it would be on. Rae, his girlfriend and her two little girls, Cesar and me all gathered around Rae's grandma's TV. Priscilla had made fresh tortillas, someone brought a crock-pot of green chile stew, and a bowl of red gelatin with marshmallows reflected the overhead light in the middle of the table. I brought what had become my stand-by for potlucks, deviled eggs. We loaded up our plates, sat on old wooden straight back kitchen chairs in front of the big screen TV and waited for our five minutes of fame. Father Rico, Anselmo and Penelope would gather at Dubs, where leftover meatloaf and mashed potatoes with red chile gravy was on the menu. With few high school sports to report, and no significant weather, the *Amigos del Las Manchas* segment would fill the gap of time between a brief weather report and even briefer sports report.

The story opened with a sweep of the area in and around the church. The cameraman had been alerted to the fallen *Welcome to Las Manchas Neighborhood* sign, half covered by weeds, and made it his close up, before cutting away to Allison Jimenez, Cesar and the volunteers hard at work restoring the graveyard. Father Rico was next, making his plea for preservation of the church and school and expressing his gratitude to those who helped, then Dub with a pullback shot of him trying to make his way to his wife and daughter's grave and another one of Priscilla loving placing plastic flowers on her husband's grave. My interview was last.

"*What made you decide to clean up this old neglected cemetery?*"

On camera, I turned and looked in back of me at the rows of headstones, taking off my cap, holding it in my hands, eyes down, then turned and faced the reporter.

"*I only came to live in Las Manchas a few months ago. I lost my own family, my two sons and my husband last year. They're buried in Santa Fe. I think about them when I'm working here. My hope is someone is doing for them what I am doing here. I think it's important to honor those who have passed, to have respect for and remember the life they lived. I can't think of a better way to do that then to keep their final resting place in a clean and honorable condition. It helps me to know they are at peace, and are remembered.*"

There was a close up of my face, a stray tear, trickled down my check, which I pushed aside with my pinkie before replacing my cap. Then the scene cut back to the reporter.

"Amigos del Las Manchas and St Ursula's parish will host an event November 2nd, All Soul's Day, here in the church and cemetery, to honor those who are buried here and mark the restoration of this historic location. All are Welcome. Channel Eight news reporting from Las Manchas Neighborhood."

All present turned and looked at me. Priscilla struggled to get up from her chair using her cane, walked over and hugged me. "Pobriceta, sé lo que es perder a su esposo e hijo."

Rae brought a chair over for his grandmother to sit on. She pulled it close beside me and held my hand.

"You never told us Blondie. You should have said something."

"It's okay. They died last year, before I came to Albuquerque. I used to visit their graves almost every day. I lost my job, things got..." I paused, fumbling for the right words, "things got difficult. I couldn't live there anymore." I sighed, put the folded tortilla I had been holding down on my plate. "I do think about them, when I'm out there cleaning the graveyard. I mean, I can't visit my sons, but I can visit someone's son's grave, here in Las Manchas. Maybe someone will remember my family too, where they are buried. At least I can hope for that."

¤ ¤ ¤

All Souls Day. Some call it the Day of the Dead. Its traditions and customs blended between ancient cultures and modern times. Like the true meaning of Christmas, the meaning of All Souls Day can be hard to fathom among the paper mache skeleton and sugared skulls decorated with bright pink and green frosting. In Las Manchas and at St. Ursula's it meant one thing: a day to remember and pray for the souls of those who have died that they may find peace in heaven.

Friday, November 2nd, All Souls Day, Father Rico held a special mass at St. Ursula, followed by a candlelight procession to the cemetery I didn't go to the mass. But I was waiting at the cemetery with Rae and boxes of candles in jelly jars, paid for by Amigos del Las Manchas. We and a handful of volunteers had spent the last two hours attaching garlands of flowers to the fence around the cemetery, and now would lay at least one artificial flower on each grave along with a candle, to mark the space between two graves. It was quite a sight, impossible to believe the transformation from a month ago when I witnessed the spirit floating through the rows. There was no ghost tonight, but a full moon just above the Sandia's cast shadows beside the gravestones and spires.

After the procession and rosary Father Rico commenced with blessing of the graves. The whole thing was attended by about three hundred people, some from the volunteer cleanup crew, but others just on-lookers and community members, curious to see the place and the people featured on the news a few days earlier. Most returned to the old school gymnasium, where a Frito Pie fundraiser and bake sale had been hastily pulled together by a local group to raise funds for the church's restoration. Young Ballet Folklorico dancers in brightly colored skirts and white peasant blouses festooned with yards and yards of lace twirled and stomped to pre-recorded guitars and the laughter of children once again filled the old gym. Speeches were made. The Archbishop himself made an appearance to thank the community for all they had done. A grand time was had by all.

I sat, quietly and alone, sideways on an old school cafeteria bench that flipped down from a low table. Father Rico bought me a Frito Pie.

"With my compliments Mrs. Roark, and a hardy thank you for your TV interview, what you said, and didn't say made a difference." He winked at me.

A man I had never seen before came over and sat beside me.

"Are you Aileen Roark, the woman who started the cemetery cleanup?"

I quickly swallowed, set down my plastic spoon. "Yes, that's me. I started it but everyone else finished, there was no way I could have done it alone."

"I'm Felix Archuleta. I write for the *New Mexico Ledger*. Have you ever read our paper?" He reached into his jacket pocket and pulled out what I thought was a cell phone, but turned out to be a small digital recorded.

"Yes of course." What I didn't tell him was that I not only read it, but used it as both blanket and mattress during my homeless days.

The *Ledger* was one of those free newspapers that had great investigative reporting on local stories and issues. Contrast that with the back pages made up almost exclusively of ads for porn shops, medical marijuana and bail bondsmen with the occasional lawyer advertisement sandwiched in between. Talk about an identity crisis.

"I'm doing a story on Las Manchas and St. Ursula's. I'd like to interview you, ask you some questions about how you came here. Do you mind if I record this?" He turned the digital recorder over, pushed a small button on the side and placed it vertically between us.

"No, it's okay. I don't mind. But I'm not the one you need to talk to. The people you should talk to are the ones who have lived here a while. They can tell you more than I can." I took another bite of the Frito Pie.

"I've already spoken with Mr. Duboski, and Rae Romero and his Grandmother. I've got an appointment set up to speak with Father Rico on Monday. You're the one I wanted to talk to. "He took out a small notebook and pencil. Gee, did reporters still take notes? I thought they just recorded everything.

"How did you come to live here in Las Manchas?"

Something about him made me open up. I don't know why. I guess that's the mark of a good reporter, they can put the person at ease and get them to talk about things they wouldn't otherwise. I found myself unloading on him, about the car accident, Sean's death, Sam's suicide, Stevie's coma, losing my job, selling my car to pay for Stevie's funeral and living on the streets. Next thing I know I'm telling him about the money I got in settlement and buying the adobe enclosed trailer at Las Manchas. I started to tell him about the ghost, but right then, as if by divine intervention, Father Rico walks up and sits down beside us.

"Mr. Archuleta, have you found out all you need to know?" Father faced outward, watching the groups of people gathering their belongings and heading for the door.

"Pretty much Father Rico, thanks." Felix Archuleta flipped off the recorded and put away his notebook. "Are we still on for Monday?"

"Absolutely young man, I am looking forward to it." Father slapped his hands on his knees.

All three of us got up. Father Rico spoke with a group of women, mothers of the dancers and youth group and they started to clean up the food.

"Can I help at all?" I offered.

"No, I think we have it all under control here. You're off duty Mrs. Roark." Father Rico waved me off with a flick of his hand.

It was past nine o'clock when I got home. I was physically tired but not sleepy. I grabbed a blanket and sat on the porch with the blanket wrapped around me for an hour, watching the candles as they gently flickered in the rows of the cemetery. I kept watch until they had all gone out.

Cesar and Rae walked slowly, single file, across the field, where a well-worn path marked the way. Each was carrying one of Rae's girlfriend's sleepy girls. They were followed by the girls' mother and one of her cousins, carrying more garland and flowers left from today's event.

Cesar called out to me. "You done good Blondie! You done good." He shifted the small child to his other shoulder.

"We, Cesar, we done good." I corrected him.

"None of this would have happened without that ghost or bogeyman or whatever it is you saw."

The small child on his shoulder picked up her head, grasped Cesar's face in both her hands. "A bogeyman, like a monster? Is there a monster in Las Manchas Uncle Cesar?"

"No hija, no monster, just grown-ups making things up."

"Are you sure?" Her small voice was serious and concerned.

"Yes hija, there are no bogeyman here, guaranteed." He reassured the sleepy child.

"And if they do show up, Uncle Cesar will pound them into the ground." Rae laughed behind him.

"Rae, cut that out. Stop scaring them." His girlfriend was not amused.

87

Monday morning, November 5th. The day my money would come in. I wanted to budget enough for a proper Thanksgiving meal. Being frugal now meant I could splurge later. Making that $525.00 stretch the entire month was still difficult, even without paying rent. But I was determined to make it work. I made a list and would go out later, by bike, to pick up what I needed. Cesar, as usual, was already up, out on his run when I went out back to feed the two hens Anselmo gave me, they were finally starting to lay eggs. Add another bag of chicken feed to that list.

A wood fire was burning in the horno oven, awaiting my first baking adventure in a mud oven. Cesar had explained the process to me, firing of the oven, raking out the coals, letting the thick adobe walls 'soak' to even out the heat, and a quick wipe down with a wet towel nailed to a broomstick. I rolled a log seat towards the oven's half oval door and sat with my tea, letting myself soak in the heat too. The Interstate traffic, only an infield hit away, rushed above me. From this perch I could discern the make and model of most cars, and read the side of the eighteen wheelers as they sped by. When the traffic lulled I heard a rustling sound coming from just over the fence that separated my and Dub's backyards from the Interstate right of way. I figured it was Little Dog, wondered how he got out through the fence, and strolled in that direction to retrieve him.

A man with a heavy backpack and thin jacket sat on the ground, leaning against Dub's side of the fence. He had a small pack of cheese and crackers, the kind they used to give out at the shelter, and was re-rolling the plastic around them with a rubber-band, holding the two he had retrieved for his breakfast in the palm of his hand.

"Good Morning." I called to him, imagined he had wondered down from the Interstate for the night.

"Morning." He popped one of the crackers in to his mouth, stood up, lifting his pack on one shoulder. "Just passing through." He started to walk parallel to the fence line.

"It's okay. I'm not worried about it." Father Rico's rescue of me came to mind. Now was my chance to pass it on. "Can I get you something to eat?"

He stopped, surprised, used his fingers to brush cracker crumbs from his beard.

"That would be really nice. I would appreciate that." It had been awhile since he had slept indoors, the dust on his face and clothes told me most of it, the fact that he hadn't bathed in a while told me the rest.

"Hop over the fence. I've got the fire going in the horno, you can sit there and warm up while I fix you something."

He tossed his pack over the fence, grabbed the edge with both hands and boosted himself over.

"Over here, you can rest over here." I motioned to the log I had just been sitting on. I went into the house and made him two fried egg sandwiches, and poured a big cup of tea into a paper cup , a handful of dollar store oatmeal cookies and a banana in one hand, I went back outside to where the traveler now rested, using a stick to draw in the sand .

"Here you go." I handed him the sandwiches, rolled a second log nearby and flipped it up to act as a table, placing the tea and a banana on top. When he reached for the tea I noticed the letters and numbers crudely tattooed across the fingers of both hands. Instinctively I studied the back of his neck where identical markings displayed his gang affiliation. No matter, if he was cold and hungry, maybe I could help. "Can I get you anything else?"

"I don't mean to be picky or anything, but do you think I could get some salt?"

I went back inside to retrieve a packet of salt. When I returned Cesar was jogging in through the side gate.

"Who the hell are you?" He stopped abruptly in front of the transient, his fists clenched, ready for a fight.

"Just passing through bro." The guy took a sip of the tea, set in down on the log table and picked up one of the egg sandwiches.

"Do you know this guy Blondie?" Cesar spoke to me without taking his eyes off the transient.

"Hey Cesar, no, I don't know him. I was just fixing him something to eat. He's been on the road as you can see."

"I can see just fine where he's been, and he's going to get on his way." Cesar was looking at the symbols inked under the skin across the guys knuckles and back of his hands, recognized them as those of a prison gang.

"Calm yourself bro, I was just eating my sandwich. I don't want any trouble with you. I'm already gone."

"You can say that again." Cesar picked up the rest of the food, stuffed it in the guy's pack and pushed it at him, glaring. "Get a move on."

The man picked up the pack and headed through the gate. Cesar followed him into the driveway and stood watch until he was out of sight.

"That was rude Cesar. All that guy wanted was a something to eat. I invited him." I was loud, argumentative.

"What are you thinking? That he's a stray dog? You give him food and take him to the shelter?" Cesar was loud back at me, yelling, getting in my face. "You think he's this sweet momma's boy lost his way? That guy's a player, a gangster. He's probably got a record."

"He was homeless, just like I've been. I was being kind." We were yelling at each other.

"You can't be like that to every gangster tramp with a rap sheet that falls off the highway. Your kindness is going to get you killed."

"My kindness is what's keeping you out of jail. My kindness is feeding you, giving you a place to live. And I wouldn't be so smug about rap sheets Mr. Chavez."

Cesar was boiling mad, the anger welled up in him. His fist were clenched, mouth pursed, ready to explode. I must say I was a little afraid I'd pushed him too far. He took a deep breath, picked up the log I had been using as a table, and with one hand pummeled it over the back fence and halfway up the hill towards the Interstate.

"Keep it. Frickin' keep it, all of it. I don't need this." Then pole vaulted himself, with one hand, over the block wall that separated my yard from Rae's.

I had gone too far. I chased away the best friend I'd ever had.

88

The day Cesar left I wasn't sure what to do. Should I leave the door unlocked? Would he come back in a few hours after an all-nighter? About eleven o'clock I looked out the window and decided he of all people knew how to cope on the streets, locked the door and went to bed. The next day there was still no sign of him, nor the next. I gathered up the few things he had left out in the camper. It didn't seem like much, tooth brush, razor, soap, towel, two shirts with the arms cut out, one pair of socks, a cast off paperback book, large plastic mug. I put it all into my JC Penny's cloth shopping bag. It didn't seem enough. I added the camouflage hoodie, the kind hunters wear, size extra large. I had found it at Las Tienda de St Martin's last bag sale. I had wanted to save it for a special occasional. I didn't realize it would be his going away party. I remembered my own hunger pangs living on the street and added two cans of potted meat and a sleeve of crackers, one of the little packs of applesauce from the dollar store, and a plastic spoon, from Wendy's of course. I remembered how he got headaches from the cold, and dumped out half the aspirin to keep for myself, leaving the rest for Cesar, closed the bottle tight and put it in the bag too. Then I hung the bag on the nail that stuck from the post of the front door and set out by bike to make the rounds. If he came by to gather his things the bag would be waiting.

When I got back the bag was gone. "I hope the hoodie fits," I said aloud, then pulled the bike and trailer around back to stack the wood pallets I would burn for heat tonight. "I'll need to get some of these done right away, there's a cold front moving in." I said aloud.

And so it went for three more days. Whether I was pulling nails, building a fire or just sitting in a chair I'd say things aloud even though I knew no one was there.

"Time for a shower, hope the water's not too cold today."

"Tomorrow I'll need to pick up a few things from the store."

"It's gonna be a cold one tonight, better load up the wood stove."

On the fourth day I got up, put some coffee on, fed the chickens, checked for eggs and turned on the radio so I could listen to NPR in the morning. There were days when the voices on the radio were the only ones I heard and I preferred the spoken word. I glanced out the front door and saw the Penny's bag hanging, empty, from the post.

I poured a steaming cup of *Choke Full of Nuts* into my World's Best Grandma mug. A gift I gave myself from the invisible grandchildren I would never have, blew roughly across it and took a sip.

"Ummmm, good coffee, good coffee." I said.

I took three steps blowing roughly across the hot coffee, took another sip, sank to the floor and started to cry.

I sat there for probably an hour, maybe two. Misery loves company and I didn't have any. I got up, reheated the coffee and made some toast. It was getting cold and I really did need to find some more wood pallets to burn. Most of my last check had been set aside for Thanksgiving. I had three more weeks in the month before my money would come in, I hoped to buy a pick-up load of scrap wood then if Rae would do the haggling for me. So I put on two sweatshirts, added "winter coat and gloves" to my list of things to look for next bag day at the thrift store and took the bike and trailer out along the main road. There was a tree nursery there that sometimes had pallets stacked by the side of the road. If I asked nicely and smiled and said I needed them to build a compost bin, maybe they would let me have them. If I told them the truth, that I needed them to burn to stay warm, the answer would have been 'No, sorry.'

There wasn't much traffic today, I was glad for that. But there were no pallets either. I stopped to ask about them, and the yard worker told me to try the hardware store past the third major intersection, it was longer than I wanted to ride, but it would be a cold night in November without wood to burn so I started up the road.

There is a small strip mall on one corner of that intersection that has an odd mix of businesses. A large chain coffee shop sits right on the corner. Beside it a high end woman's clothing and accessories store and beside that was a thrift store to benefit the animal shelter. I rarely shopped there. The prices were comparable to a consignment shop, too much for my modest budget. On the far end closest to town is the animal shelter or adoption center as they call it. They don't actually accept animals here. But they do keep a night drop box since it's the only facility on this side of town. This is where they bring the dogs and cats that pass muster. They are cleaned up, socialized, shots up to date and ready to be welcomed into the loving arms of a new owner. (Do they have a place like that for me?) In the parking lot a painted sandwich board sign was stationed near the entrance: *Today Only Adult Dogs Half Price.*

I rode to the window. Pictures of dogs, cats, puppies and kittens were taped to the door. A smiling face waved at me from inside. She came around the counter, opened the door and said, "Come in, have a look." Her name tag read Jan.

A large commercial sign hung on the wall. Tiny paw prints and cute cartoon faces of kitten and puppies framed a price list. 'Dog Adoption fee $70.00'. Who was I kidding, even at half price it would use up all but 8 dollars I had left. Besides, no dog could take the place of Peanuts, or pull me up from the deep hole of loneliness I found myself in.

I smiled sheepishly "I don't know, I'm not sure I can feed a dog right now."

Jan was a real salesperson. "We give you the first month's food. We really want to get our dogs adopted. Some of these fellows have been here a long time. Come in. At least pet a few, maybe take them for a walk, okay?"

I leaned my bike up against the glass and went in.

The dogs sensed someone new, they could smell me. Before I even entered the kennel area a cacophony of barks and growls rose from the corridor. A ring-tone of dogs barking *How much is that doggy in the window* chimed from Jan's pocket. "Pardon me; I need to take this one." She excused herself to the comparative quiet of the lobby.

I walked slowly up one side of the kennels and down the other. In most kennels there were three dogs, all about the same size. The majority were blue heeler mixes, pit bull mixes or some kind of lab. You could tell the ones who had been here a while, they didn't bark. In fact they barely raised their head as I walked by. I stopped to talk to a few of them.

"Hi sweetie. Are you a good boy?" I scratched their ears through the kennel gate.

About mid-way down the second row was a cage with two dogs. One was an obviously pregnant basset husky mix. I wonder how she got here. But the other was a small collie, or large Sheltie; not really sure which.

She was small in stature but not in girth, whatever circumstance had caused her to become homeless did not affect her appetite.

"Hi Sugar, what's your name?" She came up to the edge of the kennel and leaned her head against the open area in the gate.

"That's Flacita, she's a sweet dog. Do you want to take her out for a walk?"

A man with girth to match Flacita's stood behind me. Where did he come from? His name tag said ED. Dressed in the blue work apron worn by all the shelter volunteers, he reached behind himself for a leash, maneuvered the gate open and attached it to Flacita's collar.

"Flacita?" Somebody sure had a sense of humor; Flacita would translate Little Skinny Girl.

"There's a pet walk out that door. Take your time." Ed smiled, lips closed, encouraging, hanging his fingers on the gate after pushing it closed.

I walked Flacita down the aisle, past dozens of barking dogs; she went willingly but not enthusiastically. I'd say more of a resigned acceptance.

We went outside and I spoke softly to her.

"How ya' don' girl? Looks like they're feeding you good?"

We walked back and forth, a figure eight, u turn and every other way I could think of. Finally I sat down on the concrete bench anchored there. Flacita sat directly in front of me facing me. I petted her, scratched under her belly. She waged her tail softly a few times than stopped.

"You seem like a good girl." I cooed softly to her.

She turned her face up toward me, using her sad brown eyes to tell me her story, *I am a good girl. I always did want I was told. I was kind to people and never asked much, so how did I end up here abandoned and alone.*

I knew that look. It was what I saw every time I looked in a mirror.

Ed appeared behind me. Was I going deaf or was he just really quiet? For such a big man he had a light step.

"Well what do you think? Do you have any questions?"

"How old is she?"

"About eight."

"Has she been spayed?"

"All of our animals are spayed or neutered before they're released for adoption."

"Do you know how she got here, got to the shelter?"

"She was left in the night drop box. Such a great dog. I can't imagine why someone would do that, take off and abandon a wonderful dog like this." Ed frowned, shaking his head in mild disdain.

I was kneeling in front of Flacita, fluffing up the fur under her collar. I gently looked into her eyes and she back at me hopefully, softly wagging her tail. I stood up, turned sadly towards Ed trying to manage a weak smile.

"I'll take her," I said.

At the front desk I carefully emptied my pocket and counted out the thirty-five dollar adoption fee, I had eight dollars left. Jan printed out the pet adoption form, with the vaccination tag attached, folded them into an envelope and placed them into a Petco-cloth bag that also held a three pound bag of food, a small squeaky squirrel toy, coupons good for two more bags of free food , and discounts on other pet supplies.

"You have two weeks to return her and exchange her for another pet if she doesn't work out. After that you have thirty days to apply for a dog license from the county. You'll need to provide copies of the vaccination certificate. You can apply here, now, but the license is not transferable so you may want to wait until you decide if she's a good fit or not."

I nodded slowly, apprehensive. How was I going to get this dog home? How would I feed her when I couldn't feed myself? Was I being selfish?

Ed stood beside me. He was so amazingly quiet. He had brushed Flacita's coat making it fluffy and soft like a pillow and tied a thin pink bow around a tuft of hair behind her ear.

"Here's your new best friend. All dressed up and ready to go home." Ed grinned and handed me the thin blue braided vinyl lead.

"Can I help get her into your car? "He asked.

"I'm on my bike today, but I don't have far to go" I lied; it was going to be a struggle to get her home.

"We can hold her here for you if you want to go home and get your car? Or I can drop her off." He was genuine.

I was worried they wouldn't let me keep her if they saw where I lived.

"That's really very kind of you, but I can walk her if I need to. Really, we can manage." I smiled and lied through my teeth. "You've been so great to help me with her." That wasn't a lie.

"Stop by and see us when you're in the area. We always like to hear from our dogs' new family, see how they're doing, especially a pretty girl like this one." Ed rubbed Flacita's rear, while she leaned into his hand, her eyes sparkling and dancing like his. These two had obviously formed a bond. What a good guy.

"Thanks, we will." I took the leash from his hand and led Flacita through the door.

She paused for a minute and turned to look at Ed through the glass door. He waved at her like she was a little kid.

When we reached my bike and trailer leaning against the wall I thought I might try to load her into the two wheeled bike trailer, but didn't want to create a scene in front of the shelter. I grabbed the handle bar in the middle pulling it along on one side of me while leading Flacita with the other.

It took a while to adjust to her pace, a little tricky to balance the bike and trailer and the dog, while avoiding the obstacles beside the road.

About a quarter mile down the road an Albuquerque Open Space trail crossed the road. There was a very small dirt pull out there and a bench. Flacita was starting to drag. If I was going to get her into the trailer this was the place.

I leaned the bike up against the bench's back side. Flacita immediately sat down. Sit is the wrong word, it was more flop. She was not used to exercise.

A couple, about my age, walked along the trail. They had two golden retrievers on leash and stopped to admire Flacita

"What I pretty dog, is she a sheltie or a small collie" The woman, thin, impeccably dressed and made up even in her casual wear, held the leash of one of the retrievers who now sniffed Flacita's tail end.

"Yes." I laughed in response, insecure, uncertain and embarrassed by my own sad appearance. Once I had a future that looked like hers.

She laughed too tugging on the leash that looped through her hand. A small whirl wind picked up the leaves and small branches and scattered them on the ground in front of us.

"Well, enjoy your walk; we need to get going before the wind picks up again." The couple turned and walked away.

"You too." I studied the best way to lift the chubby dog into the trailer. There was no easy answer. I pulled the trailer around beside her and bent forward from the waist, lifting her rear end first into the back of the trailer. She used her front legs to pull herself out. This went on twice more before I tied the end of the leash to the opposite side of the bike trailer, lifted her from the middle, angled her legs into the trailer and told her sternly: "SIT!"

A young man, about the age of my older son, ran by, a few feet from where we struggled. Flacita barked at him, wanted to chase him. It surprised both of us. He turned his head slightly, the sun glinted off the mirrored lens of his glasses, and he seemed amused with my predicament.

"Good Luck with that." He kept running.

I reached into the cloth Petco bag, tore a small hole in the bag of dog food and placed a handful in the bottom of the trailer.

Flacita laid down, picking up the kibble one at a time. Now was my chance. At first, I just walked the bike, slowly, pulling the trailer with the prone dog in it, she was panting worse that when we were walking. A couple of times she struggled to get up, causing the trailer to pitch to one side, I stopped and placed another handful of kibble in the bottom of the trailer, made sure the leash was secure and kept going.

After ten minutes of slow progress, I cautiously mounted the bike and began to peddle carefully; hanging the cloth Petco bag from the handle bars so I could reach more handfuls of kibble as needed. The trailer swayed from side to side, as the nervous little collie wavered in the back. But we were moving.

I could tell people were staring. I would have stared too. After a while, Flacita got used to the ride. If a car or truck came upon us with a dog in the back she would see it and begin to bark. The other animal, in turn, barked back. It would have been funny except I was the one being laughed at.

The traffic stayed light, a small blessing. When I got to Bernalillo I turned down the short side street that headed east across the tracks into Las Manchas. I worried about crossing the tracks. If the wheels got stuck and Flacita was tied in the cart, it would be a struggle to get across quickly. I dismounted the bike, untied her, lifted her out of the trailer and began to cross the first of four sets of tracks.

Rae and his grandma pulled up beside me in the old pickup. Priscilla was driving, propped up on pillows, barely able to see above the wheel.

"Hey Aileen, what are you doing with that dog? Going to start your own circus?" Rae yelled out the window.

"Qué perro bonito." Priscilla's little poodle nervously jumped around the dashboard. "Mira Kiko un Lassie, que cute." She held her nervous dog up to the window. Flacita barked at her.

"My new best friend if I can get her home." I smiled broadly. We were still in the middle of the railroad tracks.

Rae jumped down from his side of the truck. "Hop in. I'll load the bike in the back."

"Hey thanks."

I lead Flacita back around to the passenger side, picked her up, she was still barking, and pushed her into the cab. Priscilla's scruffy poodle immediately began licking Flacita's mouth.

Rae lowered the back and lifted the front wheel of the bike onto the extended tailgate.

"Need help." I stepped up with one foot onto the floorboard of the pickup.

"Nah I got it. Holy mother of," he cursed.

The tracks begin to vibrate. In unison, we looked south toward a slight curve in the track that revealed the Roadrunner train bearing down on us. Like many such crossings, this little used lane had neither a gate nor warning lights, only the old style crossed lines on a round sign.

"Shit!" Rae panicked. He jumped up onto the bed of the truck, holding the bike front with one hand while pounding on the glass of the cab with the other. "Floor it Nina!" he yelled at Priscilla.

Priscilla, her eyes popping wide from behind thick lenses like Mr. Magoo, pushed as hard on the gas pedal as her four foot nine frame would allow. We didn't move.

"Come on Nina, we gotta move now, put it in gear."

"!Ay Ay, Raenaldo, The truck no va!" Priscilla shook her hands in the air.

I jumped all the way into the cab and pushed my way over to the driver's side squashing Priscilla against the door. The passenger side door was still open and I could see the engine of the train and hear the blasts of the horn as they tried to warn us off the track. I looked at the dash and saw the thin red line hover in the middle of the N. Priscilla had not moved the lever over far enough when she took it out of park. Flacita barked in my ear while Priscilla's poodle jumped up onto the dashboard in front of the steering wheel .The engine continued to race while Priscilla slide down low as she could pushing the gas pedal all the way to the floor. Reaching over to the gear shift on the column I pulled the lever forward and moved it into drive.

We took off, gravel flying, poodle flying , side door slamming, Rae hanging on to one side of the truck bed, hovering almost horizontally as we propelled forward, my bike and trailer dragging behind us as Rae used his other hand to hold onto its handle bars. We cleared the tracks.

"Brakes, Nina, Brakes!" Rae yelled as we continued to race down the road.

Quickly, I used one hand to steer and my other to move Priscilla's leg from the gas pedal and my foot onto the brakes, a little too hard. We skidded sideways this time. By now Rae had let go of the bike and was just holding on. Both dogs had been propelled to one side of the truck cab, the door of which had slammed closed. Like most such events, everything happened in slow motion.

If we had had air bags I'm sure they would have gone off, but Rae, tired of spending hundreds of dollars to replace the air bags every time his grandma bumped into something, had installed a cutoff switch which was almost always left in the off position.

By the time we came to rest we were facing the opposite direction. My bike and trailer lay in front of us, the trailer turned upside down, frame bent, the bike on its side. At least it seemed to be in one piece.

I hugged Priscilla, looked over at the dogs who were licking each other, realized my heart was beating about a million miles an hour. I opened the driver's side door and maneuvered myself over Priscilla, and out the door, quickly hitting the ground and hanging my upper arms on the side bed of the truck, looking for Rae.

"Rae! Are you all right? Are you hurt?"

He lay on his back in the bed of the truck, looking up at the sky, one hand on his stomach and one in the air, a small stream of blood trickled from his forearm, and he began to laugh.

Priscilla got out of the truck too, peered over the side, her eyes and nose barely rising over the edge, and started giggling.

"That was a close one Nina." Rae continued to laugh

"Sí, sí, muy." Priscilla clapped her hands rhythmically "Choo-Choo-Choo,"she said, imitating the train through her mischievous laugh.

Rae sat up and joined her. "Choo-Choo Choo."

Apparently this had happened before.

Rae walked around the front which now faced backwards, disconnected my bike from the trailer and lifted them both into the bed of the truck.

"I'm pretty sure I can fix the trailer. I have a bar I can replace the bent one with. If I just bend it back it's likely to break again, but you'll have to leave it with me for a few days."

"Are you sure you're all right? Is your grandma all right?"

"Oh yeah. This just keeps things interesting. I can't tell you how many times one of us, Grandma and me, Father Rico, Dub-0 has almost been hit by that train. We used to call it in but just got the run around. They don't think enough people use this crossing to put up a regular gate with lights and all. Of course knowing Nina she would just drive around it." Rae was still smiling.

"Do you want me to write a letter or something? I could ask Billy Dean, my lawyer, to look into it?" I put my hand on his forearm where a small gash proved to be the source of the red streak.

"No don't bother. It would just annoy the heck out of my Aunt Beulah if we got a crossing put in. She still wants to take over the land, develop it. Has this idea for some shopping center or condo office business park or something. She's even tried to have it condemned. Especially Dub's place, that's why she hates you so much, your buying Dub's place means there's one piece of land she can't control." Rae took the bandana from around his forehead and tied it tightly around his arm.

"Really? I thought she just didn't like me."

"Well that too. No, it's about money. She sees you as taking away her money. She doesn't want Las Manchas because it belonged to her family, or to pass it to her heirs. None of her husbands could stand her. She doesn't have any heirs except me. She wants to sell the place, make money off of it."

"I didn't know."

I thought about this a minute or two. No wonder she was annoyed when I cleaned up the cemetery. It meant the land wasn't neglected or abandoned. Restoring the church and school would put a hold on her plans to acquire the property cheaply. "Yeah, I can spare the trailer. I was going for some wood pallets. I need something to keep my wood stove going."

"I'll get you a load of wood I'll lend you a wheel barrel full to get through the night and go get some tomorrow." Rae dabbed at his arm, the bleeding had stopped.

Priscilla was back in the truck cab. She gathered up her little poodle and sat stroking Kiko's head, cooing at him as she sat behind the wheel. Flacita had cuddle up against her. Rae reached in and pulled the keys from the ignition.

"I can't pay right now. I won't get my check until the fifth of next month."

"It's okay. I know where you live." Rae looked over his shoulder at the railroad tracks then back at his Grandmother behind the wheel. "But you drive, okay?" He tossed me the keys.

89

Tuesday before Thanksgiving was one of those unbelievably beautiful New Mexico days. Clear blue sky, crisp but not freezing. The reds and tans of the mountains made them pop in 3D even more than they normally did. It was late fall, the cranes flew low to the ground, taking a final rest before the last hundred mile flight to the south. I could hear them as I set out on my final trek to pick up what I would need to make Thanksgiving a success. I stopped several times to look for the cranes when I heard their familiar call, finally spying them as they flew just above the Rio Grande, keeping a tight V shape. That's what I need, I said to myself, a whole flock to lift my wings when I am tired.

My destination, as usual, was the dollar store. A few serving dishes at a dollar each, another pan to steam the green beans in, maybe a couple packs of plastic knives, forks and spoons, would be enough to get me through Thanksgiving. I was approaching the intersection where the Animal Shelter that once housed Flacita was. Another sandwich board was out today, this one advertised a "Terrific Tuesday Three Dollar a Bag" special at the re-sale shop next to the shelter. I never could resist a bag day sale. Besides, if I could find what I needed here instead of the dollar store I'd be ahead a few bucks. I rode up onto the sidewalk, locked the bike to a post and went in.

I loved looking here, things were neatly arranged, easy to find, but the prices always seemed high. Re-sale shops that support a non-profit almost always charge more, so I rarely shopped there unless a special bag day sale like today. One corner of the large space was set up as a Unique Boutique area, better quality clothes, accessories and collectables were displayed with the same flair as a high end shop. A donated manikin greeted anyone who stepped into the small carpeted store within a store, elegantly dressed in full skirt, and silk blouse. A gorgeous, ruby pink, purple and gray mohair shawl was draped around the manikin's shoulders. I could really go for that, I removed it to check for wear and tear. This would be the first thing in my three dollar bag. Soft, long and well loved, a pulled it around my shoulders absorbing its' warmth.

"That is a beautiful scarf. It suits you to a T." A deep voice shook from behind me.

I spun around and there was Ed, from the Animal Shelter. How on earth did this guy move so quietly, I never heard him approach.

"Hi, remember me? You helped me when I adopted a dog a couple weeks ago." I took the shawl off and folded it in thirds, hoping to place it in my bag.

"Of course, little Flacita, how is she doing? Such a sweet dog." Ed was smiling as he leaned his hand on a nearby shelf.

"She is a sweetie. A great dog, great company. I am so happy to have her." I smiled back at him.

"You volunteer here too?"

"You bet, anywhere they need me, they asked me to help out today on account of the Bag Sale."

"Yes, I saw the sign, that's why I came in. I'm really looking for some serving dishes and a pan or two, but this shawl caught my eye." I patted the shawl as it lay over my arm.

"That is a beautiful color, looks good on you, but unfortunately the boutique items aren't included in the bag sale." Ed's eyes were apologetic.

I spread out the shawl and gently draped it back around the manikin, at ten dollars it was a bargain, but I only had ten dollars to spend today for everything I needed. "Oh, well, another time then."

"Are you sure? It'd make a great gift for someone?" He was as much a salesman here as he was at the animal shelter.

"I do like it, but today I really need to see if you have some pans and dishes."

Ed bowed slightly, "Right this way." He led me over to the kitchen area. "Take your time, I'll be up front if you need anything." He walked up to the cash register.

The pots were a little dented, but just a little. Two pots, a couple of serving bowls and some silverware, all went into the bag. At the last minute I stuffed in an old tablecloth I thought would cover the boards I had propped up to make a dining table. Good, this is good, all for three dollars. I went up to the checkout where Ed was helping sort bags of donated goods while another volunteer worked the register.

"Find what you needed?" Ed asked as he pushed a plastic crate of donated used paperbacks under the counter. He certainly was friendly. "Can't talk you into that shawl?"

"Yes, I did find everything and no, I'm afraid the shawl's not in my budget today, much to my regret." I handed the cashier my three dollars.

Ed watched as I transferred the paper bag to my shopping bag, and buttoned my sweater.

"Getting ready for Thanksgiving?" he asked, trying to make conversation.

"Yes, I'm having some neighbors over this year. I'm sure Flacita will love it, she is so friendly."

I lifted the bag up onto my shoulder as I took a step away from him. "And you?"

"Me? Well, I'll probably have something quick. I'm on Thanksgiving duty at the shelter."

"Oh, I guess I didn't realize someone had to be there."

"Not all day, just go in and feed 'em, twice, late morning and again in the evening, check things, make sure it's all good." Ed came around the counter towards me, rubbed the palms of his hands together in front of him and looked over his shoulder at the cashier then back at me. "Got time for a cup of coffee? I'll buy?"

I started to decline, to say I was busy, I needed to get going, but I stopped and took a step back. It had been a long time since I had coffee with someone, to sit and talk and enjoy a cup of coffee in a real coffee shop not a soup kitchen.

"I'd like that." I said.

Ed was a great guy. The last of the true gentlemen. He opened the door to the coffee shop next door, pulled my chair out, and returned with two coffees and two pumpkin spice scones. It felt good sitting here with him. I didn't think about how poor I was or how was I going to stay warm tonight or anything. I just sat sipping my coffee, making conversation with him.

"How long have you been volunteering?" I stirred a little more real cream into my coffee, a luxury.

"This is my fifth year. I started out when I was still working, before I retired. I just love the animals. We get so many of them it's heartbreaking."

"Do you have a dog?"

"Me? No, I moved to a condo after my divorce, no pets allowed. Wife got the house and dog. I guess that's one of the reason's I started volunteering. In a way I have a hundred dogs, not just one or two." Ed looked at the window as the cars flew by.

"I had another dog before Flacita, my son's dog really, but well, he's with someone else now too. I miss him, but Flacita helps." I broke off a piece of the scone dipped it in my coffee. Maybe I should change the subject. "Where did you work before you retired?"

"Sandia, the lab. I was there for thirty five years." He sat back in his chair and adjusted his collar.

"A scientist?" He did have that wise look about him. I could picture him in front of a computer or setting at a lab bench doing experiments.

"Now why does everyone think that?" He was genuinely perplexed. "I was a welder. The scientists would design things, or describe things really and I'd build them. Once they called me in the middle of the night, needed a set of pipes used for cooling some experiment mended or they'd have to start over. They had sent these out special, built off site, and second time they tried to use them the welds didn't hold. I stuck with it half the night getting those suckers fixed. You know what they say about welders." Ed smiled at me slyly, head tilted, and finished the rest of his coffee.

"No, what?" I was through with my coffee too and started gathering up the trash to throw away. "What do they say about welders?"

"We can fix anything from the crack of dawn to a broken heart." Ed stood up. "Thanks for your company. I don't get a chance to sit and have coffee with folks anymore, especially a lovely lady like you."

What a nice guy! "Thank you, I enjoyed it too." I said and pushed back the chair.

We walked to the door, which Ed held upon for me. I unlocked my bike, got on and was about to ride away when the thought hit me.

"Ed, can I invite you to dinner on Thanksgiving?"

90

The sound of a truck air brake, a JAKE Brake, woke me from a very sound sleep Thanksgiving morning. It was almost five o'clock. The only light I could see came from the I-25 street light high above, and the occasional passing of a semi-tractor trailer. I had slept well, refreshed enough to get up and get the day started. There was much to do.

It had been six years since I had hosted a Thanksgiving meal. In my BH (before homeless) time my house was the place to be for Thanksgiving, neighbors, friends and even distant cousins on my husband's side would start calling around the middle of October to be sure they were on the guest list. One year saw twenty six souls gathering around the table for the main event, adding another seven for desert only owing to in-law obligations at other homes. That year I cooked two turkeys, twenty pounds of mashed potatoes, four pumpkin, three apple and one cranberry peach pie and the obligatory green bean casserole times four. Guests were requested to bring appetizers, bread, wine, salads and I never turned down an extra desert. Everyone who showed up got a plate. During Stevie's college years, he would bring home roommates and girlfriends and girlfriends' brothers, you get the idea.

It was always a sit down meal and always together, the table would be extended on both ends by doors on sawhorses, card tables, a picnic table, all of uneven height, covered by yards of dark brown fabric bought and hemmed especially for this purpose. We would have to set it up on the diagonal extending into the living room so that half the guest were in there and the other end into the kitchen. It was my favorite holiday. No children's table. We were all in this together.

But AH, after homeless, Thanksgiving became difficult. The first year I helped at the Medical Center where Stevie lay in a coma, then at the local soup kitchen. Last year had been the Thanksgiving take out pot luck at the Rest-Inn. I wondered where Mr. Gonzales and Junior were. I especially worried about Cesar, hoped he had found a place to stay. It made me realize it wasn't the food that made it special but the company.

So, when store windows painted with yellow leaves and cornucopia and cartoon turkeys began to appear everywhere I knew what I had to do, organize a Thanksgiving feast for Las Manchas.

I talked to Raenaldo first, walked over with Flacita in tow, to the open bay door of his garage. I could hear a drill in use.

"Hey, Rae," I called out, the sound stopped and I started toward the back where a 67 El Camino, its hood up, was waiting for a carburetor rebuild. Before I got three steps Rae bounded up from behind me. "Oh! I thought I heard someone inside the garage."

"Um, it's my cousin. He's helping me out some, staying here for a while until he gets his own place." Rae was bobbing around from foot to foot, watching behind me. Twice I glanced over my shoulder to see what he was looking at.

"Well, I came to invite you to Thanksgiving Dinner. I didn't know if you had plans or not."

"I usually take my Grandma to the buffet at the casino, it's not bad. They cook up a special menu for Thanksgiving, but, yes, okay. Can I bring my girlfriend and her two kids?" Rae looked hopeful. I don't think spending Thanksgiving at the casino, with its heavy smoke filled gaming room, and preponderance of dour faces was high on his list.

"Of course, and your cousin and grandma too".

"Um, he's kind of shy, I'm not sure he'll come." He was looking behind me again as if for confirmation from someone in the garage bay.

"But I know my Nina will go."

"Okay if I go up to the house and to talk to her? I want to see if we can use your oven to roast the turkey. I still don't have an oven, or hot water." I started toward the house.

"Umm, sure, but I got me one of those turkey fryers. We used it last year when we went hunting." Rae reached behind his head with a wrench and scratched his neck. "I could cook the turkey in that."

I'd never had deep fried turkey. "That would be great .See you there then." I turned back up the gravel drive. Flacita was no longer with me.

Rae was in the garage bay by the front of the car, talking to someone in a low hushed way. As soon as he heard my shuffling feet on the gravel he turned, banging his head on the corner of the raised hood.

"What's up?" he said, dabbing at his bleeding forehead.

"You're hurt?" I hurried toward him grabbing a clean shop rag from the tool cart pushed up against the metal frame of the building.

Rae was quicker, with only two long bounding steps was in front of me.

"I'm okay, it's not bad. See it's already stopped." He pulled his hand away from his head for me to see.

"Oh well I can't find Flacita. Did you see where she went?"

Flacita, wagging her tail and swishing her rear, waddled slowly around from the front of the El Camino.

"Where you been? Let's go." She keeps wagging her tail and looking back toward the El Camino.

I reach down, giving her a gentle nudge in the other direction and she dutifully followed be my side.

"See you there. Come around two. I like to eat at three, but you can come earlier if you want. I'll just put everyone to work on the food".

"Great, I can't wait."

And so it went. The other invites went just as easily. Dub would bring chips and dip, Penelope and Anselmo would bring chile both green and red. If there is one thing I have learned from living in New Mexico for more than 30 years it's this: If you invite someone to your home they expect that chile will be served no matter what else is on the menu, mashed potatoes and chile, spinach and chile, even lobster and chile.

The only person who asked about the guest list was Father Rico. I wasn't raised a Catholic so I wasn't exactly sure what his responsibilities were on this day. But he let me know that each parish could celebrate Thanksgiving in its own fashion, it was not an "Official" day of worship.

He was walking amongst the pews, checking to make sure each prayer rail worked, and each bench held at least one copy of the liturgy. Since the Cemetery Cleanup and the Creation of the Historic Las Manchas Neighborhood Association there had been an increase in church attendance. I think they were there more to see what profits could be made from reviving the old church, (a tourist attraction, conversion to a brew pub?) then to seek communion with God. Once I asked Father Rico if this bothered him. He only smiled and said "I am thankful for whatever brings someone into God's house to hear his word. The lord works in many ways."

"So both Mrs. Romero and Mrs. Atencio are coming?" He looked at me with a raised eyebrow.

"Yes, at least I think they are. I know they both need help walking and getting around but I think we can all manage." I sighed. Someday I would need that help. Who would be there for me?

"Well Mrs. Roark, in that case I will bring the wine. You'll need it." He looked at me and blinked.

Now what could he possibly mean by that?

91

Thanksgiving Day arrived. Today I was thankful to wake in a bed in a house, to be warm, to have food to eat and soon friends to share it with. I was thankful for all which had been given me.

After my usual routine, chickens, coffee, feed the dog, I went outside and started the fire in the horno. This was the only oven I had. I learned to use it little by little. Cesar had plastered it, did the first firing, but had made a quick exit before I got a chance to learn much from him. Through trial and error and a few words of advice from Anselmo, I figured it out. First you must build a nice fire, not too big and not too small and let it burn down mop out the ash with some old soaked cotton rags and seal it up to even the temperature. The thick walls of the mud oven would do the rest, enough heat for pies, potatoes and a couple of loaves of bread. It took a little while to get the fire started. It had rained ever so lightly the night before and the wood was damp. I stood in front of the door, letting the light and heat of the fire enfold me and sipped coffee. Flacita decided it was too damp for her and curled up on her rug under the metal roof of the portal.

Above me a few cars sped along the interstate, less than an average Thursday. I imagined the people driving those cars, families eager to reach Grandma's house or college kids trying to make it home for a meal. I reflected on this with sadness. I would never have grandkids or again feel the rush of pride as my son burst through the door home for the weekend from college. It was the only pity I allowed myself that day. The commuters, in turn were probably looking down on me right now with pity. Not knowing that the modest accommodations of Las Manchas were appreciated by the inhabitants. Enough of that, I thought. Time to get busy I told myself.

I told everyone else to come early and they did, except for the Romero's. Rae dropped off the turkey, oil still dripping, wrapped heavily in foil and covered by a towel, then left to pick up his girlfriend and her kids.

"Is your Nina coming?" I lifted the dangerously hot turkey out if his hands.

"She's driving me." Rae used his chin to point at the truck parked out front. Priscilla's hands rested on the wheel only slightly above her head. Her four foot nine inch frame was raised by a pillow and she barely could manage the pedals.

In less than fifteen minutes, Rae, his grandmother, and Rae's girlfriend Alicia appeared at the door. Alicia handed me a huge bag of soft rolls and stick of butter. Alicia's two young daughters, dressed alike in black track pant and pink mermaid hoodies bounded in the door. The girls, hair tightly braided, both clutched a doll dressed just like they were, and one carried a board game.

Father Rico arrived carrying a cardboard box that he slid from the back of the old Mercedes. Two gallons of homemade wine wedged in place and heavy white plates, cups and bowls, overfilled the box.

"From the church kitchen," he said. "No one has been in there in years. I thought you could use these too." He pulled knives, forks, spoons, even some serving pieces from his coat pockets.

Much better than the cheap dollar store utensils I had carefully wrapped in thin embossed paper napkins and tied with left over garden string, just the way the church youth groups had done for the shelter meals. I took the box from his hands and hustled over to the table, scooping up my carefully prepared plastic wear bundles before anyone could see them.

It took quite a bit of experimenting, but I had managed to cobble together a table from cement blocks, boards and stacked crates, covered by a dark rose bag day tablecloth. It almost looked pretty. The log bench from the portal, plastic chairs scrubbed clean and a few more crates and boards completed the seating. Dollar store votive candles in jelly jars along the center, juniper branches wound around them graced the center. If I was a hippie I would be impressed.

Rae and Father walked next door and gathered Dub along with a large bag of chips and three containers of sour cream and ranch dip. I put the chips in bowls, set out napkins, and got punch for the little girls and wine and beer for the rest of us.

"Does this thing work?" Rae knelt in from of my ancient ten dollar yard sale TV.

"Some channels. Sometimes you have to move the antenna on the roof around, that digital box is connected to it. Cesar used to do it for me. I haven't been up there since." I passed around my famous deviled eggs. "Hope Cesar is okay, if I knew how to get in touch with him I would have invited him."

Father looked at Rae eyebrows raised. Rae shook his head ever so slightly and looked away.

"Padre, you stay here and flip channels. I'll go up and move that thing around." Rae stepped out the door and hopped on to the roof.

Father Rico changed the channels until a fuzzy Dallas linebacker filled the screen. Wisconsin, home team, had the ball. You couldn't really tell if the snow was from the TV reception or the weather on the field.

"How about now?" Rae called from outside.

Alicia relayed the information back inside.

"How is it Father?" Her bright pink lipstick matched the girls pink mermaid outfits and reminded me of Bert's sleeping bag.

"Better, better, no that's worse," Father answered.

"He says it's worse." Alicia called out the door.

"Try it now."-Rae

"How about now?"-Alicia

"Good, maybe a little more. The picture is a little hazy."-Father

"Still a little hazy Rae."-Alicia

"Oh No No No." Father and Dub shouted in unison.

"What? What is it?"-Rae

"Ignore them Rae."-Alicia- "Packers just scored."

"Son of a...." Rae jumped off roof and in through the door in time to see the field goal.

Everyone settled in to watch the game, lined up on the old futon couch, pulling the white plastic chairs away from the table, while Alicia's two girls, Ashley and Amanda, sat on the floor playing with Flacita and Little Dog, using the pink ribbons from their own braids to tie bows behind the dogs' ears, and peppered me with questions.

"How come she's so fat? Why does she bark all the time?"

"Does she like kids?"

"She smells."

"What kind of dog is she?"

"Can we take her for a walk after dinner?"

I went outside to check on the food in the horno, just done. I pulled the roasted vegetables from the oven using the edge of my sweatshirt to protect my hands from the heat and headed inside. A car I didn't recognize, a Silver Prius, pulled into the driveway. Who was this?

I went in the back door, set the pans on the kitchen counter and clambered down the cement block steps to the main room.

Rae was already opening the door, a large man grasping flowers and a bakery box filled the doorway "Can I help you?"

"I was looking for Aileen Roark. Maybe I have the wrong address."

"Ed, you made it." I rushed to the door, took the box from his left hand, grasped his right in mine and quickly introduced him.

"Ed, this is Rae my neighbor, his grandmother Priscilla and girlfriend Alicia, my other neighbors Dub and Father Rico."

Ed politely shook hands, still holding the flowers, stopping over the girls "And who are these young ladies?"

"I'm Ashley and this is Amanda." Ashley's toothless smile could charm the moon from the stars.

"And this is Flacita and Little Dog, but he's a boy." Amanda's smile was missing only one tooth, but two more were loose, she proudly demonstrated.

"How do you do Ashley, Amanda?" Ed reached down and extended his hand to each giggling girl.

"Well Flacita, you are looking particularly lovely," he said playfully tugging at the bow behind one ear. Flacita remembered Ed. She got up and pranced around the room, almost knocking the tubs of dip from the table, swishing her tail.

"I wasn't sure you would come, but I'm so glad you did," I said.

"I try not to miss a home cooked meal. It was so wonderful to have the invitation, these are for you? Do you have a vase?"

Alicia offered to take his jacket. "Make yourself at home. We've got the game on."

Father poured wine into one of the plastic cups. "Try this Ed; I made it myself, grapes from the churchyard. It was a particularly good year."

"Ah, a vintner extraordinaire. Do you have your own label?"

"Maybe soon, Las Manchas Vineyards, we'll put a picture of the bell tower on the label, has a nice ring to it don't you think?" Father chuckled but everyone else groaned at the often told joke.

"What's the score?" Ed pulled one of my two real dining chairs into the living area and sat beside Priscilla who greeted him warmly. One of the gang in less than two minutes, I envied the ease with which he fit in. I've never been like that, even when times were good.

I retreated to the kitchen to find something for the flowers. A red and yellow coffee can was all I could come up with. I emptied the coffee into a plastic bag, rinsed out the can, added the flowers and brought them to the table, carefully placed between the votive candles, which the girls begged me to light. Alicia got up and helped each with the matches.

"Do you need any more help?" Alicia asked "Maybe Rae can carve the turkey."

"That would be great. I've got some more food out in the horno. Maybe you could help me bring it in. As soon as Anselmo and Penelope get here we can eat"

"Qué?" Priscilla's ears perked up.

Rae looked at Dub who looked at Father who looked at me all with eyebrows raised. The shuffling sound of a walker and footsteps could be heard on the flagstone outside.

"Here they are now." I opened the door and in came Penelope, walker first, coat unbuttoned, followed my Anselmo, head bent forward as usually, carrying a speckled blue pot filled with Red Chile. They both greeted me in Spanish, "Buenas tardes, gracias por la invitación."

Priscilla, up on her feet, using her cane, moved as quickly as she could toward Penelope. "You little flirt, how dare you set your foot in here. You are nothing but a floozy. How could you? How dare you," she said at the top of her voice, than lifted her hands to slap at Priscilla like they were playing a game of patty cakes.

Penelope moved the walker between them trying to push back at Priscilla and stay at arm's length. "You were always a sore loser, just jealous because he liked me better."

"How dare you show your cara feo here." Priscilla shook her cane in the air.

"Look who's talking, you should look in a mirror." Penelope tried to lift her walker but was caught off balance and took two steps forward toward Priscilla. They both had to grab onto each other just to stay standing.

Anselmo bowed his head even lower and tried to duck behind Father Rico. Dub and Rae were laughing hysterically. Father came between the two. The dogs, caught up in the excitement, began barking and nipping at both of the elderly women's feet.

I looked from one to the other; they both had the same dimple in their chin, the same double wave on the side of their hair, the same slant to their shoulders and curve of the neck. Oh my god, they were twins.

"You didn't tell her?" Father looked to Rae.

"Tell her what?" Rae kept laughing "It had to happen sometime Padre. They just can't go on for sixty plus years holding a grudge."

Ed was totally bewildered. What had he gotten himself into? He grabbed both dogs by their collars and hustled them out the back door.

Father became peacekeeper. "Mrs. Atencio, Mrs. Romero cálmate. Estás hermanas, familia. This is no way to treat each other."

"She started it." Priscilla pouted, stomping her cane on the floor.

"Well you kept it going." It was Penelope who kept it going now, shuffling her walker to turn sideways so as not to look at her sister.

"It's time to put this to rest. You need to practice forgiveness. It is what our Holy Mother teaches us. Sixty years is a long time to hold this anger inside of you." Both ladies looked down, knowing they were in for a scolding.

"Anselmo come over here. You are part of this too."

Anselmo reluctantly walked to Father Rico, his wife and sister-in-law.

"Anselmo this is your wife whom you love and your wife's sister, who you must care for like your own sister. It is time for each of you to apologize to the other."

"I haven't done anything to apologize for." Penelope was not giving up easy.

This was turning into a Telenovela.

Priscilla spoke. "How could you pick her over me Anselmo. Why? Why did you marry her and not me?"

"You were so beautiful, so lovely and kind. I didn't know who I loved more. I went to your father for advice."

"Sí, and did he tell you to marry me and not Priscilla?" Penelope sounded exactly like her sister. If you couldn't see lips move you wouldn't know who was speaking.

"No." Anselmo looked terrified, almost crying.

Father put his hand on his shoulder. "Courage my friend, time for the truth."

"So he told you to marry me." Priscilla swished her skirt like a teenager.

"No." Anselmo's voice grew weaker with each question.

"What did he tell you then?" Both said in unison.

"We flipped a coin." His voice was barely audible.

"You flipped a coin!" A duet with one voice.

"Heads it was Priscilla, tails Penelope. It was tails." Anselmo took a handkerchief from his back pocket and blew his nose.

"That's it? You flipped a coin? You decided who to marry because you flipped a coin?"

"Sí."

Both ladies turned to each other clucking in Spanish like hens. "How could he do that to us? Let him use a coin to pick." They locked arms and turned away from Anselmo, who blew his nose again, eyes watering heavily.

Father spoke to Anselmo. "Anselmo you must end this. Do not let it go on. You and your wife are one in God's eyes, do not forget that."

Anselmo used the table to steady himself, and moved in front of the two sisters cutting them off as they clung to each other, blocking their path. Like a knight from King Arthur's court he struggled down to one knee, looking sideways and up as far as his bent back would allow. He took a hand from each lady.

Tears streaming down his eighty five year old cheeks Anselmo begged them, "Forgive me. I loved you both so. It was the only way to decide. Please Penelope, Priscilla forgive me."

Now the sisters were crying, speaking in Spanish. "We forgive you Anselmo we forgive you."

Father was beside them, grabbing Anselmo by the elbow, pulled him to his feet, embraced all three.

Rae, still half laughing, walked towards them arms stretched out "Group hug." He pulled Alicia and the girls into the circle. Dub wheeled his chair over patting Anselmo on the back. "Mi familia."

I stood there a minute. Dub extended his other hand towards me. Ashley and Amanda pushed Ed towards the circle and joined our two hands. Amanda and Ashley ran to the back door and let the barking dogs into the house. We all stood there, half laughing half crying, all hugging and holding hands.

Dub was the first to break free. "Let's eat, it's halftime."

So we did. The turkey was carved, the potatoes served, the pies divided, wine glasses were filled and filled again. More food than I had eaten in years. My face grew warm from the wine.

After dinner Alicia helped clear the table. Ed followed her into the kitchen carrying the large pot of water I had let heat on the wood stove to pour over the dishes.

"That's quite a circle of friends you have." Ed's eyes twinkled.

"Yeah, ain't I lucky?"

"You bet. That was the best Thanksgiving I've had in years. I'm so glad you invited me. I wasn't sure if you really meant for me to come."

"I wasn't sure you would come. Do you want some leftovers?" I filled a foil pie tin with turkey and stuffing.

"Boy that would be great. Since my wife and I called it splits I haven't had a real home cooked meal. This has been great." He folded the dish towel over the edge of a drawer to dry. "Can I call you?"

"You could if I had a phone. "

"Seriously? You don't have a phone?" The topic of my struggles with homelessness had never come up.

"Yeah, well, I have a very modest income, in case you couldn't tell." I picked up one of the mismatched plates and pots stacked by the sink.

Ed looked around, seeing the yellow linoleum tiled trailer's kitchen and adobe addition for what it was.

"Money isn't everything." He shrugged his shoulders.

"But it does help." I laughed. "I'll come by the shop next time you're working. Grab some coffee again?"

"Great, sounds like a date." Ed clapped his hands once.

A date? Did I have a date?

We stepped down from the trailer's kitchen into the adobe living area.

"Sorry to leave you good folks, but I'm pulling night duty at the shelter. Got to check on things one last time, make sure it's okay. It has been wonderful meeting all of you."

Alicia got Ed's sport coat from the row of hooks Cesar had nailed by the backdoor.

"So glad to meet you Ed." Dub wheeled over and shook his hand.

"Happy Thanksgiving." Penelope and Priscilla, twins once more, answered in unison.

"Delighted, Señor, delighted." Father Rico patted him on the back.

"Hope to see you again, primo." Rae reached his hand out from the futon sofa, where he sat reading a book to his girlfriend's daughters.

I walked Ed to his car. "How do you like your Prius?"

"Great. Great on gas, a little slow up hill, but I don't go uphill that much. What do you drive?"

I pointed to MaryIsabelle's bicycle leaning up against the side wall. "Drives same as yours. Slow up hill, good on gas."

Ed laughed, "Really Aileen, I had a great time."

I wasn't sure if he was serious or not. "Thanks, I'm glad you came. See you next Thursday?"

"Terrific, I'll buy." Ed backed out and pulled slowly down the road. His car was as quiet as he was, you couldn't hear either of them coming or going.

A light drizzle started up again. I wrapped my arms around myself to keep warm. I'd have to use all my wood to stoke up the wood stove to keep the place warm. When I opened the door Rae had beat me two it.

"I'll bring you some wood tomorrow, this won't last the weekend."

"Can't pay you until after the fifth of the month Rae."

"It's okay, you're good for it. I keep telling you, I know where you live."

The football was over. Greenbay came from behind in the third quarter, a great disappointment to the Cowboy crowd. To ease this new sorrow Father poured more wine and pulled a ukulele out from somewhere. We gathered our chairs in a circle and sang every song we could remember: *You Are My Sunshine; Yellow Rose of Texas; Daisy Daisy* and some in Spanish; *De Colores; Cielo Lindo*; a few the girls had learned in school. It was getting late, almost ten o'clock.

"My friends," Father addressed us. "I have wonderful news. We are getting an assistant priest, the Archdioceses has seen our little church grow. They were most interested in the little gathering we held for All Souls Day and the way we have come together to renew the area. There is even talk of a charter school re-opening in the old school."

"Qué Bueno." Priscilla clapped her hands, "Los niños aquí, en la escuela y la iglesia."

"That's great Father. I know how you worried on it." Dub said.

"We must plan something to celebrate. A way to give thanks and praise for our community. Something for the holidays that brings us all together."

"How about Los Posada?" Penelope said excitedly.

"Yes, Yes. Las Posada, Christmas Eve services that could work." Father strummed the ukulele.

"We could dance the Matachine, like we used to." Anselmo stood up, raised his hand up like a politician.

"Yes, we might manage that. Well that is a lot to think about, especially on a full stomach." Father paused to let it sink in. "My friends, do you think we can do this?"

A jumbled response, "Yes Father," "Sí," "You bet." All agreed.

Even Rae was enthusiastic. He hadn't seen Las Matachine danced here since he was eight years old, it would be his chance to learn the dance.

"My friends let us toast to each other, our Church, Santa Ursula, and to Las Manchas." Father Rico raised his glass.

"To Las Manchas." We all seconded.

Father began to strum the ukulele louder and sing. *Dream an Impossible Dream.*

Everyone was singing, off key and out of time, some a little drunk, but all singing, making it up as we went along. With each crazy verse we got louder.

"We have a quest. Reach for a star; it may be close or it may be far, keep going when you have sorrow, es claro; tenemos busqueda; impossible dream."

As we hit the final note, at that exact moment, a loud knock sounded from the door.

Everyone looked. I got up to answer it not knowing who to expect. I barely turned the knob when the door burst open.

"Is it the ghost of Las Manchas? The bogeyman?" little Ashley asked.

Close. It was Beulah.

92

The thing about uninvited guests is when they do show up, any guilt you might have had about not inviting them is instantly dissolved. Within thirty seconds Beulah was through the door and stomping around the room. Even though she stood no more than five foot tall, she was difficult to ignore. A man in a gray sport coat trailed her, acting as sentry by the door, which I quickly closed to ward off the cold damp air.

"I don't know what you're trying to pull here but you won't get away with it." She stood in front of me giving her best scowl. She looked comical not menacing. All I could do was raise my eyebrows and smile, give my classic unrehearsed response.

"Oh?" I said.

"Don't pretend you don't know what I'm talking about." She pushed a rolled up newspaper into my chest.

Father stood up, ukulele in hand and came to my defense.

"Beulah, we must remember our manners. We are guests in Mrs. Roark's home this Thanksgiving." He spoke in a calm but firm voice.

"Oh for crying out loud Father, no disrespect towards the cloth but you are in this too. Well you won't get away with it either." She clenched her teeth.

"Beulah." Priscilla grasped her cane and pushed herself up. "Beulah, you may not talk to Father that way, hija." She was speaking to a naughty child.

Penelope was on her feet too, using her walker to propel herself in Beulah's direction. Priscilla took her sister's arm and they scurried as fast as two elderly sisters could go.

"Sí, Beulah, we do not talk to the priest like that, and you must remember your manners, you are a guest in this home."

Beulah glared at her reunited aunts, who clung to each other, then turned her evil eye on me, then at Father , and finally at the empty jug of wine setting on the dining table, and the half full jug beside it. Her eyes grew wide then narrow as she surmised the situation.

"You're drunk, both of you." Beulah barked at her two aunts, and then at me "You've gotten them drunk." She turned to her companion, "Are you seeing this Mr. Lujan? Look at this, she has gotten them drunk."

Anselmo was not going to help matters. "Beulah, try some, it will relax you, and you need relaxing." He held up one of the jugs of Father Rico's home brew and poured it into a plastic cup, offering it to his niece in-law.

"Witness this Mr. Lujan, witness this. These people are all drunk. Children are present and they are all drunk."

Beulah's companion stood in silence beside her, nodding his head. I wasn't sure if he was friend or employee.

"Beulah, calm down, we are all friends here, enjoying a Thanksgiving meal. My dear you must calm yourself." Father again tried to appease her.

"Calm myself? I come to check on my elderly housebound aunt and uncle, bring them a plate of food for Thanksgiving and I find them over here so intoxicated they don't know what they're doing? Look at them, they haven't spoken in sixty years, and now they act like nothing ever happened. They're drunk." Just like that day beside the river when the Sheriff had Cesar face down in the dirt, Beulah danced around and demanded to run the show.

"And you," she again turned to me, pointing her finger at my chest. "You are responsible."

Rae, who up until now had remained silent, could take no more. "Stop it Aunt Beulah. I'm not drunk." He stepped between Beulah and me. "Everyone here is having a nice time, celebrating Thanksgiving like a family should, together. This is what a family is about." Little Ashley and Amanda, upset by the arguing, clung to Rae's leg. Alicia, their mother, put her arms around all three.

"I'm not going to allow this to happen." Beulah wagged her finger at Rae.

"Allow what Beulah? Allow what to happen?" Rae stared down his nose at his aunt, easy to do.   "Stop pretending like you don't know." She stomped her foot, tried pulling herself taller, realizing, for the first time ever, her nephew might win this one.

"I'll tell you what I know; I know we live her Aunt Beulah. Nina and I and Aunt Nellie and Uncle Anselmo, I know we live here like a family. Dub lives here. Father Rico lives here. This is our home. One day I hope to make this a home for my family too." Rae picked Ashley up in one arm and Amanda in the other. "This is our home and we intend to keep it."

Rae had never stood up to his aunt before. In retreat and not happy about it Beulah shifted her focus on a new foe, me. Eyes glowing yellow, wagging her finger in my face she raged at me.

"You won't get away with this. I will see to that. I will use every means possible to see you out of here." Then she spoke to her companion, "Mr. Lujan, help me escort my aunts and uncle home, will you please?"

After Beulah had ushered almost everyone out the door I helped Father to his Mercedes, but held fast to his keys.

"Father Rico I really don't think you should drive. I know it's only a block away but you've had quite a bit of wine and Beulah is watching." There was no way I would let him drive. I kept thinking about Sam and my boys.

"Yes, yes you're right of course." Father fumbled for his keys not realizing I still had them.

"I'll drive you and walk back."

"That is a lot to ask Mrs. Roark, but I am grateful for your offer."

"It's okay, I'll get my sweater." I ran inside to retrieve it.

Father Rico moved to the passenger side and I scooted in behind the wheel. It was a very short drive, no more than two or three minutes around the circle. I helped Father out of the car and into the living room/den attached to the quarters. No sooner had I closed the door against the chill wind than he collapsed into a recliner in one corner.

"It's cold in here Father, where is the thermostat?" I glanced around the modest room looking for the dial.

"I haven't got the furnace lit yet Mrs. Roark. I've yet to call and get it done." He had settled back into the chair.

"Do you have wood? I'll get your fireplace going."

"Don't trouble yourself Mrs. Roark." He had put his legs up and closed his eyes.

"It's okay. I know what it's like to be cold."

He opened one eye and looked at my sympathetically. I brought some wood in from the patio, stuffed paper around it and glanced around for some matches.

"There are some in the desk drawer Mrs. Roark, top drawer on the left."

I had thought he was asleep. I retrieved them and lit the fire blowing gently to get a good flame.

"Mrs. Roark. I must confess something to you." Father Rico tilted the chair even further back and again closed his eyes.

"I'm not sure I should hear your confession Father. For one thing, I keep telling you I'm not Catholic." I re-lit the flame and blew gently.

He smiled half asleep. "Do you remember the day we went fishing and the car broke down in front of the cemetery that night when we drove back?"

"How could I forget? That was the night Cesar almost got arrested." I wondered where Cesar was now, was Father Rico sheltering him? Was that his confession?

"Yes, and do you remember how you told me about the spirit you had seen calling you to the cemetery?" His hands were folded across his stomach, breathing heavily, almost snoring.

"Wait, you saw it too?" I knew I wasn't nuts, there really was a ghost.

"No, Mrs. Roark. No I didn't see it. I was the spirit."

"What?" I stood abruptly.

"I went back to try and get the car started that night. I squirted some lighter fluid into the starter. It exploded. That cloud you saw, it was me or rather the car. I'm sorry I let you believe otherwise."

I turned to look at him, he was almost asleep.

"Why didn't you tell me before?"

"Think about it Mrs. Roark, everything has a reason." His eyes closed once again, asleep, snoring loudly.

The fire was blazing, warming the room with an orange glow. I left the parsonage, locking the door behind me, walking the block to my little home, thankful I had one.

93

I spent the next morning picking up the pieces of the yesterday's meal, rearranged things and took the improvised benches and table out back to the porch. I skipped breakfast, something I rarely did since it was the one really cheap meal of the day. I had eaten so much yesterday it was afternoon before I felt the urge to sit with a plate of leftovers. I picked up the newspaper Beulah pressed into my chest the night before and tried to figure out what she was ranting about.

I unrolled the newspaper flat on the table in front of me. It was slightly damp. The New Mexico Ledger, special Thanksgiving edition, lay before me. A picture of St Ursula's Mission Church adorned the front page with the headline *Will Las Manchas Be Erased?,* a clever play on words.

Felix Archuleta, the man who interviewed me a month before, had the byline. It was a nice story, well written. It was really five stories. The first told the history of the tiny village's four hundred year old church, hacienda and old apple and grape orchards; how the coming of first the rail road, Route 66, the Interstate and finally the Rail Runner commuter train had served to isolate the community instead of unite it with the much larger Albuquerque to the south and town of Bernalillo to the north. The last few paragraphs described the efforts of developers to raze the ancient adobes and much less ancient mobile home parks to make way for townhouses and business plazas with loft studios.

The next four segments of the story, each on its own half page, told of one of us, each pictured in front of the church or cemetery. The first was a picture of Father Rico with St Ursula's bell towers in the background. Father Rico's story told of his escape by boat from Castro's Cuba, his assignment to St Ursula in the seventies and his desire to rebuild the parish school and church. Next, Rae and Priscilla's life together was explored. Priscilla described her struggles as a grandmother raising her grandchild in a fast changing world. Rae spoke of a grandson who now cared for his grandmother while trying to make a living as an independent mechanic at his Las Manchas's Garage. Rae spoke with passion about his desire to raise a family in Las Manchas as he was raised, with relatives and neighbors who looked out for each other.

Dub's story followed and was most compelling. His picture was taken in front of his wife and daughter's monument. The silly raven that shadowed him could be seen on the post in back of where he sat in his wheelchair. The author wrote of the sixteen year old Dub's survival of the Bataan Death March, return to the United States, and his quest to New Mexico to deliver a grieving father his son's last words. Dub expressed a desire to live out his last days here, in the community that had adopted him and when the time came, to be buried in the Las Manchas's cemetery beside his wife and daughter.

My story was last. If it hadn't been about me, and been my sons who died, my job lost, if it hadn't been me sleeping on the ground, hungry, alone and finally finding a home, I probably would have cried. But it was about me, so I knew how it ended, or sort of because it wasn't exactly over. I had told Felix Archuleta a lot, and he packed a lot in a few paragraphs. I'd tell you more, but you already know the story. It ended with my saying how grateful I was to have found my neighbors in Las Manchas.

No wonder Beulah was mad as heck. While her name was not mentioned, it certainly portrayed the developers as bogeymen. A story like this could shy off the investors she had lined up. She could feel the property's control slipping away from her and saw me as the instigator. Was I? All I wanted was a place to come in from the cold. I re-rolled the paper, and held it in my hand, wondering what to do with it. In the end, I used it to kindle my wood stove and watched the paper's small flame catch the large logs on fire.

94

*C*hristmas arrived. I spent time helping Priscilla and Penelope dig out the old clothing used for Las Matachines dancers. We raided thrift stores and yard sales for the rest. Bandannas, old scarves, bells and ribbons, were used to festoon the dancers in their high crowned masks. Rae's girlfriend, Alicia and her cousin helped. A few of the other ladies from the church came forward too. We met regularly in the fellowship hall to prepare the finery. It was encouraging when some of the older woman came with daughters and granddaughters wanting the chance to see how things were done. We came up with two tridents and three rattles, the rest would have to be handmade. Rae and his buddies got right to work. I offered to play the fiddle for the dancers, but was told, in no uncertain terms, it was "Not a suitable thing for a woman to do." End of story.

Christmas Eve, Dub, Ed and I lined the circular road, church yard and cemetery with farolitos. Setting up the sand filled paper bags and candles wasn't hard; it was getting them lit in the wind and light snow. Darkness came. It looked striking, like a postcard or page from a tourist magazine. The glowing farolitos lit the path from the old adobe church up to the heavy wooden gates that marked entrance to the church yard and encircled the road around Las Manchas. Ed once again volunteered for night duty at the animal shelter and had to leave before everything started, but not before pushing a small package wrapped in red tissue paper into my hands.

"Merry Christmas Aileen," he said 'er he drove out of sight.

It was nearly eight o'clock. A larger than expected crowd had gathered to watch the traditional dance and walk the farolito lined streets and church yards of Las Manchas. I skipped mass, the first one at St Ursula's lead by Father Dru. A young priest he had only recently left Serbia. Like Father Rico, he had come into adulthood when a civil war and unrest troubled his homeland. Father Rico was considered the most suitable host to help Father Dru adjust to life in the U.S.

As the novena was recited inside I stood outside, scurrying to relight the candles blown out by the December wind. The prayers ended, doors opened and the procession began. It was exciting. Slowly the fiddle started its haunting tune. Eight men, dressed in dark wool sport coats with bright blue and red scarves tied on their sleeves wore high domed headpieces. Their faces were obscured by handkerchiefs, bandanas and dense layers of long silky fringe. The men formed two lines, started the rhythmic march down the lane, occasionally stopping to spin and wave the trident and rattle they each carried. In the middle, Amanda, Alicia's oldest daughter, took the part of Malincha, dressed in white like a first communion a pink parka had been zipped around her to shield her from the cold. Rae danced beside her, guardian to her innocence. Anselmo choose the part of the devil, counterpoint to the solemnness of the dance. He walked slowly in and out of the dancers and crowd. Sometimes the bull or devil carried a whip to crack the air, sometimes a loud noise maker to startle the non-believers back into the faith. Anselmo chose the latter part and now pulled his hood up tight around him, leaning heavily on a long stick wrapped in velvet and tied with ribbons. He shook his head and growled while he worked the crowd.

"Boy, he don't even need a mask." Dub laughed as Anselmo's carra charged us.

Ba Bam!

Gunshots rang out, echoing off the church towers.

Father Dru, woefully familiar with the sound of gunfire, dove behind the cemetery wall. Rae gathered up the little dancer he had vowed to protect and ran into the church. Father Rico stood in the midst of everyone trying to bring calm. Everyone else in the crowd ran in a thousand directions, confused and terrified, screaming. Dub's raven fell from the sky, its left wing tip shot, bending the feathers at a right angle. The bird landed a few feet from where I stood in back of Dub, urgently trying to navigate his wheelchair through the gravel on the road.

One dancer, with massive shoulders and a familiar gait did not run. He pulled off his headdress and bandanna mask, walked rapidly towards the sound of the shot and yanked away the velvet wrapped rifle Anselmo had just fired into the air.

"You can't shoot that thing here old man!" Cesar angrily told him

"Por qué? It's how we did it in the old days?" The innocent Anselmo responded.

The police came. Cesar made himself scarce, his parole forbade any contact with firearms. No one questioned was able to say which of the eight dancers finally took the gun away from Anselmo. It was a mistake, a misunderstanding, everyone pleaded. Still, we made the nightly news, again, and not in a good way. Beulah, of course was delighted.

There was one more mass to be said that Christmas Eve, at midnight. This time I went, sitting alone in the back of the church. I stood when they stood, knelt when they knelt and bowed my head in prayer at the appropriate time. My eyes were closed in prayer when someone slipped in the pew beside me and grasped my hand as the giving of peace fellowship was announced.

"Merry Christmas Blondie," Cesar said. "Peace be with you."

¤ ¤ ¤

December 26th was cold and clear. I bundled up, intent on collecting the brown paper bags and spent candles that lined the drive Christmas Eve and Day, but someone had beat me to it. I stopped by Dub's to check on his raven. Father Dru and I had used duct tape and paper towels to mend his wing. The cranky bird was none too pleased about it but was somewhat placated by the nuggets of dog food Dub fed to him out of a white plastic dairy whip tub.

The raven was unable to fly. Cesar and Rae bent chicken wire into a small enclosure, protection for the earth bound raven from coyotes and skunks that wandered at night. A four foot section of a cottonwood branch served as its perch. The raven squawked to announce me. Dub sat in his wheelchair beside the chicken wire bird cage at the top of the ramp attached to his double wide, a blanket wrapped around him. Dub fussed over the raven, who hopped from branch to branch trying to get Little Dog to chase him.

"Good morning Dub, merry day after Christmas." I reached into the cage to retrieve the cake pan that served as water dish, dumping out the ice that remained in it. "Shall I fill it up?" I held the empty metal pan up for him to see.

Dub held a dog food nugget between the chicken wire, coaxing the raven to take it from him. "That'd be good of you Blondie."

Uh-oh, I knew what that meant. "Where's Cesar?"

"He's inside, be out shortly I expect." Dub scratched Little Dog under the chin and passed the jealous canine a dog bone. "He's been here the whole time you know, after he left your place."

"You're kidding. I'm surprised I never found out." The raven tried in vain to flap his broken wing and lift off, settling, instead for a high hop onto his perch.

"That's because you're so predictable." Cesar stood at the open door behind me, holding a red tissue paper wrapped package in his hands. "Here, I think this is yours. I found it when I cleaned up the farolitos last night." He traded the package for the empty pan.

"Oh, I must have dropped it with all the excitement Christmas Eve. Thanks, I forgot about it with all the confusion." I kneaded the soft package in my hands. "It's from Ed."

"Ain't you going to open it?" Dub wheeled his chair back, looked up at me.

I tore the tape from the back and unfolded the package. The mohair shawl I had admired at the Animal Shelter's resale shop was rolled tightly inside. My face softened immediately. I wrapped it around my shoulders. What a sweet gift.

"It is sweet, looks good on you too." Dub reached up and smoothed the fringe through his fingers.

Did I say that out loud? That's what happens when you live alone, you don't know when you're talking to yourself.

Cesar came back out the double wide's door, carrying the pan of water, and carefully set it inside the raven's enclosure.

"It does look good on you. You two must be sweet on each other." Cesar winked at Dub.

"He' just a friend, Cesar, we have coffee and talk, he's a nice guy."

"I'm sure he is." Cesar winked again at Dub, picked up a broom and began sweeping the wooden deck of the dirt and leaves the wind had blown there.

"What did you mean, I'm so predictable. Why do you say that?"

Little Dog pushed under the chicken wire and began running in circles under the Raven's tree branch. The Raven hopped around after him.

"Watch those two. The raven knows exactly which way Little Dog will go, when he will turn and when he will stop. That's why the dog will never catch the raven." Cesar stopped sweeping and stood beside Dub, watching the show.

"But, ya see, don't ya, that Raven could catch Little Dog anytime he wants, he just don't want to." Dub smiled, snapping his fingers inside the cage calling his dog over.

"You got it buddy." This time Cesar winked at me.

Was I really that predictable?

The Theme from Rocky sounded from Cesar's pocket. "Hello?" He moved away from us. I thought he'd go inside to take the call but instead walked towards me, "She's right her. I'll pass the phone over."

"It's Billy Dean." Cesar said and went back to sweeping.

"Aileen Roark? Is this Aileen Roark?" Billy Dean's voice, too loud, came from the phone.

"Yes Mr. Dean, it's me. Aileen."

"Aileen Roark?" He triple checked.

"Yes, it's Aileen Roark, Merry Christmas by the way. What's up?"

"I need you to come to Santa Fe, next week, January 3rd. We have a court date." Billy sounded serious.

"Next week? Yes I can make it, but I thought we settled everything with the School District. Why do we need to go to court now? Do they want their money back or something?"

"No, it's the hospital, St. Mary's Mother of Light, they filed suit, a claim on your settlement money to pay your son's medical bills." Billy spoke rapidly.

"What? How? Why? How did you find out?" Holy smokes, this was upsetting. I started trembling.

"I have a guy who does my leg work for me, investigates things. On contract to follow the legal ads, monitors if any of my clients' names are mentioned. Yours was. We only just caught it in time. Court date is next week. If you don't show the court can issue judgment in claimants favor automatically. We need to respond. You need to be here."

"How did they know about the settlement? Why now? It's almost a year later. Who's behind all this?" My hands were shaking so much I could barely hold the phone.

"Who's Beulah?" Billy asked.

95

The next few days were predictable as Cesar would say, coffee with Ed, rides to the library and dollar store shopping. But the worry over my court date distracted me. Even the weekly Women's gathering couldn't push the thought of living on the streets again from my mind. I had begun to enjoy the Women's fellowship at St Ursula's. It was more social than bible study. We met every Tuesday, weather permitting, to quilt, knit and drink very weak coffee. A new, younger bunch of stay at home moms joined the group, encouraged by the cemetery cleanup project and recent publicity. Their energy and ideas, along with able hands brought shared concerns and dreams for the Las Manchas neighborhood: a community garden, a gathering place for children and teens, a safer Rail-Runner Crossing, a school nearby where parental involvement was more than notification of what the state had already mandated.

New Year's Eve, Ed took us all to the Animal Shelter's Gala Fund Raiser. Appetizers and champagne, dancing to New Mexico rockabilly, country blues with a Latino bend. Rae and Alicia double dated with Cesar and Alicia's cousin. I left right after Ed did, early. He again volunteered to do night duty at the shelter. I'm told the party only got better. Truth was I had become so consumed by worry about my court date I hadn't been sleeping. Could they really take away my settlement? My home? I hadn't told anyone but Cesar what was going on.

Three days later when I rode out early to catch the Rail-Runner to Santa Fe, he was waiting by my gate to wish me well.

"Things will work out Blondie. It may take a while, but Billy did right by me, and he'll do right by you too. Look, I'm free. No more reporting in, no more restrictions, I'm my own man. Have faith." He handed me a paper bag with a ham sandwich and orange in it.

"What's this?" I asked as I peered into the bag.

"Lunch, I know your check doesn't come in until the fifth, something to tide you over."

"Thanks, you didn't have to go to so much trouble for me." I put the bag into my cloth shopping bag. I guess I didn't think about where I would eat up there, and Cesar was right. My pocket was empty and the cupboard bare.

"I was fixing them for Dub anyway. That's what I do for him you know, help him around the house, cooking, shopping. It's worked out. I get a place to stay and he has the help he needs to keep living there." Cesar walked beside me as I wheeled my bike onto the road. "I've got an application in at the VA, help with patient transport. I hope to hear on that soon."

"That's good then, good for both of you." What he didn't say was living in Dub's double wide, with its hot water, heat, cable TV and his own bedroom was a huge step up from the camper set on blocks he stayed in when he lived with me.

"How's the winged patient?" I asked. We removed the splint and duct tape from the raven's wing the day before, but the bird still hobbled around, awkwardly walking after Little Dog in the yard, refusing to fly.

"Good, bird's doing good. Still won't fly though. We put him up at night, but he hops around on the ground outside all day." Cesar stopped, waited for me to get on the bike.

"Good Luck Blondie. I'll be thinking of you." He waved me off and returned to Dub's yard.

The train to Santa Fe was crowded. I found a seat on the aisle and tried to read a discarded paper. I got off at the Rail Yard stop this time and as arranged, met Billy Dean outside the courthouse at the appointed time.

"Aileen, you are looking well." Billy shook my hand and led me by the elbow up the courthouse steps hurrying things along. "I know we haven't had a chance to review this, but we are going to ask for two things: one, full dismal of the suit, it is without merit and the hospital has no claim, which, frankly I do not think will be granted; and two, reschedule. This is only discovery, the judge tries to see if there is enough reason to keep the suit going. The judge will want a settlement, he won't want us to go to trial, we don't want that, we want a trial. Today, our position is that St. Mary's hasn't tried to negotiate a settlement. I'm counting on them sending one of their junior members alone to this session. I'm pretty sure they don't expect us to show up and think the judge will issue a summary judgment in their favor. But we are here. It will throw them. They won't be prepared to negotiate. The person they send won't have the authority to negotiate. That's when we ask for a new date, and they send someone who has the authority, preferably the hospital CEO." Billy was talking rapidly, leading me into the courthouse.

"Do you really think we can ask the CEO to show up?" Wow, Billy had big plans.

"He will if we demand it, if I can convince the judge that only the CEO has the authority to approve an agreement without trial." Billy was confident.

"Can you do that?" I asked in disbelief.

Billy didn't say anything. He opened the door to the courtroom and ushered me in, raised both eyebrows a couple of times like Groucho Marks and rolled his eyes.

The hearing was rescheduled, February 14th, Valentine's Day, my birthday.

¤ ¤ ¤

King's Day, January 6th. A special mass was scheduled, followed by fellowship in St. Ursula's common room. We had been blessed with a whole week of clear blue sky, cold mornings and colder nights. This morning, the sky were filled with huge white clouds that would gather by nightfall, snow was forecast. Cesar helped me load wood into the horno. I would bake the King's Day cakes in the round adobe oven. This afternoon, the dense fruited cakes would be dunked into coffee at the Fellowship Hall. Dub sat on his deck, binoculars to his eyes, scanning the tree line by the river for the pair of nesting eagles in winter residence there. Little Dog ran around the yard, begging the raven, who still refused to fly, to chase him.

"That should do it Blondie, let it burn down a while then we'll mop it out," he said as he propped the metal sheet in front of the half oval door with a cement block.

"Great, I'll get started on the cake batter." I handed him a fresh cup of coffee and we both paused a minute to absorb the warmth of the fire.

"Don't forget to put the baby in," he said to remind me.

A little plastic doll was baked into the cake, bringing good luck to who ever found it buried in their slice. Priscilla had given me the one used for fifty years by her family to bury in the sweet dough. I pulled it out of my pocket. "Got it right here Cesar, don't have to check up on me so much you know."

"That's what you think Blondie."

Rush hour traffic sped by on the Interstate above. It was that time of the morning, around seven thirty, the traffic backed up from Albuquerque to the section above us. Cars and trucks went from seventy five or eighty miles an hour to a standstill in just a few seconds. I had gotten so used to the screaming brakes and squealing tires when this happened I rarely looked up anymore. But something about this one sounded different. We heard the thud, scream of brakes and loud sound of bare metal hitting the pavement. Cesar and I both looked at the same time. A tractor trailer's rear wheel had come loose. Free of its axle, the huge wheel bounced and rolled down the incline from the Interstate at light speed, or at least so fast we couldn't keep it in our sight. It bounced thirty feet into the air, came down, bounced again and continued its rapid descent, headed straight for Dub.

"Dub, look out!" I screamed.

Cesar dropped the coffee cup and jumped over the fence. "Dub, Dub, watch out!"

The enormous truck tire bounced one last time and hurled itself forward.

Dub sat, stunned, unable to react.

The raven, in one heroic leap, spread its wings and flew at Dub, causing Dub's wheel chair to fall backwards, off the edge of the deck, while the tire flashed and spun and rolled right at them.

Sometime you pray really hard, try to make bargains with God, to let everything be okay, to not let something bad happen. You make promises to God to grant this one wish and vow to never ask for anything ever again. Sometimes you pray and wonder why God didn't listen. But sometimes, God does hear you.

Dub didn't die. He broke a wrist, dislocated his shoulder, but he didn't die. The tire missed him but the three foot fall off the deck was enough to break his elderly thin bones. He would have to spend a few weeks at the VA, but would eventually make it home. Cesar rode to the hospital with him in the ambulance. I borrowed Father's Mercedes and followed.

"That was way too close." Cesar said as we drove away from the VA. "That could have killed him."

"No kidding." I said as we pulled into the supermarket. "So what happens now? "

"Now? Don't know for sure. I'll stay on, but he may need more care than that, a nurse or something." Cesar looked over his shoulder realizing we were in a grocery store parking lot.

"What are we doing here?"

"King's Day cake, remember?" I bought three coffee cakes, poked a hole with my thumb in one and inserted the plastic baby. "Let's hope someone we know gets this slice."

When we got back to Las Manchas, the horno fire burned down, enough heat left to bake a small cake. I pulled the thick round cake, studded with raisins and nuts, out of the oven, broke it in two and gave half to the raven.

"King for a day, Mr. Bird, king for a day." The bold bird picked the chunk of cake up in its beak and flew unsteadily to the top of a fence post, where it feasted for an hour or more occasionally dropping a piece on the ground for Little Dog.

96

*F*ebruary 14th arrived with a cold front, down to minus two last night. I slept on the futon, still folded up into a sofa, in front of the wood stove for warmth. I think Flacita would have liked to curl up with me there but her girth prevented her from making the leap up. She coiled up on the shag throw rug just to the side of the futon. If my rest was fitful, hers was deep. She snored loudly and didn't flinch the two times I reached over to ruffle her fur. Three times during the night I got up, checked the faucet to be sure the pipes weren't frozen and loaded scrap wood to stoke the stove. The fourth time, about four in the morning, I stayed up.

The heavy draft through the door's jam told me more than the TV weather. A young meteorologist was reviewing the weather warnings and predictions for snow, which would come from the northwest and move in rapidly before stalling over the area, leaving the entire upper third of New Mexico caught in one huge blizzard. As if I didn't have enough to worry about. The sky was dark and clear now, but you could already make out the deep gray profile of a thick layer of clouds building to the west.

I made tea, oatmeal, opened a can of mandarin oranges, fishing out six of the little wedges and a spoonful of the thin syrup they were packed in to flavor the porridge. I sat at my make shift table with a blanket wrapped around my legs, dreading the icy cold shower I would need to take before I headed out the door to catch the 6:30 a.m. Rail-Runner train to Santa Fe. I considered skipping the shower, but not smelling like a campfire would definitely be an advantage, and I needed all the help I could get.

Flacita woke, waged her tail softly as she sat beside me, eating the dollar store kibble I put in the little pink dish, part of her Starter Pack from the animal shelter. Should I leave her in or out? It was so cold out and snow was predicted, plus if I wound up stranded in Santa Fe she would be outside on what could be one of the colder nights of the winter. If I left her inside I risked her soiling the rugs and chewing up anything she could reach.

I already had to scrounge up twenty eight bucks, half a month's food budget, for a well chewed library book. Ultimately, I put newspapers down in her favored dump station location and picked up everything she might chew on, placing it just out of reach. But I did want to get her out in the yard for a while before I left so, despite her objections, I made her go outside. Every time I tried to go back in, she rushed the door, so I stayed out with her, blanket wrapped about me and folding my arms tightly in front of me for warmth.

Someone in a hooded sweatshirt wearing orange socks for gloves came jogging up the road. Cesar began jogging in a twenty foot circle in front of my gate. He was wearing the camouflage hoodie I had given him when he walked out months earlier.

"You're up early Blondie." His breath was heavy, leaving clouds of ice as he exhaled from his mouth.

"Morning, Cesar, so are you. I didn't know you still ran. I seem to remember you doing three rounds a night a while back."

"Only one a night now, I try to do five miles five days a week. Early mornings, old habits. Never knew you an early riser?" He continued to jog, slowing with each circle.

"Today's my court date, pretrial hearing. I have to catch the Rail Runner and be in Santa Fe by eight thirty. I want to get there earlier so I can pull myself together first." I rubbed one foot against the other, stupid me was still just in socks.

"Oh, that's right, that's right. You're standing up with Billy Dean aren't you?"

"Yeah, the initial hearing was back in January, but Billy insisted the Hospital CEO had to be there for some reason. I don't know why, he was just so determined that he had to come to the hearing. It was rescheduled for today. I guess with the holidays and stuff this was the first available date."

"Trust in Billy, Blondie. He sometimes seems a little off but it's all an act, part of his strategy, that's why so many of the prosecutors can't stand him." Cesar paused and grabbed hold of the gate, using it as a brace while he stretched.

"I guess so. To be honest I am a little worried. They want to take away my settlement money, most of which went into this place. I don't know what I would do if I had to live on the streets again." I hung my head, called Flacita over to me. "I've got to go. I'm not looking forward to the cold shower I have to take. I still don't have hot water."

"Keep the faith Blondie." He frowned, leaned forward and changed legs, reaching in back of him to stretch out his quads. "Let me know if I can do anything okay?" He looked up at me, sweat dripping from his nose almost turning to icicles.

Flacita was trying to pull me back into the warm house.

"I could use some help. I'm worried about Flacita being inside all day. I'd leave her out but they're predicting snow and it's going to stay cold. If you could come over around lunch time or so and let her out for a while that would be great.

"You got it. Do you still stash the key on the nail under the portal?"

"Yes, it's there."

"Shame on you." He pointed at me. "Didn't I tell you not to do that?"

"Yeah but..."

"Yeah but, yeah but, never mind, try not to worry about things here. I'll keep the home fires burning."

"Oh that'd be great too there's a stack of wood outside the back door."

Cesar had already started jogging towards the back of Rae's auto shop. "It's a figure of speech Blondie, a figure of speech."

It was nearly five now. I had to get myself in gear. I decided to shower first give myself time to warm up a little before I started the icy bike ride to the commuter station.

It was FREEZING. I made it quick, didn't wash my hair even though it needed it, jumped out and ran to the main room to dry and dress in front of the wood stove. On Billy's advice I wore that same black skirt he bought when I was a person of interest in Bert's stabbing. It hung mid-calf, was fairly warm and I could pull on a pair of long men's trouser socks to cover the gap between shoes and skirt hem. I debated on shoes or boots, not fashion boots, work boots. If it snowed much I would need more than the thin flats Billy also picked out for me from the thrift store. In the end, I wore the shoes, and added the boots to the cloth Penny's bag I still carried. If needed, I could change into them. At the last minute I pulled the shawl Ed gave me around my shoulders and looked in the mirror. If only I had a little make-up, I might have looked like a real person.

I fried up two eggs, slide them each between a couple slices of white bread, added some mayo from the packets I still collected in a cottage cheese container inside the fridge door and wrapped them separately in wax paper, added the least bruised banana and a couple of lemon dollar store cookies wrapped in a reused piece of foil and filled a small plastic water bottle. Everything was packed into that tote bag of mine.

Well this is it. I looked around my place, my dwelling. How would I manage once the hospital took this all away? I started to cry thinking about the hungry lonely nights I spent sleeping on cardboard on top of concrete, behind retaining walls. My mind flashed on Sam's and MaryIsabelle's suicide. I wonder if it hurts? How hard would be to do? Flacita nuzzled my hand, looking up at me with those loving brown eyes and pulled me back from the edge.

When I opened the door a strong breeze came through, knocking the papers and magazines off the high counter where I had placed them so Flacita wouldn't use them for entertainment. I knelt down and gathered up the stack. My old composition notebook fell to the floor. When I bent over Flacita licked my face and sniffed the notebook's pages still held together by a rubber band. I don't know why, other than not wanting Flacita to chew it up, but I added it to the cloth shopping bag that rested on my arm and headed out the door.

Oh, did I mention it was my birthday?

¤ ¤ ¤

The train ride was uneventful, full but not crowded. The 6:30 a.m. was for commuters, not tourists or day trippers. All the regular bike spots were already taken at the park and ride lot. I had to chain it to a fence. I wondered what the later riders did with their bikes. When we pulled into the Santa Fe Rail-yard Station it was just starting to snow large wet flakes.

I clambered down the steps, walked to the north end of the station, up Guadalupe Street and started the twenty minute walk to Billy Dean's office.

Once upon a time this had been a residential area for people of modest means. Fifty years ago, Billy Dean's mom made the down payment on the little adobe, brushing off the objections of her family. How could she raise an eight year old here alone, without her extended family? But Genoviva Castillo Dean had an independent streak. She found the thick walled six room casita the perfect spot. From here she could walk to her teaching job at the nearby elementary (she would later become principal), the library, grocer and post office. What more did you need? The young Billy would thrive in this environment. No longer bullied and teased by his cousins and relieved of the Castillo family legacy his teachers' no longer had anyone to compare him to. This suited Billy just fine. By the time he was a teenager he had exceeded any of his northern cousins in academic awards.

Now, the front two rooms of the house served as his law office. It was a three block walk to either the courthouse or the jail, just a five block walk to the federal building. All around him, old adobe and pen-tile houses had been tastefully updated. Where he once played *Go*, celebrated first communions and mourned the dead, pastel mud colored buildings now housed high end boutiques, art association offices and galleries. But Billy held out. The rough cracked brown stucco and narrow single car garage out back begged to be historically preserved. As long as the property was still held in the family, Billy was free to ignore the repeated complaints of any new entrepreneurs that the building was an eyesore.

I stepped on Billy's front walk at a minute to eight, half an hour early. Billy was nowhere to be found. A very thin layer of snow dusted the walls and old two track driveway alongside the modest building. I headed around back, peered in the window, hands cupped. The place was piled high with boxes of cosmetics sold door to door by commission, Cheery Day Cosmetics, with a heart shaped red cherry on the side of each box.

Oh, so this is where Yolinda organized her stuff.

Two rusted corrugated panels, hammered to pine posts, jutted at right angles a few feet away, protecting a utility door on the side of the house. A third sheet served as a roof. The wind picked up. Thick wet flakes that turned to water on contact pelted the ground. I maneuvered under the metal enclosure. The only thing that looks and smells worse than an old dog is an old wet dog. I didn't want to become one. I sat on a rusted wire milk crate, leaning into the wall, away from the thick snow. Before I knew it I was fast asleep.

¤ ¤ ¤

"Mrs. Roark? Aileen, Aileen? Wake up darlin', Aileen?" Billy Dean shook me gently.

"Sorry, I...sorry. I was worried about getting wet." I was barely coherent.

"You didn't spend the night here did you?" His hand was still on my shoulder as he peered down at me.

"No. Just a bad night's sleep last night .What time is it? Is it late?"

"No. It's 8:30 a.m., right on time. Come inside and warm up. I'll make coffee." Billy took the bag from my arm and grabbed my bent elbow to left me up from the low crate. I struggled to stand, distressed by how stuff my legs had gotten by such a short time out in the elements.

"How did you know I was here?"

He put his finger beside his nose, "Great detective work."

"What?"

"Your foot prints dear, in the snow. See?" He pointed to them, laughing softly. He was rubbing my hands between his, feeling how cold they were.

We went inside the small house and Billy reached for the thermostat on the wall, turning it up sharply. "It's going to be a cold one I'm afraid." He passed through the low cove opening into the kitchen area, filled a carafe for coffee.

I stood in the front room and looked around. It was cluttered, but not messy. A couple of old retablos on the wall, St Thomas Moore, Patron Saint of Attorneys; San Martin de Porres, with a strand of rosary beads draped around his middle and a frosted pillar candle burned softly on a ledge.

"Nice place you got here."

"It was my mothers, lived here since I was eight. Had lots of offers on it, but I'm kind of attached to the place."

"Do you live here?"

"No, no, Yolinda and I have a place in the Hills, it's to the east of town it's...."

"I know where it is." I was a little too sharp in this response. It was where I lived when I still had a family and a home.

Startled, his tone softened, "Yes, of course, sorry I forgot." He grabbed three mugs from the cupboard.

"Cream? Sugar? "

"Cream would be nice." I was still standing in the middle of the front room, unsure what to do.

"The little girls' room is down the hall to the right, why don't you freshen up while the coffee brews." Billy opened the fridge and removed a pint carton of half and half.

I walked down the hall and pushed the door. Cheery Day boxes and diminutive pink and white bags were stacked floor to ceiling in the bathtub. I redid the braid in my hair. The wet snow turned it into dirty red-gray spirals which fought to escape the rubber-band I fastened around the end. Give up, Aileen. You can't do anything about it now. I washed my hands, smoothed the top of my head and left.

Yolinda was in the kitchen with Billy Dean when I came out. She was on her cell phone, arranging pick up and deliveries of the cosmetics she sold. Billy filled three cups of coffee, poured cream in two, handed one to me and left one on the counter in front of Yolinda.

"Let's sit a while and discuss what you should expect." Billy guided me back to the front room. A round glass table and four chairs in one corner served as his conference table.

He pulled keys from his pocket and used them to unlock a hall closet door. Odd. You don't usually put a solid core door and deadbolt on a closet. Once the door was opened I could see why. The compact space was filled with a huge filing cabinet and shelves where file boxes where neatly arranged alphabetically. The organization was in sharp contrast to the rest of the office. I recalled Cesar's comment about Billy putting on an act.

Billy pulled a file box folder and papers clearly in a space they were meant to be from a shelf, walked over to the table and set it down.

"This is a pre-trail hearing. A lot of times the judge directs both parties to negotiate an agreement rather than go to trial."

"Okay, we negotiate." I sipped the hot coffee.

"No, we don't want that. As I told you in January, we want a trial." Billy pulled several documents from the file box and clipped them together.

"Why?"

"We want this case to be heard by a jury. We want Sigfredo Jacquez there, in the courtroom, in front of the jury."

"Who's he again?"

"St. Mary's CEO, do you know what that is?" Billy was so used to dealing with people with limited schooling he forgot I had once been a teacher.

"Yes I do. Does he have to be there?"

"Probably not, but I convinced the judge that he does. We want him there."

"Why, what for?"

Billy hesitated, his face softened and he smiled slightly, scanning my face, turning his head side to side. "Look, no offense darling, the past couple of years have not been good to you and it shows. We want a jury to see you as a very sympathetic figure. A woman who has lost her sons and husband, abandoned, homeless and now the CEO in the three piece suit with a six figure income is coming after you. We want this to go to a jury; either that or they drop the case and pay my legal fees."

I hung my head and pulled the soft mohair of the shawl tightly around me. "I didn't realize I looked that bad. I tried to clean up, took a shower, a cold one, but I took one. I haven't been sleeping well."

Billy picked up his mug, drinking half, turned towards the kitchen. "Yolinda, do you have a minute?"

Yolinda came in, setting down a large box of cosmetics on the chair beside me.

"Sorry Aileen I could have said hello. I've been busy with Valentine's Day. I have so many orders to get out." Yolinda extended her hand to me.

"Can you spare five minutes with Aileen here?" Billy sipped his coffee.

"Sure honey what do you need?" Aileen looked at me then back at Billy.

"I'm not sure. You ladies figure it out." Billy continued to sip his coffee and flip through the stack of papers he had pulled from the file box.

I looked up again at Yolinda, who looked back at me, bewildered.

"What do you mean Billy love?" she said.

"You know what I mean." Billy raised his hand, fingers spread, moved it in circles over his face. "You know, the face, the things you do, lipstick maybe."

"Oh! I know Aileen! Let's start with a moisturizing cleanser." Aileen went to the back room and brought back a pink and blue case.

"No. Not cleanser, her face is clean for god's sake, you know, the other stuff."

"Billy we always start with a moisturizing cleanser." Yolinda said and corrected her spouse.

"Well make it quick. We've got to head over in twenty minutes."

"But what about the hearing, shouldn't I know more?" I relaxed my grip on the shawl.

"I can tell you what you need to know on the walk over. But basically don't say anything. Let me do the talking. They may say or do things that offend you or try to goad you about something. Just let it roll off your back. Look sad. Do that, act sad."

"That's not much of an act." I mumbled eyes downcast.

Yolinda opened her sample case and began using a pre-moistened towelette to gently wipe the side of my face.

"How does that feel?" Her tone was calm and soft.

"Good, I can't remember the last time I used something like this." This was true.

Yolinda made quick work of my mini-makeover, a light tinted moisturizer, a touch of eye-cream "This will help with the dark circles and puffiness." She used the tips of her fingers to dot on the thick fragrant paste.

When Yolanda began sharpening a steel blue eye pencil Billy stopped her. "Don't make her look too good."

"Too late for that Billy, see what a difference a little Cheery Day can make?" Yolinda smiled broadly.

Yolinda gave me a hand mirror, opened a small sample blister pack of lipstick and dipped her pinkie finger in. She held my chin in her hand and with two swipes I had on the first lipstick I'd worn in over two years.

"I'll call you at lunchtime sweetheart. Can you squeeze me in between your deliveries?"

"I can always squeeze you Billy my love" Yolinda giggled, reached over and kneaded Billy's pot belly. "Give my special love to Sigfredo for me won't you?"

"Oh absolutely dearest you know I will. Time to go Aileen. Finish your coffee and let's head out."

It was snowing steadily now. The streets and sidewalks were still clear, but snow gathered on the bare ground and canvas overhangs. I pulled on my jacket, picked up my bag and followed Billy, cardboard file folder wrapped inside a white plastic garbage bag under his arm. We headed east, towards the old post office.

"Was Yolinda talking about Sigfredo Jacquez, the guy you want at the hearing?"

"Yes, yes she was." Billy walked confidently up the side walk.

"Do they know each other?"

"He's her ex."

"What?"

"Her ex, her first husband."

"Isn't that a problem?"

"Not if we work it. It's an advantage."

"How so?"

"You'll see. Keep the faith."

"Everyone keeps telling me that."

"Well it's true. What is it you worry most about Aileen?"

"That I'll lose my home and end up on the streets again. I don't think I'd survive this time."

Billy stopped, put his arm around my shoulder, "I promise you, I intend to do everything in my power to keep that from happening. But, you have to trust me."

I nodded, didn't say anything. We started up the street again.

"How did you and Yolinda meet?"

"High school sweethearts, broke up when I went to college. Sigfredo was a classmate of ours. When I was away he swept Yolinda off her feet. She was a real beauty, still is. In those days Siggy was different, a deceit fellow. That was before the money and power got hold of him."

"How did you and Yolinda get back together?"

"Long story, I was her divorce layer. Mr. CEO decided he needed a trophy wife to go with his six figure income." We were approaching the steps to the courthouse door. "He doesn't realize it, but I'm the one who got the solid gold trophy, his is made of plastic." Billy grinned madly, obviously deeply in love with his wife.

"You're a lucky man."

"Yes I am." Billy held the door for me.

A security guard sat at the small table by the door flirting with a receptionist. He looked up long enough to wave us through. We walked up the steps at the far end of the hall to a small courtroom on the second floor.

Two lawyers, one of whom I met at the December hearing, were already milling outside the door.

"Well Evie, Mr. Gallagher, happy Valentine's Day to you both." Billy extended his hand to them. Only John Gallagher shook it.

"What's the matter Evie? Got an anti-social disease?" Billy looked directly at Evelyn Lucero.

"Not today, Billy. I don't even know why we're here; this should have been taken care of back in January."

"We're here because your man didn't bother to attend the first hearing. Is he going to make it today?" Billy peered around; no one else was in the hall.

Evelyn Lucero had her cell phone out "He just got dropped off and is waiting for the elevator. He'll be up here in thirty seconds."

Billy turned around and took three steps away from them, dragging me with him and pulled out his cell phone, pushing speed dial.

"I need you to call me in exactly twenty seconds, okay? Bye. Love you too." Billy pulled me by the elbow back towards the courtroom door.

"Don't pay any attention to Evie, she's my cousin."

"Your cousin?" John Gallagher overheard.

"Don't you see the family resemblance?" Billy stood in a mock profile, lifting his chin skyward.

John Gallagher looked from Billy to Evelyn, who was on her cell phone making a hair appointment. The elevator doors opened. Out walked Sigfredo Jacquez in a dark blue three piece suit, with a diamond and turquoise bolo tie on, cashmere overcoat draped over one arm. He walked towards us as Billy Dean's phone rang. Instead of the familiar *Let Me Call You Sweetheart* ring tone the voices of two people obviously engaged in a sex act sounded. One, a woman, had a distinct French accent while the man's deep guttural moans sounded suspiciously like Sigfredo Jacquez.

Sigfredo charged Billy.

"How dare you! How dare you!" he shouted, shoving Billy into the wall. John Gallagher jumped forward and grabbed Sigfredo around the waist pulling him away and guiding him back down the hall, picking up the discarded coat on the way.

Billy quickly answered the phone, stopping the sound of the recorded moans "Thanks, that was perfect, tell you about it later. Love you too." He spoke quickly into the phone and just as quickly snapped it back in his pocket.

Evelyn pulled her phone away from her ear. "You've crossed the line Billy. You've gone too far this time"

"You have no idea how far I'm prepared to go Evie. Say Hi to Aunt Estella for me."

97

Billy pushed past her and pulled me by the arm into the empty courtroom and up to a long table towards the front of the room.

"Sit, make yourself comfortable. This could be a long day." He pulled out a chair.

"What was that about?" I asked, nervous, it was not easy to keep the faith.

Billy laughed. "Remember I told you Jacquez was Yolinda's ex?"

"Yes." I unzipped my sweatshirt and pulled the red shawl from my shoulders, carefully folded it up and placed it inside the cloth bag.

"Siggy was having an affair with their grandkids' Montessori teacher. The two were, let's say, doing a little experiential learning, Sig butt dialed, literally, Yolinda's cell and left what you just heard as voice mail." Billy busied himself with his own down jacket.

I was shocked; maybe he had crossed the line.

"There's more. Want to hear it?" He offered his phone.

"No." I had to call him on it. "Are you sure that was the right thing to do Mr. Dean?

"Billy, call me Billy. Listen, he comes in here all suave, thinks nobody can touch him. I needed to do something to shake him up a bit. We want him to come off as the scum bag he is. Anything we can do to unnerve him is good."

I looked at the floor, exhaling deeply.

"Trust me Aileen, have a little faith."

Billy began to shuffle some papers on the desk in front of him, purposeful disarray. The St. Mary's Light of Mercy team came in, only John Gallagher looked at us, giving Billy the evil eye.

The Judge entered the room from a door to the side. Billy guided me to my feet. The St. Mary's group stood up too. A court reporter entered, took a seat at a small table to the left of the Judge.

"Please be seated. I hope we can keep the formalities to minimum today and try to come to a decision regarding this case without too much stalling." The judge was the same one from the December hearing.

Everyone sat down except John Gallagher, who cleared his throat lightly.

"Yes? Mr...." The judge flipped through the papers in front of him. The court reported called up to him quietly.

"Gallagher, John Gallagher representing St. Mary's Light of Mercy Medical Center."

"Yes Mr. Gallagher? Do you have something to say before we begin?" Judge Sandoval picked up a pair of reading glasses and propped them on his nose.

"Judge only moments ago it was brought to my attention that Mr. Dean, the respondent's attorney, is married to St. Mary's CEO Sigfredo Jacquez's first wife and Mr. Dean is first cousin to Ms. Lucero, part of claimants legal team. Given this knowledge I don't think we can proceed."

"Are you saying your client wishes to drop the suit?" The judge peered over his glasses at John Gallagher.

"No. No, it's just that given the fact the respondent's attorney is related to two of the principals on my client's side I don't see how we can proceed today."

"Sit down Mr. Gallagher. You can be forgiven in that you are new to Northern New Mexico. If we suspend our hearings and trials because someone is related to someone else we wouldn't have a judicial system here in New Mexico. It is my expectation that everyone here will behave in a professional manner regardless. IS that clear to you all?"

Billy Dean jumped up. "Yes your honor, absolutely." He gave a mischievous glance towards his opponents table.

"Ms. Lucero? Mr. Gallagher?"

They looked down tentatively. "Yes your honor." They reluctantly committed.

The hearing commenced.

It was almost ten o'clock and snowing heavily. Huge white globs of the stuff were melting then freezing on the high windows. To be honest, I really wasn't paying as much attention as I probably should have. I kept thinking about what would become of me when I lost, as I thought we were sure too given Billy's prank with Sigfredo Jacquez in the hall. I was vaguely aware the St Mary's legal team was bringing forth documents and walking them up to the Judge who handed them to the clerk, who walked them over to Billy who took them back up to the Judge. It seemed like lot of passing around of pieces of paper. I surmised they were copies of all the medical bills, judgments and mediation, requests for payment, things the St. Mary's team felt would make their case open and shut. Billy didn't seem to say much, every once in a while he would ask a question about a certain paper, make a note on his pad, then return the paper to the judge. This went on for a good ninety minutes.

"Mr. Dean, do you have discovery documents you wish to share?" The judge turned to Billy.

"A few your honor, a few. But most of my evidence will come from questioning of Mr. Jacquez."

"Is it your intent to call Mr. Jacquez to testify?" The judge spoke to Billy directly.

"Is that really necessary? I don't see what I can say that will be relevant to this case." Mr. Jacquez who had spent most of this time sitting, leg crossed, looking annoyed, spoke up.

Evelyn Lucero stood up, taking over for him.

"Your honor Mr. Dean doesn't have a case, he is fishing. He has no defense against the recovery of the debt incurred by Mrs. Roark. And the debt is substantial as you can see from the documents we have provided."

"I'm not the one unable to build a case Ms. Lucero; the only way you've won most of your cases was ex parte." The two glared at each other.

"You two approach the bench. Mr. Gallagher you too."

All three lawyers walked up to the front of the room where the judge sat at the raised podium, leaving Siggy and myself still seated at counsels' tables. Even though we were several feet away it was easy to overhear them.

"I've already warned you about this. You will conduct yourselves in a professional manner in here or I will find you all in contempt. Am I clear on that point?"

"Yes Judge. I am doing the best I can to represent my client. Ms. Lucero is the one objecting to my calling Mr. Jacquez to testify. Ms. Lucero had hoped that my client would not show up today. She intended to win this settlement exparte, in her favor, she is surprised that we aren't rolling over and submitting. You know as well as I do that any negotiation made here today would have to be approved by St. Mary's CEO and or Board. Without requiring Mr. Jacquez's presence all the work we accomplish today could potentially be for naught."

"Judge, Mr. Dean is trying to use courtroom time as part of a personal vendetta against his wife's ex, that's why he insisted he be here. Mr. Jacquez is a very busy man with major responsibilities to a multi-million dollar non-profit medical group. His time is valuable. Mr. Dean's client on the other hand can easily attend these proceedings, she's unemployed with no visible vocation, how she supports herself god knows, she...."

Billy interrupted her before she could say anymore, "If you know she has no money why are you suing her for half a million?"

"Enough, Mr. Dean. I am in agreement with you. Mr. Jacquez as representative of the Medical Center may have testimony that is relevant to this situation. However I am going to allow Ms. Lucero and Mr. Gallagher five minutes to convince me otherwise."

"I really don't want to listen to this judge." Billy's candor surprised me given the scolding he'd just gotten.

"Then you may return to your seat Mr. Dean."

Billy turned around and started walking back to our table. When he was four steps away, he turned ever so slightly in Siggy's direction and flipped over the lapel of his sport coat revealing one of those campaign style buttons that can flicker in two positions as it moves. But this one was obscene. It had a can- can girl sans panties. When you moved the button she gave a little kick and, well, you know what showed. Billy had replaced the smiling face of the dancer with a head shot of Jacquez taken from the Medical Center's web page. As he covertly flicked the button two or three times sending the tiny dancer's legs high into the air, he whispered 'Ooh La La!' to Sigfredo.

"You son of a bitch." Sigfredo jumped up and lunged for Billy Dean. A side punch caught Billy under the chin and he fell back, making an exaggerated fall, pushing the table and chairs into me.

I immediately dropped to the floor and hovered over Billy before Sigfredo could take another swing. The court reporter ran into the hall yelling for security and John Gallagher once again grabbed his client by the waist and pulled him away.

As I knelt on the floor beside him, Billy reached over pretending to use me as a brace to help himself up, and shoved the can-can dancer button into my skirt pocket. By the time the security guard reached the doorway both Billy and Sigfredo had composed themselves.

"Mr. Gallagher, you need to control your client. We will not have this in my courtroom."

"He goaded me Judge. He, well I'll show you what he has." Sigfredo broke free of John Gallagher's grasp and pulled Billy by the lapel towards the judge's bench, folding back the lapel on his jacket.

An I (heart) Cheery Day button was now pinned there.

"A Cheery Day button? You took a swing at him over a Cheery Day button?"

"Check his pockets, he switched them. I don't have to put up with this." Siggy grabbed at Billy Dean's sport coat forcefully trying to rip at the pockets. Billy stood still, let himself be manhandled without resistance, and raised his arms in mock surrender.

"Mr. Dean what is this about?"

"Judge I am not sure, but he's welcome to search me if you think it will help him to behave himself."

"Let go of Mr. Dean, Mr. Jacquez. If a search needs to be conducted I can see to that." The judge's words were angry.

"Judge, he had a button. It was offensive. He put it in his pocket or dropped it or something I'm sure of it." Sigfredo pointed at Billy, and then scurried over to the tables moving chairs around searching for the pornographic image.

"Mr. Dean, do you know what Mr. Jacquez is referring to?"

"I'm not sure. I do have a button," Billy reached under his lapel and removed the Cheery Day button before handing it to the Judge. "If Mr. Jacquez is offended by the button then I will by all means remove it."

"You do not have another button, either in your pocket, on your person or which you dropped on the floor."

"No Judge I do not have another button either on my person or dropped on the floor. If you think it will help the situation I offer up my coat for your examination." Billy removed his coat and began to hand it up to the judge.

Judge Sandoval nodded towards the security guard who took the jacket from him and checked the pockets, patting down the entire jacket before shaking his head no to the judge.

"His pockets then, his pants pockets..." Sigfredo stood up, smoothed his shirt and straightened his tie.

Billy turned out his pockets before the judge could speak.

"That won't be necessary. Everyone take your seat. If you could remain with us for a few minutes Earl, I want to straighten this out."

"Mr. Dean please comes up here." The judge pulled out a fresh page from the yellow pad and began to write.

Billy put on his jacket, straightening the lapels and approached the judge.

I could barely hear Judge Sandoval admonishments. "Mr. Dean there will be no more shenanigans. Do you understand me? This is not going to happen again. If it does I will not only rule in favor of the claimant without further discussion but I will recommend censure to the New Mexico Bar. Are you absolutely certain you understand me?"

"Yes Judge, I do. I apologize to the court for anything that has happened that I may have contributed to."

Judge Sandoval returned the Cheery Day button, tossed it up in the air, Billy caught it in one hand and deposited it in his pocket. He walked quickly back to our table, took his seat and winked at me.

97

Judge Sandoval ordered a two hour recess. That would include lunch. If anyone thought it was to prepare for the afternoon sessions they were mistaken. It was Valentine's Day after all. Anyone from the court who was not going out to lunch with their sweetie was otherwise engaged in last minute flower, card and chocolate shopping lest they go home empty handed.

With apologies, Billy Dean handed me a twenty dollar bill and told me he was meeting his wife, Yolinda, for lunch at La Fonda where they went every year for Valentine's Day since that first real date many years before at the hotel bar. I believe Bill Hearne was performing then and still does now.

"That's okay Mr. Dean, I brought something." I tried to hand it back to him.

"Billy, it's Billy and really, treat yourself. Actually things are going well" Why did he keep winking at me?

It was snowing pretty steadily now. What had started as fits and spits, had settled into a typical New Mexico spring storm. By 1:30 p.m. schools would start dismissing leaving uneaten cupcakes decorated with candy conversation hearts to grow stale in the classroom; by two o'clock government offices would send all out of town employees home and by three almost everyone else would join them. By four thirty the road between Albuquerque and Santa Fe would be icy and snow packed and NMDOT would put employees on "Standby" to keep roads plowed and sanded. After nightfall they would probably close I-25 and I 40, so if you weren't where you needed to be by then, expect not to make it home tonight, if you had one.

If you were homeless it was a worst case scenario. The typical places of refuge would be locked up tight. Community centers, libraries, government buildings where you could at least use the restroom and hide in the stairwell for a brief respite from the cold would be dark and tightly locked. The Presbyterians might consent to opening their fellowship hall once notified by the authorities there were no more beds at the shelter. If the Governor declared a state of emergency the National Guard and Red Cross might team up to feed and house the stranded. About midnight the Santa Fe Police Department would do a general round up of anyone still on the streets. Those unlucky enough to be part of this crowd would find themselves deposited at the hospital emergency room waiting area where the medical staff was none too pleased to be babysitting a bunch of homeless souls, some of whom would try to sneak into patients rooms or behind nurses stations to get their hands on any medications left unattended.

I watched Billy Dean walk away and the St. Mary's Light of Mercy legal team scurry off to wherever they went; I sat on the wooden steps of the second landing and pulled a fried egg sandwich from my bag. Before I had pulled back the wax paper Earl, the stern security guard, walked up the three or four steps towards where I sat. Here we go again, I was about to be told once more to move on.

"Sorry mam, no food or drink in these areas."

I had seen him when I came in this morning, right inside the front entrance not far from where I now sat. He'd been munching a breakfast burrito the receptionist brought him, while she indulged in a Chocolate Mint Croissant and cinnamon tea. A few years ago, in my 'before homeless' period, I would have brought that up and challenged him. But the time spent on the streets had served to reinforce the concept of *US* and *THEM*. I was *THEM*. I re-wrapped my sandwich and placed it back in my bag.

"Okay if I change into my boots here? I don't want to ruin my shoes in the snow." I gave him my best sad puppy look, but at my age it was more of an old sad dog, huge difference.

"If it won't take too long." Earl looked low under his cap, arms folded in front of him.

I slipped out of my shoes and loosened the ties on the brown work-boots that served as my all weather wear. When you are buying your clothes at three dollars a bagful you take what you can get. I wished I had thought to bring an extra pair of socks, the boots would have fit better and my feet stayed warmer, but oh well.

Under Earl's watchful eye, like I might have something hidden in my shoes, I pulled on the boots, laced them up and with one single motion placed the shoes in my bag, zipped up my hoodie and wrapped the shawl around my neck like a scarf. I had this bag lady look down. There was no mistaking me for anything else.

The snow was really starting to come down. Visibility was no more than thirty or forty feet. Without a real plan in mind I started walking west towards the cemetery. I trudged through the snow looking up only when I came to an alley or dumpster where I knew my former companions might seek shelter. I few were there, but most had already started to make their way to the missions or soup kitchens in hopes of a dry spot for the night. Almost all the homeless teens had been placed in a shelter by now, the dedicated staff of the Street School started making phone calls around ten thirty to find beds for the kids and their dogs. Those teens that were left would be taken in by shelter staff and their families, sleeping in heated garages on air mattresses with their canines (and a few cats), watching videos and eating boxed macaroni and cheese that only made them a little reluctant to go back to the streets.

When I came upon a street person, many of whom I knew, I would throw them a little peace sign, akin of sideways "V" and say "Peace brother" or "Stay warm friend." Most looked back at me in surprised disbelief that someone had spoken to them. Either they didn't recognize me or had forgotten all about me. Unused to being greeted by anything but rude condemnations (get a job- sober up- take a bath) they turned away as quickly as the gentile folk did when approached by a street person, trying to will away contact.

I stopped at the corner of Paseo and Catron Road. Burger Stop was just across the street. Once a Drive–In with car hops, the now unused parking sheds were a favored location to get out of the weather. The upscale Chicago Style Diner which had taken over a former car repair garage as part of the revitalization of Santa Fe had put up a six foot chain link fence topped by barbed wire around the parking lot lest they be invaded by the true local clientele.

That's where I found Lenny, dread locks covered by a bright alpaca beret. He was kind of sandwiched between the bare branches of a Chinese Elm tree and the fence, half covered by the old car canopy; an overflowing shopping cart wedged nearby. Snow was starting to build up around his encampment. He was squatting there rolling a cigarette, or trying to since the snow kept getting the papers wet.

"Lenny, Lenny, hey remember me?" I called to him.

He turned half sideways, tilting his head and squinting without standing up.

"Who is that calling my name? How do you know me sister?" He spoke with that lilting Jamaican accent I was sure was fake. He finally succeeded in getting his cigarette rolled. Now he just had to get it lit.

"It's Aileen. You remember me? Teacher Lady?" I approached him hopeful that I had at least one friend left.

He squinted again, inhaling deeply from the burning cigarette in his mouth. Wait, I don't think that's tobacco.

He stood up quickly. "Aileen, ah, yes, yes, yes, teacher lady Aileen. How do you carry yourself sister?" He removed the joint from his lips and offered it to me, the polite thing to do.

I smiled and shook my head from side to side twice. "I'm well sir and you?"

"Living in paradise sister," he laughed, "living in paradise." He inhaled again, the ash glowing bright through the snowfall.

I pulled the two sandwiches from my bag and offered him one. "Hungry?"

He took it, unwrapped and started to eat, looking longingly at the one I now held. "Where do you keep yourself?" he asked.

"Albuquerque, or close to it. I've got a place right off the Interstate, Las Manchas. I have a little space to keep a garden, some apples, you know."

Cars were starting to slip and slide down the slick street, only a few feet from where we were holding up.

He finished the sandwich. I gave him the other one. "Here take it. I'm not really that hungry."

"Taste like the ones that nun makes, the Egg Lady."

"Yeah, that's how I got the idea. She doesn't do that anymore. The Archdiocese made her stop, people were complaining."

He nodded, placing the second sandwich inside a pocket of his coat which was starting to smell like an old wet blanket as the snow soaked into it.

"What brings you back to this Holy City Teacher Aileen? Come to visit old friends?" Lenny was high, wavering from side to side, oblivious to the snow swirling around him.

"I had to go to court. I got a little money from the school that fired me. That's how I got my place in Las Manchas. The Hospital is trying to take it away, they say I owe for my son's medical bills."

"The one in a coma? Did he ever wake up?" The joint had gone out but he was trying to relight it, not an easy task in the blowing snow. He squatted down beside his shopping cart and pulled the green plastic sheeting over his head as a shield from the snow and wind.

"No, no he didn't. He died." I was overcome with grief, hit in the gut, like it just happened. "I'm going to visit his grave now. He and his brother and dad are buried over there." I extended my chin outwards towards the cemetery less than a block away, and stuffed my hands up my sleeves to keep them warm.

Lenny stood up again. Even though he was totally wasted he felt my grief. "God speed your journey sister, take my prayers with you." He reached out and kneaded my forearm, unsure if he should come closer.

"Thanks." I took his hand and we did the bro shake, hand, wrist then arm, that passes for a hug in some circles. "Stay warm Lenny." We touched finger tips as I backed away a few feet and turned towards the cemetery.

Lenny's head bobbed, listening to music only he heard. He squatted down again, pulling the green plastic almost all the way over himself like a tent, propped up on one side by the shopping cart and on the other by the branches of the elm tree.

98

I pulled the shawl up over my head. The snow was falling so hard it was impossible to see. Footprints filled instantly with the falling snow leaving only a ghostly outline of where I had walked. I crossed the street against the light; a few cars beeped at me, and entered the cemetery through a foot gate. Wood smoke from Piñon burning in hundreds of fireplaces hung in the air; I could have used some of their warmth.

I walked up hill passing the rows of pink and yellow plastic flowers pressed into the dirt beside headstones. I went to Sean and Sam's grave first. I still had a little money then so although not side by side at least you could see each headstone from the other. I was relieved the stones were still there and had not been repossessed. They were simple: Sean- Born- Died, much loved son, brother and friend; Sam- Born. Died. Rest in Peace.

There were so many things I thought I wanted to tell them, but when I got there I realized none of that mattered. I knelt down, brushed the snow from their stones and told them how much I loved them and missed them, Sam especially. I thought I might curse at him and yell and make a scene when I was there, you know like you see in the movies: 'How could you do this, how could you leave me alone to clean up your mess?' I imagined myself screaming into the earth. Now that I was here all I felt was sorrow and loneliness. "Loved you Sam, hope you knew that," I whispered.

Stevie's grave was a little harder to find as the snow deepened. It was only a few yards away from the potter's field where five or six souls might occupy a site meant for one. It was the best I could do for him. A metal plaque, like a garden marker, stood up from the ground. There were few plastic flowers here; once in a while a small headstone rose up from the earth with the least one could write. Some of them bore only one name and a year: Sanchez-1998; Garnier-2002, leaving you to wonder who was buried there, man, woman, young or old.

I found Stevie's grave, brushed the snow away to make sure I was in the right place and knelt down. The snow was five inches deep and still falling.

"Hey son," I said to him. "Sorry about your dog, he got adopted by someone. I think it's a good thing. I just couldn't take care of him anymore. I got a new dog though, a little collie. She's not too little, she's kind of fat. She's a sweetie though, you'd like her."

"I have a garden now too. I wish you were here to help me. Remember how I used your El Camino to get a load of manure? I thought you'd never forgive me."

"Sorry it's taken so long to visit. I moved to Albuquerque. I don't come up much."

I was running out of things to say but I wasn't ready to leave. Still on my knees, I bent forward, my head almost touching the snow, as if touching the earth would let me touch Stevie one more time. I looked like the round base of a snow man. I'm not sure how long I stayed like that. I kept flashing on my first nights on the streets, how I would come here when I had nowhere else to go. Things hadn't changed all that much.

Someone was standing in back of me.

"You can't stay here dear lady."

Wizard! Where had he come from? I sat up. Wizard was to the side of me. His lips were blue like a kid eating a blue snow-cone. Ice had started to build up on his beard and eyebrows.

"Wizard, how did you know to find me?"

His eyes were still brilliant blue and sparkled with the snow. "You can't stay here dear lady. You can't dwell here. Mind body or spirit you can't dwell here." He extended his arms down to help me up. His hands were unbelievably cold.

"You're freezing." I said to him and bent down to pick up my bag.

"This is no place for a dwelling." He spoke softly, walking smoothly and lightly, guiding me to the foot gate. My own plodding steps were labored and slow in what had become knee deep snow.

"I have some gloves, you can have them." I reached into my bag to retrieve the dollar store gray stripe garden gloves I had brought along but been too embarrassed to wear even in front of strangers.

He shook his head, eyes twinkling. "You can't stay here good lady, you have to move on. Your sons are at rest and your husband at peace. Build no dwelling here, mind body or spirit. This is no place for the living to dwell." He pushed me ever so gently out the graveyard gate.

The fringe of his buckskin jacket was wet, frozen and hung like icicles from his sleeve. It looked like ice was hanging from his chin too, how could he stand the cold like that? He bent down and retrieved the same old dirty red canvas pack he always carried from just inside the graveyard fence, slung it over one shoulder and headed back uphill between the grave markers toward the Potter's field, disappearing into the swirling snow.

99

I could hear the bell from St. Francis Cathedral toll one o'clock. I needed to get back to the courthouse and clean up. If there was time I'd buy a coffee at the storefront WI-FI coffee house across from the post office but there wasn't. Fewer and fewer cars slid down the road as offices closed and workers made their way home. It was easy to cross the streets. I walked up the courthouse steps just as Billy Dean came around the corner. He was smiling brightly.

"And how was your lunch? Did you visit an old favorite or find something new?" He asked.

"Um, I used the time to visit some people I used to know." It wasn't exactly a lie.

"Oh? And I hope all is well with them." He seemed surprised.

"Yeah, as well as can be expected." I pulled the shawl from my shoulders and shook off the snow that clung to it. "I better see if I can clean up a bit. My hair got a little messed in the snow."

"Well don't be late. The judge texted me at lunch he wants to wrap this up quickly and close the courts. I think we can turn this to our favor." He held the door open for me.

I scurried past Earl who was tossing plastic cups full of kitty litter on the icy walkway. I went up the steps to the second floor ladies room. The courthouse was at least sixty years old, the floors and door a heavy varnished wood. Although restroom stalls had been refurbished and fixtures replaced, everything else about the place seemed to be caught in a different century. The old chandelier light fixtures had been fitted with the new every efficient bulbs which gave only minimal light. There was little natural light coming in today from the high narrow windows that faced south towards the street. I fished a black comb out of my bag. I remembered getting it in a shelter gift bag given out two years ago. I stood in front of the mirrors, trying to smooth and re-braid my hair. I must have been crying. The makeup that Billy Dean's wife Yolinda had so carefully applied streamed in ribbons down my cheeks.

I got a paper towel and wet it with soapy water and carefully washed my face doing my best to preserve as much of the makeup as possible. There was no need to worry about anything else. The winter weather had left my already street ruddy complexion with bright red checks and forehead.

Someone in one of the three stalls flushed and clicked the door open. It was Evelyn Lucero, impeccably suited, flawless makeup and amazing stiletto heels. She barely glanced at me, leaned towards the mirror and pulled a very thin lipstick from a small leather bag. I couldn't help but do the math in my head, those shoes and that purse cost more than the thousand bucks they garnished from my check each month. It made me think about how much of the money they billed for Stevie's care actually went to the staff that cared for him. As I looked at her I realized where I had seen her before. She was the attorney I consulted about Stevie's guardianship and move to the Basic Care Unit. If she remembered me she didn't let on. Things began to click, she knew so much about Stevie because I had told it to her almost two years ago. Evelyn smoothed the corners of her lips as she reapplied the lipstick, twisted the cap on and turned to walk out. I smiled at her in the mirror. "See you in a while."

She gave a deep exasperated sigh, blinked her eyes to focus her contacts and frowned as she walked out the door smelling like Italian perfume. Apparently she had better places to be on this stormy Valentine's Day, just like that day she had sent me from her office thirty five dollars poorer, little more than a coffee break for her, but meals for a month for me.

I knew it was late. I repacked my bag laying my wet shawl on top after I took my dry shoes out. I would have to try to slip them on once I was back in the courtroom. I didn't want to give the judge cause to dismiss me by being late. I hurried down the hall behind Evelyn. She didn't bother holding the heavy wood door for me. Billy Dean gave her 'the look' as I reached for the polished handle before the door slapped me in the face. I hurried up the aisle and sat down at the table beside Billy, who was busy trying to clean a spot of red chile off his tie.

Judge Sandoval came in, we stood up, and we sat down. He reconvened the session.

"I believe I notified you that we want to try to wrap this up quickly. I have been in contact with the Department of Transportation and they have advised me that roads both in and out of Santa Fe and within the city itself are snow packed and travel is becoming extremely difficult. If we could finish up by two-thirty, one hour's time, it would be best. If not we will need to have the clerk reschedule the discovery hearing for another date. Mr. Gallagher, Mr. Dean what say you?"

I quickly untied my boots under the table and shoved them under the bench. My socks were soaking wet. If I set the shoes beside my feet I could slip them on if called on. Even though my feet were freezing, I didn't want to risk going barefoot in the court. I looked over at Billy Dean. "Will I have to get up or take the stand?" I whispered to him

"Probably not." He mouthed back.

I took off my wet socks and laid them carefully over my boots, hoping they too would dry, than bent my knees to curl my feet under the chair.

"Judge we are prepared to resolve this case quickly. However, Mr. Dean and his client are not willing to negotiate a payment plan to reimburse St Mary's Light of Mercy for Mrs. Roark's son's medical cost. We have taken all the necessary steps to notify Mrs. Roark of her fiscal responsibilities and she has not responded. That is why we have brought the legal action."

Billy Dean stood and placed his hands on the table. "Judge Mrs. Roark has been paying one thousand a month towards the over one hundred thousand in medical costs the hospital billed Mrs. Roark for her son's care." He gestured one hand in John Gallagher's direction, just like a scene from the Scopes Monkey Trial, a play I am sure he stared in many times.

"St. Mary's is attempting to nullify the mediation agreement and compel Mrs. Roark to cover the full amount billed for her son's care. Close to five hundred thousand dollars I believe."

Evelyn Lucero stood up now, "The payments are made through garnishment of

Mrs. Roark's husband's retirement account Judge. They were not voluntarily initiated by the defendant. At the time of the mediation, St. Mary's Light of Mercy was given to believe Mrs. Roark did not have the resources to cover the cost of her son's medical care, but we have been made aware her circumstances have changed and so she should be held responsible for the full amount and the mediated amount revisited. Mr. Dean and his client have been unwilling to renegotiate that amount." Evelyn Lucero placed her index fingers, tipped by an exquisitely manicured nail with a small embedded diamond on the table in front of her like a kid playing chopsticks. Evidently she had spent her lunch hour at the Blue Mesa Nail Saloon and Day Spa.

"Mrs. Roark how old is your son? Was he not covered by your insurance provider? Where is he now? And where is your husband, isn't it his money that is being garnished?" The judge peered over the bench at me.

All three lawyers and Sigfredo Jacquez bowed their heads. Billy Dean reached out and touched my elbow guiding me to stand up.

"My son died your honor, he was twenty seven. He had just started a new job. So no, he wasn't covered by insurance. My husband committed suicide after our younger son's death. I was supposed to get half his retirement, that's what they are taking the payment from now. I only get five hundred a month after they take the payment out."

"Oh, I'm very sorry for your loss. Was your son hospitalized at the time of his death?" The judge looked over his glasses at me as he shuffled through papers in front of him.

"Yes, he was in a coma. They moved him to a basic life care unit when the hospital applied for guardianship. He got an infection there, they were short staff and his IV wasn't changed correctly and he got the infection."

"Guardianship? You were not his guardian?" Judge Sandoval looked up and shuffled through the bundle of papers again.

"Object...oh, um, Mrs. Roark's son's cause of death is not relevant to the cost of medical care provided. Mrs. Roark signed fiscal responsibility forms at the time of her son's admission. Whether or not she was guardian is irrelevant to her promise and responsibility to pay for the medical service provided. Mrs. Roark is a well-educated woman. She has a responsibility to be aware of what she is signing." Siegfried Jacquez looked annoyed.

"I'll decide what is relevant, Mr. Jacquez." The judge peered over his glasses at Sigfredo, equally annoyed.

The snow was starting to pile up on the ledges outside the high windows making an already dark courtroom even darker.

"Mrs. Roark, did you not apply for available assistance in paying medical bills? Was anyone at the hospital assigned to work with you regarding your son's case management?"

"No, no one worked with me. I didn't even know they had applied for guardianship until he was moved into the Basic Life Care unit. I just showed up one day and he was gone. I tried talking to the Family Assistance Center there but they said it was routine for the hospital to apply for guardianship of someone who needed care so that they could get the disability payments."

"Objection, conversations Mrs. Roark had is hearsay." Siggy's blood pressure was going up again.

"This is not a trial Mr. Jacquez, it is discovery, and unless you are acting as St. Mary's attorney, I recommend you leave procedural processes to your counsel."

Billy Dean stepped up to the plate.

"Judge, the hospital applied for guardianship of Mrs. Roark's twenty seven year old son when they found out he was not insured. They failed to notify Mrs. Roark of their actions, yet continued to bill her for care they provided even though she was no longer given a choice in what care they did provide. And I remind St. Mary's Light of Mercy that Mrs. Roark was paying one thousand monthly on the agreed upon amount."

Evelyn stood up again, she held in her hand a copy of the garnishment order that took away most of Sam's retirement check.

"Judge Sandoval, Mrs. Roark was not making sufficient payments on the balance due on her account, it was necessary to obtain a garnishment order to collect on the debt Mrs. Roark incurred. She failed to notify St. Mary's of her current address and we were not able to track her down."

"My client had just experienced several great loses, her husband, both sons, her job and home, it isn't reasonable to expect her to notify the hospital of a change of address when she herself was uncertain of where her next address would be." Billy Dean hit the ball back to Evelyn Lucero.

The judge wavered back and forth between the two tables, occasionally he would glance at his watch then through the window to the street outside where the snow kept falling.

"Am I given to believe the hospital failed to notify Mrs. Roark of the outstanding bill and application for guardianship because they couldn't find her? Mrs. Roark did the hospital have your address?"

"I gave the nurses my new address when I had to move. I used to visit Stevie every day. I gave them the address when I moved."

"We have supporting documentation of the address Mrs. Roark provided St. Mary's. The notification of garnishment was sent by registered mail, and it was returned as undeliverable." Evelyn held up a business size envelope with the green self-stick return receipt requested post card still attached.

"I got some mail. They sent me a sympathy card when Stevie died. I got that, it had the correct address." I retrieved the composition notebook from my bag, removed the rubber band holding it together and leafed to the back where I kept the card, still in its envelope tucked between the pages. I pulled the card out and handed it to Billy Dean.

Billy looked at me with absolute disbelief. Evelyn looked at the envelope in her own hands then at the one Billy Dean held. This was unexpected.

"Please bring me both documents." The judge removed his glasses and accepted the sympathy card Billy Dean presented with his left hand and the returned notification from Evelyn Lucero in his right. He placed both envelops side by side on the desk in front of him and removed his glasses.

"They have different addresses." He jotted down something on the pad in front of him.

He picked them up and turned them over, handed the garnishment notice to Billy Dean and the sympathy card to Evelyn Lucero.

Evelyn immediately spoke out. "Judge this card is not an official document it was obviously hand addressed by the nurses, they were not acting as agents of St. Mary's when they sent this card. The official address, the one of record, is the one on the garnishment notification which was returned as undeliverable, the administration of St. Mary's was not made aware that there was a change of address."

Billy reached for the card, taking it from Evelyn's hands.

"It has an official St. Mary's return address printed on the envelope." He flipped it back and forth several times "The sticker sealing the envelope is identical to the ones St. Mary's uses on its donor thank -you cards."

Billy Dean was really in his element, like an elaborate debate, spun around first to look at Sigfredo Jacquez, then back at Evelyn Lucero returning the card, still in its envelope to her. John Gallagher waited, stood without moving, unsure what his next move should be. He was new to New Mexico courtrooms, and the drama filled years that had preceded him, and probably succeed him too.

Sigfredo sat down, shaking his head, extending his hands like he was giving a lecture to a group of incoming freshman.

"Judge Sandoval, the nurses and medical staff, as a matter of respect and sympathy towards the deceased, routinely sign and send a condolence card to the family of the deceased, but the administration is not notified when such as card is sent, or to whom."

It was my turn to look at Sigfredo with disdain.

"You signed it." I spoke directly to him.

"What?" Billy Dean spun around and studied me, at the same time taking the card back from Evelyn's hand. Evelyn and John Gallagher both stared at Sigfredo with alarm.

"He, Mr. Jacquez signed the card. Look on the inside." Billy Dean handed me the card. I slipped it out of the envelope, opened it up and pointed to where Sigfredo had signed.

Our sincere condolences on your loss, Sigfredo Jacquez, CEO St. Mary's Light of Mercy Medical Center.

Billy Dean took the card to Sigfredo, "Is this your signature Mr. Jacquez?"

Sigfredo barely glanced at it. "I sign dozens of things like this every day. It is a routine part of my responsibilities." He waved Billy Dean off.

Evelyn and John, in unison, blinked twice and put their hands to their forehead.

"Please let me see the card Mr. Dean." The judge looked curious. Billy handed it to him, still open, thumb slightly to the left of Sigfredo's signature.

"So it is your signature Mr. Jacques?" The judge scrutinized it and the other signatures made by the nursing staff and med techs.

Billy Dean answered for him, "Mr. Jacquez is the CEO of St. Mary's. If he was aware of Mrs. Roark's address, he had a responsibility to assure all correspondence is correctly addressed. Mr. Jacquez is a well-educated man. He has a responsibility to be aware of what he is signing." Billy Dean looked sideways at Siggy again. I hoped they weren't setting up for another boxing match.

John Gallagher tried to salvage what he could. He stood up, hands on hips, jacket pushed back and pivoted from the waist in all directions without moving his feet. I swear he could have been in the movies.

"Judge, Mr. Jacquez as CEO of St. Mary's, does not concern himself in the routine billing of medical services, he does not proof read billing notification forms for correct address prior to mailing, Mrs. Roark had a responsibly to notify the business office. She did not, and an action of garnishment was initiated by St. Mary's business office. We are here to request full reimbursement for services provided to Mrs. Roark's son, not to argue over when she changed her address."

Billy Dean still held the notice of garnishment. He flipped quickly through the sheets of paper while John spoke, paused on one of the pages.

"Siggy signed the garnishment notice too." He walked quickly up to the judge's desk, still looking down at the papers in his hand, and presented them to Judge Sandoval, to reveal the signature once more.

All the documents were lined up in front of the judge. Sigfredo, for the first time looked a little worried. John Gallagher looked perplexed, and Evelyn looked annoyed. This was not her first court case with her cousin across the aisle and she did not like to be bested by such a disheveled mess.

I still had my notebook out, flipping nervously through the pages. I stopped in the middle, right where I had sketched a picture of Peanuts lying beside Stevie's grave marker. It was one that I had done on that first day at the Rest Inn, when I had sat covered only by newspapers all day and night, waiting for my clothes to dry. The wax of the crayons I had used to color it had started to flake off and cling to another envelope stuck to the opposite page. In it were copies of the guardianship request along with the receipt Evelyn Lucero had given me two years ago when I visited her office. Twenty five minutes, thirty five dollars.

Now or never.

"He signed the guardianship papers too." I pulled my copy of them out of the envelope walked over to the judge and handed them to him. The judge kept staring at my feet.

Oops. I was barefoot.

"Sorry judge, my shoes and socks were wet, I went walking at lunch."

"Not the best weather for a walk was it Mrs. Roark?" he said.

"I went to visit my husband and sons' graves. They're buried over in the cemetery off of Paseo, the snow there was a little deep. Sorry, I'll put them back on." I returned to my seat and tried to slip the wet socks and shoes on. The judge's eyes followed me back to my seat.

Billy Dean's eyes kept staring at me with wonder. It was not an act. He decided to match John Gallagher's body language a tactic I had seen him use during Cesar's court hearing. It annoyed the heck out of the other team who were already pretty annoyed. What should have been an open and shut case over medical expenses had turned into a major courtroom showdown with lots of old history and hard feelings coming into play. Billy placed his hands on his hips and pivoted around trying to read the judges mind. But, Billy's girth was no match for the twice daily ab-buster workouts of John Gallagher. Billy looked just like one of those animated Santa's dancing in a Hawaiian shirt.

It was a little after two o'clock. Outside the courtroom we could hear the other judicial staff trying to turn out lights and close and lock doors. By two thirty everyone would need to be on their way. The snow kept falling.

"Again, I sign dozens of such forms each day. The guardianship order is not germane to the current proceeding." Sigfredo was livid. As a CEO he was not accustomed to having his actions so intricately scrutinized.

"I'm not going to caution you again Mr. Jacquez it is not your role, by policy or by practice to determine what is relevant to these proceedings."

"Judge, Mr. Jacquez has been trying to disavow responsibility for his signature on three separate documents which are all central to Mrs. Roark's alleged financial responsibility for her son's medical care. Yet the plaintiff is basing the entirety of the case on one signature, Mrs. Roark's, on one form, signed when she was under the duress of having lost her younger son and learning her older son had been critically injured. Why is Mrs. Roark being held accountable for her signature yet Mr. Jacquez, who admits to signing multiple forms each day in the comfort of his office with staff to advise him, why is Mr. Jacquez not also held accountable? Shouldn't such a well-educated man know what he is signing?" Billy was really rubbing it in. His voice was forceful and clear. He held out his hands and paced the room like a Shakespeare actor.

"Save your performance for Dinner Theater Mr. Dean. I am inclined to agree with Mr. Gallagher regarding guardianship. I am not sure it is germane to the current action." Judge Sandoval handed the guardianship papers back to Billy Dean.

Billy was crest fallen his brilliant performance had gone unappreciated.

Billy walked over and placed the documents on the table, pushing them towards me. I pushed them back.

The papers were dated October twenty third, almost six months before Stevie died.

"They kept billing me for Stevie's care even after they had guardianship. The date of guardianship is October twenty third, but they billed me through March fifth." I spoke softly, directly to Billy Dean, my feet were freezing and so was the rest of me. I was worried where I would spend tonight if the Rail-Runner was canceled.

"What?" Billy Dean blinked, pivoted both his feet and waist and bent slightly, leaning on the table. "What did you say?"

I spoke louder this time.

"They're trying to get me to pay for when they already were Stevie's guardian. Look at the paper, look at the dates. They had guardianship those last few months. They were getting the benefits but they still billed me."

Billy picked the papers back up. "Judge, St. Mary's was aware..."

"I heard her Billy, bring those papers back up here."

John Gallagher stood up. "Mrs. Roark had the opportunity to contest the dates of guardianship on several occasions. This is the first time she has brought this issue up. St. Mary's is not responsible for Mrs. Roark's failure to seek advice regarding her son's guardianship. The services to be billed were delineated during the mediation for amount due."

Billy Dean jumped on that. Everyone was speaking so fast I was having a difficult time keeping up with what was going on. The Judge kept looking at his watch.

"Judge Sandoval, St. Mary's initiated the request to overturn the mediated amount, not my client. If the plaintiff is requesting the binding mediated amount be set aside, they should be aware the amount can be reduced as well as increased."

Evelyn already tasting the Irish Coffee with a dash of red chile she would order over at the Palace Bar, rejoined the foray. She couldn't believe how much time this was taking.

"St. Mary's is seeking to set aside the mediation agreement on the basis that full disclosure did not occur at the time of mediation and Mrs. Roark's financial resources have changed. She did not act in good faith."

Billy Dean picked up that gauntlet. "My client would also like to set aside the mediation. It was St. Mary's that did not negotiate in good faith regarding the guardianship of Stevie Roark and the time period during which Mrs. Roark was financially responsible for his care. We are requesting the amount due be voided, and a new itemized bill which accounts for guardianship be prepared."

Evelyn Lucero was matching Billy's body language now, grabbing her lapels and pivoting around in one spot. "Look Billy, none of us knew the date of guardianship at the time mediation occurred, your client, on the other hand, was fully aware of her financial obligation at the time."

"Ms. Lucero knew. I told her." I said it softly, almost to myself. I was resting my head on one hand, leaning forward on the table. Billy once again starred at me with eyes wide.

"What did you say?" His voiced cracked. He said it again "Can you explain what you just said?"

"Oh for crying out loud." Evelyn Lucero stomped her foot, throwing her hands up in the air before looking at her watch and returning to her chair.

Judge Valdez looked at me, "Do you have information to share Mrs. Roark?" His voice was stern.

"I went to see Mrs. Lucero two years ago. I had a prepaid legal plan though my work. I went to see her about trying to regain Stevie's guardianship. After I told her everything that happened, showed her the papers, the guardianship papers and the garnishment papers, she made copies of some of them. Then she told me she couldn't represent me because her firm was already on contract to represent the hospital, but that it was probably better to allow the hospital to become guardian so they could apply for Social Security and Medical benefits on Stevie's behalf."

"Really?" Billy Dean was grinning. He looked over his shoulder, first to Sigfredo, then Evelyn. John Gallagher, still standing up, stared from one to the other, still pivoting at the waist without moving his feet.

Immediately Evelyn jumped up. "I have no remembrance of this conversation Judge." She hesitated. It was starting to come back to her.

Flustered she started to walk towards me but caught her heel on the edge of carpet that had been placed under both counsel's tables, she went flying toward the bench, caught by her cousin Billy.

John Gallagher stepped forward. He was still trying to turn this around. "Mrs. Roark has no evidence to substantiate her claim. If and I do mean if she had a conversation with Ms. Lucero regarding Guardianship it is hearsay."

"I have a receipt." I said it softly, a hoarse whisper and reached back into the pages of my book. There, in the envelope which up until a few minutes ago held the guardianship papers, was the CU Legal Benefits Group Claim for Reimbursement form with receipt attached. Reason for visit: Adult Guardianship consultation; pay garnishment inquiry. It was signed by Evelyn Lucero and date stamped by the law firm clerk.

"I have a receipt." I said again clearing my throat lightly. My stomach growled and I remembered I hadn't eaten lunch. Boy were my feet cold.

Billy Dean was smirking, eyes squinted, pounding his fists lightly on the table in front of me. "You have a receipt." He turned to face the judge. "She has a receipt."

"Mrs. Lucero signed it." I said.

Billy was trying so hard not to laugh. He took the thin yellow paper from my hand.

"Evelyn did you sign this?" He presented it to her pushing it inches from her face, lips clamped tightly together, he knew that part of being a showman was knowing when to keep silent and now was the time.

"Oh for God's sake Billy." She pulled the paper down and away from her face letting it fly to the floor. Billy picked it up and took it up to the judge then turned and rapidly walked back to the chair beside me blinking twice, holding his hands together in a kind of victory shake, he sat down.

A woman, the receptionist I had seen downstairs, came in from a side door and spoke quietly to the judge, she already had on her coat and a scarf wrapped halfway around her neck.

"Judge we would like to request a brief recess." John Gallagher was the only one still trying to hold it together.

"Very brief Mr. Gallagher. Court will be closing in twenty minutes. I have been informed that the DOT and Santa Fe Police will be closing all roads in and out of the city by three thirty and we have to give every one time to be on their way. I'll give you ten minutes."

Evelyn Lucero, John Gallagher and Sigfredo Jacquez all filed out of the room. To avoid making any comments, Billy Dean drank from a small bottle of water, tipping it up as the three walked by. I stared down at my notebook. As soon as the door closed behind them Billy turned to me.

"This is good, this is very good. The tides are with us, the stars in our sign, the fates smile on us." He was giddy. "I'm going to the restroom, now's a good time if you need a break too, but don't frolic, I mean delay, I mean be quick- we really want to keep the judge on our side." He left the courtroom with a rise in his step.

It kept getting darker inside as well as out. Snow was building up so high on the windows that whatever light remained outside was not enough to make its way in. There were a couple of steep pitches on the gable above the windows and the weight of the snow caused a mini-avalanche to slide past with a distinctive thud. I shuddered to think about where I might sleep if couldn't make it home. I remembered Wizard, maybe if I went back to the graveyard I could find him again. Or maybe I could find a way into the garage turned cosmetics storage locker behind Billy Dean's office.

I kept flipping through the pages of the notebook, here a little haiku that was really bad writing but at the time it seemed great, on another a comic clipped from on old newspaper, *Agnes* eating fried chicken while a Christmas movie played on the motel TV could have been my life. I was struck by how without meaning to I had told the story of my journey over the past couple of years. You would have thought the saddest part was when Stevie died. It wasn't. I knew Stevie wasn't going to make if for a long time. The saddest part was when I had to push Peanuts into the night drop box at the animal shelter. That was the day I gave up. Jesus, I was going to start crying all over again. I had to stop. I slapped the book closed, replaced the rubber band around it and put it into my bag. I wished my feet were warm.

Billy Dean came back in, one look at my face and he could tell I was upset.

"Hey, really, this is going to be good. It's going to work out. Please just trust me." He tried to console me.

St Mary's Light of Mercy trio came back, retook their seats at the table. John Gallagher had taken over. Evelyn Lucero and Sigfredo Jacquez sat, hands folded on the table, eyes looking down. John stood between them.

Judge Sandoval came into the room. We stood up, we sat down. The Judge called out John Gallagher.

"Mr. Gallagher, I am given to understand you have decided to negotiate a settlement with Mrs. Roark."

"Yes Judge, we are prepared to re-examine the medical billing for any possible errors taking into account the date of guardianship and adjust the amount due accordingly."

"Mr. Gallagher just so everyone is clear on this, if it appears Mrs. Roark was over billed, and I am anticipating your financial department will find that is the case, a refund would be expected based on the amount she has already paid. Am I clear enough on that point?"

John was not expecting this, neither was Evelyn or Sigfredo They had not taken Billy's comments seriously or considered the possibility they might owe money instead of collect it. Not coming to a settlement that the Judge would approve would mean a costly trial. They knew, as did Billy Dean, I would present a much more sympathetic figure to a jury then I did here to the jaded legal team. Billy was sure to bring up the issue of all the signatures from both Jacquez and Evelyn Lucero, especially the sympathy card which Sig had described as routine. Not to mention my struggles with homelessness.

John looked over at Sigfredo, who still sat with hands folded in front of him. He continued to look down as he nodded his head in agreement. Yes, money would be refunded.

"And Mr. Dean, your client is agreeable to this?" Judge Sandoval spoke quickly, he wanted to go home.

"Well Judge, there are my legal fees." Billy's voice trailed off.

The Judge glared at him with an 'I should have known' look.

"Very well then, Mr. Gallagher, it is my expectation that after St. Mary's Light of Mercy has had the opportunity to review all relevant material, the adjusted bill and refund due to Mrs. Roark and a sufficient amount to provide reasonable compensation for services rendered by Mr. Dean will be agreed upon?"

Both Siggy and Evelyn's face drew up into a pucker like they had sipped a bad margarita. But Siggy again nodded, waving the back of his hand slightly towards John, still not saying anything.

"Yes judge, we are clear on the expectations for settlement." They had surrendered.

"Then in six weeks' time we will reconvene to review and approve the proposed settlement, at which time I will vacate the binding mediation agreement. Until that time, St. Mary's Light of Mercy is to immediately suspend the garnishment of Mrs. Roark's account. We are dismissing this session and closing the courthouse for the day. You may call the clerk in the morning, if weather permits us to open, to request a court date be set. Ladies and gentleman, have a safe trip home."

Judge Sandoval rose to leave. Everyone, except me, was still standing.

I turned to Billy Dean, "Wait, I don't understand."

Billy smiled at me as he packed up his papers. "It's good. The Judge thinks you deserve a refund, that there is a billing error and St. Mary's has agreed."

"A refund?" I stood up, all the anger and frustration that had stayed inside of me for three years whipped up like wildfire on a windy day.

"A refund? I lost my son, my job, my home, my car and you offer a refund?" I turned to look, really look at Evelyn and Siggy for the first time.

"Mr. Dean, see to your client." The judge sat down again.

"Please Aileen, please." Billy Dean tried to quiet me.

But I was not to be stopped.

"A refund? I slept on the ground, under trees, in parks, under bridges, ate in soup kitchens if I ate at all. And now I'm entitled to a refund?" My tone is sarcastic. I was shaking and my voice getting louder with each proclamation.

"Mr. Dean, Mrs. Roark needs to calm down. See to your client." The judge was trying to find his gavel, but it had already been stowed, so he just slapped his hand on his desk three times.

"Please Aileen, we won, we won." Billy pleads with me.

"I wore the same filthy dirty clothes day and night without washing them for two months because of your billing, I had to defecate behind dumpsters; I was cited for vagrancy." With each word I paused to be sure they were hearing what I said. "I had to leave my dog...give up my beautiful dog, all I had left of my sons, my family, in the night drop box of the animal shelter because of your billing error, and all you have to say is 'you're due a refund'?" I closed my eyes, all I could envision was Peanuts whining desperately, scratching at the door, inside that concrete cubical at the animal shelter and me watching helplessly from across the street.

There was a clap of thunder, thunder-snow the weatherman call it, and the lights blinked quickly off then back on again.

The St. Mary's trio turned their heads to look away, the way people do when a homeless person asks for spare change. I closed my eyes and shook my head.

I could sense someone beside me. I was pretty sure it was security guard Earl to escort me off the premises. When I opened my eyes Wizard was standing by my elbow. How did he get in? Why hadn't Earl stopped him? His lips were still purple and blue, his touch cold. He reached out and placed his hand on my arm.

"Do not dwell here, dear lady, mind body or spirit do not dwell here." He looked deeply into my eyes. I stared back transfixed. "You can't stay here. Build no dwelling."

'Build no dwelling here,' his whisper echoed. I was dazed. His words were spiraling in my brain.

"I will not dwell here, mind body or spirit, I will build no dwelling here." I whispered back. I twisted away from Wizard so I was facing everyone else in the court. I understood what Wizard meant now; I looked sadly from face to face. "I will not dwell here." I repeated again and turned back towards Wizard but he wasn't there. How had he gotten in and out so quickly? I hurried to the window to see if I could catch sight of him. Only the receptionist stood on the street outside the building waiting for her carpool. Another clap of thunder and another blink of the lights, it's over.

The others in the room watched me with slight alarm. I knew what they were thinking- 'what would this crazy bag lady do next.' But I took my promise to Wizard to heart. I would not dwell here. In three steps I was back, picked up my cloth bag and headed out the door.

100

I knew it would be a long ride home, if I still had a way there. I stopped in the same restroom where Evelyn Lucero scorned me. I would need a few minutes to compose myself if I was ever going to make it to the train station. I hoped the three forty-five train was still running and I could catch it at the rail yard, if not I would have to try the shelters. The twenty bucks Billy Dean had given me along with the leftover train ticket money would not be enough for a motel room. I sat on the pot longer than needed, just to rest my legs really, although I had been sitting most of the day. I was shaking and unsteady. I came out, washed hands and face and slipped a stack of paper towels into my bag. I wondered if could find any old newspapers. I might need them to cover up with tonight.

There was a tap at the door. Billy Dean cautiously poked his head in.

"I'm right out here when you're ready. But really, we need to get going. They're kicking us all out," he said. His face at ease, and manner gentler then I had known it before.

I wrapped the shawl, still damp, over my head and shoulders, pulled on the hoodie and walked out the door. I was freezing and not outside yet. Billy turned towards me taking both my shoulders in his hands walking backwards down the hall.

"Aileen, we won. We Won. You do understand that? They are not going to get your settlement money, they have to refund some of the money you already paid, and they can't touch what your husband left you anymore. You get the full monthly amount effective immediately. We won. '

I nodded, looking up at him. "Yes, we won. Thank you. Thank you for everything."

We started down the stairs.

"Look, let's be honest, you were the one who kept those papers. Without the sympathy card or the guardianship papers things might not have gone so well. But especially that receipt, with Evie's god-damn signature no less. She didn't know what hit here. Whatever made you save that stuff?"

"I don't know. Holding out hope things would change I guess. I don't know." My voice and my knees were still shaking.

"What was that deal about dwelling you were going on about? Where did you come up with that?"

"Wizard. Didn't you hear him? He kept saying it over and over 'don't dwell here'." Billy Dean was almost as close to Wizard as I was, how could he not have heard?

"Wizard? Old hippie? Wears a buckskin jacket and cowboy hat?"

"Well yeah. He was right there. You must have heard him."

"Where was this? When?"

"Just now, in the courtroom. He was right there beside me. How could you..."

Billy looked at me with concern. "Aileen, there, I..."

We were half way down the steps.

"I forgot my boots. Meet you outside." I turned and ran back up the stairs praying the door to the courtroom wasn't locked yet. The lights were off and the room dark, like twilight. I hoped to sneak in and get my boots before anyone saw me. Wrong.

Judge Sandoval stood beside one of the tables sorting through some papers.

"Yes? May I help you Mrs. Roark?" Surprised but not annoyed.

"Sorry Judge, I left my boots. I changed them when I got back from lunch."

"Yes, the barefoot defendant." He chuckled.

"Is it okay if I put them on now, here I mean?"

"Yes, of course."

I sat down and struggled to get out of my shoes and pull the boots on over wet socks.

"You don't remember me do you Mrs. Roark?" Judge Sandoval continued to sort through the papers.

"No. No I don't." I shook my head.

"A year ago Thanksgiving Friday you returned my wallet to me outside a coffee shop in Albuquerque. I dropped it in restroom. Were you homeless then?"

I studied him for a minute or two, his face did seem familiar. "I remember, followed you almost a block before I caught up. I was sort of homeless. I was living in one of those motels on Central that rents by the month."

"Over a thousand dollars was inside the wallet. Did you know that?"

"Yeah, I figured you were Christmas shopping, you know Black Friday Specials?" I laced up my boots.

"You gave it back." It was a simple declarative statement.

"What else would I have done?"

"I gave you a reward, ten dollars I believe." He folded his arms in front of his chest, holding the papers in one hand, and leaned back against the table, amused.

"Yes, it was ten dollars."

"Do you remember what you did with it?"

"Am I under oath?" I stood up and zipped up my jacket.

"Always." He smiled lightly.

"I put it in the Salvation Army kettle."

"That's right. I was watching. You put it in the Salvation Army kettle. What possessed you, living in a cheap motel, with limited means, to do that, to give ten dollars away?"

"I don't know judge." I shrugged my shoulders. "It just seemed like the right thing to do at the time, to help someone who needed it."

"The right thing to do, you gave it away because it felt like the right thing to do." He put the papers down. "You are a remarkable woman Mrs. Roark, you have my utmost respect."

"Thanks judge." I tied my other boot and headed for the door. "Have a safe trip home "

"You too, Mrs. Roark."

I hustled down the stairs, out the doors and heard them click as Earl locked them.

Billy Dean was outside trying to escape the snow by standing under the small foyer overhang on one side, while the St. Mary's Group stood on the other. All three of them were on cell phones, awkwardly turning their backs to Billy. I started down the slippery front steps and onto the sidewalk. Billy came after me sliding sideways.

"Hey, what's your hurry?"

"I need to get to the rail-yard and try to catch the train. I hope it's still running. I have to get home."

"Wait, I'll give you a ride. I called my wife, she'll be right here."

"That's kind of you-but really, I'm okay."

"Aileen will you stop for a minute and let someone help you. You're not alone you know, you've got friends. People do care about you. Wait, we'll give you a ride." He put his hand in front of me, stopping me from moving forward.

I nodded, sad, worried, cold, the snow stinging my face. I licked my lips, tasted their salt, unaware I had been crying the whole time until then. He was right. I needed to let him help me through this. We continued to walk together to the end of the walkway, pausing near the curb. A snowplow had already pulled through the street once, leaving a mound of snow beneath the curb.

A bronze *Porsche Cayenne* pulled up, a young man, about twenty, got out of the driver's side. Evelyn Lucero, heels clicking, still talking on her cell phone, scurried past us, stepping over the snow mound, hopped into the open door of the *Cayenne*, and drove away, leaving the kid standing there.

The Otto, Gallegos and Lucero Law firm used a parking valet service, situated about seven blocks from the courthouse. The lawyers would call and one of the valets would meet them at the courthouse to pick up and drop off the cars. The more empathetic lawyers, of which John Gallagher was one, would tip them a few bucks and give them a ride back to the lot. The rest, like Evelyn would slam the car door in their face, convinced the monthly parking fee was adequate compensation for their services, and the valet would have to huff it back.

John Gallagher's Silver *Lexus* SUV arrived next, quickly followed by Sigfredo Jacquez's *Land Cruiser*, driven by his young French wife, who, despite being yards away from the police station in a town where cell phone use while driving was prohibited, had a cell phone plastered to her ear. When Sigfredo walked over to the driver's side to take over she waved him off, refusing to relinquish control and continuing to speak into the cell phone; vexed, Sigfredo made his way through the slushy snow around the car and got in the passenger side.

John Gallagher shouted towards the kid his law partner had left behind, motioning him to climb in and you could see him apologizing to the two young valets for her rudeness. He would never make partner with that firm, nor did he want to.

Next up was Billy's baby powder blue 1978 two door *Ford LTD*, a classic with a magnetic 'I LOVE CHEERY DAY' cosmetics sign tacked to the side. It would have made a great low rider. Yolinda behind the wheel waved and grinned at us as the sedan slid back and forth around the slippery corner. Both John Gallagher and Sigfredo Jacquez stared back in alarm, unsure if she could stop. But stop she did, inches from the back of her ex's *Land Cruiser*.

Unlike the SUV's which had been swept clean of snow, de-iced and defrosted prior to arrival, the *LTD* was capped by a half foot of snow on the roof, trunk and hood. Its windows fogged except where Yolinda had used a gloved hand to wipe the condensation away. The half-moons made by the windshield wipers prominently marked the progress of the snow.

"Ah, our chariot has arrived." Billy grinned and extended his hand toward the *LTD*. He gave me his other hand to steady my walk.

"I'll bet you're wondering why a successful lawyer, such as myself, doesn't drive a luxury SUV, like a *Lexus* or *Escalade*?" He turned to face me walking backwards a little, but didn't wait for me to respond.

"Well the answer is I really do love Cheery Day." He winked at me. We were at the car and he opened the passenger side then pulled the seat forward so I could climb into the back with the boxes of skin cleanser, moisturizers and glossy red gift bags filled with Valentine cosmetics still to be delivered. He jumped in, closed the door, leaned over and kissed Yolinda, resting his hand on her leg. Yolinda put her foot on the gas and spun the tires a little before they gripped. She headed down the street, fishtailing side to side every few yards, leaving the others in the snow.

101

"Where to?" Yolanda skidded through the stop sign at the corner of Paseo.

"I need to catch the Rail Runner back to Albuquerque down at the Rail-Yard. Can you drop me there?" I fumbled to find the seat belts under the piles of boxes and bags on the back seat.

"Yes, but it's a little early, you'll have a wait. Want to stop anywhere in between?" Yolinda glanced in the rear view mirror and cranked up the heat, it blew cold.

"Listen Aileen, why don't you catch the train down at the South Complex, let me pick up a few things, that'll give us about 45 minutes. What say you my love?" Billy turned to Yolinda and smiled.

"Sounds good to me Billy Boy." Yolinda turned south onto Guadalupe Street and passed the train stop. Only a few brave souls and the homeless now walked the streets. The radio announced a long list of closures and delays, one of them the Rail Runner, would be making its last run of the day at four. I had to be on that train.

The parking lot was surprisingly busy considering the weather conditions. I don't know why I was surprised. The state offices across the intersection had just closed for the day, and workers where stocking up for a Valentine's dinner at home. I saw lots of bouquets and bottles of wine walk through the door.

"Thanks for the ride. You two have been so kind to me. I'm going to head over to the train stop. I want to be sure to catch it since it's the last one." I gathered my things and leaned forward to step out.

"Don't be silly, you have plenty of time and you'll freeze if you have to wait that long. We'll take you over. Come into the store with us." Yolinda zipped her coat and pulled its furry hood close around her.

I looked longingly at the ads posted on the front for cheese and produce. It had been years since I had been able to shop at this store. "Thanks, but maybe I'll just run up to the dollar store. I could use a few things."

"Suit yourself, be back in twenty, we'll drive you over." Billy opened the door and held up the seat.

I watched, more than a little jealous, as Billy and Yolinda walked hand in hand, laughing and smiling, catching snowflakes on their tongues.

The dollar store was half up the walkway, which had already been swept and salted as each store tried to keep up with the falling snow. Few of the stores had more than one or two customers. But the dollar store was packed. I made a quick mental list of what to get with my twenty dollar bill. Top on the list was a dry pair of socks.

Everyone smiled at me as I walked in, exclaiming about the snow, and urging caution. I found a pair of fluffy red and white snug socks infused with aloe hanging from a rack by the check-outs, a Valentine's birthday gift I would give myself along with generic dry boxes of mac and cheese, oatmeal, some prepackaged cheese and crackers and a bag of dog treats for Flacita. At the last minute I threw in a packaged pound cake and small bag of candy hearts. If I made it home tonight I would celebrate my birthday. Everything fit into my cloth bag. I headed out the door.

Billy and Yolinda were already in the car. Yolinda handed me a glossy red gift bag of Cheery Day Cosmetics, and Billy passed over a Trader Joe's bag of just what I had longed for; cheese, apples, oranges, bread and some prepackaged dinners. "Wow," was all I could think to say.

"For the ride home, and Happy Birthday." Billy smiled sheepishly as he handed it over.

"How did you know?" I looked up. Did lawyers really celebrate their clients' Birthdays?

"Yolinda told me. She keeps track of these things." Billy laughed gruffly and glanced over at his wife. "It's why I keep her around."

Yolinda rolled her eyes.

Billy pulled the seat forward and I again climbed in. The parking lot had cleared and we easily pulled onto the street which connected directly with the train stop. I could hear the signal guards as the train approached the intersection, and nervously gathered everything onto my arms praying I hadn't missed the train.

"We'll get you there." Billy reassured me. "Do you have a way home once you arrive at the Bernalillo station?"

"I left my bike there. Hopefully it hasn't snowed as much down there. It's really not that far. I'll be all right." Yolinda and Billy exchanged a glance again.

"Well, be careful. I'll contact you in a few days, or you can call me. We'll set up a time to meet. Hopefully I'll know the court date by then."

I couldn't speak, just nodded, looked out the window at the ever deepening snow and blinked back more tears.

Billy reached back and put his hand on my fore arm, "Aileen it's going to be okay.

We won. Really, things will be much better for you from now on. Keep the faith."

About twenty people were waiting for the train and thirty more already on it. I maneuvered out of the car. Billy hugged me. "I'll get a message to you about the next meeting."

Yolinda, still in the driver's seat, called after me, "Be careful Aileen, stay warm."

"Thank you both. I don't know what else to say, or how to thank you."

"Don't. I made money on this deal." Billy winked. "And Yolinda always relishes the chance to stick it to her ex."

I climbed on the train. Most days one car is designated a quiet car, but today it was quiet all around. The snow muffled the sounds. People spoke in soft hushed tones if they spoke at all. The sky was getting very dark, almost like nightfall so the interior lights glowed from the train. I settled into a window seat on the right side of the train, shook the snow from my shawl and pulled my red and white aloe socks out. My feet where wet, cold, and starting to turn blue. I slipped on the socks and wrapped my shawl around them before stretching my legs out as far as I could toward a small floor vent that sent heat into the train car.

The train started to move, pulled slowly away from the platform. Two men with scraggly beards, thin fleece jackets and heavy packs walked a few yards from the train tracks. I said a prayer for them "Please God, let them find a warm place for the night."

A slight jerk as the engine shifted gears caused me to fall back in the seat and we were on our way.

The ride home was uneventful. Along the way I looked out the window at the forgotten backyards and few cars and trucks still struggling in the snow. I realized how hungry I was and smuggled an apple out of the bag Billy Dean had given me. It was the first fresh apple I had eaten since last October when the last of the apples from my tree turned to mush and became compost for next year's garden. It tasted very sweet. I kept gazing out the window, sometimes catching sight of the sad old lady I had become reflected back. Did I really look like that now?

The train pulled into the Bernalillo Station. My hope of an easy bike ride home was dashed by the sight of at least half a foot of snow already on the ground and a furious on-slot of large wet flakes still coming down. It was past five o'clock, darker than it should have been. I could tell by the slow pace of cars on the Interstate to the east of us the roads were icy. I would have to walk my bike the five miles home, something I was not looking forward to. Considering the conditions, if I put my head down and didn't think about it, I might be home before seven thirty. Then, I reasoned, I would celebrate with a bowl of canned soup and piece of dollar store pound cake. Not to mention a cup of hot tea.

I trudged slowly and carefully down the stairs of the train platform to the parking area along with the dozen or so other passengers anxious to get home. The spot where I had chained my bike to a fence post was empty. It wasn't there, the bike wasn't there. Panicked, I spun frantically around. Was it stolen or confiscated as abandoned? God, oh God, I had come to depend on that bike for everything. Even Flacita had become excited about her rides in the trailer. My head sunk even lower into my chest as I tried to keep the blowing snow out of my eyes.

"Blondie. Hey Blondie, over here." It was Cesar, leaning out the window of Rae's Ford pickup, his blue knit beanie pulled low to just above his eyebrows.

"Aileen this way." Ed was with him, waved at me through the snow.

Cesar stopped the truck in the passenger pickup area where two hopeful souls waited for their ride home. Ed jumped out, taking the two bags from me.

"Climb in. We've been waiting." Flacita's head and sausage roll shape appeared from the middle of the seat. "Move over girl." She pulled her ears back and licked me.

"Boy am I glad to see you two or three I should say." I reached over to scratch Flacita's belly. "My bikes missing, someone must have taken it. I thought I was going to have to walk home."

Ed laughed, "Take a look in the back Aileen. It's there."

"You really should get a better lock Blondie." Cesar drummed his fingers on the steering wheel.

Should I yell or thank him. "How did you know to be here?"

"Billy Dean called Rae. He was worried about you. He said things went well, but you didn't seem yourself." Cesar rolled down the window and used his hand to clear the layer of snow that the wipers just couldn't catch.

"Yes. Yes, sort of. Billy said I won. They aren't going after my money anymore. I have to go back in a couple of weeks to see what Billy has worked out. He said it would be okay." The events of the last couple of years had left me more than a little skeptical about happy endings.

"Listen Aileen," (Uh oh, Cesar never called me by my real name) "if Billy said it was going to be okay, it is. People don't give him credit. He's pretty good at what he does." Cesar reassured me as we pulled out into traffic and headed west towards the old Route 66.

"I'm just glad to be home and really glad to see you guys. My feet were so cold they were turning blue. Are the roads very icy?" I reached down and rubbed my ankles trying to get the circulation back into them.

"They're getting that way, but we'll make it. I need to make a stop first okay? I promised Rae's girlfriend I'd pick up a pizza for her girls." We pulled into the strip mall where Sunny's Pizza, sold by the pie or by the slice, occupied one of four stores. In good weather and even in not so good weather, you could find someone wearing a lucha dora mask standing on the street corner flipping a sign announcing today's specials. But today, only the large yellow sign that was Sunny's trademark could be seen taped to the metal post of the stop sign. It was a Sweetheart Special, two heart shaped pepperoni, sausage or cheese pizza's fourteen dollars. Only the zeros were replace by lopsided hearts.

Cesar pulled past the store and backed around so he faced out from the parking spot. He hopped out and left the engine running.

"If I didn't know better I'd say you were setting up to rob the place Cesar. You know a quick get-away." I couldn't resist the ribbing.

"Don't even go there Blondie." He wagged his finger in front of me. "I'll only be a minute."

Ed and I sat on the bench seat, listening to the radio. He leaned back in his seat and put his arm around my shoulder. "Hey, happy Valentine's Day. Forgive me for not getting you a card. I'm new to this you know. Or almost new, it's been I don't know how many years since I did this. I'll make it up to you this weekend, coffee? Pie? Maybe even a movie. Please?"

New to this? Did he mean sweethearts on Valentine's Day?

"That'd be great Ed. Sorry I didn't get you anything either. A lot's been happening."

"I know, I know." He reached out and took my hand, pulling it close to his chest, holding it there with both hands. I could feel his heartbeat. I reached out with my other hand and held on tight remembering what tenderness felt like.

Cesar pulled open the door, using his gloved hand to wipe condensation from the inside of the windshield. "Okay you two love birds. Save it for later. You've got this place steaming." He pushed the two pizzas onto my lap.

It was snowing even harder when we pulled up the lane that led to Las Manchas. All the lights were on at may place and smoke puffed from the chimney. Father Rico's *Mercedes* was parked in the driveway, as was Rae's girlfriend's old red *Camry*.

"Why's everyone here? Did I leave that many lights on?" We pulled in the drive way. Cesar placed the truck in park and grabbed the pizzas.

"We wanted to be sure the place was warmed up. Make sure the pipes wouldn't freeze."

Ed opened the passenger's side and lifted Flacita to the ground before extending his hand to me. "Let's go in and see what's up."

All the lights blinked out. Oh no, not again.

Ed held open the door for me.

"Surprise!" The lights flicked on. Alisa's two little girls, decked out in red and white Kitty sweat shirts appeared in front of me holding either side of a yellow sheet cake, eight birthday candles burning bright.

"Wow, Wow." I started to cry.

"Blow out the candles," the girls exclaimed, jumping up, almost overturning the cake. Alisa's cousin Lynissa had to reach out and steady the pan.

"Esperan. Esperan, tenemos que cantar." Penelope called out.

In terrible harmony, everyone off key and out of time, all eleven present sang Happy Birthday. It was the most beautiful singing I ever heard.

"Make a wish," the girls yelled.

I wished for peace. I wished for warmth and a safe harbor for all those who needed one. I wished I could save this moment forever.

"Come and eat. Mira, we have enchilidas, posole." Father Rico pulled us together. Interrupted by Father Dru, we bowed our heads and gave a quick blessing.

"Pizza," the girls said in unison.

"Hice biscochitos. Felize Compleanos Aileen." The frail Priscilla used one shaky hand to pull my arm close to her and the other to present me with a container filled with the sweet anise and cinnamon cookies she was known for. She had topped the lid with a leftover Christmas bow, red and white candy canes stamped on the wide silver of the ribbon. I put my arm around her, still crying and she kissed my check.

Anselmo handed me a small box of chocolate covered cherries, the kind you get for ninety nine cents. "These are from Priscilla and I. Happy Birthday." I took the box from him, grabbed both of his hands and lightly embraced them, lest I make his arthritis worse.

I walked over to Penelope, balancing two plates on her arm she filled them with Jello salad and pizza for the excited girls. I hugged her lightly. She grinned sheepishly. "De nada, de nada," she said and handed Ashley her plate.

We filled our plates and sat around the table and on the futon sofa. The girls pulled up pillows and sat on the floor in front of the fuzzy light of the TV, watching the steady blue streamer of school closings pass across the bottom of the screen.

Father Rico was in the kitchen heating some of his homemade Concord grape wine with a stick of cinnamon, honey and slices of lemon peel. "Don't forget this will be ready soon," he said sticking his head out the door.

Father came out of the kitchen and joined us. I hadn't noticed the other men leave the room. The four ladies and two little girls hovered around me. Father Rico addressed us.

"We have one final gift for you Mrs. Roark. We all chipped in. We hope you like it."

The back door opened. Cesar, Rae and Ed, carrying a large box, filed in. They propped the box in front of me.

"A hot water heater. Oh my goodness, a hot water heater, this is so wonderful, thank you thank you." I jumped up and ran my hand down the side of the box. It really was wonderful, but all I could think about was where I would get the money to have it installed. I lot of good it would do me in a box. Of all the people there Cesar knew me best and read my mind.

"Don't worry Blondie this is the old piece of junk that was in there. We already put the new one in." He accepted a beer from Father Dru.

"Yeah," Rae spoke up. "Alissa's brother is a plumber. He came over and helped us this afternoon. Well mostly helped Ed put it in, he's the one that did the work."

I walked over to Alissa and hugged her. "Thank you so much. Tell your brother thank you. This is so wonderful."

I put my arms around Ed, who blushed profusely unable to overcome his sudden shyness. "Later," he said softly

A glimmer through the window caught my eye. A man stood outside the gate, holding onto it with both hands. It was hard to see him through the falling snow.

I paused, wiped away the condensation from the glass and cupped my hands. Wizard! He was smiling at me, his blue eyes reflecting the porch light. I ran to the door, glad to see him, wanting to welcome him in for cake, posole, hot water for God's sake. I ran outside slipping on the ice.

"Wizard, come in. Come in. How did you get here?"

"Dear lady, it looks like you found the right place." He was backing up.

"What? Wait, come inside." I struggled to break the ice that had formed around the gate's hinge making it difficult to push open.

He shook his head. "You've found it," he said. "You've found the right place for a dwelling."

"Wait, Wizard, wait." I finally yanked the gate open.

Flacita came running out, along with Little Dog and Priscilla's dog KiKo. The three dogs pushed out the gate barking at the figure as it faded into night.

I heard a high pitched cheer inside. The girl's school finally scrolled across the ever growing list of closures. They would have no school tomorrow.

The girls ran outside, coats only half on, celebrating the occasion. Everyone else followed. Ed began throwing snowballs to the three dogs. The canines raced furiously after them, barking and returning to the yard.

Cesar, Alissa, Lynisa and Rae came outside holding cups of hot spiced wine, laughed and joked on the porch, watching the circus unfold.

The young Father Dru came outside too, fell to his knees and started to help the girls roll large snow balls for a snowman. They were soon joined by Rae and Alissa.

Even the two elderly twins and Anselmo made their way outside.

I looked around at them, bewildered. Hadn't anyone else seen Wizard?

"Have you tried your hot water yet?" Lynisa asked me, her arm around Cesar's waist.

"Yeah Blondie, you know we all chipped in on that, but Ed made up the difference. I think you might have something going there." Cesar raised his eyebrows and made a little clicking noise.

"No, I haven't tried it yet. I'll go in now and see. I want some of that wine of Father's."

"Better hurry it's going fast." Cesar raised his cup to his lips and took a long sip.

I went inside, gathered a few of the empty plates scattered around and took them to the sink, turned on the hot water tap and held my hand under the running water. It soon turned hot. What an amazing invention.

Father Rico stood over the stove, stirring cinnamon sticks into a pan of deep red wine. "You know, you have to wait, have patience for things. You have to stir them a little, ignore them a little, add just the right amount of sugar, the right amount of heat, a little sour, a little spice. But when it's right it's right." He lifted a spoon to his lips and tasted. "Tonight it's very right."

Father picked up a paper cup from the stack beside the stove and filled it three fourths full with the burgundy mix using an old ceramic mug as a ladle. He handed it to me and I sipped gently.

"We have a lot to be thankful for you and I. God does listen to our prayer. Sometimes we don't get the answer we are expecting, but he always answers in due time."

I set the cup down and began to wash the plates, appreciating the hot sudsy water.

"Take me for instance. I prayed for guidance in leading my church, my community. I wanted to bring back our school, help our parishioners renew their faith and rebuild our mission. Now we have a start. The charter school will open next fall in the old St Ursula's building, the Las Manchas's Neighborhood Association has taken on rebuilding of our Church as a Historic site and," he paused here, "they sent us Father Dru. You know I'll be eighty three next birthday. Now maybe I can take it a little easier. Go on more fishing trips, perfect my wine." He chuckled, looked content.

I nodded, rinsing the suds from my hands with the blessedly warm water, uncertainty, sadness and confusion over the day's events still inside me. I was just starting to grasp what was happening.

One of the girls came running in, cheeks rosy with the cold, she stopped between us, excited beyond belief, wet snow melting onto the floor. Her back, including her hair, was covered by thick clots of snow.

"Tia Aileen, Father Rico, come outside. Come outside and see. Quick! You need to see what we're doing, pleeease?"

She grasped both of our hands and pulled us out to the yard. There, lying on their backs in the snow were her older sister, her mother, Rae and the young Father Dru, waving their arms and legs into wing shaped imprints in the sparkling snow. The tiniest angel silhouette amongst them was now empty of its maker.

Priscilla and Penelope joined hands and ventured into the yard, sticking their tongues out like five year olds catching snowflakes. Anselmo leaned heavily on his cane, turned sideways and watched them both lovingly. I surveyed them, witnessed them delight in each other, watched Ed throw yet another snowball for the three dogs to chase, and caught sight as Cesar sneaked a kiss with Lynisa while they leaned against the hood of the truck.

"See Tia, see? Angels in the Snow." The little girl released my hand and pointed to the scene unfolding in the yard in front of us. Then she fell into the fresh snow waving her arms and legs.

"Do you see the Angels?" she asked.

I looked out at all of them, then down at her.

"Yes. Yes I do."

Readers Guide

1. Think about your engagement with the book. Were you drawn into the book right away or did it take a few chapters? Did the book start to feel real to you? When? What made it seem real or why did you have a hard time believing things like this happen?

2. No Handbook for the Homeless tells the story of a middle class woman who has her life forever changed by a drunk driver, her husband. Yet she stands by him. Why? What other choices could she have made? How would her life have been different?

3. Aileen repeatedly laments her alienation from those around because of the tragedy; even her only brother refuses to return her calls. Were they right to blame her?

4. The classroom scenes in the book are both funny and poignant. Students are refused lunch when they are minutes late to the cafeteria or are not allowed to attend a school fun day because they didn't meet a sales quota from the fund raising catalog. What do you think about these situations? Are all school rules fair? Are they equally enforced? Should they be? Do schools have a double standard for the haves and have nots as portrayed in the book? When students are placed in these unwinnable situations and act out, how much of the blame for their actions and behaviors does the school or teacher share?

4. The title of the book comes from Aileen's lament, "There is no handbook for the homeless..., at best, if you haven't burned all your karma you'll find a spirit guide, more likely the guide will find you." Who were her spirit guides? How did each help her? Which of the spirit guides did you find most compelling? Who would you want to know more about?

5. When people think about programs to help the homeless they tend to think about shelters and meal sites, yet much of Aileen's help came in small ways. Think about the small things, small kindnesses extended to her. How did this change her life?

6. Aileen is continually chased off or told to move on. Where could she have gone?

7. Peanuts is a pivotal character in the book. Was Aileen right to keep Peanuts with her for so long or should she have surrendered him to an animal shelter soon after the accident? Would either Peanuts or Aileen been better off if she had?

8. Did anything about Aileen's story surprise or dismay you? Pick one or two events that you found noteworthy and explain how they affected you.

9. Think about Aileen's relationship with MaryIsabelle. Could Aileen have done more to help her? What do you think about Billy Dean's advice to stay out of MaryIsabelle situation?

10. The story presents both the good and bad sides of the police and the homeless. How can the police balance the demands of merchants and residents versus the situation the homeless face? Aileen tells one officer "I'm local too, I live here too." How do you feel about that statement?

11. Aileen and Cesar have an uneasy on again, off again friendship. How does it change over the course of the book? How could their relationship been different?

12. Great detail is given to specific settings in the book, such as the motel room at the Steer Inn, or the smells in the back of the police car. Did this add to or distract from the story? Pick a descriptive part of the book, what parts of the description needed to be expanded, what could have been left out?

13. La Mancha is an arid portion of Spain, the setting for Cervantes novel and basis for a musical play. A literal translation is a spot, stain or patch as in a spot on one's character, a blemish or hitting a rough patch. Yet, Cervantes novel is filled with one man's quest to right wrongs, both real and imagined. Relate why the author picked this name for the neighborhood Aileen finds to dwell in.

13. Why was Aileen upset at the end of her hearing when she is told she will get a refund?

14. Was Ed's character necessary to a happy ending?

15. Some people are considered chronically homeless, like Wizard. Others, such as Aileen are overcome by economic circumstances and are trying to find a way out; still others have mental health or substance abuse problems. Here's the final question: Is homelessness a choice?

NOTE: The author suggests you use your reading of this book as an opportunity to support a program that helps the homeless in your community. Consider a food, blanket or toiletries drive, volunteering at a shelter or meal site or becoming an advocate for the homeless in your area.

www.ingramcontent.com/pod-product-compliance
Lightning Source LLC
Chambersburg PA
CBHW021845010726
47493CB00005B/1563